The
Hawaiian Romance
of Laieikawai

The Hawaiian Romance of Laieikawai was first published in 1918.

This edition published by Mint Editions 2021.

ISBN 9781513290737 | E-ISBN 9781513293585

Published by Mint Editions®

 MINT
EDITIONS

minteditionbooks.com

Publishing Director: Jennifer Newens
Design & Production: Rachel Lopez Metzger
Project Manager: Micaela Clark
Translated By: Martha W. Beckwith
Typesetting: Westchester Publishing Services

The Hawaiian Romance of Laieikawai

S. N. Hale'ole

MINT EDITIONS

Contents

---

* The titles of chapters are added for convenience in reference and are not found in the text.

PREFACE

This work of translation has been undertaken out of love for the land of Hawaii and for the Hawaiian people. To all those who have generously aided to further the study I wish to express my grateful thanks. I am indebted to the curator and trustees of the Bishop Museum for so kindly placing at my disposal the valuable manuscripts in the museum collection, and to Dr. Brigham, Mr. Stokes, and other members of the museum staff for their help and suggestions, as well as to those scholars of Hawaiian who have patiently answered my questions or lent me valuable material—to Mr. Henry Parker, Mr. Thomas Thrum, Mr. William Rowell, Miss Laura Green, Mr. Stephen Desha, Judge Hazelden of Waiohinu, Mr. Curtis Iaukea, Mr. Edward Lilikalani, and Mrs. Emma Nawahi. Especially am I indebted to Mr. Joseph Emerson, not only for the generous gift of his time but for free access to his entire collection of manuscript notes. My thanks are also due to the hosts and hostesses through whose courtesy I was able to study in the field, and to Miss Ethel Damon for her substantial aid in proof reading. Nor would I forget to record with grateful appreciation those Hawaiian interpreters whose skill and patience made possible the rendering into English of their native romance—Mrs. Pokini Robinson of Maui, Mr. and Mrs. Kamakaiwi of Pahoa, Hawaii, Mrs. Kama and Mrs. Supé of Kalapana, and Mrs. Julia Bowers of Honolulu. I wish also to express my thanks to those scholars in this country who have kindly helped me with their criticism—to Dr. Ashley Thorndike, Dr. W.W. Lawrence, Dr. A.C.L. Brown, and Dr. A.A. Goldenweiser. I am indebted also to Dr. Roland Dixon for bibliographical notes. Above all, thanks are due to Dr. Franz Boas, without whose wise and helpful enthusiasm this study would never have been undertaken.

MARTHA WARREN BECKWITH.
COLUMBIA UNIVERSITY,
October, 1917.

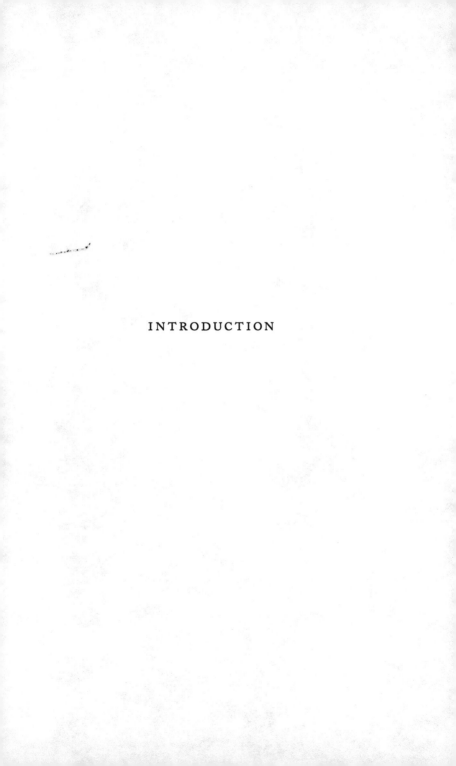

INTRODUCTION

I

THE BOOK AND ITS WRITER; SCOPE OF THE PRESENT EDITION

The *Laieikawai* is a Hawaiian romance which recounts the wooing of a native chiefess of high rank and her final deification among the gods. The story was handed down orally from ancient times in the form of a *kaao*, a narrative rehearsed in prose interspersed with song, in which form old tales are still recited by Hawaiian story-tellers.[1] It was put into writing by a native Hawaiian, Haleole by name, who hoped thus to awaken in his countrymen an interest in genuine native story-telling based upon the folklore of their race and preserving its ancient customs—already fast disappearing since Cook's rediscovery of the group in 1778 opened the way to foreign influence—and by this means to inspire in them old ideals of racial glory. Haleole was born about the time of the death of Kaméhaméha I, a year or two before the arrival of the first American missionaries and the establishment of the Protestant mission in Hawaii. In 1834 he entered the mission school at Lahainaluna, Maui, where his interest in the ancient history of his people was stimulated and trained under the teaching of Lorrin Andrews, compiler of the Hawaiian dictionary, published in 1865, and Sheldon Dibble, under whose direction David Malo prepared his collection of "Hawaiian Antiquities," and whose History of the Sandwich Islands (1843) is an authentic source for the early history of the mission. Such early Hawaiian writers as Malo, Kamakau, and John Ii were among Haleole's fellow students. After leaving school he became first a teacher, then an editor. In the early sixties he brought out the *Laieikawai*, first as a serial in the Hawaiian newspaper, the *Kuokoa*, then, in 1863, in book form.[2] Later, in 1885, two part-Hawaiian editors, Bolster and

---

1. Compare the Fijian story quoted by Thomson (p. 6).
2. Daggett calls the story "a supernatural folklore legend of the fourteenth century," and includes an excellent abstract of the romance, prepared by Dr. W.D. Alexander, in his collection of Hawaiian legends. Andrews says of it (Islander, 1875, p. 27): "We have seen that a Hawaiian Kaao or legend was composed ages ago, recited and kept in memory merely by repetition, until a short time since it was reduced to writing by a Hawaiian and printed, making a duodecimo volume of 220 pages, and that, too, with the poetical parts

Meheula, revised and reprinted the story, this time in pamphlet form, together with several other romances culled from Hawaiian journals, as the initial volumes of a series of Hawaiian reprints, a venture which ended in financial failure.[3] The romance of *Laieikawai* therefore remains

---

mostly left out. It is said that this legend took six hours in the recital." In prefacing his dictionary he says: "The Kaao of Laieikawai is almost the only specimen of that species of language which has been laid before the public. Many fine specimens have been printed in the Hawaiian periodicals, but are neither seen nor regarded by the foreign community."
3. The changes introduced by these editors have not been followed in this edition, except in a few unimportant omissions, but the popular song printed below appears first in its pages:

"*Aia Laie-i-ka-wai*
I ka uka wale la o Pali-uli;
O ka nani, o ka nani,
Helu ekahi o ia uka.

"*E nanea e walea ana paha,*
I ka leo nahenahe o na manu.

"*Kau mai Laie-i-ka-wai*
I ka eheu la o na manu;
O ka nani, o ka nani,
Helu ekahi o Pali-uli.

"*E nanea, etc.*

"*Ua lohe paha i ka hone mai,*
O ka pu lau-i a Malio;
Honehone, honehone,
Helu ekahi o Hopoe.

"*E nanea, etc.*"

Behold Laieikawai
On the uplands of Paliuli;
Beautiful, beautiful,
The storied one of the uplands.

REF.—Perhaps resting at peace,
To the melodious voice of the birds.

Laieikawai rests here
On the wings of the birds;
Beautiful, beautiful,
The storied one of the uplands.

She has heard perhaps the playing
Of Malio's ti-leaf trumpet;
Playfully, playfully,
The storied one of Hopoe.

the sole piece of Hawaiian, imaginative writing to reach book form. Not only this, but it represents the single composition of a Polynesian mind working upon the material of an old legend and eager to create a genuine national literature. As such it claims a kind of classic interest.

The language, although retaining many old words unfamiliar to the Hawaiian of to-day, and proverbs and expressions whose meaning is now doubtful, is that employed since the time of the reduction of the speech to writing in 1820, and is easily read at the present day. Andrews incorporated the vocabulary of this romance into his dictionary, and in only a few cases is his interpretation to be questioned. The songs, though highly figurative, present few difficulties. So far as the meaning is concerned, therefore, the translation is sufficiently accurate. But as regards style the problem is much more difficult. To convey not only the meaning but exactly the Hawaiian way of seeing things, in such form as to get the spirit of the original, is hardly possible to our language. The brevity of primitive speech must be sacrificed, thus accentuating the tedious repetition of detail—a trait sufficiently characteristic of Hawaiian story-telling. Then, too, common words for which we have but one form, in the original employ a variety of synonyms. "Say" and "see" are conspicuous examples. Other words identical in form convey to the Polynesian mind a variety of ideas according to the connection in which they are used—a play upon words impossible to translate in a foreign idiom. Again, certain relations that the Polynesian conceives with exactness, like those of direction and the relation of the person addressed to the group referred to, are foreign to our own idiom; others, like that of time, which we have more fully developed, the Polynesian recognizes but feebly. In face of these difficulties the translator has reluctantly foregone any effort to heighten the charm of the strange tale by using a fictitious idiom or by condensing and invigorating its deliberation. Haleole wrote his tale painstakingly, at times dramatically, but for the most part concerned for its historic interest. We gather from his own statement and from the breaks in the story that his material may have been collected from different sources. It seems to have been common to incorporate a *Laieikawai* episode into the popular romances, and of these episodes Haleole may have availed himself. But we shall have something more to say of his sources later; with his particular style we are not concerned. The only reason for presenting the romance complete in all its original dullness and unmodified to foreign taste is with the definite object of showing as nearly as possible from the native angle the genuine Polynesian imagination at work upon its own material, reconstructing in this strange tale of the "Woman of the Twilight" its own objective world, the social interests which regulate its actions and desires, and by this means to portray the actual character of the Polynesian mind.

This exact thing has not before been done for Hawaiian story and I do not recall any considerable romance in a Polynesian tongue so rendered.[4] Admirable collections of the folk tales of Hawaii have been gathered by Thrum, Remy, Daggett, Emerson, and Westervelt, to which should be added the manuscript tales collected by Fornander, translated by John Wise, and now edited by Thrum for the Bishop Museum, from which are drawn the examples accompanying this paper. But in these collections the lengthy recitals which may last several hours in the telling or run for a couple of years as serial in some Hawaiian newspaper are of necessity cut down to a summary narrative, sufficiently suggesting the flavor of the original, but not picturing fully the way in which the image is formed in the mind of the native story-teller. Foreigners and Hawaiians have expended much ingenuity in rendering the *mélé* or chant with exactness,[5] but the much simpler if less important matter of putting into literal English a Hawaiian *kaao* has never been attempted.

To the text such ethnological notes have been added as are needed to make the context clear. These were collected in the field. Some were gathered directly from the people themselves; others from those who had lived long enough among them to understand their customs; others still from observation of their ways and of the localities mentioned in the story; others are derived from published texts. An index of characters, a brief description of the local background, and an abstract of the story itself prefaces the text; appended to it is a series of abstracts from the Fornander collection, of Hawaiian folk stories, all of which

---

4. Dr. N. B. Emerson's rendering of the myth of *Pele and Hiiaka* quotes only the poetical portions. Her Majesty Queen Liliuokalani interested herself in providing a translation of the *Laieikawai,* and the Hon. Sanford B. Dole secured a partial translation of the story; but neither of these copies has reached the publisher's hands.

5. The most important of these chants translated from the Hawaiian are the "Song of Creation," prepared by Liliuokalani; the "Song of Kualii," translated by both Lyons and Wise, and the prophetic song beginning *"Haui ka lani,"* translated by Andrews and edited by Dole. To these should be added the important songs cited by Fornander, in full or in part, which relate the origin of the group, and perhaps the name song beginning "The fish ponds of Mana," quoted in Fornander's tale of *Lonoikamakahiki*, the canoe-chant in *Kana*, and the wind chants in *Pakaa*.

were collected by Judge Fornander in the native tongue and later rendered into English by a native translator. These abstracts illustrate the general character of Hawaiian story-telling, but specific references should be examined in the full text, now being edited by the Bishop Museum. The index to references includes all the Hawaiian material in available form essential to the study of romance, together with the more useful Polynesian material for comparative reference. It by no means comprises a bibliography of the entire subject.

II

Nature and the Gods as Reflected in the Story

1. Polynesian Origin of Hawaiian Romance

Truly to interpret Hawaiian romance we must realize at the start its relation to the past of that people, to their origin and migrations, their social inheritance, and the kind of physical world to which their experience has been confined. Now, the real body of Hawaiian folklore belongs to no isolated group, but to the whole Polynesian area. From New Zealand through the Tongan, Ellice, Samoan, Society, Rarotongan, Marquesan, and Hawaiian groups, fringing upon the Fijian and the Micronesian, the same physical characteristics, the same language, customs, habits of life prevail; the same arts, the same form of worship, the same gods. And a common stock of tradition has passed from mouth to mouth over the same area. In New Zealand, as in Hawaii, men tell the story of Maui's fishing and the theft of fire.[1] A close comparative study of the tales from each group should reveal local characteristics, but for our purpose the Polynesian race is one, and its common stock of tradition, which at the dispersal and during the subsequent periods of migration was carried as common treasure-trove of the imagination as far as New Zealand on the south and Hawaii on the north, and from the western Fiji to the Marquesas on the east, repeats the same adventures among similar surroundings and colored by the same interests and desires. This means, in the first place, that the race must have developed for a long period of time in some common home of origin before the dispersal came, which sent family groups migrating

---

1. Bastian In Samoanische Schöpfungssage (p. 8) says: "Oceanien (im Zusammenbegriff von Polynesien und Mikronesien) repräsentirt (bei vorläufigem Ausschluss von Melanesien schon) einen Flächenraum, der alles Aehnliche auf dem Globus intellectualis weit übertrifft (von Hawaii bis Neu-Seeland, von der Oster-Insel bis zu den Marianen), und wenn es sich hier um Inseln handelt durch Meeresweiten getrennt, ist aus solch insularer Differenzirung gerade das Hilfsmittel comparativer Methode geboten für die Induction, um dasselbe, wie biologiseh sonst, hier auf psychologischem Arbeitsfelde zur Verwendung zu bringen." Compare: Krämer, p. 394; Finck, in Royal Scientific Society of Göttingen, 1909.

along the roads of ocean after some fresh land for settlement;[2] in the second place, it reflects a period of long voyaging which brought about interchange of culture between far distant groups.[3] As the Crusades were the great exchange for west European folk stories, so the days of the voyagers were the Polynesian crusading days. The roadway through the seas was traveled by singing bards who carried their tribal songs as a race heritage into the new land of their wanderings. Their inns for hostelry were islets where the boats drew up along the beach and the weary oarsmen grouped about the ovens where their hosts prepared cooked food for feasting. Tales traveled thus from group to group with a readiness which only a common tongue, common interests, and a common delight could foster, coupled with the constant competition of family rivalries.

Hawaiian tradition reflects these days of wandering.[4] A chief vows to wed no woman of his own group but only one fetched from "the land of good women." An ambitious priest seeks overseas a leader of divine ancestry. A chief insulted by his superior leads his followers into exile on some foreign shore. There is exchange of culture-gifts, intermarriage, tribute, war. Romance echoes with the canoe song and the invocation

---

2. Lesson says of the Polynesian groups (I, 378): "On sait. . . que tous ont, pour loi civile et religieuse, la même interdiction; que leurs institutions, leurs cérémonies sont semblables; que leurs croyances sont foncièrement identiques; qu'ils ont le même culte, les mêmes coutumes, les mêmes usages principaux; qu'ils ont enfin les mêmes moeurs et les mêmes traditions. Tout semble donc, a priori, annoncer que, quelque soit leur éloignement les uns des autres, les Polynesiens ont tiré d'une même source cette communauté d'idées et de langage; qu'ils ne sont, par consequent, que les tribus disperses d'une même nation, et que ces tribus ne se sont séparées qu'à une epoque où la langue et les idées politiques et religieuses de cette nation étaient déja fixées."

3. Compare: Stair, Old Samoa, p. 271; White, I, 176; Fison, pp. 1, 19; Smith, Hawaiki, p. 123; Lesson, II, 207, 209; Grey, pp. 108–234; Baessler, Neue Südsee-Bilder, p. 113; Thomson, p. 15.

4. Lesson (II, 190) enumerates eleven small islands, covering 40 degrees of latitude, scattered between Hawaii and the islands to the south, four showing traces of ancient habitation, which he believes to mark the old route from Hawaii to the islands to the southeast. According to Hawaiian tradition, which is by no means historically accurate, what is called the second migration period to Hawaii seems to have occurred between the eleventh and fourteenth centuries (dated from the arrival of the high priest Paao at Kohala, Hawaii, 18 generations before Kaméhaméha); to have come from the southeast; to have introduced a sacerdotal system whose priesthood, symbols, and temple structure persisted up to the time of the abandoning of the old faith in 1819. Compare Alexander's History, ch. III; Malo, pp. 25, 323; Lesson, II, 160–169.

to the confines of Kahiki[5]—this in spite of the fact that intercourse seems to have been long closed between this northern group and its neighbors south and east. When Cook put in first at the island of Kauai, most western of the group, perhaps guided by Spanish charts, perhaps by Tahitian navigators who had preserved the tradition of ancient voyages,[6] for hundreds of years none but chance boats had driven upon its shores.[7] But the old tales remained, fast bedded at the foundation of Hawaiian imaginative literature. As now recited they take the form of chants or of long monotonous recitals like the *Laieikawai*, which take on the heightened form of poetry only in dialogue or on occasions when the emotional stress requires set song. Episodes are passed along, from one hero cycle to another, localities and names vary, and a fixed form in matter of detail relieves the stretch of invention; in fact, they show exactly the same phenomena of fixing and reshaping, that all story-telling whose object is to please exhibits in transference from mouth to mouth. Nevertheless, they are jealously retentive of incident. The story-teller, generally to be found among the old people of any locality, who can relate the legends as they were handed down to him from the past is known and respected in the community. We find the same story[8] told in New Zealand and in Hawaii scarcely changed, even in name.

2. Polynesian Cosmogony

IN THEME THE BODY OF Polynesian folk tale is not unlike that of other primitive and story-loving people. It includes primitive philosophy—stories of cosmogony and of heroes who shaped the earth; primitive annals—migration stories, tales of culture heroes, of conquest and overrule. There is primitive romances—tales of competition, of vengeance, and of love; primitive wit—of drolls and tricksters; and primitive fear in tales of spirits and the power of ghosts. These divisions are not individual to Polynesia; they belong to universal delight; but the form each takes is shaped and determined by the background, either of real life or of life among the gods, familiar to the Polynesian mind.

---

5. *Kahiki*, in Hawaiian chants, is the term used to designate a "foreign land" in general and does not refer especially to the island of Tahiti in the Society Group.
6. Lesson, II, 152.
7. Ibid., 170.
8. Ibid., 178.

The conception of the heavens is purely objective, corresponding, in fact, to Anaxagoras's sketch of the universe. Earth is a plain, walled about far as the horizon, where, according to Hawaiian expression, rise the confines of Kahiki, *Kukulu o Kahiki*.[9] From this point the heavens are superimposed one upon the other like cones, in number varying in different groups from 8 to 14; below lies the underworld, sometimes divided into two or three worlds ruled by deified ancestors and inhabited by the spirits of the dead, or even by the gods[10]—the whole inclosed from chaos like an egg in a shell.[11] Ordinarily the gods seem to be conceived as inhabiting the heavens. As in other mythologies, heaven and the life the gods live there are merely a reproduction or copy of earth and its ways. In heaven the gods are ranged by rank; in the highest heaven dwells the chief god alone enjoying his supreme right of silence, *tabu moe*; others inhabit the lower heavens in gradually descending grade corresponding to the social ranks recognized among the Polynesian chiefs on earth. This physical world is again the prototype for the activities of the gods, its multitudinous manifestations representing the forms and forces employed by the myriad gods in making known their presence on earth. They are not these forms themselves, but have them at their disposal, to use as transformation bodies in their appearances on earth, or they may transfer them to their offspring on earth. This is due

---

9. In the Polynesian picture of the universe the wall of heaven is conceived as shutting down about each group, so that boats traveling from one group to another "break through" this barrier wall. The *Kukulu o Kahiki* in Hawaii seems to represent some such confine. Emerson says (in Malo, 30): "Kukulu was a wall or vertical erection such as was supposed to stand at the limits of the horizon and support the dome of heaven." Points of the compass were named accordingly *Kukulu hikina, Kukulu komohana, Kukulu hema, Kukulu akau*—east, west, south, north. The horizon was called *Kukulu-o-ka-honua*—"the compass-of-the-earth." The planes inclosed by such confines, on the other hand, are named *Kahiki*. The circle of the sky which bends upward from the horizon is called *Kahiki-ku* or "vertical." That through which, the eye travels in reaching the horizon, *Kahiki-moe*, or "horizontal."

10. The Rarotongan world of spirits is an underworld. (See Gill's Myths and Songs.) The Hawaiians believed in a subterranean world of the dead divided into two regions, in the upper of which Wakea reigned; in the lower, Milu. Those who had not been sufficiently religious "must lie under the spreading *Kou* trees of Milu's world, drink its waters and eat lizards and butterflies for food." Traditional points from which the soul took its leap into this underworld are to be found at the northern point of Hawaii, the west end of Maui, the south and the northwest points of Oahu, and, most famous of all, at the mouth of the great Waipio Valley on Hawaii. Compare Thomson's account from Fiji of the "pathway of the shade." p. 119.

11. White, I, chart; Gill, Myths and Songs, pp. 3, 4; Ellis, III, 168–170.

to the fact that the gods people earth, and from them man is descended. Chiefs rank, in fact, according to their claim to direct descent from the ancient gods.[12]

Just how this came about is not altogether uniformly explained. In the Polynesian creation story[13] three things are significant—a monistic idea of a god existing before creation;[14] a progressive order of creation out of the limitless and chaotic from lower to higher forms, actuated by desire, which is represented by the duality of sex generation in a long line of ancestry through specific pairs of forms from the inanimate world—rocks and earth, plants of land and sea forms—to the animate—fish, insects, reptiles, and birds;[15] and the special analysis of the soul of man into "breath," which constitutes life; "feeling," located in the heart; "desire" in the intestines; and "thought" out of which springs doubt—the whole constituting *akamai* or "knowledge." In Hawaii the creation story lays emphasis upon progressive sex generation of natural forms.

Individual islands of a group are popularly described as rocks dropped down out of heaven or fished up from below sea as resting places for the gods;[16] or they are named as offspring of the divine ancestors of the

---

12. Gill says of the Hervey Islanders (p. 17 of notes): "The state is conceived of as a long house standing east and west, chiefs from the north and south sides of the island representing left and right; under chiefs the rafters; individuals the leaves of the thatch. These are the counterpart of the actual house (of the gods) in the spirit world." Compare Stair, p. 210.

13. Bastian, Samoanische Schöpfungs-Sage; Ellis, I, 321; White, vol. I; Turner, Samoa, 3; Gill, Myths and Songs, pp. 1–20; Moerenhout I, 419 et seq.; Liliuokalani, translation of the Hawaiian "Song of Creation"; Dixon, Oceanic Mythology.

14. Moerenhout translates (I, 419): "He was, *Taaroa* (Kanaloa) was his name. He dwelt in immensity. Earth was not. *Taaroa*, called, but nothing responded to him, and, existing alone, he changed himself into the universe. The pivots (axes or orbits), this is *Taaroa*; the rocks, this is he. *Taaroa* is the sand, so is he named. *Taaroa* is the day. *Taaroa* is the center. *Taaroa* is the germ. *Taaroa* is the base. *Taaroa* is the invincible, who created the universe, the sacred universe, the shell for *Taaroa*, the life, life of the universe."

15. Moerenhout, I, 423: "*Taaroa* slept with the woman called *Hina* of the sea. Black clouds, white clouds, rain are born. *Taaroa* slept with the woman of the uplands; the first-germ is born. Afterwards is born all that grows upon the earth. Afterwards is born the mist of the mountain. Afterwards is born the one called strong. Afterwards Is born the woman, the beautiful adorned one," etc.

16. Grey, pp. 38–45; Krämer, Samoa Inseln, pp. 395–400; Fison, pp. 139–146; Mariner, I, 228; White, II, 75; Gill, Myths and Songs, p. 48.

S. N. HALE'OLE

group.[17] The idea seems to be that they are a part of the divine fabric, connected in kind with the original source of the race.

3. The Demigod as Hero

As NATURAL FORMS MULTIPLIED, so multiplied the gods who wedded and gave them birth. Thus the half-gods were born, the *kupua* or demigods as distinguished from *akua* or spirits who are pure divinities.[18] The nature of the Polynesian *kupua* is well described in the romance of *Laieikawai*, in Chapter XXIX, when the sisters of Aiwohikupua try to relieve their mistress's fright about marrying a divine one from the heavens. "He is no god—*Aole ia he Akua*—" they say, "he is a man like us, yet in his nature and appearance godlike. And he was the first-born of us; he was greatly beloved by our parents; to him was given superhuman power—*ka mana*—which we have not. . . Only his taboo rank remains, Therefore fear not; when he comes you will see that he is only a man like us." It is such a character, born of godlike ancestors and inheriting through the favor of this god, or some member of his family group, godlike power or *mana*, generally in some particular form, who appears as the typical hero of early Hawaiian romance. His rank as a god is gained by competitive tests with a rival *kupua/* or with the ancestor from whom he demands recognition and endowment. He has the power of transformation into the shape of some specific animal, object, or physical phenomenon which serves as the "sign" or "body" in which the god presents himself to man, and hence he controls all objects of this class. Not only the heavenly bodies, clouds, storms, and the appearances in the heavens, but perfumes and notes of birds serve to announce his divinity, and special kinds of birds, or fish, or reptiles, or of animals like the rat, pig, or dog, are recognized as peculiarly likely to be the habitation of a god. This is the form in which *aumakua*, or

---

17. In Fornander's collection of origin chants the Hawaiian group is described as the offspring of the ancestors Wakea and Papa, or Hina.
18. Mariner, II, 103; Turner, Nineteen Tears in Polynesia, pp. 238–242; Ibid., Samoa, pp. 23–77; Ellis, I, 334; Gracia, pp. 41–44; Krämer (Samoa Inseln, p. 22) and Stair (p. 211) distinguished *akua* as the original gods, *aiku* as their descendants, the demonic beings who appear in animal forms and act as helpers to man; and *kupua* as deified human beings.

guardian spirits of a family, appear to watch over the safety of the household they protect.[19]

Besides this power of transformation the *kupua* has other supernatural gifts, as the power of flight,[20] of contraction and expansion at will, of seeing what is going on at a distance, and of bringing the dead to life. As a man on earth he is often miraculously born or miraculously preserved at birth, which event is heralded by portents in the heavens. He is often brought up by some supernatural guardian, grows with marvelous rapidity, has an enormous appetite—a proof of godlike strain, because only the chief in Polynesian economic life has the resources freely to indulge his animal appetite—and phenomenal beauty or prodigious skill, strength, or subtlety in meeting every competitor. His adventures follow the general type of mythical hero tales. Often he journeys to the heavens to seek some gift of his ancestors, the ingenious fancy keeping always before it an objective picture of this heavenly superstructure—bearing him thither upon a cloud or bird, on the path of a cobweb, a trailing vine, or a rainbow, or swung thither on the tip of a bamboo stalk. Arrived in the region of air, by means of tokens or by name chants, he proves his ancestry and often substantiates his claim in tests of power, ability thus sharing with blood the determining of family values. If his deeds are among men, they are of a marvelous nature. Often his godlike nature is displayed by apparent sloth and indolence on his part, his followers performing miraculous feats while he remains inactive; hence

---

19. When a Polynesian invokes a god he prays to the spirit of some dead ancestor who acts as his supernatural helper. A spirit is much stronger than a human being—hence the custom of covering the grave with a great heap of stone or modern masonry to keep down the ghost. Its strength may be increased through prayer and sacrifice, called "feeding" the god. See Fornander's stories of *Pumaia*, and *Nihoalaki*. In Fison's story of Mantandua the mother has died of exhaustion in rescuing her child. As he grows up her spirit acts as his supernatural helper, and appears to him in dreams to direct his course. He accordingly achieves prodigies through her aid. In *Kuapakaa* the boy manages the winds through his grandmother's bones, which he keeps in a calabash. In *Pamano*, the supernatural helper appears in bird shape. The Fornander stories of *Kamapua'a*, the pig god, and of *Pikoiakaalala*, who belongs to the rat family, illustrate the *kupua* in animal shape. Malo, pp. 113–115. Compare Mariner, II, 87, 100; Ellis, I, 281.

20. Bird-bodied gods of low grade in the theogony of the heavens act as messengers for the higher gods. In Stair (p. 214) Tuli, the plover, is the bird messenger of Tagaloa. The commonest messenger birds named in Hawaiian stories are the plover, wandering tattler, and turnstone, all migratory from about April to August, and hence naturally fastened upon by the imagination as suitable messengers to lands beyond common ken. Gill (Myths and Songs, p. 35) says that formerly the gods spoke through small land birds, as in the story of Laieikawai's visit to Kauakahialii.

he is reproached for idleness by the unwitting. Sometimes he acts as a transformer, changing the form of mountains and valleys with a step or stroke; sometimes as a culture hero bringing gifts to mankind and teaching them the arts learned from the gods, or supplying food by making great hauls of fish by means of a miraculous hook, or planting rich crops; sometimes he is an avenger, pitting his strength against a rival demigod who has done injury to a relative or patron of his own, or even by tricks outwitting the mischievous *akua*. Finally, he remains on earth only when, by transgressing some *kupua* custom or in contest with a superior *kupua*, he is turned into stone, many rock formations about the islands being thus explained and consequently worshiped as dwelling places of gods. Otherwise he is deified in the heavens, or goes to dwell in the underworld with the gods, from whence he may still direct and inspire his descendants on earth if they worship him, or even at times appear to them again on earth in some objective form.[21]

4. The Earthly Paradise; Divinity in Man and Nature

FOR ACCORDING TO THE OLD myth, Sky and Earth were nearer of access in the days when the first gods brought forth their children—the winds, the root plants, trees, and the inhabitants of the sea, but the younger gods rent them apart to give room to walk upright;[22] so gods and men walked together in the early myths, but in the later traditions, called historical, the heavens do actually get pushed farther away from man and the gods retreat thither. The fabulous demigods depart one by one from Hawaii; first the great gods—Kane, Ku, Lono, and Kanaloa; then the demigods, save Pele of the volcano. The supernatural race of the dragons and other beast gods who came from "the shining heavens" to people Hawaii, the gods and goddesses who governed the appearances in the heavens, and the myriad race of divine helpers who dwelt in the tiniest forms of the forest and did in a night the task of months of labor, all those god men who shaped the islands and named their peaks and valleys, rocks, and crevices as they trampled hollows with a spring and thrust their spears through mountains, were superseded by

21. With the stories quoted from Fornander may be compared such wonder tales as are to be found in Krämer, pp. 108, 116, 121, 413–419; Fison, pp. 32, 49, 99; Grey, p. 59; Turner, Samoa, p. 209; White I, 82, etc.
22. Grey, pp. 1–15; White, I, 46; Baessler, Neue Südsee-Bilder, pp. 244, 245; Gill, Myths and Songs, pp. 58–60.

a humaner race of heroes who ruled the islands by subtlety and skill, and instead of climbing the heavens after the fiery drink of the gods or searching the underworld for ancestral hearth fires, voyaged to other groups of islands for courtship or barter. Then even the long voyages ceased and chiefs made adventure out of canoe trips about their own group, never save by night out of sight of land. They set about the care of their property from rival chiefs. Thus constantly in jeopardy from each other, sharpening, too, their observation of what lay directly about them and of the rational way to get on in life, they accepted the limits of a man's power and prayed to the gods, who were their great ancestors, for gifts beyond their reach.[23]

And during this transfer of attention from heaven to earth the objective picture of a paradise in the heavens or of an underworld inhabited by spirits of the dead got mixed up with that of a land of origin on earth, an earthly paradise called Hawaiki or Bulotu or "the lost land of *Kane*"—a land about which clustered those same wistful longings which men of other races have pictured in their visions of an earthly paradise—the "talking tree of knowledge," the well of life, and plenty without labor.[24] "Thus they dwelt at Paliuli," says Haleole of the

---

23. Compare Krämer's Samoan story (in Samoa Inseln, p. 413) of the quest after the pearl fishhooks kept by Night and Day in the twofold heavens with the Hawaiian stories collected by Fornander of *Aiai* and *Nihoalaki*. Krämer's story begins:

> "Aloalo went to his father
> To appease Sina's longing;
> He sent him to the twofold heavens,
> To his grandparents, Night and Day,
> To the house whence drops fall spear-shaped,
> To hear their counsel and return.
> Aloalo entered the house,
> Took not the unlucky fishhook,
> Brought away that of good luck,"
> etc.

24. Krämer, Samoa Inseln, pp. 44, 115; Fison, pp. 16, 139–161, 163; Lesson, II, 272, 483 (see index); Mariner, II, 100, 102, 115, et seq.; Moerenhout, I, 432; Gracia, p. 40; Turner, Nineteen Years in Polynesia, p. 237; Gill, Myths and Songs, pp. 152–172.

In Fison's story (p. 139) the gods dwell in Bulotu, "where the sky meets the waters in the climbing path of the sun." The story goes: "In the beginning there was no land save that on which the gods lived; no dry land was there for men to dwell upon; all was sea; the sky covered it above and bounded it on every side. There was neither day nor night, but a mild light shone continually through the sky upon the water, like the shining of the moon when its face is hidden by a white cloud."

sisters' life with Laieikawai, "and while they dwelt there never did they weary of life. Never did they even see the person who prepared their food, nor the food itself save when, at mealtimes, the birds brought them food and cleared away the remnants when they had finished. So Paliuli became to them a land beloved."

Gods and men are, in fact, to the Polynesian mind, one family under different forms, the gods having superior control over certain phenomena, a control which they may impart to their offspring on earth. As he surveys the world about him the Polynesian supposes the signs of the gods who rule the heavens to appear on earth, which formerly they visited, traveling thither as cloud or bird or storm or perfume to effect some marriage alliance or govern mankind. In these forms, or transformed themselves into men, they dwelt on earth and shaped the social customs of mankind. Hence we have in such a romance as the *Laieikawai* a realistic picture, first, of the activities of the gods in the heavens and on earth, second, of the social ideas and activities of the people among whom the tale is told. The supernatural blends into the natural in exactly the same way as to the Polynesian mind gods relate themselves to men, facts about one being regarded as, even though removed to the heavens, quite as objective as those which belong to the other, and being employed to explain social customs and physical appearances in actual experience. In the light of such story-telling even the Polynesian creation myth may become a literal genealogy, and the dividing line between folklore and traditional history, a mere shift of attention and no actual change in the conception itself of the nature of the material universe and the relations between gods and men.

5. The Story: Its Mythical Character

THESE MYTHICAL TALES OF THE gods are reflected in Haleole's romance of *Laieikawai*. Localized upon Hawaii, it is nevertheless familiar with regions of the heavens. Paliuli, the home of Laieikawai, and Pihanakalani, home of the flute-playing high chief of Kauai, are evidently earthly paradises.[25] Ask a native where either of these places

---

25. As such Paliuli occurs in other Hawaiian folk tales:

1. At Paliuli grew the mythical trees Makali'i, male and female, which have the power to draw fish. The female was cut down and taken to Kailua, Oahu, hence the chant:

> "*Kupu ka laau ona a Makali'i,*
> *O Makali'i, laau Kaulana mai ka pomai.*"

is to be found and he will say, smiling, "In the heavens." The long lists of local place names express the Polynesian interest in local journeyings. The legend of *Waiopuka* is a modern or at least adapted legend. But the route which the little sister follows to the heavens corresponds with Polynesian cosmogonic conceptions, and is true to ancient stories of the home of the gods.

The action of the story, too, is clearly concerned with a family of demigods. This is more evident if we compare a parallel story translated by Westervelt in "Gods and Ghosts," page 116, which, however, confused and fragmentary, is clearly made up of some of the same material as Haleole's version.[26]

---

2. In the Fornander notes from Kepelino and Kamakau, Paliuli is the land given to the first man and is called "hidden land of Kane" and "great land of the gods." 3. In Fornander's story of *Kepakailiula*, the gods assign Paliuli to be the hero's home. To reach it the party start at second cockcrow from Keaau (as in the *Laieikawai*) and arrive in the morning. It is "a good land, flat, fertile, filled with many things desired by man." The native apples are as large as breadfruit. They see a pond "lying within the land stocked with all kinds of fish of the sea except the whale and the shark." Here "the sugar cane grew until it lay flat, the hogs until the tusks were long, the chickens until the spurs were long and sharp, and the dogs until their backs were flattened out." They leave Paliuli to travel over Hawaii, and "no man has ever seen it since."

4. In Fornander's story of *Kana*, Uli, the grandmother of Kana, goes up to Paliuli to dig up the double canoe Kaumaielieli in which Kana is to sail to recover his mother. The chant in which this canoe is described is used to-day by practicers of sorcery to exorcise an enemy.

26. The gods Kane and Kanaloa, who live in the mountains of Oahu, back of Honolulu, prepare a home for the first-born son of Ku and Hina, whom they send Rainbow to fetch from Nuumealani. The messenger, first gaining the consent of the lizard guardian at Kuaihelani, brings back Child-adopted-by-the-gods to the gods on Oahu. Again Hina bears a child, a daughter. For this girl also the gods send two sister messengers, who bring Paliuli to Waka, where she cares for the birds in the forests of Puna. Here a beautiful home is prepared for the girl and a garden planted with two magical food-producing trees, Makalei, brought from Nuumealani to provide fish and prepared food in abundance. These two children, brother and sister, are the most beautiful pair on earth, and the gods arrange their marriage. Kane precedes the boy, dressed in his lightning body, and the tree people come to dance and sing before Paliuli. Some say that the goddess Laka, patroness of the *hula* dance, accompanied them. For a time all goes well, then the boy is beguiled by Poliahu (Cold-bosom) on the mountain. Paliuli, aware of her lover's infidelity, sends Waka to bring him back, but Cold-bosom prevents his approach, by spreading the mountain with snow. Paliuli wanders away to Oahu, then to Kauai, learning dances on the way which she teaches to the trees in the forest on her return.

Meanwhile another child is born to Ku and Hina. The lizard guardian draws this lovely girl from the head of Hina, calls her Keaomelemele, Golden-cloud, and sets her to rule the clouds in the Shining-heavens. Among these clouds is Kaonohiokala, the Eyeball-of-the-sun, who knows what is going on at a distance. From the lizard guardian

The main situation in this story furnishes a close parallel to the *Laieikawai* A beautiful girl of high rank is taken from her parents and brought up apart in an earthly paradise by a supernatural guardian, Waka, where she is waited upon by birds. A great lizard acts as her protector. She is wedded to a high taboo chief who is fetched thither from the gods, and who later is seduced from his fidelity by the beauty of another woman. This woman of the mountain, Poliahu, though identical in name and nature, plays a minor part in Haleole's story. In other details the stories show discrepancies.[27] It is pretty clear that Haleole's version has suppressed, out of deference to foreign-taught proprieties, the original relationship of brother and sister retained in the Westervelt story. This may be inferred from the fact that other unpublished Hawaiian romances of the same type preserve this relation, and that, according to Hawaiian genealogists, the highest divine rank is ascribed to such a union. Restoring this connection, the story describes the doings of a single family, gods or of godlike descent.[28]

In the Westervelt story, on the whole, the action is treated mythically to explain how things came to be as they are—how the gods peopled the islands, how the *hula* dances and the lore of the clouds were taught in Hawaii. The reason for the localization is apparent. The deep

---

Golden-cloud learns of her sister Paliuli's distress, and she comes to earth to effect a reconciliation. There she learns all the dances that the gods can teach.

Now, Ku and Hina, having learned the lore of the clouds, choose other mates and each, bears a child, one a boy called Kaumailiula, Twilight-resting-in-the-sky, the other a girl named Kaulanaikipokii.

The boy is brought to Oahu, riding in a red canoe befitting a chief, to be Goldencloud's husband. His sister follows with her maidens riding in shells, which they pick up and put in their pockets when they come to land. Ku, Hina, and the lizard family also migrate to Oahu to join the gods, Kane and Kanaloa, for the marriage festival. Thus these early gods came to Oahu.

27. Although the earthly paradise has the same location in both stories, the name Paliuli in Westervelt's version belongs to the heroine herself. The name of the younger sister, too, who acts no part in this story, appears again in the tale collected by Fornander of *Kaulanapokii*, where, like the wise little sister of Haleole's story, she is the leader and spokesman of her four Maile sisters, and carries her part as avenger by much more magical means than in Haleole's naturalistic conception. The character who bears the name of Haleole's sungod, Kaonohiokala, plays only an incidental part in Westervelt's story.

28. First generation: Waka, Kihanuilulumoku, Lanalananuiaimakua.

Second generation: Moanalihaikawaokele, Laukieleula; Mokukeleikahiki and Kaeloikamalama (brothers to Laukieleula).

Third generation: Kaonohiokala m. Laieikawai, Laielohelohe (m. Kekalukaluokewaii), Aiwohikupua, Mailehaiwale, Mailekaluhea, Mailelaulii, Mailepakaha, Kahalaomapuana.

forests of Puna, long dedicated to the gods, with their singing birds, their forest trees whose leaves dance in the wind, their sweet-scented *maile* vine, with those fine mists which still perpetually shroud the landscape and give the name Haleohu, House-of-mist, to the district, and above all the rainbows so constantly arching over the land, make an appropriate setting for the activities of some family of demigods. Strange and fairylike as much of the incident appears, allegorical as it seems, upon the face of it, the Polynesian mind observes objectively the activities of nature and of man as if they proceeded from the same sort of consciousness.

So, in Haleole's more naturalistic tale the mythical rendering is inwrought into the style of the narrative. Storm weds Perfume. Their children are the Sun-at-high-noon; a second son, possibly Lightning; twin daughters called after two varieties of the forest vine, *ieie*, perhaps symbols of Rainbow and Twilight; and five sweet-smelling daughters— the four varieties of *maile* vine and the scented *hala* blossom. The first-born son is of such divine character that he dwells highest in the heavens. Noonday, like a bird, bears visitors to his gate, and guards of the shade—Moving-cloud and Great-bright-moon—close it to shut out his brightness. The three regions below him are guarded by maternal uncles and by his father, who never comes near the taboo house, which only his mother shares with him. His signs are those of the rainstorm—thunder, lightning, torrents of "red rain," high seas, and long-continued mists—these he inherits from his father. An ancestress rears Rainbow in the forests of Puna. Birds bear her upon their wings and serve her with abundance of food prepared without labor, and of their golden feathers her royal house is built; sweet-scented vines and blossoms surround her; mists shroud her when she goes abroad. Earthquake guards her dwelling, saves Rainbow from Lightning, who seeks to destroy her, and bears a messenger to fetch the Sun-at-high-noon as bridegroom for the beautiful Rainbow. The Sun god comes to earth and bears Rainbow away with him to the heavens, but later he loves her sister Twilight, follows her to earth, and is doomed to sink into Night.

6. The Story as a Reflection of Aristocratic Social Life

SUCH IS THE BARE OUTLINE of the myth, but notice how, in humanizing the gods, the action presents a lively picture of the ordinary course of Polynesian life. Such episodes as the concealment of the child to preserve its life, the boxing and surfing contests, all the business of love-making—its jealousies and subterfuges, the sisters to act as go-betweens, the bet at checkers and the *Kilu* games at night, the marriage cortege and the public festival; love for music, too, especially the wonder and curiosity over a new instrument, and the love of sweet odors; again, the picture of the social group—the daughter of a high chief, mistress of a group of young virgins, in a house apart which is forbidden to men, and attended by an old woman and a humpbacked servant; the chief's establishment with its soothsayers, paddlers, soldiers, executioner, chief counselor, and the group of under chiefs fed at his table; the ceremonial wailing at his reception, the *awa* drink passed about at the feast, the taboo signs, feather cloak, and wedding paraphernalia, the power over life and death, and the choice among virgins. Then, on the other hand, the wonder and delight of the common people, their curious spying into the chief's affairs, the treacherous paddlers, the different orders of landowners; in the temple, the human sacrifices, prayers, visions; the prophet's search for a patron, his wrestling with the god, his affection for his chief, his desire to be remembered to posterity by the saying "the daughters of Hulumaniani"—all these incidents reflect the course of everyday life in aristocratic Polynesian society and hence belong to the common stock of Hawaiian romance.

Such being the material of Polynesian romance—a world in which gods and men play their part; a world which includes the heavens yet reflects naturalistically the beliefs and customs of everyday life, let us next consider how the style of the story-teller has been shaped by his manner of observing nature and by the social requirements which determine his art—by the world of nature and the world of man. And in the first place let us see under what social conditions Polynesia has gained for itself so high a place, on the whole, among primitive story-telling people for the richness, variety, and beauty of its conceptions.[29]

Polynesian romance reflects its own social world—a world based upon the fundamental conception of social rank. The family tie and the inherited rights and titles derived from it determine a man's place in the community. The families of chiefs claim these rights and titles

29. J.A. Macculloch (in Childhood of Fiction, p. 2) says, comparing the literary ability of primitive people: "Those who possess the most elaborate and imaginative tales are the Red Indians and Polynesians."

from the gods who are their ancestors.[30] They consist not only in land and property rights but in certain privileges in administering the affairs of a group, and in certain acknowledged forms of etiquette equivalent to the worship paid to a god. These rights are administered through a system of taboo.[31]

A taboo depends for its force upon the belief that it is divinely ordained and that to break it means to bring down the anger of the gods upon the offender. In the case, therefore, of a violation of taboo, the community forestalls the god's wrath, which might otherwise extend to the whole number, by visiting the punishment directly upon the guilty offender, his family or tribe. But it is always understood that back of the community disapproval is the unappeased challenge of the gods. In the case of the Polynesian taboo, the god himself is represented in the person of the chief, whose divine right none dare challenge and who may enforce obedience within his taboo right, under the penalty of death. The limits of this right are prescribed by grade. Before some chiefs the bystander must prostrate himself, others are too sacred to be touched. So, when a chief dedicates a part of his body to the deity, for an inferior it is taboo; any act of sacrilege will throw the chief into a fury of passion. In the same way tabooed food or property of any kind is held sacred and can not be touched by the inferior. To break a taboo is to challenge a contest of strength—that is, to declare war.

As the basis of the taboo right lay in descent from the gods, lineage was of first importance in the social world. Not that rank was independent of ability—a chief must exhibit capacity who would claim possession of the divine inheritance;[32] he must keep up rigorously the

---

30. Moerenhout, II, 4, 265.

31. Gracia (p. 47) says that the taboo consists in the interdict from touching some food or object which, has been dedicated to a god. The chief by his divine descent represents the god. Compare Ellis, IV, 385; Mariner, II, 82, 173; Turner, Samoa, pp. 112, 185; Fison, pp. 1–3; Malo, p. 83; Dibble, p. 12; Moerenhout, I, 528–533. Fornander says of conditions in Hawaii: "The chiefs in the genealogy from Kane were called *Ka Hoalii* or 'anointed' (*poni ia*) with the water of Kane (*wai-niu-a-Kane*) and they became 'divine tabu chiefs' (*na lii kapu-akua*). Their genealogy is called *Iku-pau*, because it alone leads up to the beginning of all genealogies. They had two taboo rights, the ordinary taboo of the chiefs (*Kapu-alii*) and the taboo of the gods (*Kapu-akua*). The genealogy of the lower ranks of chiefs (*he lii noa*), on the other hand, was called *Iku-nuu*. Their power was temporal and they accordingly were entitled only to the ordinary taboo of chiefs (*Kapu-alii*)."

32. Compare Krämer, Samoa Inseln, p. 31; Stair, p. 75; Turner, Samoa, p. 173; White, II, 62, and the Fornander stories of *Aukele* and of *Kila*, where capacity, not precedence of birth, determines the hero's rank.

fitting etiquette or be degraded in rank. Yet even a successful warrior, to insure his family title, sought a wife from a superior rank. For this reason women held a comparatively important position in the social framework, and this place is reflected in the folk tales.[33] Many Polynesian romances are, like the *Laieikawai*, centered about the heroine of the tale. The mother, when she is of higher rank, or the maternal relatives, often protect the child. The virginity of a girl of high rank is guarded, as in the *Laieikawai*, in order to insure a suitable union.[34] Rank, also, is authority for inbreeding, the highest possible honor being paid to the child of a brother and sister of the highest chief class. Only a degree lower is the offspring of two generations, father and daughter, mother and son, uncle and niece, aunt and nephew being highly honorable alliances.[35]

Two things result as a consequence of the taboo right in the hands of a chief. In the first place, the effort is constantly to keep before his following the exclusive position of the chief and to emphasize in every possible way his divine character as descended from a god. Such is the meaning of the insignia of rank—in Hawaii, the taboo staff which warns men of his neighborhood, the royal feather cloak, the high seat apart in the double canoe, the head of the feast, the special apparel of his followers, the size of his house and of his war canoe, the superior workmanship and decoration of all his equipment, since none but the chief can command the labor for their execution. In the second place, this very effort to aggrandize him above his fellows puts every

---

33. In certain groups inheritance descends on the mother's side only. See Krämer, op. cit., pp. 15, 39; Mariner, II, 89, 98. Compare Mariner, II, 210–212; Stair, p. 222. In Fison (p. 65) the story of *Longapoa*, shows what a husband of lower rank may endure from a termagant wife of high rank.

34. Krämer (p. 32 et seq.) tells us that in Samoa the daughter of a high chief is brought up with extreme care that she may be given virgin to her husband. She is called *taupo*, "dove," and, when she comes of age, passes her time with the other girls of her own age in the *fale aualuma* or "house of the virgins," of whom she assumes the leadership. Into this house, where the girls also sleep at night, no youth dare enter.

Compare Fornander's stories of *Kapuaokaoheloai* and *Hinaaikamalama*.

See also Stair, p. 110; Mariner, II, 142, 212; Fison, p. 33.

According to Gracia (p. 62) candidates in the Marquesas for the priesthood are strictly bound to a taboo of chastity.

35. Rivers, I, 374; Malo, p. 80.

Gracia (p. 41) says that the Marquesan genealogy consists in a long line of gods and goddesses married and representing a genealogy of chiefs. To the thirtieth generation they are brothers and sisters. After this point the relation is no longer observed.

material advantage in the hands of the chief. The taboo means that he can command, at the community expense, the best of the food supply, the most splendid ornaments, equipment, and clothing. He is further able, again at the community expense, to keep dependent upon himself, because fed at his table, a large following, all held in duty bound to carry out his will. Even the land was, in Hawaii and other Polynesian communities, under the control of the chief, to be redistributed whenever a new chief came into power. The taboo system thus became the means for economic distribution, for the control of the relation between the sexes, and for the preservation of the dignity of the chief class. As such it constituted as powerful an instrument for the control of the labor and wealth of a community and the consequent enjoyment of personal ease and luxury as was ever put into the hands of an organized upper class. It profoundly influenced class distinctions, encouraged exclusiveness and the separation of the upper ranks of society from the lower.[36]

To act as intermediary with his powerful line of ancestors and perform all the ceremonials befitting the rank to which he has attained, the chief employs a priesthood, whose orders and offices are also graded according to the rank into which the priest is born and the patronage

---

36. Keaulumoku's description of a Hawaiian chief (Islander, 1875) gives a good idea of the distinction felt between the classes:

> *"A well-supplied dish is the wooden dish,*
> *The high-raftered sleeping-house with shelves;*
> *The long eating-house for women.*
> *The rushes are spread down, upon them is spread the mat,*
> *They lie on their backs, with heads raised in dignity,*
> *The fly brushers wave to and fro at the door; the door is shut,*
> *the black* tapa *is drawn up.*

> *"Haste, hide a little in refreshing sleep, dismiss fatigue.*
> *They sleep by day in the silence where noise is forbidden.*
> *If they sleep two and two, double is their sleep;*
> *Enjoyable is the fare of the large-handed man.*
> *In parrying the spear the chief is vigorous;*
> *the breaking of points is sweet.*
> *Delightful is the season of fish, the season of food;*
> *when one is filled with fish, when one is filled with food.*
> *Thou art satisfied with food, O thou common man,*
> *To be satisfied with land is for the chief."*

Compare the account of the Fiji chief in Williams and Calvert, I, 33–42.

he is able to secure for himself.[37] Even though the priest may be, when inspired by his god, for the time being treated like a god and given divine honors, as soon as the possession leaves him he returns to his old rank in the community.[38] Since chief and priest base their pretensions upon the same divine authority, each supports the other, often the one office including the other;[39] the sacerdotal influence is, therefore, while it acts as a check upon the chief, on the whole aristocratic.

The priest represented in Polynesian society what we may call the professional class in our own. Besides conducting religious ceremonials, he consulted the gods on matters of administration and state policy, read the omens, understood medicine, guarded the genealogies and the ancient lore, often acted as panegyrist and debater for the chief. All these powers were his in so far as he was directly inspired by the god who spoke through him as medium to the people.[40]

---

37. Stair, p. 220; Gracia, p. 59; Alexander, History, chap. IV; Malo, p. 210. The name used for the priesthood of Hawaii, *kahuna*, is the same as that applied in the Marquesas, according to Gracia (p. 60), to the order of chanters.
38. Gracia, p. 46; Mariner, II, 87, 101, 125; Gill, Myths and Songs, pp. 20, 21; Moerenhout, I, 474–482.
39. Malo, p. 69.
40. Ellis (III, 36) describes the art of medicine in Polynesia, and Erdland (p. 77) says that on the Marshall Islands knowledge of the stars and weather signs is handed down to a favorite child and can raise rank by attaching a man to the service of a chief.

Compare Mariner, II, 90; Moerenhout, I, 409; Williams and Calvert, I, 111.

III

THE ART OF COMPOSITION

1. Aristocratic Nature of Polynesian Art

THE ARTS OF SONG AND oratory, though practiced by all classes,[1] were considered worthy to be perfected among the chiefs themselves and those who sought their patronage. Of a chief the Polynesian says, "He speaks well."[2] Hawaiian stories tell of heroes famous in the *hoopapa*, or art of debating; in the *hula*, or art of dance and song; of chiefs who learned the lore of the heavens and the earth from some supernatural master in order to employ their skill competitively. The *oihana haku-mele*, or "business of song making," was hence an aristocratic art. The able composer, man or woman, even if of low rank, was sure of patronage as the *haku mele*, "sorter of songs," for some chief; and his name was attached to the song he composed. A single poet working alone might produce the panegyric; but for the longer and more important songs of occasion a group got together, the theme was proposed and either submitted to a single composer or required line by line from each member of the group. In this way each line as it was composed was offered for criticism lest any ominous allusion creep in to mar the whole by bringing disaster upon the person celebrated, and as it was perfected it was committed to memory by the entire group, thus insuring it against loss. Protective criticism, therefore, and exact transmission were secured by group composition.[3]

---

1. Jarves says: "Songs and chants were common among all classes, and recited by strolling musicians as panegyrics on occasions of joy, grief, or worship. Through them the knowledge of events in the lives of prominent persons or the annals of the nation were perpetuated. The chief art lay in the formation of short metrical sentences without much regard to the rhythmical terminations. Monosyllables, dissyllables, and trisyllables had each their distinct time. The natives repeat their lessons, orders received, or scraps of ancient song, or extemporize in this monotonous singsong tone for hours together, and in perfect accord."

Compare Ellis's Tour, p. 155.

2. Moerenhout, I, 411.

3. Andrews, Islander, 1875, p. 35; Emerson, Unwritten Literature, pp. 27, 38.

Exactness of reproduction was in fact regarded as a proof of divine inspiration. When the chief's sons were trained to recite the genealogical chants, those who were incapable were believed to lack a share in the divine inheritance; they were literally "less gifted" than their brothers.[4]

This distinction accorded to the arts of song and eloquence is due to their actual social value. The *mele*, or formal poetic chants which record the deeds of heroic ancestors, are of aristocratic origin and belong to the social assets of the family to which they pertain. The claim of an heir to rank depends upon his power to reproduce, letter perfect, his family chants and his "name song," composed to celebrate his birth, and hence exact transmission is a matter of extreme importance. Facility in debate is not only a competitive art, with high stakes attached, but is employed in time of war to shame an enemy,[5] quickness of retort being believed, like quickness of hand, to be a God-given power. Chants in memory of the dead are demanded of each relative at the burial ceremony.[6] Song may be used to disgrace an enemy, to avenge an insult, to predict defeat at arms. It may also be turned to more pleasing purposes—to win back an estranged patron or lover;[7] in the art of love, indeed, song is invaluable to a chief. Ability in learning and language is, therefore, a highly prized chiefly art, respected for its social value and employed to aggrandize rank. How this aristocratic patronage has affected the language of composition will be presently clear.

2. Nomenclature: Its Emotional Value

THE HAWAIIAN (OR POLYNESIAN) COMPOSER who would become a successful competitor in the fields of poetry, oratory, or disputation must store up in his memory the rather long series of names for persons, places, objects, or phases of nature which constitute the learning of the aspirant for mastery in the art of expression. He is taught, says one tale, "about everything in the earth and in the heavens"—that is, their names, their distinguishing characterstics. The classes of objects

---

4. In Fornander's story of *Lonoikamakahiki*, the chief memorizes in a single night a new chant just imported from Kauai so accurately as to establish his property right to the song.
5. Compare with Ellis, I, 286, and Williams and Calvert, I, 46, 50, the notes on the boxing contest in the text of *Laieikawai*.
6. Gill, Myths and Songs, pp. 268 et seq.
7. See Fornander's stories of *Lonoikamakahiki*, *Halemano*, and *Kuapakaa*.

thus differentiated naturally are determined by the emotional interest attached to them, and this depends upon their social or economic value to the group.

The social value of pedigree and property have encouraged genealogical and geographical enumeration. A long recitation of the genealogies of chiefs provides immense emotional satisfaction and seems in no way to overtax the reciter's memory. Missionaries tell us that "the Hawaiians will commit to memory the genealogical tables given in the Bible, and delight to repeat them as some of the choicest passages in Scripture." Examples of such genealogies are common; it is, in fact, the part of the reciter to preserve the pedigree of his chief in a formal genealogical chant.

Such a series is illustrated in the genealogy embedded in the famous song to aggrandize the family of the famous chief Kualii, which carries back the chiefly line of Hawaii through 26 generations to Wakea and Papa, ancestors of the race.

> *"Hulihonua the man,*
> *Keakahulilani the woman,*
> *Laka the man, Kepapaialeka the woman,"*

runs the song, the slight variations evidently fitting the sound to the movement of the recitative.

In the eleventh section of the "Song of Creation" the poet says:

> *She that lived up in the heavens and Piolani,*
> *She that was full of enjoyments and lived in the heavens,*
> *Lived up there with Kii and became his wife,*
> *Brought increase to the world;*

and he proceeds to the enumeration of her "increase":

> *Kamahaina was born a man,*
> *Kamamule his brother,*
> *Kamaainau was born next,*
> *Kamakulua was born, the youngest a woman.*

Following this family group come a long series, more than 650 pairs of so-called husbands and wives. After the first 400 or so, the enumeration proceeds by variations upon a single name. We have first some 50 *Kupo* (dark nights)—"of wandering," "of wrestling," "of littleness," etc.; 60 or more *Polo*; 50 *Liili*; at least 60 *Alii* (chiefs); followed by *Mua* and *Loi* in about the same proportion.

At the end of this series we read that—

> *Storm was born, Tide was born,*
> *Crash was born, and also bursts of bubbles.*
> *Confusion was born, also rushing, rumbling shaking earth.*

So closes the "second night of Wakea," which, it is interesting to note, ends like a charade in the death of Kupololiilialiimualoipo, whose nomenclature has been so vastly accumulating through the 200 or 300 last lines. Notice how the first word *Kupo* of the series opens and swallows all the other five.

Such recitative and, as it were, symbolic use of genealogical chants occurs over and over again. That the series is often of emotional rather than of historical value is suggested by the wordplays and by the fact that the hero tales do not show what is so characteristic of Icelandic saga—a care to record the ancestry of each character as it is introduced into the story. To be sure, they commonly begin with the names of the father and mother of the hero, and their setting; but in the older mythological tales these are almost invariably *Ku* and *Hina*, a convention almost equivalent to the phrase "In the olden time"; but, besides fixing the divine ancestry of the hero, carrying also with it an idea of kinship with those to whom the tale is related, which is not without its emotional value.

Geographical names, although not enumerated to such an extent in any of the tales and songs now accessible, also have an important place in Hawaiian composition. In the *Laieikawai* 76 places are mentioned by name, most of them for the mere purpose of identifying a route of travel. A popular form of folk tale is the following, told in Waianae, Oahu: "Over in Kahuku lived a high chief, Kaho'alii. He instructed his son 'Fly about Oahu while I chew the *awa*; before I have emptied it into the cup return to me and rehearse to me all that you have seen.'" The rest of the tale relates the youth's enumeration of the places he has seen on the way.

If we turn to the chants the suggestive use of place names becomes still more apparent. Dr. Hyde tells us (*Hawaiian Annual*, 1890, p. 79):

"In the Hawaiian chant (*mele*) and dirge (*kanikau*) the aim seems to be chiefly to enumerate every place associated with the subject, and to give that place some special epithet, either attached to it by commonplace repetition or especially devised for the occasion as being particularly characteristic." An example of this form of reference is to be found in the *Kualii* chant. We read:

> *Where is the battle-field*
> *Where the warrior is to fight?*
> *On the field of Kalena,*
> *At Manini, at Hanini,*
> *Where was poured the water of the god,*
> *By your work at Malamanui,*
> *At the heights of Kapapa, at Paupauwela,*
> *Where they lean and rest.*

In the play upon the words *Manini* and *Hanini* we recognize some rhetorical tinkering, but in general the purpose here is to enumerate the actual places famous in Kualii's history.

At other times a place-name is used with allusive interest, the suggested incident being meant, like certain stories alluded to in the Anglo-Saxon "Beowulf," to set off, by comparison or contrast, the present situation. It is important for the poet to know, for example, that the phrase "flowers of Paiahaa" refers to the place on Kau, Hawaii, where love-tokens cast into the sea at a point some 20 or 30 miles distant on the Puna coast, invariably find their way to shore in the current and bring their message to watchful lovers.

A third use of localization conforms exactly to our own sense of description. The Island of Kauai is sometimes visible lying off to the northwest of Oahu. At this side of the island rises the Waianae range topped by the peak Kaala. In old times the port of entry for travelers to Oahu from Kauai was the seacoast village of Waianae. Between it and the village of Waialua runs a great spur of the range, which breaks off abruptly at the sea, into the point Kaena. Kahuku point lies beyond Waialua at the northern extremity of the island. Mokuleia, with its old inland fishpond, is the first village to the west of Waialua. This is the setting for the following lines, again taken from the chant of *Kualii*, the translation varying only slightly from that edited by Thrum:

O Kauai,
Great Kauai, inherited from ancestors,
Sitting in the calm of Waianae,
A cape is Kaena,
Beyond, Kahuku,
A misty mountain back, where the winds meet, Kaala,
There below sits Waialua,
Waialua there,
Kahala is a dish for Mokuleia,
A fishpond for the shark roasted in ti-leaf,
The tail of the shark is Kaena,
The shark that goes along below Kauai,
Below Kauai, thy land,
Kauai O!

The number of such place names to be stored in the reciter's memory is considerable. Not only are they applied in lavish profusion to beach, rock, headland, brook, spring, cave, waterfall, even to an isolated tree of historic interest, and distributed to less clearly marked small land areas to name individual holdings, but, because of the importance of the weather in the fishing and seagoing life of the islander, they are affixed to the winds, the rains, and the surf or "sea" of each locality. All these descriptive appellations the composer must employ to enrich his means of place allusion. Even to-day the Hawaiian editor with a nice sense of emotional values will not, in his obituary notice, speak of a man being missed in his native district, but will express the idea in some such way as this: "Never more will the pleasant *Kupuupuu* (mist-bearing wind) dampen his brow." The songs of the pleading sisters in the romance of *Laieikawai* illustrate this conventional usage. In *Kualii*, the poet wishes to express the idea that all the sea belongs to the god Ku. He therefore enumerates the different kinds of "sea," with their locality—"the sea for surf riding," "the sea for casting the net," "the sea for going naked," "the sea for swimming," "the sea for surf riding sideways," "the sea for tossing up mullet," "the sea for small crabs," "the sea of many harbors," etc.

The most complete example of this kind of enumeration occurs in the chant of Kuapakaa, where the son of the disgraced chief chants to his lord the names of the winds and rains of all the districts about each island in succession, and then, by means of his grandmother's bones in a calabash in the bottom of the canoe (she is the Hawaiian wind-goddess) raises a storm and avenges his father's honor. He sings:

> *There they are! There they are!!*
> *There they are!!!*
> *The hard wind of Kohala,*
> *The short sharp wind of Kawaihae,*
> *The fine mist of Waimea,*
> *The wind playing in the cocoanut-leaves of Kekaha,*
> *The soft wind of Kiholo,*
> *The calm of Kona,*
> *The ghost-like wind of Kahaluu,*
> *The wind in the hala-tree of Kaawaloa,*
> *The moist wind of Kapalilua,*
> *The whirlwind of Kau,*
> *The mischievous wind of Hoolapa,*
> *The dust-driven wind of Maalehu,*
> *The smoke-laden wind of Kalauea.*

There is no doubt in this enumeration an assertion of power over the forces the reciter calls by name, as a descendant of her who has transmitted to him the magic formula.

Just so the technician in fishing gear, bark-cloth making, or in canoe or house building, the two crafts specially practiced by chiefs, acquires a very minute nomenclature useful to the reciter in word debate or riddling. The classic example in Hawaiian song is the famous canoe-chant, which, in the legend of *Kana*, Uli uses in preparing the canoe for her grandsons' war expedition against the ravisher of Hina (called the Polynesian Helen of Troy) and which is said to be still employed for exorcism by sorcerers (*Kahuna*), of whom Uli is the patron divinity. The enumeration begins thus:

> *It is the double canoe of Kaumaielieli,*
> *Keakamilo the outrigger,*
> *Halauloa the body,*
> *Luu the part under water,*
> *Aukuuikalani the bow;*

and so on to the names of the cross stick, the lashings, the sails, the bailing cup, the rowers in order, and the seat of each, his paddle, and

S. N. HALE'OLE

his "seagoing loin cloth." There is no wordplay perceptible in this chant, but it is doubtful whether the object is to record a historical occurrence or rather to exhibit inspired craftsmanship, the process of enumeration serving as the intellectual test of an inherited gift from the gods.

Besides technical interests, the social and economic life of the people centers close attention upon the plant and animal life about them, as well as upon kinds of stone useful for working. Andrews enumerates 26 varieties of edible seaweed known to the Hawaiians. The reciters avail themselves of these well-known terms, sometimes for quick comparison, often for mere enumeration. It is interesting to see how, in the "Song of Creation," in listing plant and animal life according to its supposed order of birth—first, shellfish, then seaweed and grasses, then fishes and forests plants, then insects, birds, reptiles—wordplay is employed in carrying on the enumeration. We read:

> *"The Mano (shark) was born, the Moana was born*
> *in the sea and swam,*
> *The Mau was born, the Maumau was born in the sea and swam,*
> *The Nana was born, the Mana was born in the sea and swam."*

and so on through Nake and Make, Napa and Nala, Pala and Kala, Paka (eel) and Papa (crab) and twenty-five or thirty other pairs whose signification is in most cases lost if indeed they are not entirely fictitious. Again, 16 fish names are paired with similar names of forest plants; for example:

> *"The Pahau was born in the sea,*
> *Guarded by the Lauhau that grew in the forest."*

> *"The Hee was born and lived in the sea,*
> *Guarded by the Walahee that grew in the forest."*

Here the relation between the two objects is evidently fixed by the chance likeness of name.

On the whole, the Hawaiian takes little interest in stars. The "canoe-steering star," to be sure, is useful, and the "net of Makalii" (the Pleiads) belongs to a well-known folk tale. But star stories do not appear in Hawaiian collections, and even sun and moon stories are rare, all belonging to the older and more mythical tales. Clouds, however, are very minutely observed, both as weather indicators and in the lore of signs, and appear often in song and story.[8]

Besides differentiating such visible phenomena, the Polynesian also thinks in parts of less readily distinguishable wholes. When we look toward the zenith or toward the horizon we conceive the distance as a whole; the Polynesian divides and names the space much as we divide our globe into zones. We have seen how he conceives a series of heavens above the earth, order in creation, rank in the divisions of men on earth and of gods in heaven. In the passage of time he records how the sun measures the changes from day to night; how the moon marks off the month; how the weather changes determine the seasons for planting and fishing through the year; and, observing the progress of human life

---

8. In the Hawaiian Annual, 1890, Alexander translates some notes printed by Kamakau in 1865 upon Hawaiian astronomy as related to the art of navigation. The bottom of a gourd represented the heavens, upon which were marked three lines to show the northern and southern limits of the sun's path, and the equator—called the "black shining road of Kane" and "of Kanaloa," respectively, and the "road of the spider" or "road to the navel of Wakea" (ancestor of the race). A line was drawn from the north star to Newe in the south; to the right was the "bright road of Kane," to the left the "much traveled road of Kanaloa." Within these lines were marked the positions of all the known stars, of which Kamakau names 14, besides 5 planets. For notes upon Polynesian astronomy consult Journal of the Polynesian Society, iv, 236. Hawaiian priestly hierarchies recognize special orders whose function it is to read the signs in the clouds, in dreams, or the flight of birds, or to practice some form of divination with the entrails of animals. In Hawaii, according to Fornander, the soothsayers constitute three of the ten large orders of priests, called Oneoneihonua, Kilokilo, and Nanauli, and these are subdivided into lesser orders. *Ike*, knowledge, means literally "to see with, the eyes," but it is used also to express mental vision, or knowledge with reference to the objective means by which such knowledge is obtained. So the "gourd of wisdom"—*ka ipu o ka ike*—which Laieikawai consults, brings distant objects before the eyes so that the woman "knows by seeing" what is going on below. Signs in the clouds are especially observed, both as weather indicators and to forecast the doings of chiefs. According to Westervelt's story of *Keaomelemele*, the lore is taught to mythical ancestors of the Hawaiian race by the gods themselves. The best analysis of South Sea Island weather signs is to be found in Erdland's "Marshall Insulaner," page 69. Early in the morning or in the evening is the time for making observations. Rainbows, *punohu*—doubtfully explained to me as mists touched by the end of a rainbow—and the long clouds which lie along the horizon, forecast the doings of chiefs. A pretty instance of the rainbow sign occurred in the recent history of Hawaii. When word reached Honolulu of the death of King Kalakaua, the throng pressed to the palace to greet their new monarch, and as Her Majesty Liliuokalani appeared upon the balcony to receive them, a rainbow arched across the palace and was instantly recognized as a symbol of her royal rank. In the present story the use of the rainbow symbol shows clumsy workmanship, since near its close the Sun god is represented as sending to his bride as her peculiar distinguishing mark the same sign, a rainbow, which has been hers from birth.

S. N. HALE'OLE

from infancy to old age, he names each stage until "the staff rings as you walk, the eyes are dim like a rat's, they pull you along on the mat," or "they bear you in a bag on the back."

Clearly the interest aroused by all this nomenclature is emotional, not rational. There is too much wordplay. Utility certainly plays some part, but the prevailing stimulus is that which bears directly upon the idea of rank, some divine privilege being conceived in the mere act of naming, by which a supernatural power is gained over the object named. The names, as the objects for which they stand, come from the gods. Thus in the story of *Pupuhuluena*, the culture hero propitiates two fishermen into revealing the names of their food plants and later, by reciting these correctly, tricks the spirits into conceding his right to their possession. Thus he wins tuberous food plants for his people.

For this reason, exactness of knowledge is essential. The god is irritated by mistakes.[9] To mispronounce even casually the name of the remote relative of a chief might cost a man a valuable patron or even life itself. Some chiefs are so sacred that their names are taboo; if it is a word in common use, there is chance of that word dropping out of the language and being replaced by another.

Completeness of enumeration hence has cabalistic value. When the Hawaiian propitiates his gods he concludes with an invocation to the "forty thousand, to the four hundred thousand, to the four thousand"[10] gods, in order that none escape the incantation. Direction is similarly invoked all around the compass. In the art of verbal debate—called

---

9. Moerenhout (I, 501–507) says that the Areois society in Tahiti, one of whose chief objects was "to preserve the chants and songs of antiquity," sent out an officer called the "Night-walker," *Hare-po*, whose duty it was to recite the chants all night long at the sacred places. If he hesitated a moment it was a bad omen. "Perfect memory for these chants was a gift of god and proved that a god spoke through and inspired the reciter." If a single slip was made, the whole was considered useless.

Erdland relates that a Marshall Islander who died in 1906 remembered correctly the names of officers and scholars who came to the islands in the Chamisso party when he was a boy of 8 or 10.

Fornander notes that, in collecting Hawaiian chants, of the *Kualii* dating from about the seventeenth century and containing 618 lines, one copy collected on Hawaii, another on Oahu, did not vary in a single line; of the *Hauikalani*, written just before Kamehameha's time and containing 527 lines, a copy from Hawaii and one from Maui differed only in the omission of a single word.

Tripping and stammering games were, besides, practiced to insure exact articulation. (See Turner, Samoa, p. 131; Thomson, pp. 16, 315.)

10. Emerson, Unwritten Literature, p. 24 (note).

hoopapa in Hawaii—the test is to match a rival's series with one exactly parallel in every particular or to add to a whole some undiscovered part.[11]

---

11. This is well illustrated in Fornander's story of Kaipalaoa's disputation with the orators who gathered about Kalanialiiloa on Kauai. Say the men:

> *"Kuu moku la e kuu moku,*
> *Moku kele i ka waa o Kaula,*
> *Moku kele i ka waa, Nihoa,*
> *Moku kele i ka waa, Niihau.*
> *Lehua, Kauai, Molokai, Oahu,*
> *Maui, Lanai, Kahoolawe,*
> *Moloklni, Kauiki, Mokuhano,*
> *Makaukiu, Makapu, Mokolii."*

> *My island there, my island;*
> *Island to which my canoe sails, Kaula,*
> *Island to which my canoe sails, Nihoa,*
> *Island to which my canoe sails, Niihau.*
> *Lehua, Kauai, Molokai, Oahu,*
> *Maui, Lanai, Kahoolawe,*
> *Molokini, Kauiki, Mokuhano,*
> *Makaukiu, Makapu, Mokolii.*

"You are beaten, young man; there are no islands left. We have taken up the islands to be found, none left."

Says the boy:

> *"Kuu moku e, kuu moku,*
> *O Mokuola, ulu ka ai,*
> *Ulu ka niu, ulu ka laau,*
> *Ku ka hale, holo ua holoholona."*

> *Here is my island, my island*
> Mokuola, *where grows food,*
> *The cocoanut grows, trees grow,*
> *Houses stand, animals run.*

"There is an island for you. It is an island. It is in the sea."
(This is a small island off Hilo, Hawaii.)
The men try again:

> *"He aina hau kinikini o Kohala,*
> *Na'u i helu a hookahi hau,*
> *I e hiku hau keu.*
> *O ke ama hau la akahi,*
> *O ka iaku hau la alua,*
> *O ka ilihau la akolu,*
> *O ka laau hau la aha,*
> *O ke opu hau la alima,*

S. N. HALE'OLE

A charm mentioned in folk tale is "to name every word that ends with *lau*." Certain numbers, too, have a kind of magic finality in themselves;

O ka nanuna hau la aone,
O ka hau i ka mauna la ahiku."

A land of many hau *trees is Kohala*
Out of a single hau *tree I have counted out*
And found seven hau.
The hau *for the outriggers makes one,*
The hau *for the joining piece makes two,*
The hau *bark makes three,*
The hau *wood makes four,*
The hau *bush makes five,*
The large hau *tree makes six,*
The mountain hau *makes seven.*

"Say, young man, you will have no *hau*, for we have used it all. There is none left. If you find any more, you shall live, but if you fail you shall surely die. We will twist your nose till you see the sun at Kumukena. We will poke your eyes with the *Kahili* handle, and when the water runs out, our little god of disputation shall suck it up—the god Kaneulupo."

Says the boy, "You full-grown men have found so many uses, you whose teeth are rotten with age, why can't I, a lad, find other uses, to save myself so that I may live. I shall search for some more hau, and if I fail you shall live, but if I find them you shall surely die."

"Aina hau kinikini o Kona,
Na'u i helu hookahi hau,
A ehiku hau keu.
O Honolohau la akahi,
O Lanihau la alua
O Punohau la akolu,
O Kahauloa la aha,
O Auhaukea la alima,
O Kahauiki la aono,
Holo kehau i ka waa kona la ahiku."

A land of many hau *trees is in* Kona
Out of a single hau *I have counted one,*
And found seven hau.
Honolahau makes one,
Lanihau makes two,
Punohau makes three,
Kahauloa makes four,
Auhaukea makes five,
Kahaniki makes six,
The Kehau that drives the canoe at Kona makes seven.

(All names of places in the Kona district.)
"There are seven *hau*, you men with rotten teeth."

for example, to count off an identical phrase by ten without missing a word is the charm by which Lepe tricks the spirits. In the *Kualii*, once more, Ku is extolled as the tenth chief and warrior:

> *The first chief, the second chief,*
> *The third chief, the fourth chief,*
> *The fifth chief, the sixth chief,*
> *The seventh chief, the eighth chief,*
> *The ninth, chief, the tenth chief is Ku,*
> *Ku who stood, in the path of the rain of the heaven,*
> *The first warrior, the second warrior,*
> *The third warrior, the fourth warrior,*
> *The fifth warrior, the sixth warrior,*
> *The seventh warrior, the eighth warrior,*
> *The ninth warrior, the tenth warrior*
> *Is the Chief who makes the King rub his eyes,*
> *The young warrior of all Maui.*

And there follows an enumeration of the other nine warriors. A similar use is made of counting-out lines in the famous chant of the "Mirage of Mana" in the story of *Lono*, evidently with the idea of completing an inclusive series.

Counting-out formulae reappear in story-telling in such repetitive series of incidents as those following the action of the five sisters of the unsuccessful wooer in the *Laieikawai* story. Here the interest develops, as in the lines from *Kualii*, an added emotional element, that of climax. The last place is given to the important character. Although everyone is aware that the younger sister is the most competent member of the group, the audience must not be deprived of the pleasure of seeing each one try and fail in turn before the youngest makes the attempt. The story-teller, moreover, varies the incident; he does not exactly follow his formula, which, however, it is interesting to note, is more fixed in the evidently old dialogue part of the story than in the explanatory action.

Story-telling also exhibits how the vital connection felt to exist between a person or object and the name by which it is distinguished, which gives an emotional value to the mere act of naming, is extended further to include scenes with which it is associated. The Hawaiian has a strong place sense, visible in his devotion to scenes familiar to his experience, and this is reflected in his language. In the *Laieikawai* it appears in the plaints of the five sisters as they recall their native land. In the songs in the *Halemano* which the lover sings to win his lady and the chant in *Lonoikamakahiki* with which the disgraced favorite seeks to win back his lord, those places are recalled to mind in which the friends have met hardship together, in order, if possible, to evoke the same emotions of love and loyalty which were theirs under the circumstances described. Hawaiians of all classes, in mourning their dead, will recall vividly in a wailing chant the scenes with which their lost friend has been associated. I remember on a tramp in the hills above Honolulu coming upon the grass hut of a Hawaiian lately released from serving a term for manslaughter. The place commanded a fine view—the sweep of the blue sea, the sharp rugged lines of the coast, the emerald rice patches, the wide-mouthed valleys cutting the roots of the wooded hills. "It is lonely here?" we asked the man. "*Aole! maikai keia!*" ("No, the view is excellent") he answered.

The ascription of perfection of form to divine influence may explain the Polynesian's strong sense for beauty.[12] The Polynesian sees in nature the sign of the gods. In its lesser as in its more marvelous manifestations—thunder, lightning, tempest, the "red rain," the rainbow, enveloping mist, cloud shapes, sweet odors of plants, so rare in Hawaii, at least, or the notes of birds—he reads an augury of divine indwelling. The romances glow with delight in the startling effect of personal beauty upon the beholder—a beauty seldom described in detail save occasionally by similes from nature. In the *Laieikawai* the sight of the heroine's beauty creates such an ecstasy in the heart of a mere countryman that he leaves his business to run all about the island heralding his discovery. Dreaming of the beauty of Laieikawai, the young chief feels his heart glow with passion for this "red blossom of Puna" as the fiery volcano scorches the wind that fans across its bosom. A divine hero must select a bride of faultless beauty; the heroine chooses her lover for his physical perfections. Now we can hardly fail to see that in all these cases the delight is intensified by the belief that beauty is godlike and betrays divine rank in its possessor. Rank is tested by perfection of face and form. The recognition of beauty thus becomes regulated by express rules of symmetry and surface. Color, too, is admired according to its social value. Note the delight in red, constantly associated with the accouterments of chiefs.

---

12. Thomson says that the Fijians differ from the Polynesians in their indifference to beauty in nature.

3. Analogy: Its Pictorial Quality

A SECOND SIGNIFICANT TRAIT IN the treatment of objective life, swiftness of analogy, affects the Polynesian in two ways: the first is pictorial and plays upon a likeness between objects or describes an idea or mood in metaphorical terms; the second is a mere linguistic play upon words. Much nomenclature is merely a quick picturing which fastens attention upon the special feature that attracts attention; ideas are naturally reinforced by some simple analogy. I recall a curious imported flower with twisted inner tube which the natives call, with a characteristic touch of daring drollery, "the intestines of the clergyman." Spanish moss is named from a prominent figure of the foreign community "Judge Dole's beard." Some native girls, braiding fern wreaths, called my attention to the dark, graceful fronds which grow in the shade and are prized for such work. "These are the natives," they said; then pointing slyly to the coarse, light ferns burned in the sun they added, "these are the foreigners." After the closing exercises of a mission school in Hawaii one of the parents was called upon to make an address. He said: "As I listen to the songs and recitations I am like one who walks through the forest where the birds are singing. I do not understand the words, but the sound is sweet to the ear." The boys in a certain district school on Hawaii call the weekly head inspection "playing the ukulele" in allusion to the literal interpretation of the name for the native banjo. These homely illustrations, taken from the everyday life of the people, illustrate a habit of mind which, when applied for conscious emotional effect, results in much charm of formal expression. The habit of isolating the essential feature leads to such suggestive names as "Leaping water," "White mountain," "The gathering place of the clouds," for waterfall or peak; or to such personal appellations as that applied to a visiting foreigner who had temporarily lost his voice, "The one who never speaks"; or to such a description of a large settlement as "many footprints."[13] The graphic sense of analogy applies to a mountain such a name as "House of the sun"; to the prevailing rain of a certain district the appellation "The rain with a pack on its back," "Leaping whale" or "Ghostlike"; to a valley, "The leaky canoe"; to a canoe, "Eel sleeping in the water." A

---

13. Turner, Samoa, p. 220.

man who has no brother in a family is called "A single coconut," in allusion to a tree from which hangs a single fruit.[14]

This tendency is readily illustrated in the use of synonyms. *Oili* means "to twist, roll up;" it also means "to be weary, agitated, tossed about in mind." *Hoolala* means "to branch out," as the branches of a tree; it is also applied in sailing to the deflection from a course. *Kilohana* is the name given to the outside decorated piece of tapa in a skirt of five layers; it means generally, therefore, "the very best" in contrast to that which is inferior. *Kuapaa* means literally "to harden the back" with oppressive work; it is applied to a breadfruit parched on the tree or to a rock that shows itself above water. Lilolilo means "to spread out, expand as blossom from bud;" it also applies to an open-handed person. *Nee* may mean "to hitch along from one place to another," or "to change the mind." *Palele* means "separate, put somewhere else when there is no place vacant;" it also applies to stammering. These illustrations gathered almost at random may be indefinitely multiplied. I recall a clergyman in a small hamlet on Hawaii who wished to describe the character of the people of that place. Picking up a stone of very close grain of the kind used for pounding and called *alapaa*, literally, "close-grained stone," he explained that because the people of that section were "tight" (stingy) they were called *Kaweleau alapaa*. This ready imitativeness, often converted into caricature, enters into the minutest detail of life and is the clew to many a familiar proverb like that of the canoe on the coral reef quoted in the text.[15] The chants abound in such symbols. Man is "a long-legged fish" offered to the gods. Ignorance is the "night of the mind." The cloud hanging over Kaula is a bird which flies before the wind[16]—

The blackbird begged,
The bird of Kaula begged,
Floating up there above Waahila.

The coconut leaves are "the hair of the trees, their long locks." Kailua district is "a mat spread out narrow and gray."

---

14. Ibid.; Moerenhout, I, 407–410.
15. Turner, Samoa, pp. 216–221; Williams and Calvert, I, p. 110.
16. Williams and Calvert, I, 118.

The classic example of the use of such metaphor in Hawaiian song is the famous passage in the *Hauikalani* in which chiefs at war are compared with a cockfight, the favorite Hawaiian pastime[17] being realistically described in allusion to Keoua's wars on Hawaii:

> *Hawaii is a cockpit; the trained cocks fight on the ground.*
> *The chief fights—the dark-red cock awakes at night for battle;*
> *The youth fights valiantly—Loeau, son of Keoua.*
> *He whets his spurs, he pecks as if eating;*
> *He scratches in the arena—this Hilo—the sand of Waiolama.*

> * * * * *

> *He is a well-fed cock. The chief is complete,*
> *Warmed in the smokehouse till the dried feathers rattle,*
> *With changing colors, like many-colored paddles, like piles*
> *of polished Kahili.*
> *The feathers rise and fall at the striking of the spurs.*

Here the allusions to the red color and to eating suggest a chief. The feather brushes waved over a chief and the bright-red paddles of his war fleet are compared to the motion of a fighting cock's bright feathers, the analogy resting upon the fact that the color and the motion of rising and falling are common to all three.

This last passage indicates the precise charm of Polynesian metaphor. It lies in the singer's close observation of the exact and characteristic truth which suggests the likeness, an exactness necessary to carry the allusion with his audience, and which he sharpens incessantly from the concrete facts before him. Kuapakaa sings:

> *The rain in the winter comes slanting,*
> *Taking the breath away, pressing down the hair,*
> *Parting the hair in the middle.*

The chants are full of such precise descriptions, and they furnish the rich vocabulary of epithet employed in recalling a place, person, or object. Transferred to matters of feeling or emotion, they result

---

17. Moerenhout, II, 146.

in poetical comparisons of much charm. Sings Kuapakaa (Wise's translation):

> *The pointed clouds have become fixed in the heavens,*
> *The pointed clouds grow quiet like one in pain before childbirth,*
> *Ere it comes raining heavily, without ceasing.*
> *The umbilicus of the rain is in the heavens,*
> *The streams will yet be swollen by the rain.*

Hina's song of longing for her lost lover in *Laieikawai* should be compared with the lament of Laukiamanuikahiki when, abandoned by her lover, she sees the clouds drifting in the direction he has taken:

> *The sun is up, it is up;*
> *My love is ever up before me.*
> *It is causing me great sorrow, it is pricking me in the side,*
> *For love is a burden when one is in love,*
> *And falling tears are its due.*

How vividly the mind enters into this analogy is proved, by its swift identification with the likeness presented. Originally this identification was no doubt due to ideas of magic. In romance, life in the open—in the forests or on the sea—has taken possession of the imagination. In the myths heroes climb the heavens, dwelling half in the air; again they are amphibian like their great lizard ancestors. In the *Laieikawai*, as in so many stories, note how much of the action takes place on or in the sea—canoeing, swimming, or surfing. In less humanized tales the realization is much more fantastic. To the Polynesian, mind such figurative sayings as "swift as a bird" and "swim like a fish" mean a literal transformation, his sense of identity being yet plastic, capable of uniting itself with whatever shape catches the eye. When the poet Marvel says—

> *Casting the body's vest aside,*
> *My soul into the boughs does glide;*
> *There, like a bird, it sits and sings,*
> *Then whets and combs its silver wings,*
> *And, till prepared for longer flight,*
> *Waves in its plumes the various light—*

he is merely expressing a commonplace of primitive mental experience, transformation stories being of the essence of Polynesian as of much primitive speculation about the natural objects to which his eye is drawn with wonder and delight.

4. The Double Meaning; Plays on Words

ANALOGY IS THE BASIS OF many a double meaning. There is, in fact, no lyric song describing natural scenery that may not have beneath it some implied, often indelicate, allusion whose riddle it takes an adroit and practiced mind to unravel.

This riddling tendency of figurative verse seems to be due to the aristocratic patronage of composition, whose tendency was to exalt language above the comprehension of the common people, either by obscurity, through ellipsis and allusion, or by saying one thing and meaning another. A special chief's language was thus evolved, in which the speaker might couch his secret resolves and commands unsuspected by those who stood within earshot. Quick interpretation of such symbols was the test of chiefly rank and training. On the other hand, the wish to appear innocent led him to hide his meaning in a commonplace observation. Hence nature and the objects and actions of everyday life were the symbols employed. For the heightened language of poetry the same chiefly strain was cultivated— the allusion, metaphor, the double meaning became essential to its art; and in the song of certain periods a play on words by punning and word linking became highly artificial requirements.[18]

Illustrations of this art do not fall upon a foreign ear with the force which they have in the Polynesian, because much of the skill lies in tricks with words impossible to translate, and often the jest depends upon a custom or allusion with which the foreigner is unfamiliar. It is for this reason that such an art becomes of social value, because only the chief who keeps up with the fashion and the follower who hangs upon the words of his chief can translate the allusion and parry the thrust or satisfy the request. In a Samoan tale a wandering magician requests in one village "to go dove catching," and has the laugh on his simple host because he takes him at his word instead of bringing him a wife. In a

---

18. See Moerenhout, II, 210; Jarves, p. 34; Alexander in Andrews' Dict., p. xvi; Ellis, I, 288; Gracia, p. 65; Gill, Myths and Songs, p. 42.

Tongan story[19] the chief grows hungry while out on a canoe trip, and bids his servant, "Look for a banana stalk on the weather side of the boat." As this is the side of the women, the command meant "Kill a woman for me to eat." The woman designed for slaughter is in this case wise enough to catch his meaning and save herself and child by hiding under the canoe. In Fornander's story a usurper and his accomplice plan the moment for the death of their chief over a game of *konane*, the innocent words which seem to apply to the game being uttered by the conspirators with a more sinister meaning. The language of insults and opprobrium is particularly rich in such double meanings. The pig god, wishing to insult Pélé, who has refused his advances, sings of her, innocently enough to common ears, as a "woman pounding *noni*." Now, the *noni* is the plant from which red dye is extracted; the allusion therefore is to Pélé's red eyes, and the goddess promptly resents the implication.

It is to this chiefly art of riddling that we must ascribe the stories of riddling contests that are handed down in Polynesian tales. The best Hawaiian examples are perhaps found in Fornander's *Kepakailiula*. Here the hero wins supremacy over his host by securing the answer to two riddles— "The men that stand, the men that lie down, the men that are folded," and "Plaited all around, plaited to the bottom, leaving an opening." The answer is in both cases a house, for in the first riddle "the timbers stand, the batons lie down, the grass is folded under the cords"; in the second, the process of thatching is described in general terms. In the story of *Pikoiakaala*, on the other hand; the hero puzzles his contestants by riddling with the word "rat." This word riddling is further illustrated in the story of the debater, Kaipalaoa, already quoted. His opponents produce this song:

> *The small bird chirps; it shivers in the rain, in Puna,*
> *at Keaau, at Iwainalo,*

and challenge him to "find another *nalo*." Says the boy:

> *The crow caw caws; it shines in the rain. In* Kona, *at* Honalo,
> *it is hidden* (nalo).

Thus, by using *nalo* correctly in the song in two ways, he has overmatched his rivals.

---

19. Fison, p. 100.

In the elaborated *hula* songs, such as Emerson quotes, the art can be seen in full perfection. Dangerous as all such interpretation of native art must be for a foreigner, I venture in illustration, guided by Wise's translation, the analysis of one of the songs sung by Halemano to win back his lost lady love, the beauty of Puna. The circumstances are as follows: Halemano, a Kauai chief, has wedded a famous beauty of Puna, Hawaii, who has now deserted him for a royal lover. Meanwhile a Kohala princess who loves him seeks to become his mistress, and makes a festival at which she may enjoy his company. The estranged wife is present, and during the games he sings a series of songs to reproach her infidelity. One of them runs thus:

> *Ke kua ia mai la e ke kai ka hala o Puna.*
> *E halaoa ana me he kanaka la,*
> *Lulumi iho la i kai o Hilo-e.*
> *Hanuu ke kai i luna o Mokuola.*
> *Ua ola ae nei loko i ko aloha-e.*
> *He kokua ka inaina no ke kanaka.*
> *Hele kuewa au i ke alanui e!*
> *Pela, peia, pehea au e ke aloha?*
> *Auwe kuu wahine—a!*
> *Kuu hoa o ka ulu hapapa o Kalapana.*
> *O ka la hiki anuanu ma Kumukahi.*
> *Akahi ka mea aloha o ka wahine.*
> *Ke hele neiia wela kau manawa,*
> *A huihui kuu piko i ke aloha,*
> *Ne aie kuu kino no ia la-e.*
> *Hoi mai kaua he a'u koolau keia,*
> *Kuu wahine hoi e! Hoi mai.*
> *Hoi mai kaua e hoopumehana.*
> *Ka makamaka o ia aina makua ole.*

> *Hewn down by the sea are the pandanus trees of Puna.*
> *They are standing there like men,*
> *Like a multitude in the lowlands of Hilo.*
> *Step by step the sea rises above the Isle-of-life.*
> *So life revives once more within me, for love of you.*
> *A bracer to man is wrath.*
> *As I wandered friendless over the highways, alas!*
> *That way, this way, what of me, love?*

Alas, my wife—O!
My companion of the shallow planted breadfruit of Kalapana.
Of the sun rising cold at Kumukahi.
Above all else the love of a wife.
For my temples burn,
And my heart (literally "middle") is cold for your love,
And my body is under bonds to her (the princess of Kohala).
Come back to me, a wandering Au bird of Koolau,
My love, come back.
Come back and let us warm each other with love,
Beloved one in a friendless land (literally, "without parents").

Paraphrased, the song may mean:

The sea has encroached upon the shore of Puna and Hilo so that the *hala* trees stand out in the water; still they stand firm in spite of the flood. So love floods my heart, but I am braced by anger. Alas! my wife, have you forgotten the days when we dwelt in Kalapana and saw the sun rise beyond Cape Kumukahi? I burn and freeze for your love, yet my body is engaged to the princess of Kohala, by the rules of the game. Come back to me! I am from Kauai, in the north, and here in Puna I am a stranger and friendless.

The first figure alludes to the well-known fact that the sinking of the Puna coast has left the pandanus trunks standing out in the water, which formerly grew on dry land. The poetical meaning, however, depends first upon the similarity in sound between *Ke kua*, "to cut," which begins the parallel, and *He Kokua*, which is also used to mean cutting, but implies assisting, literally "bracing the back," and carries over the image to its analogue; and, second, upon the play upon the word ola, life: "The sea floods the isle of life—yes! Life survives in spite of sorrow," may be the meaning. In the latter part of the song the epithets *anuanu*, chilly, and *hapapa*, used of seed planted in shallow soil, may be chosen in allusion to the cold and shallow nature of her love for him.

The nature of Polynesian images must now be apparent. A close observer of nature, the vocabulary of epithet and image with which it has enriched the mind is, especially in proverb or figurative verse, made use of allusively to suggest the quality of emotion or to convey a sarcasm. The quick sense of analogy, coupled with a precise nomenclature, insures its suggestive value. So we find in the language of nature vivid, naturalistic accounts of everyday happenings in fantastic reshapings, realistically conceived and ascribed to the gods who rule natural phenomena; a figurative language of signs to be read as an implied analogy; allusive use of objects, names, places, to convey the associated incident, or the description of a scene to suggest the accompanying emotion; and a sense of delight in the striking or phenomenal in sound, perfume, or appearance, which is explained as the work of a god.

5. Constructive Elements of Style

FINALLY, TO THE INFLUENCE OF song, as to the dramatic requirements of oral delivery, are perhaps due the retention of certain constructive elements of style. No one can study the form of Hawaiian poetry without observing that parallelism is at the basis of its structure. The same swing gets into the prose style. Perhaps the necessity of memorizing also had its effect. A composition was planned for oral delivery and intended to please the ear; tone values were accordingly of great importance. The variation between narrative, recitative, and formal song; the frequent dialogue, sometimes strictly dramatic; the repetitive series in which the same act is attempted by a succession of actors, or the stages of an action are described in exactly the same form, or a repetition is planned in ascending scale; the singsong value of the antithesis;[20] the suspense gained by the

---

20. The following examples are taken from the Laieikawai, where antithesis is frequent:

"Four children were mine, four are dead."
"Masters inside and outside" (to express masters over everything).
"I have seen great and small, men and women; low chiefs, men and women; high chiefs."
"When you wish to go, go; if you wish to stay, this is Hana, stay here."
"As you would do to me, so shall I to you."
"I will not touch, you, you must not touch me."
"Until day becomes night and night day."
"If it seems good I will consent; if not, I will refuse."
"Camped at some distance from A's party and A's party from them."
"Sounds only by night, . . . never by day."
"Through us the consent, through us the refusal."
"You above, our wife below."
"Thunder pealed, this was Waka's work; thunder pealed, this was Malio's work."
"Do not look back, face ahead."
"Adversity to one is adversity to all;" "we will not forsake you, do not you forsake us."
"Not to windward, go to leeward."

ejaculation[21]—all these devices contribute values to the ear which help to catch and please the sense.

"Never... any destruction before like this; never will any come hereafter."
"Everyone has a god, none is without."
"There I stood, you were gone."
"I have nothing to complain of you, you have nothing to complain of me."
The balanced sentence structure is often handled with particular skill:
"If... a daughter, let her die; however many daughters... let them die."
"The penalty is death, death to himself, death to his wife, death to all his friends."
"Drive him away; if he should tell you his desire, force him away; if he is very persistent, force him still more."
"Again they went up... again the chief waited... the chief again sent a band."
"A crest arose; he finished his prayer to the amen; again a crest arose, the second this; not long after another wave swelled."
"If she has given H. a kiss, if she has defiled herself with him, then we lose the wife, then take me to my grave without pity. But if she has hearkened... then she is a wife for you, if my grandchild has hearkened to my command."

A series of synonyms is not uncommon, or the repetition of an idea in other words:

"Do not fear, have no dread."
"Linger not, delay not your going."
"Exert your strength, all your godlike might."
"Lawless one, mischief maker, rogue of the sea."
"Princess of broad Hawaii, Laieikawai, our mistress."
"House of detention, prison-house."
"Daughter, lord, preserver."

21. In the course of the story of *Laieikawai* occur more than 50 ejaculatory phrases, more than half of these in the narrative, not the dialogue, portion:

1. The most common is used to provide suspense for what is to follow and is printed without the point—*aia hoi*, literally, "then (or there) indeed," with the force of our lo! or behold!
2. Another less common form, native to the Hawaiian manner of thought, is the contradiction of a plausible conjecture—*aole ka!* "not so!". Both these forms occur in narrative or in dialogue. The four following are found in dialogue alone:
3. *Auhea oe?* "where are you?" is used to introduce a vigorous address.
4. *Auwe!* to express surprise (common in ordinary speech), is rare in this story.
5. The expression of surprise, *he mea kupapaha*, is literally "a strange thing," like our impersonal "it is strange"
6. The vocable *e* is used to express strong emotion.
7. Add to these an occasional use, for emphasis, of the belittling question, whose answer, although generally left to be understood, may be given; for example: *A heaha la o Haua-i-liki ia Laie-i-ka-wai? he opala paha*, "What was Hauailiki to Laieikawai? 'mere chaff!'", and the expression of contempt—*ka*—with which the princess dismisses her wooer.

IV

Conclusions

1. Much of the material of Hawaiian song and story is traditional within other Polynesian groups.
2. Verse making is practiced as an aristocratic art of high social value in the households of chiefs, one in which both men and women take part.
3. In both prose and poetry, for the purpose of social aggrandizement, the theme is the individual hero exalted through his family connection and his own achievement to the rank of divinity.
4. The action of the story generally consists in a succession of contests in which is tested the hero's claim to supernatural power. These contests range from mythical encounters in the heavens to the semihistorical rivalries of chiefs.
5. The narrative may take on a high degree of complexity, involving many well-differentiated characters and a well-developed art of conversation, and in some instances, especially in revenge, trickster, or recognition motives, approaching plot tales in our sense of the word.
6. The setting of song or story, both physical and social, is distinctly realized. Stories persist and are repeated in the localities where they are localized. Highly characteristic are stories of rock transformations and of other local configurations, still pointed to as authority for the tale.
7. Different types of hero appear:
   (*a*) The hero may be a human being of high rank and of unusual power either of strength, skill, wit, or craft.
   (*b*) He may be a demigod of supernatural power, half human, half divine.
   (*c*) He may be born in shape of a beast, bird, fish, or other object, with or without the power to take human form or monstrous size.
   (*d*) He may bear some relation to the sun, moon, or stars, a form rare in Hawaii, but which, when it does occur, is treated objectively rather than allegorically.

(e) He may be a god, without human kinship, either one of the "departmental gods" who rule over the forces of nature, or of the hostile spirits who inhabited the islands before they were occupied by the present race.

(f) He may be a mere ordinary man who by means of one of these supernatural helpers achieves success.

8. Poetry and prose show a quite different process of development. In prose, connected narrative has found free expression. In poetry, the epic process is neglected. Besides the formal dirge and highly developed lyric songs (often accompanied and interpreted by dance), the characteristic form is the eulogistic hymn, designed to honor an individual by rehearsing his family's achievements, but in broken and ejaculatory panegyric rather than in connected narrative. In prose, again, the picture presented is highly realistic. The tendency is to humanize and to localize within the group the older myth and to develop later legendary tales upon a naturalistic basis. Poetry, on the other hand, develops set forms, plays with double meanings. Its character is symbolic and obscure and depends for its style upon, artificial devices.

9. Common to each are certain sources of emotional Interest such as depend upon a close interplay of ideas developed within an intimate social group. In prose occur conventional episodes, highly elaborated minor scenes, place names in profusion which have little to do with the action of the story, repetitions by a series of actors of the same incident in identical form, and in the dialogue, elaborate chants, proverbial sayings, antithesis and parallelism. In poetry, the panegyric proceeds by the enumeration of names and their qualities, particularly place or technical names; by local and legendary allusions which may develop into narrative or descriptive passages of some length; and by eulogistic comparisons drawn from nature or from social life and often elaborately developed. The interjectional expression of emotion, the rhetorical question, the use of antithesis, repetition, wordplay (puns and word-linking) and mere counting-out formulas play a striking part, and the riddling

element, both in the metaphors employed and in the use of homonyms, renders the sense obscure.

Persons in the Story

1. AIWOHI-KUPUA. A young chief of Kauai, suitor to Laie-i-ka-wai.
2. AKIKEEHIALE. The turnstone, messenger of Aiwohikupua.
3. AWAKEA. "Noonday." The bird that guards the doors of the sun.
4. HALA-ANIANI. A young rascal of Puna.
5. HALULU-I-KE-KIHE-O-KA-MALAMA. The bird who bears the visitors to the doors of the sun.
6. HATUA-I-LIKI. "Strike-in-beating." A young chief of Kauai, suitor to Laie-i-ka-wai.
7. HAUNAKA. A champion boxer of Kohala.
8. HINA-I-KA-MALAMA. A chiefess of Maui.
9. HULU-MANIANI. "Waving feather." A seer of Kauai.
10. IHU-ANU. "Cold-nose." A champion boxer of Kohala.
11. KA-ELO-I-KA-MALAMA. The "mother's brother" who guards the land of Nuumealani.
12. KA-HALA-O-MAPU-ANA. "The sweet-scented hala." The youngest sister of Aiwohikupua.
13. KAHAU-O-KAPAKA. The chief of Koolau, Oahu, father of Laie-i-ka-wai.
14. KAHOUPO'KANE. Attendant upon Poliahu.
15. KA-ILI-O-KA-LAU-O-KE-KOA. "The-skin-of-the-leaf-of-the-koa (tree)." The wife of Kauakahialii.
16. KALAHUMOKU. The fighting dog of Aiwohikupua.
17. KA-OHU-KULO-KIALEA. "The-moving-cloud-of-Kaialea." Guard of the shade at the taboo house of Kahiki.
18. KA-ONOHI-O-KA-LA. "The-eyeball-of-the-sun." A high taboo chief, who lives in Kahiki.
19. KAPUKAI-HAOA. A priest, grandfather of Laie-i-ka-wai.
20. KAUA-KAHI-ALII. The high chief of Kauai.
21. KAULAAI-LEHUA. A beautiful princess of Molokai.
22. KE-KALUKALU-O-KE-WA. Successor to Kauakahi-alii and suitor to Laic-i-ka-wai.
23. KIHA-NUI-LULU-MOKU. "Great-convulsion-shaking-the-island." A guardian spirit of Pali-uli.

24. KOAE. The tropic bird. Messenger of Aiwohikupua.
25. LAIE-I-KA-WAI. A species of the *ieie* vine. (?) The beauty of Pali-uli.
26. LAIE-LOHELOHE. Another species of the *ieie* vine. (?) Twin sister of Laie-i-ka-wai.
27. LANALANA-NUI-AI-MAKUA. "Great-ancestral-spider." The one who lets down the pathway to the heavens.
28. LAU-KIELE-ULA. "Red-kiele-leaf." The mother who attends the young chief in the taboo house at Kahiki.
29. LILI-NOE. "Fine-fog." Attendant to Poliahu.
30. MAHINA-NUI-KONANE. "Big-bright-moon." Guard of the shade at the taboo house at Kahiki.
31. MAILE-HAIWALE. "Brittle-leafed-maile-vine." Sister of Aiwohikupua.
32. MAILE-KALUHEA. "Big-leafed-maile-vine." Sister of Aiwohikupua.
33. MAILE-LAULII. "Fine-leafed-maile-vine." Sister of Aiwohikupua.
34. MAILE-PAKAHA. "Common-maile-vine." Sister of Aiwohikupua.
35. MAKA-WELI. "Terrible-eyes." A young chief of Kauai.
36. MALAEKAHANA. The mother of Laie-i-ka-wai.
37. MALIO. A sorceress, sister of the Puna rascal,
38. MOANALIHA-I-KA-WAOKELE. A powerful chief in Kahiki.
39. MOKU-KELE-KAHIKI. "Island-sailing-to-Kahiki." The mother's brother who guards the land of Ke-alohi-lani.
40. POLI-AHU. "Cold-bosom." A high chiefess who dwells on Maunakea.
41. POLOULA. A chief at Wailua, Kauai.
42. ULILI. The snipe. Messenger to Aiwohikupua.
43. WAI-AIE. "Water-mist." Attendant of Poliahu.
44. WAKA. A sorceress, grandmother of Laie-i-ka-wai.

The chief counsellor of Aiwohikupua.
The humpbacked attendant of Laie-i-ka-wai.
A canoe owner of Molokai.
A chief of Molokai, father of Kaulaailehua.
A countrywoman of Hana.
Paddlers, soldiers, and country people.

Action of the Story

TWIN SISTERS, LAIEIKAWAI AND LAIELOHELOHE, are born in Koolau, Oahu, their birth heralded by a double clap of thunder. Their father, a great chief over that district, has vowed to slay all his daughters until a son is born to him. Accordingly the mother conceals their birth and intrusts them to her parents to bring up in retirement, the priest carrying the younger sister to the temple at Kukaniloko and Waka hiding Laieikawai in the cave beside the pool Waiapuka. A prophet from Kauai who has seen the rainbow which always rests over the girl's dwelling place, desiring to attach himself to so great a chief, visits the place, but is eluded by Waka, who, warned by her husband, flies with her charge, first to Molokai, where a countryman, catching sight of the girl's face, is so transported with her beauty that he makes the tour of the island proclaiming her rank, thence to Maui and then to Hawaii, where she is directed to a spot called Paliuli on the borders of Puna, a night's journey inland through the forest from the beach at Keaau. Here she builds a house for her "grandchild" thatched with the feathers of the *oo* bird, and appoints birds to serve her, a humpbacked attendant to wait upon her, and mists to conceal her when she goes abroad.

To the island of Kauai returns its high chief, Kauakahialii, after a tour of the islands during which he has persuaded the fair mistress of Paliuli to visit him. So eloquent is his account of her beauty that the young chief Aiwohikupua, who has vowed to wed no woman from his own group, but only one from "the land of good women," believes that here he has found his wish. He makes the chief's servant his confidant, and after dreaming of the girl for a year, he sets out with his counsellor and a canoeload of paddlers for Paliuli. On the way he plays a boxing bout with the champion of Kohala, named Cold-nose, whom he dispatches with a single stroke that pierces the man through the chest and comes out on the other side. Arrived at the house in the forest at Paliuli, he is amazed to find it thatched all over with the precious royal feathers, a small cloak of which he is bearing as his suitor's gift. Realizing the girl's rank, he returns at once to Kauai to fetch his five sweet-scented sisters to act as ambassadresses and bring him honor as a wooer. Laieikawai, however, obstinately refuses the first four; and the angry lover in a rage refuses to allow the last and youngest to try her charms. Abandoning them, all to their fate in the forest, he sails back to Kauai. The youngest and favorite, indeed, he would have taken with him, but she will not abandon her sisters. By her wit and skill she gains the favor of the royal beauty, and all five are taken into the household of Laieikawai to act as guardians of her virginity and pass upon any suitors for her hand.

When Aiwohikupua, on his return, confesses his ill fortune, a handsome comrade, the best skilled in surfing over all the islands, lays a bet to win the beauty of Paliuli. He, too, returns crestfallen, the guards having proved too watchful. But Aiwohikupua is so delighted to hear of his sisters' position that he readily cancels the debt and hurries off to Puna. His sisters, however, mindful of his former cruelty, deny him access, and he returns to Kauai burning with rage, to collect a war party to lead against the obdurate girls. Only after band after band has been swallowed up in the jaws of the great lizard who guards Paliuli, and his supernatural fighting dog has returned with ears bitten off and tail between its legs, does he give over the attempt and return home disconsolate to Kauai.

Now, on his first voyage to Puna, as the chief came to land at Hana, Maui, a high chiefess named Hina fell in love with him. The two staking their love at a game of *konane*, she won him for her lover. He excused himself under pretext of a vow to first tour about Hawaii, but pledged himself to return. On the return trip he encountered and fell in love with the woman of the mountain, Poliahu or Snow-bosom, but she, knowing through her supernatural power of his affair with Hina, refused his advances. Now, however, he determines to console himself with this lady. His bird ambassadors go first astray and notify Hina, but finally the tryst is arranged, the bridal cortege arrives in state, and the bridal takes place. On their return to Kauai during certain games celebrated by the chiefs, the neglected Hina suddenly appears and demands her pledge. The jealous Poliahu disturbs the new nuptials by plaguing their couch first with freezing cold, then with burning heat, until she has driven away her rival. She then herself takes her final departure.

Kauakahialii, the high chief of Kauai, now about to die, cedes the succession to his favorite chief, Kekalukaluokewa, and bids him seek out the beauty of Paliuli for a bride. He is acceptable to both the girl and her grandmother—to the first for his good looks, to the second for his rank and power. But before the marriage can be consummated a wily rascal of Puna, through the arts of his wise sister Malio, abducts Laieikawai while she and her lover are out surfing, by his superior dexterity wins her affection, and makes off with her to Paliuli. When the grandmother discovers her grandchild's disgrace, she throws the girl over and seeks out her twin sister on Oahu to offer as bride to the great chief of Kauai. So beautiful is Laielohelohe that now the Puna rascal abandons his wife and almost tricks the new beauty out of the hands of the noble bridegroom; but this time the marriage is successfully managed, the mists clear, and bride and bridegroom appear mounted upon birds, while all the people shout, "The marriage of the chiefs!" The spectacle is witnessed by the abandoned beauty and her guardians, who have come thither riding upon the great lizard; and on this occasion Waka denounces and disgraces her disowned grandchild.

Left alone by her grandmother, lordly lover, and rascally husband, Laieikawai turns to the five virgin sisters and the great lizard to raise her fortunes. The youngest sister proposes to make a journey to Kealohilani, or the Shining-heavens, and fetch thence her oldest brother, who dwells in the "taboo house on the borders of Tahiti." As a youth of the highest divine rank, he will be a fit mate to wed her mistress. The chiefess consents, and during the absence of the ambassadress, goes journeying with her four remaining guardians. During this journey she is seen and recognized by the prophet of Kauai, who has for many years been on the lookout for the sign of the rainbow. Under his guardianship she and the four sisters travel to Kauai, to which place the scene now shifts. Here they once more face Aiwohikupua, and the prophet predicts the coming of the avenger. Meanwhile the lizard bears the youngest sister over sea. She ascends to various regions of the heavens, placating in turn her maternal uncles, father, and mother, until finally she reaches the god himself, where he lies basking in the white radiance of the noonday sun. Hearing her story, this divine one agrees to lay aside his nature as a god and descend to earth to wed his sister's benefactress and avenge the injuries done by his brother and Waka. Signs in the heavens herald his approach; he appears within the sun at the back of the mountain and finally stands before his bride, whom he takes up with him on a rainbow to the moon. At his return, as he stands upon the rainbow, a great sound of shouting is heard over the land in praise of his beauty. Thus he deals out judgment upon Laieikawai's enemies: Waka falls dead, and Aiwohikupua is dispossessed of his landed rights. Next, he rewards her friends with positions of influence, and leaving the ruling power to his wife's twin sister and her husband, returns with Laieikawai to his old home in the heavens.

In the final chapters the Sun-god himself, who is called "The eyeball-of-the-sun," proves unfaithful. He falls captive to the charms of the twin sister, sends his clever youngest sister, whose foresight he fears, to rule in the heavens, and himself goes down to earth on some pretext in pursuit of the unwilling Laielohelohe. Meanwhile his wife sees through the "gourd of knowledge" all that is passing on earth and informs his parents of his infidelity. They judge and disgrace him; the divine Sun-god becomes the first *lapu*, or ghost, doomed to be shunned by all, to live in darkness and feed upon butterflies. The beauty of Paliuli, on the other hand, returns to earth to live with her sister, where she is worshiped and later deified in the heavens as the "Woman-of-the-Twilight."

Background of the Story

WHATEVER THE ORIGINAL HOME OF the *Laieikawai* story, the action as here pictured, with the exception of two chapters, is localized on the Hawaiian group. This consists of eight volcanic islands lying in the North Pacific, where torrid and tropical zones meet, about half again nearer to America than Asia, and strung along like a cluster of beads for almost 360 miles from Kauai on the northwest to the large island of Hawaii on the southeast. Here volcanic activity, extinct from prehistoric times on the other islands, still persists. Here the land attains its greatest elevation—13,825 feet to the summit of the highest peak—and of the 6,405 square miles of land area which constitute the group 4,015 belong to Hawaii. Except in temperature, which varies only about 11 degrees mean for a year, diversity marks the physical features of these mid-sea islands. Lofty mountains where snow lies perpetually, huge valleys washed by torrential freshets, smooth sand dunes, or fluted ridges, arid plains and rain-soaked forests, fringes of white beach, or abrupt bluffs that drop sheer into the deep sea, days of liquid sunshine or fierce storms from the south that whip across the island for half a week, a rainfall varying from 287 to 19 inches in a year in different localities—these are some of the contrasts which come to pass in spite of the equable climate. A similar diversity marks the plant and sea life—only in animal, bird, and especially insect life, are varieties sparsely represented.

Most of the action of the story takes place on the four largest islands—on Oahu, where the twins are born; on Maui, the home of Hina, where the prophet builds the temple to his god; on Hawaii, where lies the fabled land of Paliuli and where the surf rolls in at Keaau; and on Kauai, whence the chiefs set forth to woo and where the last action of the story takes place. These, with Molokai and Lanai, which lie off Maui "like one long island," virtually constitute the group.

Laie, where the twins are born, is a small fishing village on the northern or Koolau side of Oahu, adjoining that region made famous by the birth and exploits of the pig god, Kamapuaa. North from Laie village, in a cane field above the Government road, is still pointed out the water hole called Waiopuka—a long oval hole like a bathtub dropping to the pool below, said by the natives to be brackish in taste and to rise and fall with the tide because of subterranean connection with the sea. On one side an outjutting rock marks the entrance to a cave said to open out beyond the pool and be reached by diving. Daggett furnishes a full description of the place in the introduction to his published synopsis of the story. The appropriateness of Laie as the birthplace of the rainbow girl is evident to anyone who has spent a week along this coast. It is one of the most picturesque on the islands, with the open sea on one side fringed with white beach, and the Koolau range rising sheer from the narrow strip of the foothills, green to the summit and fluted into fantastic shapes by the sharp edge of the showers that drive constantly down with the trade winds, gleaming with rainbow colors.

Kukaniloko, in the uplands of Wahiawa, where Laielohelohe is concealed by her foster father, is one of the most sacred places on Oahu. Its fame is coupled with that of Holoholoku in Wailua, Kauai, as one of the places set apart for the birthplace of chiefs. Tradition says that since a certain Kapawa, grandson of a chief from "Tahiti" in the far past, was born upon this spot, a special divine favor has attended the birth of chiefs upon this spot. Stones were laid out right and left with a mound for the back, the mother's face being turned to the right. Eighteen chiefs stood guard on either hand. Then the taboo drum sounded and the people assembled on the east and south to witness the event. Say the Hawaiians, "If one came in confident trust and lay properly upon the supports, the child would be born with honor; it would be called a divine chief, a burning fire."[1] Even Kaméhaméha desired that his son Liholiho's birth should take place at Kukaniloko. Situated as it is

---

1. *Kuakoa*, iv, No. 31, translated also in *Hawaiian Annual*, 1912, p. 101; Daggett, p. 70; Fornander, II, 272.

upon the breast of the bare uplands between the Koolau and Waianae Ranges, the place commands a view of surprising breadth and beauty. Though the stones have been removed, through the courtesy of the management of the Waialua plantation a fence still marks this site of ancient interest.

The famous hill Kauwiki, where the seer built the temple to his god, and where Hina watched the clouds drift toward her absent lover, lies at the extreme eastern end of Maui. About this hill clusters much mythic lore of the gods. Here the heavens lay within spear thrust to earth, and here stood Maui, whose mother is called Hina, to thrust them apart. Later, Kauwiki was the scene of the famous resistance to the warriors of Umi, and in historic times about this hill for more than half a century waged a rivalry between the warriors of Hawaii and Maui. The poet of the Kualii mentions the hill thrice—once in connection with the legend of Maui, once when he likens the coming forth of the sun at Kauwiki to the advent of Ku, and in a descriptive passage in which the abrupt height is described:

> Shooting up to heaven is Kauwiki,
> Below is the cluster of islands,
> In the sea they are gathered up,
> O Kauwiki,
> O Kauwiki, mountain bending over,
> Loosened, almost falling, Kauwiki-e.

Finally, Puna, the easternmost district of the six divisions of Hawaii, is a region rich in folklore. From the crater of Kilauea, which lies on the slope of Mauna Loa about 4,000 feet above sea level, the land slopes gradually to the Puna coast along a line of small volcanic cones, on the east scarcely a mile from the sea. The slope is heavily forested, on the uplands with tall hard-wood trees of *ohia*, on the coast with groves of pandanus. Volcanic action has tossed and distorted the whole district. The coast has sunk, leaving tree trunks erect in the sea. Above the bluffs of the south coast lie great bowlders tossed up by tidal waves. Immense earthquake fissures occur. The soil is fresh lava broken into treacherous hollows, too porous to retain water and preserving a characteristic vegetation. About this region has gathered the mysterious lore of the spirit world. "Fear to do evil in the uplands of Puna," warns the old chant, lest mischief befall from the countless wood spirits who haunt these mysterious forests. Pélé, the volcano goddess, still loves her old haunts in Puna, and many a modern native boasts a meeting with this beauty of the flaming red hair who swept to his fate the brave youth from Kauai when he raced with her down the slope to the sea during the old mythic days when the rocks and hills of Puna were forming.

TEXT AND TRANSLATION

Foreword

The editor of this book rejoices to print the first fruits of his efforts to enrich the Hawaiian people with a story book. We have previously had books of instruction on many subjects and also those enlightening us as to the right and the wrong; but this is the first book printed for us Hawaiians in story form, depicting the ancient customs of this people, for fear lest otherwise we lose some of their favorite traditions. Thus we couch in a fascinating manner the words and deeds of a certain daughter of Hawaii, beautiful and greatly beloved, that by this means there may abide in the Hawaiian people the love of their ancestors and their country.

Take it, then, this little book, for what it is worth, to read and to prize, thus showing your search after the knowledge of things Hawaiian, being ever ready to uphold them that they be not lost.

It is an important undertaking for anyone to provide us with entertaining reading matter for our moments of leisure; therefore, when the editor of this book prepared it for publication he depended upon the support of all the friends of learning in these islands; and this thought alone has encouraged him to persevere in his work throughout all the difficulties that blocked his way. Now, for the first time is given to the people of Hawaii a book of entertainment for leisure moments like those of the foreigners, a book to feed our minds with wisdom and insight. Let us all join in forwarding this little book as a means of securing to the people more books of the same nature written in their own tongue—the Hawaiian tongue.

And, therefore, to all friends of learning and to all native-born Hawaiians, from the rising to the setting sun, behold the Woman-of-the-Twilight! She comes to you with greetings of love and it is fitting to receive her with the warmest love from the heart of Hawaii. *Aloha no!*

I

This tale was told at Laie, Koolau; here they were born, and they were twins; Kahauokapaka was the father, Malaekahana the mother. Now Kahauokapaka was chief over two districts, Koolauloa and Koolaupoko, and he had great authority over these districts.

At the time when Kahauokapaka took Malaekahana to wife,[1] after their union, during those moments of bliss when they had just parted from the first embrace, Kahauokapaka declared his vow to his wife, and this was the vow:[2]

"My wife, since we are married, therefore I will tell you my vow: If we two live hereafter and bear a child and it is a son, then it shall be well with us. Our children shall live in the days of our old age, and when we die they will cover our nakedness.[3] This child shall be the one to portion out the land, if fortune is ours in our first born and it is a boy; but if the first born is a daughter, then let her die; however many daughters are born to us, let them die; only one thing shall save them, the birth of a son shall save those daughters who come after."

About the eighth year of their living as man and wife, Malaekahana conceived and bore a daughter, who was so beautiful to look upon, the mother thought that Kahauokapaka would disregard his vow; this child he would save. Not so! At the time when she was born, Kahauokapaka was away at the fishing with the men.

When Kahauokapaka returned from the fishing he was told that Malaekahana had born a daughter. The chief went to the house; the baby girl had been wrapped in swaddling clothes; Kahauokapaka at once ordered the executioner to kill it.

After a time Malaekahana conceived again and bore a second daughter, more beautiful than the first; she thought to save it. Not so! Kahauokapaka saw the baby girl in its mother's arms wrapped in swaddling clothes; then the chief at once ordered the executioner to kill it.

Afterwards Malaekahana bore more daughters, but she could not save them from being killed at birth according to the chief's vow.

When for the fifth time Malaekahana conceived a child, near the time of its birth, she went to the priest and said, "Here! Where are you? Look upon this womb of mine which is with child, for I can no longer endure my children's death; the husband is overzealous to keep his vow; four children were mine, four are dead. Therefore, look upon this womb of mine, which is with child; if you see it is to be a girl, I will kill it before it takes human shape.[4] But if you see it is to be a boy, I will not do it."

Then the priest said to Malaekahana, "Go home; just before the child is to be born come back to me that I may know what you are carrying."

At the time when the child was to be born, in the month of October, during the taboo season at the temple, Malaekahana remembered the priest's command. When the pains of childbirth were upon her, she came to the priest and said, "I come at the command of the priest, for the pains of childbirth are upon me; look and see, then, what kind of child I am carrying."

As Malaekahana talked with the priest, he said: "I will show you a sign; anything I ask of you, you must give it."

Then the priest asked Malaekahana to give him one of her hands, according to the sign used by this people, whichever hand she wished to give to the priest.

Now, when the priest asked Malaekahana to give him one of her hands she presented the left, with the palm upward. Then the priest told her the interpretation of the sign: "You will bear another daughter, for you have given me your left hand with the palm upward."

When the priest said this, the heart of Malaekahana was heavy, for she sorrowed over the slaying of the children by her husband; then Malaekahana besought the priest to devise something to help the mother and save the child.

Then the priest counseled Malaekahana, "Go back to the house; when the child is about to be born, then have a craving for the *manini* spawn,[5] and tell Kahauokapaka that he must himself go fishing, get the fish you desire with his own hand, for your husband is very fond of the young *manini* afloat in the membrane, and while he is out fishing he will not know about the birth; and when the child is born, then give it to me to take care of; when he comes back, the child will be in my charge, and if he asks, tell him it was an abortion, nothing more."

At the end of this talk, Malaekahana went back to the house, and when the pains came upon her, almost at the moment of birth, then Malaekahana remembered the priest's counsel to her.

When the pain had quieted, Malaekahana said to her husband, "Listen, Kahauokapaka! the spawn of the *manini* come before my eyes;

go after them, therefore, while they are yet afloat in the membrane; possibly when you bring the *manini* spawn, I shall be eased of the child; this is the first time my labor has been hard, and that I have craved the young of the *manini*; go quickly, therefore, to the fishing."

Then Kahauokapaka went out of the house at once and set out. While they were gone the child was born, a girl, and she was given to Waka, and they named her Laieikawai. As they were attending to the first child, a second was born, also a girl, and they named her Laielohelohe.

After the girls had been carried away in the arms of Waka and Kapukaihaoa, Kahauokapaka came back from the fishing, and asked his wife, "How are you?"

Said the woman, "I have born an abortion and have thrown it into the ocean."

Kahauokapaka already knew of the birth while he was on the ocean, for there came two claps of thunder; then he thought that the wife had given birth. At this time of Laieikawai and Laielohelohe's birth thunder first sounded in October,[6] according to the legend.

When Waka and Kapukaihaoa had taken their foster children away, Waka said to Kapukaihaoa, "How shall we hide our foster children from Kahauokapaka?"

Said the priest, "You had better hide your foster child in the water hole of Waiapuka; a cave is there which no one knows about, and it will be my business to seek a place of protection for my foster child."

Waka took Laieikawai where Kapukaihaoa had directed, and there she kept Laieikawai hidden until she was come to maturity.

Now, Kapukaihaoa took Laielohelohe to the uplands of Wahiawa, to the place called Kukaniloko.[7]

All the days that Laieikawai was at Waiapuka a rainbow arch was there constantly, in rain or calm, yet no one understood the nature of this rainbow, but such signs as attend a chief were always present wherever the twins were guarded.

Just at this time Hulumaniani was making a tour of Kauai in his character as the great seer of Kauai, and when he reached the summit of Kalalea he beheld the rainbow arching over Oahu; there he remained 20 days in order to be sure of the nature of the sign which he saw. By that time the seer saw clearly that it was the sign of a great chief—this rainbow arch and the two ends of a rainbow encircled in dark clouds.

Then the seer made up his mind to go to Oahu to make sure about the sign which he saw. He left the place and went to Anahola to bargain for a boat to go to Oahu, but he could not hire a boat to go to Oahu. Again the seer made a tour of Kauai; again he ascended Kalalea and saw again the same sign as before, just the same as at first; then he came back to Anahola.

While the seer was there he heard that Poloula owned a canoe at Wailua, for he was chief of that place, and he desired to meet Poloula to ask the chief for a canoe to go to Oahu.

When Hulumaniani met Poloula he begged of him a canoe to go to Oahu. Then the canoe and men were given to him. That night when the canoe star rose they left Kauai, 15 strong, and came first to Kamaile in Waianae.

Before the seer sailed, he first got ready a black pig, a white fowl, and a red fish.

On the day when they reached Waianae the seer ordered the rowers to wait there until he returned from making the circuit of the island.

Before the seer went he first climbed clear to the top of Maunalahilahi and saw the rainbow arching at Koolauloa, as he saw it when he was on Kalalea.

He went to Waiapuka, where Laieikawai was being guarded, and saw no place there set off for chiefs to dwell in. Now, just as the seer arrived, Waka had vanished into that place where Laieikawai was concealed.

As the seer stood looking, he saw the rippling of the water where Waka had dived. Then he said to himself: "This is a strange thing. No wind ripples the water on this pool. It is like a person bathing, who has hidden from me." After Waka had been with Laieikawai she returned, but while yet in the water she saw someone sitting above on the bank, so she retreated, for she thought it was Kahauokapaka, this person on the brink of the water hole.

Waka returned to her foster child, and came back at twilight and spied to discover where the person had gone whom she saw, but there was the seer sitting in the same place as before. So Waka went back again.

The seer remained at the edge of the pool, and slept there until morning. At daybreak, when it was dawn, he arose, saw the sign of the rainbow above Kukaniloko, forsook this place, journeyed about Oahu, first through Koolaupoko; from there to Ewa and Honouliuli, where he saw the rainbow arching over Wahiawa; ascended Kamaoha, and there slept over night; but did not see the sign he sought.

II

When the seer failed to see the sign which he was following he left Kamaoha, climbed clear to the top of Kaala, and there saw the rainbow arching over Molokai. Then the seer left the place and journeyed around Oahu; a second time he journeyed around in order to be sure of the sign he was following, for the rainbow acted strangely, resting now in that place, now in this.

On the day when the seer left Kaala and climbed to the top of Kuamooakane the rainbow bent again over Molokai, and there rested the end of the rainbow, covered out of sight with thunderclouds. Three days he remained on Kuamooakane, thickly veiled in rain and fog.

On the fourth day he secured a boat to go to Molokai. He went on board the canoe and had sailed half the distance, when the paddlers grew vexed because the prophet did nothing but sleep, while the pig squealed and the cock crowed.

So the paddler in front[8] signed to the one at the rear to turn the canoe around and take the seer back as he slept.

The paddlers turned the canoe around and sailed for Oahu. When the canoe turned back, the seer distrusted this, because the wind blew in his face; for he knew the direction of the wind when he left Oahu, and now, thought he, the wind is blowing from the seaward.

Then the seer opened his eyes and the canoe was going back to Oahu. Then the seer asked himself the reason, But just to see for himself what the canoe men were doing, he prayed to his god, to Kuikauweke, to bring a great tempest over the ocean.

As he prayed a great storm came suddenly upon them, and the paddlers were afraid.

Then they awoke him: "O you fellow asleep, wake up, there! We thought perhaps your coming on board would be a good thing for us. Not so! The man sleeps as if he were ashore."

When the seer arose, the canoe was making for Oahu.

Then he asked the paddlers: "What are you doing to me to take the canoe back again? What have I done?"

Then the men said: "We two wearied of your constant sleeping and the pig's squealing and the cock's crowing; there was such a noise; from the time we left until now the noise has kept up. You ought to have taken hold and helped paddle. Not so! Sleep was the only thing for you!"

The seer said: "You two are wrong, I think, if you say the reason for your returning to Oahu was my idleness; for I tell you the trouble was with the man above on the seat, for he sat still and did nothing."

As he spoke, the seer sprang to the stern of the canoe, took charge of the steering, and they sailed and came to Haleolono, on Molokai.

When they reached there, lo! the rainbow arched over Koolau, as he saw it from Kuamooakane; he left the paddlers, for he wished to see the sign which he was following.

He went first clear to the top of Waialala, right above Kalaupapa. Arrived there, he clearly saw the rainbow arching over Malelewaa, over a sharp ridge difficult to reach; there, in truth, was Laieikawai hidden, she and her grandmother, as Kapukaihaoa had commanded Waka in the vision.

For as the seer was sailing over the ocean, Kapukaihaoa had foreknowledge of what the prophet was doing, therefore he told Waka in a vision to carry Laieikawai away where she could not be found.

After the seer left Waialala he went to Waikolu right below Malelewaa. Sure enough, there was the rainbow arching where he could not go. Then he considered for some time how to reach the place to see the person he was seeking and offer the sacrifice he had prepared, but he could not reach it.

On the day when the seer went to Waikolu, the same night, came the command of Kapukaihaoa to Laieikawai in a dream, and when she awoke, it was a dream. Then Laieikawai roused her grandmother, and the grandmother awoke and asked her grandchild why she had roused her.

The grandchild said to her: "Kapukaihaoa has come to me in a dream and said that you should bear me away at once to Hawaii and make our home in Paliuli; there we two shall dwell; so he told me, and I awoke and wakened you."

As Laieikawai was speaking to her grandmother, the same vision came to Waka. Then they both arose at dawn and went as they had both been directed by Kapukaihaoa in a vision.

They left the place, went to Keawanui, to the place called Kaleloa, and there they met a man who was getting his canoe ready to sail for Lanai. When they met the canoe man, Waka said: "Will you let us get into the canoe with you, and take us to the place where you intend to go?"

Said the canoe man: "I will take you both with me in the canoe; the only trouble is I have no mate to paddle the canoe."

And as the man spoke this word, "a mate to paddle the canoe," Laieikawai drew aside the veil that covered her face because of her grandmother's wish completely to conceal her grandchild from being seen by anyone as they went on their way to Paliuli; but her grandchild thought otherwise.

When Laieikawai uncovered her face which her grandmother had concealed, the grandmother shook her head at her grandchild to forbid her showing it, lest the grandchild's beauty become thereafter nothing but a common thing.

Now, as Laieikawai uncovered her face, the canoe man saw that Laieikawai rivaled in beauty all the daughters of the chiefs round about Molokai and Lanai. And lo! the man was pierced through[9] with longing for the person he had seen.

Therefore, the man entreated the grandmother and said: "Unloosen the veil from your grandchild's face, for I see that she is more beautiful than all the daughters of the chiefs round about Molokai and Lanai."

The grandmother said: "I do not uncover her because she wishes to conceal herself."

At this answer of Waka to the paddler's entreaties, Laieikawai revealed herself fully, for she heard Waka say that she wished to conceal herself, when she had not wanted to at all.

And when the paddler saw Laieikawai clearly, desire came to him afresh. Then the thought sprang up within him to go and spread the news around Molokai of this person whom he longed after.

Then the paddler said to Laieikawai and her companion, "Where are you! live here in the house; everything within is yours, not a single thing is withholden from you in the house; inside and outside[10] you two are masters of this place."

When the canoe man had spoken thus, Laieikawai said, "Our host, shall you be gone long? for it looks from your charge as if you were to be away for good."

Said the host, "O daughter, not so; I shall not forsake you; but I must look for a mate to paddle you both to Lanai."

And at these words, Waka said to their host, "If that is the reason for your going away, leaving us in charge of everything in your house, then let me say, we can help you paddle."

The man was displeased at these words of Waka to him.

He said to the strangers, "Let me not think of asking you to paddle the canoe; for I hold you to be persons of importance."

Now it was not the man's intention to look for a mate to paddle the canoe with him, but as he had already determined, so now he vowed within him to go and spread around Molokai the news about Laieikawai.

When they had done speaking the paddler left them and went away as he had vowed.

As he went he came first to Kaluaaha and slept at Halawa, and here and on the way there he proclaimed, as he had vowed, the beauty of Laieikawai.

The next day, in the morning, he found a canoe sailing to Kalaupapa, got on board and went first to Pelekunu and Wailau; afterwards he came to Waikolu, where the seer was staying.

When he got to Waikolu the seer had already gone to Kalaupapa, but this man only stayed to spread the news of Laieikawai's arrival.

When he reached Kalaupapa, behold! a company had assembled for boxing; he stood outside the crowd and cried with a loud voice:[11] "O ye men of the people, husbandmen, laborers, tillers of the soil; O ye chiefs, priests, soothsayers, all men of rank in the household of the chief! All manner of men have I beheld on my way hither; I have seen the high and the low, men and women; low chiefs, the *kaukaualii*, men and women; high chiefs, the *niaupio*, and the *ohi*; but never have I beheld anyone to compare with this one whom I have seen; and I declare to you that she is more beautiful than any of the daughters of the chiefs on Molokai or even in this assembly."

Now when he shouted, he could not be heard, for his voice was smothered in the clamor of the crowd and the noise of the onset.

And wishing his words to be heard aright, he advanced into the midst of the throng, stood before the assembly, and held up the border of his garment and repeated the words he had just spoken.

Now the high chief of Molokai heard his voice plainly, so the chief quieted the crowd and listened to what the stranger was shouting about, for as he looked at the man he saw that his face was full of joy and gladness.

At the chief's command the man was summoned before the chief and he asked, "What news do you proclaim aloud with glad face before the assembly?"

Then the man told why he shouted and why his face was glad in the presence of the chief: "In the early morning yesterday, while I was working over the canoe, intending to sail to Lanai, a certain woman came with her daughter, but I could not see plainly the daughter's face. But while we were talking the girl unveiled her face. Behold! I saw a girl of incomparable beauty who rivaled all the daughters of the chiefs of Molokai."

When the chief heard these words he said, "If she is as good looking as my daughter, then she is beautiful indeed."

At this saying of the chief, the man begged that the chiefess be shown to him, and Kaulaailehua, the daughter of the chief, was brought thither. Said the man, "Your daughter must be in four points more beautiful than she is to compare with that other."

Replied the chief, "She must be beautiful indeed that you scorn our beauty here, who is the handsomest girl in Molokai."

Then the man said fearlessly to the chief, "Of my judgment of beauty I can speak with confidence."[12]

As the man was talking with the chief, the seer remained listening to the conversation; it just came to him that this was the one whom he was seeking.

So the seer moved slowly toward him, got near, and seized the man by the arm, and drew him quietly after him.

When they were alone, the seer asked the man directly, "Did you know that girl before about whom you were telling the chief?"

The man denied it and said, "No; I had never seen her before; this was the very first time; she was a stranger to me."

So the seer thought that this must be the person he was seeking, and he questioned the man closely where they were living, and the man told him exactly.

After the talk, he took everything that he had prepared for sacrifice when they should meet and departed.

III

When the seer set out after meeting that man, he went first up Kawela; there he saw the rainbow arching over the place which the man had described to him; so he was sure that this was the person he was following.

He went to Kaamola, the district adjoining Keawanui, where Laieikawai and her companion were awaiting the paddler. By this time it was very dark; he could not see the sign he saw from Kawela; but the seer slept there that night, thinking that at daybreak he would see the person he was seeking.

That night, while the seer was sleeping at Kaamola, then came the command of Kapukaihaoa to Laieikawai in a dream, just as he had directed them at Malelewaa.

At dawn they found a canoe sailing to Lanai, got on board, and went and lived for some time at Maunalei.

After Laieikawai and her companion had left Kalaeloa, at daybreak, the seer arose and saw that clouds and falling rain obscrued the sea between Molokai and Lanai with a thick veil of fog and mist.

Three days the veil of mist hid the sea, and on the fourth day the seer's stay at Kaamola, in the very early morning, he saw an end of the rainbow standing right above Maunalei. Now the seer regretted deeply not finding the person he was seeking; nevertheless he was not discouraged into dropping the quest.

About 10 days passed at Molokai before he saw the end of the rainbow standing over Haleakala; he left Molokai, went first to Haleakala, to the fire pit, but did not see the person he was seeking.

When the seer reached there, he looked toward Hawaii; the land was veiled thick in cloud and mist. He left the place, went to Kauwiki, and there built a place of worship[13] to call upon his god as the only one to guide him to the person he was seeking.

Whenever the seer stopped in his journeying he directed the people, if they found the person he was following, to search him out wherever he might be.

At the end of the days of consecration of the temple, while the seer was at Kauwiki, near the night of the gods Kane and Lono,[14] the land of Hawaii cleared and he saw to the summit of the mountains.

Many days the seer remained at Kauwiki, nearly a year or more, but he never saw the sign he had followed thither.

One day in June, during the first days of the month, very early in the morning, he caught a glimpse of something like a rainbow at Koolau on Hawaii; he grew excited, his pulse beat quickly, but he waited long and patiently to see what the rainbow was doing. The whole month passed in patient waiting; and in the next month, on the second day of the month, in the evening, before the sun had gone down, he entered the place of worship prepared for his god and prayed.

As he prayed, in the midst of the place appeared to the seer the spirit forms[15] of Laieikawai and her grandmother; so he left off praying, nor did those spirits leave him as long as it was light.

That night, in his sleep, his god came to him in a vision and said: "I have seen the pains and the patience with which you have striven to find Waka's grandchild, thinking to gain honor through her grandchild. Your prayers have moved me to show you that Laieikawai dwells between Puna and Hilo in the midst of the forest, in a house made of the yellow feathers of the *oo* bird[16]; therefore, to-morrow, rise and go."

He awoke from sleep; it was only a dream, so he doubted and did not sleep the rest of the night until morning.

And when it was day, in the early morning, as he was on Kauwiki, he saw the flapping of the sail of a canoe down at Kaihalulu. He ran quickly and came to the landing, and asked the man where the boat was going. The man said, "It is going to Hawaii"; thereupon he entreated the man to take him, and the latter consented.

The seer returned up Kauwiki and brought his luggage, the things he had got ready for sacrifice.

When he reached the shore he first made a bargain with them: "You paddlers, tell me what you expect of me on this trip; whatever you demand, I will accede to; for I was not well treated by the men who brought me here from Oahu, so I will first make a bargain with you men, lest you should be like them."

The men promised to do nothing amiss on this trip, and the talk ended; he boarded the canoe and set out.

On the way they landed first at Mahukona in Kohala, slept there that night, and in the morning the seer left the paddlers, ascended to Lamaloloa, and entered the temple of Pahauna,[17] an ancient temple belonging to olden times and preserved until to-day.

Many days he remained there without seeing the sign he sought; but in his character as seer he continued praying to his god as when he was on Kauwiki, and in answer to the seer's prayer, he had again the same sign that was shown to him on Kauwiki.

At this, he left the place and traversed Hawaii, starting from Hamakua, and the journey lasted until the little pig he started with had grown too big to be carried.

Having arrived at Hamakua, he dwelt in the Waipio Valley at the temple of Pakaalana but did not stay there long.

The seer left that place, went to Laupahoehoe, and thence to Kaiwilahilahi, and there remained some years.

HERE WE WILL LEAVE THE story of the seer's search. It will be well to tell of the return of Kauakahialii to Kauai with Kailiokalauokekoa.[18] As we know, Laieikawai is at Paliuli.

In the first part of the story we saw that Kapukaihaoa commanded Waka in a dream to take Laieikawai to Paliuli, as the seer saw.

The command was carried out. Laieikawai dwelt at Paliuli until she was grown to maidenhood.

When Kauakahialii and Kailiokalauokekoa returned to Kauai after their meeting with the "beauty of Paliuli" there were gathered together the high chiefs, the low chiefs, and the country aristocracy as well, to see the strangers who came with Kailiokalauokekoa's party. Aiwohikupua came with the rest of the chiefs to wail for the strangers.

After the wailing the chiefs asked Kauakahialii, "How did your journey go after your marriage with Kailiokalauokekoa?"

Then Kauakahialii told of his journey as follows: "Seeking hence after the love of woman, I traversed Oahu and Maui, but found no other woman to compare with this Kailiokalauokekoa here. I went to Hawaii, traveled all about the island, touched first at Kohala, went on to Kona, Kau, and came to Keaau, in Puna, and there I tarried, and there I met another woman surpassingly beautiful, more so than this woman here (Kailiokalauokekoa), more than all the beauties of this whole group of islands."

During this speech Aiwohikupua seemed to see before him the lovely form of that woman.

Then said Kauakahialii: "On the first night that she met my man she told him at what time she would reach the place where we were staying and the signs of her coming, for my man told her I was to be her husband and entreated her to come down with him; but she said: 'Go back to this ward of yours who is to be my husband and tell him this night I will come. When rings the note of the *oo* bird I am not in that sound, or the *alala*, I am not in that sound; when rings the note of the *elepaio* then am I making ready to descend; when the note of the *apapane* sounds, then am I without the door of my house; if you hear the note of the *iiwipolena*[19] then am I without your ward's house; seek me, you two, and find me without; that is your ward's chance to meet me.' So my man told me.

"When the night came that she had promised she did not come; we waited until morning; she did not come; only the birds sang. I thought my man had lied. Kailiokalauokekoa and her friends were spending the night at Punahoa with friends. Thinking my man had lied, I ordered the executioner to bind ropes about him; but he had left me for the uplands of Paliuli to ask the woman why she had not come down that night and to tell her he was to die.

"When he had told Laieikawai all these things the woman said to him, 'You return, and to-night I will come as I promised the night before, so will I surely do.'

"That night, the night on which the woman was expected, Kailiokalauokekoa's party had returned and she was recounting her adventures, when just at the edge of the evening rang the note of the *oo*; at 9 in the evening rang the note of the *alala*; at midnight rang the note of the *elepaio*; at dawn rang the note of the *apapane*; and at the first streak of light rang the note of the *iiwipolena*; as soon as it sounded there fell the shadow of a figure at the door of the house. Behold! the room was thick with mist, and when it passed away she lay resting on the wings of birds in all her beauty."

At these words of Kauakahialii to the chiefs, all the body of Aiwohikupua pricked with desire, and he asked, "What was the woman's name?"

They told him it was Laieikawai, and such was Aiwohikupua's longing for the woman of whom Kauakahialii spoke that he thought to make her his wife, but he wondered who this woman might be. Then he said to Kauakahialii: "I marvel what this woman may be, for I am a man who has made the whole circuit of the islands, but I never saw any woman resting on the wings of birds. It may be she is come hither from the borders of Tahiti, from within Moaulanuiakea."[20]

Since Aiwohikupua thought Laieikawai must be from Moaulanuiakea, he determined to get her for his wife. For before he had heard all this story Aiwohikupua had vowed not to take any woman of these islands to wife; he said that he wanted a woman of Moaulanuiakea.

The chiefs' reception was ended and the accustomed ceremonies on the arrival of strangers performed. And soon after those days Aiwohikupua took Kauakahialii's man to minister in his presence, thinking that this man would be the means to attain his desire.

Therefore Aiwohikupua exalted this man to be head over all things, over all the chief's land, over all the men, chiefs, and common people, as his high counsellor.

As this man became great, jealous grew the former favorites of Aiwohikupua, but this was nothing to the chief.

IV

After this man had become great before the chief, even his high counsellor, they consulted constantly together about those matters which pleased the chief, while the people thought they discussed the administration of the land and of the substance which pertained to the chief; but it was about Laieikawai that the two talked and very seldom about anything else.

Even before Aiwohikupua heard from Kauakahialii about Laieikawai he had made a vow before his food companions, his sisters, and before all the men of rank in his household: "Where are you, O chiefs, O my sisters, all my food companions! From this day until my last I will take no woman of all these islands to be my wife, even from Kauai unto Hawaii, no matter how beautiful she is reported to be, nor will I get into mischief with a woman, not with anyone at all. For I have been ill-treated by women from my youth up. She shall be my wife who comes hither from other islands, even from Moaulanuiakea, a place of kind women, I have heard; so that is the sort of woman I desire to marry."

When Aiwohikupua had heard Kauakahialii's story, after conferring long with his high counsellor about Laieikawai, then the chief was convinced that this was the woman from Tahiti.

Next day, at midday, the chief slept and Laieikawai came to Aiwohikupua in a dream[21] and he saw her in the dream as Kauakahialii had described her.

When he awoke, lo! he sorrowed after the vision of Laieikawai, because he had awakened so soon out of sleep; therefore he wished to prolong his midday nap in order to see again her whom he had beheld in his dream.

The chief again slept, and again Laieikawai came to him for a moment, but he could not see her distinctly; barely had he seen her face when he waked out of sleep.

For this reason his mind was troubled and the chief made oath before all his people:

"Where are you? Do not talk while I am sleeping; if one even whispers, if he is chief over a district he shall lose his chiefship; if he is chief over part of a district, he shall lose his chiefship; and if a tenant farmer break my command, death is the penalty."

The chief took this oath because of his strong desire to sleep longer in order to make Laieikawai's acquaintance in his dream.

After speaking all these words, he tried once more to sleep, but he could not get to sleep until the sun went down.

During all this time he did not tell anyone about what he saw in the dream; the chief hid it from his usual confidant, thinking when it came again, then he would tell his chief counsellor.

And because of the chief's longing to dream often, he commanded his chief counsellor to chew *awa*.

So the counsellor summoned the chief's *awa* chewers and made ready what the chief commanded, and he brought it to him, and the chief drank with his counsellor and drunkenness possessed him. Then close above the chief rested the beloved image of Laieikawai as if they were already lovers. Then he raised his voice in song, as follows:[22]

> *"Rising fondly before me,*
> *The recollection of the lehua blossom of Puna,*
> *Brought hither on the tip of the wind,*
> *By the light keen wind of the fiery pit.*
> *Wakeful—sleepless with heart longing,*
> *With desire—O!"*

Said the counsellor, to the chief, after he had ended his singing, "This is strange! You have had no woman since we two have been living here, yet in your song you chanted as if you had a woman here."

Said the chief, "Cut short your talk, for I am cut off by the drink." Then the chief fell into a deep sleep and that ended it, for so heavy was the chief's sleep that he saw nothing of what he had desired.

A night and a day the chief slept while the effects of the *awa* lasted. Said the chief to his counsellor, "No good at all has come from this *awa* drinking of ours."

The counsellor answered, "What is the good of *awa* drinking? I thought the good of drinking was that admirable scaly look of the skin?"[23]

Said the chief, "Not so, but to see Laieikawai, that is the good of *awa* drinking."

After this the chief kept on drinking *awa* many days, perhaps a year, but he gained nothing by it, so he quit it.

It was only after he quit *awa* drinking that he told anyone how Laieikawai had come to him in the dream and why he had drunk the *awa*, and also why he had laid the command upon them not to talk while he slept.

After talking over all these things, then the chief fully decided to go to Hawaii to see Laieikawai. At this time they began to talk about getting Laieikawai for a wife.

At the close of the rough season and the coming of good weather for sailing, the counsellor ordered the chief's sailing masters to make the double canoe ready to sail for Hawaii that very night; and at the same time he appointed the best paddlers out of the chief's personal attendants.

Before the going down of the sun the steersmen and soothsayers were ordered to observe the look of the clouds and the ocean to see whether the chief could go or not on his journey, according to the signs. And the steersmen as well as soothsayers saw plainly that he might go on his journey.

And in the early morning at the rising of the canoe-steering star the chief went on board with his counsellor and his sixteen paddlers and two steersmen, twenty of them altogether in the double canoe, and set sail.

As they sailed, they came first to Nanakuli at Waianae. In the early morning they left this place and went first to Mokapu and stayed there ten days, for they were delayed by a storm and could not go to Molokai. After ten days they saw that it was calm to seaward. That night and the next day they sailed to Polihua, on Lanai, and from there to Ukumehame, and as the wind was unfavorable, remained there, and the next day left that place and went to Kipahulu.

At Kipahulu the chief said he would go along the coast afoot and the men by boat. Now, wherever they went the people applauded the beauty of Aiwohikupua.

They left Kipahulu and went to Hana, the chief and his counsellor by land, the men by canoe. On the way a crowd followed them for admiration of Aiwohikupua.

When they reached the canoe landing at Haneoo at Hana the people crowded to behold the chief, because of his exceeding beauty.

When the party reached there the men and women were out surf riding in the waves of Puhele, and among them was one noted princess of Hana, Hinaikamalama by name. When they saw the princess of Hana, the chief and his counsellor conceived a passion for her; that was the reason why Aiwohikupua stayed there that day.

When the people of the place had ended surfing and Hinaikamalama rode her last breaker, as she came in, the princess pointed her board straight at the stream of Kumaka where Aiwohikupua and his companion had stopped.

While the princess was bathing in the water of Kumaka the chief and his counsellor desired her, so the chief's counsellor pinched Aiwohikupua quietly to withdraw from the place where Hinaikamalama was bathing, but their state of mind got them into trouble.

When Aiwohikupua and his companion had put some distance between themselves and the princess's bathing place, the princess called, "O chiefs, why do you two run away? Why not throw off your garment, jump in, and join us, then go to the house and sleep? There is fish and a place to sleep. That is the wealth of the people of this place. When you wish to go, go; if you wish to stay, this is Hana, stay here."

At these words of the princess the counsellor said to Aiwohikupua, "Ah! the princess would like you for her lover! for she has taken a great fancy to you."

Said Aiwohikupua, "I should like to be her lover, for I see well that she is more beautiful than all the other women who have tempted me; but you have heard my vow not to take any woman of these islands to wife."

At these words his counsellor said, "You are bound by that vow of yours; better, therefore, that this woman be mine."

After this little parley, they went out surf riding and as they rode, behold! the princess conceived a passion for Aiwohikupua, and many others took a violent liking to the chief.

After the bath, they returned to the canoe thinking to go aboard and set out, but Aiwohikupua saw the princess playing *konane*[24] and the stranger chief thought he would play a game with her; now, the princess had first called them to come and play.

So Aiwohikupua joined the princess; they placed the pebbles on the board, and the princess asked, "What will the stranger stake if the game is lost to the woman of Hana?"

Said Aiwohikupua, "I will stake my double canoe afloat here on the sea, that is my wager with you."

Said the princess, "Your wager, stranger, is not well—a still lighter stake would be our persons; if I lose to you then I become yours and will do whatever you tell me just as we have agreed, and if you lose to me, then you are mine; as you would do to me, so shall I to you, and you shall dwell here on Maui."

The chief readily agreed to the princess's words. In the first game, Aiwohikupua lost.

Then said the princess, "I have won over you; you have nothing more to put up, unless it be your younger brother; in that case I will bet with you again."

To this jesting offer of the princess, Aiwohikupua readily gave his word of assent.

During the talk, Aiwohikupua gave to the princess this counsel. "Although I belong to you, and this is well, yet let us not at once become lovers, not until I return from my journey about Hawaii; for I vowed before sailing hither to know no woman until I had made the circuit of Hawaii; after that I will do what you please as we have agreed. So I lay my command upon you before I go, to live in complete purity, not to consent to any others, not to do the least thing to disturb our compact; and when I return from sight-seeing, then the princess's stake shall be paid. If when I return you have not remained pure, not obeyed my commands, then there is an end of it."

Now, this was not Aiwohikupua's real intention. After laying his commands upon Hinaikamalama, they left Maui and went to Kapakai at Kohala.

The next day they left Kapakai and sailed along by Kauhola, and Aiwohikupua saw a crowd of men gathering mountainward of Kapaau.

Then Aiwohikupua ordered the boatmen to paddle inshore, for he wanted to see why the crowd was gathering.

When they had come close in to the landing at Kauhola the chief asked why the crowd was gathering; then a native of the place said they were coming together for a boxing match.

At once Aiwohikupua trembled with eagerness to go and see the boxing match; they made the canoe fast, and Aiwohikupua, with his counsellor and the two steersmen, four in number, went ashore.

When they came to Hinakahua, where the field was cleared for boxing, the crowd saw that the youth from Kauai surpassed in beauty all the natives of the place, and they raised a tumult.

After the excitement the boxing field again settled into order; then Aiwohikupua leaned against the trunk of a *milo* tree to watch the attack begin.

As Aiwohikupua stood there, Cold-nose entered the open space and stood in the midst to show himself off to the crowd, and he called out in a loud voice: "What man on that side will come and box?" But no one dared to come and stand before Cold-nose, for the fellow was the strongest boxer in Kohala.

As Cold-nose showed himself off he turned and saw Aiwohikupua and called out, "How are you, stranger? Will you have some fun?"

When Aiwohikupua heard the voice of Cold-nose calling him, he came forward and stood in front of the boxing field while he bound his red loin cloth[25] about him in the fashion of a chief's bodyguard, and he answered his opponent:

"O native born, you have asked me to have some fun with you, and this is what I ask of you: Take two on your side with you, three of you together, to satisfy the stranger."

When Cold-nose heard Aiwohikupua, he said, "You are the greatest boaster in the crowd![26] I am the best man here, and yet you talk of three from this side; and what are you compared to me?"

Answered Aiwohikupua, "I will not accept the challenge without others on your side, and what are you compared to me! Now, I promise you, I can turn this crowd into nothing with one hand."

At Aiwohikupua's words, one of Cold-nose's backers came up behind Aiwohikupua and said: "Here! do not speak to Cold-nose; he is the best man in Kohala; the heavy weights of Kohala can not master that man."[27]

Then Aiwohikupua turned and gave the man at his back a push, and he fell down dead.[28]

V

When all the players on the boxing field saw how strong Aiwohikupua was to kill the man with just a push;

Then Cold-nose's backers went to him and said: "Here, Cold-nose, I see pretty plainly now our side will never get the best of it; I am sure that the stranger will beat us, for you see how our man was killed by just a push from his hand; when he gives a real blow the man will fly into bits. Now, I advise you to dismiss the contestants and put an end to the game and stop challenging the stranger. So, you go up to the stranger and shake hands,[29] you two, and welcome him, to let the people see that the fight is altogether hushed up."

These words roused Cold-nose to hot wrath and he said: "Here! you backers of mine, don't be afraid, don't get frightened because that man of ours was killed by a push from his hand. Didn't I do the same thing here some days ago? Then what are you afraid of? And now I tell you if you fear the stranger, then hide your eyes in the blue sky. When you hear that Cold-nose has conquered, then remember my blow called *The-end-that-sang*, the fruit of the tree which you have never tasted, the master's stroke which you have never learned. By this sign I know that he will never get the better of me, the end of my girdle sang to-day."[30]

At these words of Cold-nose his supporters said, "Where are you! We say no more; there is nothing left to do; we are silent before the fruit of this tree of yours which you say we have never tasted, and you say, too, that the end of your girdle has sung; maybe you will win through your girdle!" Then his backers moved away from the crowd.

While Cold-nose was boasting to his backers how he would overcome Aiwohikupua, then Aiwohikupua moved up and cocked his eye at Cold-nose, flapped with his arms against his side like a cock getting ready to crow, and said to Cold-nose, "Here, Cold-nose! strike me right in the stomach, four time four blows!"

When Cold-nose heard Aiwohikupua's boasting challenge to strike, then he glanced around the crowd and saw someone holding a very little child; then said Cold-nose to Aiwohikupua, "I am not the man to strike you; that little youngster there, let him strike you and let him be your opponent."

These words enraged Aiwohikupua. Then a flush rose all over his body as if he had been dipped in the blood of a lamb.[31] He turned right to the crowd and said, "Who will dare to defy the Kauai boy, for I say to him, my god can give me victory over this man, and my god will deliver the head of this mighty one to be a plaything for my paddlers."

Then Aiwohikupua knelt down and prayed to his gods as follows: "O you Heavens, Lightning, and Rain, O Air, O Thunder and Earthquake! Look upon me this day, the only child of yours left upon this earth. Give this day all your strength unto your child; by your might turn aside his fists from smiting your child, and I beseech you to give me the head of Ihuanu into my hand to be a plaything for my paddlers, that all this assembly may see that I have power over this uncircumcised[32] one. Amen."[33]

At the close of this prayer Aiwohikupua stood up with confident face and asked Cold-nose, "Are you ready yet to strike me?"

Cold-nose answered, "I am not ready to strike you; you strike me first!"

When Cold-nose's master heard these words he went to Cold-nose's side and said, "You are foolish, my pupil. If he orders you forward again then deliver the strongest blow you can give, for when he gives you the order to strike he himself begins the fight." So Cold-nose was satisfied.

After this, Aiwohikupua again asked Cold-nose, "Are you ready yet to strike me? Strike my face, if you want to!"

Then Cold-nose instantly delivered a blow like the whiz of the wind at Aiwohikupua's face, but Aiwohikupua dodged and he missed it.

As the blow missed, Aiwohikupua instantly sent his blow, struck right on the chest and pierced to his back; then Aiwohikupua lifted the man on his arm and swung him to and fro before the crowd, and threw him outside the field, and Aiwohikupua overcame Cold-nose, and all who looked on shouted.

When Cold-nose was dead his supporters came to where he was lying, those who had warned him to end the fight, and cried, "Aha! Cold-nose, could the fruit we have never tasted save you? Will you fight a second time with that man of might?" These were the scornful words of his supporters.

As the host were crowding about the dead body of their champion and wailing, Aiwohikupua came and cut off Cold-nose's head with the man's own war club[34] and threw it contemptuously to his followers; thus was his prayer fulfilled. This ended, Aiwohikupua left the company, got aboard the canoe, and departed; and the report of the deed spread through Kohala, Hamakua, and all around Hawaii.

They sailed and touched at Honokaape at Waipio, then came off Paauhau and saw a cloud of dust rising landward. Aiwohikupua asked his counsellor, "Why is that crowd gathering on land? Perhaps it is a boxing match; let us go again to look on!"

His counsellor answered, "Break off that notion, for we are not taking this journey for boxing contests, but to seek a wife."

Said Aiwohikupua to his counsellor, "Call to the steersman to turn the canoe straight ashore to hear what the crowd is for." The chief's wish was obeyed, they went alongside the cliff and asked the women gathering shellfish, "What is that crowd inland for?"

The women answered, "They are standing up to a boxing match, and whoever is the strongest, he will be sent to box with the Kauai man who fought here with Cold-nose and killed Cold-nose; that is what all the shouting is about."

So Aiwohikupua instantly gave orders to anchor the canoe, and Aiwohikupua landed with his counsellor and the two steersmen, and they went up to the boxing match; there they stood at a distance watching the people.

Then came one of the natives of the place to where they stood and Aiwohikupua asked what the people were doing, and the man answered as the women had said.

Aiwohikupua said to the man, "You go and say I am a fellow to have some fun with the boxers, but not with anyone who is not strong."

The man answered, "Haunaka is the only strong one in this crowd, and he is to be sent to Kohala to fight with the Kauai man."

Said Aiwohikupua, "Go ahead and tell Haunaka that we two will have some fun together."

When the man found Haunaka, and Haunaka heard these words, he clapped his hands, struck his chest, and stamped his feet, and beckoned to Aiwohikupua to come inside the field, and Aiwohikupua came, took off his cape,[35] and bound it about his waist.

When Aiwohikupua was on the field he said to Haunaka, "You can never hurt the Kauai boy; he is a choice branch of the tree that stands upon the steep."[36]

As Aiwohikupua was speaking a man called out from outside the crowd, who had seen Aiwohikupua fighting with Cold-nose, "O Haunaka and all of you gathered here, you will never outdo this man; his fist is like a spear! Only one blow at Cold-nose and the fist went through to his back. This is the very man who killed Cold-nose."

Then Haunaka seized Aiwohikupua's hand and welcomed him, and the end of it was they made friends and the players mixed with the crowd, and they left the place; Aiwohikupua's party went with their friends and boarded the canoes, and went on and landed at Laupahoehoe.

VI

In Chapter V of this story we have seen how Aiwohikupua got to Laupahoehoe. Here we shall say a word about Hulumaniani, the seer who followed Laieikawai hither from Kauai, as described in the first chapter of this story.

On the day when Aiwohikupua's party left Paauhau, at Hamakua, on the same day as he sailed and came to Laupahoehoe, the prophet foresaw it all on the evening before he arrived, and it happened thus:

That evening before sunset, as the seer was sitting at the door of the house, he saw long clouds standing against the horizon where the signs in the clouds appear, according to the soothsayers of old days even until now.

Said the seer, "A chief's canoe comes hither, 19 men, 1 high chief, a double canoe."

The men sitting with the chief started up at once, but could see no canoe coming. Then the people with him asked, "Where is the canoe which you said was a chief's canoe coming?"

Said the prophet, "Not a real canoe; in the clouds I find it; to-morrow you will see the chief's canoe."

A night and a day passed; toward evening he again saw the cloud rise on the ocean in the form which the seer recognized as Aiwohikupua's—perhaps as we recognize the crown of any chief that comes to us, so Aiwohikupua's cloud sign looked to the seer.

When the prophet saw that sign he arose and caught a little pig and a black cock, and pulled a bundle of *awa* root to prepare for Aiwohikupua's coming.

The people wondered at his action and asked, "Are you going away that you make these things ready?"

The seer said, "I am making ready for my chief, Aiwohikupua; he is the one I told you about last evening; for he comes hither over the ocean, his sign is on the ocean, and his mist covers it."

As Aiwohikupua's party drew near to the harbor of Laupahoehoe, 20 peals of thunder sounded, the people of Hilo crowded together, and as soon as it was quiet all saw the double canoe coming to land carrying above it the taboo sign[37] of a chief. Then the seer's prediction was fulfilled.

When the canoe came to land the seer was standing at the landing; he advanced from Kaiwilahilahi, threw the pig before the chief, and prayed in the name of the gods of Aiwohikupua, and this was his prayer:

"O Heavens, Lightning, and Rain; O Air, Thunder, and Earthquake; O gods of my chief, my beloved, my sacred taboo chief, who will bury these bones! Here is a pig, a black cock, *awa*, a priest, a sacrifice, an offering to the chief from your servant here; look upon your servant, Hulumaniani; bring to him life, a great life, a long life, to live forever, until the staff rings as he walks, until he is dragged upon a mat, until the eyes are dim.[38] Amen, it is finished, flown away."

As the chief listened to the prophet's prayer, Aiwohikupua recognized his own prophet, and his heart yearned with love toward him; for he had been gone a long while; he could not tell how long it was since he had seen him.

As soon as the prayer was ended, Aiwohikupua commanded his counsellor to "present the seer's gifts to the gods."

Instantly the seer ran and clasped the chief's feet and climbed upward to his neck and wept, and Aiwohikupua hugged his servant's shoulders and wailed out his virtues.

After the wailing the chief asked his servant: "Why are you living here, and how long have you been gone?"

The servant told him all that we have read about in former chapters. When the seer had told the business on which he had come and his reason for it, that was enough. Then it was the seer's turn to question Aiwohikupua, but the chief told only half the story, saying that he was on a sight-seeing tour.

The chief stayed with the seer that night until at daybreak they made ready the canoe and sailed.

They left Laupahoehoe and got off Makahanaloa when one of the men, the one who is called the counsellor, saw the rainbow arching over Paliuli.

He said to the chief: "Look! Where are you! See that rainbow arch? Laieikawai is there, the one whom you want to find and there is where I found her."

Said Aiwohikupua: "I do not think Laieikawai is there; that is not her rainbow, for rainbows are common to all rainy places. But let us wait until it is pleasant and see whether the rainbow is there then; then we shall know it is her sign."

At the chief's proposal they anchored their canoes in the sea, and Aiwohikupua went up with his counsellor to Kukululaumania to the houses of the natives of the place and stayed there waiting for pleasant weather. After four days it cleared over Hilo; the whole country was plainly visible, and Panaewa lay bare.

On this fourth day in the early morning Aiwohikupua awoke and went out of the house, lo! the rainbow arching where they had seen it before; long the chief waited until the sun came, then he went in and aroused his counsellor and said to him: "Here! perhaps you were right; I myself rose early while it was still dark, and went outside and actually saw the rainbow arching in the place you had pointed out to me, and I waited until sunrise—still the rainbow! And I came in to awaken you."

The man said: "That is what I told you; if we had gone we should have been staying up there in Paliuli all these days where she is."

That morning they left Makahanaloa and sailed out to the harbor of Keaau.

They sailed until evening, made shore at Keaau and saw Kauakahialii's houses standing there and the people of the place out surf riding. When they arrived, the people of the place admired Aiwohikupua as much as ever.

The strangers remained at Keaau until evening, then Aiwohikupua ordered the steersmen and rowers to stay quietly until the two of them returned from their search for a wife, only they two alone.

At sunset Aiwohikupua caught up his feather cloak and gave it to the other to carry, and they ascended.

They made way with difficulty through high forest trees and thickets of tangled brush, until, at a place close to Paliuli, they heard the crow of a cock. The man said to his chief: "We are almost out."

They went on climbing, and heard a second time the cock crow (the cock's second crow this). They went on climbing until a great light shone.

The man said to his chief, "Here! we are out; there is Laieikawai's grandmother calling together the chickens as usual."[39]

Asked Aiwohikupua, "Where is the princess's house?"

Said the man, "When we get well out of the garden patch here, then we can see the house clearly."

When Aiwohikupua saw that they were approaching Laieikawai's house, he asked for the feather cloak to hold in his hand when they met the princess of Paliuli.

The garden patch passed, they beheld Laieikawai's house covered with the yellow feathers of the *oo* bird, as the seer had seen in his vision from the god on Kauwiki.

When Aiwohikupua saw the house of the princess of Paliuli, he felt strangely perplexed and abashed, and for the first time he felt doubtful of his success.

And by reason of this doubt within him he said to his companion, "Where are you? We have come boldly after my wife. I supposed her just an ordinary woman. Not so! The princess's house has no equal for workmanship; therefore, let us return without making ourselves known."

Said his counsellor, "This is strange, after we have reached the woman's house for whom we have swum eight seas, here you are begging to go back. Let us go and make her acquaintance, whether for failure or success; for, even if she should refuse, keep at it; we men must expect to meet such rebuffs; a canoe will break on a coral reef."[40]

"Where are you?" answered Aiwohikupua. "We will not meet the princess, and we shall certainly not win her, for I see now the house is no ordinary one. I have brought my cloak wrought with feathers for a gift to the princess of Paliuli and I behold them here as thatch for the princess's house; yet you know, for that matter, even a cloak of feathers is owned by none but the highest chiefs; so let us return." And they went back without making themselves known.

VII

When Aiwohikupua and his companion had left Paliuli they returned and came to Keaau, made the canoe ready, and at the approach of day boarded the canoe and returned to Kauai.

On the way back Aiwohikupua would not say why he was returning until they reached Kauai; then, for the first time, his counsellor knew the reason.

On the way from Keaau they rested at Kamaee, on the rocky side of Hilo, and the next day left there, went to Humuula on the boundary between Hilo and Hamakua; now the seer saw Aiwohikupua sailing over the ocean.

After passing Humuula they stopped right off Kealakaha, and while the chief slept they saw a woman sitting on the sea cliff by the shore.

When those on board saw the woman they shouted, "Oh! what a beautiful woman!"

At this Aiwohikupua started up and asked what they were shouting about. They said, "There is a beautiful woman sitting on the sea cliff." The chief turned his head to look, and saw that the stranger was, indeed, a charming woman.

So the chief ordered the boatmen to row straight to the place where the woman was sitting, and as they approached they first encountered a man fishing with a line, and asked, "Who is that woman sitting up there on the bank directly above you?"

He answered, "It is Poliahu, Cold-bosom.".

As the chief had a great desire to see the woman, she was beckoned to; and she approached with her cloak all covered with snow and gave her greeting to Aiwohikupua, and he greeted her in return by shaking hands.

After meeting the stranger, Aiwohikupua said, "O Poliahu, fair mistress of the coast, happily are we met here; and therefore, O princess of the cliff, I wish you to take me and try me for your husband, and I will be the servant under you; whatever commands you utter I will obey. If you consent to take me as I beseech you, then come on board the canoe and go to Kauai. Why not do so?"

The woman answered, "I am not mistress of this coast. I come from inland; from the summit of that mountain, which is clothed in a white garment like this I am wearing; and how did you find out my name so quickly?"

Said Aiwohikupua, "This is the first I knew about your coming from the White Mountain, but we found out your name readily from that fisherman yonder."

"As to what the chief desires of me," said Poliahu, "I will take you for my husband; and now let me ask you, are you not the chief who stood up and vowed in the name of your gods not to take any woman of these islands from Hawaii to Kauai to wife—only a woman who comes from Moaulanuiakea? Are you not betrothed to Hinaikamalama, the famous princess of Hana? After this trip around Hawaii, then are you not returning for your marriage? And as to your wishing our union, I assure you, until you have made an end of your first vow it is not my part to take you, but yours to take me with you as you desire."

At Poliahu's words Aiwohikupua marveled and was abashed; and after a while a little question escaped him: "How have you ever heard of these deeds of mine you tell of? It is true, Poliahu, all that you say; I have done as you have described; tell me who has told you."

"No one has told me these things, O chief; I knew them for myself," said the princess; "for I was born, like you, with godlike powers, and, like you, my knowledge comes to me from the gods of my fathers, who inspire me; and through these gods I showed you what I have told you. As you were setting out at Humuula I saw your canoe, and so knew who you were."

At these words Aiwohikupua knelt and did reverence to Poliahu and begged to become Poliahu's betrothed and asked her to go with him to Kauai.

"We shall not go together to Kauai," said the woman, "but I will go on board with you to Kohala, then I will return, while you go on."

Now, the chiefs met and conversed on the deck of the canoe.

Before setting out the woman said to Aiwohikupua and his companion, "We sail together; let me be alone, apart from you two, fix bounds between us. You must not touch me, I will not touch you until we reach Kohala; let us remain under a sacred taboo;" and this request pleased them.

As they sailed and came to Kohala they did not touch each other.

They reached Kohala, and on the day when Aiwohikupua's party left, Poliahu took her garment of snow and gave it to Aiwohikupua, saying, "Here is my snow mantle, the mantle my parents strictly forbade my giving to anyone else; it was to be for myself alone; but as we are betrothed, you to me and I to you, therefore I give away this mantle until the day when you remember our vows, then you must seek me, and you will find me above on the White Mountain; show it to me there, then we shall be united."

When Aiwohikupua heard these things the chief's heart was glad, and his counsellor and the paddlers with him.

Then Aiwohikupua took out his feather cloak, brought it and threw it over Poliahu with the words, "As you have said to me before giving me the snow mantle, so do you guard this until our promised union."

When their talk was ended, at the approach of day, they parted from the woman of the mountain and sailed and came to Hana and met Hinaikamalama.

VIII

When Aiwohikupua reached Hana, after parting with Poliahu at Kohala, his boat approached the canoe landing at Haneoo, where they had been before, where Hinaikamalama was living.

When Aiwohikupua reached the landing the canoe floated on the water; and as it floated there Hinaikamalama saw that it was Aiwohikupua's canoe; joyful was she with the thought of their meeting; but still the boat floated gently on the water.

Hinaikamalama came thither where Aiwohikupua and his men floated. Said the woman, "This is strange! What is all this that the canoe is kept afloat? Joyous was I at the sight of you, believing you were coming to land. Not so! Now, tell me, shall you float there until you leave?"

"Yes," answered Aiwohikupua.

"You can not," said the woman, "for I will order the executioner to hold you fast; you became mine at *konane* and our vows are spoken, and I have lived apart and undefiled until your return."

"O princess, not so!" said Aiwohikupua. "It is not to end our vow— that still holds; but the time has not come for its fulfillment. For I said to you, 'When I have sailed about Hawaii then the princess's bet shall be paid;' now, I went meaning to sail about Hawaii, but did not; still at Hilo I got a message from Kauai that the family was in trouble at home, so I turned back; I have stopped in here to tell you all this; and therefore, live apart, and on my next return our vow shall be fulfilled."

At these words of Aiwohikupua the princess's faith returned.

After this they left Hana and sailed and came to Oahu, and on the sea halfway between Oahu and Kauai he laid his command upon the oarsmen and the steersmen, as follows: "Where are you? I charge you, when you come to Kauai, do not say that you have been to Hawaii to seek a wife lest I be shamed; if this is heard about, it will be heard through you, and the penalty to anyone who tells of the journey to Hawaii, it is death, death to himself, death to his wife, death to all his friends; this is the debt he shall pay." This was the charge the chief laid upon the men who sailed with him to Hawaii. Aiwohikupua reached Kauai at sunset and met his sisters. Then he spoke thus to his sisters: "Perhaps you wondered when I went on my journey, because I did not tell you my reason, not even the place where I was to go; and now I tell it to you in secret, my sisters, to you alone. To Hawaii I disappeared to fetch Laieikawai for my wife, after hearing Kauakahialii's story the day when his party returned here. But when I came there I did not get sight of the woman's face; I did not see Laieikawai, but my eyes beheld her house thatched with the yellow feathers of the *oo* bird, so I thought I could not win her and came back here unsuccessful. And as I thought of my failure, then I thought of you sisters,[41] who have won my wishes for me in the days gone by; therefore I came for you to go to Hawaii, the very ones to win what I wish, and at dawn let us rise up and go." Then they were pleased with their brother's words to them.

As Aiwohikupua talked with his sisters, his counsellor for the first time understood the reason for their return to Kauai.

The next day Aiwohikupua picked out fresh paddlers, for the chief knew that the first were tired out. When all was ready for sailing, that very night the chief took on board 14 paddlers, 2 steersmen, the 5 sisters, Mailehaiwale, Mailekaluhea, Mailelaulii, Mailepakaha, and the youngest, Kahalaomapuana, the chief himself, and his counsellor, 23 in all. That night, at the approach of day, they left Kauai, came to Puuloa, and there rested at Hanauma; the next day they lay off Molokai at Kaunakakai, from there they went ashore at Mala at Lahaina; and they left the place, went to Keoneoio in Honuaula, and there they stayed 30 days.

For it was very rough weather on the ocean; when the rough weather was over, then there was good sailing.

Then they left Honuaula and sailed and came to Kaelehuluhulu, at Kona, Hawaii.

As Aiwohikupua's party were on the way from Maui thither, Poliahu knew of their setting sail and coming to Kaelehuluhulu.

Then Poliahu made herself ready to come to wed Aiwohikupua; one month she waited for the promised meeting, but Aiwohikupua was at Hilo after Laieikawai.

Then was revealed to Poliahu the knowledge of Aiwohikupua's doings; through her supernatural power she saw it all; so the woman laid it up in her mind until they should meet, then she showed what she saw Aiwohikupua doing.

From Kaelehuluhulu, Aiwohikupua went direct to Keaau, but many days and nights the voyage lasted.

At noon one day they came to Keaau, and after putting to rights the canoe and the baggage, the chief at once began urging his sisters and his counsellor to go up to Paliuli; and they readily assented to the chief's wish.

Before going up to Paliuli, Aiwohikupua told the steersmen and the paddlers, "While we go on our way to seek her whom I have so longed to see face to face, do you remain here quietly, doing nothing but guard the canoes. If you wait until this night becomes day and day becomes night, then we prosper; but if we come back to-morrow early in the morning, then my wishes have failed, then face about and turn the course to Kauai;" so the chief ordered.

After the chief's orders to the men they ascended half the night, reaching Paliuli. Said Aiwohikupua to the sisters: "This is Paliuli where Laieikawai is, your sister-in-law. See what you are worth."

Then Aiwohikupua took Mailehaiwale, the first born; she stood right at the door of Laieikawai's house, and as she stood there she sent forth a fragrance which filled the house; and within was Laieikawai with her nurse fast asleep; but they could no longer sleep, because they were wakened by the scent of Mailehaiwale.

And starting out of sleep, they two marveled what this wonderful fragrance could be, and because of this marvel Laieikawai cried out in a voice of delight to her grandmother:

LAIEIKAWAI: "O Waka! O Waka—O!"

WAKA: "Heigh-yo! why waken in the middle of the night?"

LAIEIKAWAI: "A fragrance is here, a strange fragrance, a cool fragrance, a chilling fragrance; it goes to my heart."

WAKA: "That is no strange fragrance; it is certainly Mailehaiwale, the sweet-smelling sister of Aiwohikupua, who has come to get you for his wife, you for the wife and he for the husband; here is the man for you to marry."

LAIEIKAWAI: "Bah! I will not marry him." [42]

When Aiwohikupua heard Laieikawai's refusal to take Aiwohikupua for her husband, then he was abashed, for they heard her refusal quite plainly.

IX

After this refusal, then Aiwohikupua said to his counsellor, "You and I will go home and let my sisters stay up here; as for them, let them live as they can, for they are worthless; they have failed to gain my wish."

Said the counsellor, "This is very strange! I thought before we left Kauai you told me that your sisters were the only ones to get your wish, and you have seen now what one of them can do; you have ordered Mailehaiwale to do her part, and we have heard, too, the refusal of Laieikawai. Is this your sisters' fault, that we should go and leave them? But without her you have four sisters left; it may be one of them will succeed."

Said Aiwohikupua, "If the first-born fails, the others perhaps will be worthless."

His counsellor, spoke again, "My lord, have patience; let Mailekaluhea try her luck, and if she fails then we will go."

Now, this saying pleased the chief; said Aiwohikupua, "Suppose you try your luck, and if you fail, all is over."

Mailekaluhea went and stood at the door of the chief-house and gave out a perfume; the fragrance entered and touched the rafters within the house, from the rafters it reached Laieikawai and her companion; then they were startled from sleep.

Said Laieikawai to her nurse, "This is a different perfume, not like the first, it is better than that; perhaps it comes from a man."

The nurse said, "Call out to your grandmother to tell you the meaning of the fragrance."

Laieikawai called:

LAIEIKAWAI: "O Waka! O Waka—O!"

WAKA: "Heigh-yo! why waken in the middle of the night?"

LAIEIKAWAI: "Here is a fragrance, a strange fragrance, a cool fragrance, a chilling fragrance; it goes to my heart."

WAKA. "That is no strange fragrance, it is Mailekaluhea, the sweet-smelling sister of Aiwohikupua, who has come to make you his wife to marry him."

LAIEIKAWAI: "Bah! I will not marry him!"

Said Aiwohikupua to his counsellor, "See! did you hear the princess's refusal?"

"Yes, I heard it; what of her refusing! it is only their scent she does not like; perhaps she will yield to Mailelaulii."

"You are persistent," said Aiwohikupua. "Did I not tell you I wanted to go back, but you refused—you would not consent!"

"We have not tried all the sisters; two are out; three remain," said his counsellor. "Let all your sisters take a chance; this will be best; perhaps you are too hasty in going home; when you reach Keaau and say you have not succeeded, your other sisters will say: 'If you had let us try, Laieikawai would have consented;' so, then, they get something to talk about; let them all try."

"Where are you, my counsellor!" said Aiwohikupua. "It is not you who bears the shame; I am the one. If the grandchild thought as Waka does all would be well."

"Let us bear the shame," said his counsellor. "You know we men must expect such rebuffs; 'a canoe will break on a coral reef;' and if she should refuse, who will tell of it? We are the only ones to hear it. Let us try what Mailelaulii can do."

And because the counsellor urged so strongly the chief gave his consent.

Mailelaulii went right to the door of the chief-house; she gave out her perfume as the others had done; again Laieikawai was startled from sleep and said to her nurse, "This is an entirely different fragrance—not like those before."

Said the nurse, "Call out to Waka."

LAIEIKAWAI: "O Waka! O Waka—O!"

WAKA: "Heigh-yo! Why waken in the middle of the night?"

LAIEIKAWAI: "Here is a fragrance, a strange fragrance, a cool fragrance, a chilling fragrance; it goes to my heart."

WAKA: "That is no strange fragrance; it is Mailelaulii, one of the sweet-smelling sisters of Aiwohikupua, who has come to get you for his wife; he is the husband, the husband for you to marry."

LAIEIKAWAI: "Bah! I will not marry him!"

"One refusal is enough," said Aiwohikupua, "without getting four more! You have brought this shame upon us both, my comrade."

"Let us endure the shame," said his counsellor, "and if our sisters do not succeed, then I will go and enter the house and tell her to take you for her husband as you desire."

S. N. HALE'OLE

Then the chief's heart rejoiced, for Kauakahialii had told him how this same man had got Laieikawai to come down to Keaau, so Aiwohikupua readily assented to his servant's plea.

Then Aiwohikupua quickly ordered Mailepakaha to go and stand at the door of the chief-house; she gave forth her perfume, and Laieikawai was startled from sleep, and again smelled the fragrance. She said to her nurse, "Here is this fragrance again, sweeter than before."

Said the nurse again, "Call Waka."

LAIEIKAWAI: "O Waka! O Waka—O!"

WAKA: "Heigh-yo! Why waken in the middle of the night?"

LAIEIKAWAI: "Here is a fragrance, a strange fragrance, not like the others, a sweet fragrance, a pleasant fragrance; it goes to my heart."

WAKA: "That is no strange fragrance; it is Mailepakaha, the sweet-smelling sister of Aiwohikupua, who has come to get you for a wife to marry him."

LAIEIKAWAI: "Bah! I will not marry him! No matter who comes I will not sleep with him. Do not force Aiwohikupua on me again."

When Aiwohikupua heard this fresh refusal from Laieikawai, his counsellor said, "My lord, it is useless! There is nothing more to be done except one thing; better put off trying the youngest sister and, if she is refused, my going myself, since we have heard her vehement refusal and the sharp chiding she gave her grandmother. And now I have only one thing to advise; it is for me to speak and for you to decide."

"Advise away," said Aiwohikupua, "If it seems good, I will consent; but if not, I will refuse."

"Let us go to the grandmother," said his counsellor, "and ask her; maybe we can get the consent from her."

Said Aiwohikupua, "There is nothing left to be done; it is over; only one word more—our sisters, let them stay here in the jungle, for they are worthless."

Then Aiwohikupua said to his sisters, "You are to stay here; my cherished hope has failed in bringing you here; the forest is your dwelling hereafter." It was then pretty near dawn.

At Aiwohikupua's words all the sisters bowed their heads and wailed.

When Aiwohikupua and his companion started to go, Kahalaomapuana, the youngest sister, called out, "O you two there! Wait! Had we known in Kauai that you were bringing us to leave us in this place, we would never have come. It is only fair that I, too, should have had a chance to win Laieikawai, and had I failed then you would have a right to leave me; we are all together, the guilty with the guiltless; you know me well, I have gained all your wishes."

When Aiwohikupua heard his youngest sister, he felt himself to blame.

Aiwohikupua called to his sister, "You shall come with me; your older sisters must stay here."

"I will not go," answered the youngest sister, "unless we all go together, only then will I go home."

X

At these words of his youngest sister[43] Aiwohikupua said, "Stay here, then, with your sisters and go with them wherever you wish, but I am going home."

Aiwohikupua turned to go, and as the two were still on the way, sang the song of Mailehaiwale, as follows:

> *My divine brother,*
> *My heart's highest,*
> *Go and look*
> *Into the eyes of our parents, say*
> *We abide here,*
> *Fed upon the fruit of sin.[44]*
> *Is constancy perhaps a sin?*

Aiwohikupua turned and looked back at his younger sisters and said, "Constancy is not a sin; haven't I told you that I leave you because you are worthless? If you had gained for me my desire you would not have to stay here; that was what you were brought here for." The two turned and went on and did not listen to the sisters any longer.

When Aiwohikupua and his companion had departed, the sisters conferred together and agreed to follow him, thinking he could be pacified.

They descended and came to the coast at Keaau, where the canoe was making ready for sailing. At the landing the sisters sat waiting to be called; all had gone aboard the canoe, there was no summons at all, the party began to move off; then rang out the song of Mailekaluhea, as follows:

> *My divine brother,*
> *My heart's highest—turn hither,*
> *Look upon your little sisters,*
> *Those who have followed you over the way,*
> *Over the high way, over the low way,*
> *In the rain with a pack on its back,*
> *Like one carrying a child,*

In the rain that roars in the hala trees,
That roars in the hala trees of Hanalei.
How is it with us?
Why did you not leave us,
Leave us at home,
When you went on the journey?
You will look,
Look into the eyes,
The eyes of our parents,
Fare you well!

While Mailekaluhea was singing not once did their brother compassionately look toward them, and the canoe having departed, the sisters sat conferring, then one of them, Kahalaomapuana, the youngest, began to speak.

These were her words: "It is clear that our brother chief is not pacified by the entreaties of Mailehaiwale and Mailekaluhea. Let us, better, go by land to their landing place, then it will be Mailelaulii's turn to sing. It may be he will show affection for her." And they did as she advised.

They left Keaau, came first to Punahoa, to a place called Kanoakapa, and sat down there until Aiwohikupua's party arrived.

When Aiwohikupua and his companions had almost come to land where the sisters were sitting, Aiwohikupua suddenly called out to the paddlers and the steersmen, "Let us leave this harbor; those women have chased us all this way; we had better look for another landing place."

As they left the sisters sitting there, Mailelaulii sang a song, as follows:

My divine brother,
My heart's highest,
What is our great fault?
The eyes of our chief are turned away in displeasure,
The sound of chanting is forbidden,
The chant of your little ones
Of your little sisters.
Have compassion upon us,
Have compassion upon the comrades who have followed you,

The comrades who climbed the cliffs of Haena,
Crept over the cliff where the way was rugged,
The rugged ladder-way up Nualolo
The rough cliff-way up Makana,
It is there—return hither,
Give a kiss to your sisters,
And go on your way,
On the home journey—heartless.
Farewell-to you, you shall look
Look, in our native land,
Into the eyes of our parents.
Fare you well!

As Aiwohikupua heard the sister's voice, they let the canoe float gently; then said Kahalaomapuana, "That is good for us; this is the only time they have let the canoe float; now we shall hear them calling to us, and go on board the canoe, then we shall be safe."

After letting the canoe float a little while, the whole party turned and made off, and had not the least compassion.

When they had left, the sisters consulted afresh what they should do. Kahalaomapuana gave her advice.

She said to her sisters, "There are two of us left, I and Mailepakaha."

Answered Mailepakaha, "He will have no compassion for me, for he had none on any of our sisters; it may be worse with me. I think you had better plead with him as you are the little one, it may be he will take pity on you."

But the youngest would not consent; then they drew lots by pulling the flower stems of grass; the one who pulled the longest, she was the one to plead with the brother; now when they drew, the lot fell to Kahalaomapuana.

When this was done, they left Punahoa, again followed their brother and came to Honolii, where Aiwohikupua's party had already arrived. Here they camped at some distance from Aiwohikupua's party, and Aiwohikupua's party from them.

At Honolii that night they arranged that the others should sleep and a single one keep watch, and to this all consented. They kept watch according to age and gave the morning watch to the youngest. This was in order to see Aiwohikupua's start, for on their journey from Kauai the party had always set out at dawn.

The sisters stood guard that night, until in Mailepakaha's watch Aiwohikupua's party made the canoes ready to start; she awakened the others, and all awoke together.

As the sisters crouched there Kahalaomapuana's watch came, and the party boarded the canoe. The sisters followed down to the landing, and Kahalaomapuana ran and clung to the back of the canoe and called to them in song, as follows:

> Our brother and lord,
> Divine brother,
> Highest and closest!
> Where are you, oh! where?
> You and we, here and there,
> You, the voyager,
> We, the followers.
> Along the cliffs, swimming 'round the steeps,
> Bathing at Waihalau,
> Waihalau at Wailua;
> No longer are we beloved.
> Do you no longer love us?
> The comrades who followed you over the ocean,
> Over the great waves, the little waves,
> Over the long waves, the short waves,
> Over the long-backed waves of the ocean,
> Comrades who followed you inland,
> Far through the jungle,
> Through, the night, sacred and dreadful,
> Oh, turn back!
> Oh, turn back and have pity,
> Listen to my pleading,
> Me the littlest of your sisters.
> Why will you abandon,
> Abandon us
> In this desolation?
> You have opened the highway before us,
> After you we followed,
> We are known as your little sisters,
> Then forsake your anger,
> The wrath, the loveless heart,

S. N. HALEʻOLE

Give a kiss to your little ones,
Fare you well!

When, his youngest sister raised this lamentation to Aiwohikupua, then the brother's heart glowed with love and longing for his sister.

And because of his great love for his little sister, he took her in his arms, set her on his lap, and wept.

When Kahalaomapuana was in her brother's lap, Aiwohikupua ordered the canoemen to paddle with all their might; then the other sisters were left far behind and the canoe went ahead.

As they went, Kahalaomapuana was troubled in mind for her sisters.

Then Kahalaomapuana wept for her sisters and besought Aiwohikupua to restore her to her sisters; but Aiwohikupua would not take pity on her.

"O Aiwohikupua," said his sister, "I will not let you take me by myself without taking my sisters with me, for you called me to you before when we were at Paliuli, but I would not consent to your taking me alone."

And because of Aiwohikupua's stubbornness in refusing to let his sister go, then Kahalaomapuana jumped from the canoe into the sea. Then, for the last time she spoke to her brother in a song, as follows:

You go home and look,
Look into the eyes,
Into the eyes of our parents.
Love to our native land,
My kindred and our friends,
I am going back to your little sisters,
To my older sisters I return.

XI

During this very last song of Kahalaomapuana's, Aiwohikupua's heart filled with love, and he called out for the canoe to back up, but Kahalaomapuana had been left far behind, so swiftly were the men paddling, and by the time the canoe had turned about to pick her up she was not to be found.

Here we must leave Aiwohikupua for a little and tell about his sisters, then speak again about Aiwohikupua.

When Aiwohikupua's party forsook his sisters at Honolii and took Kahalaomapuana with them, the girls mourned for love of their younger sister, for they loved Kahalaomapuana better than their parents or their native land.

While they were still mourning Kahalaomapuana appeared by the cliff; then their sorrow was at an end.

They crowded about their younger sister, and she told them what had happened to her and why she had returned, as has been told in the chapter before.

After talking of all these things, they consulted together where they might best live, and agreed to go back to Paliuli.

After their council they left Honolii and returned to the uplands of Paliuli, to a place near Laieikawai's house, and lived there inside of hollow trees.

And because they wished so much to see Laieikawai they spied out for her from day to day, and after many days of spying they had not had the least sight of her, for every day the door was fast closed.

So they consulted how to get sight of Laieikawai, and after seeking many days after some way to see the princess of Paliuli they found none.

During this debate their younger sister did not speak, so one of her older sisters said, "Kahalaomapuana, all of us have tried to devise a way to see Laieikawai, but we have not found one; perhaps you have something in mind. Speak."

"Yes" said, their younger sister, "let us burn a fire every night, and let the oldest sing, then the next, and so on until the last of us, only one of us sing each night, then I will come the last night; perhaps the fire burning every night will annoy the princess so she will come to find out about us, then perhaps we shall see Laieikawai."

Kahalaomapuana's words pleased them.

The next night they lighted the fire and Mailehaiwale sang that night, as they had agreed, and the next night Mailekaluhea; so they did every night, and the fourth night passed; but Laieikawai gave them no concern. The princess had, in fact, heard the singing and seen the fire burning constantly, but what was that to the princess!

On the fifth night, Kahalaomapuana's night, the last night of all, they lighted the fire, and at midnight Kahalaomapuana made a trumpet of a *ti* leaf[45] and played on it.

Then for the first time Laieikawai felt pleasure in the music, but the princess paid no attention to it. And just before daylight Kahalaomapuana played again on her *ti* leaf trumpet as before, then this delighted the princess. Only two times Kahalaomapuana blew on it that night.

The second night Kahalaomapuana did the same thing again; she began early in the evening to play, but the princess took no notice.

Just before daylight that night she played a second time. Then Laieikawai's sleep was disturbed, and this night she was even more delighted.

And, her interest aroused, she sent her attendant to see where the musical instrument was which was played so near her.

Then the princess's attendant went out of the door of the chief-house and saw the fire which the girls had lighted, crept along until she came to the place where the fire was, and stood at a distance where she was out of sight of those about the fire.

And having seen, she returned to Laieikawai, and the princess inquired about it.

The attendant told the princess what she had seen. "When I went outside the door of the house I saw a fire burning near, and I went and came and stood at a distance without being myself seen. There, behold! I saw five girls sitting around the fire, very beautiful girls; all looked alike, but one of them was very little and she was the one who played the sweet music that we heard."

When the princess heard this she said to her attendant, "Go and get the smallest of them, tell her to come here and amuse us."

At these words of the princess, the nurse went and came to the place where the sisters were and they saw her, and she said, "I am a messenger sent hither by my chief to fetch whichever one of you I want to take; so I take the smallest of you to go and visit my princess as she has commanded."

When Kahalaomapuana was carried away, the hearts of the sisters sang for joy, for they thought to win fortune thereafter.

And their sister went into the presence of Laieikawai.

When they had come to the house, the attendant opened the door; then, Kahalaomapuana was terrified to see Laieikawai resting on the wings of birds as was her custom; two scarlet *iiwi* birds were perched on the shoulders of the princess and shook the dew from red *lehua* blossoms upon her head.

And when Kahalaomapuana saw this, then it seemed marvelous to the stranger girl, and she fell to the ground with trembling heart.

The princess's attendant came and asked, "What is the matter, daughter?"

And twice she asked, then the girl arose and said to the princess's attendant as follows: "Permit me to return to my sisters, to the place from which you took me, for I tremble with fear at the marvelous nature of your princess."

Said the princess's attendant, "Do not fear, have no dread, arise and enter to meet my princess as she has commanded you."

"I am afraid," said the girl.

When the princess heard their low voices, she arose and called to Kahalaomapuana; then the girl's distress was at an end, and the stranger entered to visit the princess.

Said Laieikawai, "Is the merry instrument yours that sounded here last night and this?"

"Yes; it is mine," said Kahalaomapuana.

"Go on," said Laieikawai, "play it."

Kahalaomapuana took her *ti* leaf trumpet from behind her ear, and played before the princess; then Laieikawai was delighted. This was the first time the princess had seen this kind of instrument.

XII

Now, Laieikawai became fascinated with the merry instrument upon which the girl played, so she bade her sound it again.

Said the girl, "I can not sound it again, for it is now daylight, and this instrument is a kind that sounds only by night; it will never sound by day."

Laieikawai was surprised at these words, thinking the girl was lying. So she snatched the trumpet out of the girl's hand and played upon it, and because she was unpracticed in playing the trumpet the thing made no sound; then the princess believed that the trumpet would not sound by day.

Said Laieikawai to Kahalapmapuana, "Let us two be friends, and you shall live here in my house and become my favorite, and your work will be to amuse me."

Said Kahalaomapuana, "O princess, you have spoken well; but it would grieve me to live with you and perhaps gain happiness for myself while my sisters might be suffering."

"How many of you are there?" asked Laieikawai, "and how did you come here?"

Said Kahalaomapuana, "There are six of us born of the same parents; one of the six is a boy and five of us are his younger sisters, and the boy is the oldest, and I am the youngest born. And we journeyed hither with our brother, and because we failed to gain for him his wish, therefore he has abandoned us and has gone back with his favorite companion, and we live here in distress."

Laieikawai asked, "Where do you come from?"

"From Kauai," answered Kahalaomapuana.

"And what is your brother's name?"

"Aiwohikupua," replied the girl.

Again Laieikawai asked, "What are the names of each of you?"

Then she told them all.

Then Laieikawai understood that these were the persons who came that first night.

Said Laieikawai, "Your sisters and your brother I know well, if it was really you who came to me that night; but you I did not hear."

"Yes; we were the ones," said Kahalaomapuana.

Said Laieikawai, "If you were the ones who came that night, who guided you here? For the place is unfrequented, not a single person comes here."

The girl said, "We had a native of the place to guide us, the same man who spoke to you in behalf of Kauakahialii." Then it was clear he was a fellow countryman of theirs.

The end of all this talk was that Laieikawai bade her grandmother to prepare a house for the sisters of Aiwohikupua.

Then, through the supernatural power of her grandmother, Waka, the matter was quickly dispatched, the house was made ready.

When the house was prepared Laieikawai gave orders to Kahalaomapuana: "You return, and to-night come here with all your sisters; when I have seen them then you shall play to us on your merry instrument."

When Kahalaomapuana rejoined her sisters they asked what she had done—what kind of interview she had had with the princess.

Answered the girl, "When I reached the door of the palace a hunchback opened the door to receive me, and when I saw the princess resting on the wings of birds, at the sight I trembled with fear and fell down to the earth. For this reason when I was taken in to talk with the princess I did just what she wished, and she asked about us and I told her everything. The result is, fortune is ours; she has commanded us all to go to her to-night."

When they heard this the sisters were joyful.

At the time the princess had directed they left the hollow tree where they had lived as fugitives.

They went and stood at the door of the chief-house. Laieikawai's attendant opened the door, and they saw just what their sister had described to them.

But when they actually saw Laieikawai, then they were filled with dread, and all except Kahalaomapuana ran trembling with fear and fell to the ground.

And at the princess's command the strangers were brought into the presence of the princess, and the princess was pleased with them.

And at this interview with the princess she promised them her protection, as follows:

"I have heard from your younger sister that you are all of the same parentage and the same blood; therefore I shall treat you all as one blood with me, and we shall protect each other. Whatever one says, the others shall do. Whatever trouble comes to one, the others shall share; and for this reason I have asked our grandmother to furnish you a home where you may live virgin like myself, no one taking a husband without the others' consent. So shall it be well with us from this time on."[46]

To these conditions the stranger girls agreed; the younger sister answered the princess for them all:

"O princess, we are happy that you receive us; happy, too, that you take us to be your sisters as you have said; and so we obey. Only one thing we ask of you: All of us sisters have been set apart by our parents to take no delight in men; and it is their wish that we remain virgin until the end of our days; and so we, your servants, beseech you not to defile us with any man, according to the princess's pleasure, but to allow us to live virgin according to our parents' vow."

And this request of the strangers seemed good to the princess.

After talking with the princess concerning all these things, they were dismissed to the house prepared for them.

As soon as the girls went to live in the house they consulted how they should obey the princess's commands, and they appointed their younger sister to speak to the princess about what they had agreed upon.

One afternoon, just as the princess woke from sleep, came Kahalaomapuana to amuse the princess by playing on the trumpet until the princess wished it no longer.

Then she told Laieikawai what the sisters had agreed upon and said, "O princess, we have consulted together how to protect you, and all five of us have agreed to become the bodyguard for your house; ours shall be the consent, ours the refusal. If anyone wishes to see you, be he a man, or maybe a woman, or even a chief, he shall not see you without our approval. Therefore I pray the princess to consent to what we have agreed."

Said Laieikawai, "I consent to your agreement, and yours shall be the guardianship over all the land of Paliuli."

Now the girls' main purpose in becoming guardians of Paliuli was, if Aiwohikupua should again enter Paliuli, to have power to bar their enemy.

Thus they dwelt in Paliuli, and while they dwelt there never did they weary of life. Never did they even see the person who prepared them food, nor the food itself, save when, at mealtimes, the birds brought them food and cleared away the remnants when they had done. So

Paliuli became to them a land beloved, and there they dwelt until the trouble came upon them which was wrought by Halaaniani.

Here, O reader, we leave speaking of the sisters of Aiwohikupua, and in Chapter XIII of this tale will speak again of Aiwohikupua and his coming to Kauai.

XIII

At the time when Kahalaomapuana leaped from the canoe into the sea it was going very swiftly, so she fell far behind. The canoe turned back to recover Kahalaomapuana, but the party did not find her; then Aiwohikupua abandoned his young sister and sailed straight for Kauai.

As Aiwohikupua sailed away from Hawaii, between Oahu and Kauai he spoke to his paddlers as follows: "When we get back to Kauai let no one tell that we have been to Hawaii after Laieikawai, lest shame come to me and I be spoken of jeeringly; and therefore I lay my commands upon you. Whoever speaks of this journey of ours and I hear of it, his penalty is death, his and all his offspring, as I vowed to those paddlers of mine before."

They returned to Kauai. A few days afterwards Aiwohikupua, the chief, wished to make a feast for the chiefs and for all his friends on Kauai.

While the feast was being made ready the chief gave word to fetch the feasters; with all the male chiefs, only one woman of rank was allowed to come to the celebration; this was Kailiokalauokekoa.[47]

On the day of the feast all the guests assembled, the food was ready spread, and the drink at the feast was the *awa*.

Before eating, all the guests together took up their cups of *awa* and drank. During the feasting, the *awa* had not the least effect upon them.

And because the *awa* had no effect, the chief hastily urged his *awa* chewers to chew the *awa* a second time. When the chief's command was carried out, the guests and the chief himself took up their cups of *awa* all together and drank. When this cup of *awa* was drained the effect of the *awa* overcame them. But the one who felt the effects most was the chief who gave the feast.

Now, while the chief was drunk, the oath which he swore at sea to the rowers was not forgotten; not from one of his own men was the forbidden story told, but from the mouth of Aiwohikupua himself was the chief's secret heard.

While under the influence of the *awa*, Aiwohikupua turned right around upon Kauakahialii, who was sitting near, and said: "O Kauakahialii, when you were talking to us about Laieikawai, straightway there entered into me desire after that woman; then sleepless were my nights with the wish, to see her; so I sailed and came to Hawaii, two of us went up, until at daylight we reached the uplands of Paliuli; when I went to see the chief's house, it was very beautiful, I was ashamed; therefore I returned here. I returned, in fact, thinking that the little sisters were the ones to get my wish; I fetched them, made the journey with the girls to the house of the princess, let them do their best; when, as it happened, they were all refused, all four sisters except the youngest; for shame I returned. Surely that woman is the most stubborn of all, she has no equal."

While Aiwohikupua talked of Laieikawai's stubbornness, Hauailiki was sitting at the feast, the young singer of Mana, a chief of high rank on the father's side and of unrivaled beauty.

He arose and said to Aiwohikupua, "You managed the affair awkwardly. I do not believe her to be a stubborn woman; give me a chance to stand before her eyes; I should not have to speak, she would come of her own free will to meet me, then you would see us together."

Said Aiwohikupua, "Hauailiki, I wish you would go to Hawaii; if you get Laieikawai, you are a lucky fellow, and I will send men with you and a double canoe; and should you lose in this journey then your lands become mine, and if you return with Laieikawai then all my lands are yours."

After Aiwohikupua had finished speaking, that very night, Hauailiki boarded the double canoe and set sail, but many days passed on the journey.

As they sailed they stood off Makahanaloa, and, looking out, saw the rainbow arching above the beach of Keaau. Said Aiwohikupua's chief counsellor to Hauailiki, "Look well at that rainbow arching the beach there at Keaau. There is Laieikawai watching the surf riding."

Said Hauailiki, "I thought Paliuli was where she lived."

And on the next day, in the afternoon, when they reached Keaau, Laieikawai had just returned with Aiwohikupua's sisters to Paliuli.

When Hauailiki's party arrived, behold many persons came to see this youth who rivaled Kauakahialii and Aiwohikupua in beauty, and all the people of Keaau praised him exceedingly.

Next day at sunrise the mist and fog covered all Keaau, and when it cleared, behold! seven girls were sitting at the landing place of Keaau, one of whom was more beautiful than the rest. This was the very first time that the sisters of Aiwohikupua had come down with Laieikawai, according to their compact.

As Laieikawai and her companions were sitting there that morning, Hauailiki stood up and walked about before them, showing off his good looks to gain the notice of the princess of Paliuli. But what was Hauailiki to Laieikawai? Mere chaff!

Four days Laieikawai came to Keaau after Hauailiki's entering the harbor; and four days Hauailiki showed himself off before Laieikawai, and she took no notice at all of him.

On the fifth day of her coming, Hauailiki thought to display before the beloved one his skill with the surf board;[48] the truth is Hauailiki surpassed any one else on Kauai as an expert in surf riding, he surpassed all others in his day, and he was famous for this skill as well as for his good looks.

That day, at daybreak, the natives of the place, men and women, were out in the breakers.

While the people were gathering for surfing, Hauailiki undid his garment, got his surf board, of the kind made out of a thick piece of *wili-wili* wood, went directly to the place where Laieikawai's party sat, and stood there for some minutes; then it was that the sisters of Aiwohikupua took a liking to Hauailiki.

Said Mailehaiwale to Laieikawai, "If we had not been set apart by our parents, I would take Hauailiki for my husband."

Said Laieikawai, "I like him, too; but I, too, have been set apart by my grandmother, so that my liking is useless."

"We are all alike," said Mailehaiwale.

When Hauailiki had showed himself off for some minutes, Hauailiki leaped with his surf board into the sea and swam out into the breakers.

When Hauailiki was out in the surf, one of the girls called out, "Land now!"

"Land away!" answered Hauailiki, for he did not wish to ride in on the same breaker with the crowd. He wished to make himself conspicuous on a separate breaker, in order that Laieikawai should see his skill in surf riding and maybe take a liking to him. Not so!

When the others had gone in a little wave budded and swelled, then Hauailiki rode the wave. As he rode, the natives cheered and the sisters of Aiwohikupua also. What was that to Laieikawai?

When Hauailiki heard the cheering, then he thought surely Laieikawai's voice would join the shouting. Not so! He kept on surfing until the fifth wave had passed; it was the same; he got no call whatever; then Hauailiki first felt discouragement, with the proof of Aiwohikupua's saying about the "stubbornness of Laieikawai."

XIV

When Hauailiki saw that Laieikawai still paid no attention to him he made up his mind to come in on the surf without the board.

He left it and swam out to the breakers. As he was swimming Laieikawai said, "Hauailiki must be crazy."

Her companions said, "Perhaps he will ride in on the surf without a board."

When Hauailiki got to the breakers, just as the crest rose and broke at his back, he stood on its edge, the foam rose on each side of his neck like boars' tusks. Then all on shore shouted and for the first time Laieikawai smiled; the feat was new to her eyes and to her guardians also.

When Hauailiki saw Laieikawai smiling to herself he thought she had taken a liking to him because of this feat, so he kept on repeating it until five breakers had come in; no summons came to him from Laieikawai.

Then Hauailiki was heavy-hearted because Laieikawai took no notice of him, and he felt ashamed because of his boast to Aiwohikupua, as we have seen in the last chapter.

So he floated gently on the waves, and as he floated the time drew near for Laieikawai's party to return to Paliuli. Then Laieikawai beckoned to Hauailiki.

When Hauailiki saw the signal the burden was lifted from his mind; Hauailiki boasted to himself, "You wanted me all the time; you just delayed."

And at the signal of the princess of Paliuli he lay upon the breaker and landed right where Laieikawai and her companions were sitting; then Laieikawai threw a *lehua* wreath around Hauailiki's neck, as she always did for those who showed skill in surf riding. And soon after the mist and fog covered the land, and when it passed away nothing was to be seen of Laieikawai and her party; they were at Paliuli.

This was the last time that Laieikawai's party came to Keaau while Hauailiki was there; after Hauailiki's return to Kauai, then Laieikawai came again to Keaau.

After Laieikawai's party were gone to the uplands of Paliuli, Hauailiki left off surf riding and joined his guide, the chief counsellor of Aiwohikupua. Said he, "I think she is the only one who is impregnable;

what, Aiwohikupua said is true. There is no luck in my beauty or my skill in surf riding; only one way is left, for us to foot it to Paliuli tonight." To this proposal of Hauailiki his comrade assented.

In the afternoon, after dinner, the two went up inland and entered the forest where it was densely overgrown with underbrush. As they went on, they met Mailehaiwale, the princess's first guardian. When she saw them approaching from a distance, she cried, "O Hauailiki, you two go back from there, you two have no business to come up here, for I am the outpost of the princess's guards and it is my business to drive back all who come here; so turn back, you two, without delay."

Said Hauailiki, "Just let us go take a look at the princess's house."

Said Mailehaiwale, "I will not let you; for I am put here to drive off everybody who comes up here like you two."

But because they urged her with such persuasive words, she did consent.

As they went on, after Mailehaiwale let them pass, they soon encountered Mailekaluhea, the second of the princess's guardians.

Said Mailekaluhea, "Here! you two go back, you two have no right to come up here. How did you get permission to pass here?"

Said they, "We came to see the princess."

"You two have no such right," said Mailekaluhea, "for we guards are stationed here to drive off everybody who comes to this place; so, you two go back."

But to Mailekaluhea's command they answered so craftily with flattering words that they were allowed to pass.

As the two went on they met Mailelaulii and with the same words they had used to the first, so they addressed Mailelaulii.

And because of their great craft in persuasion, the two were allowed to pass Mailelaulii's front. And they went on, and met Mailepakaha, the fourth guardian.

When they came before Mailepakaha this guardian was not at all pleased at their having been let slip by the first guards, but so crafty was their speech that they were allowed to pass.

And they went on, and behold! they came upon Kahalaomapuana, the guardian at the door of the chief-house, who was resting on the wings of birds, and when they saw how strange was the workmanship of the chief-house, then Hauailiki fell to the earth with trembling heart.

When Kahalaomapuana saw them she was angry, and she called out to them authoritatively, as the princess's war chief, "O Hauailiki! haste and go back, for you two have no business here; if you persist, then I will call hither the birds of Paliuli to eat your flesh; only your spirits will return to Kauai."

At these terrible words of Kahalaomapuana, Hauailiki's courage entirely left him; he arose and ran swiftly until he reached Keaau in the early morning.

For weariness of the journey up to Paliuli, they fell down and slept.

While Hauailiki slept, Laieikawai came to him in a dream, and they met together; and on Hauailiki's starting from sleep, behold! it was a dream.

Hauailiki slept again; again he had the dream as at first; four nights and four days the dream was repeated to Hauailiki, and his mind was troubled.

On the fifth night after the dream had come to Hauailiki so repeatedly, after dark, he arose and ascended to the uplands of Paliuli without his comrade's knowledge.

In going up, he did not follow the road the two had taken before, but close to Mailehaiwale he took a new path and escaped the eyes of the princess's guardians.

When he got outside the chief-house Kahalaomapuana was fast asleep, so he tiptoed up secretly, unfastened the covering at the entrance to the house, which was wrought with feather work, and behold! he saw Laieikawai resting on the wings of birds, fast asleep also.

When he had entered and stood where the princess was sleeping, he caught hold of the princess's head and shook her. Then Laieikawai started up from' sleep, and behold! Hauailiki standing at her head, and her mind was troubled.

Then Laieikawai spoke softly to Hauailiki, "Go away now, for death and life have been left with my guardians, and therefore I pity you; arise and go; do not wait."

Hauailiki said, "O Princess, let us kiss[49] one another, for a few nights ago I came up and got here without seeing you; we were driven away by the power of your guards, and on our reaching the coast, exhausted, I fell asleep; while I slept we two met together in a dream and we were united, and many days and nights the same dream came; therefore I have come up here again to fulfill what was done in the dream."

Laieikawai said, "Return; what you say is no concern of mine; for the same thing has come to me in a dream and it happened to me as it happened to you, and what is that to me? Go! return!"

As Kahalaomapuana slept, she heard low talking in the house, and she started up from sleep and called out, "O Laieikawai, who is the confidant who is whispering to you?"

When she heard the questioner, Laieikawai ceased speaking.

Soon Kahalaomapuana arose and entered the house, and behold! Hauailiki was in the house with Laieikawai.

Kahalaomapuana said, "O Hauailiki, arise and go; you have no right to enter here; I told you before that you had no business in this place, and I say the same thing to-night as on that first night, so arise and return to the coast."

And at these words of Kahalaomapuana Hauailiki arose with shame in his heart, and returned to the beach at Keaau and told his comrades about his journey to Paliuli.

When Hauailiki saw that he had no further chance to win Laieikawai, then he made the canoe ready to go back to Kauai, and with the dawn left Keaau and sailed thither.

When Hauailiki's party returned to Kauai and came to Wailua, he saw a great company of the high chiefs and low chiefs of the court, and Kauakahialii and Kailiokalauokekoa with them.

As Hauailiki and his party were nearing the mouth of the river at Wailua, he saw Aiwohikupua and called out, "I have lost."

When Hauailiki landed and told Aiwohikupua the story of his journey and how his sisters had become the princess's guardians, then Aiwohikupua rejoiced.

He declared to Hauailiki, "There's an end to our bet, for it was made while we were drunk with *awa*."

While Hauailiki was telling how Aiwohikupua's sisters had become guardians to Laieikawai, then Aiwohikupua conceived afresh the hope of sailing to Hawaii to get Laieikawai, as he had before desired.

XV

S aid Aiwohikupua, "How fortunate I am to have left my sisters on Hawaii, and so I shall attain my desire, for I have heard that my sisters are guardians to the one on whom I have set my heart."

Now, while all the chiefs were gathered at Wailua, then Aiwohikupua stood up and declared his intention in presence of the chiefs: "Where are you! I shall go again to Hawaii, I shall not fail of my desire; for my sisters are now guardians of her on whom I have set my heart."

At these words of Aiwohikupua, Hauailiki said, "You will not succeed, for I saw that the princess was taboo, and your sisters also put on reserved airs; one of them, indeed, was furious, the smallest of them; so my belief is you will not succeed, and if you go near you will get paid for it."

To Hauailiki's words Aiwohikupua paid no attention, for he was hopeful because of what he had heard of his sisters' guarding the princess.

After this he summoned the bravest of his fighting men, his bodyguard, all his chiefly array, and the chief arranged for paddlers; then he commanded the counsellor to make the canoes ready.

The counsellor chose the proper canoes for the trip, twenty double canoes, and twice forty single canoes, these for the chiefs and the bodyguard, and forty provision canoes for the chief's supplies; and as for the chief himself and his counsellor, they were on board of a triple canoe.

When everything was ready for such a journey they set out.

Many days they sailed. When they came to Kohala, for the first time the Kohala people recognized Aiwohikupua, a magician renowned all over the islands. And because the chief came in disguise to Kohala when he fought with Cold-nose, this was why they had not recognized him.

They left Kohala and went to Keaau. Just as they reached there, Laieikawai and the sisters of Aiwohikupua returned to Paliuli.

When Laieikawai and her companions returned, on the day when Aiwohikupua's party arrived, their grandmother had already foreseen Aiwohikupua's arrival at Keaau.

Said Waka, "Aiwohikupua has come again to Keaau, so let the guard be watchful, look out for yourselves, do not go down to the sea, stay here on the mountain until Aiwohikupua returns to Kauai."

When the princess's head guard heard the grandmother's words, then Kahalaomapuana immediately ordered Kihanuilulumoku,[50] their god, to come near the home of the chief and prepare for battle.

As the princess's chief guard, she ordered her sisters to consult what would be the best way to act in behalf of the princess.

When they met and consulted what was best to be done, all agreed to what Kahalaomapuana, the princess's chief guard, proposed, as follows: "You, Mailehaiwale, if Aiwohikupua should come hither, and you two meet, drive him away, for you are the first guard; and if he should plead his cause force him away: and if he is very persistent, because he is a brother, resist him still more forcibly; and if he still insists then despatch one of the guardian birds to me, then we will all meet at the same place, and I myself will drive him away. If he threatens to harm us, then I will command our god, Kihanuilulumoku, who will destroy him."

After all the council had assented they stationed themselves at a distance from each other to guard the princess as before.

At dawn that night arrived Aiwohikupua with his counsellor. When they saw the taboo sign—the hollow post covered with white *tapa*—then they knew that the road to the princess's dwelling was taboo. But Aiwohikupua would not believe it taboo because of having heard that his sisters had the guardian power.

So they went right on and found another taboo sign like the first which they had found, for one sign was set up for each of the sisters.

After passing the fourth taboo sign, they approached at a distance the fifth sign; this was Kahalaomapuana's. This was the most terrible of all, and then it began to be light; but they could not see in the dark how terrible it was.

They left the sign, went a little way and met Mailehaiwale; overjoyed was Aiwohikupua to see his sister. At that instant Mailehaiwale cried, "Back, you two, this place is taboo."

Aiwohikupua supposed this was in sport; both again began to approach Mailehaiwale; again the guardian told them to go. "Back at once, you two! What business have you up here and who will befriend you?"

"What is this, my sister?" asked Aiwohikupua. "Are you not my friends here, and through you shall I not get my desire?"

Then Mailehaiwale sent one of her guardian birds to Kahalaomapuana; in less than no time the four met at the place guarded by Mailekaluhea, where they expected to meet Aiwohikupua.

XVI

And they were ready and were sent for and came. When Aiwohikupua saw Kahalaomapuana resting on the wings of birds, as commander in chief, this was a great surprise to Aiwohikupua and his companion. Said the head guard, "Return at once, linger not, delay not your going, for the princess is taboo, you have not the least business in this place; and never let the idea come to you that we are your sisters; that time has passed." Kahalaomapuana arose and disappeared.

Then the hot wrath of Aiwohikupua was kindled and his anger grew. He decided at that time to go back to the sea to Keaau, then send his warriors to destroy the younger sisters.

When they turned back and came to Kahalaomapuana's taboo sign, behold! the tail of the great lizard protruded above the taboo sign, which was covered with white *tapa* wound with the *ieie* vine and the sweet-scented fern,[51] and it was a terrible thing to see.

As soon as Aiwohikupua and his companion reached the sea at Keaau, Aiwohikupua's counsellor dispatched the chief's picked fighting men to go up and destroy the sisters, according to the chief's command.

That very day Waka foresaw what Aiwohikupua's intention was. So Waka went and met Kahalaomapuana, the princess's commander in chief, and said: "Kahalaomapuana, I have seen what your brother intends to do. He is preparing ten strong men to come up here and destroy you, for your brother is wrathful because you drove him away this morning; so let us be ready in the name of our god."

Then she sent for Kihanuilulumoku, the great lizard of Paliuli, their god. And the lizard came and she commanded him: "O our god, Kihanuilulumoku, see to this lawless one, this mischief-maker, this rogue of the sea; if they send a force here, slaughter them all, let no messenger escape, keep on until the last one is taken, and beware of Kalahumoku, Aiwohikupua's great strong dog;[52] if you blunder, there is an end of us, we shall not escape; exert your strength, all your godlike might over Aiwohikupua. Amen, it is finished, flown away." This was Kahalaomapuana's charge to their god.

That night the ten men chosen by the chief went up to destroy the sisters of Aiwohikupua, and the assistant counsellor made the eleventh in place of the chief counsellor.

At the first dawn they approached Paliuli. Then they heard the humming of the wind in the thicket from the tongue of that great lizard, Kihanuilulumoku, coming for them, but they did not see the creature, so they went on; soon they saw the upper jaw of the lizard hanging right over them; they were just between the lizard's jaws; then the assistant counsellor leaped quickly back, could not make the distance; it snapped them up; not a messenger was left.

Two days passed; there was no one to tell of the disaster to Aiwohikupua's party, and because he wondered why they did not return the chief was angry.

So the chief again chose a party of warriors, twenty of them, from the strongest of his men, to go up and destroy the sisters; and the counsellor appointed an assistant counsellor to go for him with the men.

Again they went up until they came clear to the place where the first band had disappeared; these also disappeared in the lizard; not a messenger was left.

Again the chief waited; they came not back. The chief again sent a band of forty; all were killed. So it went on until eight times forty warriors had disappeared.

Then Aiwohikupua consulted with his counsellor as to the reason for none of the men who had been sent returning.

Said Aiwohikupua to his counsellor, "How is it that these warriors who are sent do not return?"

Said his counsellor, "It may be when they get to the uplands and see the beauty of the place they remain, and if not, they have all been killed by your sisters."

"How can they be killed by those helpless girls, whom I intended to kill?" So said Aiwohikupua.

And because of the chief's anxiety to know why his warriors did not come back he agreed with his counsellor to send messengers to see what the men were doing.

At the chief's command the counsellor sent the Snipe and the Turnstone, Aiwohikupua's swiftest messengers, to go up and find out the truth about his men.

Not long after they had left they met another man, a bird catcher from the uplands of Olaa;[53] he asked, "Where are you two going?"

The runners said, "We are going up to find out the truth about our people who are living at Paliuli; eight times forty men have been sent— not one returned."

"They are done for," said the bird catcher, "in the great lizard, Kihanuilulumoku; they have not been spared."

When they heard this they kept on going up; not long after they heard the sighing of the wind and the humming of the trees bending back and forth; then they remembered the bird catcher's words, "If the wind hums, that is from the lizard."

They knew then this must be the lizard; they flew in their bird bodies. They flew high and looked about. There right above them was the upper jaw shutting down upon them, and only by quickness of flight in their bird bodies did they escape.

XVII

As they flew far upward and were lost to sight on high, Snipe and his companion looked down at the lower jaw of the lizard plowing the earth like a shovel, and it was a fearful thing to see. It was plain their fellows must all be dead, and they returned and told Aiwohikupua what they had seen.

Then Kalahumoku, Aiwohikupua's great man-eating dog, was fetched to go and kill the lizard, then to destroy the sisters of Aiwohikupua.

When Kalahumoku, the man-eating dog from Tahiti, came into the presence of his grandchild (Aiwohikupua), "Go up this very day and destroy my sisters," said Aiwohikupua, "and bring Laieikawai."

Before the dog went up to destroy Aiwohikupua's sisters the dog first instructed the chief, and the chiefs under him, and all the men, as follows: "Where are you? While I am away, you watch the uplands. When the clouds rise straight up, if they turn leeward then I have met Kihanuilulumoku and you will know that we have made friends. But if the clouds turn to the windward, there is trouble; I have fought with that lizard. Then pray to your god, to Lanipipili; if you see the clouds turn, seaward, the lizard is the victor; but when the clouds ascend and turn toward the mountain top, then the lizard has melted away; we have prevailed.[54] Then keep on praying until I return."[55]

After giving his instructions, the dog set out up the mountain, and Aiwohikupua sent with him Snipe and Turnstone as messengers to report the deeds of the dog and the lizard.

When the dog had come close to Paliuli, Kihanuilulumoku was asleep at the time; he was suddenly startled from sleep; he was awakened by the scent of a dog. By that time the lizard was too late for the dog, who went on until he reached the princess's first guardian.

Then the lizard took a sniff, the guardian god of Paliuli, and recognized Kalahumoku, the marvel of Tahiti; then the lizard lifted his upper jaw to begin the fight with Kalahumoku.

Instantly the dog showed his teeth at the lizard, and the fight began; then the lizard was victor over Kalahumoku and the dog just escaped without ears or tail.

At the beginning of the fight the messengers returned to tell Aiwohikupua of this terrible battle.

When they heard from Snipe and his companion of this battle between the lizard and the dog, Aiwohikupua looked toward the mountain.

As they looked the clouds rose straight up, and no short time after turned seaward, then Aiwohikupua knew that the lizard had prevailed and Aiwohikupua regretted the defeat of their side.

In the evening of the day of the fight between the two marvelous creatures Kalahumoku came limping back exhausted; when the chief looked him over, gone were the ears and tail inside the lizard.

So Aiwohikupua resolved to depart, since they were vanquished. They departed and came to Kauai and told the story of the journey and of the victory of the lizard over them. (This was the third time that Aiwohikupua had been to Paliuli after Laieikawai without fulfilling his mission.)

Having returned to Kauai without Laieikawai, Aiwohikupua gave up thinking about Laieikawai and resolved to carry out the commands of Poliahu.

At this time Aiwohikupua, with his underchiefs and the women of his household, clapped hands in prayer before Lanipipili, his god, to annul his vow.

And he obtained favor in the presence of his god, and was released from his sinful vow "not to take any woman of these islands to wife," as has been shown in the former chapters of this story.

After the ceremonies at Kauai, he sent his messengers, the Snipe and the Turnstone, to go and announce before Poliahu the demands of the chief.

In their bird bodies they flew swiftly to Hinaikamalama's home at Hana and came and asked the people of the place, "Where is the woman who is betrothed to the chief of Kauai?"

"She is here," answered the natives of the place.

They went to meet the princess of Hana.

The messengers said to the princess, "We have been sent hither to tell you the command of your betrothed husband. You have three months to prepare for the marriage, and in February, on the night of the seventeenth, the night of Kulu, he will come to meet you, according to the oath between you."

When the princess had heard these words the messengers returned and came to Aiwohikupua.

Asked the chief, "Did you two meet Poliahu?"

"Yes," said the messengers, "we told her, as you commanded, to prepare herself; Poliahu inquired, 'Does he still remember the game of *konane* between us?'"

"Perhaps so," answered the messengers.

When Aiwohikupua heard the messengers' words he suspected that they had not gone to Poliahu; then Aiwohikupua asked to make sure, "How did you two fly?"

Said they, "We flew past an island, flew on to some long islands—a large, island like the one we first passed, two little islands like one long island, and a very little island; we flew along the east coast of that island and came to a house below the hills covered with shade; there we found Poliahu; that was how it was."

Said Aiwohikupua, "You did not find Poliahu; this was Hinaikainalama."

Now for this mistake of the messengers the rage of Aiwohikupua was stirred against his messengers, and they ceased to be among his favorites.

At this, Snipe and his companion decided to tell the secrets prohibited to the two by their master. Now how they carried out their intrigue, you will see in Chapter XVIII.

XVIII

After the dismissal of Snipe and his fellow, the chief dispatched Frigate-bird, one of his nimble messengers, with the same errand as before.

Frigate-bird went to Poliahu; when they met, Frigate-bird gave the chief's command, according to the words spoken in Chapter XVII of this story. Having given his message, the messenger returned and reported aright; then his lord was pleased.

Aiwohikupua waited until the end of the third month; the chief took his underchiefs and his favorites and the women of his household and other companions suitable to go with their renowned lord in all his royal splendor on an expedition for the marriage of chiefs.

On the twenty-fourth day of the month Aiwohikupua left Kauai, sailed with 40 double canoes, twice 40 single canoes, and 20 provision boats.

Some nights before that set for the marriage, the eleventh night of the month, the night of Huna, they came to Kawaihae; then he sent his messenger, Frigate-bird, to get Poliahu to come thither to meet Aiwohikupua on the day set for the marriage.

When the messenger returned from Poliahu, he told Poliahu's reply: "Your wife commands that the marriage take place at Waiulaula. When you look out early in the morning of the seventeenth, the day of Kulu, and the snow clothes the summit of Maunakea, Maunaloa, and Hualalai,[56] clear to Waiulaula, then they have reached the place where you are to be wed; then set out, so she says."

Then Aiwohikupua got ready to present himself with the splendor of a chief.

Aiwohikupua clothed the chiefs and chiefesses and his two favorites in feather capes and the women of his household in braided mats of Kauai. Aiwohikupua clothed himself in his snow mantle that Poliahu had given him, put on the helmet of *ie* vine wrought with feathers of the red *iiwi* bird. He clothed his oarsmen and steersmen in red and white *tapa* as attendants of a chief; so were all his bodyguard arrayed.

On the high seat of the double canoe in which the chief sailed was set up a canopied couch covered with feather capes, and right above the couch the taboo signs of a chief, and below the sacred symbols sat Aiwohikupua.

Following the chief and surrounding his canoe came ten double canoes filled with expert dancers. So was Aiwohikupua arrayed to meet Poliahu.

On the seventeenth day, the day of Kulu, in the early morning, a little later than sunrise, Aiwohikupua and his party saw the snow begin to hide the summits of the mountain clear to the place of meeting.

Already had Poliahu, Lilinoe, Waiaie, and Kahoupokane arrived for the chief's marriage.

Then Aiwohikupua set out to join the woman of the mountain. He went in the state described above.

As Aiwohikupua was sailing from Kawaihae, Lilinoe rejoiced to see the unrivaled splendor of the chief.

When they came to Waiulaula they were shivering with cold, so Aiwohikupua sent his messenger to tell Poliahu, "They can not come for the cold."

Then Poliahu laid off her mantle of snow and the mountain dwellers put on their sun mantles, and the snow retreated to its usual place.

When Aiwohikupua and his party reached Poliahu's party the princess was more than delighted with the music from the dancers accompanying the chief's canoe and she praised his splendid appearance; it was beautiful.

When they met both showed the robes given them before in token of their vow.

Then the chiefs were united and became one flesh, and they returned and lived in Kauai, in the uplands of Honopuwai.

Now Aiwohikupua's messengers, Snipe and Turnstone, went to tell Hinaikamalama of the union of Aiwohikupua with Poliahu.

When Hinaikamalama heard about it, then she asked her parents to let her go on a visit to Kauai, and the request pleased her parents.

The parents hastened the preparation of canoes for Hinaikamalama's voyage to Kauai, and selected a suitable cortege for the princess's journey, as is customary on the journey of a chief.

When all was ready Hinaikamalama went on board the double canoe and sailed and came to Kauai.

When she arrived Aiwohikupua was with Poliahu and others at Mana, where all the chiefs were gathered for the sport between Hauailiki and Makaweli.

That night was a festival night, the game of *kilu* and the dance *kaeke* being the sports of the night.[57]

During the rejoicings in the middle of the night came Hinaikamalama and sat in the midst of the festive gathering, and all marveled at this strange girl.

When she came into their midst Aiwohikupua did not see her, for his attention was taken by the dance.

As Hinaikamalama sat there, behold! Hauailiki conceived a passion for her.

Then Hauailiki went and said to the master of ceremonies, "Go and tell Aiwohikupua to stop the dance and play at spin-the-gourd; when the game begins, then you go up and draw the stranger for my partner to-night."

At the request of the one for whom the sports were given the dance was ended.

Then Hauailiki played at spin-the-gourd with Poliahu until the gourd had been spun ten times. Then the master of ceremonies arose and made the circuit of the assembly, returned and touched Hauailiki with his *maile* wand and sang a song, and Hauailiki arose.

Then the master of ceremonies took the wand back and touched Hinaikamalama's head and she arose.

As she stood there she requested the master of the sports to let her speak, and he nodded.

Hinaikamalama asked for whom the sports were given, and they told her for Hauailiki and Makaweli.

And Hinaikamalama turned right around and said to Hauailiki, "O chief of this festal gathering (since I have heard this is all in your honor), your sport master has matched us two, O chief, to bring us together for a little; now I put off the match which the master of ceremonies has chosen. But let me explain my object in coming so far as Kauai. That fellow there, Aiwohikupua, is my reason for coming to this land, because I heard that he was married to Poliahu; therefore I came here to see how he had lied to me. For that man there came to Hana on Maui while we were surf riding. The two of them were the last to surf, and when they were through, they came home to play *konane* with me. He wanted to play *konane*. We set up the board again; I asked what he would bet; he pointed to his double canoe. I said I did not like his bet; then I told the bet I liked, our persons; if he beat me at *konane*, then I would become his and do everything that he told me to do, and the same if he lost to me, then he was to do for me as I to him; and we made this bargain. And in the game in a little while my piece blocked the game, and he was beaten. I said to him, 'You have lost; you ought to stay with me as we have wagered.' Said that fellow, 'I will wait to carry out the bet until I return, from a touring trip. Then I will fulfill the bet, O princess.' And because of his fine speeches we agreed upon this, and for this reason, I have lived apart under a taboo until now. And when I heard that he had a wife, I came to Kauai and entered the festal gathering. O chief, that is how it was."

Then the men at the gathering all around the *kilu* shelter were roused and blamed Aiwohikupua. Then at Hinaikamalama's story, Poliahu was filled with hot anger; and she went back to White Mountain and is there to this day.

Soon after Hinaikamalama's speech the games began again; the game was between Aiwohikupua and Makaweli.

Then the master of ceremonies stood up and touched Hauailiki and Hinaikamalama with the wand, and Hauailiki arose and Hinaikamalama also. This time Hinaikamalama said to Hauailiki, "O chief, we have been matched by the sport master as is usual in this game. But I must delay my consent; when Aiwohikupua has consented to carry out our vow, after that, at the chief's next festival night, this night's match shall be fulfilled." Then Hauailiki was very well pleased.

And because of Hinaikamalama's words, Aiwohikupua took Hinaikamalama to carry out their vow.

That very night as they rested comfortably in the fulfillment of their bargain, Hinaikamalama grew numb with cold, for Poliahu had spread her cold snow mantle over her enemy.

Then Hinaikamalama raised a short chant—

Cold, ah! cold,
A very strange cold,
My heart is afraid.
Perhaps sin dwells within the house,
My heart begins to fear,
Perhaps the house dweller has sinned.
O my comrade, it is cold.

XIX

When Hinaikamalama ceased chanting, she said to Aiwohikupua, "Where are you? Embrace me close to make me warm; I am cold all over; no warmth at all."

Then Aiwohikupua obeyed her, and she grew as warm as before.

As they began to take their ease in fulfillment of their vow at the betrothal, then the cold came a second time upon Hinaikamalama.

Then she raised a chant, as follows:

> *O my comrade, it is cold,*
> *Cold as the snow on the mountain top,*
> *The cold lies at the soles of my feet,*
> *It presses upon my heart,*
> *The cold wakens me*
> *In my night of sleep.*

This time Hinaikamalama said to Aiwohikupua, "Do you not know any reason for our being cold? If you know the reason, then tell me; do not hide it."

Said Aiwohikupua, "This cold comes from your rival; she is perhaps angry with us, so she wears her snow mantle; therefore we are cold."

Hinaikamalama answered, "We must part, for we have met and our vow is fulfilled."

Said Aiwohikupua, "We will break off this time; let us separate; to-morrow at noon, then we will carry out the vow."

"Yes," said Hinaikamalama.

After they had parted then Hinaikamalama slept pleasantly the rest of the night until morning.

At noon Aiwohikupua again took her in fulfillment of the agreement of the night before.

As those two reposed accordingly, Poliahu was displeased.

Then Poliahu took her sun mantle and covered herself; this time it was the heat Poliahu sent to Hinaikamalama. Then she raised a short song, as follows:

> *The heat, ah! the heat,*
> *The heat of my love stifles me,*

> *It burns my body,*
> *It draws sweat from my heart,*
> *Perhaps this heat is my lover's—ah!*

Said Aiwohikupua, "It is not my doing; perhaps Poliahu causes this heat; perhaps she is angry with us."

Said Hinaikamalama, "Let us still have patience and if the heat comes over us again, then leave me."

After this, they again met in fulfillment of their vow.

Then again the heat settled over them, then she raised again the chant:

> *The heat, ah! the heat,*
> *The heat of my love stifles me.*
> *Its quivering touch scorches my heart,*
> *The sick old heat of the winter,*
> *The fiery heat of summer,*
> *The dripping heat of the summer season,*
> *The heat compels me to go,*
> *I must go.*

Then Hinaikamalama arose to go.

Said Aiwohikupua, "You might give me a kiss before you go."

Said Hinaikamalama, "I will not give you a kiss; the heat from that wife of yours will come again, it will never do. Fare you well!"

Let us leave off here telling about Aiwohikupua. It is well to speak briefly of Hinaikamalama.

After leaving Aiwohikupua, she came and stayed at the house of a native of the place.

This very night there was again a festivity for Hauailiki and the chiefs at Puuopapai.

This night Hinaikamalama remembered her promise to Hauailiki after the game of spin-the-gourd, before she met Aiwohikupua.

This was the second night of the festival; then Hinaikamalama went and sat outside the group.

Now, the first game of spin-the-gourd was between Kauakahialii and Kailiokalauokekoa. Afterward Kailiokalauokekoa and Makaweli had the second game.

During the game Poliahu entered the assembly. To Hauailiki and Poliahu went the last game of the night.

And as the master of ceremonies had not seen Hinaikamalama early that night, he had not done his duty. For on the former night the first game this night had been promised to Hauailiki and Hinaikamalama, but not seeing her he gave the first game to others.

Close on morning the sport master searched the gathering for Hinaikamalama and found her.

Then the sport master stood up in the midst of the assembly, while Hauailiki and Poliahu were playing, then he sang a song while fluttering the end of the wand over Hauailiki and took away the wand and Hauailiki stood up. The sport master went over to Hinaikamalama, touched her with the wand and withdrew it. Then Hinaikamalama stood in the midst of the circle of players.

When Poliahu saw Hinaikamalama, she frowned at the sight of her rival.

And Hauailiki and Hinaikamalama withdrew where they could take their pleasure.

When they met, said Hinaikamalama to Hauailiki, "If you take me only for a little while, then there is an end of it, for my parents do not wish me to give up my virginity thus. But if you intend to take me as your wife, then I will give myself altogether to you as my parents desire."

To the woman's words Hauailiki answered, "Your idea is a good one; you think as I do; but let us first meet according to the choice of the sport master, then afterwards we will marry."

"Not so," said Hinaikamalama, "let me be virgin until you are ready to come and get me at Hana."

On the third night of Hauailiki's festivities, when the chiefs and others were assembled, that night Lilinoe and Poliahu, Waiaie and Kahoupokane met, for the three had come to find Poliahu, thinking that Aiwohikupua was living with her.

This night, while Aiwohikupua and Makaweli were playing spin-the-gourd, in the midst of the sport, the women of the mountain entered the place of assembly.

As Poliahu and the others stood in their mantles of snow, sparkling in the light, the group of players were in an uproar because of these women, because of the strange garments they wore; at the same time cold penetrated the whole *kilu* shelter and lasted until morning, when Poliahu and her companions left Kauai. At the same time Hinaikamalama left Kauai.

When we get to Laieikawai's coming to Kauai after Kekalukaluokewa's marriage with Laieikawai, then we will begin again the story of Hinaikamalama; at this place let us tell of Kauakahialii's command to his friend, and so on until he meets Laieikawai.

After their return from Hawaii, Kauakahialii lived with Kailiokalauokekoa at Pihanakalani.[58] Now the end of their days was near.

Then Kauakahialii laid a blessing upon his friend, Kekalukaluokewa, and this it was:

"Ah! my friend, greatly beloved, I give you my blessing, for the end of my days is near, and I am going back to the other side of the earth.

"Only one thing for you to guard, our wife.[59] When I fall dead, there where sight of you and our wife comes not back, then do you rule over the island, you above, and our wife below; as we two ruled over the island, so will you and our wife do.

"It may be when I am dead you will think of taking a wife; do not take our wife; by no means think of her as your wife, for she belongs to us two.

"The woman for you to take is the wife left on Hawaii, Laieikawai. If you take her for your wife it will be well with you, you will be renowned. Would you get her, guard one thing, our flute, guard well the flute,[60] then the woman is yours, this is my charge to you."

Kauakahialii's charge pleased his friend.

In the end Kauakahialii died; the chief, his friend, took the rule, and their wife was the counsellor.

Afterwards, when Kailiokalauokekoa's last days drew near, she prayed her husband to guard Kanikawi, their sacred flute, according to Kauakahialii's command:

"My husband, here is the flute; guard it; it is a wonderful flute; whatever things you desire it can do; if you go to get the wife your friend charged you to, this will be the means of your meeting. You must guard it forever; wherever you go to dwell, never leave the flute at all, for you well know what your friend did when you two came to get me when I was almost dead for love of your friend. It was this flute that saved me from the other side of the grave; therefore, listen and guard well my sayings."

XX

After Kailiokalauokekoa's death, the chief's house and all things else became Kekalukaluokewa's, and he portioned out the land[61] and set up his court.

After apportioning the land and setting up his court, Kekalukaluokewa bethought him of his friend's charge concerning Laieikawai.

Then he commanded his counsellor to make ready 4,000 canoes for the journey to Hawaii after a wife, according to the custom of a chief.

When the chief's command was carried out, the chief took two favorites, a suitable retinue of chiefs, and all the embalmed bodies of his ancestors.

In the month called "the first twin," when the sea was calm, they left Kauai and came to Hawaii. Many days passed on the voyage.

As they sailed, they arrived in the early morning at Makahanaloa in Hilo. Then said the man who had seen Laieikawai before to the chief, "See that rainbow arching over the uplands; that is Paliuli, where I found her." Now the rain was sweeping Hilo at the time when they came to Makahanaloa.

At the man's words, the chief answered, "I will wait before believing that a sign for Laieikawai; for the rainbow is common in rainy weather; so, my proposal is, let us anchor the canoes and wait until the rain has cleared, then if the rainbow remains when there is no rain, it must be a sign for Laieikawai." The chief's proposal was the same as Aiwohikupua's.

So they remained there as the chief desired. In ten days and two it cleared over Hilo, and the country was plainly visible.

In the early morning of the twelfth day the chief went out of the house, and lo! the rainbow persisted as before; a little later in the day the rainbow was at the seacoast of Keaau; Laieikawai had gone to the coast (as in the narrative before of Aiwohikupua's story).

That day there was no longer any doubt of the sign, and they sailed and came to Keaau. When they arrived, Laieikawai had gone up to Paliuli.

When they arrived the people crowded to see Kekalukaluokewa and exclaimed, "Kauai for handsome men!"

On the day when Kekalukaluokewa sailed and came to Keaau, Waka foresaw this Kekalukaluokewa.

Said Waka to her grandchild, "Do not go again to the coast, for Kekalukaluokewa has come to Keaau to get you for his wife. Kauakahialii is dead, and has charged his favorite to take you to wife; therefore this is your husband. If you accept this man you will rule the island, surely preserve these bones. Therefore wait up here four days, then go down, and if you like him, then return and tell me your pleasure."

So Laieikawai waited four days as her grandmother commanded.

In the early morning of the fourth day of retirement, she arose and went down with her hunchbacked attendant to Keaau.

When she arrived close to the village, lo! Kekalukaluokewa was already out surf riding; three youths rose in the surf, the chief and his favorites.

As Laieikawai and her companion spied out for Kekalukaluokewa, they did not know which man the grandmother wanted.

Said Laieikawai to her nurse, "How are we to know the man whom my grandmother said was here?"

Her nurse said, "Better wait until they are through surfing, and the one who comes back without a board, he is the chief."

So they sat and waited.

Then, the surf riding ended and the surfers came back to shore.

Then they saw some men carrying the boards of the favorites, but the chief's board the favorites bore on their shoulders, and Kekalukaluokewa came without anything. So Laieikawai looked upon her husband.

When they had seen what they had come for, they returned to Paliuli and told their grandmother what they had seen.

Asked the grandmother, "Were you pleased with the man?"

"Yes," answered Laieikawai.

Said Waka, "To-morrow at daybreak Kekalukaluokewa goes surfing alone; at that time I will cover all the land of Puna with a mist, and in this mist I will send you on the wings of birds to meet Kekalukaluokewa without your being seen. When the mist clears, then all shall see you riding on the wave with Kekalukaluokewa; that is the time to give a kiss to the Kauai youth. So when you go out of the house, speak no word to anyone, man or woman, until you have given a kiss to Kekalukaluokewa, then you may speak to the others. After the surf riding, then I will send the birds and a mist over the land; that is the time for you to return with your husband to your house, become one flesh according to your wish."

When all this had been told Laieikawai, she returned to the chief-house with her nurse.

Afterward, when they were in the house, she sent her nurse to bring Mailehaiwale, Mailekaluhea, Mailelaulii, Mailepakaha, and Kahalaomapuana, her counsellors, as they had agreed.

When the counsellors came, her body guard, Laieikawai said, "Where are you, my comrades? I have taken counsel with our grandmother about my marriage, so I sent my nurse to bring you, as we agreed when we met here. My grandmother wishes Kekalukaluokewa to be my husband. What do you say? What you all agree, I will do. If you consent, well; if not, it shall be just as you think." Kahalaomapuana said, "It is well; marry him as your grandmother wishes; not a word from us. Only when you marry a husband do not forsake us, as we have agreed; where you go, let us go with you; if you are in trouble, we will share it."

"I will not forsake you," said Laieikawai.

Now we have seen in former chapters, in the story of Hauailiki and the story of Aiwohikupua's second trip to Hawaii, that it was customary for Laieikawai to go down to Keaau, and it was the same when Kekalukaluokewa came to Hawaii.

Every time Laieikawai came to Keaau the youth Halaaniani saw her without knowing where she came from; from that time the wicked purpose never left his mind to win Laieikawai, but he was ashamed to approach her and never spoke to her.

As to this Halaaniani, he was Malio's brother, a youth famous throughout Puna for his good looks, but a profligate fellow.

During the four days of Laieikawai's retirement Halaaniani brooded jealously over her absence. She came no more to Keaau.

In the village he heard that Laieikawai was to be Kekalukaluokewa's. Then quickly he went to consult his sister, to Malio.[62]

Said her brother, "Malio, I have come to you to gain my desire. All those days I was absent I was at Keaau to behold a certain beautiful woman, for my passion forced me to go again and again to see this woman. To-day I heard that to-morrow she is to be the chief's of Kauai; therefore let us exert all our arts over her to win her to me."

Said his sister, "She is no other than Waka's grandchild, Laieikawai, whom the grandmother has given to the great chief of Kauai; to-morrow is the marriage. Therefore, as you desire, go home, and in the dark of evening return, and we will sleep here on the mountain; that is the time for us to determine whether you lose or win."

According to Malio's directions to her brother, Halaaniani returned to his house at Kula.

He came at the time his sister had commanded.

Before they slept, Malio said to Halaaniani, "If you get a dream when you sleep, tell it to me, and I will do the same."

They slept until toward morning. Halaaniani awoke, he could not sleep, and Malio awoke at the same time.

XXI

Malio asked Halaaniani, "What did you dream?"

Said Halaaniani, "I dreamed nothing, as I slept I knew nothing, had not the least dream until I awoke just now."

Halaaniani asked his sister, "How was it with you?"

Said his sister, "I had a dream; as we slept we went into the thicket; you slept in your hollow tree and I in mine; my spirit saw a little bird building its nest; when it was completed the bird whose the nest was flew away out of sight. And by-and-by another bird flew hither and sat upon the nest, but I saw not that bird come again whose the nest was."

Asked Halaaniani of the dream, "What is the meaning of this dream?"

His sister told him the true meaning of the dream. "You will prosper; for the first bird whose the nest was, that is Kekalukaluokewa, and the nest, that is Laieikawai, and the last bird who sat in the nest, that is you. Therefore this very morning the woman shall be yours. When Waka sends Laieikawai on the wings of the birds for the marriage with Kekalukaluokewa, mist and fog will cover the land; when it clears, then you three will appear riding on the crest of the wave, then you shall see that I have power to veil Waka's face from seeing what I am doing for you; so let us arise and get near to the place where Laieikawai weds."

After Malio's explanation of the dream was ended they went right to the place where the others were.

Now Malio had power to do supernatural deeds; it was to secure this power that she lived apart.

When they came to Keaau they saw Kekalukaluokewa swimming out for surf riding.

Malio said to Halaaniani, "You listen to me! When you get on the back of the wave and glide along with the breaker, do not ride—lose the wave; this for four waves; and the fifth wave, this is their last. Maybe they will wonder at your not riding ashore and ask the reason, then you answer you are not accustomed to surfing on the short waves, and when they ask you what long waves you surf on say on the *Huia*.[63] If they pay no attention to you, and prepare to ride in on their last wave, as they ride you must seize hold of Laieikawai's feet while Kekalukaluokewa rides in alone. When you have the woman, carry her far out to sea; look over to the coast where Kumukahi[64] swims in the billows, then this is the place for surfing; then pray in my name and I will send a wave over you; this is the wave you want; it is yours."

While they were talking Waka covered the land with a mist. Then the thunder pealed and there was Laieikawai on the crest of the wave. This was Waka's work. Again the thunder pealed a second peal. This was Malio's work. When the mist cleared three persons floated on the crest of the wave, and this was a surprise to the onlookers.

As Waka had commanded her grandchild, "speak to no one until you have kissed Kekalukaluokewa, then speak to others," the grandchild obeyed her command.

While they rode the surf not one word was heard between them.

As they stood on the first wave Kekalukaluokewa said, "Let us ride." Then they lay resting upon their boards; Halaaniani let his drop back, the other two rode in; then it was that Laieikawai and Kekalukaluokewa kissed as the grandmother had directed.

Three waves they rode, three times they went ashore, and three times Halaaniani dropped back.

At the fourth wave, for the first time Laieikawai questioned Halaaniani: "Why do you not ride? This is the fourth wave you have not ridden; what is your reason for not riding?"

"Because I am not used to the short waves," said Halaaniani, "the long wave is mine."

He spoke as his sister had directed.

The fifth wave, this was the last for Laieikawai and Kekalukaluokewa.

As Kekalukaluokewa and Laieikawai lay resting on the wave, Halaaniani caught Laieikawai by the soles of her feet and got his arm around her, and Laieikawai's surf board was lost. Kekalukaluokewa rode in alone and landed on the dry beach.

When Laieikawai was in Halaaniani's arms she said, "This is strange! my board is gone."

Said Halaaniani, "Your board is all right, woman; a man will bring it back."

While they were speaking Laieikawai's surf board floated to where they were.

Said Laieikawai to Halaaniani, "Where is your wave that you have kept me back here for?"

At this question of the princess they swam, and while they swam Halaaniani bade the princess, "As we swim do not look back, face ahead; when my crest is here, then I will tell you."

They swam, and after a long time Laieikawai began to wonder; then she said, "This is a strange wave, man! We are swimming out where there are no waves at all; we are in the deep ocean; a wave here would be strange; there are only swells out here."

Said Halaaniani, "You listen well; at my first word to you there will be something for us."

Laieikawai listened for the word of her surfing comrade.

They swam until Halaaniani thought they could get the crest, then Halaaniani said to his surfing comrade, "Look toward the coast."

Laieikawai replied, "The land has vanished, Kumukahi comes bobbing on the wave."

"This is our crest," said Halaaniani. "I warn you when the first wave breaks, do not ride that wave, or the second; the third wave is ours. When the wave breaks and scatters, keep on, do not leave the board which keeps you floating; if you leave the board, then you will not see me again."

At the close of this speech Halaaniani prayed to their god in the name of his sister, as Malio had directed.

Halaaniani was half through his prayer; a crest arose; he finished the prayer to the amen; again a crest arose, the second this; not long after another wave swelled.

This time Halaaniani called out, "Let us ride."

Then Laieikawai quickly lay down on the board and with Halaaniani's help rode toward the shore.

Now, when Laieikawai was deep under the wave, the crest broke finely; Laieikawai glanced about to see how things were; Halaaniani was not with her. Laieikawai looked again; Halaaniani with great dexterity was resting on the very tip of the wave. That was when Laieikawai began to give way to Halaaniani.

Waka saw them returning from surf riding and supposed Laieikawai's companion was Kekalukaluokewa.

Malio, the sister of Halaaniani, as is seen in the story of her life, can do many marvelous things, and in Chapters XXII and XXIII you will see what great deeds she had power to perform.

XXII

While Laieikawai was surfing ashore with Halaaniani, Waka's supernatural gift was overshadowed by Malio's superior skill, and she did not see what was being done to her grandchild.

Just as Laieikawai came to land, Waka sent the birds in the mist, and when the mist passed off only the surf boards remained; Laieikawai was with Halaaniani in her house up at Paliuli. There Halaaniani took Laieikawai to wife.

The night passed, day came, and it was midday; Waka thought this strange, for before sending her grandchild to meet Kekalukaluokewa she had said to her:

"Go, to-day, and meet Kekalukaluokewa, then return to the uplands, you two, and after your flesh has become defiled come to me; I will take care of you until the pollution is past." Now, this was the custom with a favorite daughter.

Because Waka was surprised, at midday of the second day after Laieikawai joined Halaaniani, the grandmother went to look after her grandchild.

When the grandmother came to them, they were both fast asleep, like new lovers, as if the nights were the time for waking.

As Laieikawai lay asleep, her grandmother looked and saw that the man sleeping with her grandchild was not the one she had chosen for her.

Then Waka wakened the grandchild, and when she awoke the grandmother asked, "Who is this?"

Answered the grandchild, "Kekalukaluokewa, of course."

Said the grandmother in a rage, "This is no Kekalukaluokewa; this is Halaaniani, the brother of Malio. Therefore, I give you my oath never to see your face again, my grandchild, from this time until I die, for you have disobeyed me. I thought to hide you away until you could care for me. But now, live with your husband for the future; keep your beauty, your supernatural power is yours no longer; that you must look for from your husband; work with your own hands; let your husband be your fortune and your pride."

After this Waka made ready to build another house like that she had built for Laieikawai. And by Waka's art the house was speedily completed.

When the house was ready, Waka went herself to meet Kekalukaluokewa in person, for her heart yearned with love for Kakalukaluokewa.

When Waka reached Kekalukaluokewa's place, she clasped his feet and said, with sorrowful heart: "Great is my grief and my love for you, O chief, for I desired you for my grandchild as the man to save these bones. I thought my grandchild was a good girl, not so! I saw her sleeping with Halaaniani, not the man I had chosen for her. Therefore, I come to beseech you to give me a canoe and men also, and I will go and get the foster child of Kapukaihaoa, Laielohelohe,[66] who is like Laieikawai, for they are twins."

And for this journey Kekalukaluokewa gave a double canoe with men and all the equipment.

Before Waka went after Laielohelohe she commanded Kekalukaluokewa as follows: "I shall be gone three times ten days and three days over, then I shall return. Keep watch, and if the mist rises on the ocean, then you will know that I am returning with your wife, then purify yourself for two days before the marriage."

According to her determination, Waka sailed to Oahu, where the canoes landed at Honouliuli and Waka saw the rainbow arching up at Wahiawa.

She took a little pig to sacrifice before Kapukaihaoa, the priest who took care of Laielohelohe, and went up thither.

Waka went up and reached Kukaniloko; she draw near the place where Laielohelohe was hidden, held the pig out to the priest and prayed, and came to the amen, then she let the pig go.

The priest asked, "Why do you bring me the pig? What can I do for you?"

Said Waka, "My foster child has sinned, she is not a good girl; I wished to have the chief of Kauai for her husband, but she would not listen to me, she became Halaaniani's; therefore, I come to take your foster child to be the wife of Kekalukaluokewa, the chief of Kauai. We two shall be provided for, he will preserve our bones in the days of our old age until we die, and when that chief is ours my foster child will be supplanted, and she will realize how she has sinned."

Said Kapukaihaoa, "The pig is well, therefore I give you my foster child to care for, and if you succeed well, and I hear of your prosperity, then I will come to seek you."

Then Waka entered with Kapukaihaoa the taboo place where Laielohelohe was hidden; Waka waited and the priest went still farther into the place and brought her to Waka, then Waka knelt before Laielohelohe and did her reverence.

On the day when Laielohelohe went on board the canoe, then the priest took his foster child's umbilical cord[66] and wore it about his neck. But he did not sorrow for Laielohelohe, thinking how good fortune had come to her.

From the time Laielohelohe was taken on board, not one of the paddlers had the least glimpse of her until they came to Hawaii.

Kekalukaluokewa waited during the time appointed.

The next day, in the early morning, when the chief awoke from sleep, he saw the sign which Waka had promised, for there was the colored cloud on the ocean.

Kekalukaluokewa prepared for Laielohelohe's arrival, expecting to see her first at that time. Not so!

In the afternoon, when the double canoes came in sight, all the people crowded to the landing place to see the chief, thinking she would come ashore and meet her husband.

When the canoe approached the shore, then fog and mist covered the land from Paliuli to the sea.

Then Laielohelohe and Waka were borne under cover of the mist on the birds to Paliuli, and Laielohelohe was placed in the house prepared for her and stayed there until Halaaniani took her.

Three days was Waka at Paliuli after returning from Oahu. Then she came down with Kekalukaluokewa for the marriage of the chiefs.

Then Waka came to Kekalukaluokewa and said, "Your wife has come, so prepare yourself in forty days; summon all the people to assemble at the place where you two shall meet; make a *kilu* shelter; there disgrace Laieikawai, that she may see what wrong she has done."

At the time when Waka took away her supernatural protection from Laieikawai, Aiwohikupua's sisters took counsel as to what they had better do; and they agreed upon what they should say to Laieikawai.

Kahalaomapuana came to Laieikawai, and she said: "We became your bodyguard while Waka still protected you; now she has removed her guardianship and left you. Therefore, as we agreed in former days, 'Adversity to one is adversity to all;' now that you are in trouble, we will share your trouble. As we will not forsake you, so do not you forsake us until our death; this is what we have agreed."

When Laieikawai heard these words her tears fell for love of her comrades, and she said, "I supposed you would forsake me when fortune was taken from me; not so! What does it matter! Should fortune come to me hereafter, then I will place you far above myself."

Halaaniani and Laieikawai lived as man and wife and Aiwohikupua's sisters acted as her servants.

Perhaps the fourth month of their union, one day at noon when Halaaniani opened the door and went outside the house, he saw Laielohelohe going out of her taboo house. Then once more longing seized Halaaniani.

He returned with his mind fixed upon doing a mischief to the girl, determined to get her and pollute her.

As he was at that time living on good terms with Laieikawai, Halaaniani sought some pretext for parting from Laieikawai in order to carry out his purpose.

That night Halaaniani deceived Laieikawai, saying, "Ever since we have lived up here, my delight in surf riding has never ceased; at noon the longing seizes me; it is the same every day; so I propose to-morrow we go down to Keaau surf riding, and return here."

The wife agreed.

Early in the morning Laieikawai sought her counsellors, the sisters of Aiwohikupua, and told them what the husband had proposed that night, and this pleased her counsellors.

Laieikawai said to them, "We two are going to the sea, as our husband wishes. You wait; do not be anxious if ten days pass and our husband has not had enough of the sport of surf riding; but if more than ten days pass, some evil has befallen us; then come to my help."

They departed and came to a place just above Keaau; then Halaaniani began to make trouble for Laieikawai, saying, "You go ahead to the coast and I will go up and see your sister-in-law, Malio, and return. And if you wait for me until day follows night, and night again that day, and, again the day succeeds the night, then you will know that I am dead; then marry another husband."

This proposal of her husband's did not please the wife, and she proposed their going up together, but the slippery fellow used all his cunning, and she was deceived.

Halaaniani left her. Laieikawai went on to Keaau, and at a place not close to Kekalukaluokewa, there she remained; and night fell, and the husband did not return; day came, and he did not return. She waited that day until night; it was no better; then she thought her husband was dead, and she began to pour out her grief.

XXIII

Very heavy hearted was Laieikawai at her husband's death, so she mourned ten days and two (twelve days) for love of him.

While Laieikawai mourned, her counsellors wondered, for Laieikawai had given them her charge before going to Keaau.

"Wait for me ten days, and should I not return," she had bidden them as told in Chapter XXII; so clearly she was in trouble.

And the time having passed which Laieikawai charged her companions to wait, Aiwohikupua's sisters awoke early in the morning of the twelfth day and went to look after their comrade.

They went to Keaau, and as they approached and Laieikawai spied her counsellors she poured out her grief with wailing.

Now her counsellors marveled at her wailing and remembered her saying "some evil has befallen"; at her wailing and at her gestures of distress, for Laieikawai was kneeling on the ground with one hand clapped across her back and the other at her forehead, and she wailed aloud as follows:

O you who come to me—alas!
Here I am,
My heart is trembling,
There is a rushing at my heart for love.
Because the man is gone—my close companion!
He has departed.

He has departed, my lehua blossom, spicy kookoolau,
With his soft pantings,
Tremulous, thick gaspings,
Proud flower of my heart,
Behold—alas!

Behold me desolate—
The first faint fear branches and grows—I can not bear it!
My heart is darkened
With love.
Alas, my husband!

When her companions heard Laieikawai wailing, they all wailed with her.

After their lament, said Kahalaomapuana, "This is a strange way to cry; you open your mouth wide, but no tears run; you seem to be dried up, as if the tears were shut off."

Said the sisters, "What do you mean?"

Kahalaomapuana replied, "As if there were nothing the matter with our husband."

Said Laieikawai, "He is dead, for on the way down, just above here, he said, 'You go ahead and I will go up and see your sister-in-law, and if you wait for me until day follows night and night day and day again that night, then I am dead,' so he charged me. I waited here; the appointed time passed; I thought he was dead; here I stayed until you came and found me wailing."

Said Kahalaomapuana, "He is not dead; wait a day; stop wailing!"

Because of Kahalaomapuana's words they waited four days, but nothing happened. Then Laieikawai began to wail again until evening of the third day, and this night, at dawn, for the first time she fell asleep.

Just as sleep came to her Halaaniani stood before her with another woman, and Laieikawai started up, and it was only a dream!

At the same time Mailehaiwale had a vision. She awoke and told her dream to Mailelaulii and Mailekaluhea.

As they were talking about it Laieikawai awoke and told her dream.

Said Mailelaulii, "We are just talking of Mailehaiwale's dream."

As they discussed the dreams Kahalaomapuana awoke from sleep and asked what they were talking about.

Mailehaiwale told the dream that had come to her: "It was up at Paliuli, Halaaniani came and took you, Kahalaomapuana, and you two went away somewhere; my spirit stood and watched you, and the excitement awoke me."

Laieikawai also told her dream, and Kahalaomapuana said, "Halaaniani is not dead; we will wait; do not weep; waste no tears."

Then Laieikawai stopped wailing, and they returned to Paliuli.

At this place we shall tell of Halaaniani, and here we shall see his clever trickery.

When Halaaniani told Laieikawai he was going up to see Malio, this was in order to get away from her after giving her his commands.

The fellow went up and met Malio. His sister asked. "What have you come up here for?"

Said Halaaniani, "I have come up here to you once more to show you what I desire; for I have again seen a beautiful woman with a face like Laieikawai's.

"Yesterday morning when I went outside my house I saw this young girl with the lovely face; then a great longing took possession of me.

"And because I remembered that you were the one who fulfilled my wishes, therefore I have come up here again."

Said Malio to her brother, "That is Laielohelohe, another of Waka's grandchildren; she is betrothed to Kekalukaluokewa, to be his wife. Therefore go and watch the girl's house without being seen for four days, and see what she does; then come back and tell me; then I will send you to seduce the girl. I can not do it by my power, for they are two."

At these words of Malio, Halaaniani went to spy outside of Laielohelohe's house without being seen; almost twice ten days he lay in wait; then he saw Laielohelohe stringing *lehua* blossoms. He came repeatedly many days; there she was stringing *lehua* blossoms.

Halaaniani returned to his sister as he had been directed, and told her what he had seen of Laielohelohe.

When Malio heard the story she told her brother what to do to win Laielohelohe, and said to Halaaniani, "Go now, and in the middle of the night come up here to me, and we two will go to Laielohelohe's place."

Halaaniani went away, and close to the appointed time, then he arose and joined his sister. His sister took a *ti*-leaf trumpet and went with her brother, and came close to the place where Laielohelohe was wont to string *lehua* blossoms.

Then Malio said to Halaaniani, "You climb up in the *lehua* tree where you can see Laielohelohe, and there you stay. Listen to me play on the *ti*-leaf trumpet; when I have blown five times, if you see her turn her eyes to the place where the sound comes from, then we shall surely win, but if she does not look toward where I am playing, then we shall not win to-day."

As they were speaking there was a crackling in the bushes at the place where Laielohelohe strung *lehua* blossoms, and when they looked, there was Laielohelohe breaking *lehua* blossoms.

Then Halaaniani climbed up the trunk of a tree and kept watch. When he was up the tree, Malio's trumpet sounded, again it sounded a second time, so on until the fifth time, but Halaaniani did not see the girl turn her eyes or listen to the sound.

Malio waited for Halaaniani to return and tell what he had seen, but as he did not return, Malio again blew on the trumpet five times; still Halaaniani did not see Laielohelohe pay the least attention until she went away altogether.

Halaaniani came back and told his sister, and his sister said, "We have not won her with the trumpet; shall we try my nose flute?"

The two returned home, and very early in the morning, they came again to the same place where they had lain in ambush before.

No sooner were they arrived than Laielohelohe arrived also at her customary station. Malio had already instructed her brother, as follows:

"Take *lehua* flowers, bind them into a cluster, when you hear me playing the nose flute, then drop the bunch of flowers right over her; maybe she will be curious about this."

Halaaniani climbed the tree right over where Laielohelohe was wont to sit. Just as Malio's nose flute sounded, Halaaniani dropped the bunch of *lehua* flowers down from the tree, and it fell directly in front of Laielohelohe. Then Laielohelohe turned her eyes right upward, saying, "If you are a man who has sent me this gift and this music of the flute, then you are mine: if you are a woman, then you shall be my intimate friend."

When Halaaniani heard this speech, he waited not a moment to descend and join his sister.

To Malio's question he told her what he had seen.

Said Malio to Halaaniani, "We will go home and early in the morning come here again, then we shall find out her intentions."

They went home and returned early in the morning. When they had taken their stations, Laielohelohe came as usual to string *lehua* blossoms.

Then Malio sounded the flute, as Laielohelohe began to snip the *lehua* blossoms, and she stopped, for her attention was attracted to the music.

Three times Malio sounded the nose flute.

Then said Laielohelohe, "If you are a woman who sounds the flute, then let us two kiss."

At Laielohelohe's words, Malio approached Laielohelohe and the girl saw her, and she was a stranger to Laielohelohe's eyes.

Then she started to kiss her.

And as the girl was about to give the promised kiss, Malio said, "Let our kiss wait, first give my brother a kiss; when you two have done, then we will kiss."

Then said Laielohelohe, "You and your brother may go away, do not bring him into my presence; you both go back to your own place and do not come here again. For it was only you I promised to greet with a kiss, no one else; should I do as you desire, I should disobey my good guardian's command."

When Malio heard this she returned to her brother and said, "We have failed to-day, but I will try my supernatural arts to fulfill your desire."

They went back to the house, then she directed Halaaniani to go and spy upon Laieikawai.

When Halaaniani came to Keaau as his sister directed, he neither saw nor heard of Laieikawai.

XXIV

On his arrival there, Halaaniani heard there was to be a great day for Kakalukaluokewa, a day of celebration for the marriage of Laielohelohe with Kekalukaluokewa. And when he had carefully noted the day for the chief's wedding feast he returned and told his sister this thing.

When Malio heard it she said to her brother, "On the marriage day of Kekalukaluokewa with Laielohelohe, on that day Laielohelohe shall be yours."

Now Aiwohikupua's sisters were wont to go down to the sea at Keaau to keep watch for their husband, to make sure if he were dead or not.

As Aiwohikupua's sisters were on the way to Keaau, they heard of the festival for Kekalukaluokewa and Laielohelohe.

When the great day drew near, Waka went down from Paliuli to meet Kekalukaluokewa, and Waka said to Kekalukaluokewa: "To-morrow at sunrise call together all the people and the chiefs of the household to the place prepared for the celebration; there let all be assembled. Then go and show yourself first among them and near midday return to your house until day declines, then I will send a mist to cover the land, and the place where the people are assembled.

"When the mist begins to close down over the land, then wait until you hear the birds singing and they cease; wait again until you hear the birds singing and they cease.

"And after that I will lift the mist over the land. Then you will see up to Paliuli where the cloud rises and covers the mountain top, then the mist will fall again as before.

"Wait this time until you hear the cry of the *alae* bird, and the *ewaewaiki* calling; then come out of the house and stand before the assembly.

"Wait, and when the *oo* birds call and cease, then I am prepared to send Laielohelohe.

"When the voice of the *iiwipolena* sounds, your wife is on the left side of the place of meeting. Soon after this, you will hear the land snails[67] singing, then do you two meet apart from the assembly.

"And when you two meet, a single peal of thunder will crash, the earth tremble, the whole place of assembly shall shake. Then I will send you two on the birds, the clouds and mist shall rise, and there will be you two resting upon the birds in all your splendor. Then comes Laieikawai's disgrace, when she sees her shame and goes off afoot like a captive slave."

After all this was arranged, Waka returned to Paliuli.

Already has Halaaniani's expedition been described to look after his wife Laieikawai at Keaau, and already has it been told how he heard of the marriage celebration of Kekalukaluokewa and Laielohelohe.

On the day when Waka went to Keaau to meet Kekalukaluokewa, as we have seen above,

On that very day, Malio told Halaaniani to get ready to go down to the festival, saying: "To-morrow, at the marriage celebration of Kekalukaluokewa and Laielohelohe, then Laielohelohe shall be yours. For them shall crash the thunder, but when the clouds and mist clear away, then all present at the place of meeting shall behold you and Laielohelohe resting together upon the wings of birds."

Early in the morning of the next day, the day of the chief's marriage celebration, Kihanuilulumoku was summoned into the presence of Aiwohikupua's sisters, the servants who guarded Laieikawai.

When the lizard came, Kahalaomapuana said, "You have been summoned to take us down to the sea at Keaau to see Kekalukaluokewa's wedding feast. Be ready to take us down soon after the sun begins to decline."

Kihanuilulumoku went away until the time appointed, then he came to them.

And as the lizard started to come into his mistress's presence, lo! the land was veiled thick with mist up there at Paliuli, and all around, but Kihanuilulumoku did not hurry to his mistresses, for he knew when the chiefs' meeting was to take place.

When Kekalukaluokewa saw this mist begin to descend over the land, then he remembered Waka's charge.

He waited for the remaining signs. After hearing the voices of the *ewaewaiki* and the land shells, then Kekalukaluokewa came out of his house and stood apart from the assembly.

Just at that moment, Kihanuilulumoku stuck out his tongue as a seat for Laieikawai and Aiwohikupua's sisters.

And when the voice of the thunder crashed, clouds and mist covered the land, and when it cleared, the place of meeting was to be seen; and there were Laielohelohe and Halaaniani resting upon the birds.

S. N. HALE'OLE

Then also were seen Laieikawai and Aiwohikupua's sisters seated upon the tongue of Kihanuilulumoku, the great lizard of Paliuli.

Now they arrived at the same instant as those for whom the day was celebrated; lo! Laieikawai saw that Halaaniani was not dead, and she remembered Kahalaomapuana's prediction.

When Kekalukaluokewa saw Halaaniani and Laielohelohe resting on the birds, he thought he had lost Laielohelohe.

So Kekalukaluokewa went up to Paliuli to tell Waka.

And Kekalukaluokewa told Waka all these things, saying: "Halaaniani got Laielohelohe; there she was at the time set, she and Halaaniani seated together!"

Said Waka, "He shall never get her; but let us go down and I will get close to the place of meeting; if she has given Halaaniani a kiss, the thing which I forbade her to grant, for to you alone is my grandchild's kiss devoted—if she has defiled herself with him, then we lose the wife, then take me to my grave without pity. But if she has harkened to my command not to trust anyone else; not even to open her lips to Halaaniani, then she is your wife, if my grandchild has harkened to my command."

As they approached, Waka sent the clouds and mist over the assembly, and they could not distinguish one from another.

Then Waka sent Kekalukaluokewa upon the birds, and when the clouds cleared, lo! Laielohelohe and Kekalukaluokewa sat together upon the birds. Then the congregation shouted all about the place of assembly: "The marriage of the chiefs! The marriage of the chiefs!"[68]

When Waka heard the sound of shouting, then Waka came into the presence of the assembly and stood in the midst of the congregation and taunted Laieikawai.

When Laieikawai heard Waka's taunts, her heart smarted and the hearts of every one of Aiwohikupua's sisters with her; then Kihanuilulumoku bore them back on his tongue to dwell in the uplands of Olaa; thus did Laieikawai begin to burn with shame at Waka's words, and she and her companions went away together.

On that day, Kekalukaluokewa wedded Laielohelohe, and they went up to the uplands of Paliuli until their return to Kauai. And Halaaniani became a vagabond; nothing more remains to be said about him.

And when the chief resolved to return to Kauai, he took his wife and their grandmother to Kauai, and the men together with them.

When they were ready to return, they left Keaau, went first to Honouliuli on Oahu and there took Kapukaihaoa with them to Kauai;

and they went to Kauai, to Pihanakalani, and turned over the rule over the land and its divisions to Kapukaihaoa, and Waka was made the third heir to the chief's seat.

At this place let us tell of Laieikawai and her meeting with the prophet, Hulumaniani.

Laieikawai was at Olaa as beautiful as ever, but the art of resting on the wings of birds was taken away from her; nevertheless some of her former power remained and the signs of her chiefly rank, according to the authority the sisters of Aiwohikupua had over the lizard.

XXV

When Laieikawai returned from Keaau after Waka had disgraced her, and dwelt at Olaa, then Aiwohikupua's sisters consulted how to comfort the heavy heart of the princess, Laieikawai, for her shame at Waka's reproaches.

They went and told Laieikawai their decision, saying:

"O princess of peace, we have agreed upon something to relieve your burden of shame, for not you alone bear the burden; all of us share your trouble.

"Therefore, princess, we beseech you, best ease your heart of sorrow; good fortune shall be yours hereafter.

"We have agreed here to share your fortune; our younger sister has consented to go and get Kaonohiokala for your husband, the boy chief who dwells in the taboo house at the borders of Tahiti, a brother of ours, through whom Aiwohikupua gained the rank of chief.

"If you will consent to your brother being fetched, then we shall win greater honor than was ours before, and you will become a sacred person of great dignity so that you can not associate with us; now this is what we have thought of; you consent, then your reproach is lifted, Waka is put to shame."

Said Laieikawai, "Indeed I would consent to ease my burden of shame, only one thing I will not consent to—my becoming your brother's wife; for you say he is a taboo chief, and if we should be united, I should not see you again, so high a chief is he, and this I should regret exceedingly, our friendship together."

Said her companions, "Do not think of us; consider your grandmother's taunts; when her reproach is lifted, then we are happy, for we think first of you."

And for this reason Laieikawai gave her consent.

Then Kahalaomapuana left directions with Laieikawai and her sisters, saying: "I go to get our brother as husband for the princess; your duty is to take good care of our mistress; wherever she goes, there you go, whatever she wishes, that is yours to fulfill; but let her body be kept pure until I return with our brother."

After saying all this, Kahalaomapuana left her sisters and was borne on the back of the big lizard Kihanuilulumoku and went to fetch Kaonohiokala.

At this place we will leave off speaking of this journey; we must tell about Laieikawai and her meeting with the prophet who followed her from Kauai hither, as related in the first two chapters of this story.

After Kahalaomapuana left her sisters, the desire grew within Laieikawai's mind to travel around Hawaii.

So her companions carried out the chief's wish and they set out to travel around about Hawaii.

On the princess's journey around Hawaii they went first to Kau, then Kona, until they reached Kaiopae in Kohala, on the right-hand side of Kawaihae, about five miles distant; there they stayed several days for the princess to rest.

During the days they were there the seer saw the rainbow arching over the sea as if right at Kawaihae. The uplands of Ouli at Waimea was the place the seer looked from.

For in former chapters it has been told how the seer came to Hilo, to Kaiwilahilahi, and lived there some years waiting for the sign he was seeking.

But when it did not come to the seer as he waited for the sign he was seeking, then he waited and sought no longer for the sign he had followed from Kauai to this place.

So he left Hilo, intending to go all the way back to Kauai, and he set out. On his return, he did not leave the offerings which he had brought from Kauai thither, the pig and the cock.

When he reached Waimea, at Ouli, there he saw the rainbow arching over the sea at Kawaihae.

And the seer was so weary he was not quick to recognize the rainbow, but he stayed there, and on the next day he did not see the sign again.

Next day the seer left the place, the very day when Laieikawai's party left Kaiopae, and came back above Kahuwa and stopped at Moolau.

When the seer reached Puuloa from Waimea, he saw the rainbow arching over Moolau; then the seer began to wonder, "Can that be the sign I came to seek?"

The seer kept right on up to the summit of Palalahuakii. There he saw the rainbow plainly and recognized it, and knew it was the sign he was seeking.

Then he prayed to his god to interpret the rainbow to him, but his god did not answer his prayer.

The seer left that place, went to Waika and stayed there, for it was then dark.

In the early morning, lo! the rainbow arched over the sea at Kaiopae, for Laieikawai had gone back there.

Then the seer went away to the place where he had seen the rainbow, and, approaching, he saw Laieikawai plainly, strolling along the sea beach. A strange sight the beautiful woman was, and there, directly above the girl, the rainbow bent.

Then the seer prayed to his god to show him whether this woman was the one he was seeking or not, but he got no answer that day. Therefore, the seer did not lay down his offering before Laieikawai. The seer returned and stayed above Waika.

The next day the seer left the place, went to Lamaloloa and remained there. Then he went repeatedly into the temple of Pahauna and there prayed unceasingly to his god. After a number of days at Moolau, Laieikawai and her companions left that place.

They came and stayed at Puakea and, because the people of the place were surf riding, gladly remained.

The next day at noon, when the sun shone clear over the land, the prophet went outside the temple after his prayer.

Lo! he saw the rainbow bending over the sea at Puakea, and he went away thither, and saw the same girl whom he had seen before at Kaiopae.

So he fell back to a distance to pray again to his god to show him if this was the one he was seeking, but he got no answer that day; and, because his god did not answer his petition, he almost swore at his god, but still he persevered.

He approached the place where Laieikawai and her sisters were sitting.

The seer was greatly disturbed at seeing Laieikawai, and when he had reached the spot, he asked Laieikawai and her companions, "Why do you sit here? Why do you not go surfing with the natives of the place?"

The princess answered, "We can not go; it is better to watch the others."

The seer asked again, "What are you doing here?"

"We are sitting here, waiting for a canoe to carry us to Maui, Molokai, Oahu, and to Kauai, then we shall set sail," so they answered.

To this the seer replied, "If you are going to Kauai, then here is my canoe, a canoe without pay."

Said Laieikawai, "If we go on board your canoe, do you require anything of us?"

The seer answered, "Where are you? Do not suppose I have asked you on board my canoe in order to defile you; but my wish is to take you all as my daughters; such daughters as you can make my name famous, for my name will live in the saying, 'The daughters of Hulumaniani,' so my name shall live; is not this enough to desire?"

Then the seer sought a canoe and found a double canoe with men to man it.

Early in the morning of the next day they went on board the canoe and sailed and rested at Honuaula on Maui, and from there to Lahaina, and the next day to Molokai; they left Molokai, went to Laie, Koolauloa, and stayed there some days.

On the day of their arrival at Laie, that night, Laieikawai said to her companions and to her foster father:

"I have heard from my grandmother that this is my birthplace; we were twins, and because our father had killed the first children our mother bore, because they were girls, when we also were born girls, then I was hidden within a pool of water; there I was brought up by my grandmother.

"And my twin, the priest guarded her, and because the priest who guarded my companion saw the prophet who had come here from Kauai to see us, therefore the priest commanded my grandmother to flee far away; and this was why I was carried away to Paliuli and why we met there."

XXVI

When the seer heard this story the seer saw plainly that this was the very one he sought. But in order to make sure, the seer withdrew to a distance and prayed to his god to confirm the girl's story.

After praying he came back and went to sleep, and as he slept the seer received the assurance in a vision from his god, saying, "The time has come to fulfill your wishes, to free you from the weariness of your long search. She is here—the one who told you her story; this is the one you are seeking.

"Therefore arise and take the offering you have prepared and lay it before her, having blessed her in the name of your god.

"This done, linger not; carry them at once to Kauai, this very night, and let them dwell on the cliffs of Haena in the uplands of Honopuwaiakua."

At this the seer awoke from his dream; he arose and brought the pig and the cock and held them out to Laieikawai, saying, "Blessed am I, my mistress, that my god has shown you to me, for long have I followed you to win a blessing from you.

"And therefore I beseech you to guard these bones under your special favor, my mistress, and to leave this trust to your descendants unto the last generation."

Laieikawai answered, "Father, the time of my prosperity has passed, for Waka has taken her favor from me; but hereafter I shall win honor beyond my former honor and glory; then you shall also rise to prosperity with us."

And after these things the prophet did as his god commanded— sailed that night and dwelt in the place commanded.

Many days the seer lived here with his daughter above Honopuwaiakua. At one time the seer made one of his customary journeys.

As he traveled in his character as seer he came to Wailua. Lo! all the virgin daughters of Kauai were gathered together, all of the rank of chief with the girls of well-to-do families, at the command of Aiwohikupua to bring the virgins before the chief, the one who pleased the chief to become the wife of Aiwohikupua.

When the seer came within the crowd, lo! the maidens were assembled in one place before the chief.

The seer asked some one in the crowd, "What is this assembly for and why are all these maidens standing in a circle before the chief?"

He was told, "All the virgins have been summoned by the chief's command, and the two who please Aiwohikupua, these he will take for his wives in place of Poliahu and Hinaikamalama, and their parents are to be clothed in feather cloaks."

Then the seer stood before the chiefs and all the assembly and cried in a loud voice:

"O chiefs, it is a wise and good thing for the chief to take whichever one of these virgins pleases him, but not one of these can fill the loss of Poliahu and Hinaikamalama.

"If any one of these virgins here could compare in beauty with the left leg of my daughters, then she would be worth it. These are pretty enough, but not like my daughters."

Said Aiwohikupua in an angry voice, "When did we ever know that you had daughters!"

And those who had brought their daughters before the chief looked upon the seer as an enemy.

And to the chief's angry words the seer replied, "Did I not seek diligently and alone for a ruler over all these islands? And this lord of the land, she is my daughter, and my other daughters, they are my lord's sisters.

"Should my daughter come hither and stand upon the sea, the ocean would be in tumult; if on land, the wind would blow, the sun be darkened, the rain fall, the thunder crash, the lightning flash, the mountain tremble, the land would be flooded, the ocean reddened, at the coming of my daughter and lord."

And the seer's words spread, fear through the assembly. But those whose virgin daughters were present were not pleased.

They strongly urged the chief, therefore, to bind him within the house of detention, the prison house, where the chief's enemies were wont to be imprisoned.

Through the persistence of his enemies, it was decided to make the seer fast within that place and let him stay there until he died.

On the day of his imprisonment, that night at dawn, he prayed to his god. And at early daybreak the door of the house was opened for him and he went out without being seen.

In the morning the chief sent the executioner to go and see how the prophet fared in prison.

When the executioner came to the outside of the prison, he called with a loud voice:

"O Hulumaniani! O Hulumaniani! Prophet of God! How are you? Are you dead?" Three times the executioner called, but heard not a sound from within.

The executioner returned to the chief and said, "The prophet is dead."

Then the chief commanded the head man of the temple to make ready for the day of sacrifice and flay the prophet on the place of sacrifice before the altar.

Now the seer heard this command from some distance away, and in the night he took a banana plant covered with *tapa* like a human figure and put it inside the place where he had been imprisoned, and went back and joined his daughters and told them all about his troubles.

And near the day of sacrifice at the temple, the seer took Laieikawai and her companions on board of the double canoe.

In the very early morning of the day of sacrifice at the temple the man was to be brought for sacrifice, and when the head men of the temple entered the prison, lo! the body was tightly wrapped up, and it was brought and laid within the temple.

And close to the hour when the man was to be laid upon the altar all the people assembled and the chief with them; and the chief went up on the high place, the banana plant was brought and laid directly under the altar.

Said the chief to his head men, "Unwrap the *tapa* from the body and place it upon the altar prepared for it."

When it was unwrapped there was a banana plant inside, not the prophet, as was expected. "This is a banana plant! Where is the prophet?" exclaimed the chief.

Great was the chief's anger against the keeper of the prison where the prophet was confined.

Then all the keepers were called to trial. While the chief's keepers were being examined, the seer arrived with his daughters in a double canoe and floated outside the mouth of the inlet.

The seer stood on one canoe and Aiwohikupua's sisters on the other, and Laieikawai stood on the high seat between, under the symbols of a taboo chief.

As they stood there with Laieikawai, the wind blew, the sun was darkened, the sea grew rough, the ocean was reddened, the streams went back and stopped at their sources, no water flowed into the sea.[69]

After this the seer took Laieikawai's skirt[70] and laid it down on the land; then the thunder crashed, the temple fell, the altar crumbled.

After all these signs had been displayed, Aiwohikupua and the others saw Laieikawai standing above the canoes under the symbol of a taboo chief. Then the assembly shouted aloud, "O the beautiful woman! O the beautiful woman! How stately she stands!"

Then the men ran in flocks from the land down to the sea beach; one trampled on another in order to see.

Then the seer called out to Aiwohikupua, "Your keepers are not guilty; not by their means was I freed from prison, but by my god, who has saved me from many perils; and this is my lord.

"I spoke truly; this is my daughter, my lord, whom I went to seek, my preserver."

And when Aiwohikupua looked upon Laieikawai his heart trembled, and he fell to the ground as if dead.

When the chief recovered he commanded his head man to bring the seer and his daughter to fill the place of Poliahu and Hinaikamalama.

The head man went and called out to the seer on the canoe and told him the chief's word.

When the seer heard it he said to the head man, "Return and tell the chief, my lord indeed, that my lordly daughter shall never become his wife; she is chief over all the islands."

The head man went away; the seer, too, went away with his daughters, nor was he seen again after that at Wailua; they returned and dwelt at Honopuwaiakua.

XXVII

In this chapter we will tell how Kahalaomapuana went to get Kaonohiokala, the Eyeball-of-the-Sun, the betrothed husband of Laieikawai, and of her return.

After Kahalaomapuana had laid her commands upon her sisters she made preparation for the journey.

At the rising of the sun Kahalaomapuana entered inside Kihanuilulumoku and swam through the ocean and came to The Shining Heavens; in four months and ten days they reached Kealohilani.

When they arrived they did not see Mokukelekahiki, the guard who watches over Kaonohiokala's wealth, his chief counsellor in The Shining Heavens; twice ten days they waited for Mokukelekahiki to return from his garden patch.

Mokukelekahiki returned while the lizard was asleep inside the house; the head alone filled that great house of Mokukelekahiki's, the body and tail of the lizard were still in the sea.

A terrible sight to Mokukelekahiki to see that lizard; he flew away up to Nuumealani, the Raised Place in the Heavens; there was Kaeloikamalama, the magician who closes the door of the taboo house on the borders of Tahiti, where Kaonohiokala was hidden.

Mokukelekahiki told Kaeloikamalama how he had seen the lizard. Then Kaeloikamalama flew down with Mokukelekahiki from the heights of Nuumealani, the land in the air.

As Mokukelekahiki and his companion approached the house where the lizard was sleeping, then said Kihanuilulumoku to Kahalaomapuana, "When those men get here who are flying toward us, then I will throw you out and land you on Kaeloikamalama's neck, and when he questions you, then tell him you are a child of theirs, and when he asks what our journey is for, then tell him."

Not long after, Mokukelekahiki and Kaeloikamalama thundered at the door of the house.

When the lizard looked, there stood Kaeloikamalama with the digging spade called Kapahaelihonua, The Knife-that-cuts-the-earth, twenty fathoms its length, four men to span it. Thought the lizard, "A slaughterer this." There was Kaeloikamalama swinging the digging spade in his fingers.

Then Kihanuililulumoku lifted his tail out of the water, the sea swelled, the waves overwhelmed the cliffs from their foundations as high waves sweep the coast in February; the spume of the sea rose high, the sun was darkened, white sand was flung on the shore.

Then fear fell upon Kaeloikamalama and his companion, and they started to run away from before the face of the lizard.

Then Kihanuililulumoku threw out Kahalaomapuana, and she fell upon Kaeloikamalama's neck.[71]

Kaeloikamalama asked, "Whose child are you?"

Said Kahalaomapuana, "The child of Mokuekelekahiki, of Kaeloikamalama, of the magicians who guard the taboo house on the borders of Tahiti."[72]

The two asked, "On what journey, my child, do you come hither?"

Kahalaomapuana answered, "A journey to seek one from the heavens."

Again they asked, "To seek what one from the heavens?"

"Kaonohiokala," replied Kahalaomapuana, "the high taboo one of Kaeloikamalama and Mokukelekahiki."

Again they asked, "Kaonohiokala found, what is he to do?"

Said Kahalaomapuana, "To be husband to the princess of broad Hawaii, to Laieikawai, our mistress."

Again they asked, "Who are you?"

She told them, "Kahalaomapuana, the youngest daughter of Moanalihaikawaokele and Laukieleula."[73]

When Mokukelekahiki and Kaeloikamalama heard she was their own child, then they released her from Kaeloikamalama's neck and kissed their daughter.

For Mokukelekahiki and Kaeloikamalama were brothers of Laukieleula, Aiwohikupua's mother.

Said Kaeloikamalama, "We will show you the road, then you shall ascend."

For ten days they journeyed before they reached the place to go up; Kaeloikamalama called out, "O Lanalananuiaimakua! Great ancestral spider. Let down the road here for me to go up!! There is trouble below!!!"

Not long after, Great ancestral spider let down a spider-web that made a network in the air.

Then Kaeloikamalama instructed her, saying, "Here is your way, ascend to the top, and you will see a house standing alone in a garden patch; there is Moanalihaikawaokele; the country is Kahakaekaea.

"When you see an old man with long gray hair, that is Moanalihaikawaokele; if he is sitting up, don't be hasty; should he spy you first, you will die, he will not listen to you, he will take you for another.

"Wait until he is asleep; should he turn his face down he is not asleep, but when you see him with the face turned up, he is really asleep; then approach not the windward, go to the leeward, and sit upon his breast, holding tight to his beard, then call out:

> *"O Moanalihaikawaokele—O!*
> *Here am I—your child,*
> *Child of Laukieleula,*
> *Child of Mokukelekahiki,*
> *Child of Kaeloikamalama,*
> *The brothers of my mother,*
> *Mother, mother,*
> *Of me and my older sisters*
> *And my brother, Aiwohikupua,*
> *Grant me the sight, the long sight, the deep sight,*
> *Release the one in the heavens,*
> *My brother and lord,*
> *Awake! Arise!*

"So you must call to him, and if he questions you, then, tell him about your journey here.

"On the way up, if fine rain covers you, that is your mother's doings; if cold comes, do not be afraid. Keep on up; and if you smell a fragrance, that too is your mother's, it is her fragrance, then all is well, you are almost to the top; keep on up, and if the sun's rays pierce and the heat strikes you, do not fear when you feel the sun's hot breath; try to bear it and you will enter the shadow of the moon; then you will not die, you have entered Kahakaekaea."

When they had finished talking, Kahalaomapuana climbed up, and in the evening she was covered with fine rain; this she thought was her father's doings; at night until dawn she smelled the fragrance of the *kiele* plant; this she thought was her mother's art; from dawn until the sun was high she was in the heat of the sun, she thought this was her brother's doing.

Then she longed to reach the shadow of the moon, and at evening she came into the shadow of the moon; she knew then that she had entered the land called Kahakaekaea.

She saw the big house standing, it was then night. She approached to the leeward; lo! Moanalihaikawaokele was still awake; she waited at a distance for him to go to sleep, as Kaeloikamalama had instructed her. Still Moanalihaikawaokele did not sleep.

When at dawn she went, Moanalihaikawaokele's face was turned upwards, she knew he was asleep; she ran quickly and seized her father's beard and called to him in the words taught her by Kaeloikamalama, as shown above.

Moanalihaikawaokele awoke; his beard, the place where his strength lay, was held fast; he struggled to free himself; Kahalaomapuana held the beard tight; he kept on twisting here and there until his breath was exhausted.

He asked, "Whose child are you?"

Said she, "Yours."

Again he asked, "Mine by whom?"

She answered, "Yours by Laukieleula."

Again he asked, "Who are you?"

"It is Kahalaomapuana."

Said the father, "Let go my beard; you are indeed my child."

She let go, and the father arose and set her upon his lap and wailed, and when he had ended wailing, the father asked, "On what journey do you come hither?"

"A journey to seek one from the heavens," answered Kahalaomapuana.

"To seek what one from the heavens?"

"Kaonohiokala," the girl answered.

"The high one found, what is he to do?"

Said Kahalaomapuana, "I have come to get my brother and lord to be the husband to the princess of broad Hawaii, to Laieikawai, our royal friend, the one who protects us."

She related all that her brother had done, and their friend.

Said Moanalihaikawaokele, "The consent is not mine to give, your mother is the only one to grant it, the one who has charge of the chief; she lives there in the taboo place prohibited to me. When your mother is unclean, she returns to me, and when her days of uncleanness are over, then she leaves me, she goes back to the chief.

"Therefore, wait until the time comes when your mother returns, then tell her on what journey you have come hither."

They waited seven days; it was Laukieleula's time of uncleanness.

Said Moanalihaikawaokele, "It is almost time for your mother to come, so to-night, get to the taboo house first and sleep there; in the early morning when she comes, you will be sleeping in the house; there is no place for her to go to get away from you, because she is unclean. If she questions you, tell her exactly what you have told me."

That night Moanalihaikawaokele sent Kahalaomapuana into the house set apart for women.

XXVIII

Very early in the morning came Laukieleula; when she saw someone sleeping there, she could not go away because she was unclean and that house was the only one open to her. "Who are you, lawless one, mischief-maker, who have entered my taboo house, the place prohibited to any other?" So spoke the mistress of the house.

Said the stranger, "I am Kahalaomapuana, the last fruit of your womb."

Said the mother, "Alas! my ruler, return to your father. I can not see you, for my days of uncleanness have come; when they are ended, we will visit together a little, then go."

So Kahalaomapuana went back to Moanalihaikawaokele; the father asked, "How was it?"

The daughter said, "She told me to return to you until her days of uncleanness were ended, then she would come to see me."

Three days the two stayed there; close to the time when Laukieleula's uncleanness would end, Moanalihaikawaokele said to his daughter, "Come! for your mother's days are almost ended; to-morrow, early in the morning before daylight, go and sit by the water hole where she washes herself; do not show yourself, and when she jumps into the pool and dives under the water, then run and bring hither her skirt and her polluted clothes; when she has bathed and returns for the clothes, they will be gone; then she will think that I have taken them; when she comes to the house, then you can get what you wish.

"If you two weep and cease weeping and she asks you if I have taken her clothes, then tell her you have them, and she will be ashamed and shrink from you because she has defiled you; then she will have nothing great enough to recompense you for your defilement, only one thing will be great enough, to get you the high one; then when she asks you what you desire, tell her; then you shall see your brother; we shall both see him, for I see him only once a year; he peeps out and disappears."

At the time the father had said, the daughter arose very early in the morning before daylight, and went as her father had directed.

When she arrived, she hid close to the water hole; not long after, the mother came, took off her polluted clothes and sprang into the water.

Then the girl took the things as directed and returned to her father.

She had not been there long; the mother came in a rage; Moanalihaikawaokele absented himself and only the daughter remained in the house.

"O Moanalihaikawaokele, give me back my polluted clothes, let me take them to wash in the water." No answer; three times she called, not once an answer; she peeped into the house where Kahalaomapuana lay sleeping, her head covered with a clean piece of *tapa*.

She called, "O Moanalihaikawaokele, give me back my polluted skirt; let me take it to wash in the water."

Then Kahalaomapuana started up as if she had been asleep and said to her mother, "My mother and ruler, he has gone; only I am in the house; that polluted skirt of yours, here it is."

"Alas! my ruler. I shrink with fear of evil for you, because you have guarded my skirt that was polluted; what recompense is there for the evil I fear for you, my ruler?"

She embraced the girl and wailed out the words in the line above.

When she had ceased wailing, the mother asked, "On what journey do you come hither to us?"

"I come to get my older brother for a husband for our friend, the princess of the great broad land of Hawaii, Laieikawai, our protector when we were lovelessly deserted by our older brother; therefore we are ashamed; we have no way to repay the princess for her protection; and for this reason permit me and my princely brother to go down below and bring Laieikawai up here." These were Kahalaomapuana's words to her mother.

The mother said, "I grant it in recompense for your guarding my polluted garment.

"If anyone else had come to get him, I would not have consented; since you come in person, I will not keep him back.

"Indeed, your brother has said that you are the one he loves best and thinks the most of; so let us go up and see your brother.

"Now you wait here; let me call the bird guardian of you two, who will bear us to the taboo house at the borders of Tahiti."

Then the mother called:

> *O Halulu at the edge of the light,*
> *The bird who covers the sun,*
> *The heat returns to Kealohilani.*
> *The bird who stops up the rain,*

The stream-heads are dry of Nuumealani.
The bird who holds back the clouds above,
The painted clouds move across the ocean,
The islands are flooded,
Kahakaekaea trembles,
The heavens flood not the earth.
O the lawless ones, the mischief makers!
O Mokukelekahiki!
O Kaeloikamalama!
The lawless ones who close the taboo house at the borders of Tahiti,
Here is one from the heavens, a child of yours,
Come and receive her, take her above to Awakea, the noonday.

Then that bird[71] drooped its wings down and its body remained aloft, then Laukieleula and Kahalaomapuana rested upon the bird's wings and it flew and came to Awakea, the Noonday, the one who opens the door of the sun where Kaonohiokala lived.

At the time they arrived, the entrance to the chief's house was blocked by thunderclouds.

Then Laukieleula ordered Noonday, "Open the way to the chief's place!"

Then Noonday put forth her heat and the clouds melted before her; lo! the chief appeared sleeping right in the eye of the sun in the fire of its intensest heat, so he was named after this custom The Eye of the Sun.

Then Laukieleula seized hold of one of the sun's rays and held it. Then the chief awoke.

When Kohalaomapuana looked upon her brother his eyes were like lightning and his skin all over his body was like the heat, of the furnace where iron is melted.

Laukieleula cried out, "O my heavenly one, here is your sister, Kahalaomapuana, the one you love best, here she is come to seek you."

When Kaonohiokala heard he awoke from sleep and signed with his eyes to Laukieleula to call the guards of the shade. She called:

O big bright moon,
O moving cloud of Kaialea,
Guards of the shadows, present yourselves before the chief.

Then the guards of the shade came and stood before the chief. Lo! the heat of the sun left the chief.

When the shadows came over the place where the chief lay, then he called his sister, and went to her, and wept over her, for his heart fainted with love for his youngest sister, and long had been the days of their separation.

When their wailing was ended he asked, "Whose child are you?"

Said the sister, "Mokukelekahiki's, Kaeloikamalama's, Moanalihaikawaokele's through Laukieleula."

Again the brother asked, "What is your journey for?"

Then she told him the same thing she had told the mother.

When the chief heard these things, he turned to their mother and asked, "Laukieleula, do you consent to my going to get the one whom she speaks of for my wife?"

"I have already given you, as she requested me; if anyone else had brought her to get you, if she had not come to us two, she might have stayed below; grant your little sister's request, for you first opened the pathway, she closed it; no one came before, none after her." Thus the mother.

After this answer Kaonohiokala asked further about her sisters and her brother.

Then said Kahalaomapuana, "My brother has not done right; he has opposed our living with this woman whom I am come to get you for. When he first went to woo this woman he came back again after us; we went with him and came to the woman's house, the princess of whom I speak. That night we went to the uplands; in the midst of the forest there she dwelt with her grandmother. We stood outside and looked at the workmanship of Laieikawai's house, inwrought with the yellow feathers of the *oo* bird.

"Mailehaiwale went to woo her, gained nothing, the woman refused; Mailekaluhea went, gained nothing at all; Mailelaulii went, gained nothing at all; Mailepakaha went, gained nothing at all; she refused them all; I remained, I never went to woo her; he went away in a rage leaving us in the jungle.

"When he left us, we followed; our brother's rage waxed as if we had denied his wish.

"Then it was we returned to where he left us, and the princess protected us, until I left to come hither; that is how we live."

When Kaonohiokala heard this story, he was angry. Then he said to Kahalaomapuana, "Return to your sisters and to your friend, the princess; my wife she shall be; wait, and when the rain falls and floods the land, I am still here.

"When the ocean billows swell and the surf throws white sand on the shore, I am still here; when the wind whips the air and for ten days lies calm, when thunder peals without rain, then I am at Kahakaekaea.

"When the dry thunder peals again, then ceases, I have left the taboo house at the borders of Tahiti. I am at Kealohilani, my divine body is laid aside, only the nature of a taboo chief remains, and I am become a human being like you.

"After this, hearken, and when the thunder rolls, the rain pours down, the ocean swells, the land is flooded, the lightning flashes, a mist overhangs, a rainbow arches, a colored cloud rises on the ocean, for one month bad weather closes down,[75] when the storm clears, there I am behind the mountain in the shadow of the dawn.

"Wait here and at daybreak, when I leave the summit of the mountain, then you shall see me sitting within the sun in the center of its ring of light, encircled by the rainbow of a chief.

"Still we shall not yet meet; our meeting shall be in the dusk of evening, when the moon rises on the night of full moon; then I will meet my wife.

"After our marriage, then I will bring destruction over the earth upon those who have done you wrong.

"Therefore, take a sign for Laieikawai, a rainbow; thus shall I know my wife."

These words ended, she returned by the same way that she had climbed up, and within one month found Kihanuilulumoku and told all briefly, "We are all right; we have prospered."

She entered into Kihanuilulumoku and swam over the ocean; as many days as they were in going, so many were they in returning.

They came to Olaa. Laieikawai and her companions were gone; the lizard smelled all about Hawaii; nothing. They went to Maui; the lizard smelled about; not a trace.

He sniffed about Kahoolawe, Lanai, Molokai. Just the same. They came to Kauai; the lizard sniffed about the coast, found nothing; sniffed inland; there they were, living at Honopuwaiakua, and Kihanuilulumoku threw forth Kahalaomapuana.

The princess and her sisters saw her and rejoiced, but a stranger to the seer was this younger sister, and he was terrified at sight of the lizard; but because he was a prophet, he stilled his fear.

Eleven months, ten days, and four days over it was since Kahalaomapuana left Laieikawai and her companions until their return from The-shining-heavens.

XXIX

When Kahalaomapuana returned from Kealohilani, from her journey in search of a chief, she related the story of her trip, of its windings and twistings, and all the things she had seen while she was away.

When she recited the charge given her by Kaonohiokala, Laieikawai said to her companions, "O comrades, as Kahalaomapuana tells me the message of your brother and my husband, a strange foreboding weighs upon me, and I am amazed; I supposed him to be a man, a mighty god that! When I think of seeing him, however I may desire it, I am ready to die with fear before he has even come to us."

Her companions answered, "He is no god; he is a man like us, yet in his nature and appearance godlike. He was the first-born of us; he was greatly beloved by our parents; to him was given superhuman powers which we have not, except Kahalaomapuana; only they two were given this power; his taboo rank still remains; therefore, do not fear; when he comes, you will see he is only a man like us."

Now, before Kahalaomapuana's return from Kealohilani, the seer foresaw what was to take place, one month before her return. Then the seer prophesied, in these words: "A blessing descends upon us from the heavens when the nights of full moon come.

"When we hear the thunder peal in dry weather and in wet, then we shall see over the earth rain and lightning, billows swell on the ocean, freshets on the land, land and sea covered thick with fog, fine mist and rain, and the beating of the ocean rain.

"When this passes, on the day of full moon, in the dusk of the early morning, at the time when the sun's rays strike the mountain tops, then the earth shall behold a youth sitting within the eye of the sun, one like the taboo child of my god. Afterwards the earth shall behold a great destruction and shall see all the haughty snatched away out of the land; then we shall be blessed, and our seed."

When his daughters heard the seer's prophecy, they wondered within themselves that he should prophesy at this distance, without knowing anything about their sister's mission for which they waited.

As a prophet it was his privilege to proclaim about Kauai those things which he saw would come to pass.

So, before leaving his daughters, he commanded them and said,

"My daughters, I am giving you my instructions before leaving you, not, indeed, for long; but I go to announce those things which I have told you, and shall return hither. Therefore, dwell here in this place, which my god has pointed out to me, and keep yourselves pure until my prophecy is fulfilled."

The prophet went away, as he had determined, and he went into the presence of the chiefs and men of position, at the place where the chiefs were assembled; there he proclaimed what he had seen.

And first he came to Aiwohikupua and said, "From this day, erect flag signals around your dwelling, and bring inside all whom you love.

"For there comes shortly a destruction over the earth; never has any destruction been seen before like this which is to come; never will any come hereafter when this destruction of which I tell is ended.

"Before the coming of the wonder-worker he will give you a sign of destruction, not over all the people of the land, but over you yourself and your people; then the high ones of earth shall lie down before him and your pride shall be taken from you.

"If you listen to my word, then you will be spared from the destruction that is verily to come; therefore, prepare yourselves at once."

And because of the seer's words, he was driven away from before the face of the chief.

Thus he proclaimed to all the chiefs on Kauai, and the chiefs who listened to the seer, they were spared.

He went to Kekalukaluokewa, with his wife and all in their company.

And as he said to Aiwohikupua, so he said to Kekalukaluokewa, and he believed him.

But Waka would not listen, and answered, "If a god is the one to bring destruction, then I have another god to save me and my chiefs."

And at Waka's words the seer turned to the chiefs and said, "Do not listen to your grandmother, for a great destruction is coming over the chiefs. Plant flag signals at once around you, and bring all dear to you inside the signals you have set up, and whoever will not believe me, let them fall in the great day of destruction.

"When that day comes, the old women will lie down before the soles of the feet of that mighty youth, and plead for life, and not get it, because they have disbelieved the words of the prophet."

And because Kekalukaluokewa knew that his former prophecies had been fulfilled, therefore he rejected the old woman's counsel. When the seer left the chief planted flag signals all around the palace and stayed within the protected place as the prophet had commanded.

At the end of his circuit, the seer returned and dwelt with his daughters.

For no other reason than love did the seer go to tell those things which he saw. He had been back one day with his daughters at Honopuwaiakua when Kahalaomapuana arrived, as described in the chapter before.

XXX

Ten days after Kahalaomapuana's return from Kealohilani came the first of their brother's promised signs.

So the signs began little by little during five days, and on the sixth day the thunder cracked, the rain poured down, the ocean billows swelled, the land was flooded, the lightning flashed, the mist closed down, the rainbow arched, the colored cloud rose over the ocean.

Then the seer said, "My daughters, the time is come when my prophecy is fulfilled as I declared it to you."

The daughters answered, "This is what we have been whispering about, for first you told us these things while Kahalaomapuana had not yet returned, and since her return she has told us the same thing again."

Said Laieikawai, "I tremble and am astonished, and how can my fear be stilled?"

"Fear not; be not astonished; we shall prosper and become mighty ones among the islands round about; none shall be above us; and you shall rule over the land, and those who have done evil against you shall flee from you and be chiefs no more.

"For this have I followed you persistently through danger and cost and through hard weariness, and I see prosperity for me and for my seed to be mine through you."

One month of bad weather over the land as the last sign; in the early morning when the rays of the sun rose above the mountain, Kaonohiokala was seen sitting within the smoking heat of the sun, right in the middle of the sun's ring, encircled with rainbows and a red mist.

Then the sound of shouting was heard all over Kauai at the sight of the beloved child of Moanalihaikawaokele and Laukieleula, the great high chief of Kahakaekaea and Nuumealani.

Behold! a voice shouting, "The beloved of Hulumaniani! the wonderful prophet! Hulumaniani! Give us life!"

From morning until evening the shouting lasted, until they were hoarse and could only point with their hands and nod their heads, for they were hoarse with shouting for Kaonohiokala.

Now, as Kaonohiokala looked down upon the earth, lo! Laieikawai was clothed in the rainbow garment his sister, Kahalaomapuana, had brought her; then through this sign he recognized Laieikawai as his betrothed wife.

In the dusk of the evening, at the rising of the bright full moon, he entered the prophet's inclosure.

When he came, all his sisters bowed down before him, and the prophet before the Beloved.

And Laieikawai was about to do the same; when, the Beloved saw Laieikawai about to kneel he cried out, "O my wife and ruler! O Laieikawai! do not kneel, we are equals."

"My lord, I am amazed and tremble, and if you desire to take my life, it is well; for never have I met before with anyone so terrible as this!" answered Laieikawai.

"I have not come to take your life, but on my sister's visit to me I gave her a sign for me to know you by and recognize you as my betrothed wife; and therefore have I come to fulfill her mission," so said Kaonohiokala.

When his sisters and the seer heard, then they shouted with joyful voices, "Amen! Amen! Amen! it is finished, flown beyond!". They rose up with joy in their eyes.

Then he called to his sisters, "I take my wife and at this time of the night will come again hither." Then his wife was caught away out of sight of her companions, but the prophet had a glimpse of her being carried on the rainbow to dwell within the moon; there they took in pledge their moments of bliss.

And the next night when the moon shone bright, at the time when its light decreased, a rainbow was let down, fastened to the moon and reaching to the earth; when the moon was directly over Honopuwaiakua, then the chiefs appeared above in the sky in their majesty and stood before the prophet, saying: "Go and summon all the people for ten days to gather together in one place; then I will declare my wrath against those who have done you wrong.

"At the end of ten days, then we shall meet again, and I will tell you what is well for you to do, and my sisters with you."

When these words were ended the seer went away, and when he had departed the five sisters were taken up to dwell with the wife in the shelter of the moon.

On the seer's circuit, according to the command of the Beloved, he did not encounter a single person, for all had gone up to Pihanakalani, the place where it had been predicted that victory should be accomplished.

After ten days the seer returned to Honopuwaiakua; lo! it was deserted.

Then Kaonohiokala met him, and the seer told him about the circuit he had made at the Beloved's command.

Then the prophet was taken up also to dwell in the moon.

And in the morning of the next day, at sunrise, when the hot rays of the sun rose over the mountains,

Then the Beloved began to punish Aiwohikupua and Waka. To Waka he meted out death, and Aiwohikupua was punished by being deprived of all his wealth, to wander like a vagrant over the earth until the end of his days.

At the request of Laieikawai to spare Laielohelohe and her husband, the danger passed them by, and they became rulers over the land thereafter.

Now in the early morning of the day of Aiwohikupua's and Waka's downfall, lo! the multitude assembled at Pihanakalani saw a rainbow let down from the moon to earth, trembling in the hot rays of the sun.

Then, as they all crowded together, the seer and the five girls stood on the ladder way, and Kaonohiokala and Laieikawai apart, and the soles of their feet were like fire. This was the time when Aiwohikupua and Waka fell to the ground, and the seer's prophecy was fulfilled.

When the chief had avenged them upon their enemies, the chief placed Kahalaomapuana as ruler over them and stationed his other sisters over separate islands. And Kekalukaluokewa was chief counsellor under Laielohelohe, and the seer was their companion in council, with the power of chief counsellor.

After all these things were put in order and well established, Laieikawai and her husband were taken on the rainbow to the land within the clouds and dwelt in the husband's home.

In case her sisters should do wrong then, it was Kahalaomapuana's duty to bring word to the chief.

But there was no fault to be found with his sisters until they left this world.

XXXI

After the marriage of Laieikawai and Kaonohiokala, when his sisters and the seer and Kekalukaluokewa and his wife were well established, after all this had been set in order, they returned to the country in the heavens called Kahakaekaea and dwelt in the taboo house on the borders of Tahiti.

And when she became wife under the marriage bond, all power was given her as a god except that to see hidden things and those obscure deeds which were done at a distance; only her husband had this power.

Before they left Kauai to return to the heavens, a certain agreement was made in their assembly at the government council.

Lo! on that day, the rainbow pathway was let down from Nuumealani and Kaonohiokala and Laieikawai mounted upon that way, and she laid her last commands upon her sisters, the seer, and Laielohelohe; these were her words:

"My companions and our father the prophet, my sister born with me in the womb and your husband, I return according to our agreement! leave you and return to that place where you will not soon come to see me; therefore, live in peace, for each alike has prospered, not one of you lacks fortune. But Kaonohiokala will visit you to look after your welfare."

After these words they were borne away out of sight. And as to her saying Kaonohiokala would come to look after the welfare of her companions, this was the sole source of disturbance in Laieikawai's life with her husband.

While Laieikawai lived at home with her husband it was Kaonohiokala's custom to come down from time to time to look after his sisters' welfare and that of his young wife three times every year.

They had lived perhaps five years under the marriage contract, and about the sixth year of Laieikawai's happy life with her husband, Kaonohiokala fell into sin with Laielohelohe without anyone knowing of his falling into sin.

After Laieikawai had lived three months above, Kaonohiokala went down to look after his sister's welfare, and returned to Laieikawai; so he did until the third year, and after three years of going below to see after his sisters, lo! Laielohelohe was full-grown and her beauty had increased and surpassed that of her sister, Laieikawai's.

Not at this time, however, did Kaonohiokala fall into sin, but his sinful longing had its beginning.

On every trip Kaonohiokala took to do his work below, for four years, lo! Laielohelohe's loveliness grew beyond what he had seen before, and his sinful lust increased mightily, but by his nature as a child of god he persisted in checking his lust; for perhaps a minute the lust flew from him, then it clung to him once more.

In the fifth year, at the end of the first quarter, Kaonohiokala went away to do his work below.

At that time virtue departed far from the mind of Kaonohiokala and he fell into sin.

Now at this time, when he met his sisters, the prophet and his *punalua* and their wife (Laielohelohe), Kaonohiokala began to redistribute the land, so he called a fresh council.

And to carry out his evil purpose, he transferred his sisters to be guards over the land called Kealohilani, and arranged that they should live with Mokukelekahiki and have charge of the land with him.

When some of his sisters saw how much greater the honor was to become chiefs in a land they had never visited, and serve with Mokukelekahiki there, they agreed to consent to their brother's plan.

But Kahalaomapuana would not consent to return to Kealohilani, for she cared more for her former post of honor than to return to Kealohilani.

And in refusing, she spoke to her brother as follows: "My high one, as to your sending us to Kealohilani, let them go and I will remain here, living as you first placed me; for I love the land and the people and am accustomed to the life; and if I stay below here and you above and they between, then all will be well, just as we were born of our mother; for you broke the way, your little sisters followed you, and I stopped it up; that was the end, and so it was."

Now he knew that his youngest sister had spoken well; but because of Kaonohiokala's great desire to get her away so that she would not detect his mischievous doings, therefore he cast lots upon his sisters, and the one upon whom, the lot rested must go back to Kealohilani.

Said Kaonohiokala to his sisters, "Go and pull a grass flower; do not go together, every one by herself, then the oldest return and give it to me, in the order of your birth, and the one who has the longest grass stem, she shall go to Kealohilani."

Every one went separately and returned as they had been told.

The first one went and pulled one about two inches in length, and the second one pulled and broke her flower perhaps three inches and a half; and the third, she pulled her grass stem about two inches long; and the fourth of them, hers was about one inch long; and Kahalaomapuana did not pull the tall flowers, she pulled a very short one, about three feet long hers was, and she cut off half and came back, thinking her grass stem was the shortest.

But in comparing them, the oldest laid hers down before her brother. Kahalaomapuana saw it and was much surprised, so she secretly broke hers inside her clothing; but her brother saw her doing it and said, "Kahalaomapuana, no fooling! leave your grass stem as it is."

The others laid down theirs, but Kahalaomapuana did not show hers; said he, "The lot rests upon you."

Then she begged her brother to draw the lot again; again they drew lots, again the lot rested upon Kahalaomapuana; Kahalaomapuana had nothing left to say, for the lot rested upon her.

Lo! she was sorrowful at separating herself from her own chief-house and the people of the land; darkened was the princess's heart by the unwelcome lot that sent her back to Kealohilani.

And on the day when Kahalaomapuana was to depart for Kealohilani, the rainbow was let down from above the earth.

Then she said to her brother, "Let the pathway of my high one wait ten days, and let the chiefs be gathered together and all the people of the land, that I may show them my great love before you take me away."

When Kaonohiokala saw that his sister's words were well, he granted her wish; then the pathway was taken up again with her brother.

And on the tenth day, the pathway was let down again before the assembly, and Kahalaomapuana mounted upon the ladder way prepared for her and turned with heavy heart, her eyes filled with a flood of tears, the water drops of Kulanihakoi, and said: "O chiefs and people, I am leaving you to return to a land unknown to you; only I and my older sisters have visited it; it was not my wish to go back to this land; but my hand decided my leaving you according to the lot laid by my divine brother. But I know that every one of us has a god, no one is without; now, therefore, do you pray to your god and I will pray to my god, and if our prayer has might, then shall we meet again hereafter. Love to you all, love to the land, we cease and disappear."

Then she caught hold of her garment and held it up to her eyes before the assembly to hide her feeling for the people and the land.

And she was borne by the rainbow to the land above the clouds, to Lanikuakaa, the heavens higher up.

The great reason why Kaonohiokala wished to separate Kahalaomapuana in Kealohilani was to hide his evil doings with Laielohelohe, for Kahalaomapuana was the only one who could see things done in secret; and she was a resolute girl, not one to give in. Kaonohiokala thought she might disclose to Moanalihaikawaokele this evil doing; so he got his sister away, and by his supernatural arts he made the lot fall to Kahalaomapuana.

When his sister had gone, about the end of the second quarter of the fifth year, he went away below to carry out his lustful design upon Laielohelohe.

Not just at that time, but he made things right with Kekalukaluokewa by putting him in Kahalaomapuana's place and the seer as his chief counsellor.

Mailehaiwale was made governor on Kauai, Mailekaluhea on Oahu, Mailelaulii on Maui and the other islands, Mailepakaha on Hawaii.

XXXII

When Kekalukaluokewa became head over the group, then Kaonohiokala sent him to make a tour of the islands and perform the functions of a ruler, and he put Laielohelohe in Kekalukaluokewa's place as his substitute.

And for this reason Kekalukaluokewa took his chief counsellor (the prophet) with him on the circuit.

So Kekalukaluokewa left Pihanakalani and started on the business of visiting the group; the same day Kaonohiokala left those below.

When Kaonohiokala started to return he did not go all the way up, but just watched that day the sailing of Kekalukaluokewa's canoes over the ocean.

Then Kaonohiokala came back down and sought the companionship of Laielohelohe, but not just then was the sin committed.

When the two met, Kaonohiokala asked Laielohelohe to separate herself from the rest, and at the high chief's command the princess's retainers withdrew.

When Laielohelohe and Kaonohiokala were alone he said, "This is the third year that I have desired you, for your beauty has grown and overshadowed your sister's, Laieikawai's. Now at last my patience no longer avails to turn away my passion from you."

"O my high one," said Laielohelohe, "how can you rid yourself of your passion? And what does my high one see fit to do?"

"Let us know one another," said Kaonohiokala, "this is the only thing to be done for me."

Said Laielohelohe, "We can not touch one another, my high one, for the one who brought me up from the time I was born until I found my husband, he has strictly bound me not to defile my flesh with anyone; and, therefore, my high one, it is his to grant your wish."

When Kaonohiokala heard this, then he had some check to his passion, then he returned to the heavens to his wife, Laieikawai. He had not been ten days there when, he was again thick-pressed by the thunders of his evil lust, and he could not hold out against it.

To ease this passion he was again forced down below to meet Laielohelohe.

And having heard that her guardian who bound her must give his

S. N. HALEʻOLE

consent, he first sought Kapukaihaoa and asked his consent to the chief's purpose.

So he went first and said to Kapukaihaoa: "I wish to unite myself with Laielohelohe for a time, not to take her away altogether, but to ease my heavy heart of its lust after your foster child; for I first begged my boon of her, but she sent me for your consent, and so I have come to you."

Said Kapukaihaoa: "High one of the highest, I grant your request, my high one; it is well for you to go in to my foster child; for no good has come to me from my charge. It was our strong desire, mine and hers who took care of your wife Laieikawai, that Kekalukaluokewa should be our foster child's husband; very good, but in settling the rule over the islands, the gain has gone to others and I have nothing. For he has given all the islands to your sisters, and I have nothing, the one who provided him with his wife; so it will be well, in order to avoid a second misfortune, that you have the wife for the two of you."

At the end of their secret conference, Kapukaihaoa went with the chief to Laielohelohe.

Said he, "My ward, here is the husband, be ruled by him; heavens above, earth beneath; a solid fortune, nothing can shake its foundation; and look to the one who bore the burden."

Then Laielohelohe dismissed her doubts; and Kaonohiokala took Laielohelohe and they took their pleasure together.

Three days after, Kaonohiokala returned to Kahakaekaea.

And after he had been some days absent, the pangs of love caught him fast, and changed his usual appearance.

Then on the fourth day of their separation, he told a lie to Laieikawai and said, "This was a strange night for me, I never slept, there was a drumming all night long."

Said Laieikawai, "What was it?"

Said Kaonohiokala, "Perhaps the people below are in trouble."

"Perhaps so," said Laieikawai. "Why not go down and see?"

And at his wife's mere suggestion, in less than no time Kaonohiokala was below in the companionship of Laielohelohe. But Laielohelohe never thought of harm; what was that to her mind!

When they met at the chief's wish. Laielohelohe did not love Kaonohiokala, for the princess did not wish to commit sin with the great chief from the heavens, but to satisfy her guardian's greed.

After perhaps ten days of these evil doings, Kaonohiokala returned above.

Then Laielohelohe's love for Kekalukaluokewa waxed and grew because she had fallen into sin with Kaonohiokala.

One day in the evening Laielohelohe said to Kapukaihaoa, "My good guard and protector, I am sorry for my sin with Kaonohiokala, and love grows within me for Kekalukaluokewa, my husband; good and happy has been our life together, and I sinned not by my own wish, but through your wish alone. What harm had you refused? I referred the matter to you because of your binding me not to keep companionship with anyone; I thought you would keep your oath; not so!"

Said Kapukaihaoa, "I allowed you to be another's because your husband gave me no gifts; for in my very face your husband's gifts were given to others; there I stood, then you were gone. Little he thought of me from whom he got his wife."

Said Laielohelohe to her foster father, "If that is why you have given me over to sin with Kaonohiokala, then you have done very wrong, for you know the rulers over the islands were not appointed by Kekalukaluokewa, but by Kaonohiokala; and therefore to-morrow I will go on board a double canoe and set sail to seek my husband."

That very evening she commanded her retainers, those who guarded the chief's canoe, to get the canoe ready to set sail to seek the husband.

And not wishing to meet Kaonohiokala, she hid inside the country people's houses where he would not come, lest Kaonohiokala should come again and sin with her against her wish; so she fled to the country people's houses, but he did not come until that night when she had left and was out at sea.

When she sailed, she came to Oahu and stayed in the country people's houses. So she journeyed until her meeting with Kekalukaluokewa.

About the time that Laielohelohe was come to Oahu, that next day Kaonohiokala came again to visit Laielohelohe; but on his arrival, no Laielohelohe at the chief's house; he did not question the guard for fear of his suspecting his sin with Laielohelohe. Now Laielohelohe had secretly told the guard of the chief's house why she was going. And failing in his desires he returned above.

The report of his lord's falling into sin had reached the ears of the chief through some of his retainers and he had heard also of Laielohelohe's displeasure.

Now the vagabond, Aiwohikupua, was one of the chief's retainers, he was the one who heard these things. And when he heard Laielohelohe's reason for setting sail to seek her husband, then he said to the palace guard, "If Kaonohiokala returns again, and asks for Laielohelohe, tell him she is ill, then he will not come back, for she would pollute Kaonohiokala and our parents; when the uncleanness is over, then the deeds of Venus may be done."

When Kaonohiokala came again and questioned the guard then he was told as Aiwohikupua had said, and he went back up again.

XXXIII

I n Chapter XXXII of this story the reason was told why Laielohelohe went in search of her husband.

Now, she followed him from Kauai to Oahu and to Maui; she came to Lahaina, heard Kekalukaluokewa was in Hana, having returned from Hawaii.

She sailed by canoe and came to Honuaula; there they heard that Hinaikamalama was Kekalukaluokewa's wife; the Honuaula people did not know that this was his wife.

When Laielohelohe heard this news, they hurried forward at once and came to Kaupo and Kipahulu. There was substantiated the news they heard first at Honuaula, and there they beached the canoe at Kapohue, left it, went to Waiohonu and heard that Kekalukaluokewa and Hinaikamalama had gone to Kauwiki, and they came to Kauwiki; Kekalukaluokewa and his companion had gone on to Honokalani; many days they had been on the way.

On their arrival at Kauwiki, that afternoon, Laielohelohe asked a native of the place how much farther it was to Honokalani, where Kekalukaluokewa and Hinaikamalama were staying.

Said the native, "You can arrive by sundown."

They went on, accompanied by the natives, and at dusk reached Honokalani; there Laielohelohe sent the natives to see where the chiefs were staying.

The natives went and saw the chiefs drinking *awa*, and returned and told them.

Then Laielohelohe sent the natives again to go and see the chiefs, saying, "You go and find out where the chiefs sleep, then return to us."

And at her command, the natives went and found out where the chiefs slept, and returned and told Laielohelohe.

Then for the first time she told the natives that she was Kekalukaluokewa's married wife.

Before Laielohelohe's meeting with Kekalukaluokewa he had heard of her falling into sin with Kaonohiokala; he heard it from one of Kauakahialii's men, the one who became Aiwohikupua's chief counsellor; and, because of that man's hearing about Laielohelohe, he came there to tell Kekalukaluokewa.

When Laielohelohe and her companions came to the house where Kekalukaluokewa was staying, lo! they lay sleeping in the same place under one covering, drunk with *awa*.

Laielohelohe entered and sat down at their heads, kissed him and wept quietly over him; but the fountain of her tears overflowed when she saw another woman sleeping by her husband, nor did they know this; for they were drunk with *awa*.

Then Laielohelohe did not stay her anger against Hinaikamalama. So she got between them, pushed Hinaikamalama away, took Kekalukaluokewa and embraced him, and wakened him.

Then Kekalukaluokewa started from his sleep and saw his wife; just then, Hinaikamalama waked suddenly from sleep and saw this strange woman with them; she ran away from them in a rage, not knowing this was Kekalukaluokewa's wife.

When Kekalukaluokewa saw the anger in Hinaikamalama's eyes as she went, then he said, "O Hinaikamalama, will you run to people with angry eyes? Do not take this woman for a stranger, she is my wedded wife." Then her rage left her and shame and fear took the place of rage.

When Kekalukaluokewa awoke from his drunken sleep and saw his wife Laielohelohe, they kissed as strangers meet.

Then he said to his wife, "Laielohelohe, I have heard about your falling into sin with our lord, Kaonohiokala, and now this is well for you and him, and well for me to rule under you two; for from him this honor comes, and life and death are with him; if I should object, he would kill me; therefore, whatever our lord wishes it is best for us to obey; it was not for my pleasure that I gave you up, but for fear of death."

Then Laielohelohe said to her husband, "Where are you, husband of my childhood? What you have heard is true, and it is true that I have fallen into sin with the lord of the land, not many times, only twice have we sinned; but, my husband, it was not I who consented to defile my body with our lord, but it was my guardian who permitted the sin; for on the day when you went away, that very day our lord asked me to defile myself; but I did not wish it, therefore I referred my refusal to him; but on his return from above he asked Kapukaihaoa, and so we met twice; and because I did not like it, I hid myself in the country people's houses, and for the same reason have I left the seat appointed me, and have sought you; and when I arrived, I found you with that woman. Therefore we are square; I have nothing to complain of your you have nothing to complain of me; therefore, leave this woman this very night."

Now his wife's words seemed right to her husband; but at Laielohelohe's last request to separate them from their sinful companionship, then was kindled the fire of Hinaikamalama's hot love for Kekalukaluokewa.

Hinaikamalama returned home to Haneoo to live; every day that Hinaikamalama stayed at her chief-house, she was wont to sit at the door of the house and turn her face to Kauwiki, for the hot love that wrapped her about.

One day, as the princess sought to ease the love she bore to Kekalukaluokewa, she climbed Kaiwiopele with her attendants, and sat there with her face turned toward Kauwiki, facing Kahalaoaka, and as the clouds rested there right above Honokalahi then the heart of the princess was benumbed with love for her lover; then she chanted a little song, as follows:

> *Like a gathering cloud love settles upon me,*
> *Thick darkness wraps my heart.*
> *A stranger perhaps at the door of the house,*
> *My eyes dance.*
> *It may be they weep, alas!*
> *I shall be weeping for you.*
> *As flies the sea spray of Hanualele,*
> *Right over the heights of Honokalani.*
> *My high one! So it is I feel.*

After this song she wept, and seeing her weep, her attendants wept with her.

They sat there until evening, then they returned to the house; her parents and her attendants commanded her to eat, but she had no appetite for food because of her love.

It was the same with Kekalukaluokewa, for when Hinaikamalama left Kekalukaluokewa that night, when Laielohelohe came, the chief was not happy, but he endured it for some days after their separation.

And on the day when Hinaikamalama went up on Kaiwiopele, that same night, he went to Hinaikamalama without Laielohelohe's knowledge, for she was asleep.

While Hinaikamalama lay awake, sleepless for love, entered Kekalukaluokewa, without the knowledge of anyone in the chief's house.

S. N. HALE'OLE

When Kekalukaluokewa came, he went right to the place where the princess slept, took the woman by the head and wakened her.

Then Hinaikamalama's heart leaped with the hope it was her lover; now when she seized him it was in truth the one she had hoped for. Then she called out to the attendants to light the lamps, and at dawn Kekalukaluokewa returned to his true wife, Laielohelohe. After that, Kekalukaluokewa went to Hinaikamalama every night without being seen; ten whole days passed that the two did evil together without the wife knowing it; for in order to carry out her husband's desire Laielohelohe's senses were darkened by the effects of *awa*.

One day one of the native-born women of the place felt pity for Laielohelohe, therefore the woman went to visit the princess.

While Kekalukaluokewa was in the fiber-combing house with the men, the woman visited with Laielohelohe, and she said mysteriously, "How is your husband? Does he not struggle and groan sometimes for the woman?"

Said Laielohelohe, "No; all is well with us."

Said the woman again, "It may be he is deceiving you."

"Perhaps so," answered Laielohelohe, "but so far as I see we are living very happily."

Then the woman told her plainly, "Where are you? Our garden patch is right on the edge of the road; my husband gets up to dig in our garden. As he was digging, Kekalukaluokewa came along from Haneoo; my husband thought at once he had been with Hinaikamalama; my husband returned and told me, but I was not sure. On the next night, at moonrise, I got up with my husband, and we went to fish for red fish in the sea at Haneoo; as we came to the edge of the gulch, we saw some one appear above the rise we had just left; then we turned aside and hid; it was Kekalukaluokewa coming; then we followed his footsteps until we came close to Hinaikamalama's house; here Kekalukaluokewa entered. After we had fished and returned to the place where we met him first, we met him going back, and we did not speak to him nor he to us; that is all, and this day Hinaikamalama's own guard told me—my husband's sister she is—ten days the chiefs have been together; that is my secret; and therefore my husband and I took pity on you and I came to tell you."

XXXIV

A nd at the woman's words, the princess's mind was moved; not at once did she show her rage; but she waited but to make sure. She said to the woman, "No wonder my husband forces me to drink *awa* so that when I am asleep under the influence of the *awa*, he can go; but to-night I will follow him."

That night Kekalukaluokewa again gave her the *awa*, then she obeyed him, but after she had drunk it all, she went outside the house immediately and threw it up; and afterwards her husband did not know of his wife's guile, and she returned to the house, and Laielohelohe lay down and pretended to sleep.

When Kekalukaluokewa thought that his wife was fast asleep under the effects of the *awa*, then he started to make his usual visit to Hinaikamalama.

When Laielohelohe saw that he had left her, she arose and followed Kekalukaluokewa without being seen.

Thus following, lo! she found her husband with Hinaikamalama.

Then Laielohelohe said to Kekalukaluokewa, when she came to Hinaikamalama's house where they were sleeping, "My husband, you have deceived me; no wonder you compelled me to drink *awa*, you had something to do; now I have found you two, I tell you it is not right to endure this any longer. We had best return to Kauai; we must go at once."

Her husband saw that the princess was right; they arose and returned to Honokalani and next day the canoes were hastily prepared to fulfill Laielohelohe's demand, thinking to sail that night; but they did not, for Kekalukaluokewa pretended to be ill, and they postponed going that night. The next day he did the same thing again, so Laielohelohe gave up her love for her husband and returned to Kauai with her canoe, without thinking again of Kekalukaluokewa.

The next day after Laielohelohe reached Kauai after leaving her husband, Kaonohiokala arrived again from Kahakaekaea, and met with Laielohelohe.

Four months passed of their amorous meetings; this long absence of Kaonohiokala's seemed strange to Laieikawai, he had been away four months; and as Laieikawai wondered at the long absence, Kaonohiokala returned.

Laieikawai asked, "Why were you gone four months? You have not done so before."

Said Kaonohiokala, "Laielohelohe has had trouble with her husband; Kekalukaluokewa has taken a stranger to wife, and this is why I was so long away."

Then Laieikawai said to her husband, "Get your wife and bring her up here and let us live together."

Therefore, Kaonohiokala left Laieikawai and went away, as Laieikawai thought, to carry out her command. Not so!

On this journey Kaonohiokala stayed away a year; now Laieikawai did not think her husband's long stay strange, she laid it to Laielohelohe's troubles with Kekalukaluokewa.

Then she longed to see how it was with her sister, so Laieikawai went to her father-in-law and asked, "How can I see how it is with my sister, for I have heard from my husband and high one that Laielohelohe is having trouble with Kekalukaluokewa, and so I have sent Kaonohiokala to fetch the woman and return hither; but he has not come back, and it is a year since he went, so give me power to see to that distant place to know how it is with my relatives."

Then said Moanalihaikawaokele, her father-in-law, "Go home and look for your mother-in-law; if she is asleep, then go into the taboo temple; if you see a gourd plaited with straw and feathers mounted on the edge of the cover, that is the gourd. Do not be afraid of the great birds that stand on either side of the gourd, they are not real birds, only wooden birds; they are plaited with straw and inwrought with feathers. And when you come to where the gourd is standing take off the cover, then put your head into the mouth of the gourd and call out the name of the gourd, 'Laukapalili, Trembling Leaf, give me wisdom.' Then you shall see your sister and all that is happening below. Only when you call do not call in a loud voice; it might resound; your mother-in-law, Laukieleula, might hear, the one who guards the gourd of wisdom."

Laukieleula was wont to watch the gourd of wisdom, at night, and by day she slept.

Very early next morning, at the time when the sun's warmth began to spread over the earth, she went to spy out Laukieleula; she was just asleep.

When she saw she was asleep Laieikawai did as Moanalihaikawaokele had directed, and she went as he had instructed her.

When she came to the gourd, the one called "the gourd of wisdom," she lifted the cover from the gourd and bent her head to the mouth of the gourd, and she called the name of the gourd, then she began to see all that was happening at a distance.

At noon Laieikawai's eyes glanced downward, lo! Kaonohiokala sinned with Laielohelohe.

Then Laieikawai went and told Moanalihaikawaokele about it, saying, "I have employed the power you gave me, but while I was looking my high lord sinned; he did evil with my sister; for the first time I understand why his business takes him so long down below."

Then Moanalihaikawaokele's wrath was kindled, and Laukieleula heard it also, and her parents-in-law went to the gourd—lo! they plainly saw the sin committed as Laieikawai had said.

That day they all came together, Laieikawai and her parents-in-law, to see what to do about Kaonohiokala, and they came to their decision.

Then the pathway was let down from Kahakaekaea and dropped before Kaonohiokala; then Kaonohiokala's heart beat with fear, because the road dropped before him; not for long was Kaonohiokala left to wonder.

Then the air was darkened and it was filled with the cry of wailing spirits and the voice of lamentation—"The divine one has fallen! The divine one has fallen!!" And when the darkness was over, lo! Moanalihaikawaokele and Laukieleula and Laieikawai sat above the rainbow pathway.

And Moanalihaikawaokele said to Kaonohiokala, "You have sinned, O Kaonohiokala, for you have defiled yourself and, therefore, you shall no longer have a place to dwell within Kahakaekaea, and the penalty you shall pay, to become a fearsome thing on the highway and at the doors of houses, and your name is Lapu, Vanity, and for your food you shall eat moths; and thus shall you live and your posterity."

Then was the pathway taken from him through his father's supernatural might. Then they returned to Kahakaekaea.

In this story it is told how Kaonohiokala was the first ghost on these islands, and from his day to this, the ghosts wander from place to place, and they resemble evil spirits in their nature.[76]

On the way back after Kaonohiokala's punishment, they encountered Kahalaomapuana in Kealohilani, and for the first time discovered she was there.

And at this discovery, Kahalaomapuana told the story of her dismissal, as we saw in Chapter XXVII of this story, and at the end Kahalaomapuana was taken to fill Kaonohiokala's place.

At Kahakaekaea, sometimes Laieikawai longed for Laielohelohe, but she could do nothing; often she wept for her sister, and her parents-in-law thought it strange to see Laieikawai's eyes looking as if she had wept.

Moanalihaikawaokele asked the reason for this; then she told him she wept for her sister.

Said Moanalihaikawaokele, "Your sister can not live here with us, for she is defiled with Kaonohiokala; but if you want your sister, then you go and fill Kekalukaluokewa's place." Now Laieikawai readily assented to this plan.

And on the day when Laieikawai was let down, Moanalihaikawaokele said, "Return to your sister and live virgin until your death, and from this time forth your name shall be no longer called Laieikawai, but your name shall be 'The Woman of the Twilight,' and by this name shall all your kin bow down to you and you shall be like a god to them."

And after this command, Moanalihaikawaokele took her, and both together mounted upon the pathway and returned below.

Then, Moanalihaikawaokele said all these things told above, and when he had ended he returned to the heavens and dwelt in the taboo house on the borders of Tahiti.

Then, The Woman of the Twilight placed the government upon the seer; so did Laieikawai, the one called The Woman of the Twilight, and she lived as a god, and to her the seer bowed down and her kindred, according to Moanalihaikawaokele's word to her. And so Laieikawai lived until her death.

And from that time to this she is still worshiped as The Woman of the Twilight.

(The End)

Notes on the Text

Preface

1. For the translation of Haleole's foreword, which is in a much more ornate and involved style than the narrative itself, I am indebted to Miss Laura Green, of Honolulu.

I

1. Haleole uses the foreign form for wife, *wahine mare*, literally "married woman," a relation which in Hawaiian is represented by the verb *hoao*. A temporary affair of the kind is expressed in Waka's advice to her granddaughter, "*O ke kane ia moeia*," literally, "the man this to be slept with."

2. The chief's vow, *olelo paa*, or "fixed word," to slay all his daughters, would not be regarded as savage by a Polynesian audience, among whom infanticide was commonly practiced. In the early years of the mission on Hawaii, Dibble estimated that two-thirds of the children born perished at the hands of their parents. They were at the slightest provocation strangled or burned alive, often within the house. The powerful Areois society of Tahiti bound its members to slay every child born to them. The chief's preference for a son, however, is not so common, girls being prized as the means to alliances of rank. It is an interesting fact that in the last census the proportion of male and female full-blooded Hawaiians was about equal.

3. The phrase *nalo no hoi na wahi huna*, which means literally "conceal the secret parts," has a significance akin to the Hebrew rendering "to cover his nakedness," and probably refers to the duty of a favorite to see that no enemy after death does insult to his patron's body. So the bodies of ancient chiefs are sewed into a kind of bag of fine woven coconut work, preserving the shape of the head and bust, or embalmed and wrapped in many folds of native cloth and hidden away in natural tombs, the secret of whose entrance is intrusted to only one or two followers, whose superstitious dread prevents their revealing the secret, even when offered large bribes. These bodies, if worshiped, may be repossessed by the spirit and act as supernatural guardians of the house. See page 494, where the Kauai chief sets out on his wedding embassy with "the embalmed bodies of his ancestors." Compare, for the service itself, Waka's wish that the Kauai

chief might be the one to hide her bones, the prayer of Aiwohikupua's seer that his master might, in return for his lifelong service, "bury his bones"—"*e kalua keai mau iwi*," and his request of Laieikawai, that she would "leave this trust to your descendants unto the last generation."

4. Prenatal infanticide, *omilomilo*, was practiced in various forms throughout Polynesia even in such communities as rejected infanticide after birth. The skeleton of a woman, who evidently died during the operation, is preserved in the Bishop Museum to attest the practice, were not testimony of language and authority conclusive.

5. The *manini* (*Tenthis sandvicensis*, Street) is a flat-shaped striped fish common in Hawaiian waters. The spawn, called *ohua*, float in a jellylike mass on the surface of the water. It is considered a great delicacy and must be fished for in the early morning before the sun touches the water and releases the spawn, which instantly begin to feed and lose their rare transparency.

6. The month *Ikuwa* is variously placed in the calendar year. According to Malo, on Hawaii it corresponds to our October; on Molokai and Maui, to January; on Oahu, to August; on Kauai, to April.

7. The adoption by their grandparents and hiding away of the twins must be compared with a large number of concealed birth tales in which relatives of superior supernatural power preserve the hero or heroine at birth and train and endow their foster children for a life of adventure. This motive reflects Polynesian custom. Adoption was by no means uncommon among Polynesians, and many a man owed his preservation from death to the fancy of some distant relative who had literally picked him off the rubbish heap to make a pet of. The secret amours of chiefs, too, led, according to Malo (p. 82), to the theme of the high chief's son brought up in disguise, who later proves his rank, a theme as dear to the Polynesian as to romance lovers of other lands.

II

8. The *iako* of a canoe are the two arched sticks which hold the outrigger. The *kua iako* are the points at which they are bound to the canoe, or rest upon it, aft and abaft of the canoe.

9. The verb *hookuiia* means literally "cause to be pierced" as with a needle or other sharp instrument. *Kui* describes the act of piercing, *hoo* is the causative prefix, *ia* the passive particle, which was, in old Hawaiian, commonly attached to the verb as a suffix. The Hawaiian speech expresses

much more exactly than our own the delicate distinction between the subject in its active and passive relation to an action, hence the passive is vastly more common. Mr. J.S. Emerson points out to me a classic example of the passive used as an imperative—an old form unknown to-day—in the story of the rock, Lekia, the "pohaku o Lekia" which overlooks the famous Green Lake at Kapoho, Puna. Lekia, the demigod, was attacked by the magician, Kaleikini, and when almost overcome, was encouraged by her mother, who called out, "*Pohaku o Lekia, onia a paa*"—"be planted firm." This the demigod effected so successfully as never again to be shaken from her position.

10. Hawaiian challenge stories bring out a strongly felt distinction in the Polynesian mind between these two provinces, *maloko a mawaho*, "inside and outside" of a house. When the boy Kalapana comes to challenge his oppressor he is told to stay outside; inside is for the chief. "Very well," answers the hero, "I choose the outside; anyone who comes out does so at his peril." So he proves that he has the better of the exclusive company.

11. In his invocation the man recognizes the two classes of Hawaiian society, chiefs and common people, and names certain distinctive ranks. The commoners are the farming class, *hu, makaainu, lopakuakea, lopahoopiliwale* referring to different grades of tenant farmers. Priests and soothsayers are ranked with chiefs, whose households, *aialo*, are made up of hangers-on of lower rank—courtiers as distinguished from the low-ranking countrymen—*makaaina*—who remain on the land. Chiefs of the highest rank, *niaupio*, claim descent within the single family of a high chief. All high-class chiefs must claim parentage at least of a mother of the highest rank; the low chiefs, *kaukaualii*, rise to rank through marriage (Malo, p. 82). The *ohi* are perhaps the *wohi*, high chiefs who are of the highest rank on the father's side and but a step lower on the mother's.

12. With this judgment of beauty should be compared Fornander's story of *Kepakailiula*, where "mother's brothers" search for a woman beautiful enough to wed their protegé, but find a flaw in each candidate; and the episode of the match of beauty in the tale of *Kalanimanuia*.

III

13. The building of a *heiau*, or temple, was a common means of propitiating a deity and winning his help for a cause. Ellis records (1825) that on the journey from Kailua to Kealakekua he passed at

least one *heiau* to every half mile. The classic instance in Hawaiian history is the building of the great temple of Puukohala at Kawaihae by Kamehamaha, in order to propitiate his war god, and the tolling thither of his rival, Keoua, to present as the first victim upon the altar, a treachery which practically concluded the conquest of Hawaii. Malo (p. 210) describes the "days of consecration of the temple."

14. The nights of Kane and of Lono follow each other on the 27th and 28th of the month and constitute the days of taboo for the god Kane. Four such taboo seasons occur during the month, each lasting from two to three days and dedicated to the gods Ku, Kanaloa, and Kane, and to Hua at the time of full moon. The night Kukahi names the first night of the taboo for Ku, the highest god of Hawaii.

15. By *kahoaka* the Hawaiians designate "the spirit or soul of a person still living," in distinction from the *uhane*, which may be the spirit of the dead. *Aka* means shadow, likeness; *akaku*, that kind of reflection in the mists which we call the "specter in the brocken." *Hoakaku* means "to have a vision," a power which seers possess. Since the spirit may go abroad independently of the body, such romantic shifts as the vision of a dream lover, so magically introduced into more sophisticated romance, are attended with no difficulties of plausibility to a Polynesian mind. It is in a dream that Halemano first sees the beauty of Puna. In a Samoan story (Taylor, I, 98) the sisters catch the image of their brother in a bottle and throw it upon the princess's bathing pool. When the youth turns over at home, the image turns in the water.

16. The feathers of the *oo* bird (*Moho nobilis*), with which the princess's house is thatched, are the precious yellow feathers used for the manufacture of cloaks for chiefs of rank. The *mamo* (*Drepanis pacifica*) yields feathers of a richer color, but so distributed that they can not be plucked from the living bird. This bird is therefore almost extinct in Hawaiian forests, while the *oo* is fast recovering itself under the present strict hunting laws. Among all the royal capes preserved in the Bishop Museum, only one is made of the *mamo* feathers.

17. The reference to the temple of Pahauna is one of a number of passages which concern themselves with antiquarian interest. In these and the transition passages the hand of the writer is directly visible.

18. The whole treatment of the Kauakahialii episode suggests an inthrust. The flute, whose playing won for the chief his first bride, plays no part at all

in the wooing of Laieikawai and hence is inconsistently emphasized. Given a widely sung hero like Kauakahialii, whose flute playing is so popularly connected with his love making, and a celebrated heroine like the beauty who dwelt among the birds of Paliuli, and the story-tellers are almost certain to couple their names in a tale, confused as regards the flute, to be sure, but whose classic character is perhaps attested by the grace of the description. The Hebraic form in which the story of the approach of the divine beauty is couched can not escape the reader, and may be compared with the advent of the Sun god later in the story. There is nothing in the content of this story to justify the idea that the chief had lost his first wife, Kailiokalauokekoa, unless it be the fact that he is searching Hawaii for another beauty. Perhaps, like the heroine of *Halemano*, the truant wife returns to her husband through jealousy of her rival's attractions. A special relation seems to exist in Hawaiian story between Kauai and the distant Puna on Hawaii, at the two extremes of the island group: it is here that *Halemano* from Kauai weds the beauty of his dream, and it is a Kauai boy who runs the sled race with Pele in the famous myth of *Kalewalo*. With the Kauakahialii tale (found in *Hawaiian Annual*, 1907, and Paradise of the Pacific, 1911) compare Grey's New Zealand story (p. 235) of Tu Tanekai and Tiki playing the horn and the pipe to attract Hinemoa, the maiden of Rotorua. In Malo, p. 117, one of the popular stories of this chief is recorded, a tale that resembles Gill's of the spirit meeting of Watea and Papa.

19. These are all wood birds, in which form Gill tells us (Myths and Songs, p. 35) the gods spoke to man in former times. Henshaw tells us that the *oo* (*Moho nobilis*) has "a long shaking note with ventriloquial powers." The *alala* is the Hawaiian crow (*Corvus hawaiiensis*), whose note is higher than in our species. If, as Henshaw says, its range is limited to the dry Kona and Kau sections, the chief could hardly hear its note in the rainy uplands of Puna. But among the forest trees of Puna the crimson *apapane* (*Himatione sanguinea*) still sounds its "sweet monotonous note;" the bright vermillion *iiwipolena* (*Vectiaria coccinea*) hunts insects and trills its "sweet continual song;" the "four liquid notes" of the little rufous-patched *elepaio* (*Eopsaltria sandvicensis*), beloved of the canoe builder, is commonly to be heard. Of the birds described in the Laielohelohe series the cluck of the *alae* (*Gallinula sandricensis*) I have heard only in low marshes by the sea, and the *ewaewaiki* I am unable to identify. Andrews calls it the cry of a spirit.

20. *Moaulanuiakea* means literally "Great-broad-red-cock," and is the name of Moikeka's house in Tahiti, where he built the temple Lanikeha

near a mountain Kapaahu. His son Kila journeys thither to fetch his older brother, and finds it "grand, majestic, lofty, thatched with the feathers of birds, battened with bird bones, timbered with *kauila* wood." (See Fornander's *Kila*.)

IV

21. Compare Gill's story of the first god, Watea, who dreams of a lovely woman and finds that she is Papa, of the underworld, who visits him in dreams to win him as her lover. (Myths and Songs, p. 8.)

22. In the song the girl is likened to the lovely *lehua*, blossom, so common to the Puna forests, and the lover's longing to the fiery crater, Kilauea, that lies upon their edge. The wind is the carrier of the vision as it blows over the blossoming forest and scorches its wing across the flaming pit. In the *Halemano* story the chief describes his vision as follows: "She is very beautiful. Her eyes and form are perfect. She has long, straight, black hair and she seems to be of high rank, like a princess. Her garment seems scented with the *pele* and *mahuna* of Kauai, her skirt is made of some very light material dyed red. She wears a *hala* wreath on her head and a *lehua* wreath around her neck."

23. No other intoxicating liquor save *awa* was known to the early Hawaiians, and this was sacred to the use of chiefs. So high is the percentage of free alcohol in this root that it has become an article of export to Germany for use in drug making. Vancouver, describing the famous Maui chief, Kahekili, says: "His age I suppose must have exceeded 60. He was greatly debilitated and emaciated, and from the color of his skin I judged his feebleness to have been brought on by excessive use of *awa*."

21. In the Hawaiian form of checkers, called *konane*, the board, *papamu*, is a flat surface of stone or wood, of irregular shape, marked with depressions if of stone, often by bone set in if of wood; these depressions of no definite number, but arranged ordinarily at right angles. The pieces are beach pebbles, coral for white, lava for black. The smallest board in the museum collection holds 96, the largest, of wood, 180 men. The board is set up, leaving one space empty, and the game is played by jumping, the color remaining longest on the board winning the game. *Konane* was considered a pastime for chiefs and was accompanied by reckless betting. An old native conducting me up a valley in Kau district,

Hawaii, pointed out a series of such evenly set depressions on the flat rock floor of the valley and assured me that this must once have been a chief's dwelling place.

25. The *malo* is a loin cloth 3 or 4 yards long and a foot wide, one end of which passes between the legs and fastens in front. The red *malo* is the chief's badge, and his bodyguard, says Malo, wear the girdle higher than common and belted tight as if ready for instant service. Aiwohikupua evidently travels in disguise as the mere follower of a chief.

28. In Hawaiian warfare, the biggest boaster was the best man, and to shame an antagonist by taunts was to score success. In the ceremonial boxing contest at the Makahiki festivities for Lono, god of the boxers, as described by Malo, the "reviling recitative" is part of the program. In the story of *Kawelo*, when his antagonist, punning on his grandfather's name of "cock," calls him a "mere chicken that scratches after roaches," Kawelo's sense of disgrace is so keen that he rolls down the hill for shame, but luckily bethinking himself that the cock roosts higher than the chief (compare the Arab etiquette that allows none higher than the king), and that out of its feathers, brushes are made which sweep the chief's back, he returns to the charge with a handsome retort which sends his antagonist in ignominious retreat. In the story of Lono, when the nephews of the rival chiefs meet, a sparring contest of wit is set up, depending on the fact that one is short and fat, the other long and lanky, "A little shelf for the rats," jeers the tall one. "Little like the smooth quoit that runs the full course," responds the short one, and retorts "Long and lanky, he will go down in the gale like a banana tree." "Like the *ea* banana that takes long to ripen," is the quick reply. Compare also the derisive chants with which Kuapakaa drives home the chiefs of the six districts of Hawaii who have got his father out of favor, and Lono's taunts against the revolting chiefs of Hawaii.

27. The idiomatic passages "*aohe puko momona o Kohala*," etc., and (on page 387) "*e huna oukou i ko oukou mau maka i ke aouli*" are of doubtful interpretation.

28. This boast of downing an antagonist with a single blow is illustrated in the story of *Kawelo*. His adversary, Kahapaloa, has struck him down and is leaving him for dead. "Strike again, he may revive," urge his supporters. Kahapaloa's refusal is couched in these words:

> *"He is dead; for it is a blow from the young,*
> *The young must kill with a blow*
> *Else will the fellow go down to Milu*
> *And say Kahapaloa struck frim twice,*
> *Thus was the fighter slain."*

All Hawaiian stories of demigods emphasize the ease of achievement as a sign of divine rather than human capacity.

V

29. Shaking hands was of foreign introduction and marks one of the several inconsistencies in Haleole's local coloring, of which "the deeds of Venus" is the most glaring. He not only uses such foreign coined words as *wati*, "watch," and *mare*, "marry," but terms which are late Hawaiian, such as the triple canoe, *pukolu*, and provision boat, *pelehu*, said to have been introduced in the reign of Kaméhaméha I.

30. Famous Hawaiian boxing teachers kept master strokes in reserve for the pupils, upon whose success depended their own reputation. These strokes were known by name. Compare Kawelo, who before setting out to recapture Kauai sends his wife to secure from his father-in-law the stroke called *wahieloa*. The phrase *"Ka ai a ke kumu i ao oleia ia oukou"* has been translated with a double-punning meaning, literal and figurative, according to the interpretation of the words. Cold-nose's faith in his girdle parodies the far-fetched dependence upon name signs common to this punning race. The snapping of the end of his loin cloth is a good omen for the success of a stroke named "End-that-sounds"! Even his supporters jeer at him.

31. Few similes are used in the story. This figure of the "blood of a lamb," the "blow like the whiz of the wind," the *moo* ploughing the earth with his jaw "like a shovel," a picture of the surf rider—"foam rose on each side of his neck like a boar's tusks," and the appearance of the Sun god's skin, "like a furnace where iron is melted," will, perhaps, cover them all. In each the figure is exact, but ornamental, evidently used to heighten the effect. Images are occasionally elaborated with exact realization of the bodily sensation produced. The rainbow "trembling in the hot rays of the sun" is an example, and those passages which convey the lover's sensations—"his heart fainted with love," "thick pressed with thunders of love," or such an image as "the burden of his mind was

lifted." Sometimes the image carries the comparison into another field, as in "the windings and twistings of his journey"—a habit of mind well illustrated in the occasional proverbs, and in the highly figurative songs.

32. The Polynesians, like the ancient Hebrews, practiced circumcision with strict ceremonial observances.

33. The gods invoked by Aiwohikupua are not translated with certainty, but they evidently represent such forces of the elements as we see later belong among the family deities of the Aiwohikupua household. Prayer as an invocation to the gods who are called upon for help is one of the most characteristic features of native ritual, and the termination *amama*, generally accompanied by the finishing phrases *ua noa*, "it is finished," and *lele wale aku la*, "flown away," is genuine Polynesian. Literally *mama* means "to chew," but not for the purpose of swallowing like food, but to spit out of the mouth, as in the preparation of *awa*. The term may therefore, authorities say, be connected with the ceremonial chewing of *awa* in the ritualistic invocations to the gods. A similar prayer quoted by Gill (Myths and Songs, 120) he ascribes to the antiquity of the story.

34. The *laau palau*, literally "wood-that-cuts," which Wise translates "war club," has not been identified on Hawaii in the Bishop Museum, but is described from other groups. Gill, from the Hervey Islands, calls it a sharpened digging stick, used also as a weapon. The gigantic dimensions of these sticks and their appellations are emphasized in the hero tales.

35. The Hawaiian cloak or *kihei* is a large square, 2 yards in size, made of bark cloth worn over the shoulders and joined by two corners on one side in a knot.

36. The meaning of the idiomatic boast *he lala kamahele no ka laau ku i ka pali* is uncertain. I take it to be a punning reference to the Pali family from whom the chief sprang, but it may simply be a way of saying "I am a very high chief." Kamahele is a term applied to a favorite and petted child, as, in later religious apostrophe, to Christ himself.

VI

37. The *puloulou* is said to have been introduced by Paao some five hundred years ago, together with the ceremonial taboo of which it is the symbol. Since for a person of low rank to approach a sacred place or person was death to the intruder, it was necessary to guard against

accidental offences by the use of a sign. The *puloulou* consisted of a ball-shaped bundle of white bark cloth attached to the end of a staff. This symbol is to be seen represented upon the Hawaiian coat of arms; and Kalakaua's *puloulou*, a gilded wooden ball on the end of a long staff, is preserved in the Bishop Museum.

38. Long life was the Polynesian idea of divine blessing. Of Kualii the chanter boasts that he "lived to be carried to battle in a net." The word is *kaikoko*, "to carry on the back in a net," as in the case of old and feeble persons. Polynesian dialects contain a full vocabulary of age terms from infancy to old age.

39. Chickens were a valuable part of a chief's wealth, since from their feathers were formed the beautiful fly brushes, *kahili*, used to wave over chiefs of rank and carried in ceremonial processions. The entrance to the rock cave is still shown, at the mouth of Kaliuwaa valley, where Kamapuaa's grandmother shut up her chickens at night, and it was for robbing his uncle's henroost that this rascally pig-god was chased away from Oahu. This reference is therefore one of many indications that the Laieikawai tale belongs with those of the ancient demigods.

40. Mr. Meheula suggested to me this translation of the idiomatic allusions to the canoe and the coral reef.

VIII

41. A peculiarly close family relation between brother and sister is reflected in Polynesian tales, as in those of Celtic, Finnish, and Scandinavian countries. Each serves as messenger or go-between for the other in matters of love or revenge, and guards the other's safety by magic arts. Such a condition represents a society in which the family group is closely bound together. For such illustrations compare the Fornander stories of *Halemano, Hinaikamalama, Kalanimanuia, Nihoalaki, Kaulanapokii, Pamano*. The character of accomplished sorceress belongs especially to the helpful sister, a woman of the Malio or Kahalaomapuana type, whose art depends upon a life of solitary virginity. She knows spells, she can see what is going on at a distance, and she can restore the dead to life. In the older stories she generally appears in bird form. In more human tales she wins her brother's wishes by strategy. This is particularly true of the characters in this story, who win their way by wit rather than magic. In this respect the youngest sister of Aiwohikupua should be compared

with her prototype, Kaulanapokii, who weaves spells over plants and brings her slain brothers back to life. Kahalaomapuana never performs any such tasks, but she is pictured as invincible in persuasion; she never fails in sagacity, and is always right and always successful. She is, in fact, the most attractive character in the story. It is rather odd, since modern folk belief is firmly convinced of the power of love spells, that none appear in the recorded stories. All is accomplished by strategy.

42. For the translation of this dialogue I am indebted, to the late Dr. Alexander, to whose abstract of the story I was fortunate enough to have access.

X

43. To express the interrelation between brothers and sisters two pairs of kinship terms are used, depending upon the age and sex. Sisters speak of brothers as *kaikunane*, and brothers of sisters as *kaikuahine*, but within the same sex *kaikuaana* for the elder and *kaikaina* for the younger is used. So on page 431 Aiwohikupua deserts his sisters—*kaikuahine*—and the girls lament for their younger sister—*kaikaina*. After their reunion her older sisters—*kaikuaana*—ask her counsel. Notice, too, that when, on page 423, the brother bids his youngest sister—*kaikuahine opiopio*—stay with "her sisters" he uses the word *kaikuaana*, because he is thinking of her relation to them, not of his own. The word *pokii*,—"little sister"—is an endearing term used to good effect where the younger sister sings—

> "I am going back to your little sisters (me o'u pokii)
> To my older sisters (kaikuaana) I return."

44. The line translated "Fed upon the fruit of sin" contains one of those poetic plays upon words so frequent in Polynesian song, so difficult to reproduce in translation. Literally it might read "Sheltering under the great *hala* tree." But *hala*, also means "sin." This meaning is therefore caught up and employed in the next line—"is constancy then a sin?"—a repetition which is lost in translation. *Malu*, shade, is a doubtful word, which may, according to Andrews, mean "protected," or may stand for "wet and uncomfortable," a doubt evidently depending upon the nature of the case, which adds to the riddling character of the message. In their songs the sisters call up the natural scenery, place names, and childhood experiences of their native home on Kauai. The images used attempt actual description. The slant of the rain, the actual ladder of wood which helps scale the steep footpath up Nualolo Valley (compare *Song of Kualii*,

line 269, Lyons' version), the rugged cliffs which are more easily rounded by sea—"swimming 'round the steeps"—picture actual conditions on the island. Notice especially how the song of the youngest sister reiterates the constant theme of the "follow your leader" relation between the brother and his younger sisters. Thus far they have unhesitatingly followed his lead; how, then, can he leave them leaderless? is the plea: first, in their sports at home; next, in this adventure over sea and through the forest; last, in that divine mystery of birth when he first opened the roadway and they, his little sisters, followed after.

XI

45. This *ti*-leaf trumpet is constructed from the thin, dry, lilylike leaf of the wild *ti* much as children make whistles out of grass. It must be recalled that musical instruments were attributed to gods and awakened wonder and awe in Polynesian minds.

XII

46. In the story of *Kapuaokaoheloai* we read that the daughter of the king of Kuaihelani, the younger brother of Hina, has a daughter who lives apart under a sacred taboo, with a bathing pool in which only virgins can safely bathe, and "ministered to by birds." Samoan accounts say that the chiefs kept tame birds in their houses as pets, which fluttered freely about the rafters. A stranger unaccustomed to such a sight might find in it something wonderful and hence supernatural.

XIII

47. A strict taboo between man and woman forbade eating together on ordinary occasions. Such were the taboo restrictions that a well-regulated, household must set up at least six separate houses: a temple for the household gods, *heiau*; an eating house for the men, *hale mua*, which was taboo to the women; and four houses especially for the women—the living house, *hale noa*, which the husband might enter; the eating house, *hale aina*; the house of retirement at certain periods, which was taboo for the husband, *hale pea*; and the *kua*, where she beat out tapa. The food also must be cooked in two separate ovens and prepared separately in different food vessels.

48. The place of surf riding in Hawaiian song and story reflects its popularity as a sport. It inspires chants to charm the sea into good surfing—an end also attained by lashing the water with the convolvulus vine of the sea beach; forms the background for many an amorous or competitive adventure; and leaves a number of words in the language descriptive of the surfing technique or of the surf itself at particular localities famous for the sport, as, for example, the "Makaiwa crest" in Moikeha's chant, or the "Huia" of this story. Three kinds of surfing are indulged in—riding the crest in a canoe, called *pa ka waa*; standing or lying flat upon a board, which is cut long, rounded at the front end and square at the back, with slightly convex surfaces, and highly polished; and, most difficult feat of all, riding the wave without support, body submerged and head and shoulders erect. The sport begins out where the high waves form. The foundation of the wave, *honua*, the crest side, *muku*, and the rear, *lala*, are all distinguished. The art of the surfer lies in catching the crest by active paddling and then allowing it to bear him in swift as a race horse to the *hua*, where the wave breaks near the beach. All swimmers know that three or four high waves follow in succession. As the first of these, called the *kulana*, is generally "a high crest which rolls in from end to end of the beach and falls over bodily," the surfer seldom takes it, but waits for the *ohu* or *opuu*, which is "low, smooth and strong." For other details, see the article by a Hawaiian from Kona, published in the *Hawaiian Annual*, 1896, page 106.

XIV

49. *Honi*, to kiss, means to "touch" or "smell," and describes the Polynesian embrace, which is performed by rubbing noses. Williams (I, 152) describes it as "one smelling the other with a strong sniff."

XV

50. The abrupt entrance of the great *moo*, as of its disappearance later in the story, is evidently due to the humanized and patched-together form in which we get the old romance. The *moo* is the animal form which the god takes who serves Aiwohikupua's sisters, and represents the helpful beast of Polynesian folk tale, whose appearance is a natural result of the transformation power ascribed to the true demigod, or *kupua*, in the wilder mythical tales. The myths of the coming of the *moo* to Hawaii in the days of the gods, and of their subjection by Hiiaka, sister of Pele,

are recounted in Westervelt's "Legends of Honolulu" and in Emerson's "Pele and Hiiaka." Malo (p. 114) places Waka also among the lizard gods. These gods seem to have been connected] with the coming of the Pali family to Hawaii as recounted in Liliuokalani's "Song of Creation" and in Malo, page 20. The ritual of the god Lono, whose priests are inferior to those of Ku, is called that of "Paliku" (Malo, 210), a name also applied to the northern part of Hilo district on Hawaii with which this story deals. The name means "vertical precipice," according to Emerson, and refers to the rending by earthquakes. In fact, the description in this story of the approach of the great lizard, as well as his name—the word *kiha* referring to the writhing convulsions of the body preparatory to sneezing—identify the monster with the earthquakes so common to the Puna and Hilo districts of Hawaii, which border upon the active volcano, Kilauea. Natives say that a great lizard is the guardian spirit or *aumakua* of this section. At Kalapana is a pool of brackish water in which, they assert, lies the tail of a *moo* whose head is to be seen at the bottom of a pool a mile and a half distant, at Punaluu; and bathers in this latter place always dive and touch the head in order to avert harm. As the lizard guardians of folk tale are to be found "at the bottom of a pit" (see Fornander's story of *Aukele*), so the little gecko of Hawaii make their homes in cracks along cuts in the *pali*, and the natives fear to harm their eggs lest they "fall off a precipice" according to popular belief. When we consider the ready contractility of Polynesian demigods, the size of the monster dragons of the fabulous tales is no difficulty in the way of their identification with these tiny creatures, the largest of which found on Hawaii is 144 millimeters. By a plausible analogy, then, the earthquake which rends the earth is attributed to the god who clothes himself in the form of a lizard; still further, such a convulsion of nature may have been used to figure the arrival of some warlike band who peopled Hawaii, perhaps settling in this very Hilo region and forcing their cult upon the older form of worship.

XVI

51. The *ieie* vine and the sweet-scented fern are, like the *maile* vine, common in the Olaa forests, and are considered sacred plants dedicated to ceremonial purposes.

52. The fight between two *kupua*, one in lizard form, the other in the form of a dog, occurs in Hawaiian story. Again, when Wahanui goes to

Tahiti he touches a land where men are gathering coral for the food of the dead. This island takes the form of a dog to frighten travelers, and is named Kanehunamoku.

53. The season for the bird catcher, *kanaka kia manu*, lay between March and May, when the *lehua* flowers were in bloom in the upland forest, where the birds of bright plumage congregated, especially the honey eaters, with their long-curved bill, shaped like an insect's proboscis. He armed himself with gum, snares of twisted fiber, and tough wooden spears shaped like long fishing poles, which were the *kia manu*. Having laid his snare and spread it with gum, he tolled the birds to it by decorating it with honey flowers or even transplanting a strange tree to attract their curiosity; he imitated the exact note of the bird he wished to trap or used a tamed bird in a cage as a decoy. All these practical devices must be accompanied by prayer. Emerson translates the following bird charm:

> *Na aumakua i ka Po,*
> *Na aumakua i ka Ao,*
> *Ia Kane i ka Po,*
> *Ia Kanaloa i ka Po,*
> *Ia Hoomeha i ka Po,*
> *I ko'u mau kapuna a pau loa i ka Po.*

> *Spirits of darkness primeval,*
> *Spirits of light,*
> *To Kane the eternal,*
> *To Kanaloa the eternal,*
> *To Hoomeha the eternal,*
> *To all my ancestors from eternity.*

> *Ia Ku-huluhulumanu i ka Po,*
> *Ia pale i ka Po,*
> *A puka i ke Ao,*
> *Owau, o Eleele, ka mea iaia ka mana,*
> *Homai he iki,*
> *Homai he loaa nui,*
> *Pii oukou a ke kuahiwi,*
> *A ke kualono,*
> *Ho'a mai oukou i ka manu a pau,*
> *Hooili oukou iluna o ke kepau kahi e pili ni,*
> *Amama! Ua noa.*

To Kuhuluhulumanu, the eternal.
That you may banish the darkness.
That we may enter the light.
To me, Eleele, give divine power.
Give intelligence.
Give great success.
Climb to the wooded mountains.
To the mountain ridges.
Gather all the birds.
Bring them to my gum to be held fast.
Amen, it is finished.

XVII

54. For the cloud sign compare the story of Kualii's battles and in Westervelt's *Lepeamoa* (Legends of Honolulu, p. 217), the fight with the water monster.

55. Of Hawaiians at prayer Dibble says: "The people were in the habit of praying every morning to the gods, clapping their hands as they muttered a set form of words in a singsong voice."

XVIII

56. The three mountain domes of Hawaii rise from 13,000 to 8,000 feet above the sea, and the two highest are in the wintertime often capped with snow.

57. The games of *kilu* and *ume*, which furnished the popular evening entertainment of chiefs, were in form much like our "Spin the plate" and "Forfeits." *Kilu* was played with "a funnel-shaped toy fashioned from the upper portion of a drinking gourd, adorned with the *pawehe* ornamentation characteristic of Niihau calabashes." The player must spin the gourd in such a way as to hit the stake set up for his side. Each hit counted 5, 40 scoring a game. Each player sang a song before trying his hand, and the forfeit of a *hula* dance was exacted for a miss, the successful spinner claiming for his forfeit the favor of one of the women on the other side. *Ume* was merely a method of choosing partners by the master of ceremonies touching with a wand, called the *maile*, the couple selected for the forfeit, while he sang a jesting song. The sudden

personal turn at the close of many of the *oli* may perhaps be accounted for by their composition for this game. The *kaeke* dance is that form of *hula* in which the beat is made on a *kaekeeke* instrument, a hollow bamboo cylinder struck upon the ground with a clear hollow sound, said to have been introduced by Laamaikahiki, the son of Moikeha, from Tahiti.

XIX

58. In the story of Kauakahialii, his home at Pihanakalani is located in the mountains of Kauai back of the ridge Kuamoo, where, in spite of its inland position, he possesses a fishpond well stocked with fish.

59. The Hawaiian custom of group marriages between brothers or sisters is clearly brought out in this and other passages in the story. "Guard our wife"—*Ka wahine a kaua*—says the Kauai chief to his comrade, "she belongs to us two"—*ia ia kaua*. The sisters of Aiwohikupua call their mistress's husband "our husband"—*ka kakou kane*. So Laieikawai's younger sister is called the "young wife"—*wahine opio*—of Laieikawai's husband, and her husband is called his *punalua*, which is a term used between friends who have wives in common, or women who have common husbands.

60. The Hawaiian flute is believed to be of ancient origin. It is made of a bamboo joint pierced with holes and blown through the nose while the right hand plays the stops. The range is said to comprise five notes. The name Kanikawi means "changing sound" and is the same as that given to Kaponohu's supernatural spear.

XX

61. At the accession of a new chief in Hawaii the land is redistributed among his followers.

62. The names of Malio and Halaaniani are still to be found in Puna. Ellis (1825) notes the name Malio as one of three hills (evidently transformed demigods), which, according to tradition, joined at the base to block an immense flow of lava at Pualaa, Puna. Off the coast between Kalapana and Kahawalea lies a rock shaped like a headless human form and called Halaaniani, although its legend retains no trace of the Puna rascal.

XXI

63. The *huia* is a specially high wave formed by the meeting of two crests, and is said to be characteristic of the surf at Kaipalaoa, Hawaii.

64. Kumukahi is a bold cape of black lava on the extreme easterly point of the group. Beyond this cape stretches the limitless, landless Pacific. Against its fissured sides seethes and booms the swell from the ocean, in a dash of foaming spray. Piles of rocks mark the visits of chiefs to this sacred spot, and tombs of the dead abut upon its level heights. A visitor to this spot sees a magnificent horizon circling the wide heavens, hears the constant boom of the tides pulling across the measureless waters. It is one of the noteworthy places of Puna, often sung in ancient lays.

XXII

65. The name of Laieikawai occurs in no old chants with which I am familiar. But in the story of *Umi*, the mother of his wife, Piikea, is called Laielohelohe. She is wife of Piilani and has four children who "have possession on the edge of the tabu," of whom Piikea is the first-born, and the famous rival chiefs of Maui, Lonopili, and Kihapiilani, are the next two; the last is Kalanilonoakea, who is described in the chant quoted by Fornander as white-skinned and wearing a white loin cloth. Umi's wife is traditionally descended from the Spaniards wrecked on the coast of Hawaii (see Lesson). The "Song of Creation" repeats the same genealogy and calls Laielohelohe the daughter of Keleanuinohoonaapiapi. In the "ninth era" of the same song Lohelohe is "the last one born of Lailai" and is "a woman of dark skin," who lived in Nuumealani.

66. To preserve the umbilical cord in order to lengthen the life of a child was one of the first duties of a guardian. J.S. Emerson says that the *piko* was saved in a bottle or salted and wrapped in tapa until a suitable time came to deposit it in some sacred place. Such a depository was to be found on Oahu, according to Westervelt, in two rocks in the Nuuanu valley, the transformed *moo* women, Hauola and Haupuu. In Hawaii, in Puna district, on the north and south boundaries of Apuki, lie two smooth lava mounds whose surfaces are marked with cup hollows curiously ringed. Pictographs cover other surfaces. These are named Puuloa and Puumahawalea, or "Hill of long life" and "Hill that brings together with rejoicing," and the natives tell me that within their own lifetime pilgrimages have been made to this

spot to deposit the *piko* within some hollow, cover it with a stone, and thus insure long life to the newborn infant.

XXIV

67. More than 470 species of land snails of a single genus, *Achatinella*, are to be found in the mountains of Hawaii, a fact of marked interest to science in observing environmental effect upon the differentiation of species. One of these the natives call *pupu kani oi* or "shrill voiced snail," averring that a certain cricketlike chirp that rings through the stillness of the almost insectless valleys is the voice of this particular species. Emerson says that the name *kahuli* is applied to the land snail to describe the peculiar tilting motion as the snail crawls first to one side and then to the other of the leaf. He quotes a little song that runs:

> *Kahuli aku, kahuli mai,*
> *Kahuli lei ula, lei akolea.*
> *Kolea, kolea, e kii ka wai,*
> *Wai akolea.*

> *Tilting this way and that*
> *Tilts the red fern-plume.*
> *Plover, plover, bring me dew,*
> *Dew from the fern-plume.*

68. This incident is unsatisfactorily treated. We never know how Waka circumvented Malio and restored her grandchild to the husband designed for her. The whole thing sounds like a dramatic innovation with farcical import, which appeared in the tale without motivation for the reason that it had none in its inception. The oral narrator is rather an actor than a composer; he may have introduced this episode as a surprise, and its success as farce perpetuated it as romance.

XXVI

69. This episode of the storm is another inconsistency in the story. The storm signs belong to the gods of Aiwohikupua and his brother, the Sun god, not to Laieikawai, and were certainly not hers when Waka deserted her. If they were given her for protection by Kahalaomapuana or through the influence of the seer with the Kauai family, the story-teller does not inform us of the fact.

70. The *pa-u* is a woman's main garment, and consists of five thicknesses of bark cloth 4 yards long and 3 or 4 feet wide, the outer printed in colors, and worn wrapped about the loins, reaching the knees.

XXVII

71. In mythical quest stories the hero or heroine seeks, by proving his relationship, generally on the mother's side, to gain the favor of the supernatural guardian of whatever treasure he seeks. By breaking down the taboo he proclaims his rank, and by forcing the attention of the relative before the angry god (or chief) has a chance to kill him (compare the story of *Kalaniamanuia*, where the father recognizes too late the son whom he has slain), he gains time to reveal himself. In this episode the father's beard is, like the locks of Dionysus in Euripides' line, dedicated to the god, hence to seize it was a supreme act of lawlessness.

72. According to the old Polynesian system of age groups, the "mother's brother" bears the relation to the child of *makua* equally with his real parents. Kahalaomapuana says to her father:

> *"I am your child (kama),*
> *The child of Laukieleula,*
> *The child of Mokukelekahiki,*
> *The child of Kaeloikamalama."*

thus claiming rank from all four sources. Owing to inbreeding and this multiple method of inheriting title, Polynesian children may be of higher rank than either parent. The form of colloquy which follows each encounter (compare Kila's journey to Tahiti) is merely the customary salutation in meeting a stranger, according to Hawaiian etiquette.

73. The name Laukieleula means "Red-kiele-leaf." The kiele, Andrews says, is "a sweet-scented flower growing in the forest," and is identified by some natives with the gardenia, of which there are two varieties native in Hawaii; but the form does not occur in any chants with which I am familiar. It is probably selected to express the idea of fragrance, which seems to be the *kupua* property of the mother's side of the family. It is the rareness of fragrant plants indigenous to the islands, coupled with sensuous delight in odor, which gives to perfume the attributes of deity, and to those few varieties which possess distinct scent like the *maile* and *hala*, a conspicuous place in religious ceremonial.

The name of Moanalihaikawaokele, on the other hand, appears in the "Song of Creation," in the eighth era where the generations of Uli are sung. In the time of calm is born the woman Lailai, and after her the gods Kii, Kane, and Kanaloa, and it is day. Then

> *"The drums are born,*
> *Called Moanaliha,*
> *Kawaomaaukele came next,*
> *The last was Kupololiilialiimuaoloipo,*
> *A man of long life and very high rank."*

There follow 34 pages devoted to the history and generations of this family before the death of this last chief is recorded. Now it is clear that out of the first two names, Moanaliha and Kawao(maau)kele, is compounded that of the storm god. This would place him in the era of the gods as the father of Ku and ancestor of the Uli line.

XXVIII

74. The story of the slaying of Halulu in the legend of *Aukelenuiaiku* is a close parallel to the Indian account of the adventure with the thunder bird. (See Matthews's "Navajo legends.") The thunder bird is often mentioned in Hawaiian chants. In the "Song of Creation" the last stanza of the third or bird era points out

> *"—the leaping point of the bird Halulu,*
> *Of Kiwaa, the bird of many notes,*
> *And of those birds that fly close together and shade the sun."*

75. The divine approach marked by thunder and lightning, shaken by earthquake and storm, indicates the *kupua* bodies in which the Sun god travels in his descent to earth. There are many parallels to be found in the folk stories. When the sister of Halemano sets out to woo the beauty of Puna she says: "When the lightning flashes, I am at Maui; when it thunders I am at Kohala; when the earth quakes, at Hamakua; when freshets stain the streams red, I am at Puna." When Hoamakeikekula, the beauty of Kohala, weds, "thunder was heard, lightning flashed, rain came down in torrents, hills were covered with fog; for ten days mist covered the earth." When Uweuwelekehau, son of Ku and Hula, is born "thunder, lightning, earthquake, water, floods and rain" attend his birth. In Aukelenuiaiku, when the wife of Makalii comes out of her house her beauty overshadows the rays of the sun, "darkness covered the land, the

red rain, fog, and fine rain followed each other, then freshets flowed and lightning played in the heavens; after this the form of the woman, was seen coming along over the tips of the fingers of her servants, in all her beauty, the sun shone at her back and the rainbow was as though it were her footstool." In the prayer to the god Lono, quoted by Fornander, II, 352, we read:

> *"These are the sacred signs of the assembly;*
> *Bursting forth is the voice of the thunder;*
> *Striking are the rays of the lightning;*
> *Shaking the earth is the earthquake;*
> *Coming is the dark cloud and the rainbow;*
> *Wildly comes the rain and the wind;*
> *Whirlwinds sweep over the earth;*
> *Rolling down are the rocks of the ravines;*
> *The red mountain streams are rushing to the sea;*
> *Here the waterspouts;*
> *Tumbled about are the clustering clouds of heaven;*
> *Gushing forth are the springs of the mountains."*

XXXIV

75. Kaonohiokala, Mr. Emerson tells me, is the name of one of the evil spirits invoked by the priest in the art of *po'iuhane* or "soul-catching." The spirit is sent by the priest to entice the soul of an enemy while its owner sleeps, in order that he may catch it in a coconut gourd and crush it to death between his hands. "*Lapu lapuwale*" is the Hawaiian rendering of Solomon's ejaculation "Vanity of vanities!"

APPENDIX
HAWAIIAN STORIES
ABSTRACTS FROM THE TALES COLLECTED
BY FORNANDER AND EDITED
BY THOMAS G. THRUM.
THE BISHOP MUSEUM, HONOLULU

I. Song of Creation, as translated by Liliuokalani

II. Chants Relating to the Origin of the Group:

From the Fornander manuscript:

A. Kahakuikamoana
B. Pakui
C. Kamahualele
D. Opukahonua
E. Kukailani
F. Kualii

III. Hawaiian Folktales, Romances, or Moolelo:

From the Fornander manuscript:

A. Hero tales primarily of Oahu and Kauai
   1. Aukelenuiaiku
   2. Hinaaikamalama
   3. Kaulu
   4. Palila
   5. Aiai
   6. Puniaiki
   7. Pikoiakaalala
   8. Kawelo
   9. Kualii
   10. Opelemoemoe
   11. Kalelealuaka

B. Hero tales primarily of Hawaii
   1. Wahanui
   2. Kamapuaa
   3. Kana
   4. Kapunohu
   5. Kepakailiula
   6. Kaipalaoa
   7. Moikeha
   8. Kila
   9. Umi

10. Kihapiilani (of Maui)
11. Pakaa and Kuapakaa
12. Kalaepuni
13. Kalaehina
14. Lonoikamakahiki
15. Keaweikekahialii (an incident)
16. Kekuhaupio (an incident)

C. Love stories
1. Halemano
2. Uweuwelekehau
3. Laukiamanuikahiki
4. Hoamakeikekula
5. Kapunokaoheloai

D. Ghost stories and tales of men brought to life
1. Oahu stories
    Kahalaopuna
    Kalanimanuia
    Pumaia
    Nihoalaki
2. Maui stories
    Eleio
    Pamano
3. Hawaii stories
    Kaulanapokii
    Pupuhuluena
    Hiku and Kawelu

E. Trickster stories
1. Thefts
    Iwa
    Maniniholokuaua
    Pupualenalena
2. Contests with spirits
    Kaululaau (see Eleio)
    Lepe
    Hanaaumoe
    Punia
    Wakaina

3. Stories of modern cunning
   Kulepe
   Kawaunuiaola
   Maiauhaalenalenaupena
   Waawaaikinaaupo and Waawaaikinaanao
   Kuauamoa

I

Song of Creation (Hekumulipo)

The "account of the creation of the world according to Hawaiian tradition" is said to celebrate Lonoikamakahiki, also called Kaiimamao, who was the father of Kalaniopuu, king of Hawaii at the time of Cook's visit. The song was "composed by Keaulumoku in 1700" and handed down by the chanters of the royal line since that day. It was translated by "Liliuokalani of Hawaii" in 1895–1897, and published in Boston, 1897.

From the Sea-bottom (?) (the male) and Darkness (the female) are born the coral insect, the starfish, sea urchin, and the shellfish. Next seaweed and grasses are born. Meanwhile land has arisen, and in the next era fishes of the sea and plants of the forest appear. Next are born the generations of insects and birds; after these the reptiles—all the "rolling, clinging" creatures. In the fifth era is born a creature half pig, half man; the races of men also appear (?). In the sixth come the rats; in the seventh, dogs and bats; in the eighth is born the woman Lailai (calmness), the man Kii, and the gods Kane and "the great octopus" Kanaloa. Lailai flies to heaven, rests upon "the boughs of the *aoa* tree in Nuumealani," and bears the earth. She weds Kii and begets a generation of gods and demigods.

In the course of these appear Wakea and his three wives, Haumea, Papa, and Hoohokukalani. Wakea, becoming unfaithful to Papa, changes the feast days and establishes the taboo. Later the stars are hung in the heavens. Wakea seeks in the sea for "seeds from Hina," with which to strew the heavens. Hina floats up from the bottom of the sea and bears sea creatures and volcanic rocks. Haumea, a stranger of high rank from Kuaihelani at Paliuli, marries her own sons and grandsons. To her line belong Waolena and his wife Mafuie, whose grandchild, Maui, is born in the shape of a fowl. The brothers of his mother, Hina, are angry and fight Maui, but are thrown. They send him to fetch a branch from the sacred *awa* bush; this, too, he achieves. He desires to learn the art of fishing, and his mother gives him a hook and line with which he catches "the royal fish Pimoe." He "scratches the eight eyes" of the bat who abducts Hina. He nooses the sun and so wins summer. He conquers (?) Hawaii, Maui, Kauai, and Oahu. From him descends "the only high chief of the island."

II

Chants Relating to the Origin
of the Group

A. Kahakuikamoana

This famous priest chants the history of "the row of islands from Nuumea; the group of islands from the entrance to Kahiki." First Hawaii is born, "out of darkness," then Maui, then Molokai "of royal lineage." Lanai is a foster child, Kahoolawe a foundling, of whose afterbirth is formed the rock island Molokini. Oahu and Kauai have the same mother but different fathers. Another pair bear the triplets, the islets Niihau, Kaulu, and Nihoa.

B. Pakui

According to this high priest and historian of Kamehameha I, from Wakea and Papa are born Kahikiku, Kahikimoe ("the foundation stones," "the stones of heaven"), Hawaii, and Maui. While Papa is on a visit to Kahiki, Wakea takes another wife and begets Lanai, then takes Hina to wife and begets Molokai. The plover tells Papa on her return, and she in revenge bears to Lua the child Oahu. After this she returns to Wakea and bears Kauai and its neighboring islets.

C. Kamahualele

The foster son of Moikeha accompanies this chief on the journey to Hawaii and Kauai. On sighting land at Hawaii he chants a song in honor of his chief in which he calls Hawaii a "man," "child of Kahiki," and "royal offspring from Kapaahu."

D. Opukahonua

This man with his two brothers and a woman peopled Hawaii 95 generations before Kamehameha. According to his chant, the islands are fished up from Kapaahu by Kapuheeuanui, who brings up one piece of coral after another, and, offering sacrifices and prayers to each, throws it back into the ocean, so creating in succession Hawaii, Maui, Kauai, and the rest of the islands of the group.

E. Kukailani

A POWERFUL PRIEST, 75 GENERATIONS from Opukahonua, on the occasion of the sacrifice in the temple of the rebel Iwikauikana by Kenaloakuaana, king of Maui, chants the genealogies, dividing them into the time from the migration from Kahiki to Pili, Pili to Wakea, Wakea to Waia, and Waia to Liloa.

F. Kualii

THE SONG OF KUALII WAS composed about 1700 to celebrate the royal conqueror of Oahu. It opens with an obscure allusion to the fishing up by Maui from the hill Kauwiki, of the island of Hawaii, out of the bottom of the sea, and the fetching of the gods Kane and Kanaloa, Kauakahi and Maliu, to these islands.

III

Hawaiian Folk Tales, Romances, or Moolelo

A. Hero Tales Primarily of Oahu and Kauai

1. Aukelenuiaiku[1]

THE ELEVENTH CHILD OF IKU and Kapapaiakea in Kuaihelani is his father's favorite, and to him Iku wills his rank and his kingdom. The brothers are jealous and seek to kill him. They go through the Hawaiian group to compete in boxing and wrestling, defeat Kealohikikaupea, the strong man of Kauai; Kaikipaananea, Kupukupukehaikalani, and Kupukupukehaiaiku, three strong men of Oahu, and King Kakaalaneo of Maui; but are afraid when they hear of Kepakailiula, the strong man of Hawaii, and return to Kuaihelani.

Aukelenuiaiku has grown straight and faultless. "His skin is like the ripe banana and his eyeballs like the blood of the banana as it first appears." He wants to join his brothers in a wrestling match, but is forbidden by the father, who fears their jealousy. He steals away and shoots an arrow into their midst; it is a twisted arrow, theirs are jointed. The brothers are angry, but when one of them strikes the lad, his own arm is broken. The younger brother takes up each one in turn and throws him into the sea. The brothers pretend friendship and invite him into the house, but only to throw him into the pit Kamooinanea, where lives the lizard grandmother who devours men. She saves her grandchild and instructs him how to reach the queen, Namakaokahai. For the journey she furnishes him with a box for his god, Lonoikoualii; a leaf, *laukahi*, to satisfy his hunger; an ax and a knife; her own tail, in which lies the strength of her body; and her feather skirt and *kahili*, by shaking which he can reduce his enemies to ashes.

When his brothers see him return safe from the pit they determine to flee to foreign lands. They make one more attempt to kill him by shutting him into a water hole, but one soft-hearted brother lets

---

1. Compare Westervelt's Gods and Ghosts, p. 66.

him out. The hero then persuades the brothers to let him accompany them. On the way he feeds them with "food and meat" from his club, Kaiwakaapu. They sail eight months, touch at Holaniku, where they get *awa*, sugar cane, bananas, and coconuts, and arrive in four months more at Lalakeenuiakane, the land of Queen Namakaokahai. The queen is guarded by four brothers in bird form, Kanemoe, Kaneapua, Leapua and Kahaumana, by two maid servants in animal form, and by a dog, Moela. The whole party is reduced to ashes at the shaking of the queen's skirt, except the hero, who escapes and by his good looks and quick wit wins the friendship of the queen's maids and her brothers. When he approaches the queen he must encounter certain tests. The dog he turns into ashes; to befriend him the maids run away and the bird brothers transform themselves into a rock, a log, a coral rock, and a hard blue rock, in order to hide themselves. He escapes poisoned food set before him. Then he worships each one by name, and they are astounded at his knowledge. The queen therefore takes him as her husband. She is part human, part divine; the moon is her grandfather, the thunder-and-lightning-bolt is her uncle. Aukelanuiaiku must know her taboos, eat where she bids him, not come to her unless she leads him in.

The bird Halulu with feathers on her forehead, called Hinawaikolii, who is the queen's cousin, carries the hero away to her nest in the cliff, but he kills her with his ax, and her mate, Kiwaha, lets him down on a rainbow.

The two live happily. Their first child is to be called Kauwilanuimakehaikalani, "the lightning seen in a rainstorm," and for him sugar cane, potato, banana and taro are tabooed. The queen can return to life if cut to pieces; can turn herself into a cliff, a roaring fire, and a great ocean; and has the power of flight. All her tricks the queen and her brothers teach to the hero. Then she sends him with her brothers to meet her relatives. He goes ahead of his guides, encounters Kuwahailo, who sends against him two bolts of fire, Kukuena and Mahuia, and two thunder rocks, Ikuwa and Welehu, all of which he wards off like a puff of wind. Next they meet Makalii and his wife, the beautiful Malanaikuaheahea.

The next adventure is after the water of life with which to restore the brothers to life. The first trip is unsuccessful. Instead of flying in a straight line between the sky (*lewa*) and space (*nenelu*—literally, mud) the hero falls into space and is obliged to cling to the moon for support. Meanwhile his wife thinks him dead and has summoned

Night, Day, Sun, Stars, Thunder, Rainbow, Lightning, Water-spout, Fog, Fine rain, etc., to mourn for him. Then, through her supernatural knowledge she hears him declare to the moon, her grandfather, Kaukihikamalama, his birth and ancestry, and learns for the first time that they are related. On the next trip he reaches a deep pit, at the bottom of which is the well of everlasting life, the property of Kamohoalii. It is guarded by two maternal uncles of the hero, Kanenaiau and Hawewe and a maternal aunt, Luahinekaikapu, the sister of the lizard grandmother, who is blind. The hero steals the bananas she is roasting, dodges her anger, and restores her sight. She paints up his hands to look like Kamohoalii's and the guards at the well hand him the gourd Huawaiakaula with its string network called Paleaikaahalanalana. The rustling of the *lama* trees, the *loulou* palms and the bamboo, as Aukelenuiaiku retreats, wakens Kamohoalii, who pursues; but with a start of one year and six months, the hero can not be overtaken.

The brothers are restored to life and the hero hands over to them his wife and kingdom and lives humbly. When he woos Pele and Hiiaka, his wife drives them over seas until they come to Maunaloa, Hawaii. Then the brothers leave for Kuaihelani, and Aukelenuiaiku desires also to see his native land again. There he finds the lizard grandmother overgrown with coral and his parents gone to Kauai.

2. Hinaaikamalama

KAIULI AND KAIKEA ARE GODS who change into *Paoo* fish and live in the bottom of the sea in Kahikihonuakele. They have two children, the girl Hinaluaikoa and the boy Kukeapua. These two have 10 children, Hinaakeahi, Hinaaimalama, Hinapaleaoana, Hinaluaimoa, all girls, Iheihe, a boy, Moahelehaku, Kiimaluhaku, and Kanikaea, girls, and the boys Kipapalaula and Luaehu. As Hinaaikamalama is the most beautiful she is placed under strict taboo under guard of her brother Kipapalaula. He is banished for neglect of duty, crawls through a crack at Kawaluna at the edge of the great ocean. The king treats him kindly, hence he returns and gets his sister to be the king's wife. In her calabash, called Kipapalaulu, she carries the moon for food and the stars for fish.

King Konikonia and Hinaaikamalama have 10 children, the youngest of whom, the boy Maikoha, is found to be guilty of sacrilege and banished. He goes to Kaupo and changes into the *wauke* plant. His sisters coming in search of him, land at Oahu and turn into fish ponds—Kaihuopalaai into Kapapaapuhi pond at Ewa; Kaihukoa into Kaena at Waianae; Kawailoa into Ihukoko at Waialua, and Ihukuuna into Laniloa at Laie. Kaneaukai, their brother, comes to look for them in the form of a log. It drifts ashore at Kealia, Waialua, changes into a man, and becomes fish god for two old men at Kapaeloa.[2]

3. Kaulu

KUKAOHIALAKA AND HINAULUOHIA LIVE IN Kailua, Oahu, with their two sons, Kaeha and Kamano. A third, Kaulu, remains five years unborn because he has heard Kamano threaten to kill him. Then he is born in the shape of a rope, and Kaeho puts him on an upper shelf until he grows into a boy. Meanwhile Kaeha is carried away by spirits to Lewanuu and Lewalani where Kane and Kanaloa live, and Kaulu goes in search of him. On the way he defeats and breaks into bits the opposing surfs and the dog Kuililoloa, hence surf and dogs remain small. In the spirit land he fools the spirits, then visits the land where their food is raised, Monowaikeoo, guarded by Uweleki and Uweleka, Maaleka, and Maalaki. He fools these guards into promising him all he can eat, and devours everything, even obscuring the rays of the sun. In revenge the shark Kukamaulunuiakea swallows his brother. Kaulu drinks the sea dry in search for him, catches a thunder rock on his *poi* finger, and forces Makalii to tell him where Kaeho is. Then he spits out the sea and this is why the sea is salt. The dead shark becomes the milky way. The brothers return to Oahu, and Kaulu kills Haumea, a female spirit, at Niuhelewai, by catching her in a net got from Makalii. Next he kills Lonokaeho, also called Piokeanuenue, king of Koolau, by singing an incantation which makes his forehead fast to the ground on the hill of Olomana.[3] After Kaeha's death, Kaulu marries Kekele, but they have no children.

---

2. The rock called Kaneaukai, "Man-floating-on-the-sea," on the shore below Waimea, Oahu, is still worshiped with offerings. The local story tells how two old men fish up the same rock three times. Then they say, "It is a god," and, in spite of the weight of the rock, carry it inshore and place it where it now stands and make it their fish god. Thrum tells this, story, p. 250.

3. See *Kamapuaa*, where the same feat is described.

4. Palila

PALILA, SON OF KALUAPALENA, CHIEF over one-half of Kauai, and of Mahinui the daughter of Hina, is born at Kamooloa, Koloa, Kauai, in the form of a cord and cast out upon the rubbish heap whence he is rescued by Hina and brought up in the temple of Alanapo among the spirits, where he is fed upon nothing but bananas. The other chief of Kauai, Namakaokalani, is at war with his father. Hina sends Palila to offer his services. With his war club he fells forests as he travels and makes hollows in the ground. When he arrives before his father, all fall on their faces until Hina rolls over their bodies to make Palila laugh and thus remove the taboo. As he stands on a rise of ground, Maunakalika, with his robe Hakaula, and his mat Ikuwa, she circumcises Palila and returns with him to Alanapo. When Palila leaves home to fight monsters, he travels by throwing his club and hanging to one end. The first throw is to Uualolo cliff on Kamaile, the next to Kaena Point, Oahu, thence to Kalena, to Pohakea, Maunauna, Kanehoa, Keahumoa, and finally to Waikele. The king of Oahu, Ahuapau, offers the rule of Oahu to anyone who can slay the shark man, Kamaikaakui. After effecting this, Palila (who has inherited the nature of a spirit from his mother), is carried to the temple and made all human, in order to wed the king's daughter. He slays Olomana, the greatest warrior on Oahu, goes fishing successfully with Kahului, with war club for paddle and fishhook, then, with his club to aid him, springs to Molokai, Lanai, Maui, and thence to Kaula, Hawaii. Hina's sister Lupea becomes his attendant. She is a *hau* tree, and where Palila's malo is hung no *hau* tree grows to this day, through the power of Ku, Palila's god. The kings of Hilo and Hamakua districts, Kulukulua and Wanua, are at war. Palila fights secretly, known only by a voice which at each victim calls "slain by me, Palila, by the offspring of Walewale, by the word of Lupea, by the *oo* bird that sings in the forest, by the mighty god Ku." Finally he makes himself known and kills Moananuikalehua, whose war club, Koholalele, takes 700 men to carry; Kumunuiaiake, whose spear of *mamane* wood from Kawaihae can be thrown farther than one *ahupuaa*; and Puupuukaamai, whose spear of hard *koaie* wood can kill 1,200 at a stroke. The jaw bones of these heroes he hangs on the tree Kahakaauhae. Kulukulua is made ruler; finally Palila becomes king of Hilo.

5. Aiai

KUULA AND HINA LIVE AT Molopa, Nuuanu. They possess a pearl fish hook called Kanoi, guarded by the bird Kamanuwai, who lives upon the *aku* fish caught by the magic hook. When Kipapalaulu, king of Honolulu, steals the hook, the bird sleeps from hunger, hence the name of the locality. Kaumakapili, "perching with closed eyes." Hina bears an abortive child which she throws into the water. It drifts to a rock below the Hoolilimanu bridge and floats there. This child is Aiai. The king's daughter discovers it, brings up the child, and when he becomes a handsome youth, she marries him. One day she craves the *aku* fish. Her husband, Aiai, persuades her to beg the stolen hook of her father. Thus he secures the hook and returns it to its bird guardian.[4]

6. Puniaiki

THE HANDSOME SON OF KUUPIA and of Halekou of Kaneohe, Oahu, who nurses Uhumakaikai, the parent of all the fishes, is furnished with whatever fish he wants. He marries Kaalaea, a handsome and well-behaved woman of the district, who brings him no dowry, but to whom he and his father make gifts according to custom. With his mother's permission he goes to live in her home, but the aunt insults him because he does nothing but sleep. The family offer to kill her, but he broods over his wrong, leaves for Kauai, and, on a wager, bids his mother use her influence to send the fish thither. They come just in time to save his life and to win for him the island of Kauai. But his pet fish laments his unfaithfulness to his home, he takes it up and kisses it and returns to Oahu.

7. Pikoiakaalala

RAVEN IS THE FATHER, KOUKOU the mother, Hat and Bat the sisters, and Pikoiakaalala the brother of the rat family of Wailua, Kauai, who change into human beings. The sisters marry men of note. Pikoiakaalala

---

4. Compare the fishhook Pahuhu in *Nihoalaki*; the *leho* shells in *Iwa*, and the pearl fishhook of Kona in *Kaulanapokii*. In Thrum's story from Moke Manu (p. 230) Aiai is the son of the fish god, Kuula, and, like his father, acts as a culture hero who locates the fishing grounds and teaches the art of making fish nets for various kinds of fishes. The hero of this story is Aiai's son, Puniaiki.

wins in his first attempt to float the *Koieie* board, then follows it down the rapids and swims to Oahu. Here he beats Mainele, the champion rat shooter, by summoning the rats in a chant and then shooting ten rats and one bat at once. Then he defeats him in a riddling contest in which the play turns upon the word rat. On Hawaii the king, Keawenuiaumi, wants the birds shot because they deceive his canoe builders and prevent any trees from being felled. Pikoiakaalala succeeds in shooting them by watching their reflection in a basin of water.

8. Kawelo

WHEN KAWELO IS BORN TO Maihuna and Malaiakalani in Hanamaulu, Kauai, the fourth of five children, the maternal grandparents foresee that he is to be a wonder, and they offer to bring him up at Wailua, where Aikanaka, the king's son, and Kauahoa of Hanalei are his companions. Later the parents take him to Oahu, where Kakuhewa is king, and live at Waikiki, where Kawelo marries Kanewahineikiaoha, daughter of a famous warrior, Kalonaikahailaau, from whom he learns the art of war. Fishing he learns from Maakuakeke. On his parents' return to Kauai they are abused of their property, and summon Kawelo to redress their wrongs. He sends his' wife to fetch the stroke Wahieloa from his father-in-law, who heaps abuse upon the son-in-law, not aware that Kawelo hears all his derisive comments through his god Kalanikilo. A fight follows in which the son-in-law knocks out the old man and proves his competence as a pupil. The Oahu king furnishes a canoe in which Kawelo sets out for Kauai with his wife, his brother, Kamalama, and other followers, of whom Kalaumeki and Kaeleha are chief. On Kauai he and his brother defeat all the champions of Aikanaka, with their followers, one after the other, finally slaying his old playmate Kauahoa, this with the aid of his wife, who tangles her *pikoi* ball in the end of his opponent's war club.

In the division of land that follows this victory Kona falls to his brother and Koolau and Puna to his two chief warriors. But Kaelehu visits Aikanaka at Hanapepe, falls in love with his daughter, and persuades himself that he could do better by taking up the cause of the defeated chief. Knowing that Kawelo has never learned the art of dodging stones, they bury him in a shower of rocks, beat him with a club, and leave him, for dead. He revives when carried to the temple for sacrifice, rises, and slays them all; not one escapes.

9. Kualii

KUALII'S FIRST BATTLE HAPPENS BEFORE he is a man, when he and his father dedicate the temple on Kawaluna, Oahu, as an act of rebellion. The chiefs of Oahu come against him with three armies, but Kualii, with his warriors, Maheleana and Malanaihaehae, and his war club, Manaiakalani, slays the enemy chiefs and beats back 12,000 men at Kalena. Later he conducts a successful campaign in Hawaii, establishes Paepae against the rebel faction of Molokai, and pacifies Haloalena, who is rebelling against the king of Maui. In this campaign he secures the bold and mischievous Kauhi as his follower, who is in time his chief warrior. As Kualii grows stronger, he goes in disguise to battle, kills the bravest chief, secures his feather cloak, and runs home with it. A lad who sees him pass each day runs after and cuts a finger from the dead enemy, after the battle of Kalakoa, and reveals the true hero of the day.[5] The chant to Kualii is composed by two brothers, Kapaahulani and Kamakaaulani, who are in search of a new lord. On the day of battle at Kaahumoa one joins each army; one brother leads Kualii's forces to an appointed spot and the other attempts to pacify the chief with the prearranged chant, in which he is successful; the brothers are raised to honor and peace is declared. Kualii lives to old age, when he is "carried to battle in a net of strings." His genealogical tree carries his ancestry back to Kane, and Kualii himself has the knowledge and attributes of a god.

10. Opelemoemoe

A MAN OF KALAUAO, EWA, Oahu, has a habit of falling into a supernatural sleep for a month at a time. In such a sleep he is taken to be sacrificed at the temple of Polomauna, Kauai, but waking at the sound of thunder, he goes to Waimea, where he marries, and cultivates land. When the time comes for his sleep, he warns his wife, but she and her brothers and servants decide to drop him into the sea. When the month is up, it thunders, he wakens, finds himself tied in the bottom of the sea, breaks loose and comes back to his wife. Before their son is born he leaves her and returns to Oahu. The child is born, is abused by his stepfather, and finding he has a different father, follows Opelemoemoe to Oahu. The rest of his story is told under Kalelealuaka.

---

5. Compare *Kalelealuaka*.

11. Kalelealuaka

KAKUHIHEWA, KING OF EWA, ON Oahu, and Pueonui, king from Moanalua to Makapuu, are at war with each other. Kalelealuaka, son of Opelemoemoe, the sleeper, lives with his companion, Keinohoomanawanui, at Oahunui. He is a dreamer; that is, a man who wants everything without working for it. One night the two chant their wishes. His companion desires a good meal and success in his daily avocations, but Kalelealuaka wishes for the king's food served by the king himself, and the king's daughter for his wife. Now Kakuhihewa has night after night seen the men's light and wondered who it might be. This night he comes to the hut, overhears the wish, and making himself known to the daring man, fulfills his wish to the, letter. Thus Kalelealuaka becomes the king's son-in-law. When the battle is on with the rival king, Kalelealuaka's companion goes off to war, but Kalelealuaka remains at home. When all are gone, he runs off like the wind, slays Pueo's best captain and brings home his feather cloak, while his friend gets the praise for the deed. Finally he is discovered, he brings out the feather cloaks and is made king of Oahu, Kakuhihewa serving under him.

B. Hero Tales Primarily of Hawaii

1. Wahanui

WAHANUI, KING OF HAWAII, MAKES a vow to "trample the breasts of Kane and Kanaloa."[6] He takes his prophet, Kilohi, and starts for Kahiki. Kane and Kanaloa have left their younger brother, Kaneapua, on Lanai, because he made their spring water filthy. He forces himself upon Wahanui, and saves him from the dangers of the way—from the land of Kanehunamoku, which takes the shape of Hina's dog; from the two demigod hills, Paliuli and Palikea, sent against them by Kane and Kanaloa; and from a 10 days' storm loosened from the calabash

---

6. This means literally "to travel over land and sea." (See Malo, p. 316.) The song runs:

> *"Wahilani, king of Oahu.*
> *Who sailed away to Kahiki,*
> *To the islands of Moananuiakea,*
> *To trample the breasts of Kane and Kanaloa."*

of Laamaomao, which they escape by making their boat fast to the intestines of Kamapuaa's grandmother under the sea. When Wahanui has fulfilled his quest and sets out to return, Kaneapua gives him his double-bodied god, Pilikua, and warns him not to show it until he gets to Hawaii. He displays it at Kauai, and the Kauai people kill him in order to get the god. The Hawaii people hear of it, invite the Kauai people to see them, and slaughter them in revenge.

2. Kamapuaa

THIS DEMIGOD, HALF MAN, HALF hog, lives in Kaliuwaa valley, Oahu, in the reign of Olopana.[7] His father is Kahikiula, his mother, Hina, his brother, Kahikihonuakele. He robs Olopana's chicken roosts, is captured, swung on a stick, and carried in triumph until his grandmother sings a chant which gives him supernatural strength to slay his enemies. Four times he is captured and four times escapes, killing all of Olopana's men but Makalii. Then he flees up the valley Kaliuwaa and lets his followers climb up over his back to the top of the cliff, except his grandmother, who insists upon climbing up his front. He flees to Wahiawa, loses his strength by eating food spelled with the letters *lau*, but eventually becomes lord of Oahu. In Kahiki, his father-in-law, Kowea, has a rival, Lonokaeho, who in his supernatural form has eight foreheads as sharp as an ax. Kamapuaa chants to his gods, and the weeds Puaakukui, Puaatihaloa, and Puaamaumau grow over the foreheads. Thus snared, Lonokaeho is slain. Kamapuaa also defeats Kuilioloa, who has the form of a dog.

The story next describes the struggle between Pele and the pig god. Kamapuaa goes to Kilauea on Hawaii and stands on a point of land overlooking the pit called Akanikolea. Below sit Pele and her sisters stringing wreaths. Kamapuaa derides Pele's red eyes and she in revenge tells him he is a hog, his nose pierced with a cord, his face turned to the ground and a tail that wags behind. When he retaliates she is so angry that she calls out to her brothers to start the fires. Kamapuaa's love-making god, Lonoikiaweawealoha, decoys the brothers to the lowlands. Then Pele bids her sisters and uncles to keep up the fire, but Kamapuaa's sister, Keliiomakahanaloa, protects him with cloud and rain. Kamapuaa takes his hog form, and hogs overrun the place; Pele is almost dead.

---

7. This is not the Olopana of Hawaii.

Then the love-making god restores her, she fills up the pit again with fire; but Kamapuaa calls for the same plants as before, which are his supernatural bodies, to choke out the flames. At length peace is declared and Pele takes Puna, Kau, and Kona districts, while Kamapuaa takes Hilo, Hamakua, and Kohala. (Hence the former districts are overrun with lava flows; the latter escape.)

Next Kamapuaa gets Kahikikolo for a war club. Makalii, king of Kauai, is fighting Kaneiki. After Kamapuaa has killed two warriors and driven away two spear throwers, he reveals himself to Makalii, who prostrates himself. Kamapuaa recounts the names of over fifty heroes whom he has slain and boasts of his amours. He spares Makalii on condition that he chant the name song in his honor, and spares his own father, brother, and mother. Later he pays a visit to his parents at Kalalau, but has to chant his name song to gain recognition. This angers him so much that he can be pacified only when Hina, his mother, chants all the songs in honor of his name. By and by he goes away to Kahiki with Kowea.[8]

3. Kaina

THE FIRST-BORN OF HAKALANILEO AND Hina is born in the form of a rope at Hamakualoa, Maui, in the house Halauoloolo, and brought up by his grandmother, Uli, at Piihonua, Hilo. He grows so long that the house has to be lengthened from mountain to sea to hold him. When the bold Kapepeekauila, who lives on the strong fortress of Haupu, Molokai, carries away Hina on his floating hill, Hakalanileo seeks first his younger son, Niheu, the trickster, then his terrible son Kana, to beseech their aid in recovering her. From Uli, Kana secures the canoe Kaumaielieli, which is buried at Paliuli, and the expedition sets forth, bearing Kana stretched in the canoe like a long package to conceal his presence, Niheu with his war club Wawaikalani, and the father Hakalanileo, with their equipment of paddlers. The Molokai chief has been warned by his priest Moi's dream of defeat, but, refusing to believe him, sends Kolea and Ulili to act as scouts. As the canoe approaches, he sends the scoutfish Keauleinakahi to stop it, but Niheu

---

8. This is only a fragment of the very popular story of the pig god. For Pele, see Ellis, IV. For both Pele and Kamapuaa, Emerson, *Unwritten Literature*, pp. 25, 85, 180, 228; and *Pele and Hiiaka*; Thrum, pp. 36, 193; and Daggett, who places the beginning of the Pele worship in the twelfth century.

kills the warrior with his club. When a rock is rolled down the cliff to swamp it, Kana stops it with his hand and slips a small stone under to hold it up. Niheu meanwhile climbs the cliff, enters the house Halehuki, seizes Hina and makes off with her. But Hina has told her new lover that Niheu's strength lies, in his hair, so Kolea and Ulili fly after and lay hold of the intruder's hair. Niheu releases Hina and returns unsuccessful. Kana next tries his skill. He stretches upward, but the hill rises also until he is spun out into a mere cobweb and is famishing with hunger. Niheu advises him to lean over to Hawaii that his grandmother may feed him. After three days, this advice reaches his ear and he bends over Haleakala mountain on Maui, where the groove remains to this day, and puts his head in at the door of his grandmother's house in Hawaii, where he is fed until he is fat again. Niheu, left behind in the boat, sees his brother's feet growing fat, and finally cuts off one to remind Kana of the business in hand. Now the hill Haupu is really a turtle. Uli tells Kana that if he breaks the turtle's flippers it can no longer grow higher. Thus Kana succeeds in destroying the hill Haupu and winning Hina back to his father.[9]

4. Kapunohu

KUKUIPAHU AND NIULII ARE CHIEFS of Kohala when Kapunohu, the great warrior, is born in Kukuipahu. Kanikaa is his god, and Kanikawi his spear. Insulted by Kukuipahu, he goes to the uplands to test his strength, and sends his spear through 800 *wili-wili* trees at once. Two men he meets on the way are offered as much land as they can run over in a certain time; thus the upland districts of Pioholowai and Kukuikiikii are formed. Kapunohu makes a conquest of a number of women, before joining Niulii against Kukuipahu. In the battle that follows at Kapaau 3,200 men are killed and trophies taken, and Kukuipahu falls. Kapunohu, armed with Kanikawi, kills Paopele at Lamakee, whose huge war club 4,000 men carry. After this feat he goes to Oahu, where his sister has married Olopana, who is at war with Kakuhihewa. Kapunohu pulls eight patches of taro at one time for food, then joins his brother-in-law and slays Kakuhihewa. Next

---

9. Rev. A.O. Forbes's version of this story is printed in Thrum, p. 63. See also Daggett. They differ only in minor detail. Uli's chant of the canoe is used by sorcerers to exorcise the spirits, and Uli is the special god of the priests who use sorcery.

he wins against Kemano, chief of Kauai, in a throwing contest, spear against sling stone, and becomes ruler over Kauai. His skill in riddles brings him wealth in a tour about Hawaii, but two young men of Kau finally outdo him in a contest of wit.

5. Kepakailiula

WHEN THIS SON OF KU and Hina is born in Keaau, Puna, in the form of an egg, the maternal uncles, Kiinoho and Kiikele, who are chiefs of high rank, steal him away and carry him to live in Paliuli, where in 10 days' time he becomes a beautiful child; in 40 days he has eyes and skin, as red as the feather cape in which h& is wrapped, and eats nothing but bananas, a bunch at a meal. The foster parents travel about Hawaii to find a bride of matchless beauty for their favorite, and finally choose Makolea, the daughter of Keauhou and Kahaluu, who live in Kona. Thither they take the boy, leaving Paliuli forever, and this place has never since been seen by man. The girl is, however, betrothed to Kakaalaneo, king of Maui, and when her parents discover her amour with Kepakailiula they send her off to her husband, who is a famous spearsman. Kepakailiula now moves to Kohala and marries the pretty daughter of its king. Two successive nights he slips over to Maui, fools the drunken king, and enjoys his bride. Then he persuades his father-in-law, Kukuipahu, to send a friendly expedition to Maui, which he turns into a war venture, and slays the chief Kakaalaneo and so many men that his father-in-law is obliged to put a stop to the slaughter by running in front of him with his wife in his arms. He then makes Kukuipahu king over Maui and goes on to Oahu, where Kakuhihewa hastens to make peace. One day when Makolea is out surf riding, messengers of the king of Kauai, Kaikipaananea, steal her away and she becomes this king's wife. Kepakailiula follows her to Kauai and defeats the king in boxing. One more contest is prepared; the king has two riddles, the failure to answer which will mean death. Only one man knows the answers, Kukaea, the public crier, and he is an outcast who has lived on nothing but filth air his life. Kepakailiula invites him in, feeds, and clothes him. For this attention, the man reveals the riddles, Kepakailiula answers them correctly, and bakes the king in his own oven. The riddles are:

1. "Plaited all around, plaited to the bottom, leaving an opening. Answer: A house, thatched all around and leaving a door."

2. "The men that stand, the men that lie down, the men that are
   folded. Answer: A house, the timbers that stand, the battens
   laid down, the grass and cords folded."

6. Kaipalaoa

THE BOY SKILLED IN THE art of disputation, or *hoopapa*, lives in
Waiakea, Hilo, Hawaii. In the days of Pueonuiokona, king of Kauai, his
father, Halepaki, has been killed in a riddling contest with Kalanialiiloa,
the taboo chief of Kauai, whose house is almost surrounded by a fence
of human bones from the victims he has defeated in this art. Kaipalaoa's
mother teaches him all she knows, then his aunt, Kalenaihaleauau, wife
of Kukuipahu, trains him until he is an expert. He meets Kalanialiiloa,
riddles against all his champions, and defeats them. They are killed,
cooked in the oven, and the flesh stripped from their bones. Thus
Kaipalaoa avenges his father's death.

7. Moikeha

OLOPANA AND HIS WIFE LUUKIA, during the flood at Waipio, are
swept out to sea, and sail, or swim, to Tahiti, where Moikeha is king.
Olopana becomes chief counsellor, and Luukia becomes Moikeha's
mistress. Mua, who also loves Luukia, sows discord by reporting to
her that Moikeha is boasting in public of her favors. She repulses
Moikeha and he, out of grief, sails away to Hawaii. The lashing used
for water bottles and for the binding of canoes is called the *pauoluukia*
("skirt of Luukia") because she thus bound herself against the chief's
approaches.

Moikeha touches at various points on the islands. At Hilo, Hawaii,
he leaves his younger brothers Kumukahi and Haehae; at Kohala, his
priests Mookini and Kaluawilinae; at Maui, a follower, Honuaula;
at Oahu his sisters Makapuu and Makaaoa. With the rest—his
foster son Kamahualele, his paddlers Kapahi and Moanaikaiaiwe,
Kipunuiaiakamau and his fellow, and two spies, Kaukaukamunolea
and his fellow—he reaches Wailua, Kauai, at the beach Kamakaiwa.
He has dark reddish hair and a commanding figure, and the king of
Kauai's two daughters fall in love with and marry him. He becomes
king of Kauai and by them has five sons, Umalehu, Kaialea, Kila,
Kekaihawewe, Laukapalala. How his bones are buried first in the

cliff of Haena and later removed to Tahiti is told in the story of Kila.[10]

8. Kila

MOIKEHA, WISHING TO SEND A messenger to fetch his oldest son from Tahiti, summons his five sons and tests them to know by a sign which boy to send. The lot falls upon Kila, the youngest. On his journey Kila encounters dangers and calls upon his supernatural relatives. The monsters Keaumiki and Keauka draw him down to the coral beds, but Kakakauhanui saves him. His rat aunt, Kanepohihi, befriends him, and when he goes to his uncle Makalii,[11] who has all the food fastened up in his net, she nibbles the net and the food falls out. At Tahiti he first kills Mua, who caused his father's exile. Then his warriors are matched with the Tahiti champions and he himself faces Makalii, whose club is Naulukohelewalewa. Kila, with the club Kahikikolo stuns his uncle "long enough to cook two ovens of food." The spirits of Moikeha's slain followers appear and join their praises to those of the crowd assembled, together with ants, birds, pebbles, shells, grass, smoke, and thunder. Kila goes to his father's house, Moaulanuiakea, thatched with birds' feathers, and built of *kauila* wood. All is desolate. The man whom he seeks, Laamaikahiki, is hidden in the temple of Kapaahu. On a strict taboo night Kila conceals himself and, when the brother comes to beat the drum, delivers his message. Kila succeeds in bringing his brother to Hawaii, who later returns to Kahiki from Kahoolawe, hence the name "The road to Tahiti" for the ocean west of that island. When Laamaikahiki revisits Hawaii to get the bones of his father, he brings the *hula* drum and *kaeke* flute. Meanwhile Kila has become king, after his father's death. The jealous brothers entice him to Waipio, Hawaii, where they abandon him to slavery. The priest of the temple adopts him. He gains influence and introduces the tenant system of working a number of days for the landlord, and is beloved

---

10. See Daggett's account, who places Moikeha's role in the eleventh century.

11. Kaulu meets the wizard Makalii in rat form and kills him by carrying him up in the air and letting him drop. Makalii means "little eyes" and refers to a certain mesh of fish net. One form of cat's cradle has this name. It also names the six summer months, the Pleiades, and the trees of plenty planted in Paliuli. "Plenty of fish" seems to be the root idea of the symbol.

for his industry. At the time of famine in the days of Hua,[12] one of his brothers comes to Waipo to get food. Kila has him thrown into prison, but each time he is taken out to be killed, Kila imitates the call of a mud hen and the sacrifice is postponed. Finally the mother and other brothers are summoned, Kila makes himself known, and the mother demands the brothers' death. Kila offers himself as the first to be killed, and reconciliation follows. Later he goes with Laamaikahiki back to Tahiti to carry their father's bones.

9. Umi

THE GREAT CHIEF OF HAWAII, Liloa, has a son by Piena, named Hakau. On a journey to dedicate the temple of Manini at Kohalalele, Liloa sees Akahiakuleana bathing in the Hoea stream at Kaawikiwiki and falls in love with her. Some authorities claim she was of low birth, others make her a relative of Liloa. He leaves with her the customary tokens by which to recognize his child. When their boy Umi is grown, having quarreled with his supposed father, he takes the tokens and, by his mother's direction, goes to seek Liloa in Waipio valley. Two boys, Omaokamao and Piimaiwaa, whom he meets on the way, accompany him. Umi enters the sacred inclosure of the chief and sits in his father's lap, who, recognizing the trophies, pardons the sacrilege and sending for his gods, performs certain ceremonies. At his death he wills his lands and men to Hakau, but his gods and temples to Umi.

Hakau is of a cruel and jealous disposition. Umi is obliged to leave him and go to farming with his two companions and a third, Koi, whom he meets on the way. He marries two girls, but their parents complain that he is lazy and gets no fish. Racing with Paiea at Laupahoehoe, he gets crowded against the rocks. This is a breach of etiquette and he nurses his revenge. Finally, by a rainbow sign and by the fact that a pig offered in sacrifice walks toward Umi, his chiefly blood is proved to the priest Kaoleioku. The priest considers how Umi may win the kingdom away from the unpopular Hakau. Umi studies animal raising and farming. He builds four large houses, holding 160 men each, and these are filled in no time with men training in the arts of war. A couple of disaffected old men, Nunu and Kakohe, are won over to Umi's cause, and they advise Hakau to prepare for war with

---

12. Daggett tells the story of *Hua*, priest of Maui.

Umi. While all the king's men are gone to the forests to get feathers for the war god, Umi and his followers start, on the day of Olekulua, and on the day of Lono they surprise and kill Hakau and his few attendants, who thought they were men from the outdistricts come with their taxes. So Umi becomes king. Kaoleioku is chief priest, and Nunu and Kakohe are high in authority. The land he divides among his followers, giving Kau to Omaokamau, Hilo to Kaoleioku, Hamakua to Piimaiwaa, Kahala to Koi, Kona to Ehu, and Puna to another friend. To prove how long Umi will hold his kingdom, he is placed 8 fathoms away from a warrior who hurls his spear at the king's middle, using the thrust known as Wahie. Umi wards it off, catches it by the handle and holds it. This is a sign that he will hold his kingdom successfully— "your son, your grandson, your issue, your offspring until the very last of your blood."

Umi now makes a tour of the island for two years. He slays Paiea. He sends Omaokamau to Piilani of Maui to arrange a marriage with Piikea. After 20 days, Piikea sets sail for Hawaii with a fleet of 400 canoes, and a rainbow "like a feather helmet" stands out at sea signaling her approach. The rest of the story has to do with the adventures of Umi's three warriors, Omaokamau who is right-handed, Koi who is left-handed, and Piimaiwae, who is ambidextrous, during the campaign on Maui, undertaken at Piikea's plea to gain for her brother, Kihapiilani, the rule over Maui. The son and successor of Umi is Keawenuiaumi, father of Lonoikamakahiki.

10. Kihapilani

LONOAPII, KING OF MAUI, HAS two sisters, Piikea, the wife of Umi, and Kihawahine, named for the lizard god, and a younger brother, Kihapiilani, with whom he quarrels. Kihapiilani nurses his revenge as he plants potatoes in Kula. Later he escapes to Umi in Hawaii, and his sister Piikea persuades her husband to aid his cause with a fleet of war canoes that make a bridge from Kohala to Kauwiki. Hoolae defends the fort at Kauwiki. Umi's greatest warriors, Piimaiwae, Omaokamau, and Koi, attack in vain by day. At night a giant appears and frightens away intruders. One night Piimaiwaa discovers that the giant is only a wooden image called Kawalakii, and knocks it over with his club. Lonoapii is slain and Kihapiilani becomes king. He builds a paved road from Kawaipapa to Kahalaoaka and a shell road on Molokai.

11. Pakaa and Kuapakaa[13]

PAKAA, THE FAVORITE OF KEAWENUIAUMI, king of Hawaii, regulates the distribution of land, has charge of the king's household, keeps his personal effects, and is sailing master for his double canoe. The king gives him land in the six districts of Hawaii. He owns the paddle, Lapakahoe, and the wooden calabash with netted cover in which are the bones of his mother, Laamaomao, whose voice the winds obey.

Two men, Hookeleiholo and Hookeleipuna, ruin him with the king. So, taking the king's effects, his paddle and calabash, he sails away to Molokai where he marries a high chiefess and has a son, Kuapakaa, named after the king's cracked skin from drinking *awa*. He plants fields in the uplands marked out like the districts of Hawaii, and trains his son in all the lore of Hawaii.

The king dreams that Pakaa reveals to him his residence in Kaula. His love for the man returns and he sets out with a great retinue to seek him. Pakaa foresees the king's arrival and goes to meet him and bring him to land. He conceals his own face under the pretense of fishing, and leaves the son to question the expedition. First pass the six canoes of the district chiefs of Hawaii, and Kuapakaa sings a derisive chant for each, calling him by name. Then he inquires their destination and sings a prophecy of storm. The king's sailing masters, priests, and prophets deny the danger, but the boy again and again repeats the warning. He names the winds of all the islands in turn, then calls the names of the king's paddlers. Finally he uncovers the calabash, and the canoes are swamped and the whole party is obliged to come ashore. Pakaa brings the king the loin cloth and scented tapa he has had in keeping, prepares his food in the old way, and makes him so comfortable that the king regrets his old servant. The party is weather-bound four months. As they proceed, they carry the boy Kuapakaa with them. He blows up a storm in which the two sailing masters are drowned, and carries the rest of the party safe back to Kawaihae, Kohala. Here the boy is forgotten, but by a great racing feat, in which he wins against his contestants by riding in near shore in the eddy caused by their flying canoes, thus coming to the last stretch unwearied, he gets the lives of his father's last enemies. Then he makes known to the king his parentage, and Pakaa is returned to all his former honors.

---

13. This story Fornander calls "the most famous in Hawaiian history."

12. Kalaepuni

THE OLDER BROTHER OF KALAEHINA and son of Kalanipo and Kamelekapu, is born and raised in Holualoa, Kona, in the reign of Keawenuiaumi. He is mischievous and without fear. At 6 he can outdo all his playmates, at 20 he is fully developed, kills sharks with his hands and pulls up a *kou* tree as if it were a blade of grass. The king hides himself, and Kalaepuni rules Hawaii. The priest Mokupane plots his death. He has a pit dug on Kahoolawe, presided over by two old people who are told to look out for a very large man with long hair like bunches of *olona* fiber. Once Kalaepuni goes out shark killing and drifts to this island. The old people give him fish to eat, but send him to the pit to get water; then throw down stones on his head until he dies, at the place called Keanapou.

13. Kalaehina

THE YOUNGER BROTHER OF KALAEPUNI can throw a canoe into the sea as if it were a spear, and split wood with his head. He proves his worth by getting six canoes for his brother out of a place where they were stuck, in the uplands of Kapua, South Kona, Hawaii. He makes a conquest of the island of Maui; its king, Kamalalawalu, flees and hides himself when Kalaehina defies his taboo. There he rules until Kapakohana, the strong usurper of Kauai, wrestles with him and pushes him over the cliff Kaihalulu and kills him.[14]

14. Lonoikamakahike

LONOIKAMAKAHIKE WAS KING OF HAWAII after Keawenuiaumi, his father, 64 generations from Wakea. According to the story, he is born

---

14. One of the most popular heroes of the Puna, Kau, and Kona coast of Hawaii to-day is the *kupua* or "magician," Kalaekini. His power, *mana*, works through a rod of *kauila* wood, and his object seems to be to change the established order of things, some say for good, others for the worse. The stories tell of his efforts to overturn the rock called Pohaku o Lekia (rock of Lekia), of the bubbling spring of Punaluu, whose flow he stops, and the blowhole called Kapuhiokalaekini, which he chokes with cross-sticks of *kauila* wood. The double character of this magician, whom one native paints as a benevolent god, another, not 10 miles distant, as a boaster and mischief-maker, is an instructive example of the effect of local coloring upon the interpretation of folklore. Daggett describes this hero. He seems to be identical with the Kalaehina of Fornander.

and brought up at Napoopo, Hawaii, by the priests Loli and Hauna. He learns spear throwing from Kanaloakuaana; at the test he dodges 3 times 40 spears at one time. He discards sports, but becomes expert in the use of the spear and the sling, in wrestling, and in the art of riddling disputation, the *hoopapa*. He also promotes the worship of the gods. While yet a boy he marries his cousin Kaikilani, a woman of high rank who has been Kanaloakuaana's wife, and gives her rule over the island until he comes of age. Then they rule together, and so wisely that everything prospers.

Kaikilani has a lover, Heakekoa, who follows them as they set out on a tour of the islands. While detained on Molokai by the weather, Lonoikamakahike and his wife are playing checkers when the lover sings a chant from the cliff above Kalaupapa. Lonoikamakahike suspects treachery and strikes his wife to the ground with the board. Fearful of the revenge of her friends he travels on to Kailua on Oahu to Kekuhihewa's court, which he visits incognito. Reproached because he has no name song, he secures from a visiting chiefess of Kauai the chant called "The Mirage of Mana." In the series of bets which follow, Lonoikamakahike wins from Kakuhihewa all Oahu and is about to win his daughter for a wife when Kaikilani arrives, and a reconciliation follows. The betting continues, concluded by a riddling match, in all of which Lonoikamakahike is successful.

But his wife brings word that the chiefs of Hawaii, enraged by his insult to her person, have rebelled against him, only the district of Kau remaining faithful. In a series of battles at Puuanahulu, called Kaheawai; at Kaunooa; at Puupea; at Puukohola, called Kawaluna because imdertaken at night and achieved by the strategy of lighting torches to make the appearance of numbers; at Kahua, called Kaiopae; at Halelua, called Kaiopihi from a warrior slain in the battle; finally at Puumaneo, his success is complete, and Hawaii becomes his.

Lonoikamakahike sails to Maui with his younger brother and chief counsellor, Pupuakea, to visit King Kamalalawalu, whose younger brother is Makakuikalani: In the contest of wit, Lonoikamakahike is successful. The king of Maui wishes to make war on Hawaii and sends his son to spy out the land, who gains false intelligence. At the same time Lonoikamakahike sends to the king two chiefs who pretend disaffection and egg him on to ruin. In spite of Lanikaula's prophecy of disaster, Kamalalawalu sails to Hawaii with a fleet that reaches from

Hamoa, Hana, to Puakea, Kohala; he and his brother are killed at Puuoaoaka, and their bodies offered in sacrifice.[15]

Lonoikamakahike, desiring to view "the trunkless tree Kahihikolo," puts his kingdom in charge of his wife and sails for Kauai. Such are the hardships of the journey that his followers desert him, only one stranger, Kapaihiahilani, accompanying him and serving him in his wanderings. This man therefore on his return is made chief counsellor and favorite. But he becomes the queen's lover, and after an absence on Kauai, finds himself disgraced at court. Standing without the king's door, he chants a song recalling their wanderings together; the king relents, the informers are put to death, and he remains the first man in the kingdom until his death. Nor are there any further wars on Hawaii until the days of Keoua.

15. Keaweikekahialii

THIS CHIEF, BORN IN KAILUA, Kona, has a faithful servant, Mao, who studies how his master may usurp the chief ship of Hawaii. One day while Keaweikekahialii plays at checkers with King Keliiokaloa, Mao approaches, and while speaking apparently about the moves of the game, conveys to him the intelligence that now is the time to strike. Mao kills the king by a blow on the neck, and they further slay all the 800 chiefs of Hawaii save Kalapanakuioiomoa, whose daughter Keaweikekahialii marries, thus handing down the high chief blood of Hawaii to this day.

16. Kekuhaupio

ONE OF THE MOST FAMOUS warriors and chiefs in the days of Kalaniopuu and of Kamehameha, kings of Hawaii, was Kekuhaupio, who taught the latter the art of war. He could face a whole army of men and ward off 400 to 4,000 spears at once. In the battle at Waikapu between Kalaniopuu of Hawaii and Kahekili of Maui, the Hawaii men are put to flight. As they flee over Kamoamoa, Kekuhaupio faces the Maui warriors alone. Weapons lie about him in heaps, still he is not wounded. The Maui hero, Oulu, encounters him with his sling; the

---

15. Mr. Stokes found on the rocks at Kahaluu, near the *heiau* of Keeku, a petroglyph which the natives point to as the beheaded figure of Kamalalawalu.

first stone misses, the god Lono in answer to prayer averts the next. Kekuhaupio then demands with the third a hand-to-hand conflict, in which he kills Oulu.

C. Love Stories

1. Halemano

THE SON OF WAHIAWA AND Kukaniloko is born in Halemano, Waianae, and brought up in Kaau by his grandmother, Kaukaalii. Dreaming one day of Kamalalawalu, the beauty of Puna, he dies for love of her, but his sister Laenihi, who has supernatural power, restores him to life and wins the beauty for her brother. First she goes to visit her and fetches back her wreath and skirt to Halemano. Then she shows him how to toll the girl on board his red canoe by means of wooden idols, kites, and other toys made to please her favorite brother.

The king of Oahu, Aikanaka, desires Halemano's death in order to enjoy the beauty of Puna. They flee and live as castaways, first on Molokai, then Maui, then Hawaii, at Waiakea, Hilo. Here the two are estranged. The chief of Puna seduces her, then, after a reconciliation, the Kohala chief, Kumoho, wins her affection. Halemano dies of grief, and his spirit appears to his sister as she is surfing in the Makaiwi surf at Wailua, Kauai. She restores him to life with a chant.

In order to win back his bride, Halemano makes himself an adept in the art of singing and dancing (the *hula*). His fame travels about Kohala and the young chiefess Kikekaala falls in love with him. Meanwhile the seduced wife has overheard his wonderful singing and her love is restored. When his new mistress gives a *kilu* singing match, she is present, and when Halemano, after singing eight chants commemorating their life of love together, goes off with the new enchantress, she tries in vain to win him back by chanting songs which in turn deride the girl and recall herself to her lover. He soon wearies of the girl and escapes from her to Kauai, where his old love follows him. But they do not agree. Kamalalawalu leaves for Oahu, where she becomes wife to Waiahole at Kualoa. Two Hawaii chiefs, Huaa and Kuhukulua, come with a fleet of 8,000 canoes, make great slaughter at Waiahole, and win the beauty of Puna for their own.

2. Uweuwelekehau

Olopana, king of Kauai, has decreed that his daughter, Luukia, shall marry none but Uweuwelekehau, the son of Ku and Hina in Hilo, and that he shall be known when he comes by his chiefly equipment, red canoe, red sails, etc. Thunder, lightning, and floods have heralded this child's birth, and he is kept under the chiefly taboo. One day he goes to the Kalopulepule River to sail a boat; floods wash him out to sea; and in the form of a fish he swims to Kauai, is brought to Luukia and, changing into a man, becomes her lover. When Olopana hears this, he banishes the two to Mana, where only the gods dwell. These supply their needs, however, and the country becomes so fertile that the two steal the hearts of the people with kindness, and all go to live at Mana. Finally Olopana recognizes his son-in-law and they become king and queen of Kauai, plant the coconut grove at Kaunalewa, and build the temple of Lolomauna.

3. Laukiamanuikahiki

Makiioeoe, king of Kuaihelani, has an amour with Hina on Kauai and, returning home, leaves with Hina his whale-tooth necklace and feather cloak to recognize the child by, and bids that his daughter be sent to him with the full equipment of a chief. Meanwhile he prepares a bathing pool, plants a garden, and taboos both for his daughter's arrival. Laukiamanuikahiki is abused by her supposed father, and, discovering the truth, starts out under her mother's direction to find her real father. With the help of her grandmother she reaches Kuaihelani. Here she bathes in the taboo pool and plucks the taboo flowers. She is about to be slain for this act when her aunt, in the form of an owl, proclaims her name, and the chief recognizes his daughter. Her beauty shines like a light. Kahikiula, her half brother, on a visit to his father, becomes her lover. When he returns to his wife, Kahalaokolepuupuu in Kahikiku, she follows in the shape of an old woman called Lupewale. Although her lover recognizes her, she is treated like a servant. In revenge she calls upon the gods to set fire to the dance house, and burns all inside. Kahikiula now begs her to stay, but she leaves him and returns to Kuaihelani.

4. Hoamakeikekula

"Companion-in-suffering-on-the-plain" is a beautiful woman of Kohala, Hawaii, born at Oioiapaiho, of parents of high rank, Hooleipalaoa and Pili. As she is in the form of an *ala* stone, she is cast out upon the trash; but her aunt has a dream, rescues her through a rainbow which guides her to the place, and wraps her in red *tapa* cloth. In 20 days she is a beautiful child. Until she is 20 she lives under a strict taboo; then, as she strings *lehua* blossoms in the woods, the *elepaio* bird comes in the form of a handsome man and carries her away in a fog to be the bride of Kalamaula, chief's son of Kawaihae. She asks for 30 days to consider it, and dreams each night of a handsome man, with whom she falls in love. She runs away and, accompanied by a rainbow, wanders in the uplands of Pahulumoa until Puuhue finds her and carries her home to his lord, the king of Kohala, Puuonale, who turns out to be the man of her dream. Her first child is the image Alelekinakina.

5. Kapuaokaoheloai

When Ku and Hina are living at Waiakea, Hilo, they have two children, a boy called Hookaakaaikapakaakaua and a lovely girl named Kapuaokaoheloai. They are brought up apart and virgin, without being permitted to see each other, until one day the sister discovers the brother by the bright light that shines from his house, and outwits the attendants. The two are discovered and banished. Attendants of the king of Kuaihelani find the girl and, because she is so beautiful, carry her back with them to be the king's wife. Her virginity is tested and she slips on the platform, is wounded in the virgin's bathing pool, and slips on the bank getting out. Her guilt thus proved, she is about to be slain when a soothsayer reveals her high rank as the child of Hina, older sister to the king, and the king forgives and marries her. His daughter, Kapuaokaohelo, who is ministered to by birds, hearing Kapuaokaoheloai tell of her brother on Hawaii, falls in love with him and determines to go in search of him. When she reaches Punahoa harbor at Kumukahi, Hawaii, where she has been directed, she finds no handsome youth, for the boy has grown ill pining for his sister. In two days, however, he regains his youth and good looks, and the two are married.

D. Ghost Stories and Tales of Men Brought to Life

1. Oahu Stories

Kahalaopuna

During the days of Kakuhihewa, king of Oahu, there is born in Manoa, Oahu, a beautiful girl named Kahalaomapuana. Kauakuahine is her father, Kahioamano her mother. Her house stands at Kahoiwai. Kauhi, her husband, hears her slandered, and believing her guilty, takes her to Pohakea on the Kaala mountain, and, in spite of her chant of innocence, beats her to death under a great *lehua* tree, covers the body with leaves, and returns. Her spirit flies to the top of the tree and chants the news of her death. Thus she is found and restored to life, but she will have nothing more to do with Kauhi.[16]

Kalanimanuia

The son of Ku, king of Lihue, through a secret amour with Kaunoa, is brought up at Kukaniloko, where he incurs the anger of his supposed father by giving food away recklessly. He therefore runs away to his real father, carrying the king's spear and malo; but Ku, not recognizing them, throws him into the sea at Kualoa point. The spirit comes night after night to the temple, where the priests worship it until it becomes strong enough to appear in human form. In this shape Ku recognizes his son and snares the spirit in a net. At first it takes the shape of a rat, then almost assumes human form. Kalanimanuia's sister, Ihiawaawa, has three lovers, Hala, Kumuniaiake, and Aholenuimakiukai. Kalanimanuia sings a derisive chant, and they determine upon a test of beauty. A cord is arranged to fall of itself at the appearance of the most handsome contestant. The night before the match, Kalanimanuia hears a knocking at the door and there enter his soles, knees, thighs, hair, and eyes. Now he is a handsome fellow. Wind, rain, thunder, and lightning attend his advent, and the cord falls of itself.

---

16. This story is much amplified by Mrs. Nakuina in Thrum, p. 118. Here mythical details are added to the girl's parentage, and the ghost fabric related in full, in connection with her restoration to life and revenge upon Kauhi. The Fornander version is, on the whole, very bare. See also Daggett.

Pumaia

King Kualii of Oahu demands from the hog raiser, Pumaia, of Pukoula, one hog after another in sacrifice. At last Pumaia has but one favorite hog left. This he refuses to give up, since he has vowed it shall die a natural death, and he kills all Kualii's men, sparing only the king and his god. The king prays to his god, and Pumaia is caught, bound, and sacrificed in the temple Kapua. Pumaia's spirit directs his wife to collect the bones out of the bone pit in the temple and flee with her daughter to a cave overlooking Nuuanu pali. Here the spirit brings them food and riches robbed from Kualii's men. In order to stop these deprivations, Kualii is advised by his priest to build three houses at Waikiki, one for the wife, one for the daughter, and one for the bones of Pumaia. (In one version, Pumaia is then brought back to life.)

Nihoalaki

Nihoalaki is this man's spirit name. He is born at Keauhou, Kona, Hawaii, and goes to Waianae, Oahu, where he marries and becomes chief, under the name of Kaehaikiaholeha, because of his famous *aku*-catching hook called Pahuhu (see Aiai). He goes on to Waimea, Kauai, and becomes ruler of that island, dies, and his body is brought back to Waianae. The parents place the body in a small house built of poles in the shape of a pyramid and worship it until it is strong enough to become a man again. Then he goes back to Waimea, under the new name of Nihoalaki. Here his supernatural sister, in the shape of a small black bird, Noio, has guarded the fishhook. When Nihoalaki is reproached for his indolence, he takes the hook and his old canoe and, going out, secures an enormous haul of *aku* fish. As all eat, the "person with dropsy living at Waiahulu," Kamapuaa, who is a friend of Nihoalaki's, comes to have his share and the two go off together, diving under the sea to Waianae. A Kauai chief, who follows them, is turned into the rock Pohakuokauai outside Waianae. Nihoalaki goes into his burial house at Waianae and disappears. Kamapuaa marries the sister.

2. Maui Stories

Eleio

Eleio runs so swiftly that he can make three circuits of Maui in a day. When King Kakaalaneo of Lahaina is almost ready for a meal, Eleio sets out for Hana to fetch fish for the king, and always returns before the king sits down to eat. Three times a spirit chases him for the fish, so he takes a new route. Passing Kaupo, he sees a beautiful spirit, brings her to life, and finds that she is a woman of rank from another island, named Kanikaniaula. She gives him a feather cape, until then unknown on Maui. The king, angry at his runner's delay, has prepared an oven to cook him in at his return, but at sight of the feather cape he is mollified, and marries the restored chiefess. Their child is Kaululaau. (See under Trickster stories.)

Pamano

In Kahikinui, Maui, in the village of Kaipolohua, in the days of King Kaiuli, is born Pamano, child of Lono and Kenia. His uncle is Waipu, his sisters are spirits named Nakinowailua and Hokiolele. Pamano studies the art of the *hula*, and becomes a famous dancer, then comes to the uplands of Mokulau in Kaupo, where the king adopts him, but places a taboo between him and his daughter, Keaka. Keaka, however, entices Pamano into her house. Now Pamano and his friend, Hoolau, have agreed not to make love to Keaka without the other's consent. Koolau, not knowing it is the girl's doing, reports his friend to the king, and he and his wife decide that Pamano must die. They entice him in from surf riding, get him drunk with *awa* in spite of his spirit sisters' warnings, and chop him to pieces. The sisters restore him to life. At a *kilu* game given by Keaka and Koolau. Pamano reveals himself in a chant and orders his three enemies slain before he will return to Keaka.

3. Hawaii Stories

Kaulanapokii

Kaumalumalu and Lanihau of Holualoa, Kona, Hawaii, have five sons and five daughters. The boys are Mumu, Wawa, Ahewahewa, Lulukaina and Kalino; their sisters are Mailelaulii, Mailekaluhea, Mailepakaha, Mailehaiwale, and Kaulanapokii, who is endowed with gifts of magic. The girls go sight-seeing along the coast of Kohala, and Mailelaulii weds the king of Kohala, Hikapoloa. He gets them to send for the supernatural pearl fishhook with which their brothers catch *aku* fish, but the hook sent proves a sham, and the angry chief determines to induce the brothers thither on a visit and then kill them in revenge. When the five arrive with a boatload of *aku*, the sisters are shut up in the woman's house composing a name song for the first-born. Each brother in turn comes up to the king's house and thrusts his head in at the door, only to have it chopped off and the body burnt in a special kind of wood fire, *opiko*, *aaka*, *mamane*, *pua* and *alani*. The youngest sister, however, is aware of the event, and the sisters determine to slay Hikapoloa. When he comes in to see his child, Kaulanapokii sings an incantation to the rains and seas, the *ie* and *maile* vines, to block the house. Thus the chief is killed. Then Kaulanapokii sings an incantation to the various fires burning her brothers' flesh, to tell her where their bones are concealed. With the bones she brings her brothers to life, and they all return to Kona, abandoning "the proud land of Kohala and its favorite wind, the Aeloa."

Pupuhuluena

The spirits have potatoes, yam, and taro at Kalae Point, Kau, but the Kohala people have none. Pupuhuluena goes fishing from Kohala off Makaukiu, and the fishes collect under his canoe. As he sails he leaves certain kinds of fish as he goes until he comes just below Kalae. Here Ieiea and Poopulu, the fishermen of Makalii, have a dragnet. By oiling the water with chewed *kukui* nut, he calms it enough to see the fishes entering their net, and this art pleases the fishermen. By giving them the nut he wins their friendship, hence when he goes ashore, one prompts him with the names of the food plants which are new to him. Then he stands the spirits on their heads, so shaming them that they give him the plants to take to Kohala.

Hiku and Kawelu[17]

The son of Keaauolu and Lanihau, who live in Kaumalumalu, Kona, once sends his arrow, called Puane, into the hut of Kawelu, a chiefess of Kona. She falls violently in love with the stranger who follows to seek it, and will not let him depart. He escapes, and she dies of grief for him, her spirit descending to Milu. Hiku, hearing of her death, determines to fetch her thence. He goes out into mid-ocean, lets down a *koali*

---

17. See Thrum, p. 43.

vine, smears himself with rancid *kukui* oil to cover the smell of a live person, and lowers himself on another vine. Arrived in the lower world, he tempts the spirits to swing on his vines. At last he catches Kawelu, signals to his friends above, and brings her back with him to the upper world. Arrived at the house where the body lies, he crowds the spirit in from the feet up. After some days the spirit gets clear in. Kawelu crows like a rooster and is taken up, warmed, and restored.

E. Trickster Stories

1. Thefts

Iwa

At Keaau, Puna, lives Keaau, who catches squid by means of two famous *leho* shells, Kalokuna, which the squid follow into the canoe. Umi, the king, hears about them and demands them. Keaau, mourning their loss, seeks some one clever enough to steal them back from Umi. He is directed to a grove of *kukui* trees between Mokapu Point and Bird Island, on Oahu, where lives Kukui and his thieving son Iwa. This child, "while yet in his mother's womb used to go out stealing." He was the greatest thief of his day. Keaau engages his services and they start out. With one dip of Iwa's paddle, Kapahi, they are at the next island. So they go until they find Umi fishing off Kailua, Hawaii. Iwa swims 3 miles under water, steals the shells, and fastens the hooks to the coral at the bottom of the sea 400 fathoms below. Later, Iwa steals back the shells from Keaau for Umi.

Iwa's next feat is the stealing of Umi's ax, Waipu, which is kept under strict taboo in the temple of Pakaalana, in Waipio, on Hawaii. It hangs on a rope whose ends are fastened to the necks of two old women. A crier runs back and forth without the temple to proclaim the taboo. Iwa takes the place of the crier, persuades the old women to let him touch the ax, and escapes with it.

Umi arranges a contest to prove who is the champion thief. Iwa is pitted against the six champions from each of the six districts of Hawaii. The test is to see which can fill a house fullest in a single night. The six thieves go to work, but Iwa sleeps until cockcrow, when he rises and steals all the things out of the other thieves' house. He also steals sleeping men, women, and children from the king's own house to fill his own. The championship is his, and the other six thieves are killed.

Maniniholokuaua

This skillful thief lives at Kaunakahakai on Molokai, where he is noted for strength and fleetness. In a cave at Kalamaula, in the uplands, his lizard guardian keeps all the valuables that he steals from strangers who land on his shore. This cave opens and shuts at his call. Maniniholokuaua steals the canoe of the famous Oahu runner, Keliimalolo, who can make three circuits of Oahu in a day, and this man secures the help of two supernatural runners from Niihau, Kamaakauluohia (or Kaneulohia), and Kamaakamikioi (or Kaneikamikioi), sons of Halulu, who can make ten circuits of Kauai in a day. In spite of his grandmother's warning, Maniniholokuaua steals from them also, and they pursue him to his cave, where he is, caught between the jaws in his haste.

Pupualenalena

This marvelous dog named Pupualenalena fetches *awa* from Hakau's food patches in Waipio, Hawaii, to his master in Puako. Hakau has the dog tracked, and is about to kill both dog and master when he bethinks himself. He has been troubled by the blowing of a conch shell, Kuana, by the spirits above Waipio, and he now promises life if the dog will bring him the shell. This the dog effects in the night, though breaking a piece in his flight, and the king, delighted, rewards the master with land in Waipio.

2. Contests with Spirits

THE SON OF KAKAALANEO, KING of Maui and Kanikaniaula, uproots all the breadfruit trees of Lahaina to get the fruit that is out of reach, and does so much mischief with the other children born on the same day with him, who are brought to court for his companions, that they are sent home, and he is abandoned on the island of Lanai to be eaten by the spirits. His god shows him a secret cave to hide in. Each night the spirits run about trying to find him, but every time he tricks them until they get so overworked that all die except Pahulu and a few others. Finally his parents, seeing his light still burning, send a double canoe to fetch him home with honor. This is how Lanai was cleared of spirits.[18]

---

18. Daggett tells this story.

Lepe

A trickster named Lepe lives at Hilo, Hawaii, calls up the spirits by means of an incantation, and then fools them in every possible way.

Hanaaumoe

Halalii is the king of the spirits on Oahu. The ghost of Hawaii is Kanikaa; that of Maui, Kaahualii; of Lanai, Pahulu; of Molokai, Kahiole. The great flatterer of the ghosts, Hanaaumoe, persuades the Kauai chief, Kahaookamoku, and his men to land with the promise of lodging, food, and wives. When they are well asleep, the ghost come and eat them up—"they made but one smack and the men disappeared." But one man, Kaneopa, has suspected mischief and hidden under the doorsill where the king of the spirits sat, so no one found him. He returns and tells the Kauai king, who makes wooden images, brings them with him to Oahu, puts them in place of his men in the house; while they hide without, and while the ghosts are trying to eat these fresh victims, burns down the house and consumes all but the flatterer, who manages to escape.

Punia

The artful son of Hina in Kohala goes to the cave of lobsters and by lying speech tricks the shark who guard it under their king, Kaialeale. He pretends to dive, throws in a stone, and dives in another place. Then he accuses one shark after another as his accomplice, and its companions kill it, until only the king is left. The king is tricked into swallowing him whole instead of cutting him into bits. There he remains until he is bald—"serves him right, the rascal!"—but finally he persuades the shark to bring him to land, and the shark is caught and Punia escapes. Next he kills a parcel of ghosts by pretending that this is an old fishing ground of his and enticing them out to sea two by two, when he puts them to death, all but one.

Wakaina

A cunning ghost of Waiapuka, North Kohala, disguises himself as a dancer and approaches a party of people. He shows off his skill, then calls for feather cloak, helmet, bamboo flute, skirt, and various other valuable things with which to display his art. When he has them secure, he flies off with them, and the audience never see him or their property again.[19]

3. Stories of Modern Cunning

Kulepe

A cunning man and great thinker lives on Oahu in the days of Peleioholani. He travels to Kalaupapa, Molokai, is hungry, and, seeing some people bent over their food, chants a song that deceives them into believing him a soldier and man of the court. They become friendly at once and invite him to eat.

Kawaunuiaola

A woman of Kula, Maui, whose husband deserts her for another woman, makes herself taboo, returns to her house, and offers prayers and invents conversations as if she had a new husband. The news quickly spreads, and Hoeu starts at once for home. In this cunning manner she regains her husband.

Maiauhaalenalenaupena

The upland peddlers bring sugar cane, bananas, gourds, etc., to sea to peddle for fish. Maiauhaalenalenaupena pretends to be a fisherman. He spreads out his net as if just driven in from sea by the rough weather. The peddlers trust him with their goods until he has better luck; but he really is no fisherman and never gives them anything.

Waawaaikinaaupo and Waawaaikinaanao

One day these two brothers go out snaring birds. The older brother suggests that they divide the spoils thus: He will take all those with holes on each side of the beak. The unobservant younger brother consents, thinking this number will be few, and the older wins the whole catch.

---

19. Gill tells this same story from the Hervey group. Myths and Songs, p. 88.

Kuauamoa

At Kawaihae, Kohala, lives the great trickster, Kuauamoa. He knows Davis and Young after they are made prisoners by the natives, and thus learns some English words. On the plains of Alawawai he meets some men going to sell rope to the whites and they ask him to instruct them what to say. He teaches them to swear at the whites. When the white men are about to beat the peddlers, they drop the rope and run away.

THE ORIGINAL HAWAIIAN TEXT

Olelo Hoakaka

Ua hoopuka ka mea nana i pai keia buke me ka olioli nui, ka makamua o ka hoao ana e hoolako i buke hoonanea na na kanaka Hawaii. Ua loaa mua mai ia kakou na buke kula o na ano he nui wale, a he nui no hoi na buke i hoolakoia mai na kakou, e hoike mai ana ia kakou i ka pono a me ka hewa; aka, o ka buke mua nae keia i paiia na ka poe Hawaii nei, ma ke ano hoikeike ma ke Kaao i na mea kahiko a keia lahui kanaka, me ka aua mai hoi mai ka nalowale loa ana'ku o kekahi o na moolelo punihei a lakou. E hoike ana iloko o na huaolelo maikai wale i na olelo a me na hana a kekahi o ko Hawaii kaikamahine wahine maikai a punahele no hoi, a na ia mea no hoi e kokua mai i ka noho mau ana o ke aloha o na poe o Hawaii nei, no ko lakou mau kupuna a me ko lakou aina.

E lawe hoi ano, i keia wahi buke uuku, a e hoike ia ia ma ke ano o kona loaa ana mai, e heluhelu, a e malama hoi ia ia, e hoike ana i kou iini i ka naauao Hawaii, me kou makaukau mau no hoi e kokua aku ia mea, i ku mau ai.

He mea nui no ka hapai ana i ka mea nana e hoomaamaa mai ia kakou ma ka heluhelu ana, me ka hoonanea pu mai no hoi i na minute noho hana ole o ko kakou noho ana; nolaila, i ka hoomaka ana a ka mea nana i pai i keia buke, e hoomakaukau ia ia no ka hele ana'ku imua o keia lahui, ua hilinai oia i ke kokua nui mai o na makamaka a pau o ka naauao iwaena o keia mau pae moku; a na ia manao wale iho no i hooikaika mai ia ia ma ke kupaa ana mamuli o kana mea i manaolana'i e hana aku, iloko o na pilikia he nui wale e alai mai ana. Akahi no a haawiia i ka lahui Hawaii, ka buke e pili ana i ka hoonanea'ku i ka noho ana, e like me ka na haole, he mea ia nana e hanai mai i ko kakou mau manao i ka ike a me ka naauao. Ua hiki ia kakou a pau ke hui mai ma ka malama ana a me ka hooholomua aku hoi i keia wahi buke, he kumu ia e hapai hou ia mai ai i mau buke hou na keia lahui, ma kana olelo iho—ka olelo Hawaii. A nolaila la, e na makamaka a pau o ka naauao a me na keiki kupa no hoi o Hawaii nei, mai ka la hiki a ka la kau, eia mai Kawahineokaliula, ke hele aku la imua o oukou me ke aloha, a e pono hoi ke hookipa ia ia me ka aloha makamae o ka puuwai Hawaii. ALOHA NO!

Mokuna I

I ke kamailio ana i keia kaao, ua oleloia ma Laie, Koolau, kona wahi i hanau ai, a he mau mahoe laua, o Kahauokapaka ka makuakane, o Malaekahana ka makuahine. O Kahauokapaka nae, oia ke Alii nona na okana elua, o Koolauloa a me Koolaupoko, a ia ia ka mana nui maluna o kela mau okana.

I ka manawa i lawe ai o Kahauokapaka ia Malaekahana'i wahine mare nana (hoao) mahope iho o ko laua hoao ana, hai mua o Kahauokapaka i kana olelo paa imua o kana wahine, o laua wale no ma ke kaawale, oiai iloko o ko laua mau minute oluolu, a eia ua olelo paa la:

"E kuu wahine, he nani ia ua mare ae nei kaua, a nolaila, ke hai nei au i kuu olelo paa ia oe; i noho aku auanei kaua, a i loaa ka kaua keiki, a he keikikane, alaila pomaikai kaua, ola na iwi iloko o ko kaua mau la elemakule, a haule aku i ka make, nalo no hoi na wahi huna: na ia keiki e nai na moku e pau ai, ke loaa hoi ia kaua ke keiki mua a he keikikane; aka hoi, ina he kaikamahine ke hanau mua mai, alaila e make, a ina he mau kaikamahine wale no ka kaua ke hanau mai e make no, aia no ke ola a hanau mai a he keikikane, ola na hanau mui i na he mau kaikamahine."

I ka ewalu paha o na makahiki o ko laua noho ana he kane a he wahine, hapai ae la o Malaekahana, a hanau mai la he kaikamahine, ua maikai na helehelena i ka nana aku, a no ka maikai o na helehelena o ua kaikamahine nei, manao iho la ka makuahine o ke kumu la hoi ia e lilo ai ka olelo paa a Kahauokapaka i mea ole, ola la hoi ua kaikamahine nei, aole ka! Ia manawa i hanau ai, aia nae o Kahauokapaka i ka lawai-a me na kanaka.

A hoi mai o Kahauokapaka mai ka lawai-a mai, haiia aku la ua hanau o Malaekahana he kaikamahine. A hiki ke alii i ka hale, ua wahiia ke kaikamahine i ke kapa keiki, kena koke ae la o Kahauokapaka i ka Ilamuku e pepehi.

Ma ia hope iho hapai hou o Malaekahana, a hanau hou mai la he kaikamahine, o keia nae ke kaikamahine oi aku o ka maikai mamua o kela kaikamahine mua, manao iho la e ola la hoi, aole ka! Ike ae la o Kahauokapaka i ke kaikamahine e hiiia mai ana, ua hoaahuia i ke kapa keiki, ia manawa, kena koke ae la ke alii i ka Ilamuku e pepehi.

Mahope mai, ua hapai wale no o Malaekahana, he mau kaikamahine wale no, aole nae i ola iki kekahi oia mau hanau ana o Malaekahana, ua pau wale no i ka pepehiia e like me ka olelo paa a ke alii.

A i ka hapai hou ana o Malaekahana i ke keiki, o ka lima ia, a kokoke i na la hanau, hele aku la kela a imua o ke Kahuna, a olelo aku la, "E! auhea oe? E nana mai oe i keia opu o'u e hapai nei, no ka mea, ua pauaho ae nei hoi i ka pau o na keiki i ka make i ka pakela pepehi a ke kane, aha ae nei a maua keiki, aha no i ka make; nolaila, e nana mai oe i keia opu o'u e hapai nei, ina i ike oe he kaikamahine, e omilomio ae au, oiai aole i hookanaka ae ke keiki. Aka hoi, ina i ike mai hoi oe i keia opu o'u e hapai nei a he keikikane, aole ana."

Alaila, olelo mai ke Kahuna ia Malaekahana, "O hoi, a kokoke i ko la hanau, alaila, hele mai oe i o'u nei, i nana aku au i keia hapai ana."

A kokoke i na la hanau, i ka malama o Ikuwa, i na la kapu heiau, hoomanao ae la o Malaekahana i ke kauoha a ke Kahuna. Ia ianei e nahunahu ana, hele aku la keia imua o ke Kahuna, me ka olelo aku, "I hele mai nei au ma ke kauoha a ke Kahuna, no ka mea, ke hoomaka mai nei ka nahunahu hanau keiki ana; nolaila, ano oe e nana mai oe i kuu keiki e hapai nei."

Ia Malaekahana me ke Kahuna e kamailio ana no keia mau mea, alaila, hai aku la ke Kahuna i kana olelo ia Malaekahana, "E hailona aku au ia oe, ma ka mea a'u e noi aku ai, e haawi mai oe."

Ia manawa, nonoi aku la ke Kahuna ia Malaekahana e haawi mai i kekahi lima imua o ke alo o ke Kahuna, e like no me ka hailona mau o keia lahui, ma ka lima no nae ana e makemake ai e haawi aku imua o ke Kahuna.

Ia manawa a ke Kahuna i noi aku ai i kekahi lima, haawi mai la o Malaekahana i ka lima hema, me ka hoohuliia o ke alo o ka lima iluna. Alaila, hai aku la ke Kahuna i ka hailona i ku i kana ike, "E hanau hou ana no oe he kaikamahine, no ka mea, ua haawi mai nei oe i kou lima hema ia'u, me ka huli nae o ke alo o ka lima iluna."

A no keia olelo a ke Kahuna, kaumaha loa iho la ka naau o Malaekahana, no ka mea, ua kumakena mau kela i ka pepehi mau a kana kane i na keiki mua; nolaila, noi aku la o Malekahana i ke Kahuna e noonoo mai i mea e pono ai ka wahine, a e ola ai hoi ke keiki.

Alaila, hai aku la ke Kahuna i kana mau olelo ia Malaekahana, "E hoi oe a ka hale, ina e hiki i ka wa e aneane hanau ai, alaila ea, e ono ae oe i ka ohua, me ka olelo aku ia Kahauokapaka, nana ponoi no e lawai-a, o ka i-a ponoi no e loaa ana ma kona lima oia kau i-a e ono ai; no ka mea, he kanaka puni kaalauohua hoi ko kane, i lilo ai kela i ka lawai-a, ike ole ia i kou hanau ana, a ina e hanau ae, alaila, na'u e malama ke keiki, i hoi mai ia ua lilo ia'u ke keiki, a ina e niuau mai, hai aku oe he heiki alualu, alaila pau wale."

A pau ka laua kamailio ana no keia mau mea, hoi aku la o Malaekahana a hiki i ka hale, in manawa, nui loa mai la ka nahunahu ana a aneane e hanau, alaila, hoomanao ae la o Malaekahana i na olelo a ke Kahuna i a-oa-o mai ai ia ia.

A i ka mao ana'e o ka eha no ka aneane hanau, olelo aku la o Malaekahana i kana kane, "E Kahauokapaka e! ke kau mai nei i ko'u mau maka ka ohuapalemo; nolaila, e holo aku oe i ke kaalauohua, me he mea'la a loaa mai ka ohuapalemo, alaila hemo kuu keiki, akahi wale no o'u hanau ino ana, a me ka ono o'u i ka ohua; nolaila, e hele koke aku oe me na kanaka i ka lawai-a."

Ia manawa, puka koke aku o Kahauokapaka a hele aku la. Ia lakou e hele ana, hanau ae la ua keiki nei he kaikamahine, a lilo ae la ia Waka ka hanai, a kapa iho la i ka inoa o Laieikawai. Ia lakou no hoi e lawelawe ana i ke keiki mua, hanau hou mai la he kaikamahine no, a lilo ae la ia Kapukaihaoa, a kapa iho la i ka inoa o ka muli o Laielohelohe.

A lilo na kaikamahine ma ka lima o Waka a me Kapukaihaoa me ke kaawale, hoi mai la o Kahauokapaka mai ka lawai-a mai, ninau iho la i ka wahine, "Pehea oe?"

I mai la ka wahine, "Ua hanau ae nei au he keiki alualu, ua kiola ia aku nei i ka moana."

Ua akaka mua no nae ia Kahauokapaka ka hanau ia lakou i ka moana; no ka mea, elua hekili o ke kui ana, manao ae la no hoi o Kahauokapaka ua hanau ka wahine; mai ka hanau ana o Laieikawai me Laielohelohe, oia ka hoomaka ana o ka hekili e kani iloko o Ikuwa, pela i olelo ia iloko o keia moolelo.

Ia Waka me Kapukaihaoa ma ke kaa wale me na hanai a laua, olelo aku la o Waka ia Kapukaihaoa, "Pehea la auanei e nalo ai na hanai a kaua ia Kahauokapaka?"

I mai la ke Kahuna, "E pono oe ke huna loa i kau hanai iloko o ke kiowai i Waiapuka, aia malaila kekahi ana i ike oleia e na mea a pau, a na'u no hoi e imi ko'u wahi e malama ai i ka'u hanai."

Lawe aku la o Waka ia Laieikawai ma kahi a Kapukaihaoa i kuhikuhi ai, a malaila oia i malama malui'ai o Laieikawai a hiki i kona manawa i hoomahuahua iki ae ai.

Mahope iho o keia mau la, lawe ae la o Kapukaihaoa ia Laielohelohe i uka o Wahiawa ma kahi i oleloia o Kukaniloko.

Iloko o ko Laieikawai mau la ma Waiapuka, ua hoomauia ka pio ana o ke anuenue ma kela wahi, iloko o ka manawa ua a me ka malie, i ka po a me ke ao; aka, aole nae i hoomaopopo na mea a pau i ke ano o keia anuenue; aka, ua hoomauia keia mau hailona alii ma na wahi i malamai'ai ua mau mahoe nei.

I kekahi manawa, ia Hulumaniani e kaahele ana ia Kauai apuni, ma kona ano Makaula nui no Kauai, a ia ia i hiki ai iluna pono o Kalalea, ike mai la oia i ka pio a keia anuenue i Oahu nei; noho iho la oia malaila he iwakalua la, i kumu e ike maopopoi'ai o ke ano o kana mea e ike nei. Ia manawa, ua, maopopo lea i ka Makaula he Alii Nui ka mea nona keia anuenue e pio nei, a me na onohi elua i hoopuniia i na ao polohiwa apuni.

Ia manawa, hooholo ae la ka Makaula i kona manao e holo i Oahu, i maopopo ai ia ia kana mea e ike nei. Haalele keia ia wahi, hiki aku la keia i Anahola, hoolimalima aku la keia i waa e holo ai i Oahu nei; aka, aole i loaa ia ia he waa e holo ai i Oahu nei. Kaapuni hou ka Makaula ia Kauai a puni, pii hou oia iluna o Kalalea, a ike hou no oia i kana mea i ike mua ai, aia no e mau ana e like no me mamua, alaila, hoi hou keia a hiki i Anahola.

I ua Makaula nei malaila, lohe keia o Poloula ka mea waa o Wailua, no ka mea, he alii ia no ia wahi, ake aku la oia e halawai me Poloula, me ka manao e noi aku i ke alii i waa e hiki ai i Oahu.

Ia Hulumaniani i halawai aku ai me Poloula, nonoi aku la oia i waa e holo ai i Oahu nei; alaila, haawiia mai la ka waa me na kanaka; ia po iho, i ka hiki ana o ka Hokuhookelewaa, haalele lakou ia Kauai, he umikumamalima ko lakou nui, hiki mua mai la lakou ma Kamaile, i Waianae.

Mamua ae nae o ko ka Makaula holo ana mai, ua hoomakaukau mua oia hookahi puaa hiwa, he moa lawa, a me ka i-a ula.

Ia la o lakou i hiki ai ma Waianae, kauoha ka Makaula i na kanaka e noho malaila a hoi mai oia mai ka huakai kaapuni ana.

I ua Makaula nei i hele ai, hiki mua keia iluna pono o Maunalahilahi, ike aku la keia i ke anuenue e pio ana ma Koolauloa, e like me kana ike ana i kona mau la iluna o Kalalea.

A hiki keia i Waiapuka, kahi i malamaia ai o Laieikawai, ike iho la oia aole he kuleana kupono o kela wahi e nohoi'ai e na'lii. I kela manawa nae a ka Makaula i hiki ai ilaila, ua nalo mua aku o Waka ma kahi i hunai'ai o Laieikawai.

I ka manawa nae a ka Makaula e kunana ana, alaila, ike aku la oia i ka aleale ana o ka wai o ko Waka luu ana aku. Olelo iho la ka Makaula iloko ona, "He mea kupanaha, aole hoi he makani o keia lua wai e kuleana ai la hoi ka aleale ana o ka wai, me he mea he mea e auau ana, a ike ae nei ia'u pee iho nei." A pau ko Waka manawa ma kahi o

Laieikawai, hoi mai la oia; aka, ike ae la keia maloko o ka wai i keia mea e noho ana maluna iho, emi hope hou aku la o Waka, no ka mea, ua manao oia o Kahauokapaka, keia mea ma kae o ka luawai.

Hoi hou aku la o Waka me kana moopuna, a hiki i ka molehulehu ana, hoomakakiu hou mai la oia me ka manao ua hele aku kela mea ana i ike ai; aka, aia no ua Makaulanei ma kana wahi i noho mua ai, nolaila, hoi hope hou o Waka.

Ua noho ua Makaula nei ma ke kae o kela luawai, a moe oia malaila a ao ia po. Ia kakahiaka ana ae, i ka manawa molehulehu, ala ae la oia, ike aku la kela i ka pio a ke anuenue i uka o Kukaniloko, haalele keia ia wahi, kaapuni keia ia Oahu nei, ma Koolaupoko kona hele mua ana, a ma Kona nei, a mai anei aku hiki ma Ewa; a hiki keia i Honouliuli, ike aku la ua Makaula nei i ka pio o ke anuenue i uka o Wahiawa, pii loa aku la oia a hiki i Kamaoha, a malaila oia i moe ai a ao ia po, aole oia i ike i kana mea i ukali mai ai.

Mokuna II

A nele ka Makaula i ka ike i kana mea e ukali nei, haalele keia ia Kamaoha, hiki keia iluna pono o Kaala, a malaila oia i ike ai e pio ana ke anuenue i Molokai; nolaila, haalele ka Makaula ia wahi, kaapuni hou ia Oahu nei; o ka lua ia o kana huakai kaapuni ana, i mea e hiki ai ia ia ke ike maopopo i kana mea e ukali nei, no ka mea, ua ano e ka hana a ke anuenue, no ka holoholoke ana i kela wahi keia wahi.

I ka la a ua Makaula nei i haalele ai ia Kaala, hiki mua aku oia iluna o Kuamooakane, aia hoi e pio ana ke anuenue i Molokai, e ku ana ka punohu i uhipaaia e na ao hekili, ekolu mau la oia nei ma Kuamooakane, ua hoomauia ka uhi paapu a ka ua a me ka noe.

I ka eha o na la oia nei malaila, loaa ia ia he waa e holo ana i Molokai; kau aku la oia maluna o ka waa, a holo aku la a like a like o ka moana, loaa ka manao ino i na mea waa, no ka mea, ua uluhua laua i ua Makaula nei no ka hiamoe, a me ka ala a mau ana o kahi puaa, a o-o-o mau no hoi o kahi moa.

A no keia mea, kunou aku la ka mea mahope o ka waa i ke kanaka iluna o kuaiako, e hoi hou ka waa i hope, a hoonoho hou i ka Makaula i Oahu nei, a ua like ka manao o na mea waa ma ia mea e hoihoi hope ka waa, e moe ana nae ka Makaula ia manawa.

Hoohuli ae la na mea waa i ka waa i hope a holo i Oahu nei; ia manawa a ka waa e hoi hope nei, hoohuoi iho la ka Makaula i ka pa ana a ka makani ma kona papalina, no ka mea, ua maopopo ia ia kahi a ka makani i pa ai i ka holo ana mai Oahu aku nei manao iho la oia, ma kai mai ka makani e pa nei.

Nolaila, kaakaa ae la na maka o ka Makaula, aia hoi e hoi hou ana ka waa i Oahu nei; ia manawa, nalu iho la ka Makaula i ke kumu o keia hoi hou ana o ka waa. Aka hoi, no ko ianei makemake e ike maopopo i ka hana a na mea waa, pule aku la oia i kona Akua ia Kuikauweke, e hooili mai i ka ino nui maluna o ka moana.

Ia ia e pule ana iloko ona iho, hiki koke mai la ka ino nui maluna o lakou, a pono ole ka manao o na mea waa.

Ia manawa, hoala ae la na mea waa ia ianei, "E keia kanaka e moe nei! e ala ae paha oe, kainoa paha he pono kau i kau mai ai maluna o ko maua waa, aole ka! oia no ka moe a nei kanaka la o uka."

Alaila, ala ae la ua Makaula nei, e hooiho ana ka waa i Oahu nei.

Alaila, ninau aku la oia i na mea waa, "Heaha iho nei keia hana a olua ia'u i hoi hope ai ka waa? A heaha kuu hewa?"

Alaila, olelo mai la na mea waa, "Ua uluhua maua no kou hiamoe, a me ka alala mau o ko wahi puaa, a me ke kani mau a ko wahi moa, nolaila kulikuli; mai ka holo ana mai nei no ka ke kulikuli a hiki i keia manawa, ua pono no la hoi ia, i na la hoi e hoe ana oe, aole ka, he moe wale iho no ka kau."

I aku la ka Makaula, "Ua hewa olua i kuu manao; ina o kuu noho wale ke kumu o ka hoi hou ana o ka waa o kakou i Oahu, alaila, ke olelo nei au, ua hewa ka mea iluna o kuaiako, no ka mea, he noho wale iho no kana, aole ana hana."

Ia lakou e kamailio ana no keia mau mea, lele aku la ka Makaula mahope o ka waa, a lilo iho la ia ia ia ka hookele, holo aku la lakou a kau ma Haleolono i Molokai.

Ia lakou i hiki aku ai malaila, aia hoi, e pio ana ke anuenue i Koolau, e like me kana ike ana i kona mau la maluna o Kuamooakane, haalele keia i na mea waa, ake aku la oia e ike i kana mea i ukali mai ai.

Ia hele ana hiki mua keia i Waialala maluna pono ae o Kalaupapa; ia ianei malaila, ike maopopo aku la oia e pio ana ke anuenue iluna o Malelewaa, ma kahi nihinihi hiki ole ke heleia. Aia nae malaila kahi i hunaia ai o Laieikawai, oia a me kona kupunawahine, e like me ke kauoha mau a Kapukaihaoa ia Waka ma ka hihio.

No ka mea, i ka Makaula e holo mai ana ma ka moana, ua ike mua e aku o Kapukaihaoa i ka Makaula, a me kana mau hana, nolaila oia i olelo mau ai ia Waka ma ka hihio e ahai mua ia Laieikawai ma kahi hiki ole ke loaa.

I ka Makaula i haalele ai ia Waialala, hiki aku keia ma Waikolu ilalo pono o Malelewaa, aia nae e pio ana ke anuenue i kahi hiki ole ia ia ke hele aku; aka, ua noonoo ka Makaula i kekahi manawa, i wahi e hiki ai e ike i kana mea e ukali nei, a waiho aku i kana kanaenae i hoomakaukau mua ai, aole nae e hiki.

I kela la a ka Makaula i hiki ai ma Waikolu, ia po iho, hiki mua ke kauoha a Kapukaihaoa ia Laieikawai ma ka moeuhane, a puoho ae la oia, he moeuhane. Alaila, hoala aku la o Laieikawai i kona kupunawahine, a ala ae la, ninau aku la ke kupunawahine i kana moopuna i ke kumu o ka hoala ana.

Hai mai la ka moopuna, "Ua hiki mai o Kapukaihaoa i o'u nei ma ka moeuhane, e olelo mai ana, e ahai loa oe ia'u i Hawaii a hoonoho ma Paliuli, a malaila kaua e noho ai, pela mai nei oia ia'u, a puoho wale ae la wau la, hoala aku la ia oe."

Ia Laieikawai nae e kamailio ana i ke kupunawahine, hiki iho la ka hihio ma o Waka la, a ua like me ka ka moopuna e olelo ana, ia manawa, ala ae la laua i ke wanaao a hele aku la e like me ke kuhikuhi a Kapukaihaoa ia laua ma ka moeuhane.

Haalele laua ia wahi, hiki aku laua ma Keawanui, kahi i kapaia o Kaleloa, a malaila laua i halawai ai me ke kanaka e hoomakaukau ana i ka waa e holo ai i Lanai. La laua i halawai aku ai me ka mea waa, olelo aku la o Waka, "E ae anei oe ia maua e kau pu aku me oe ma ko waa, a holo aku i kau wahi i manao ai e holo?"

Olelo mai la ka mea waa, "Ke ae nei wau e kau pu olua me a'u ma ka waa, aka hookahi no hewa, o ko'u kokoolua ole e hiki ai ka waa."

Ia manawa a ka mea waa i hoopuka ai i keia olelo "i kokoolua" hoewaa, wehe ae la o Laieikawai i kona mau maka i uhiia i ka aahu kapa, mamuli o ka makemake o ke kupunawahine e huna loa i kana moopuna me ka ike oleia mai e na mea e ae a hiki i ko laua hiki ana i Paliuli, aka, aole pela ko ka moopuna manao.

I ka manawa nae a Laieikawai i hoike ai i kona mau maka mai kona hunaia ana e kona kupunawahine, luliluli ae la ke poo o ke kupunawahine, aole a hoike kana moopuna ia ia iho, no ka mea, e lilo auanei ka nani o kana moopuna i mea pakuwa wale.

I ka manawa nae a Laieikawai i wehe ae ai i kona mau maka, ike aku la ka mea waa i ka oi kelakela o ko Laieikawai helehelena mamua o na kaikamahine kaukaualii o Molokai a puni, a me Lanai. Aia hoi, ua hookuiia mai ka mea waa e kona iini nui no kana mea e ike nei.

A no keia mea, noi aku la ka mea waa i ke kupunawahine, me ka olelo aku, "E kuu loa ae oe i na maka o ko moopuna mai kona hoopulouia ana, no ka mea, ke ike nei wau ua oi aku ka maikai o kau milimili, mamua o na kaikamahine kaukaualii o Molokai nei a me Lanai."

I mai la ke kupunawahine. "Aole e hiki ia'u ke wehe ae ia ia, no ka mea, o kona makemake no ka huna ia ia iho."

A no keia olelo a Waka i ka mea waa mamuli o kana noi, alaila, hoike pau loa ae la o Laieikawai ia ia mai kona hunaia ana, no ka mea, ua lohe aku la o Laieikawai i ka olelo a kona kupunawahine, o Laieikawai no ka makemake e huna ia ia; aka, ua, makemake ole keia e huna.

A no ka ike maopopo loa ana aku o ka mea waa ia Laieikawai, alaila, he nuhou ia i ka mea waa. Alaila, kupu ae la ka manao ano e iloko ona, e hele e hookaulana ia Molokai apuni, no keia mea ana e iini nei.

Alaila, olelo aku la ua mea waa nei ia Laieikawai ma, "Auhea olua, e noho olua i ka hale nei, na olua na mea a pau oloko, aole kekahi mea e koe o ka hale nei ia olua, o olua maloko a mawaho o keia wahi."

A no ka hoopuka ana o ka mea waa i keia olelo, alaila, olelo aku la o Laieikawai, "E ke kamaaina o maua, e hele loa ana anei oe? No ka mea, ke ike lea nei maua i kou kauoha honua ana, me he mea la e hele loa ana oe?"

I aku la ke kamaaina, "E ke kaikamahine, aole pela, aole au e haalele ana ia oula; aka, i manao ae nei au e huli i kokoolua no'u e hoe aku ai ia olua a pae i Lanai."

A no keia olelo a ka mea waa, i aku la o Waka i ke kamaaina o laua nei, "Ina o ke kumu ia o kou hele ana i kauoha honua ai oe i na mea a pau o kou hale ia maua; alaila, ke i aku nei wau, he hiki ia maua ke kokua ia oe ma ka hoe ana."

A ike ka mea waa he mea kaumaha keia olelo a Waka imua ona.

Olelo aku la oia imua o na malahini, "Aole o'u manao e hoounauna aku ia olua e kokua mai ia'u ma ka hoe pu ana i ka waa, no ka mea, he mea nui olua na'u."

Aka, aole pela ka manao o ka mea waa e huli i kokoolua hoe waa pu me ia, no ka mea, ua hooholo mua oia i kana olelo hooholo iloko ona, e hele e kukala aku ia Laieikawai apuni o Molokai.

A pau ke kamailio ana a lakou i keia mau olelo, haalele iho la ka mea waa ia laua nei, a hele aku la e like me ka olelo hooholo mua iloko ona.

Ia hele ana, ma Kaluaaha kona hiki mua ana, a moe aku oia i Halawa, a ma keia hele ana a ia nei, ua kukala aku oia i ka maikai o Laieikawai e like me kona manao paa.

A ma kekahi la ae, i ke kakahiaka nui, loaa ia ia ka waa e holo ana i Kalaupapa, kau aku la oia maluna o ka waa, hiki mua oia i Pelekunu, a me Wailau, a mahope hiki i Waikolu kahi a ka Makaula e noho ana.

Ia ia nae i hiki aku ai i Waikolu, ua hala mua aku ua Makaula nei i Kalaupapa, aka, o ka hana mau a ua wahi kanaka nei, ke kukala hele no Laieikawai.

A hiki keia i Kalaupapa, aia hoi, he aha mokomoko e akoakoa ana ku aku la oia mawaho o ka aha, a kahea aku la me ka leo nui, "E ka hu, e na makaainana, e ka lopakuakea, lopahoopiliwale, e na'lii, na Kahuna, na kilo, na aialo, ua ike au i na mea a pau ma keia hele ana mai nei a'u, ua ike i na mea nui, na mea liilii, na kane, na wahine, na kaukaualii kane, na kaukaualii wahine, ka niaupio, ke ohi, aole wau i ike i kekahi oi o lakou e like me ka'u mea i ike ai, a ke olelo nei au, oia ka oi mamua o na kaikamahine kaukaualii o Molokai nei apuni, a me keia aha no hoi."

Ia manawa nae a ia nei e kahea nei, aole i lohe pono mai ka aha, no ka mea, ua uhiia kona leo e ka haukamumu leo o ka aha, a me ka nene no ka hoouka kaua.

A no ko ianei manao i lohe ponoia mai kana olelo, oi pono loa aku la ia iwaena o ke anaina, ku iho la oia imua o ka aha, a kuehu ae la oia i ka lepa o kona aahu, a hai hou ae la i ka olelo ana i olelo mua ai.

Iloko o keia manawa, lohe pono loa aku la ke Alii nui o Molokai i keia leo, alaila hooki ae la ke alii i ka aha, i loheia aku ai ka olelo a keia kanaka malahini e kuhea nei; no ka mea, iloko o ko ke alii ike ana aku i ua wahi kanaka nei, ua hoopihaia kona mau maka i ka olioli, me ke ano pihoihoi.

Kaheaia aku la ua wahi kanaka nei mamuli o ke kauoha a ke alii, a hele mai la imua o ke alii, a ninau aku la, "Heaha kou mea e nui nei kou leo imua o ka aha, me ka maka olioli?"

Alaila, hai mai la kela i ke kumu o kona kahea ana, a me kona olioli imua o ke alii. "Ma ke kakahiakanui o ka la i nehinei, e lawelawe ana wau i ka waa no ka manao e holo i Lanai, hoea mai ana keia wahine me ke kaikamahine, aole nae au i ike lea i ke ano o ua kaikamahine la. Aka, iloko o ko maua wa kamailio, hoopuka mai la ke kaikamahine i kona mau maka mai kona hunaia ana, aia hoi, ike aku la wau he kaikamahine maikai, i oi aku mamua o na kaikamahine alii o Molokai nei."

A lohe ke alii i keia olelo, ninau aku la, "Ina ua like kona maikai me kuu kaikamahine nei la, alaila, ua nani io."

A no keia ninau a ke alii, noi aku la ua wahi kanaka nei e hoikeia mai ke kaikamahine alii imua ona, a laweia mai la o Kaulaailehua ke kaikamahine a ke alii.

I aku la ua wahi kanaka nei, "E ke alii! oianei la, eha kikoo i koe o ko iala maikai ia ianei, alaila, like aku me kela." I mai la ke alii, "E! nani io aku la, ke hoole ae nei oe i ka makou maikai e ike nei, no ka mea, o ko Molokai oi no keia."

Alaila, olelo aku la kahi kanaka i ke alii me ka wiwo ole, "No ko'u ike i ka maikai, ko'u mea no ia i olelo kaena ai."

Ia manawa a kahi kanaka e kamailio ana me ke alii, e noho ana ka Makaula ia manawa e hoolohe ana i ke ano o ke kamailio ana, aka, ua haupu honua ae ka Makaula, me he mea la o kana mea e ukali nei.

A no keia mea, neenee loa aku la ka Makaula a kokoke, paa aku la ma ka lima o kahi kanaka, a huki malu aku la ia ia.

Ia laua ma kahi kaawale, ninau pono aku la ka Makaula i ua wahi kanaka nei, "Ua ike no anei oe i kela kaikamahine mamua au e kamailio nei i ke alii?"

Hoole aku la ua wahi kanaka nei, me ka i aku, "Aole au i ike mamua, akahi no wau a ike, a he mea malahini ia i ko'u mau maka."

A no keia mea, manao ae la ka Makaula, o kana mea i imi mai ai, me ka ninau pono aku i kahi i noho ai, a hai ponoia mai la.

A pau ka laua kamailio ana, lawe ae la oia i na mea ana i hoomakaukau ai i mohai no ka manawa e halawai aku ai, a hele aku la.

Mokuna III

Ia hele ana o ka Makaula mahope iho o ko laua halawai ana me kahi kanaka, hiki mua keia iluna o Kawela; nana aku la oia, e pio ana ke anuenue i kahi a ua wahi kanaka nei i olelo ai ia ia; alaila, hoomaopopo lea iho la ka Makaula o kana mea no e ukali nei.

A hiki keia i Kaamola ka aina e pili pu la me Keawanui, kahi hoi a Laieikawai ma e kali nei i ka mea waa, ia manawa, ua poeleele loa iho la, ua hiki ole ia ia ke ike aku i ka mea ana i ike ai iluna o Kawela, aka, ua moe ka Makaula malaila ia po, me ka manao i kakahiaka e ike ai i kana mea e imi nei.

I kela po a ka Makaula e moe la i Kaamola, aia hoi, ua hiki ka olelo kauoha a Kapukaihaoa ia Laieikawai ma ka moeuhane, e like me ke kuhikuhi ia laua iloko o ko laua mau la ma Malelewaa.

Ia wanaao ana ae, loaa ia laua ka waa e holo ai i Lanai, a kau laua malaila a holo aku la, a ma Maunalei ko laua wahi i noho ai i kekahi mau la.

Ia Laieikawai ma i haalele ai ia Kalaeloa ia kakahiaka, ala ae la ka Makaula, e ku ana ka punohu i ka moana, a me ka ua koko, aia nae, ua uhi paapuia ka moana i ka noe a me ke awa, mawaena o Molokai, a me Lanai.

Ekolu mau la o ka uhi paapu ana o keia noe i ka moana, a i ka eha o ko ka Makaula mau la ma Kaamola, i ke kakahiaka nui, ike aku la oia e ku ana ka onohi iluna pono o Maunalei; aka, ua nui loa ka minamina o ka Makaula no ke halawai ole me kana mea e imi nei, aole nae oia i pauaho a hooki i kona manaopaa.

Ua aneane e hala na la he umi ia ia ma Molokai, ike hou aku la oia e ku ana ka punohu iluna o Haleakala; haalele keia ia Molokai, hiki mua oia iluna o Haleakala ma kela lua pele, aole nae oia i ike i kana mea e imi nei.

I ua Makaula nei nae i hiki ai malaila, ike aku la oia ia Hawaii, ua uhi paapuia ka aina i ka ohu, a me ka noe. A haalele keia ia wahi, hiki keia i Kauwiki, a malaila oia i kukulu ai i wahi heiau, kahi hoi e hoomana ai i kona Aku, ka mea hiki ke kuhikuhi i kana mea e imi nei.

I ua Makaula nei e kaapuni ana ma na wahi a pau ana i kipa aku ai, ua kauoha mua aku ka Makaula, i na e loaa kana mea e imi nei, alaila, e huli aku ia ia ma kahi e loaa ai.

A pau ke kapu heiau a ua Makaula nei ma, Kauwiki, i na po o Kane, a me Lono paha, alaila, ike maopopoia aku la ke kalae ana o ka aina a puni o Hawaii, a ua waiho pono mai na kuahiwi.

Ua nui no na la o ka Makaula ma Kauwiki, aneane makahiki a oi ae paha, aole nae oia i ike iki i ka hoailona mau ana e ukali nei.

I kekahi la, i ka malama o Kaaona, i na Ku, i ka manawa kakahiaka nui, ike aweawea aku la oia he wahi onohi ma Koolau, o Hawaii; ia manawa, puiwa koke ae la oia me ka lele o kona oili me ka maikai ole o kona noonoo ana; aka, ua kali loihi no oia me ka hoomanawanui a maopopo lea ka hana a kela wahi onohi; a pau ia malama okoa i ka hoomanawanuiia eia, a i kekahi malama ae, i ka la o Kukahi, i ke ahiahi, mamua o ka napoo ana o ka la, komo aku la oia iloko o kona wahi heiau, kahi i hoomakaukau ai no kona Akua, a pule aku la oia.

Ia ia e pule ana, a i ka waenakonu o ka manawa, ku mai la imua o ua Makaula nei ke kahoaka o Laieikawai, a me kona kupunawahine; a no keia mea, hooniau aku la oia i ka pule ana, aole nae i haalele kela kahoaka ia ia a hiki i ka maamaama ana.

Ia po iho, iloko o kona manawa hiamoe, halawai mai la kona Akua me ia ma ka hihio, i mai la, "Ua ike au i kou luhi, a me kou hoomanawanui ana, me ke ake e loaa ia oe ka moopuna a Waka, me kou manao hoi e loaa kou pomaikai no kana moopuna mai. Iloko o kau pule ana, ua hiki ia'u ke kuhikuhi, e loaa no o Laieikawai ia oe, mawaena o Puna, a me Hilo, iloko o ka ululaau, e noho ana iloko o ka hale i uhiia i na hulu melemele o ka Oo, nolaila, apopo e ku oe a hele."

Puoho ae la oia mai ka hiamoe, aia ka he hihio, a no keia mea, pono ole iho la kona manao, aole e hiki ia ia ke moe ia po a ao.

Ia po a ao ae i ke kakahiaka nui, ia ia maluna o Kauwiki, ike aku la oia i ke kilepalepa a ka pea o ka waa ilalo o Kaihalulu; holo wikiwiki aku la oia a hiki i ke awa, ninau aku la i kahi a keia waa e holo ai, haiia mai la, "E holo ana i Hawaii," a noi aku la oia e kau pu me lakou ma ka waa, a aeia mai la oia pu me lakou.

Hoi hou aku la ka Makaula iluna o Kauwiki, e lawe mai i kana mau wahi ukana, na mea ana i hoomakaukau ai i kanaenae.

Ia manawa, aia nei i hiki ai i ka waa, hai mua aku la oia i kona manao i na mea waa, "E na mea waa, e hai mai oukou i ka'u hana ma keia holo ana o kakou; ma ka oukou mea e olelo mai ai, malaila wau e hoolohe ai, no ka mea, he kanaka wau i hana pono oleia e na mea waa i ko'u holo ana mai Oahu mai, nolaila wau e hai mua aku nei ia oukou e na mea waa, malia o like oukou me laua."

A no keia olelo a ka Makaula, olelo mai la na mea waa, aole e hanaia kekahi, mea pono ole ma ia holo ana o lakou; a pau keia mau mea kau lakou ma ka waa a holo aku la.

Ma ia holo ana hiki mua lakou i Mahukona, ma Kohala, moe malaila ia po, a i ke kakahiaka ana ae, haalele ka Makaula i na mea waa, pii aku la oia a hiki i Lamaloloa, a komo aku la i Pahauna ka hoiau, he heiau kahiko kela mai ka po mai, a hiki i keia manawa.

Ua nui loa na la ona malaila o ka noho ana, aole nae oia i ike i kana mea e imi ai; aka, ma kona ano Makaula, hoomau aku la oia i ka pule i ke Akua, e like me kona mau la ma Kauwiki, a no ka pule hoomau a ua Makaula nei, ua looa hou ia ia ke kuhikuhi ana e like me kela hoike ia ia ma Kauwiki.

A no keia mea, haalele oia ia wahi, kaahele aku la oia ia Hawaii; ma Hamakua kona hiki mua ana, oi hele aku oia mai ka manawa uuku o kahi puaa a nui loa, a na ka puaa no e hele.

Ia ia i hiki ai i Hamakua, malalo o Waipio kona wahi i noho ai ma Pakaalana, aole nae he nui kona mau la malaila.

Haalele ka Makaula ia wahi, hiki aku oia i Laupahoehoe, a malaila aku a hiki i Kaiwilahilahi, a malaila oia i noho ai he mau makahiki.

(Maanei, e waiho kakou i ka moolelo no pa imi ana o ka Makaula. Pono e kamailio no ka hoi ana o Kauakahialii, i Kauai, me Kailiokalauokekoa: i ike ai kakou, aia o Laieikawai i Paliuli.)

Ma na Helu mua o keia Kaao, ua ike kakou na Kapukaihaoa i kauoha ia Waka ma ka moeuhane e hoihoi ia Laieikawai i Paliuli, mamuli o ka ike a ka Makaula.

Ua hookoia no nae e like me ke kauoha, ua noho o Laieikawai ma Paliuli, a hiki i kona hookanakamakua ana.

Ia Kauakahialii, laua o Kailiokalauokekoa i hoi ai i Kauai, mahope iho o ko laua halawai ana me ka Olali o Paliuli (Laieikawai), a hiki lakou i Kauai, mauka o Pihanakalani, kui aku la ka lono ia Kauaiapuni; akoakoa mai la na'lii, na kaukaualii, a me na makaainana a pau e ike i ka puka malahini ana aku o Kailiokalauokekoa ma, e like me ka mea mau; o Aiwohikupua nae kekahi oia poe Alii i akoakoa pu mai ma keia aha uwe o na malihini.

A pau ka uwe ana a lakou, ninau aku la na'lii ia Kauakahialii "Pehea kau hele ana aku nei mamuli o kou hoaa'ia ianei?" (Kailiokalauokekoa.)

Alaila, hai aku la o Kauakahialii i kona hele ana, penei: "I ko'u hele ana mai anei aku mamuli o ke aloha o ka wahine, a puni Oahu, a me Maui, aole i loaa ia'u kekahi wahine e like me Kailiokalauokekoa nei; a hiki au i Hawaii, kaapuni wau ia mokupuni. Ma Kohala kuu hiki mua ana. Kaahele au ma Kona, Kau, a hiki au i Keaau, a ma Puna, a malaila wau i noho ai, a malaila wau i halawai ai me kekahi wahine maikai i oi aku mamua o ianei (Kailiokalauokekoa). A o ka oi no hoi ia mamua o na wahine maikai o keia mau mokupuni a pau."

Iloko o keia olelo ana a Kauakahialii, hoomaopopo loa mai la o Aiwohikupua i ka helehelena maikai o ua wahine nei.

Alaila, hai aku la o Kauakahialii, "I ka po mua, mahope iho o ko laua halawai ana me kuu wahi kahu nei, hai mai la oia i kona manawa e hiki mai ai i kahi o ko makou wahi e noho ana, a hai mai la no hoi oia i na hoailona o kona hiki ana mai; no ka mea, ua olelo aku kuu wahi kahu nei i kane au na ua wahine nei, me ke koi aku no hoi e iho pu mai laua me ua wahi kahu nei o'u, aka, ua hai mai kela i kana olelo, 'E hoi oe a ko hanai, kuu kane hoi au e olelo mai nei, olelo aku oe ia ia, a keia po wau hiki aku, ina e kani aku ka leo o ka Ao, aole wau iloko oia leo; a kani aku ka leo o ka Alala, aole no wau iloko oia leo; i na e kani aku ka leo o ka Elepaio, hoomakaukau wau no ka iho aku; a i kani aku ka leo o ka Apapane, alaila, ua puka wau mawaho o kuu hale nei; hoolohe mai auanei oe a i kani aku ka leo o ka Iiwipolena, alaila, aia wau mawaho o ka hale o ko hanai; imi ae olua a loaa wau mawaho, oia kuu manawa e launa ai me ko hanai.' Pela mai ka olelo ua wahi kahu nei o'u.

"I ka po hoi ana e kauoha nei, aole i hiki ae, o i kali aku makou a ao ia po, aole i hiki ae; o na manu wale no kai kani mai, manao iho la wau he wahahee na kuu wahi kahu; i Punahoa nae lakou nei (Kailiokalauokekoa ma) kahi i moe ai me na aikane. No kuu manao he wahahee na kuu wahi kahu, nolaila, kauoha ae ana wau i ka Ilamuku e hoopaa i ke kaula; aka, ua hala e ua wahi kahu nei o'u i uka o Paliuli, e ninau aku i ua wahine nei i ke kumu o kona hiki ole ana i kai ia po, me ka hai aku no hoi e make ana ia.

"A pau kana olelo ana ia Laieikawai i keia mau mea, i mai la ka wahine i ua wahi kahu nei o'u, 'E hoi oe, a ma keia po hiki aku au, e like me ka'u kauoha ia oe i ka po mua, pela no wau e hiki aku ai.'

"Ia po iho, oia ka po e hiki mai ai ua wahine nei, ua puka mua ae lakou nei (Kailiokalauokekoa ma) i ke ao, i ua po nei e kaao ana no o ianei ia makou, i ke kihi o ke ahiahi, kani ana ka leo o ka Ao; i ka pili o ke ahiahi, kani ana ka leo o ka Alala; i ke kau, kani ka leo o ka Elepaio; i ka pili o ke ao, kani ana ka leo o ka Apapane; a i ka owehewhe ana o ke alaula, kani ana ka leo o ka Iiwipolena; ia kani ana no hoi, malu ana ke aka ma ka puka o ka hale, aia hoi, ua paa oloko i ka noe, a i ka mao ana ae, e kau mai ana kela iluna o ka eheu o na manu, me kona nani nui."

A no keia olelo a Kauakahialii imua o na'lii, ua hookuiia mai ko Aiwohikupua kino okoa e ka iini nui, me ka ninau aku, "Owai ka inoa oia wahine?"

Haiia aku la oia o Laieikawai; a no ka iini nui o Aiwohikupua i keia mea a Kauakahialii e olelo nei, manao iho la ia e kii i wahine mare nana, aka, ua haohao o Aiwohikupua no keia wahine. Nolaila, hai aku oia i kana olelo imua o Kauakahialii, "Ke haohao nei wau i keia wahine, no ka mea, owau ka mea nana i kaapuni keia mau mokupuni, aole wau i ike i kekahi wahine e kau mai iluna o ka eheu o na manu; me he mea la no kukulu o Tahiti mai ia wahine, noloko o Moaulanuiakea."

No ka manao o Aiwohikupua no Moaulanuiakea, o Laieikawai, oia kona mea i manao ai e kii i wahine nana. No ke mea, manua aku o kona lohe ana i keia mau mea, ua olelo paa o Aiwohikupua, aole e lawe i kekahi wahine o keia mau mokupuni i wahine mare nana; ua olelo oia, aia kana wahine makemake noloko o Moaulanuiakea.

A pau ke kamailio ana a na'lii no keia mau mea, a me ka walea ana e like me ka mea mau o ka puka malihini ana. A mahope koke iho oia mau la, lawe ae la o Aiwohikupua i kahi o Kauakahialii, i kanaka lawelawe imua o kona alo, me ka manao o Aiwohikupua o kela wahi kanaka ka mea e loaa ai ko ke Alii makemake.

A no keia kumu, hoolilo loa ae la o Aiwohikupua i ua wahi kanaka nei i poo kiekie maluna o na mea a pau, o ko ke Alii mau aina a pau, a me na kanaka a pau loa, na'lii a me na makaainana, ma kona ano Kuhina Nui.

A lilo ae la ua wahi kanaka nei i mea nui, huahua mai la na punahele mua a Aiwohikupua, aka, he mea ole lakou i ko ke Alii manao.

Mokuna IV

Mahope iho o ka lilo ana o ua wahi kanaka nei i mea nui imua o ke Alii, me he Kuhina Nui la; a oia ka hoa kuka mau o ke Alii ma na mea e lealea ai ke Alii, me ka manao aku o ka poe e, e kuka ana ma na mea pili i ka aina, a me na waiwai e like me ka mea mau i ka noho Alii ana. Eia ka o Laieikawai no ka laua kuka mau, a he uuku ke kuka ma na mea e ae.

Mamua aku nae o ko Aiwohikupua lohe ana ia Kauakahialii no Laieikawai, ua hoike e oia i kana olelo paa imua o kona mau kaukaualii, a me na kaikuahine ona, a me kona poe aialo a pau, a eia kana olelo paa, "Auhea oukou e ko'u mau kaukaualii, a me na kaikuahine o'u ko'u mau aialo a pau; mai keia la aku a hiki i ko'u mau la hope, aole loa ana wau e lawe i kekahi wahine o keia mau mokupuni i wahine mare na'u, mai Kauai nei a hala loa i Hawaii, ina i oleloia mai he mau wahine maikai, aole no hoi au e haawi i ko'u kino e komo aku ma ke ano kolohe, he oleloa no. No ka mea, he kanaka hana pono oleia wau e na wahine, mai ko'u wa opiopio mai a hiki i ko'u hookanakamakua ana. Aia no ka'u wahine ae ke kii mai, no kekahi mau aina e mai, ina noloko mai o Moaulanuiakea, kahi o na wahine oluolu a'u i lohe ai; alaila, o ka'u wahine makemake ia, i na i kiiia mai wau ma na ano elua."

Iloko o ko Aiwohikupua lohe ana ia Kauakahialii, a me ko laua kuka mau ana me kona Kuhina Nui no Laieikawai, alaila, manaopaa ae la ke Alii no Tahiti mai ua wahine la.

I kekahi la, i ke awakea, hiamoe iho la ke Alii, loaa iho la o Laieikawai ia Aiwohikupua ma ka moeuhane, ua like kana ike ana ia Laieikawai ma ka moeuhane me ka Kauakahialii olelo ana ia ia. A puoho ae la ke Alii he moeuhane kana.

Iloko oia ala ana ae, aia hoi, he mea minamina loa i ke Alii i kona ike ana ia Laieikawai ma ka moeuhane, no ka mea, ua ala e mai ka hiamoe o ke Alii; a no ia mea, makemake iho la ke Alii e loaa hou ia ia ka hiamoe loihi ana ma ia awakea, i kumu e ike hou aku ai i kana mea i ike ai ma ka moeuhane.

Hoao hou iho la ke Alii e hiamoe hou, loaa hou no o Laieikawai ma ka hihio pokole loa, aole nae oia i ike maopopo loa aku, he wahi helehelena wale no kana ike lihi ana, a hikilele ae a oia.

A no keia mea, ua ano e loa ko ke Alii manao, ia manawa ka hoopuka ana a ke Alii i olelo paa imua o kona mau mea a pau, penei no ia:

"Auhea oukou, mai walaau oukou iloko o kuu wa hiamoe, mai hamumumu, a ina e walaau, he alii aimoku, e pau kona aimoku ana; ina lie alii aiahupuaa, e pau la; a ina he konohiki, a lopa paha ka mea nana i hahai kuu olelo paa, alaila, o ka make ka uku."

Oia iho la ka olelo paa a ke Alii, no ka mea, tia makemake loa ke Alii e loaa ia ia ka hiamoe loihi i kumu e launa hou ai laua ma ka moeuhane me Laieikawai.

A pau ka ke Alii olelo ana no keia mau mea, hoomaka hou oia e hiamoe, aole nae i loaa ia ia ka hiamoe a hiki i ka napoo ana o ka la.

Iloko o keia hana a ke Alii, aole nae oia i hai aku i keia mea ana e ike nei ma ka moeuhane, ua huna loa ke Alii i kona hoa kuka mau, manao la hoi oia, aia a loaa hou aku, alaila hai aku i kona hoa Kuhina Nui.

A no ka makemake loa o ke Alii e loaa mau ia ia ka moeuhane mau no Laieikawai, kauoha ae la oia i kona Kuhina Nui e mama i awa.

A nolaila, hoolale koke ae la ke Kuhina i na mea mama awa o ke Alii e mama i ka awa, a makaukau ko ke Alii makemake, a laweia mai la, inu iho la ke Alii me kona Kuhina, a oki mai la ka ona a ka awa. Kau koke mai la nae iluna o ke Alii ka halialia aloha o Laieikawai, me he mea ala ua launa kino mamua. Alaila, hapai ae la ia i wahi olelo ma ke mele penei:

"*Kau mai ana i o'u nei*
Ka halialia nae lehua o Puna,
I lawea mai e ka lau makani,
E ka ahe makani puulena o ka lua,
Hiamoe ole loko i ka minamina,
I ka makemake—e."

I aku la ke Kuhina o ke Alii, mahope iho o ka pau, ana o ke mele ana, "He mea kupanaha, aole hoi au wahine a kaua e noho nei, aka, iloko o kau mele e heluhelu nei, me he wahine la kau."

I mai la ke Alii, "Ua oki na olelo a kaua, no ka mea, ke oki mai nei ka ona o ka awa ia'u." Iloko oia manawa, haule aku la ke Alii i ka hiamoe nui, o ke oki no ia, no ka mea, ua poina loa ka hiamoe o ke Alii, ua ike ole ke Alii i kana mea e manao ai.

Hookahi po, hookahi ao o ka moe ana mama ka ona awa o ke Alii. Olelo aku la ke Alii i kona hoa kuka, "Ma keia ona awa o kaua, aole i waiwai iki."

I mai la kona hoa kuka, "Pehea la ka hoi ka waiwai o ka ona awa? Kainoa o ka ona no kona waiwai, o ka mahuna alua."

I mai la ke Alii, "Aole hoi paha oia, o ka ike aku ka hoi paha la ia Laieikawai, alaila waiwai ka ona ana o ka awa."

Mahope iho oia manawa, hoomau aku la ke Alii i ka inu awa a hala na la he nui, ua like paha me hookahi makahiki, aole nae ke Alii i ike i ka waiwai oia hana ana, nolaila, hoopau iho la ke Alii ia hana.

Mahope iho o ko ke Alii hoopau ana no ka inu awa, akahi no a hai aku ke Alii i ka loaa ana o Laieikawai ma ka moeuhane, a me ke kumu o kona hoomau ana i ka inu awa, a hai pu aku la no hoi ke Alii i ke kumu o kona kau ana i kanawai paa, no ka mea walaau iloko o kona wa hiamoe.

Ia laua e kamailio ana no keia mau mea, alaila, hoomaopopo loa ae la ke Alii e holo i Hawaii e ike ia Laieikawai. Ia wa ka hoopuka ana o laua i olelo hooholo no ke kii ia Laieikawai i wahine mare.

I ka pau ana o na la ino, a hiki mai ka manawa kupono no ka holo moana, kauoha ae la ke Kuhina i na Kapena waa o ke Alii, e hoomakaukau i na waa no ka holo i Hawaii ia po iho, ia manawa ke koho ana a ke Alii i na hoewaa kupono ke holo pu, ko ke Alii mau Iwikuamoo ponoi.

Mamua o ka napoo ana o ka la, kauohaia ka poe nana uli o ke Alii, a me na Kilokilo e nana i na ouli o ke ao a me ka moana, i na he hiki i ke Alii ke hele, a ina he hiki ole e like me ka mea mau; aka, ua maopopo i kona poe nana uli a Kilokilo hoi, he hiki i ke Alii ke hele i kana huakai.

A i ka wanaao, i ka puka ana o ka Hokuhookelewaa, kau aku la ke Alii a me kona Kuhina, na hoewaa he umikumamaono, na hookele elua, he iwakalua ko lakou nui maluna o na kaulua, a holo aku la.

Ia holo ana a lakou ma keia holo ana, hiki mua lakou ma Nanakuli, i Waianae, ia wanaao, haalele lakou ia wahi, hiki mua lakou i Mokapu, a malaila lakou i noho ai he umi la, no ka mea, ua loohia iakou e ka ino, hiki ole ke holo i Molokai. A pau na la he umi, ike maopopoia aku la ka malie, a maikai ka moana. Ia po iho a ao, hiki lakou i Polihua, ma

Lanai, a mailaila aku hiki ma Ukumehame, a no ka makani ino ia la, ua noho lakou malaila, a i kekahi la ae, haalele lakou ia wahi, hiki lakou i Kipahulu ia la.

Ia lakou ma Kipahulu, hooholo ae la ke Alii i olelo e hele wawae mauka, a ma na waa na kanaka. Ma kahi nae a lakou i noho ai, ua nui ka poe mahalo no Aiwohikupua no ke kanaka maikai.

Haalele lakou ia Kipahulu, hiki lakou ma Hana, ma uka no ke Alii me kona Kuhina, ma na waa no na kanaka. I ke Alii nae e hele ana, he nui ka poe i ukali ia laua, no ka makemake ia Aiwohikupua.

Ia lakou i hiki aku ai ma ke awa pae waa o Haneoo i Hana, he nue ka poe i lulumi mai e makaikai i ke Alii, no ka pakela o ka maikai.

Ia Aiwohikupua ma nae i hiki aku ai, e heenalu mai ana na kane a me na wahine i ka nalu o Puhele, aia nae ilaila kekahi kaikamahine Alii maikai kaulana o Hana, o Hinaikamalama kona inoa. Iloko hoi o ko laua ike ana i ua kaikamahine Alii nei o Hana, alaila, ua hoopuniia ke Alii kane, a me kona Kuhina e na kuko; a oia no hoi ke kumu o ko Aiwohikupua ma noho ana malaila ia la.

A pau ka heenalu ana a na kamaaina, a i ka nalu pau loa o ko Hinaikamalama hee ana, o ka nalu ia i pae, hoopolilei mai la ka hee ana a ke kaikamahine Alii ma ka wai o Kumaka, kahi hoi a Aiwohikupua ma e noho mai ana.

I ke kaikamahine Alii nae e auau ana i ka wai o Kumaka, ua hoopuiwaia ke Alii kane, a me kona Kuhina e ke kuko ino. A no ia mea, iniki malu aku la ke Kuhina o ke Alii ia Aiwohikupua, e hookaawale ia lana mai kahi a Hinaikamalama e auau ana, i ole laua e pilikia ma ka manao.

Ia Aiwohikupua ma i hoomaka ai e hookaawale ia laua mai ko ke Alii wahine wahi e auau ana, alaila, pane aku la ke Alii wahine, "E na'lii! he holo ka hoi ka olua, kainoa hoi he wehe ko ke kapa, lele iho hoi he wai, hookahi hoi ka auau ana o kakou, hoi aku he hale, a moe, he ai no, he i-a no hoi, a he wahi moe no hoi, oia iho la no ka waiwai a ke kamaaina, i makemake no hoi e hele, hele no, ina he makemake e noho, o Hana no hoi nei noho iho."

A no keia olelo a ke Alii wahine, I aku la ke Kuhina i ke Alii, "E! pono ha ka manao o ke Alii wahine, no ka mea, ua makemake loa ke Alii wahine ia oe."

I mai la o Aiwohikupua, "Ua makemake au i ke Alii wahine, no ka mea, ke ike lea nei au i ka oi loa o kona maikai mamua o ka'u mau wahine mua nana i kumakaia; aka, ua lohe oe i ka'u hoohiki paa ana, aole au e lawe mai i kekahi wahine o keia mau moku i wahine na'u."

A no keia olelo a Aiwohikupua, i aku kona Kuhina, "Ua laa oe no kela hoohiki au, alaila, e aho na'u ka wahine a kaua."

A pau keia kamailio liilii ana a laua, hele aku la laua i ka heenalu. A ia laua e heenalu ana, aia hoi, ua hoopuniia mai la ke Alii wahine no Aiwohikupua, a ua nui ka poe i hoopuni paaia no ka makemake i ke Alii kane.

A pau ka auau ana a laua, hoi aku la laua me ka manao e kau maluna o na waa a holo aku; aka, ike aku la o Aiwohikupua i ke Alii wahine e konane mai ana, a manao iho la ke Alii kane malihini e hele i ke konane; aka, ua lilo mua na ke Alii wahine ke kahea e konane laua.

A hiki o Aiwohikupua ma kahi o ke Alii wahine, kau na ilili a paa ka papa, ninau mai ke Alii wahine, "Heaha ke kumu pili o ka malihini ke make i ke kamaaina?"

I aku o Aiwohikupua, "He mau waa kaulua ko'u kumu pili, aia ke lana mai la iloko o ke kai, oia ko'u kumu pili me oe."

I mai la ke Alii wahine, "Aole he maikai o kou kumu pili e ka malihini, hookahi no kumu pili mama loa, oia na kino no o kaua, ina e make au ia oe, alaila, e lilo wau nau, ma kau hana e olelo mai ai, malaila wau e hoolohe ai, a e hooko ai hoi, ma ka mea kupono nae i ka hooko aku, a ina hoi e make oe ia'u, alaila, o oe no ka'u, e like me kau hana ia'u, pela no au e hana ai ia oe, me ko noho i Maui nei."

A no keia olelo a ke Alii wahine, hooholo koke ae la ke Alii kane i ka olelo ae. I ka hahau ana a laua i ka papa mua, make o Aiwohikupua.

Alaila, i mai la ke Alii wahine, "Ua eo ia'u, aohe ou kumu e ae e pili mai ai, a ina nae he kaikaina kou, alaila ae aku au e pili hou kaua."

A no keia mau olelo maikai a ke Alii wahine imua o Aiwohikupua, alaila, hooholo koke ae la oia i kona manao ae ma ka waha wale no.

A iloko o ko laua manawa kamailio, hoopuka aku la o Aiwohikupua i kona manao imua o ke Alii wahine, "He nani hoi ia ua pili ae nei ko'u kino me oe, a ua maikai no; aka, aole kaua e launa koke, aia a hoi mai au mai kuu kuakai kaapuni ia Hawaii; no ka mea, ua hoohiki wau mamua o kuu holo ana mai nei, aole wau e launa me kekahi o na wahine e ae, aia no a puni o Hawaii, alaila, hana wau e like me kuu makemake, e like me ka kaua e kamailio nei, a oia hoi ka hookoia ana o kou makemake. Nolaila, ke kauoha mua aku nei wau ia oe mamua o kuu hele ana, e noho oe me ka maluhia loa, aole e lilo i kekahi mea e ae, aole hoi e hana iki i kekahi mea pono ole e keakea ai i ka kaua hoohiki, a hoi mai wau mai kuu huakai makaikai mai, alaila, e hookoia ke kumu pili o ka wahine Alii. Ina i hoi mai wau, aole oe i maluhia, aole hoi oe i hooko i ka'u mau kauoha, alaila, o ka pau no ia."

Aole nae keia o ko Aiwohikupua manao maoli. A pau na kauoha a Aiwohikupua ia Hinaikamalama, haalele lakou ia Maui, hiki lakou nei i Kapakai ma Kohala.

I kekahi la ae, haalele lakou ia Kapakai, holo aku la lakou a mawaho pono o Kauhola, nana aku la o Aiwohikupua i ka akoakoa lehulehu ana o na kanaka mauka o Kapaau.

Ia manawa, kauoha ae la o Aiwohikupua i na hoewaa, e hookokoke aina aku na waa, no ka mea, ua makemake ke Alii e ike i ke kumu o keia akoakoa lehulehu ana o na kanaka.

A hiki lakou i ke awa pae waa ma Kauhola, ninau aku la ke Alii i ke kumu o ka akoakoa lehulehu ana o na kanaka, alaila, hai mai la na kamaaina, he aha mokomoko ke kumu o ia lehulehu ana.

Ia manawa, okalakala koke ae la o Aiwohikupua e hele e makaikai i ka aha mokomoko, a hekau iho la na waa o lakou, pii aku la o Aiwohikupua, a me kona Kuhina, a me na hookele elua, eha ko lakou nui o ka pii ana.

A hiki lakou i Hinakahua i ke kahua mokomoko, ia manawa, ike mai la ka aha mokomoko i ke keiki Kauai, no ka oi o kona kanaka maikai mamua o na keiki kamaaina, a lilo iho la ka aha i mea haunaele.

Mahope iho o keia haunaele ana, hoomaka hou ka hoonoho o ke kahua mokomoko, ia manawa, pili aku la o Aiwohikupua ma ke kumu laau milo, e nana ana no ka hoouka kaua.

Ia Aiwohikupua nae e ku ana ma kona wahi, puka mai la o Ihuanu a ku iwaena o ke kahua mokomoko, e hoike ana ia ia iho imua o ke anaina, a kahea mai la me ka leo nui, "Owai ka mea ma kela aoao mai e hele mai e mokomoko?" Aka, aole e hiki i kekahi mea ke aa mai e ku imua o Ihuanu, no ka mea, o ko Kohala oi kelakela no ia ma ka ikaika i ke kuikui.

Ia Ihuanu e hoike ana ia ia iho, huli ae la oia, a ike ia Aiwohikupua, kahea mai la, "Pehea oe e ka malihini? E pono paha ke lealea?"

A lohe o Aiwohikupua i keia leo kahea a Ihuanu, hele aku la a ku imua o ke kahua kaua, e hawele ana me kona aahu pukohukohu, i like me ke ano mau o na Puali o ke Alii. Pane aku la oia imua o kona hoa hakaka.

"E ke kamaaina, ua noi nai oe ia'u e lealea kaua, a eia hoi ka'u noi ia oe, i elua mai ma kou aoao, huipu me oe, akolu oukou, alaila mikomiko iki iho ka malihini."

A lohe o Ihuanu i keia olelo a Aiwohikupua, i mai la oia, "He oi oe o ke kanaka nana i olelo hookano iho nei wau imua o keia aha a pau, owau no ka oi mamua o na kanaka a pau, a ke olelo mai nei hoi oe i ekolu aku ma keia aoao, a heaha la oe i mua o'u?"

Olelo mai la o Aiwohikupua, "Aole au e aa aku e hakaka me oe ma kau noi, ke ole oe e ku mai me na mea e ae ma kou aoao, a heaha hoi oe imua o'u! Nolaila, ke olelo paa nei wau ano, he hiki ia'u ke hoolilo i keia Aha i mea ole iloko o kuu lima."

A no keia olelo a Aiwohikupua, hele mai la kekahi o na puali ikaika a ma ke kua o Aiwohikupua, olelo mai la. "E! mai olelo aku oe ia Ihuanu, o ko Kohala oi no kela; aohe puko momona o Kohala nei i kela kanaka."

Ia manawa, huli ae la o Aiwohikupua, a pale ae la i ka mea nana i olelo mai ma kona kua, haula aku la ilalo a make loa.

Mokuna V

A ike mai la ka aha kanaka a pau o ke kahua mokomoko i ka oi ana o ka ikaika o Aiwohikupua, no ka make loa ana o ke kanaka ma ke pale wale ana no.

Ia manawa, hele mai la kekahi mau puali o Ihuanu, a olelo mai la ia Ihuanu penei: "E Ihuanu e! ke ike maopopo lea aku nei wau ano i keia manawa, aole e lanakila ana ko kakou aoao, a ma kuu manao paa hoi, e lanakila ana ka malihini maluna o kakou, no ka mea, ke ike maopopo aku la no oe, ua make loa ko kakou kanaka i ka welau wale no o koia la lima, ahona a kui maoli aku kela, lele liilii. Nolaila, ke noi aku nei au ia oe, e hui ka aha, e pono ke hoopau ka mokomoko ana, a me kou aa ana aku i ka malihini, a nolaila, e hele oe a i ka malihini, e lulu lima olua, a e haawi aku i kou aloha nona, i aloha pu ai olua me ka ike aku o ka aha ua hoomoe a pau wale ke kaua."

Iloko o keia olelo, alaila, ua ho-ai'a ka inaina wela o Ihuanu no keia olelo, me ka olelo aku, "E ko'u poe kokua, mai maka'u oukou, mai hopohopo no ka make ana o kela kanaka o kakou ma ke pale ana i ka welau o kona lima, aole anei wau i hana pela i kekahi mau la mamua ae nei maanei? A heaha la oukou i maka'u ai; a nolaila, ke hai aku nei wau ia oukou, ina i hopo oukou no kela malihini, alaila, e huna oukou i ko oukou mau maka i ke aouli, aia a lohe aku oukou ua lanakila o Ihuanu, alaila, hoomanao oukou i kuu puupuu ia Kanikapiha, ka ai a ke kumu i ao oleia ia oukou. No ka mea, ke ike nei wau, aole e lanakila mai oia maluna o'u, no ka mea, ua kani ka pola o kuu malo i keia la."

A no keia olelo a Ihuanu, i aku kona mau hoa hui mokomoko, "Auhea oe! Ua pau ka makou olelo, aohe hana i koe, kulia imua o ka ai a ke kumu a kakou i ao pu oleia mai ia makou, a ke olelo mai nei hoi oe, ua kani ka pola o ko malo, malia o lanakila oe i ua malo ou." Alaila, nee aku la kona mau hoa mawaho o ka aha.

Ia Ihuanu nae e olelo kaena ana ia ia iho imua o kona mau hoa no kona lanakila maluna o Aiwohikupua, alaila, oi mai la o Aiwohikupua a kokoke iki ma ke alo o Ihuanu, upoipoi ae la oia i kona mau lima ma ka poohiwi, me he moa kane la e hoomakaukau ana no ke kani ana, a olelo aku la oia ia Ihuanu, "E Ihuanu! Kuiia i kuu piko a pololei i eha kauna kui?"

A lohe o Ihuanu i keia kaena a Aiwohikupua e kui, alaila, leha ae la na maka o Ihuanu a puni ka aha, ike aku la oia e hiiia mai ana kekahi keiki opiopio loa, alaila, olelo aku la o Ihuanu ia Aiwohikupua, "Aole na'u oe e kui, na kela wahi keiki e hiiia mai la, nana oe e kui, a oia kou hoa hakaka."

A lohe o Aiwohikupua i keia olelo, he mea e kona ukiuki, ia manawa, pii ae la ka ula o Aiwohikupua a puni ke kino, me he mea la ua hooluuia i ke koko o na hipa keiki. Huli ae la oia a kupono imua o ka aha, a olelo aku la, "Owai keia kanaka i aa mai ai oia i ke keiki Kauai nei, nolaila, ke olelo nei wau i keia, he hiki i kuu Akua ke haawi mai ia'u e lanakila maluna o keia kanaka, a e hoolilo ae kuu Akua i ke poo o ko oukou ikaika i mea milimili na kuu mau hoewaa."

Alaila, kukuli iho la o Aiwohikupua a pule aku la i kona mau Akua penei: "E Lanipipili, Lanioaka, Lanikahuliomealani, e Lono, e Hekilikaakaa, a me Nakolowailani, i keia la, e ike mai oukou ia'u i ka oukou kama, ka oukou pua i koe ma ke ao nei, ma keia la, e haawi mai oukou i ka ikaika a pau maluna o ka oukou kama nei, e hiki no ia oukou ke hoohala i kana puupuu ma kona kui ana mai i ka oukou kama, a ke noi aku nei wau e haawi mai i ke poo o Ihuanu i kuu lima, i mea paani na ko'u mau hoewaa, i ike ai keia aha a pau, owau ke lanakila maluna o keia kanaka i Okipoepoe Oleia. Amene." (Amama.)

A pau kana pule ana, ku ae la o Aiwohikupua iluna me ka maka ikaika a makaukau no ka hoouka kaua, a ninau aku la ia Ihuanu, "Ua makaukau anei oe e kue mai ia'u?"

Olelo mai la o Ihuanu, "Aole au e kui aku ia oe, nau e kui mua mai ia'u."

A lohe ke kumu kui a Ihuanu i keia mau olelo, hele mai la a ma ka aoao o Ihuanu, i mai la, "Hawawa oe e kuu haumana, ina e kena hou mai kela, alaila, e hoomaka oe e kui me kou ikaika a pau, no ka mea, o kona manawa e kena mai ai e kui, oia iho la no ka hoomaka ana," a nolaila, ua pono keia ia Ihuanu.

A pau ka laua kamailio ana, ninau hou aku la o Aiwohikupua ia Ihuanu, "Ua makaukau anei oe e kui mai ia'u; ina he manao e kui, kui mai I kuu maka."

Ia manawa, i waiho koke mai ana o Ihuanu i ka puupuu, hu ka makani ma ka papalina o Aiwohikupua, aole nae i ku, no ka mea, ua alo o Aiwohikupua, oia ka mea i hala'i.

A hala ka puupuu a Ihuanu, e waiho koke ae ana o Aiwohikupua i kana puupuu, ku no i ka houpo, hula ma ke kua; ia manawa, kaikai ae la o Aiwohikupua i ke kanaka me kona lima, a kowali ae la ia Ihuanu imua o ke anaina, a kiola aku la i waho o ka aha, a lanakila iho la o Aiwohikupua maluna o Ihuanu uwauwa aku la ka pihe me ka hui o ka aha i ka poe makaikai.

A make iho la o Ihuanu, hele mai la kona mau hoa, e waiho ana, na mea hoi nana i olelo mai e hooki ka hakaka, me ka ninau iho, "E Ihuanu! ua hiki anei i ko ai i ao oleia ia makou ke hoola ia oe, e hakaka hou me kela kanaka ikaika lua ole?" Oia ke olelo henehene a kona mau hoa.

I ka lehulehu e lulumi ana no ka make o Ihuanu ko lakou Pukaua, a e uwe ana hoi, hele aku la o Aiwohikupua, a oki ae la i ke poo o Ihuanu, a me ka laau palau a Ihuanu, a kiola aku la i kona mau hookele, oia ka hooko hope loa ana o kana pule. A pau keia mau mea, haalele o Aiwohikupua i ka aha, a hoi aku la a kau iluna o na waa, a holo aku la, kui aku la ka lono o keia make a puni o Kohala, Hamakua, a puni o Hawaii.

Holo aku la lakou nei a kau i Honokaape, ma Waipio, mailaila aku a waho o Paauhau, nana ae la lakou e ku ana ka ea o ka lepo o uka, ninau aku la o Aiwohikupua i kona Kuhina, "Heaha la kela lehulehu e paapu mai nei o uka? He mokomoko no paha? Ina he aha mokomoko kela, e hele hou kaua e makaikai."

Olelo aku la kona Kuhina, "Ua oki ia manao ou, no ka mea, aole he huakai mokomoko ka kaua i hele mai nei, he huakai imi wahine ka kaua."

I mai o Aiwohikupua i ke Kuhina, "Kaheaia aku na hookele, e hooponopono ae na waa a holo pololei aku i ke awa, i lohe aku kakou i keia lehulehu." A hookoia ko ke Alii makemake, a holo aku lakou a malalo o ka pali kahakai, ninau aku la i na wahine e kuiopihi ana, "Heaha kela lehulehu o uka?"

Hai mai la na wahine ia lakou, "He aha hookuku mokomoko, a o ka mea oi o ka ikaika, alaila, oia ke hoounaia e hele e kuikui me ke kanaka

Kauai i hakaka mai nei me Ihuanu, a make mai nei ua o Ihuanu; oia ia pihe e uwa ala."

A no keia mea, kena koke ae la o Aiwohikupua e hekau na waa, a lele aku la o Aiwohikupua, o kona Kuhina aku me na hookele elua, pii aku la lakou nei a hiki i ka aha mokomoko, aia nae lakou ma kahi kaawale mai e nana ana i ka aha.

Alaila, hele mai la kekahi kamaaina ma ko lakou nei wahi e noho ana, ninau aku la o Aiwohikupua i ka hana a ka aha, haiia mai la e like me ka olelo a kela mau wahine i olelo ai.

Olelo aku la o Aiwohikupua i kahi kamaaina, "E hele oe a olelo aku, owau kekahi e lealea me keia poe, aole nae e lealea me ka poe ikaika ole."

I mai la ua wahi kamaaina nei, "Hookahi no ikaika o keia aha o Haunaka, a oia ke hoounaia ana i Kohala, e hakaka me ke kanaka Kauai."

Olelo aku la o Aiwohikupua, "E hele koke oe, a olelo aku ia Haunaka e lealea maua."

A hiki aku ua wahi kanaka kamaaina nei a halawai me Haunaka; a lohe o Haunaka i keia mau olelo, lulu iho la oia i kona mau lima, paipai ae la i ka umauma, keekeehi na wawae, a peahi mai la ia Aiwohikupua e hele aku iloko o ka aha, a hele aku la o Aiwohikupua, a wehe ae la i kona kihei, a kaei ae la ma kona puhaka.

Ia Aiwohikupua ma ka aha, olelo aku la oia imua o Haunaka, "Aole e eha ke keiki Kauai ia oe, he lala kamahele no ka laau ku i ka pali."

Ia manawa a Aiwohikupua e kamailio ana no keia mau mea, kahea mai la mawaho o ka aha he wahi kanaka i ike i ka hakaka ana a Aiwohikupua me Ihuanu, "E Haunaka, a me ka aha, aole oukou e pakele i keia kanaka, ua like ka puupuu o keia kanaka me ka pololu, hookahi no kui ia Ihuanu, hula pu ka puupuu ma ke kua, a o ke kanaka no keia i make mai nei o Ihuanu."

Ia manawa, lalau mai la o Haunaka i na lima o Aiwohikupua, a aloha mai la oia, a o ka pau no ia, hoaikane laua, hui ka aha. A haalele lakou ia wahi, hele pu aku la o Aiwohikupua ma me ke aikane a kau lakou la ma na waa, a holo aku la a pae i Laupahoehoe.

Mokuna VI

(Ma ka Mokuna V o keia Kaao, ua ike kakou ua hiki aku a Aiwohikupua ma Laupahoehoe; maanei e kamailio iki kakou no Hulumaniani ka Makaula nana i ukali mai o Laieikawai, mai Kauai mai, ka mea i olelomuaia ma ka helu mua o keia Kaao.)

I ka la a Aiwohikupua ma i haalele ai ia Paauhau, ma Hamakua, i ka la hoi i holo mai ai a hiki i Laupahoehoe, ua ike mua aku ka Makaula i na mea a pau i kekahi ahiahi iho mamua o ko Aiwohikupua hiki ana ma Laupahoehoe, a penei kona ike ana:

I ua ahiahi la, mamua o ka napoo ana o ka la, e noho ana ka Makaula ma ka puka o ka hale, nana aku la oia i ke kuku o na opua ma ka nana ana i na ouli o ke ao, a like me ka mea mau i ka poe kilokilo mai ka wa kahiko mai a hiki i keia manawa.

I aku la ua Makaula nei, "He waa Alii hoi keia e holo mai nei, he umikumamaiwa kanaka, hookahi Alii Nui, he mau waa kaulua nae."

Ia manawa, puiwa koke ae la ka lehulehu e noho pu ana me ka Makaula, a nana aku la aole he mau waa holo mai; nolaila, ninau aku la ka poe me ia, "Auhea hoi na waa au i olelo mai nei he mau waa Alii?"

Olelo aku ka Makaula, "Aole he mau waa maoli, ma ka opua ka'u ike ana aku la, apopo e ike kakou he waa Alii."

Ia po a ao ae, mahope o ka auina la ike hou aku la oia i ke ku a ka punohu i ka moana, ma ka hoailona i ku ia Aiwohikupua e like me ka mea i maa i ua Makaula nei. (E like paha me ka ike ana i ke Kalaunu Moi o kela Alii keia Alii ke hiki mai io kakou nei, pela paha ka maopopo ana o ko Aiwohikupua punohu i ikeia e ua Makaula nei.)

A no ka ike ana o ka Makaula i kela hoailona, ku ae la oia a hopu he wahi puaa, he moa lawa, me ka puawa, e hoomakaukau ana no ka hiki mai o Aiwohikupua.

A no keia hana a ka Makaula, he mea haohao loa ia i ko lakou poe, me ka ninau aku, "E hele ana oe e hoomakaukau nei keia ukana au?"

Hai mai la ka Makaula, "E hoomakaukau mua ana wau no ka hiki mai o kau Alii o Aiwohikupua, oia kela mea a'u i olelo aku ai ia oukou i ke ahiahi nei, nolaila, eia oia ke holo mai nei i ka moana, nona kela kualau i ka moana, a me keia noe e uhi nei."

A kokoke o Aiwohikupua ma i ke awa pae o Laupahoehoe, ia manawa ke kui ana o na hekili he iwakalua, pili pu na kanaka o Hilo nokeia mea, a i ka mao ana ae, ike aku la na mea a pau i keia kaulua e holo mai ana a pae i ke awa, me ka puloulou Alii iluna o na waa, alaila, maopopo ae la ka wanana a ka Makaula

I na waa e holo mai ana a pae, ku ana ka Makaula i ke awa, mai luna mai o Kaiwilahilahi, hahau iho la ka Makaula i ka puaa imua o ke Alii, a pule aku la oia ma ka inoa o na Akua o Aiwohikupua, a eia kana pule.

"E Lanipipili, e Lanioaka, e Lanikahuliomealani, e Lono, e Hekilikaakaa, e Nakolowailani. E na Akua o kuu Alii, kuu milimili, kuu ihi kapu, ka mea nana e kalua keia mau iwi. Eia ka puaa, ka moa lawa, ka awa, he makana, he mohai, he kanaenae i ke Alii na ka oukou kauwa nei, e ike i ka oukou kauwa ia Hulumaniani homai he ola, i ola nui, i ola loa, a kau i ka puaneane, a kani koo, a palalauhala, a haumakaiola, amama, ua noa, lele wale aku la."

Ia manawa a ke Alii e hoolohe ana i ka pule a ka Makaula, ike mai la o Aiwohikupua, o kana Makaula keia, ua mokumokuahua ka manawa o ke Alii i ke aloha i kana kauwa, no ka mea, ua loihi ka manawa o ka nalo ana, aole no hoi i ikeia ka manawa i nalo ai.

A pau ka pule ana a ua Makaula nei, kena koke ae ana o Aiwohikupua i kona Kuhina, "E haawi na makana a ka Makaula na na Akua."

Lele koke aku la ka Makaula a hopu i na wawae o ke Alii, a kau iho la iluna o ka a-i, a uwe iho la; a o Aiwohikupua hoi, apo aku la ma na poohiwi o kana kauwa, a uwe helu iho la.

A pau ka uwe ana, ninau iho la ke Alii i kana kauwa, "Heaha kou mea i hiki mai ai a noho ianei; a pehea ka loihi o kou hele ana."

Hai aku la ke kauwa e like me ka kakou heluhelu ana ma na Mokuna mua. Ia manawa a ka Makaula i olelo aku ai i ke Alii i na kumu a me na kuleana o kona hele ana, a pau ia. Alaila, na ka Makaula ka ninau hope ia Aiwohikupua; aka hoi, ma ka paewaewa o ka ke Alii olelo ana, me ka olelo aku, e huakai kaapuni kana.

Walea iho la ke Alii me ka Makaula ia po a wanaao, hoo makaukau na waa, a holo aku la.

Holo aku la lakou mai Laupahoehoe aku a hiki lakou i waho o Makahanaloa, nana aku la ua wahi kanaka nei (ka mea i kapaia he Kuhina), i ka pio mai a ke anuenue iuka o Paliuli.

Olelo aku la oia i ke Alii, "E! auhea oe? E nana oe i kela anuenue e pio mai la, aia ilaila o Laieikawai, ka mea a kaua e kii nei, a malaila no kahi i loaa ai ia'u."

Olelo aku la o Aiwohikupua, "Ke manao nei wau aole kela o Laieikawai, aole no nona kela anuenue, no ka mea, he mea mau no ia no na wahi ua a pau, he pio no ke anuenue. Nolaila, ke noi aku nei wau ia oe, e kali kaua a ike ia mai ka malie ana, a ikeia aku ka pio mai o ke anuenue iloko o ka manawa malie, alaila maopopo nona kela hoailona."

A ma keia olelo a ke Alii, hekau iho la na waa o lakou i ke kai, pii aku la o Aiwohikupua me kona Kuhina a hiki i Kukululaumania, ma ke kauhale o na kamaaina, a noho iho la malaila e kali ana no ka malie o ka ua. A hala na la eha malaila, haalele loa ka malie o Hilo, ike maopopoia aku la ke kalae ana mai o ka aina, a waiho wale mai o Panaewa.

I ka eha o ka la, i ke kakahiaka nui, ala ae la o Aiwohikupua, a puka aku la mawaho o ka hale, aia hoi, e pio mai ana no ke anuenue i kahi a laua i ike mua ai, kakali, loihi iho la ke Alii a hiki i ka puka ana o ka la, hoi aku la a kona Kuhina aia kela e hiamoe ana, hooala aku la, me ka i aku i ke Kuhina, "E! pono io paha kau e olelo nei, ia'u no kakahiaka poeleele, ala e aku nei no wau iwaho, ike aku nei no au, e pio mai ana ke anuenue i kahi no au i kuhikuhi ai ia'u, i ke kali mai la no wau a puka ka la, aia no ke mau la ke anuenue, hoi mai la wau hoala aku nei ia oe."

Olelo aku la ua wahi kanaka nei, "O ka'u ia e olelo aku ana ia oe, e holo kakou, i na paha aia kakou i uka o Paliuli kahi i noho ai i keia mau la."

Ia kakahiaka, haalele lakou ia Makahanaloa, holo waho na waa o lakou, o Keaau ke awa.

Ia holo ana o lakou a ahiahi, pae lakou i Keaau, nana aku la lakou e ku mai ana no na hale o Kauakahialii ma, e heenalu mai ana no hoi na kamaaina; a hiki lakou, mahalo mai la na kamaaina no Aiwohikupua e like me kona ano mau.

Noho malihini iho la lakou ia Keaau, a ahiahi, kauoha mua iho la o Aiwohikupua i na hookele a me na hoewaa, e noho malie a hoi mai laua mai ka laua huakai imi wahine mai, oiai o lakou wale no.

I ka napoo ana o ka la, hopu aku la o Aiwohikupua i kona aahu Ahuula, a haawi aku la i kahi kanaka, a pii aku la.

Pii aku la laua iloko o na ululaau loloa, i ka hihia paa o ka nahelehele, me ka luhi, a hiki laua ma kahi e kokoke ana i Paliuli, lohe laua i ka leo o ka moa. I aku la kahi kanaka i ke Alii, "Kokoke puka kaua."

Hoomau aku la no laua i ka pii a lohe hou laua i ka leo o ka moa (o ka moa kualua ia). Hoomau aku laua i ka pii a hiki i ka malamalama loa ana.

I aku la kahi kanaka i ke Alii, "E! puka kaua, aia ke kupunawahine o Laieikawai ke houluulu mai la i na moa, e like me kana hana mau."

Ninau aku la o Aiwohikupua, "Auhea ka hale o ke Alii Wahine?"

I aku la kahi kanaka, "Aia a puka lea aku kaua iwaho o ka mahinaai nei la, alaila, ike maopopo leaia aku ka hale."

A maopopo ia Aiwohikupua, ke kokoke hiki o laua i ka hale o Laieikawai, nonoi aku la oia e haawi mai kahi kanaka i ka ahuula, i paa iho ai o Aiwohikupua ia mea ma kona lima, a hiki i ko laua launa ana me ke Alii wahine o Paliuli.

A hala ka mahinaai, ike aku la laua i ka hale o Laieikawai, ua uhiia me no hulu melemele o ka Oo, e like me ka alelo a ke akua i ka Makaula, ma ka hihio iluna o Kauwiki.

Ia Aiwohikupua e nana ana i ka hale o ke Alii wahine o Paliuli, he mea e ke kahaha a me ka hilahila, ia manawa ka hoomaka ana o ko Aiwohikupua kanalua ana.

A no ke kanalua i loaa ia Aiwohikupua, olelo aku oia i kona kokoolua, "Auhea oe, ua hele mai nei kaua me ka manao ikaika no kuu wahine, kuhi iho nei wau, he wahine a lohe mai i ke ao, aole ka! i ike aku nei ka hana i ka hale o ke Alii Wahine, aole no ona lua, nolaila, ano e hoi kaua me ka launa ole."

I mai la kona Kuhina, "He mea kupanaha, a hiki ka hoi kaua i ka hale o ko wahine, ka kaua mea i au mai nei i keia mau kai ewalua, eia ka hoi he koi kau e hoi; e hele no kaua a launa, aia mai ilaila ka nele a me ka loaa; no ka mea, ina no paha ia e hoole mai, hoomano aku no, ua akaka no he waa naha i kooka ko kaua, ko ke kane."

"Auhea oe?" Wahi a Aiwohikupua, "Aole e hiki ia kaua ke hele e halawai me ke Alii wahine, a aole no hoi e Ioaa; no ka mea, ke ike nei wau, ua ano e loa ka hale. Ua lawe mai nei au i ko'u ahuula, i makana e haawi aku ai i ke Alii wahine e Paliuli nei; aka, ke nana aku nei wau o ke pili iho la ia o ka hale o ke Alii; no ka mea, ua ike no oe, o keia mea, he ahuula aole ia e loaa i na mea e ae, i na Alii aimoku wale no e loaa'i, nolaila, e hoi kaua." O ka hoi iho la no ia me ka launa ole.

Mokuna VII

Ia Aiwohikupua ma i haalele ai ia Paliuli, hoi aku la laua a hiki i Keaau, hoomakaukau na waa, a ma ia wanaao, kau maluna o na waa, a hoi i Kauai.

Ma ia hoi ana, aole nae i hai aku o Aiwohikupua i kekahi kumu o ka hoi ana, aia i ka hiki ana i Kauai, ma keia hoi ana, akahi no a ike kona Kuhina i ke kumu.

Ma keia holo ana mai Keaau mai, a kau i Kamaee, ma Hilopaliku, a ma kekahi la ae, haalele lakou ia laila, hiki lakou i Humuula, ma ka palena o Hilo, me Hamakua, ia manawa ka ike ana mai a ka Makaula ia Aiwohikupua e holo ana i ka moana.

A hala hope o Humuula ia lakou, hiki lakou mawaho pono o Kealakaha, ike mai la lakou nei i keia wahine e noho ana i ka pali kahakai, e hiamoe ana nae ke Alii ia manawa.

Ia lakou i ike aku ai i kela wahine, hooho ana lakou iluna o na waa, "E! ka wahine maikai hoi!"

A no keia, hikilele ae la ka hiamoe o Aiwohikupua, ninau ae la i ka lakou mea e walaau nei, haiia aku la, "He wahine maikai aia ke noho mai la i ka pali." Alawa ae la ke Alii, a ike aku la he mea e o ka wahine maikai.

A no keia mea, kauoha ae la ke Alii i na hoewaa e hoe pololei aku ma kahi a ka wahine e noho mai ana, a holo aku la a kokoke, halawai mua iho la lakou me ke kanaka e paeaea ana, ninau aku la, "Owai kela wahine e noho mai la iluna o ka pali maluna pono ou?"

Haiia mai la, "O Poliahu."

A no ka manao nui o ke Alii e ike i kela wahine, peahiia aku la, a iho koke mai la kela me kona aahukapa i hoopuniia i ka hau, a haawi mai la i kona aloha ia Aiwohikupua, a aloha aku la no hoi ke Alii kane i kona aloha ma ka lululima ana.

Ia laua e halawai malihini ana, i aku o Aiwohikupua "E Poliahu e! E ka wahine maikai o ka pali, pomaikai wale wau ia oe ma ko kaua halawai ana iho nei, a no aila, e ke Alii wahine o ka pali nei, ke makemake nei wau e lawe oe ia'u i kane hoao nau, a e noho kanaka lawelawe aku malalo ou, ma kau mau olelo e olelo ai, a malaile wale no wau. Ina hoi e ae oe e lawe ia'u e like me ka'u e noi aku nei ia oe, alaila, e kau kaua maluna o na waa, a holo aku i Kauai, a pehea ia?"

I mai la ka wahine, "Aole wau he wahine no keia pali, no uka lilo mai wau, mai ka piko mai o kela mauna, e aahu mau ana i na kapa keokeo e like me keia kapa a'u e aahu aku nei. A pehea la i hikiwawe ai ka loaa ana o ko'u inoa ia oe e ke Alii?"

Olelo aku la o Aiwohikupua, "Akahi no wau a maopopo no Maunakea mai oe, a ua loaa koke kou inoa ia makou ma ka haiia ana e kela kanaka paeaea."

"A no kau noi e ke Alii," wahi a Poliahu, "E lawe wau ia oe i kane na'u, a nolaila, ke hai aku nei wau ia oe, me ka ninau aku; aole anei o oe ke Alii i ku iluna a hoohiki ma ka inoa o kou mau Akua, aole oe e lawe i hookahi wahine o keia mau mokupuni, mai Hawaii nei, a Kauai; aia kau wahine lawe noloko mai o Moaulanuiakea? Aole anei oe i hoopalau me Hinaikamalama, ke kaikamahine Alii kaulana o Hana? A pau ko huakai kaapuni ia Hawaii nei, alaila, hoi aku a hoao olua? A no kau noi mai e lawe kaua ia kaua i mau mea hoohui nolaila, ke hai aku nei wau ia oe; aia a hoopau oe i kau hoohiki mua, alaila, aole na'u e lawe ia oe, nau no e lawe ia'u a hui kaua e like me kou makemake."

A no keia olelo a Poliahu, pili pu iho la ko Aiwohikupua manao me ke kaumaha no hoi; a liuliu hoopuka aku la o Aiwohikupua i wahi ninau pokole penei, "Pehea la oe i ike ai, a i lohe ai hoi no ka'u mau hana au e hai mai nei? He oiaio, e Poliahu e, o na mea a pau au e olelo mai nei, ua hana wau e like me ia nolaila, e hai mai i ka mea nana i olelo aku ia oe."

"Aole o'u mea nana i hai mai i keia mau mea, e ke Alii kane, no'u iho no ko'u ike," wahi a ke Alii wahine, "no ka mea, ua hanau kupuaia mai wau e like me oe, a ua loaa no ia'u ka ike mai ke Akua mai o ko'u mau kupuna a hooili ia'u, e like me oe, a na ia Akua wau i kuhikuhi mai e like me ka'u e olelo nei ia oukou. Ia oukou no e holo mai ana i Humuula, ua ike wau nou na waa, a pela wau i ike ai ia oe."

A no keia olelo, kukuli iho la o Aiwohikupua, a hoomaikai aku la imua o Poliahu, me ke noi aku e lilo ia i kane hoopalau na Poliahu, me ke noi aku e holo pu i Kauai.

"Aole kaua e holo pu i Kauai," wahi a ka wahine, "aka, e kau wau me oukou a Kohala, hoi mai wau, alaila hoi oukou."

Mai ka hoomaka ana e halawai na'lii a hiki i ka pau ana o na olelo a laua, iluna no o na waa keia mau kamailio ana.

Mamua o ka holo ana, olelo aku ka wahine ia Aiwohikupua, "Ke holo pu nei kakou, e hookaawale mai ko'u wahi, kaawale aku ko olua wahi, aole o na kanaka, ua akaka ko lakou wahi, mai hoopa mai oukou ia'u, aole hoi au e hoopa ia oukou a hiki wale i Kohala, e noho maluhia loa kakou a pau." A ua maikai ia mea imua o lakou.

Ia holo ana o lakou a hiki i Kohala, aole i hanaia kekahi mea iho iwaena o lakou.

Ia lakou ma Kohala, a hiki i ka la i haalele ai o Aiwohikupua ma ia Kohala, lawe ae la o Poliahu i kona kapa hau, a haawi aku la ia Aiwohikupua me ka olelo aku, "O kuu kapa hau, he kapa i papa loaia e ko'u mau makua, aole e lilo i kekahi mea e ae, ia'u wale iho no; aka, no ko kaua lawe ana ia kaua i kane hoao oe na'u, a pela hoi wau ia oe, nolaila, ke haawi lilo aku nei wau i keia kapa, a hiki i kou la e manao mai ai ia'u ma na hoohiki a kaua, alaila, loaa kou kuleana e imi ae ai ia'u a loaa, iluna o Maunakea, alaila, hoike ae oe ia'u, alaila, hui kino kaua."

A lohe o Aiwohikupua i keia mau mea, alaila, he mea olioli nui loa ia i ko ke Alii kane naau, a me kona Kuhina, a me na kanaka hoewaa.

Ia manawa, kii aku la o Aiwohikupua i kona Ahuula, lawe mai la a hoouhi aku la ia Poliahu, me ka olelo aku, "E like me kau olelo ia'u mamua o kou haawi ana mai ia'u i ke kapa hau, pela no oe e malama ai a hiki i ko kaua hui ana e like me ke kauoha."

A pau ka laua kamailio ana i ka wanaao, hookaawale lakou i ka wahine noho mauna, a holo aku la a hiki i Hana, a halawai me Hinaikamalama.

Mokuna VIII

A hiki o Aiwohikupua ma i Hana, mai Kohala aku mahope iho o ko lakou hookaawale ana ia Poliahu, ma ke awa pae waa o Haneoo ko lakou hiki mua ana, ma ko Hinaikamalama wahi e noho ana.

Ia Aiwohikupua nae i hiki aku ai ma kela awa pae waa, i ka moana no lakou i lana aku ai; a ia lakou e lana ana malaila, ike mai la o Hinaikamalama, o Aiwohikupua keia mau waa, mahamaha mai la ka wahine me ka manao e hele aku ana a halawai me ka wahine; aka, aia no lakou ke lana malie mai la i ka moana.

Hele mai o Hinaikamalama a ma kahi a Aiwohikupua ma e lana ana; I aku la ka wahine, "He mea kupanaha! heaha iho nei hoi keia o ka lana ana o na waa iloko o ke kai? Mahamaha mai nei keia i ka ike ana mai nei ia oukou, kainoa la hoi he holo mai a pae ae, aole ka! Nolaila, ke ninau aku nei wau ia oe; malaila no anei oukou e lana ai a holo aku?"

"Ae," wahi a Aiwohikupua.

"Aole oukou e hiki," wahi a ka wahine "no ka mea, e kauoha no wau i ka Ilamuku e hoopaa ia oe, ua lilo oe ia'u i ke konaneia, a ke waiho nei no ia hoohiki a kaua, a ua noho maluhia wau me ka malu loa a hiki i kou hoi ana mai la."

"E ke Alii Wahine, aole pela," wahi a Aiwohikupua, "aole au i hoopau i ka kaua hoohiki, ke mau nei no ia, aole no i hiki i ka manawa e hookoia ai ia hoohiki a kaua, no ka mea, ua hai mua aku wau ia oe, aia a puni o Hawaii ia'u, alaila, hookoia kou kumu pili e ke Alii wahine. Nolaila, holo aku nei wau me ka manao e puni o Hawaii, aole nae i puni, a Hilo no, loaa ae nei i ka uhai mai Kauai mai no ka pilikia o ko ka hale poe, nolaila, hoi mai nei; i kipa mai nei i ou la e hai aku no keia mau mea ia oe, a nolaila, e noho malu oe a hiki i kuu hoi hou ana mai, hookoia ka hoohiki."

A no keia olelo a Aiwohikupua, hoi mai la ka manao o ke Alii wahine, a like me mamua.

A pau keia mau mea, haalele lakou ia Hana, a holo mai lakou a hiki i Oahu nei, a mai anei aku a like a like o ka moana o Oahu nei, a me Kauai, hai aku la oia i kana olelo i na hoewaa, a me na hookele, penei: "Auhea oukou, ke hai aku nei wau i kuu olelo paa; ina i hiki kakou i Kauai, mai olelo oukou i Hawaii aku nei kakou i ka imi wahine, o lilo auanei ia i mea hoohilahila ia'u, i na e loheia ma keia hope aku, alaila, i loheia no ia oukou, a o ka uku o ka mea nana e hai keia olelo no ka holo ana i Hawaii, o ka makemake ka mea nana e olelo, make mai kana wahine, o ka ohi no ia o ka make a ka mea hoaikane mai." Oia ke kanawai paa a ke Alii i kau ai no ka poe i holo pu me ia i Hawaii.

A hiki lakou i Kauai, ma ka napoo ana o ka la, a halawai me na kaikuahine. Ia manawa ka hoopuka ana i olelo i kona mau kaikuahine, penei: "Ia'u i hele aku nei i ka'u huakai hele, ua haohao paha oukou, no ka mea, aole wau i hai aku ia oukou i ke kumu o ia hele ana, aole no hoi wau i hai aku i ka'u wahi e hele ai; a nolaila, ke hai malu aku nei wau ia oukou e o'u mau kaikuahine o kakou wale. I Hawaii aku nei makou i nalo iho nei, i kii aku nei wau ia Laieikawai i wahine mare (hoao) na'u, no ko'u lohe ana no ia Kauakahialii e olelo ana i ka la a lakou i hiki mai ai. I ka hele ana aku nei hoi, aole no hoi i kanamai a ke ano-e o ka wahine; aole nae au i ike aku ia Laieikawai; aka, o ka hale ka'u i ike maka aku, ua uhiia mai i ka hulu melemele o na manu Oo; nolaila, manao no au aole e loaa, hoi okoa mai nei me ka nele. A no ia manao o'u, aole e loaa ia'u, manao ae au ia oukou e na kaikuahine, ka poe no e loaa ai ko'u makemake i na la i hala, nolaila, kii mai nei au ia oukou e holo i Hawaii, o oukou no ka poe e loaa ai ko'u makemake, a ma keia wanaao, e ku kakou a e hele." Alaila, he mea maikai keia olelo a ko lakou kaikunane ia lakou.

Iloko o keia manawa a Aiwohikupua e olelo ana me na kaikuahine, akahi no a maopopo i kona Kuhina, oia ka ke kumu o ka hoi wikiwiki ana ia Kauai.

I kekahi la ae, wae ae la o Aiwohikupua i mau hoewaa hou, no ka mea, ua maopopo i ke Alii ua luhi na hoewaa mua; a makaukau ka holo ana, ia po iho, lawe ae la ke Alii he umikumamaha hoewaa, elua hookele, o na kaikuahine elima, o Mailehaiwale, o Mailekaluhea, o Mailelaulii, o Mailepakaha, a me ko lakou muli loa o Kahalaomapuana, o ke Alii a me kona Kuhina, he iwakalua-kumakolu ko lakou nui. I ka wanaao oia po, haalele lakou ia Kauai, hiki ma Puuloa, a mailaila aku a kau ma Hanauma, i kekahi la ae kau i Molokai, ma Kaunakakai; mailaila aku a pae i Mala, ma Lahaina; a haalele lakou ia wahi, hiki lakou i Keoneoio, ma Honuaula; a malaila i noho loihi ai ekolu anahulu.

No ka mea, ua nui ka ino ma ka moana, a pau na la ino, alaila, ua ikeia mai ka maikai o ka moana.

Ia manawa ko lakou haalele ana ia Honuaula, a holo aku la a hiki ma Kaelehuluhulu, ma Kona, Hawaii.

Ia Aiwohikupua ma i holo aku ai mai Maui aku a hiki i kela wahi, ua ike mua mai o Poliahu i ko lakou holo ana a me ka hiki ana i Kaelehuluhulu.

Nolaila, hoomakaukau mua o Poliahu ia ia no ka hiki aku o Aiwohikupua, alaila hoao; hookahi malama ke kali ano o Poliahu no ko laua hoao e like me ka laua hoohiki ana; aka, ua hala o Aiwohikupua ma Hilo, no ke kii no ia Laieikawai.

I kekahi manawa, ku mai ia Poliahu ka ike no ka Aiwohikupua mau hana; ma ko Poliahu ano kupua keia ike ana, a no ia mea, waiho wale no iloko o ka wahine kona manao, aia a halawai laua, alaila, hoike aku i kana mea e ike nei no ka Aiwohikupua mau hana.

Ma keia holo ana a Aiwohikupua, mai Kaelehuluhulu aku, hiki mua lakou ma Keaau, aka, ua nui no na la, a me na po o keia hele ana.

I ke awakea o kekahi la, hiki aku lakou ma Keaau, a pau na waa i ka hooponopono, a me na ukana o lakou, ia wa no, hoolale koke ae ana ke Alii i na kaikuahine, a me kona Kuhina e pii i uka o Paliuli; a ua hooholo koke lakou ia manao o ke Alii.

Mamua o ko lakou pii ana i Paliuli, kauoha iho la o Aiwohikupua i na hookele, a me na hoewaa, "Eia makou ke hele nei i ka makou huakai hele, ka mea hoi a kuu manao i kau nui ai a halawai maka, e noho malie loa oukou, aia no ka oukou mea malama o na waa; i kali oukou a i ao keia po, a i po ka la apopo, alaila, ua waiwai makou; aka, i hoi kakahiaka mai makou i ka la apopo, alaila, ua nele no ka'u mea i manao ai, alaila, o Kauai ke alo, huli aku hoi." Oia ke kauoha a ke Alii.

A pau ke kauoha a ke Alii i na kanaka, pii aku la a like a like o ka po, hiki lakou i Paliuli. Olelo aku la o Aiwohikupua i na kaikuahine, "O Paliuli keia, eia ianei o Laieikawai, ko oukou kaikoeke, nolaila, imiia ka oukou pono."

Alaila, lawe ae la o Aiwohikupua ia Mailehaiwale, i ka hanau mua o lakou e like me ko lakou hanau ana. Ku iho la ma ka puka ponoi o ka hale o Laieikawai, ia Mailehaiwale e ku la ma ka puka o ka Halealii, kuu aku ana keia i ke ala, po oloko i ke ala, aia nae o Laieikawai me kona kahu ua pauhiaia e ka hiamoe nui; aka, aole nae e hiki ke hiamoe i kela manawa, no ka mea ua hoalaia e ke ala o Mailehaiwale.

Ia puoho ana ae o laua mai ka hiamoe, haohao ana laua nei i keia ala launa ole; a no keia haohao, kahea aku la o Laieikawai me ka leo oluolu i kona kupunawahine penei:

LAIEIKAWAI: "E Waka, e Waka—e."
WAKA: "E-o, heaha kau o ka po e ala nei?"
LAIEIKAWAI: "He ala, eia—la, he ala e wale no keia, he ala anuanu, he ala huihui, eia la i ka houpo i ka manawa o maua."

Waka: "Aole no he ala e, o Mailehaiwale aku la na, o na kaikuahine aala o Aiwohikupua i kii mai la ia oe i wahine oe, a i wahine oe, a i kane ia; o ke kane ia moeia."

Laieikawai: "Ka! aole au e moe ia ia."

A lohe aku la o Aiwohikupua i ka hoole ana mai a Laieikawai, no ka makemake ole e lawe ia Aiwohikupua i kane mare, alaila, he mea e ka hilahila, no ka mea, ua lohe maopopo aku la lakou nei i ka hoole ana mai.

Mokuna IX

Mahope iho o ka manawa i hooleia ai ko ke Alii kane makemake; alaila, olelo aku la o Aiwohikupua i kona Kuhina, "E hoi kaua, a e noho na kaikuahine o'u iuka nei, a na lakou no e imi ae ko lakou wahi e noho ai, no ka mea, aole a lakou waiwai, ua nele ae la no ka mea i manaoia ai e loaa ia lakou."

I mai la kona Kuhina, "He mea kupanaha loa ia oe, kainoa, ua olelo oe ia'u mamua o ko kakou la i haalele ai ia Kauai; o na kaikuahine wale no ou ka mea nana e kii kou makemake, a ua ike no hoi oe i ke ko ana o ka lakou mau hana; ua kena ae nei oe ia Mailehaiwale i kana loaa, a ua lohe aku la no hoi kakou i ka hoole ana mai a Laieikawai, aole paha no ko kaikuahine ia hewa, e hiki ai ia kaua ke haalele ia lakou. Nolaila, hele ae la ia ia, eha ou mau kaikuahine i koe, malia paha o loaa i kekahi o lakou."

I aku la o Aiwohikupua, "Nele ae la ka i ka hanau mua, okiloa aku paha lakou."

I hou aku kona Kuhina, "E kuu Haku, e hoomanawanui hou kaua, e hoao ae o Mailekaluhea i kana loaa, a i nele, alaila, hoi kakou."

Alaila, ua maikai iki ia olelo i ke Alii, olelo aku la o Aiwohikupua, "E hoao aku hoi oe i kau loaa, a i nele oia iho la no."

Hele aku la o Mailekaluhea, a ma ka puka o ka Halealii, ku iho la, kuu aku la i ke ala, oia hele no o ke ala a pa i kaupoku maloko o ka hale, mai kaupoku ka hoi ana iho loaa ia Laieikawai ma, ia manawa, hikilele hou ae laua mai ka hiamoe ae.

I aku la o Laieikawai i kahi kahu, "He ala okoa hoi keia, aole hoi e like me ke ala mua iho nei, he oi nae hoi keia mamua o kela iho nei, he kane paha ka mea nona, keia ala."

Olelo aku kahi kahu, "Kaheaia ko kupunawahine, e hai mai i ke ano o keia ala."

Kahea aku la o Laieikawai.

LAIEIKAWAI: "E Waka, e Waka—e."

WAKA: "E—o, heaha kau o ka po e ala nei?"

LAIEIKAWAI: "Eia la he ala, he ala e wale no keia, he ala anuanu, he ala huihui, eia la i ka houpo i ka manawa o maua."

WAKA: "Aole na he ala e, o Mailekaluhea aku la, o kekahi kaikuahine aala o Aiwohikupua, i kii mai la ia oe i wahine oe i kane ia, o ke kane ia moeia."

LAIEIKAWAI: "Ka! aole au e moe ia ia."

I aku la o Aiwohikupua i ua wahi Kuhina nei ona, "E! ke lohe pono aku la oe i ka hoole ana ae la a ke Alii wahine."

"Ae, ua loke, heaha la auanei ko ia hoole ana ae la, o ko laua aala no kai makemake oleia ae la, malia hoi o ae ia Mailelaulii."

"Hoopaa no hoi oe," wahi a Aiwohikupua, "kainoa ua hai mua iho nei wau ia oe i ko'u manao e hoi kakou, eia kau he hoololohe, hoololohe iho la oe la, aeia mai la."

"Aole ka hoi i pau na kaikuahine o kaua, alua i hala, ekolu i koe," wahi a kona Kuhina, "kuuia aku paha i pau, he nani ia, ua pau na kaikuahine o kaua i ke kii, wikiwiki auanei hoi paha oe e hoi, a hiki kakou i kai o Keaau, olelo kakou no ka loaa ole, e olelo ae auanei ka poe kaikuahine ou i koe; ina no ia makou ka olelo ana mai e kii, ina no ua ae mai o Laieikawai, aia la, loaa ka lakou mea e kamailio ai, kuuia aku i pau."

"Auhea oe e kuu Kuhina," wahi a Aiwohikupua, "aole o oe ke hilahila ana, owau no, ina e like ana ka manao o ka moopuna me ko Waka la, ina ua pono."

"Kuuia aku paha i ka hilahila," wahi a kona Kuhina, "kainoa ua ike no oe, he waa naha i kooka ko kaua ko ke kane, a hoole mai aunei ia nawai e olelo kana hoole ana, kainoa o kakou wale no kai lohe, hoaoia'ku paha o Mailelaulii."

A no ka ikaika loa o ua wahi Kuhina nei ona i ke koi, hooholo ke Alii i ka ae.

Hele aku la o Mailelaulii a kupono i ka puka o ka Halealii, kuu aku ana oia i kona aala e like me na mea mua, hikilele hou mai la o Laieikawai mai ka hiamoe, a olelo aku la i kahi kahu, "He wahi ala okoa wale no hoi keia, aole hoi e like me kela mau mea mua."

I mai la kahi kahu, "Kaheaia o Waka."

LAIEIKAWAI: "E Waka, e Waka—e."

WAKA: "E—o, heaha la kau o ka po e ala nei?"

LAIEIKAWAI: "Eia la he ala, he ala e wale no keia, he ala anuanu, he ala huihui, eia la i ka houpo i ka manawa o maua."

WAKA: "Aole na he ala e, o Mailelaulii aku la na o na kaikuahine aala o Aiwohikupua, i kii mai la ia oe i wahine oe i kane ia, o ke kane ia moeia."

LAIEIKAWAI: "Ka! aole au e moe ia ia."

"I hookahi no hoi hoole ana o ka pono," wahi a Aiwohikupua, "o ka hele ka ia he kauna wale ae no koe o ka hoole, makena no hoi ua hilahila ia oe e ke hoa."

"Kuuia aku paha i ka hilahila," wahi a kona Kuhina, "a i ole e loaa i na kaikuahine o kaua, alaila, na'u e kii a loaa iloko o ka hale, a olelo aku wau e lawe ia oe i kane hoao nana e like me kou makemake."

A no keia olelo a kona Kuhina, alaila, ua hoopihaia ko ke Alii naau i ka olioli, no ka mea, ua lohe kela ia Kauakahialii i ka loaa ana i ua wahi kanaka nei o Laieikawai, i hiki ai i kai o Keaau.

Ia manawa, kena koke ae la o Aiwohikupua ia Mailepakaha, hele aku la a ku ma ka puka o ka Halealii; kuu aku la i kona aala, a hikilele mai la ko Laieikawai hiamoe, honi hou ana no i ke ala. I hou aku keia i kahi kahu, "Eia hou no keia ala, he wahi ala nohea hoi keia."

Olelo hou aku kahi kahu, "Kaheaia o Waka."

LAIEIKAWAI: "E Waka, e Waka—e."

WAKA: "E—o, heaha kau o ka po e ala nei?"

LAIEIKAWAI: "Eia la he ala, he ala okoa hoi keia, aole hoi i like me na ala mua iho nei, he ala maikai keia, he ala nohea, eia la i ka houpo i ka manawa o maua."

WAKA: "Aole na he ala e, o Mailepakaha aku la o ke kaikuahine aala o Aiwohikupua, i kii mai la ia oe i wahine oe i kane ia, o ke kane ia moeia."

LAIEIKAWAI: "Ka! aole au e moe ia ia, ina i kii mai kekahi mea e ia'u, aole no wau e ae ana! Mai hoomoe hou oe ia'u ia Aiwohikupua."

A lohe o Aiwohikupua, a me kona Kuhina i keia hoole hou ana o Laieikawai, i aku ua Kuhina nei ona, "E kuu Haku, pale ka pono! aohe pono i koe, hookahi no pono o ka hoi wale no koe o kakou; kaukai aku nei hoi ka pono i ko kaikuahine muli la hoi, i ole ae hoi ia lakou, ia'u aku la hoi, i lohe aku nei ka hana, e hoole loa ae ana no kela, me ka nuku maoli ae la no i ke kupunawahine; a eia nae hoi ka'u wahi olelo i koe ia oe, o ka olelo no auanei ka'u, o ka ae no kau."

"Oleloia ana," wahi a Aiwohikupua, "a i ike aku au he kupono i ka ae, alaila ae aku, i na he kupono ole, aole no au e ae aku."

"E kii kaua ma o ke kupunawahine la," wahi a ua Kuhina nei, "e noi aku ia ia, malia o ae mai kela."

Olelo aku o Aiwohikupua, "Aole a kakou hana i koe, ua pau, eia wale no ka olelo i koe, o na kaikuahine o kaua, e noho lakou i ka nahelehele nei, no ka mea, aohe a lakou waiwai."

Alaila, huli aku la o Aiwohikupua a olelo aku la i na kaikuahine, "E noho oukou, ua nele ae la no ka'u mea i makemake ai e lawe mai ia oukou, o ka nahele no nei noho iho." Ke hele aku nei e maamaama.

A pau ka Aiwohikupua olelo ana i na kaikuahine; kulou like iho la ke poo o na kaikuahine i kahi hookahi, e uwe ana.

Kaha aku la o Aiwohikupua ma iho, kahea aku la o Kahalaomapuana, ke kaikuahine muli loa, i aku la, "E laua la! ku iho, e lohe mua makou i Kauai, e lawe ana oe a haalele ia makou i keia wahi, i na aole makou e hiki mai. Pono no la hoi ia, ina owau kekahi i kii aku nei ia Laieikawai, a nele ana la hoi, alaila, pono kau haalele ana ia'u, pau pu no o ka mea i hewa, a me ka mea hewa ole. Aole oe he malihini ia'u, ia'u wale no e ko ai kau mau mea a pau."

A lohe o Aiwohikupua i keia olelo a kona kaikuahine opio, hoohewa iho la oia ia ia iho.

Kahea mai la o Aiwohikupua i ke kaikuahine opiopio, "Iho mai kaua, ou mau kaikuaana ke noho aku."

"Aole wau e hiki aku," wahi a kona kaikuahine opiopio, "aia a pau loa makou i ka hoi pu me oe, alaila, hoi aku au."

A no keia olelo a kona kaikauhine opiopio, alaila i aku o Aiwohikupua, "O noho mamuli ou mau kaikuaana, a nau no e huli ae me ko mau kaikuaana i ka oukou wahi e hele ai, eia wau ke hoi nei."

Huli aku la o Aiwohikupua ma e hoi, ia laua e hele ana ma ke ala, kani aku la ke oli a Mailehaiwale, penei:

> *"Kuu kaikunane kapu,*
> *Laniihikapu o ka manawa—e, e hoi—e;*
> *E hoi oe a ike aku*
> *I ka maka o na makua, hai aku,*
> *Eia makou ianei,*
> *E malu ana i ka hala nui,*
> *He hooumau hala paha?"*

Huli mai la o Aiwohikupua nana hope aku la i na kaikuahine, me ka i aku, "Aole he hala hoomau, kainoa ua hai mua iho nei no wau ia oukou, no ka oukou waiwai ole, oia kuu mea i haalele ai ia oukou, ina i loaa iho nei kuu makemake ia oukou, alaila, aole oukou e noho, oia iho la no ko oukou mea i laweia mai ai." Huli aku la no laua hoi, pau ka ike ana i na kaikuahine.

A hala aku la o Aiwohikupua ma, kuka iho la na kaikuahine i ko lakou manao, a hooholo iho la lakou, e ukali mahope o ke kaikuane, me ka manao e maliu mai.

Iho aku la lakou a hiki i kai o Keaau, e hoomakaukau ana na waa; noho iho la na kaikuahine ma ke awa, e kali ana no ke kaheaia mai, a pau lakou i ke kau maluna o na waa, aole nae kaheaia mai, ia lakou i hoomaka ai e holo, kani aku la ke oli a Mailekaluhea, penei:

"*Kuu kaikunane kapu,*
Laniihikapu o ka manawa, e huli mai,
E nana mai i ou mau pokii,
I na hoa ukali o ke ala,
O ke ala nui, ala iki,
O ka ua haawe kua,
Me he keiki la;
O ka na hookamumu hala,
Hookamumu hala o Hanalei—e.
Pehea makou—e,
I hea no la hoi kau haalele,
Haalele oe i ka hale,
Hele oe i kau huakai.
Ike aku—e,
Ike aku i ka maka,
I ka maka o na makua,
Aloha wale—e."

Iloko o keia oli ana a Mailekaluhea, aole nae i maliu iki mai ko lakou kaikunane, a hala aku la lakou la ma na waa, noho iho la na kaikuahine, kuka iho la i manao no lakou, hookahi mea nana i hoopuka ka lakou olelo, o Kahalaomapuana, ko lakou muli loa.

Eia kana olelo, "He nani ia ua maliu ole mai la ko kakou kaikunane alii, i ka Mailehaiwale a me Mailekaluhea, i ka laua uwalo aku, e aho e hele no kakou mauka a kahi e pae ae ai lakou, alaila, na Mailelaulii e kaukau aku i ko kakou kaikuahine, malia o aloha mai ia kakou." A ua holo like ae la ia manao ia lakou.

A haalele lakou ia Keaau, hiki mua na kaikuahine i Punahoa, ma kahi i kapaia o Kanoakapa, noho iho lakou malaila; hiki hope o Aiwohikupua ma.

Ia Aiwohikupua ma i aneane ai e pae mai ma kahi a na kaikuahine e noho aku ana, ike mai la o Aiwohikupua e noho aku ana kona mau kaikuahine, kahea koke ae la o Aiwohikupua i na hoewaa a me na hookele, "E haalele kakou i keia awa; no ka mea, eia no ua poe uhai loloa nei, e pono kakou ke imi aku i awa e ae e pae aku ai."

Ia lakou i haalele ai i kahi a na kaikuahine e noho ana, hea aku la o Mailelaulii mahope, ma ke mele, penei:

"Kuu kaikunane kapu,
Laniihikapu o kuu manawa—e!
Heaha ka hala nui?
I paweo ai na maka o kuu haku,
I kapu ai ka leo i ka uwalo,
Ka uwalo hoi a kou mau pokii,
Kou mau pokii kaikuahine hoi,
E maliu mai.
E maliu mai i na hoa ukali,
Na hoa pii pali o Haena,
Kokolo pali o ke ala haka,
Alahaka ulili o Nualolo,
Pali kui—e! kui o Makana,
E iala—e, hoi mai—e.
Homai ka ihu i ou pokii,
A hele aku i kau huakai,
I ka huakai hoi a ke aloha ole—e.
Aloha oe, ike aku,
Ike aku i ka aina,
I ka maka o na makua—e."

A lohe o Aiwohikupua ma i ka leo o keia kaikuahine, lana malie iho la na waa, alaila, i aku la o Kahalaomapuana, "Pono io kakou, akahi no hea ana i lana malie ai na waa, hoolohe aku kakou o ka leo o ke kahea mai, a kau kakou maluna o na waa, alaila, palekana."

A liuliu ka lakou la hoolana ana i na waa, o ka huli aku la no ia o Aiwohikupua ma e holo, aole wahi mea a maliu iki mai.

A hala aku la lakou la, kuka hou iho la na kaikuahine i olelo hou na lakou. O Kahalaomapuana no ko lakou mea manao.

I mai la oia i kona mau kaikuaana, "Elua maua i koe, owau a me Mailepakaha."

Olelo mai hoi o Mailepakaha, "Aole no e maliu mai ia'u; no ka mea, ke maliu ole ae la ka hoi i ko kaua mau kaikuaana, oki loa aku paha wau, i ko'u manao, e aho nau e hoalohaloha'ku na kahi mea uuku o kakou, malia o maliu mai ia oe."

Aole nae he ae o kahi muli loa, alaila, hoailona iho la lakou, ma ka huhuki ana i na pua mauu, o ka mea loihi o ka mauu, oia ka mea nana e hoalohaloha ko lakou kaikunane; aka, i ka hoailona ana, ku ia Kahalaomapuana ka hoailona.

A pau ka lakou hana ana no keia mau mea, haalele lakou ia Punahoa, hele ukali hou mai Ia lakou ma kahi e loaa ai ko lakou kaikunane, ia hele ana, hiki lakou i Honolii, ua hiki mua o Aiwohikupua ma i Honolii, noho mai la lakou nei ma kahi kaawale, a pela no hoi o Aiwohikupua ma ma kahi kaawale.

Ia lakou ma Honolii ia po, kuka iho la lakou e moe kekahi poe, a e ala hookahi, a holo ia mea ia lakou. Hoomaka ko lakou wati e like me ko lakou hanau ana, a i ko lakou kaikaina ka wati wanaao o ke ku ana. O ke kumu o ia hana ana a lakou pela, i ikeia ka manawa holo o Aiwohikupua ma; no ka mea, ua maa kona mau kaikuahine i ka holo ana mai, mai Kauai mai, ma ka wanaao e holo ai.

Ku aku la na kaikuahine i ka po, a hiki i ko Mailepakaha wati e ku ana, hoomakaukau o Aiwohikupua ma i na waa no ka holo ana, hoala aku la ia i kekahi poe o lakou, a ala like mai lakou a pau.

Ia lakou e okuu nui ana, o ka Kahalaomapuana wati ia, a kau lakou ma na waa, hookokoke aku la kona mau kaikuahine ma ke awa, a o Kahalaomapuana ka mea i hele loa aku a paa mahope o na waa, a kahea aku ma ke mele, penei:

> *"Ko makou kaikunane haku,*
> *Kaikunane kapu,*
> *Laniihikapu o kuu piko—e!*
> *Auhea oe, o o o—e,*
> *O oe, o makou, i o ianei hoi,*

Nau ka huakai,
Ukali aku makou,
I na pali i ka hulaana kakou,
Au aku o ka Waihalau,
Waihalau i Wailua—e;
He aloha ole—e.
He aloha ole paha kou ia makou,
Na hoa ukali o ka moana,
O ka ale nui, ale iki,
O ka ale loa, ale poko,
O ka ale kua loloa o ka moana,
Hoa ukali o kela uka,
O kela nahele liuliu,
O ka po iu anoano,
E huli mai.
E huli mai, a e maliu mai,
E hoolono mai ka i uwalo a'u,
A'u hoi a kou pokii muli loa.
Ihea la hoi kau haalele
Haalele iho ia makou
I kahi haiki,
Nau i waele ke alanui mamua,
Mahope aku makou ou,
Ike'a ai he mau pokii,
Ilaila la haalele aku ka huhu,
Ka inaina, ka opu aloha ole,
Homai ka ihu i ou mau pokii,
Aloha wale—e."

Ia manawa a kona kaikuahine muli loa e hapai ana i keia leo kaukau imua o Aiohikupua, alaila, ua hoomaeeleia ka naau o ko lakou kaikunane i ke aloha kaumaha no kona kaikuahine.

A no ka nui loa o ke aloha o Aiwohikupua i ko lakou pokii, lalau mai la a hoonoho iho la iluna o kona uha, a uwe iho la.

Ia Kahalaomapuana e kau ana i ka uha o kona kaikunane, kena ae la o Aiwohikupua i na hoewaa, i hoe ikaika; ia manawa, ua hala hope loa kekahi mau kaikuahine, a hala mua lakou la.

Ia lakou e holo ana, alaila, ua pono ole ka manao o Kahalaomapuana i kona mau kaikuaana.

Ia Kahalaomapuana e uwe ana no kona mau kaikuaana, ia manawa kona noi ana'ku ia Aiwohikupua, e hoihoi ia ia me kona mau kaikuaana; aka, aole no he maliu mai o Aiwohikupua.

"E Aiwohikupua," wahi a kona kaikuahine, "aole wau e ae e lawe oe ia'u owau wale, ke ole oe e lawe pu me ko'u mau kaikuaana; no ka mea, ua kahea mua ae no oe ia'u i ko kakou wa i Paliuli; aka, aole wau i ae mai, no kou lawe ia'u owau wale."

A no ka paakiki loa o Aiwohikupua aole e hookuu i kona kaikuahine, ia manawa, lele aku la o Kahalaomapuana mai luna aku o ka waa a haule iloko o ke kai. Ia manawa, hoopuka aku la kona kaikuahine i olelo hope, ma ke mele, penei:

"Ke hoi la oe a ike aku,
Ike aku i ka maka,
I ka maka o na makua,
Aloha aku i ka aina,
I ka nui a me na makamaka,
Ke hoi nei wau me o'u pokii,
Me o'u kaikuaana hoi—e."

Mokuna XI

Iloko o keia kaukau hope loa a Kahalaomapuana, ua hoopihaia ko Aiwohikupua naau i ke aloha nui; a kahea ae la oia e hooemi hope na waa, aka, ua hala hope loa o Kahalaomapuana i hope, no ka ikaika loa o ka holo o na waa; a i ka wa i huli hope ai na waa e kii hou i kona kaikuahine, aole nae i loaa.

(Maanei e waiho iki i ke kamailio ana no Aiwohikupua, e pono ke kamailio hou no kona mau kaikuahine; alaila, e kamailio hou no Aiwohikupua.)

Ia manawa a Aiwohikupua ma i haalele aku ai i na kaikuahine ma Honolii, a lawe pu aku ia Kahalaomapuana; nui loa iho la ke aloha, a me ka uwe ana no ko lakou kaikaina, ua oi aku ko lakou aloha ia Kahalaomapuana, mamua o ko lakou aloha i ko lakou mau makua, a me ka aina.

Ia lakou no e uwe ana, hoea mai ana o Kahalaomapuana ma ka pali mai, alaila, ua kuuia ka naau kaumaha o kona mau kaikuaana.

A hui ae la lakou me ko lakou kaikaina, a hai aku la oia i kana hana, a me ke kumu o kona hoi ana mai e like me ka mea i olelo muaia ae nei ma keia Mokuna.

A pau ka lakou kamailio ana no keia mau mea, kuka iho la lakou i ka pono o ko lakou noho ana, a hooholo ae la lakou e hoi hou lakou i Paliuli.

Mahope iho o ko lakou kuka ana no lakou iho, haalele lakou ia Honolii, hoi aku la a uka o Paliuli, ma kahi e kokoke aku ana i ka hale o Laieikawai, noho iho la lakou maloko o na puha laau.

A no ko lakou makemake nui e ike ia Laieikawai, hoohalua mau lakou i keia la keia la, a nui na la o lakou i hoohalua ai, aole lakou i ike iki no ka lakou mea e hoohalua nei, no ka mea, ua paa mau ka puka o ka hale i na la a pau.

A no ia mea, kukakuka ae la lakou i mea e ike aku ai lakou ia Laieikawai, a nui na la o ko lakou imi ana i mea e ike aku ai no ke Alii wahine o Paliuli, aole loaa.

Iloko o kela mau la kuka o lakou, aole i pane iki ko lakou kaikaina, a no ia mea, olelo aku kekahi o kona mau kaikuaana, "E Kahalaomapuana, o makou wale no ia e noonoo nei i mea no kakou e ike aku ai ia Laieikawai, aole nae he loaa; malia paha, aia ia oe kekahi mea e hiki ai, e olelo ae oe."

"Ae," wahi a ko lakou kaikaina, "e ho-a kakou i ahima kela po keia po, a e oli aku ka hanau mua, alaila, i ka muli iho, pela a pau kakou, i hookahi no olioli ana a ka mea hookahi ma ka po, alaila, ia'u ka po hope loa; malia paha o lilo ka a-a mau ana a ke ahi i na po a pau i mea no ke Alii e uluhua ai, alaila, hele mai e nana ia kakou, alaila, pela paha e ike ai kakou ia Laieikawai."

A ma keia olelo a Kahalaomapuana, ua pono ia imua o lakou.

I ka po mua, ho-a ae la lakou i ahi, a ia Mailehaiwale ke oli ana ia po, e like me ka lakou hooholo like ana. A i kekahi po mai ia Mailekaluhea, pela mau lakou i hana ai a hala no po eha, aole nae i loaa ia Laieikawai ka hoouluhuaia, ua loho no nae ke Alii wahine i ke oli, a ua ike no hoi i ka *a-a* mau ana a ke ahi; a heaha la ia mea i ke Alii wahine.

I ka lima o ka po, oia ko Kahalaomapuana po, o ka hope loa no hoi ia; ho-a iho la ke ahi, a ma ka waenakonu o ka po, hana iho la o Kahalaomapuana he pu la-i, a hookani aku la.

Iloko oia manawa, akahi no a komo iloko o Laieikawai ka lealea no kela leo e kani nei, aole nae i hoouluhuaia ke Alii wahine. A ma ka pili o ke ao, hookani hou aku la o Kahalaomapuana i kana pu la-i e like me ke kani mua ana, alaila, ua lilo iho la no ia i mea lealea no ke Alii; elua wale no puhi ana a Kahalaomapuana ia po.

I ka lua o ka po, hana hou no o Kahalaomapuana i kana hana; ma ka pili nae o ke ahiahi kana hoomaka ana e hookani, aole nae i uluhua ke Alii.

Ma ka pili o ka wanaao oia po no, ka lua ia o ka hookani ana. Ia manawa, ua hoouluhuaia ko Laieikawai manawa hiamoe; a o ka oi no hoi keia o ka po lealea loa o ke Alii.

A no ka uluhua o Laieikawai, kena ae la oia i kona wahi kahu e hele e nana i kahi i kani mai ai keia mea kani.

Ia manawa, puka ae la ua wahi kahu nei o ke Alii iwaho o ka Halealii, a ike aku la i ke ahi a ua poe kaikamahine nei e aa mai ana, hookolo aku la oia a hiki i kahi o ke ahi e a ana, ma ke kaawale nae keia kahi i ku aku ai me ka ike ole mai a lakou la ia ianei.

A ike keia, hoi aku la a ia Laieikawai, ninau mai la ke Alii.

Hai aku la kahi kahu i kana mea i ike ai, mamuli o ka ninau a ke Alii, "Ia'u i puka aku ai mai ka hale aku nei, ike aku la wau he ahi e aa mai ana, hele aku nei wau a hiki, a ma ke kaawale ko'u ku ana aku, me ka ike ole mai o lakou la ia'u. Aia hoi, ike aku la wau he mau kaikamahine elima, e noho ana a puni ke ahi, he mau kaikamahine maikai wale no lakou, ua like wale no na ano, hookahi nae o lakou wahi mea uuku loa, a nana ka mea kani lealea a kaua e lohe aku nei."

A lohe ke Alii i keia mea, olelo aku la oia i kona kahu, "E kii oe a kahi mea uuku o lakou, olelo aku oe e hele mai ianei, i hana mai ai oia i kana mea hoolealea imua o kaua."

A no keia olelo a ke Alii, hele aku la kahi kahu a hiki i kahi o na kaikamahine, a ike mai la lakou i keia mea, hai aku la oia, "He alele wau i hoounaia mai nei e kuu Alii e kii mai i kekahi o oukou e like me ka'u mea e manao ai e lawe, nolaila, ke lawe nei wau i kahi mea uuku o oukou e hele e launa pu me kuu Alii e like me kana kauoha."

A Iaweia aku la o Kahalaomapuana, alaila, ua hoohauoliia ka naau o kona mau kaikuaana, no ka manao no e loaa ana ka pomaikai mahope.

A hiki aku la ua wahi kaikaina nei o lakou imua o Laieikawai.

Ia ia nae i hiki aku ai a ka hale, wehe ae la ke kahu o ke Alii i ka puka o ka Halealii, ia manawa, ua hoopuiwa kokeia ko Kahalaomapuana lunamanao, no ka ike ana aku ia Laieikawai e kau mai ana iluna o ka eheu o na manu e like me kona ano mau, elua hoi mau manu Iiwipolena e kau ana ma na poohiwi o ke Alii, e lu ana i na wai ala lehua ma ke poo o ke Alii.

A no ka ike ana aku o Kahalaomapuana i keia mau mea, a he mea kupanaha ia imua o ke Kaikamahine malihini, haule aku la oia i ka honua me ka naau eehia.

Hele aku la ke kahu o ke Alii, a ninau aku la, "Heaha keia e ke kaikamahine?"

A palua kana ninau ana, alaila, ala ae la ke kaikamahine, a olelo aku la i ke kahu o ke Alii me ka i aku, "E ae mai oe ia'u e hoi au me ou kaikuaana, ma kahi i loaa ai wau ia oe, no ka mea, ua eehia wau i ka maka'u no ke ano e loa o kau Alii."

Olelo mai la ke kahu o ke Alii, "Mai maka'u oe, mai hopohopo, e ku oe a e komo aku e halawai me kuu Alii e like me kana kauoha ia oe."

"He maka'u," wahi a ke kaikamahine.

A lohe mai la ke Alii i ka laua haukamumu, ala ae la oia a hea aku la ia Kahalaomapuana, alaila, ua hoopauia ko ke kaikamahine naau kaumaha, a komo aku la ka malihini e launa me ke Alii.

I mai la o Laieikawai, "Nau anei ka mea kani lealea i kani mai ai i kela po, a me keia po?"

"Ae, na'u," wahi a Kahalaomapuana.

"O i ana," wahi a Laieikawai, "hookani ia ana."

Lalau ae la o Kahalaomapuana i kana pu la-i ma kona pepeiao, a hookani aku la imua o ke Alii; alaila, ua hoolealeaia o Laieikawai. Oia ka makamua o ko ke Alii ike ana i keia mea kani.

Mokuna XII

A no ka lilo loa o ko Laieikawai manawa i ka olioli no ka mea kani lealea a ke kaikamahine; alaila, kena ae la o Laieikawai i ke kaikamahine e hookani hou.

I aku la ke kaikamahine, "Aole e kani ke hookani hou; no ka mea ua malamalama loa, he mea mau ia, ma ka po wale no e kani ai nei mea kani, aole e pono ma ke ao."

A no keia olelo a ke kaikamahine, kahaha loa iho la o Laieikawai me ka manao he wahahee na ke kaikamahine, alaila, lalau aku la o Laieikawai i ka pu la-i ma ka lima o ke kaikamahine, a hookani iho la, a no ko Laieikawai maa ole i ka hookani ka pu la-i, nolaila, ua loaa ole ke kani ma ia hookani ana, alaila, he mea maopopo loa i ke Alii wahine, he mea kani ole no ka pu la-i ke hookani ma ke ao.

Olelo aku la o Laieikawai ia Kahalaomapuana, "Ke makemake nei wau e hoaikane kaua, a ma ko'u hale nei oe e noho ai, a e lilo oe i mea punahele na'u, a o kau hana ka hoolealea mai ia'u."

Olelo aku la o Kahalaomapuana, "E ke Alii e, ua pono kau olelo; aka, he mea kaumaha no'u ke noho wau me oe, a e loaa ana paha ia'u ka pomaikai, a o ko'u mau kaikuaana, e lilo paha auanei lakou i mea pilikia."

"Ehia oukou ka nui," wahi a Laieikawai, "a pehea ko oukou hiki ana maanei?"

Olelo aku la o Kahalaomapuana, "Eono makou ko makou nui a na makua hookahi o ko makou ono, he keiki kane, a elima makou na kaikuahine, o ke keiki kane no ko makou mua, a owau ko makou muli loa. A ma ka huakai a ko makou kaikunane, oia ko makou mea i hiki ai maanei, a no ka loaa ole ana ia makou o kona makemake, nolaila, ua haalele kela ia makou, a ua hoi aku la ko makou kaikunane me kona kekoolua, a ke noho nei makou me ka makamaka ole."

Ninau mai la o Laieikawai, "Nohea mai oukou?"

"No Kauai mai," wahi a Kahalaomapuana.

"A owai ka inoa o ko oukou kaikunane?"

Hai aku la kela, "O Aiwohikupua."

Ninau hou o Laieikawai, "Owai ko oukou mau inoa pakahi?"

Alaila hai aku la kela ia lakou a pau.

Alaila, hoomaopopo iho la o Laieikawai, o lakou no ka poe i hiki i kela po mua.

I aku la o Laieikawai, "O kou mau kaikuaana a me ke kaikunane o oukou kai maopopo, ina nae o oukou kai hiki mai i kela po aku nei la; aka, o oe ka'u mea i lohe ole."

"O makou no," wahi a Kahalaomapuana.

I aku la o Laieikawai, "Ina o oukou kai hiki mai i kela po, alaila, nawai i alakai ia oukou ma keia wahi? No ka mea, he wahi ike oleia keia, akahi wale no poe i hele mai i keia wahi."

I aku keia, "He kamaaina no ko makou mea nana i alakai mai, oia hoi kela wahi kanaka nana i olelo mai ia oe no Kauakahialii." Alaila, ua maopopo he kamaaina ko lakou.

A pau ka laua kamailio ana no keia mau mea, kauoha ae la oia i kona kupunawahine, e hoomakaukau i hale no na kaikuahine o Aiwohikupua.

Alaila, ma ka mana o Waka, kona kupunawahine, ua hikiwawe loa, ua paa ka hale.

A makaukau ka hale, kena aku la o Laieikawai ia, Kahalaomapuana, "E hoi oe, a kela po aku, pii mai oe me ou mau kaikuaana mai, i ike aku wau ia lakou, alaila, e lealea mai oe ia kakou, i kau mea kani lealea."

A hala aku la o Kahalaomapuana, a hui me kona mau kaikuaana, ninau mai la nae kona mau kaikuaana i kana hana, a me ke ano o ko laua halawai ana me ke Alii.

Hai aku la kela, "Ia'u i hiki aku ai a ma ka puka o ka hale o ke Alii, wehe aku la kahi kuapuu nana i kii mai nei ia'u, a i kuu ike ana aku nei i ke Alii e kau mai ana iluna o ka eheu o na manu, no ia ike ana o'u, ua eehia wau me ka maka'u a haule aku la wau ilalo ma ka lepo. A no keia mea, kiiia mai la wau a komo aku la e kamailio pu me ke Alii, a hana aku wau i kona lealea, e like me ko ke Alii makemake, a ua ninau mai nei kela ia kakou, ua hai pau aku au. Nolaila, e loaa ana ia kakou ka pomaikai, ua kauoha mai nei kela, a i keia po pii aku kakou."

A lohe kona mau kaikuaana i keia mau olelo, he mea e ka olioli o lakou.

A hiki i ka manawa a ke Alii i kauoha mai ai ia lakou, haalele lakou i na puha laau, kahi a lakou i noho pio ai.

Hele aku la lakou a ku ma ka puka o ka Hale Alii, wehe ae la ke kahu o Laieikawai i ka puka, a ike aku la lakou e like me ka olelo a ko lakou kaikaina.

Ia lakou nae i ike aku ai ia Laieikawai, alaila, ua puiwa koke lakou, a holo aku la me ka haalulu eehia, a pau loa lakou i ka haule i ka honua, koe nae o Kahalaomapuana.

A ma ke kauoha a ke Alii, ua kii ia aku kele poe malihini a laweia mai la imua o ke Alii, a he mea oluolu ia i ko ke Alii manao.

Ia lakou e halawai ana me ke Alii wahine, hoopuka mai la oia imua o na malihini he olelo hoopomaikai, a penei no ia:

"Ua lohe wau i ko oukou kaikaina, he poe oukou no ka hanauna hookahi, a he poe koko like oukou; a nolaila, ke lawe nei au ia oukou ma ke ano o ke koko hookahi, e kiai kakou ia kakou iho, ma ka olelo a kekahi, malaila like kakou, iloko o kela pilikia keia pilikia, o kakou no kekahi ilaila. A no ia mea, ua kauoha wau e hoomakaukau ko kakou kupunawahine i hale no oukou e noho ai me ka maluhia, e like me a'u nei, aole e aeia kekahi e lawe i kane nana, me ka ae like ole o kakou; pela e pono ai kakou ma keia hope aku."

A no keia olelo, hooholo ae la na kaikamahine malihini, na ko lakou kaikaina e hoopuka ka lakou olelo pane aku i ke Alii.

"E ke Alii e! Pomaikai makou no kou hookipa ana ia makou, a pomaikai hoi makou, no kou lawe ana ae ia makou I mau hoahanau nou, e like me kau i olelo mai nei ia makou, a pela no makou e hoolohe ai. Hookahi nae mea a makou e hai aku ia oe, he poe kaikamahine makou i hoolaa ia e ko makou mau makua, aole he oluolu e lawe makou i kane mare, a o ka makemake o ko makou mau makua, e noho puupaa na makou a hiki i ko makou mau la hope, a nolaila, ke noi mua aku nei kau mau kauwa, mai ae oe ia makou e hoohaumia me kekahi mau kanaka, e like me ka makemake o ke Alii; nolaila, e hookuu ia makou e noho puupaa e like me ka olelo paa a ko makou mau makua."

He mea maikai nae i ko ke Alii manao ka olelo a na malihini.

A pau ka lakou olelo ana me ke Alii no keia mau mea, hoihoiia aku la lakou a ma ka hale i hoomakaukauia no lakou.

I ua mau kaikamahine nei e noho ana ma ko lakou hale, he mea mau ia lakou ke kuka mau ma na mea e pili ana ia lakou, a me ke Alii, no ko lakou noho ana, a me na hana a ke Alii e olelo mai ai. A hooholo ae la lakou e hoolilo i ko lakou kaikaina i hoa kuka no ke Alii ma na hana e pili ana i ko lakou noho ana.

I kekahi awakea, i ko ke Alii manawa ala mai ka hiamoe mai, hele aku la o Kahalaomapuana e hoolealea i ke Alii ma ka hookanikani ana i ka pu la-i, a pau ko ke Alii makemake.

Ia manawa, hai aku la oia i kana olelo imua o Laieikawai, no ka lakou mea i kuka ai me kona mau kaikuaana; i aku la, "E ke Alii, ua kuka makou i mea nou e maluhia ai, nolaila, ua hooholo makou i ko makou manao, e hoolilo makou ia makou elima i mau koa kiai no kou Halealii, a ma o makou la e ae ia ai, a ma o makou la e hooleia ai. Ina i hele mai kekahi mea makemake e ike ia oe, ina he kane, a he wahine paha, a ina he alii, aole lakou e ike ia oe ke ole makou e ae aku; nolaila, ke noi aku nei au e ae mai ke Alii e like me ka makou hooholo ana."

I mai la o Laieikawai, "Ke ae aku nei wau e like me ka oukou mau olelo hooholo, a o oukou no ka mana ma Paliuli nei a puni."

Eia nae ka manao nui o kela poe kaikamahine e lilo i kiai no ke Alii, no ko lakou manao e puka hou ana o Aiwohikupua i Paliuli, alaila, he mana ko lakou e kipaku i ko lakou enemi.

Noho iho la lakou ma Paliuli, iloko nae o ko lakou noho ana, aole lakou i ike i ko lakou luhi ma ia noho ana; aole hoi lakou i ike iki i ka mea nana e hana mai ka lakou ai. Eia wale no ko lakou manawa ike i ka lakou mau mea ai, i ka manawa makaukau o lakou e paina, ia manawa e lawe mai ai na manu i na mea ai a lakou, a na na manu no e hoihoi aku i na ukana ke pau ka lakou paina ana, a no keia mea, ua lilo o Paliuli i aina aloha loa na lakou, a malaila lakou i noho ai a hiki i ka haunaele ana ia Halaaniani.

(Maanei e ka mea heluhelu e waiho i ke kamailio ana no na kaikuahine o Aiwohikupua, a ma ka Mokuna XIII o keia Kaao e kamailio hou no Aiwohikupua no kona hoi ana i Kauai.)

Mokuna XIII

Mahope iho o ko Kahalaomapuana lele ana iloko o ke kai mai luna iho o na waa, e holo ikaika loa ana na waa ia manawa; nolaila, ua hala hope loa o Kahalaomapuana. Hoohuli hou na waa i hope e imi ia Kahalaomapuana, aole nae i loaa; nolaila, haalele loa o Aiwohikupua i kona kaikuahine opiopio, a hoi loa aku i Kauai.

Ia Aiwohikupua i hoi ai mai Hawaii mai a hiki mawaena o Oahu nei a me Kauai, olelo aku la o Aiwohikupua i kona mau hoewaa penei: "I ko kakou hoi ana anei a hiki i Kauai, mai olelo oukou, i Hawaii aku nei kakou i o Laieikawai la, o hilahila auanei au; no ka mea, he kanaka wau ua waia i ka olelo ia; a nolaila, ke hai aku nei au i ka'u olelo paa ia oukou. O ka mea nana e hai i keia hele ana o kakou, a lohe wau, alaila, o kona uku ka make, a me kona ohana a pau, pela no au i olelo ai i keia poe hoewaa mamua."

Hoi aku la lakou a Kauai. I kekahi mau la, makemake iho la ke Alii, o Aiwohikupua, e hana i Ahaaina palala me na'lii, a me kona mau hoa a puni o Kauai.

A i ka makaukau ana o ka Ahaaina palala a ke Alii, kauoha ae la ke Alii i kana olelo e kii aku i na hoa-ai; ma na alii kane wale no, a hookahi wale no, alii wahine i aeia e komo i ka Ahaaina palala, oia o Kailiokalauokekoa.

I ka la i Ahaaina ai, akoakoa mai la na hoa-ai a pau loa, ua makaukau na mea ai, a o ka awa ko lakou mea inu ma ia Ahaaina ana.

Mamua o ko lakou paina ana, lalau like na hoa i na apuawa, a inu iho la. Iloko o ko lakou manawa ai, aole i loaa ia lakou ka ona ana o ka awa.

A no ka loaa ole o ka ona o ka awa, hoolale koke ae la ke Alii i kona mau mama awa e mama hou ka awa. A makaukau ko ke Alii makemake, lalau like ae la na hoa-ai o ke Alii, a me ke Alii pu i na apuawa, a inu ae la. Ma keia inu awa hope o lakou, ua loohia mai maluna o lakou ka ona awa. Aka, hookahi mea oi aku o ka ona, o ke Alii nana ka papaaina.

Iloko o keia manawa ona o ke Alii, alaila, ua nalo ole ka olelopaa ana i olelo ai i kona mau hoewaa ma ka moana, aole nae i loheia ma o kana poe i papa ai; aka, ma ka waha ponoi no o Aiwohikupua i loheia'i olelo huna a ke Alii.

A ona iho la o Aiwohikupua, alaila, haliu pono aku la oia ma kahi a Kauakahialii e noho mai ana, olelo aku la, "E Kauakahialii e, ia oe no e kamailio ana ia makou no Laieikawai, komo koke iho la iloko o'u ka makemake no kela wahine; nolaila, moe ino ko'u mau po e ake e ike; nolaila, holo aku nei wau a hiki i Hawaii, pii aku nei maua a malamalama, puka i uka o Paliuli, i nana aku ka hana i ka hale o ke Alii, aole i kana mai, o ko'u hilahila; no ia mea, hoi mai nei. Hoi mai nei hoi wau, a manao mai o na kaikuahine hoi ka mea e loaa'i, kii mai nei, i hele aku nei ka hana me na kaikuahine a hiki i ka hale o ke Alii, kuu aku hoi i ka na kaikuahine loaa; i hana aku ka hana, i ka hoole waleia no a pau na kaikuahine eha, koe o kahi muli loa o'u, o ko'u hilahila no ia hoi mai nei, he oi no hoi kela o ka wahine kupaa nui wale, aole i ka lua."

Iloko o kela manawa a Aiwohikupua e kama ilio ana no ka paakiki o Laieikawai. Ia manawa e noho ana o Hauailiki, ke keiki puukani o Mana iloko o ka Ahaaina, he keiki kaukaualii no hoi, oia ka oi o ka maikai.

Ku ae la oia iluna, a olelo aku la ia Aiwohikupua "He hawawa aku la no kau hele ana, aole wau i manao he wahine paakiki ia, ina e ku au imua o kona mau maka, aole au e olelo aku, nana no e hele wale mai a hui maua; alaila, e ike oukou e noho aku ana maua."

I aku la o Aiwohikupua, "E Hauailiki e, ke makemake nei au e hele oe i Hawaii, ina e lilo mai o Laieikawai, he oi oe, a na'u no e hoouna me oe i mau kanaka, a ia'u na waa, a i nele oe ma keia hele ana au, alaila, lilo kou mau aina ia'u; a ina i hoi mai oe me Laieikawai, alaila, nou ko'u mau aina."

A pau ka Aiwohikupua ma olelo ana no keia mau mea, ia po iho, kau o Hauailiki ma maluna o na waa a holo aku la; aka, ua nui no na la i hala ma ia holo ana.

Ia holo ana, hiki aku lakou iwaho o Makahanaloa, i nana aku ka hana o lakou nei, e pio ana ke anuenue i kai o Keaau. Olelo aku la ke Kuhina o Aiwohikupua ia Hauailiki, "E nana oe i kela anuenue e pio mai la i kai, o Keaau no ia; a aia ilaila o Laieikawai, ua iho ae la i ka nana heenalu."

I mai la o Hauailiki, "Kainoa aia o Paliuli kona wahi noho mau."

A i kekahi la ae, ma ka auina la, hiki aku la lakou i Keaau, ua hoi aku nae o Laieikawai me na kaikuahine o Aiwohikupua i uka o Paliuli.

Ia Hauailiki ma i hiki aku ai, aia hoi ua nui na mea i hele mai e nana no keia keiki oi kelakela o ka maikai mamua o Kauakahialii a me Aiwohikupua, a he mea mahalo nui loa ia na na kamaaina o Keaau.

I kekahi la ae ma ka puka ana a ka la, uhi ana ke awa a me ka noe ma Keaau a puni, a i ka mao ana'e, aia hoi ehiku mau wahine e noho ana ma ke awa pae o Keaau, a hookahi oi oia poe. Akahi wale no a iho na kaikuahine o Aiwohikupua ma keia hele ana o Laieikawai, e like me kana olelo hoopomaikai.

Ia Laieikawai ma e noho ana ma kela kakahiaka, ku ae la o Hauailiki a holoholo ae la imua o lakou la, e hoika ana ia ia iho ma kona ano kanaka ui, me ka manao e maliuia mai e ke Alii wahine o Paliuli. A heaha la o Hauailiki ia Laieikawai? "he opala paha."

Eha na la o Laieikawai o ka hiki ana ma Keaau, mahope iho o ko Hauailiki puka ana aku; a eha no hoi la o ko Hauailiki hoike ana ia ia imua o Laieikawai, a aole nae he maliu iki ia mai.

I ka lima o ka la o ko Laieikawai hiki ana ma Keaau, manao iho la o Hauailiki e hoike ia ia iho imua o kana mea e iini nui nei no kona akamai ma ka heenalu; he oiaio, o Hauailiki no ka oi ma Kauai no ke akamai i ka heenalu a oia no ka oi iloko o kona mau la, a he keiki kaulana hoi oia ma ke akamai i ka heenalu, a kaulana, no hoi no kona ui.

I ua la la, i ka puka ana a ka la, aia na kamaaina ma kulana, nalu, na kane, a me na wahine.

I na kamaaina e akoakoa ana ma kulana heenalu, wehe ae la o Hauailiki i kona aahu kapa, hopu iho la i kona papa heenalu (he olo), a hele aku la a ma kahi e kupono ana ia Laieikawai ma, ku iho la oia no kekahi mau minute, ia manawa nae, komo mai la iloko o na kaikuahine o Aiwohikupua ka makemake no Hauailiki.

I aku la o Mailehaiwale ia Laieikawai, "Ina paha aole makou i hoolaaia e ko kakou mau makua, ina ua lawe wau ia Hauailiki i kane na'u."

I aku o Laieikawai, "Ua makemake no hoi wau, ina hoi aole wau i hoolaaia e ko'u kupunawahine, nolaila, he mea ole ko'u makemake."

"O kaua pu," wahi a Mailehaiwale.

A pau ko Hauailiki mau minute hookahakaha, lele aku la ua o Hauailiki me kona papa heenalu i ke kai, a au aku la a kulana nalu.

Ia Hauailiki ma kulana nalu, kahea mai la kekahi kaikamahine kamaaina, "Pae hoi kakou."

"Hee aku paha," wahi a Hauailiki, no ka mea, aole ona makemake, e hee pu oia me ka lehulehu ma ka nalu hookahi, makemake no oia e hookaokoa ia ia oia wale no ma ka nulu okoa, i kumu e ike mai ai o Laieikawai no kona akamai i ka heenalu, malia o makemake ia mai oia; aole ka!

A hala aku la na kamaaina, ohu mai la he wahi nalu opuu, ia manawa ka Hauailiki hee ana i kona nalu. Ia Hauailiki e hee la i ka nalu, uwa ka pihe a na kamaaina, a me na kaikuahine o Aiwohikupua: Heaha la ia ia Laieikawai?

A no ka lohe ana aku o Hauailiki i keia pihe uwa, alaila, manao iho ia ua huipu me Laieikawai i keia leo uwa, aole ka! hoomau aku la oia i ka heenalu a hala elima nalu, oia mau no. Aole nae i loaa ka heahea ia mai, nolaila, hoomaka mai la ia Hauailiki ke kaumaha, me ka hooiaio iki i kela olelo a Aiwohikupua no ka "paakiki o Laieikawai."

Mokuna XIV

A ike maopopo ae la o Hauailiki, aole i komo iloko o Laieikawai ka makemake ia Hauailiki ma ia mea, hoopau ae la oia i ka heenalu ma ka papa; manao ae la oia e kaha.

Haalele iho la oia i kona papa, a au aku la i kulana heenalu. Ia ia e au ana, olelo ae la o Laieikawai i kona mau hoa, "E! pupule o Hauailiki."

I aku la kona mau hoa, "Malia paha e kaha nalu ana."

Ia Hauailiki ma kulana nalu, i ka nalu i ea mai ai a kakala ma kona kua, ia manawa kaha mai la oia i ka nalu, pii ke kai me he niho puaa la ma o a ma o o kona a i. Ia manawa, uwa ka pihe o uka, akahi no a loaa mai ia Laieikawai ka akaaka, a he mea malihini no hoi ia i kona maka a me kona mea e ae.

A ike aku la o Hauailiki i ko Laieikawai akaaka ana iho, manao iho la oia, ua komo ka makemake i Laieikawai ma keia hana a Hauailiki, alaila, hoomau aku la oia ma ke kaha nalu, a hala elima nalu, aole i loaa ka hea mai a Laieikawai ia ia nei.

Nolaila, he mea kaumaha loa ia ia Hauailiki, ka maliu ole mai o Laieikawai ia ia nei, a he mea hilahila nui loa hoi nona, no ka mea, ua olelo kaena mua kela ia Aiwohikupua, e like me ka kakou ike ana ma na Mokuna mamua ae.

A no keia mea, lana malie iho la oia ma kulana nalu, ia ia e lana malie ana, ua kokoke mai ko Laieikawai ma manawa hoi i Paliuli. Ia manawa, peahi mai la o Laieikawai ia Hauailiki.

A ike aku la o Hauailiki i ka peahi ana mai, alaila, ua hoomohalaia kona naau kanalua. I iho la o Hauailiki oia wale no, "Aole no ka hoi oe e kala i makemake ai, hoolohi wale iho no."

A no ka peahi a ke Alii wahine o Paliuli, hoomoe iho la keia i ka nalu, a pae pono aku la ma kahi a Laieikawai ma e noho mai ana. Ia manawa, haawi mai la o Laieikawai i ka lei lehua, hoolei iho la ma ka a-i o Hauailiki, e like me kana hana mau i ka poe akamai i ka heenalu. A mahope iho oia manawa, he uhi ana na ka noe a me ka ohu, a i ka mao ana ae, aole o Laieikawai ma, aia aku la lakou la i Paliuli.

O ka iho hope ana keia a Laieikawai ma i Keaau, iloko o ko Hauailiki mau la, aia hala aku o Hauailiki ma i Kauai, alaila, hiki hou o Laieikawai i Keaau.

Ia Laieikawai ma i hala ai i uka o Paliuli, hoi aku la o Hauailiki mai ka heenalu aku, a halawai me ke Kuhina o Aiwohikupua, o kona alakai hoi. I aku la, "Kainoa o kahi paa ae nei a paa, he oiaio no ka ka Aiwohikupua e olelo nei. Nolaila, ua pau ka loaa a kuu kanaka maikai, a me kuu akamai i ka heenalu, hookahi wale no mea i koe ia kaua, o ke koele wawae no i Paliuli i neia po." A no keia olelo a Hauailiki, hooholo ae la kona hoa i ka ae.

Ma ka auina la mahope o ka aina awakea, pii aku la laua iuka, komo aku la iloko o na ululaau, i ka hihia paa o ka nahele. Ia laua i pii ai, halawai mua laua me Mailehaiwale, oia ke kiai makamua o ke Alii wahine. Ike mai la oia ia laua nei e kokoke aku ana io ia nei la, i mai la, "E Hauailiki, malaila olua hoi aku, aole o olua kuleana e pii mai ai ianei; no ka mea, ua hoonohoia mai wau maanei, he kiai makamua no ke Alii, a na'u no e hookuke aku i na mea a pau i hiki mai maanei, me ke kuleana ole; nolaila, e hoi olua me ke kali ole."

I aku la o Hauailiki, "E ae mai oe ia maua, e pii aku e ike i ka hale o ke Alii."

I mai la o Mailehaiwale, "Aole wau e ae aku i ko olua manao; no ka mea, o ko'u kuleana no ia i hoonohoia ai ma keia wahi, e kipaku aku i ka poe hele mai iuka nei e like me olua."

Aka, no ka oi aku o ko laua nei koi ana me ka olelo ikaika imua oiala, nolaila, ua ae aku la keia.

Ia Hauailiki ma i hala aku ai mahope iho o ko Mailehaiwale hookuu ana aku ia laua, halawai koke aku la laua me Mailekaluhea, ka lua o ko ke Alii wahine kiai.

I mai la o Mailekaluhea, "E! e hoi olua ano, aole he pono no olua e pii mai ianei, pehea la i aeia mai ai e hookuu mai ia olua?"

I aku la laua, "I hele mai nei maua e ike i ke Alii wahine."

"Aole olua e pono pela," wahi a Mailekaluhea, "no ka mea, ua hoonohoia mai makou he mau kiai e kipaku aku i na mea a pau i hele mai i keia wahi, nolaila, e hoi olua."

Aka, ma kela olelo a Mailekaluhea, ua oi aku ka maalea o ka laua nei olelo malimali imua oiala, nolaila, ua hookuuia'ku laua.

Ia laua i hala aku ai, halawai aku la laua me Mailelaulii, a e like no me ka olele a laua nei imua o na mea mua, pela no laua i hana ai imua o Mailelaulii.

A no ka maalea loa o laua i na olelo malimali, nolaila, ua hookuuia laua mai ko Mailelaulii alo aku. A hala aku la laua, halawai aku la me Mailepakaha, ka ha o na kiai.

Ia laua i hiki aku ai imua o Mailepakaha, aole he oluolu iki o keia kiai i ko laua hookuuia ana mai e na kiai mua; aka, no ka pakela o ka maalea ma ke kamailio ana, ua hookuuia aku la laua.

A hala aku laua, aia hoi, ike aku la laua ia Kahalaomapuana, ke kiai ma ka puka o ka Halealii, e kau mai ana iluna o ka eheu o na manu, a ike aku la no hoi i ke ano e o ka Halealii, ia manawa haule aku la o Hauailiki i ka honua, me ka naau eehia.

Ia Kahalaomapuana i ike mai ai ia laua nei, he mea e kona huhu, alaila, kahea mai la oia me kona mana, ma ke ano Alihikaua no ke Alii, "E Hauailiki e! e ku oe a hele aku; no ka mea, aole o olua kuleana o keia wahi, ina e hoopaakiki mai oe, alaila, e kauoha no wau i na manu o Paliuli nei, e ai aku i ko olua mau io, me ka hoi uhane aku hoi i Kauai."

A no keia olelo weliweli a Kahalaomapuana, alaila, ua hoopauia ko Hauailiki naau eehia, ala ae la ia a holo wikiwiki aku la a hiki ma Keaau, ma ke kahahiaka nui.

Ma keia hele ana a laua iuka o Paliali, ua nui ka luhi, a no ia luhi, haule aku la laua a hiamoe.

Iloko nae o ko Hauailiki manawa hiamoe, halawai mai la o Laieikawai me ka moeuhane, a halawai pu iho la laua, a i ko Hauailiki puoho ana ae mai ka hiamoe, aia hoi, he moeuhane kana.

Moe hou iho la no o Hauailiki, loaa hou no ia ia ka moeuhane, e like me mamua. Eha po, eha ao, o ka hoomau ana o keia mea ia Hauailiki, nolaila, ua pono ole ko Hauailiki manao.

I ka lima o ka po o ka hoomau ana o keia moeuhane ia Hauailiki, ma ka pili o ke ahiahi, ala ae la oia a pii aku la iuka o Paliuli, me ka ike ole nae o kona hoa.

Ia ia i pii aku ai, aole oia i hele aku ma ke alanui mua a laua i pii mua ai, a ma kahi e kokoke aku ana ia Mailehaiwale, hele ae la keia ma kahi kaawale, a pakele aku la i na maka o na kiai o ke Alii.

Ia ia i hiki ai mawaho o ka Hale Alii, ua hiamoe loa o Kahalaomapuana, alaila, nihi, malu aku la ko Hauailiki hele ana, a wehe ae la i ke pani o ka puka o ka Hale Alii, ua uhiia mai i ka Ahuula, aiahoi, ike aku la ia ia Laieikawai e kau mai ana iluna o ke eheu o na manu, ua hiamoe loa no hoi.

Ia ia i komo aku ai a ku ma kahi a ke Alii e moe ana, lalau aku la oia i ke poo o ke Alii, a hooluilui ae la. Ia manawa, puoho mai la o

Laieikawai mai ka hiamoe ana, aia hoi e ku ana o Hauailiki ma kona poo, a he mea pono ole ia i ko ke Alii wahine manao.

Alaila, olelo malu mai la o Laieikawai, ia Hauailiki, "E hoi oe ano i keia manawa, no ka mea, ua waihoia ka make a me ke ola i ko'u mau kiai; a nolaila, ke minamina nei wau ia oe; e ku oe a hele, mai kali."

I aku la o Hauailiki, "E ke Alii, e honi kaua, no ke mea, ia'u i pii mai ai iuka nei i keia mau po aku nei la, ua hiki mai wau iuka nei me ko ike ole; aka, ma ka mana o kou mau kiai, ua kipakuia wau, a ia maua i hiki ai i kai, a no ka maluhiluhi, haule aku la wau hiamoe. Ia'u e hiamoe ana, halawai pu iho la kaua ma ka moeuhane, a kahaule iho la kaua, a ua mui na la a me na po o ka hoomau ana ia'u o keia mea; nolaila wau i pii mai nei e hooko i ka hana i ka moeuhane."

I aku la o Laieikawai, "E hoe oe, aole o'u manao i kau mea e olelo mai nei; no ka mea, ua loaa no ia mea ia'u ma ka moeuhane, ua hana no e like me ka hana ia oe, a heaha la ia mea ia'u; nolaila, e hoi oe."

Iloko o ko Kahalaomapuana manawa hiamoe, lohe aku la oia i ka haukamumu o ka Halealii, a puoho ae la oia mai ka hiamoe ae, kahea aku la me ka ninau aku, "E Laieikawai! Owai kou hoa kamailio e haukamumu mai nei?"

A lohe laua i keia leo ninau, hoomaha iho la ke Alii aole i pane aku.

A mahope, ala ae la o Kahalaomapuana, a komo aku la i ka Halealii, aia hoi e noho mai ana o Hauailiki me Laieikawai iloko o ka Halealii.

I aku la o Kahalaomapuana, "E! e Hauailiki, e ku oe a e hele, aole i kupono kou komo ana mai nei, ua olelo aku wau ia oe i kela po mamua, aole ou kuleana ma keia wahi, ua like no ka'u olelo i keia po me ka po mua, nolaila, e ku oe a hoi aku."

A no keia olelo a Kahalaomapuana, ku ae la o Hauailiki me ka naau hilahila, a hoi aku la i kai o Keaau, a hai aku la i kona hoa no keia pii ana i Paliuli.

A ike iho la o Hauailiki, aole he kuleana hou e loaa ai o Laieikawai, alaila, hoomakaukau ae la na waa no ka hoi i Kauai, a ma ka wanaao, haalele lakou ia Keaau, a hoi aku la.

Ia Hauailiki ma i hoi aku ai i Kauai, a hiki lakou ma Wailua, ike aku la oia e akoakoa mai ana na'lii, a me na kaukaualii, a Kauakahialii, a me Kailiokalauokekoa kekahi i kela manawa.

Ia Hauailiki ma e hookokoke aku ana ma ka nuku o ka muliwai o Wailua, ike aku la oia ia Aiwohikupua, kahea aku la, "Ua eo wau ia oe."

A hiki aku la o Hauailiki, a hai aku la i ke ano o kana hele ana ia

Aiwohikupua, me ka hai aku nae i ka lilo ana o kona mau kaikuahine i mau kiai no ke Alii, alaila, he mea olioli ia ia Aiwohikupua.

I aku nae oia ia Hauailiki, "Ua pau ka pili a kaua, no ka manawa ona awa aku la no ia."

I loko nae o ko Hauailiki manawa e kamailio ana no ka lilo ana o na kaikuahine o Aiwohikupua i mau koa kiai no Laieikawai, alaila, ua manaolana hou ae la o Aiwohikupua e holo i Hawaii, no ke kii no ia Laieikawai e like no me kona manao mua.

Mokuna XV

I iho la o Aiwohikupua, "Pomaikai wau no kuu haalele ana i na kaikuahine o'u i Hawaii, a e ko auanei ko'u makemake; no ka mea, ua lohe ae nei wau, ua lilo ko'u mau kaikuahine i mau koa kiai no ka'u mea e manao nei."

I kela manawa a na'lii a pau e akoakoa nei ma Wailua, alaila, ku mai la o Aiwohikupua a hai mai la i kona manao imua o na Alii. "Auhea oukou, e holo hou ana wau i Hawaii, aole au e nele ana i ko'u makemake, no ka mea, aia'ku la i o'u mau kaikuahine ke kiai o ka'u mea e manao nei."

A no kela olelo a Aiwohikupua, pane mai la o Hauailiki, "Aole e loaa ia oe, no ka mea, ua ike aku la wau i ke kapu o ke Alii wahine, a kapukapu no hoi me ou mau kaikuahine, hookahi nae kaikuahine huhu loa, o kahi mea uuku, nolaila ko'u manao paa aole e loaa ia oe, a he uku no kou kokoke aku."

A no keia olelo a Hauailiki, aole he manao io o Aiwohikupua, no ka mea, ua manaolana loa kela no ka lohe ana o kona mau kaikuahine na kiai o ke Alii.

Mahope iho oia mau la, hoolale ae la oia i kona mau puali koa kiai, a me kona hanohano Alii a pau. A makaukau ke Alii no na kanaka, alaila, kauoha ae la oia i kona Kuhina e hoomakaukau na waa.

Wae ae la ke Kuhina i na waa kupono ke holo, he iwakalua kaulua, elua kanaha kaukahi, no na kaukaualii, a me na puali o ke Alii keia mau waa, a he kanaha peleleu, he mau waa a-ipuupuu no ke Alii ia. A o ke Alii hoi a me kona Kuhina, maluna laua o na pukolu.

A makaukau keia mau mea a pau, e like me ka wa holo mau o ke Alii, pela lakou i holo ai.

He nui na la i hala ma ia holo ana. A hiki lakou ma Kohala, ia manawa, akahi no a maopopo i ko Kohala poe o Aiwohikupua keia, ke kupua kaulana a puni na moku. A no ko ke Alii huna ana ia ia ma kela hiki ana ma Kohala, i hakaka'i me Ihuanu, oia ka mea i ike oleia ai.

Haalele lakou ia Kohala, hiki aku la lakou i Keaau. I kela manawa a lakou i hiki aku ai, ua hoi aku o Laieikawai, a me na kaikuahine pu o Aiwohikupua i Paliuli.

Ia Laieikawai ma i hoi aku ai ma kela la a Aiwohikupua ma i hiki aku ai, ua ike mua mai ko lakou kupunawahine i ko Aiwohikupua hiki ana ma Keaau.

I mai la o Waka, "Ua hiki hou mai la o Aiwohikupua ma Keaau i keia la; nolaila, e kiai oukou me ka makaukau, e makaala ia oukou iho, mai iho oukou maikai, e noho oukou mauka nei a hiki i ka hoi ana o Aiwohikupua i Kauai."

A lohe ke koa kiai Nui o ke Alii wahine i keia olelo a ko lakou kupunawahine, ia manawa, kauoha koke ae la o Kahalaomapuana ia Kihanuilulumoku ko lakou Akua, e hookokoke mai ma ka Halealii, e hoomakaukau no ka hoouka kaua.

Ma ko Kahalaomapuana ano kiai nui no ke Alii, kauoha ae la oia i kona mau kaikuaana, e kukakuka lakou ma na mea e pono ai ke Alii.

Ia lakou i akoakoa ai, kukakuka iho la lakou ma na mea kupono ia lakou. A eia ka lakou mau olelo hooholo, ma o ka noonoo la o Kahalaomapuana, ke koa kiai nui o ke Alii, "O oe e Mailehaiwale, ina e hiki mai o Aiwohikupua a halawai olua, e kipakuaku oe ia ia; no ka mea, o oe no ke kiai mua loa, a ina e hai mai i kona makemake, e hookuke aku no, a ina i paakiki loa mai ma kona ano keikikane ana, e hookuke ikaika aku ia ia, a ina i nui mai ka paakiki, alaila, e hoouna ae oe i kekahi manu kiai ou i o'u la, alaila, e hele mai au e hoohui ia kakou ma kahi hookahi, a na'u ponoi e kipaku aku ia ia. Ina he hele mai kana me ka inoino, alaila, e kauoha no wau i ko kakou Akua ia Kihanuilulumoku, nana no e luku aku ia ia."

A pau aeia ka lakou kuka ana no keia mau mea, hookaawale lakou ia lakou iho e like me mamua, oiai e kiai ana lakou i ke Alii.

Ma ka wanaao oia po iho, hiki ana o Aiwohikupua me kona Kuhina. Ia laua i ike mai ai e ku ana ka pahu kapu, ua uhiia i ka *oloa*, alaila, manao ae la laua ua kapu ke alanui e hiki aku ai i kahi o ke Alii. Aka, aole nae o Aiwohikupua manao ia kapu; no ka mea, ua lohe mua no ia, o kona mau kaikuahine ka mana kiai; nolaila, hoomau aku la laua i ka hele ana, a loaa hou he pahu kapu e like no me ka mea mua i loaa'i ia laua. Ua like no ko Aiwohikupua manao ma keia pahu kapu me kona manao mua.

Hoomau aku la no laua i ka hele ana a loaa hou ke kolu o ka pahu kapu e like me na mea mua; no ka mea, ua kukuluia no na pahu kapu e like me ka nui o kona mau kaikuahine.

A loaa ia laua ka ha o na pahu kapu, alaila, kokoke laua e hiki i ka lima o ka pahu kapu, oia no hoi ko Kahalaomapuana pahu kapu. Oia no hoi ka pahu kapu weliweli loa, ke hoomaka aeia e malamalama loa. Aka, aole nae laua i ike i ka weliweli oia pahu kapu, no ka mea, e molehulehu ana no.

Haalele laua i kela pahu, aole i liuliu ko laua hele ana aku, halawai mua no laua me ke kiai mua me Mailehaiwale, mahamaha aku la o Aiwohikupua, no ka ike ana aku i ke kaikuahine; ia wa koke no, pane aku la o Mailehaiwale. "E hoi olua ano, he kapu keia wahi."

Kuhi iho la o Aiwohikupua hoomaakaaka hoomaauea, hoomaka hou aku la laua e hookokoke aku i o Mailehaiwale, kipaku hou mai la no ke kiai. "E hoi koke olua, owai ko olua kuleana o uka nei, a o wai ko olua makamaka?"

"Heaha keia, e kuu kaikuahine?" wahi a Aiwohikupua, "Kainoa o oukou no ko'u makamaka, a ma o oukou la e loaa'i ko'u makemake."

Ia manawa, hoouna aku la o Mailehaiwale i kekahi manu kiai ona, a hiki i o Kahalaomapuana la; he manawa ole, hoohui ae la keia ia lakou a eha ma ko Mailekaluhea wahi kiai, a malaila i manao ai lakou e halawai me Aiwohikupua.

Mokuna XVI

A makaukau lakou, kii ia'ku la lakou a hiki mai la. Ia Aiwohikupua i ike aku ai ia Kahalaomapuana e kau mai ana kela iluna o ke eheu o na manu, me he Alihikaua Nui la, a he mea hou loa ia ia Aiwohikupua ma. Pane mai la ka kiai Nui, "E hoi olua ano, mai lohi, a aole hoi e kali, no ka mea, ua kapu ke Alii, aole no ou kuleana ma keia wahi, a aole no hoi e hiki ia oe ke manao mai he mau kaikuahine makou nou, ua hala ia manawa." O ke ku aku la no ia o Kahalaomapuana hoi, pau ka ike ana.

I kela manawa, ua ho-aia ka inaina wela o Aiwohikupua a mahuahua. Ma ia manawa, manao iho la oia e hoi a kai o Keaau, alaila, hoouna mai i kona mau puali koa e luku i na kaikuahine.

Ia laua i kaha aku e hoi a hiki i ka pahu kapu o Kahalaomapuana, aia hoi ilaila, ua hoopiiia ka huelo o ua moo nui nei iluna o ka pahu kapu, ua uhiia i ka *oloa*, ka ieie, a me ka palai, a he mea weliweli loa ia laua ka nana ana aku.

A hiki o Aiwohikupua ma i kai o Keaau, ia manawa, hoolale ae la ke Kuhina o Aiwohikupua i na puali koa o ke Alii e pii e luku i na kaikuahine, ma ke kauoha a ke Alii.

Ia la no, ike mua mai la no o Waka i ko Aiwohikupua manao, a me kana mau hana. A no ia mea, hele mai la o Waka a halawai me Kahalaomapuana, ko ke Alii wahine Alihikaua, olelo mai la, "E Kahalaomapuana, ua ike wau i ka manao o ko oukou kaikunane, a me kana mau hana, ke hoomakaukau la oia i umi mau kanaka ikaika, nana e kii mai e luku ia oukou, no ka mea, ua inaina ko oukou kaikunane, no ko oukou kipaku ana i kakahiaka nei; nolaila, e noho makaukau oukou ma ka inoa o ko kakou Akua."

Ia manawa, kauoha ae la oia ia Kihanuilulumoku, ka moo nui o Paliuli, ke akua o lakou nei. A hiki mai la ua moo nei, kauoha aku la oia, "E ko makou Akua, e Kihanuilulumoku, nanaia ke kupu, ka eu, ke kalohe o kai, ina e hele mai me ko lakou ikaika, pepehiia a pau, aohe ahailono, e noke oe a holo ke i olohelohe, e ao nae oe ia Kalahumoku, i ka ilio nui ikaika a Aiwohikupua, hemahema no oe, pau loa kakou, aole e pakele, kulia ko ikaika, ko mana a pau iluna o Aiwohikupua, Amama, ua noa, lele wale la." Oia ka pule kauoha a Kahalaomapuana i ko lakou Akua.

Ma ka po ana iho, pii aku la na kanaka he umi a ke Alii i wae ae e luku i na kaikuahine o Aiwohikupua, a o ka hope Kuhina ka umikumamakahi, mamuli o ka hookohu a ke Kuhina Nui i hope nona.

Ma ka pili o ka wanaao, hiki lakou i kahi e kokoke iki aku ana i Paliuli. Ia manawa, lohe aku la lakou i ka hu o ka nahele i ka makani o ke alelo o ua moo nui nei o Kihanuilulumoku, e hanu mai ana ia lakou nei, aole nae lakou i ike i keia mea, nolaila, hoomau aku la lakou i ka hele ana aole nae lakou i liuliu aku, he ike ana ka lakou i ka upoi ana iho a *kea* luna o ua moo nei maluna pono iho o lakou nei, aia nae lakou nei iwaenakonu o ka waha o ka moo, ia manawa, e lele koke aku ana ka Hope Kuhina, aole i kaawale aku, o ka muka koke ia aku la no ia pau loa, aohe ahailono.

Elua la, aohe mea nana i hai aku keia pilikia ia Aiwohikupua ma. A no ka haohao o ke Alii i ka hoi ole aku o kona mau koa alaila he mea e ka huhu o ke Alii.

A no keia mea, wae hou ae la ke Alii he mau kanaka he iwakalua e pii e luku i na kaikuahine, ma ka poe ikaika wale no; a hookohu aku la ke Kuhina i Hope Kuhina nona e hele pu me na koa.

Pii hou aku la no lakou a hiki no i kahi i pau ai kela poe mua i ka make, pau hou no i ua moo nei, aohe ahailono.

Kali hou no ke Alii aole i hoi aku. Hoouna hou aku no ke Alii hookahi kanaha koa, pau no i ka make; pela mau aku no ka make ana a hiki i ka e walu kanaha o na kanaka i pau i ka make.

Ia manawa, kukakuka ae la o Aiwohikupua me kona Kuhina i ke kumu o keia hoi ole mai o na kanaka e hoouna mauia nei.

I aku o Aiwohikupua i kona Kuhina, "Heaha keia e hoi ole mai nei na kanaka a kaua e hoouna aku nei?"

I aku la kona Kuhina, "Malia paha, ua pii no lakou a hiki iuka, a no ka ike i ka maikai o kela wahi, noho aku la no, a i ole, ua make mai la no i ou mau kaikuahine."

"Pehea auanei e make ai ia lakou, o na kaikamahine palupalu iho la ka mea e make ai o kau manao ana e make ia lakou?" pela aku o Aiwohikupua.

A no ka makemake o ke Alii e ike i ke kumu e hoi ole nei o kona mau kanaka, hooholo ae la laua me kona Kuhina e hoouna i mau elele e ike i ke kumu o keia hana a na kanaka o laua.

Ma ke kauoha a ke Alii, lawe ae la ke Kuhina ia Ulili, a me Akikeehiale, ko Aiwohikupua mau alele mama, a pii aku la e ike i ka pono o kona mau kanaka.

I ua mau elele la i hala aku ai, aole i liuliu halawai mai la me laua kekahi kanaka kia manu mai uka mai o Olaa; ninau mai la, "Mahea ka olua hele."

Olelo aku na elele, "E pii aku ana maua e ike i ka pono o ko makou poe, e noho la i Paliuli, awalu kanaha kanaka i hoounaia, aole hookahi o lakou i hoi ae."

"Pau aku la," wahi a ke kia manu, "i ka moo nui ia Kihanuilulumoku, aole e pakele mai."

A lohe laua i keia mea, hoomau aku la laua i ka pii ana, aole i upuupu, lohe aku la laua i ka hu a ka makani, a me ke kamumu o na laau e hina ana ma-o a ma-o, alaila hoomanao laua i ka olelo a ke kia manu, "ina e hu ana ka makani, o ua moo la ia."

Maopopo iho la ia laua o ua moo nei keia, e lele ae ana laua ma ko laua kino manu. Ia lele ana a kiekie laua nei, i alawa ae ka hana aia maluna pono o laua *kea* luna e poi iho ana ia laua nei, a no ko laua nei mama loa o ka lele ana ma ko laua ano kino manu, ua pakele laua.

Mokuna XVII

I kela wa, lele Kaawale loa aku la laua a hala loa i luna lilo, i nana iho ka hana o ua o Ulili ma i *kea* lalo o ua moo nei, e eku ana i ka honua me he

Oopalau la, alaila, he mea weliweli ia laua i ka nana aku, maopopo iho la ia laua, ua pau ko lakou poe kanaka i ka make, hoi aku la laua a olelo aku la ia Aiwohikupua i ka laua mea i ike ai.

Ia manawa, kiiia aku la o Kalahumoku, ka ilio nui ai kanaka a Aiwohikupua e hele e pepehi i ka moo a make, alaila, luku aku i na kaikuahine o Aiwohikupua.

I ka hiki ana o Kalahumoku ua ilio ai kanaka o Tahiti imua o kana moopuna (Aiwohikupua), "E pii oe i keia la e luku aku i o'u mau kaikuahine," wahi a Aiwohikupua, "a e lawe pu mai ia Laieikawai."

Mamua o ko ka ilio pii ana e luku i na kaikuahine o Aiwohikupua, kauoha mua ua Ilio nei i ke Alii, a me na kaukaualii, a me na kanaka a pau, a penei kana olelo kauoha: "Auhea oukou, ma keia pii ana a'u, e nana oukou i keia la iuka, ina e pii ka ohu a kupololei i luna a kiekie loa, ina e hina ka ohu ma ka lulu, alaila, ua halawai wau me Kihanuilulumoku, manao ae oukou ua hoaikane maua. Ina hoi e hina ana ka ohu i ka makani, alaila, ua hewa o uka, ua hakaka maua me ua moo nei. Alaila, o ka pule ka oukou i ke Akua ia Lanipipili, nana ae oukou i ka ohu a i hina i kai nei, ua lanakila ka moo; aka hoi, i pii ka ohu i luna a hina i luna o ke kuahiwi, alaila, ua hee ka moo; o ko kakou lanakila no hoi ia. Nolaila, e hoomau oukou i ka pule a hoi wale mai au."

I ka pau ana o keia mau kauoha, pii aku la ka ilio, hoouna pu aku la o Aiwohikupua ia Ulili laua me Akikeehiale, i mau elele na laua e hai mai ka hana a ka moo me ka Ilio.

I ka ilio i hiki aku ai iuka ma kahi kokoke i Paliuli, ua hiamoe nae o Kihanuilulumoku ia manawa. I ua moo nei e moe ana, hikilele ae la oia mai ka hiamoe ana, no ka mea, ua hoopuiwaia e ka hohono ilio, ia manawa nae, ua hala hope ka moo i ka ilio, e hele aku ana e loaa ke kiai mua o ke Alii Wahine.

Ia manawa, hanu ae la ka moo ka hookalakupua hoi o Paliuli, a ike aku la ia Kalahumoku i ke aiwaiwa o Tahiti, ia manawa, wehe ae la ua moo nei i kona a luna e hoouka no ke kaua me Kalahumoku.

I kela manawa koke no, hoike aku ana ka ilio i kona mau niho imua o ka moo. O ka hoomaka koke no ia o ke kaua, ia manawa, ua lanakila ka moo maluna o Kalahumoku, a hoi aku la ka ilio me ke ola mahunehune, ua pau na pepeiao a me ka huelo.

I ka hoomaka ana nae o ko laua hakaka, hoi aku la na elele a hai aku la ia Aiwohikupua ma i keia kaua weliweli.

A lohe aku la lakou ia Ulili ma i keia kaua a ka moo me ka ilio, a he mea mau nae ia Aiwohikupua ma ka nana ia uka.

Ia lakou no enana ana, pii ae la ka ohu a kupololei i luna aole i upuupu, hina ana ka ohu i kai, alaila, manao ae la o Aiwohikupua ua lanakila ka moo, alaila, he mea kaumaha ia Aiwohikupua no ke pio ana o ko lakou aoao.

Ma ke ahiahi o ua la hoouka kaua nei o na kupueu, hoi mai ana o Kalahumoku me ka nawaliwali, ua pau ke aho, i nana aku ka hana o ke Alii i kana ilio, ua pau na pepeiao, a me ka huelo i ka moo.

A no keia mea, manao ae la o Aiwohikupua e hoi, no ka mea, ua pio lakou. Hoi aku la lakou a hiki i Kauai, a hai aku la i ke ano o kana hele ana, a me ka lanakila o ka moo maluna o lakou. (O ke kolu keia, o ko Aiwohikupua hiki ana i Paliuli no Laieikawai, aole he ko iki o kona makemake.)

Ma keia hoi ana o Aiwohikupua i Kauai, mai ke kii hope ana ia Laieikawai, alaila, hoopau loa o Aiwohikupua i kona manao ana no Laieikawai. Ia manawa ka hooko ana a Aiwohikupua e hoo ko i ka olelo Kauohu a Poliahu.

I kela wa, papaiawa ae la o Aiwohikupua me kona mau kaukaualii, a me na haiawahine ona e hoopau i kana olelo hoohiki imua o Lanipipili kona Akua.

A loaa kona hoomaikaiia imua o kona Akua, me ke kalaia o kona hala hoohiki, "Aole e lawe i kekahi o na wahine o keia mau mokupuni i wahine hoao," e like me na mea i hoikeia ma kekahi o na Mokuna mua o keia Kaao.

A pau na la o ka papaiawa ma Kauai, hoouna aku la ia i kona mau elele ia Ulili laua me Akikeehiale, e holo aku e hai i ka olelo kauoha a ke Alii imua o Poliahu.

Ma ko laua ano kino manu, ua lele koke laua a hiki Hinaikamalama la ma Hana, a hiki laua, ninau aku i na ka maaina, "Auhea la ka wahine hoopalau a ke Alii o Kauai."

"E i ae no," wahi a ma kamaaina.

Hele aku la laua a halawai me ke Alii wahine o Hana.

Olelo aku la na elele i ke Alii wahine, "I hoounaia mai nei maua, e hai aku ia oe, ma ke kauoha a ko kane hoopalau. Ekolu malama ou e hoomakaukau ai no ka hoao o olua, a ma ka ha o ka malama i ka po i o Kulu e hiki mai ai oia a halawai olua e like me ka olua hoohiki ana."

A lohe ke Alii wahine i keia mau olelo, hoi aku la na elele a hiki i o Aiwohikupua.

Ninau mai la ke Alii, "Ua halawai olua me Poliahu?"

"Ae," wahi a na elele, "hai aku nei maua e like me ke kauoha, ke hoomakaukau la paha kela, i mai nei nae o ua Poliahu ia maua, ke hoomanao la no nae paha ia i ke konane ana a maua?"

"Ae paha," wahi a na elele.

A lohe ke Alii i keia olelo hope a na elele, manao ae la o Aiwohikupua i keia mau olelo, aole ia i hiki i o Poliahu la, alaila, hoomaopopo aku la o Aiwohikupua, "Pehea ka olua lele ana aku nei?"

Hai aku laua, "Lele aku nei maua a loaa he mokuaina lele hou aku no a he wahi mokuaina loihi, mailaila aku maua a he mokuaina nui e like me ka moku i loaa mua ia maua, elua nae mau moku liilii iho e like me kahi moku loihi, a he wahi mokuaina uuku loa iho, lele aku la maua ma ka aoao hikina o ua moku la a hiki maua he hele malalo o na puu, a he malu e uhi ana, ilaila o Poliahu i loaa'i ia maua, oia la."

I mai la o Aiwohikupua, "Aole i loaa ia olua o Poliahu, o Hinaikamalama aku la ia."

Aka, ma keia hana a na elele lalau, ua ho-aia ka inaina o ke Alii no kana mau elele, nolaila, ua hoopauia ko laua punahele.

Ma keia hoopauia ana o ua o Ulili ma, manao iho la laua, e hai i na mea huna i papaia ia laua e ko laua haku, nolaila, ua hooko laua i ka laua mea i ohumu ai, aia ma ka Mokuna XVIII, kakou e ike ai.

Mokuna XVIII

Mahope iho o ka hoopauia ana o Ulili ma; hoouna hou aku la oia ia Koae, kekahi o kana mau elele mama e like me ka olelo kauoha i na elele mua.

A hiki o Koae i o Poliahu la, halawai aku la laua, hai aku la o Koae i ke kauoha a ke Alii e like me ka mea i haiia ma na pauku hope o ka Mokuna XVII o keia Kaao; a pau na olelo a ke Alii i ka haiia, hoi aku la ko ke Alii elele, a hai aku la ma ka pololei, alaila, he mea maikai ia i kona Haku.

Noho iho la o Aiwohikupua, a i na la hope o ke kolu o ka malama; lawe ae la ke Alii i kona mau kaukaualii, a me na punahele, i na haiawahine hoi, na hoa kupono ke hele pu ma ke kahiko ana i ka hanohano Alii ke hele ma kana huakai no ka hoao o na Alii.

I na la i o Kaloa kukahi, haalele o Aiwohikupua ia Kauai, holo aku oia he kanaha kaulua, elua kanaha kaukahi, he iwahalua peleleu.

Mamua o ka po hoao o na Alii, i ka po i o Huna, hiki lakou i

Kawaihae, ia manawa, hoouna aku la oia ia koae, kona elele e kii ia Poliahu e iho mai e halawai me Aiwohikupua, i ka la i kauohaia'i e hoao.

A hiki ka elele imua o Aiwohikupua mai ke kii ana ia Poliahu, a hai mai la i kana olelo mai a Poliahu mai, "Eia ke kauoha a ko wahine, ma Waiulaula olua e hoao ai, ina e ike aku kakou ma ke kakahiaka nui o ka la o Kulu, e halii ana ka hau mai ka piko o Maunakea, Maunaloa, a me Hualalai, a hiki i Waiulaula, alaila, ua hiki lakou i kahi o olua e hoao ai, alaila, hele aku kakou, pela mai nei."

Alaila, hoomakaukau ae la o Aiwohikupua i kona hanohano Alii.

Kahiko aku la o Aiwohikupua i kona mau kaukaualii kane, a me na kaukaualii wahine, a me na punahele, i ka Ahuula, a o na haiawahine kekahi i kahikoia i ka Ahuoeno. A kahiko iho la o Aiwohikupua i kona kapa hau a Poliahu i haawi aku ai, kau iho la i ka mahiole ie i hakuia i ka hulu o na Iiwi. Kahiko aku la oia i kona mau hoewaa, a me na hookele i na kihei paiula, e like me ke kahiko ana i na hoewaa o ke Alii, pela no na hoewaa o kona puali alii a pau.

Ma na waa o ke Alii i kau ai a holo aku, ua kukuluia maluna o na pola o na waa he anuu, he wahi e noho ai ke Alii; ua hakuia ka anuu o ke Alii i na Ahuula, a maluna pono o ka anuu, he mau puloulou kapu Alii, a maloko o ka puloulou, noho iho la o Aiwohikupua.

Ma na waa ukali o ke Alii, he umi kaulua e hoopuni ana i ko ke Alii waa, a maluna o na waa ukali o ke Alii, he poe akamai i ke kaeke. Pela i kahikoia ai o Aiwohikupua i ko laua la i hoao ai me Poliahu.

Ma ka la o Kulu, ma ke kakahiaka, i ka puka ana ae o ka la a kiekie iki ae, ike aku la o Aiwohikupua ma i ka hoomaka ana o ka hau e uhi maluna o ka piko o na mauna, a hiki i kahi o laua e hoao ai.

I kela manawa, ua hiki o Poliahu, Lilinoe, Waiaie, a me Kahoupokane, i kahi e hoao ai na Alii.

Ia manawa, hoomaka o Aiwohikupua e hele e hui me ka wahine noho mauna o Maunakea. E like me ka mea i oleloia maluna, pela ko ke Alii hele ana.

Ia Aiwohikupua ma e holo aku ana i ka moana mai Kawaihae aku, he mea e ka olioli o Lilinoe i ka hanohano launa ole o ke Alii kane.

A hiki lakou i Waiulaula, ua pauhia lakou e ke anu, a nolaila, hoouna aku la o Aiwohikupua i kona elele e hai aku ia Poliahu, "Aole e hiki aku lakou no ke anu."

Ia manawa, haalele e Poliahu i kona kapa hau, lalau like ae la ka poe noho mauna i ko lakua kapa la, hoi aku la ka hau a kona wahi mau.

Ia Aiwohikupua ma i hiki aku ai ma ko Poliahu ma wahi e noho ana, he mea lealea loa i ke Alii wahine na mea kani o na waa o ke Alii kane, a he mea mahalo loa no hoi ia lakou ka ike ana i ko ke Alii kane hanohano, a maikai hoi.

Ia laua i hui ai, hoike ae la o Aiwohikupua, a me Poliahu, i na aahu o laua i haawi muaia i mau hoike no ka laua olelo ae like.

Ia manawa, hoa ae la na Alii, a lilo ae la laua i hookahi io, hoi ae la lakou a noho ma Kauai iuka o Honopuwai.

O na elele mua a Aiwohikupua, o Ulili laua me Akikeehiale, na laua i hele aku e hai ia Hinaikamalama i ka hoao ana o Aiwohikupua me Poliahu.

Ia Hinaikamalama i lohe ai i keia mau olelo no ka hoao o Aiwohikupua ma, ia manawa, noi aku la oia i kona mau makua e holo e makaikai ia Kauai, a ua pono kana noi imua o kona mau makua.

Hoolale ae la kona mau makua i na kanaka e hoomakaukau i na waa no Hinaikamalama e holo ai i Kauai, a wae ae la i mau hoahele kupono no ke Alii e like me ke ano mua o ka huakai Alii.

A makaukau ko ke Alii mau pono no ka hele ana, kau aku la o Hinaikamalama ma na waa, a holo aku la a hiki i Kauai.

Ia ianei i hiki aku ai, aia o Aiwohikupua me Poliahu ma Mana, e akoakoa ana na Alii malaila no ka la hookahakaha o Hauailiki me Makaweli.

Ia po iho, he po lealea ia no na Alii, he kilu, a he kaeke, na lealea ia po.

Ia Aiwohikupua ma e lealea ana ia manawa, ma ka waena konu o ka po, hiki aku la o Hinaikamalama a noho iloko o ka aha lealea; a he mea malihini nae i ka aha keia kaikamahine malihini.

Ia manawa aianei i komo aku ai iloko o ka aha lealea, aole nae o Aiwohikupua i ike maopopo mai ia manawa, no ka mea, ua lilo i ka hula kaeke.

Ia Hinaikamalama e noho ana iloko o ka aha lealea, aia hoi, ua komo iloko o Hauailiki ka iini nui.

Ia manawa, hele aku la o Hauailiki a i ka mea ume i aku la, "E hele oe a olelo aku ia Aiwohikupua e hoopau ka hula kaeke, i kilu ka lealea i koe, aia a kilu, alaila, kii aku oe a ume mai i ka wahine malihini, o ko'u pili ia o keia po."

Ma ke kauoha a ka mea nona ka po lealea e kilu, ua hoopauia ke kaeke.

Ia Hauailiki e kilu ana me Poliahu, a i ka umi o na hauna kilu a laua. Ia manawa, ku mai la ka mea ume a kaapuni ae la a puni ka aha, hoi mai la a kau aku la i ka maile ia Hauailiki me ke oli ana, a ku mai la o Hauailiki.

Ia manawa, kaili mai la ka mea ume i ka maile a kau aku la maluna o Hinaikamalama, a ku mai la.

Ia manawa, a Hinaikamalama i ku mai ai, nonoi aku la oia i ka mea ume e olelo ae, a kunou mai la ka mea ume.

Ninau aku la o Hinaikamalama i ka mea nona ka aha lealea, haiia mai la no Hauailiki me Makeweli.

Iloko o kela manawa, huli pono aku la o Hinaikamalama a olelo aku ia Hauailiki, "E ke Alii nona keia aha lealea, ua lohe ae la wau keia aha, ua umeia ae nei kaua e ka mea ume o ka aha lealea au, e ke Alii, no ka hoohui ana ia kaua no ka manawa pokole, alia nae wau e hooko i ka ume a ka mea nana i ume ia kaua e like me kona makemake. Aka, a hoakaka ae wau i ko'u kuleana i hiki mai ai ia Kauai nei, mai kahi loihi mai. Oiala, o Aiwohikupua ko'u kuleana i hiki ai i keia aina, no kuu lohe ana ae nei ua hoao oiala me Poliahu, nolaila i hele mai nei wau e ike i koiala hoopunipuni nui ia'u. No ka mea, hiki ae kela i Hana ma Maui, e heenalu ana makou, na laua la nae ka heenalu hope loa, a pau ka laua la heenalu ana, hoi laua la e konane ana makou, makemake no oiala i ke konane, kau hou ka papa konane a paa, ninau aku wau i kona kumu pili, kuhikuhi kela i na kaulua. Olelo aku wau, aole o'u makemake i kona kumu pili, alaila, hai aku wau i ka'u kumu pili makemake, o na kino no o maua, ina e make wau ia iala ma ke konane ana, alaila, lilo wau na iala, ma kana mau hana a pau e olelo ai ia'u, malaila wau, ma na mea kupono nae, a pela no hoi wau ina e make kela ia'u, alaila, e like me kana hana ia'u, pela no ka'u ia ia; a holo like ia maua keia olelo paa. I ke konane ana nae, aole i liuliu, paa mua ia'u na luna o ka papa konane a maua, o koiala make iho la no ia. I aku wau ia iala, ua eo oe, pono oe ke noho me a'u e like me ka kaua pili ana. I mai kela, 'Alia wau e hooko i kau kumu pili a hoi mai wau mai kuu huakai kaapuni mai, alaila, hookoia ke kumu pili au e ke Alii wahine.' A no keia olelo maikai aianei, ua holo like ia ia maua, a no keia mea, noho puupaa wau me ka maluhia a hiki mai i keia manawa. A no kuu lohe ana ae nei he wahine ka iala, oia ko'u hiki mai nei ia Kauai nei, a komo mai la i ko aha lealea e ke Alii, oia la."

Ia manawa, nene aku la ka aha kanaka a puni ka papai kilu, me ka hoohewa loa ia Aiwohikupua. Ia manawa no a Hinaikamalama a haiolelo la, alaila ua hoopihaia o Poliahu i ka huhu wela, o kona hoi no ia i Maunakea a hiki i keia la.

Mahope iho nae o ka haiolelo ana a Hinaikamalama, hoomaka hou ke kilu, ia Aiwohikupua laua me Makaweli ke kilu ia manawa.

Ia manawa, ku hou mai la ka mea ume a hooili hou i ka maile maluna o Hauailiki me Hinaikamalama, a ku ae la o Hauailiki, a ku mai la no hoi o Hinaikamalama. Ma keia ume hope, hai mai la o Hinaikamalama i kana olelo imua o Hauailiki, "E ke Alii e, ua hoohuiia kaua e ka mea ume ma ka mea mau o na aha lealea. Aka, alia wau e ae aku, aia ae mai o Aiwohikupua e hooko maua i na hoohiki a maua, a pau ko maua manawa, alaila, ma ka po lealea hou a ke Alii, e hookoia ai ka ume o keia po no kaua." Alaila, he mea maikai loa ia i ko Hauailiki manao.

A no keia olelo a Hinaikamalama, lawe ae la o Aiwohikupua ia Hinaikamalama no ka hooko i ka laua hoohiki.

Ia po no, iloko o ko laua manawa hoomaha no ka hooluolu i ka hoohiki ana, hike mai la ma o Hinaikamalama ke anu maeele loa, no ka mea, ua kuu mai la o Poliahu i ke anu o kona kapahau maluna o kona enemi.

Ia manawa, hapai ae la o Hinaikamalama he wahi mele:

"He anu e he a—nu
He anu e wale no hoi keia,
Ke ko nei i ke ano o kuu manawa,
Ua hewa ka paha loko o ka noho hale,
Ke kau mai nei ka halia i kuu manawa,
No ka noho hale paha ka hewa—e.
E kuu hoa—e, he anu—e."

Mokuna XIX

A pau ke oli ana i Hinaikamalama, olelo aku la oia ia Aiwohikupua, "Auhea oe, e apo mai oe ia'u a paa i mehana iho wau, hele mai nei kuu anu a anu, aohe wahi anu ole."

Alaila, hooko mai la o Aiwohikupua i ka ka wahine olelo, alaila, loaa mai la ka mahana e like me mamua.

A hoomakaukau iho la laua e hooluolu no ka hooko i ka laua hoohiki ma ka hoopalau ana, alaila, hiki hou mai la ke anu ia Hinaikamalama, o ka lua ia o kona loaa ana i ke anu.

Ia manawa, hapai hou ae la oia he wahi mele, penei:

"E ke hoa e, he a—nu,
Me he anu hau kuahiwi la keia,

Ke anu mai nei ma na kapuai,
Ke komi nei i kuu manawa,
Kuu manawa hiamoe—hoi,
Ke hoala mai nei ke anu ia'u,
I kuu po hiamoe—hoi."

I keia manawa, olelo aku la o Hinaikamalama ia Aiwohikupua, "Aole anei oe i ike i ke kumu o keia anu o kaua? Ina ua ike oe i ke kumu o keia anu, alaila e hai mai; mai huna oe."

I aku o Aiwohikupua, "No ko punalua keia anu, ua huhu paha ia kaua, nolaila, aahu ae la ia i ke kapa hau ona, nolaila na anu."

Pane aku la o Hinaikamalama, "Ua pau kaua, no ka mea, ua pili ae la no na kino o kaua, a ua ko ae la no ka hoohiki a kaua no ka hoopalau ana."

I mai o Aiwohikupua, "Ua oki kaua i keia manawa, e hookaawale kaua, apopo ma ke awakea, alaila, oia ka hooko ana o ka hoohiki a kaua."

"Ae," wahi a Hinaikamalama.

A kaawale aku la laua, alaila, loaa iho la ia Hinaikamalama ka moe oluolu ana ia koena po a hiki i ke ao ana.

Ma ke awakea, lawe hou ae la o Aiwohikupua e hooko i ka laua mea i olelo ai ia po iho mamua.

Iloko o ko laua manawa i hoomaka ai no ka hooko ana i ka hoohiki, alaila, ua pono ole ia mea i ko Poliahu manao.

Ia manawa, lawe ae la o Poliahu i kona kapa la, a aahu iho la, ia manawa ka hookuu ana'ku o Poliahu i ka wela maluna o Hinaikamalama. Ia manawa, hapai ae la oia he wahi mele, penei:

"He wela—e, he wela,
Ke poi mai nei ka wela a kuu ipo ia'u,
Ke hoohahana nei i kuu kino,
Ke hoonakulu nei hoi i kuu manawa,
No kuu ipo paha keia wela—e."

I aku o Aiwohikupua, "Aole no'u na wela, malia paha no Poliahu no na wela, ua huhu paha ia kaua."

I aku la o Hinaikamalama, "E hoomanawanui hou kaua, a ina i hiki hou mai ka wela maluna o kaua, alaila, haalele mai oe ia'u."

Mahope iho o keia mau mea, hoao hou ae la laua i ka laua hana no ka hooko i ka laua hoohiki.

Ia manawa, kau hou mai la no ka wela maluna o laua, alaila, hapai hou ae la oia ma ke mele:

"He wela—e he we—la,
Ke apu mai nei ka wela a ka po ia'u,
Ke ulili anapu nei i kau manawa,
Ka wela kukapu o ka hooilo,
I haoa enaena i ke kau,
Ka la wela kulu kahi o ka Makalii,
Ke hoeu mai nei ka wela ia'u e hele,
E hele no—e."

Ia manawa, ke ku ae la no ia o Hinaikamalama hele.

I mai o Aiwohikupua, "Kainoa o ka haawi mai i ka ihu, alaila hele aku."

I mai la o Hinaikamalama, "Aole e haawiia ka ihu ia oe, o ka hao ana mai ia o ka wela o ua wahine au, pono ole. Aloha oe."

(E waiho kakou i ke kamailio ana no Aiwohikupua maanei. E pono e kamailio pokole no Hinaikamalama.)

Mahope iho o kona hookaawale ana ia Aiwohikupua, hele aku oia a noho ma ka hale kamaaina.

Ia po iho, he po lealea hou ia no Hauailiki me na'lii ma Puuopapai.

Ia po, hoomanao ae la o Hinaikamalama no kana kauoha ia Hauailiki, mahope iho o ko laua umeia ana, a mamua hoi o kona hoohui ana me Aiwohikupua.

I kela po, oia ka lua o ka po lealea, alaila, hele aku la o Hinaikamalama a noho pu aku la mawaho o ka aha.

Ia manawa, na Kauakahialii laua me Kailiokalauokekoa ke kilu mua. Mahope iho, na Kailiokalauokekoa me Makaweli, ka lua o ka lealea.

Ia laua e kilu ana, komo mai la o Poliahu iloko o ka aha lealea. Ia Hauailiki me Poliahu ke kilu hope oia po.

A no ka ike ole o ka mea ume ia Hinaikamalama i kela po, nolaila, aole e hiki i ka mea ume ke hoomaka i kana hana. No ka mea, ua oleloia i ka po mua, no Hauailiki a me Hinaikamalama ka lealea mua oia po, a no ka loaa ole i ka maka o ka mea ume, ua lilo ka lealea i na mea e ae.

I ke kokoke ana e ao ua po nei, huli ae la ka mea ume iloko o ka aha ia Hinaikamalama, a loaa iho la.

IA MANAWA, KU MAI LA ka mea ume a waenakonu o ka aha, ia Hauailiki me Poliahu e kilu ana, ia manawa, kani aku la ke oli a ka mea ume, e hookolili ana i ka welau o ka maile i luna o Hauailiki, a kaili mai la ka mea ume i ka maile, alaila, ku mai la o Hauailiki. Hele aku la ua mea ume nei a loaa o Hinaikamalama, kau aku la i ka maile a kaili mai la. Ia manawa, ku mai la o Hinaikamalama mawaho o ka aha imua o ke anaina.

A ike mai la o Poliahu ia Hinaikamalama, kokoe aku la na maka, i ka ike i kona enemi.

A hala aku la o Hauailiki me Hinaikamalama ma kahi kupono ia laua e hooluolu ai.

Ia laua e hui ana, i aku la o Hinaikamalama ia Hauailiki. "Ina he lawe kou ia'u no ka manawa pokole a pau ae, alaila, ua pau kaua, no ka mea, aole pela ka makemake o ko'u mau makua, alaila, e waiho puupaa ia'u pela. Aka, ina i manao oe e lawe ia'u i wahine hoao nau, alaila, e haawi wau ia'u nau mau loa, e like me ka makemake o ko'u mau makua."

A no kela olelo a ka wahine, hai aku o Hauailiki i kona manao, "Ua pono kou manao, ua like no kou manao me ko'u; aka, e hoohui mua kaua ia kaua iho e like me ka makemake o ka mea ume, a mahope loa aku, alaila hoao loa kaua."

"Aole pela," wahi a Hinaikamalama, "e waiho puupaa ia'u pela, a hiki i kou manawa e kii ae ai ia'u, a loaa wau i Hana."

I ke kolu o ka po lealea o Hauailiki, i na'lii e akoakoa ana, a me na mea e ae, oia ka po i hui ai o Lilinoe, me Poliahu, o Waiau, a me Kahoupokane, no ka mea, ua imi mai lakou ia Poliahu, me ka manao ke pono nei ko Aiwohikupua ma noho ana me Poliahu.

Ia po, ia Aiwohikupua me Makaweli e kilu ana, a i ka waenakonu o ko laua manawa lealea, komo ana na wahine noho mauna iloko o ka aha lealea.

Ia Poliahu ma eha e ku ana me na kapa hau o lakou, he mea e ka hulali, ia manawa, nei aku la ka aha lealea no keia poe wahine, no ke ano e o ko lakou kapa. Ia manawa, popoi mai la ke anu i ka aha lealea a puni ka papai kilu, a kau mai la maluna o ka aha ka pilikia a hiki i ka wanaao, haalele o Poliahu ma ia Kauai. O keia manawa pu no hoi ka haalele ana o Hinaikamalama ia Kauai.

(Aia a hiki aku i ka hiki ana aku o Laieikawai i Kauai, mahope iho o ko Kekalukaluokewa hoao ana me Laieikawai, alaila, e hoomaka hou ke kamailio no Hinaikamalama. Ma keia wahi e kamailio no ke kauoha a Kauakahialii i kana aikane, pela aku a hiki i ka hui ana me Laieikawai.)

Ia Kauakahialii me Kailiokalauokekoa ma Pihanakalani, mahope iho o ko laua hoi ana mai Haawii mai. Oiai ua kokoke mai ko laua mau la hope.

Ia manawa, kauoha ae la o Kauakahialii i kana aikane ia Kekalukaluokewa, i kana olelo hoopomaikai maluna ona, a eia no ia:

"E kuu aikane aloha nui, ke waiho aku nei wau i olelo hoopomaikai maluna ou, no ka mea, ke kokoke mai nei ko'u mau la hope a hoi aku i ka aoao mau o ka honua.

"Hookahi no au mea malama o ka wahine a kaua, aia a haule aku wau i kahi hiki ole ia'u ke ike mai ia olua me ka wahine a kaua, alaila, ku oe i ka moku, o oe no maluna, o ka wahine a kaua malalo, e like no me ka kaua nei ana i ka moku i puni ai, pela no oe e noho aku ai me ka wahine a kaua.

"A make wau, a manao ae paha oe i wahine nau, mai lawe oe i ka kaua wahine, aole no hoi e manao oe ia ia o kau wahine ia, no ka mea, ua lilo no ia ia kaua.

"Aia kau wahine e kii o kuu wahine i haalele aku nei i Hawaii, o Laieikawai, i na o kau wahine, ia ola ke kino, a kaulana no hoi. A manao oe e kii, hookahi au mea malama o ka ohe a kaua, aia malama pono oe i ka ohe, alaila wahine oe, oia ke kauoha ia oe."

Ma keia kauoha a Kauakahialii, ua pono ia i ko ke aikane manao.

Ma ia hope mai, make aku la o Kauakahialii, lilo ka noho alii i kana aikane, a o ka laua wahine no ke Kuhina.

A ma ia hope mai, i ke kokoke ana i ko Kailiokalauokekoa mau la hope, waiho aku la oia i olelo kuoha no ka malama ana ia Kanikawi ka laua ohe kapu me kana kane, e like me ke kauoha a Kauakahialii:

"E kuu kane, eia ka ohe, malamaia, he ohe mana, o na mea a pau au e makemake ai, ina e kii oe i ka wahine a ko aikane i kauoha ai ia oe, o ka mea no keia nana e hoohui ia olua. Eia nae e malama mau loa oe, ma kau wahi e hele ai, a e noho ai, mai haalele iki i ka ohe, no ka mea, ua ike no oe i ka hana a kau aikane i ko olua manawa i kii ae ai ia'u i kuu wa e aneane aku ana i ka make, mamuli o kuu aloha i ko aikane. Na ua ohe la keia ola ana e ola aku nei mai ka luakupapau mai, nolaila, e hoolohe oe me ka malama loa e like me ka'u e olelo aku nei ia oe."

Mokuna XX

A make aku la o Kailiokalauokekoa, lilo ae la ka noho Alii a pau loa ia Kekalukaluokewa, a hooponopono aku la oia i ka aina, a me na kanaka a pau malalo o kona noho Alii.

Mahope iho o ka pau ana o kana hooponopono ana i ka aina, a me kona noho Alii ana. Ia manawa, hoomanao ae la o Kekalukaluokewa i ke kauoha a kana aikane no Laieikawai.

Ia Kekalukaluokewa i manao ai e hooko i ke kauoha a kana aikane, kauoha ae la oia i kona Kuhina, e hoomakaukau i na waa hookahi mano, no ka huakai kii wahine a ke Alii i Hawaii, e like me ke aoao mau o ke Alii.

A makaukau ka ke Alii kauoha, lawe ae la ke Alii elua mau punahele, a lawe ae la i na kaukaualii ka poe kupono ke hele pu me ke Alii, a lawe ae la oia i kona mau ialoa a pau.

I ka malama i oleloia o ka Mahoe mua, i na malama maikai o ka moana, haalele lakou ia Kauai, a holo aku i Hawaii. Ua nui na la i hala ia lakou ma ia hele ana.

Ma keia holo ana a lakou, hiki aku la ma Makahanaloa i Hilo, ma ke kakahiaka nui. Ia manawa, olelo aku kahi kanaka nana i ike mua ia Laieikawai i ke Alii, "E nana oe i kela anuenue e pio la iuka, o Paliuli no ia, oia no ua wahi la, malaila no kahi i loaa'i ia'u." E nee ana nae ka ua o Hilo ia mau la a lakou i hiki aku ai ma Makahanaloa.

A no keia olelo a kahi kanaka, i aku ke Alii, "Alia wau e manaoio i kau no Laieikawai kela hoailona, no ka mea, he mea mau iloko o ka wa ua ka pio o ke anuenue, nolaila, i kuu manao, e hekau na waa, a e kali kakou a malie ka ua, alaila, i pio mai ke anuenue iloko o ka wa ua ole, alaila maopopo no Laieikawai ka hoailona." Ua like ko ke Alii manao ana ma keia mea me ko Aiwohikupua.

A no keia mea, noho iho la lakou malaila e like me ko ke Alii makemake. Hookahi anahulu me elua la keu, haalele ka malie o Hilo, ike maikaiia aku la ka aina.

I ke kakahiaka nui o ka la umikumamalua, puka aku la ke Alii iwaho mai ka hale ae. Aia hoi e hoomau ana ke anuenue e like me mamua, ma ke kiekie iki ana'e o ka la, aia e pio ana ke anuenue i kai o Keaau, ua hala ae la o Laieikawai i kai. (E like me ka kakou kamailio ana mamua ma ko Aiwohikupua moolelo.)

Ma kela la, pau ko ke Alii kanalua ana no kela hoailona, a holo aku la a hiki i Keaau. Ia lakou i hiki aku ai ma Keaau, ua hoi aku o Laieikawai iuka o Paliuli.

Ia lakou i hiki aku ai, ua nui na kamaaina i lulumi mai e makaikai ia Kekalukaluokewa; me ka olelo mai o na kamaaina, "Akahi no ka aina kanaka maikai o Kauai."

I kela la a Kekalukaluokewa ma i holo aku ai a hiki i Keaau. Ua ike mua mai o Waka o Kekalukaluokewa keia.

Olelo mai o Waka i kana moopuna, "Mai iho hou oe i kai, no ka mea, ua hiki mai la o Kekalukaluokewa i Keaau, i kii mai la ia oe i wahine oe. Make aku la o Kauakahialii, kauoha ae la i ke aikane e kii mai ia oe i wahine, nolaila o kau kane ia. A ae oe o kau kane ia, ku oe i ka moku, ola no hoi na iwi. Nolaila, e noho oe iuka nei, a hala na la eha, alaila iho aku oe, a ina ua makemake oe, alaila, hoi mai oe a hai mai i kou makemake ia'u."

Noho iho la o Laieikawai a hala na la eha e like me ke kauoha a kona kupunawahine.

Ma ke kakahiaka nui o ka ha o ko Laieikawai mau la hoomalu, ala ae la oia, a me kona kahu kuapuu, a iho aku la i Keaau.

La laua i hiki aku ai, ma kahi kokoke iki e nana aku ai i kauhale; aia hoi, ua hiki mua aku o Kekalukaluokewa ma kulana heenalu mamua o ko laua hiki ana aku, ekolu nae mau keiki e ku ana ma kulana heenalu o ke Alii a me na punahele elua.

Ia Laieikawai ma e noho ana ma kahi a laua e hoohalua ana no Kekalukaluokewa, aole nae laua i like i ke kane a ke kupunawahine i makemake ai.

I aku o Laieikawai i kona wahi kahu, "Pehea la kaua e ike ai i ke kane a'u a kuu kupunawahine i olelo mai nei?"

Olelo aku kona kahu, "Pono kaua ke kali a pau ka lakou heenalu ana, a o ka mea e hele wale mai ana, aole he paa i ka papa heenalu, alaila, o ke Alii no ia, o ko kane no ka hoi ia."

Ma ka olelo a ko Laieikawai kahu, noho iho la laua malaila, e kali ana.

Ia manawa, hoopau ae la na heenalu i ko lakou manawa heenalu, a hoi mai la a pae iuka.

Ia wa, ike aku la laua i ke kiiia ana mai o na papa o na punahele e na kanaka, a laweia aku la. O ka papa heenalu hoi o ke Alii, na na punahele i auamo aku, a hele wale mai la o Kekalukaluokewa, pela i ike ai o Laieikawai i kana kane.

A maopopo iho la ia laua ka laua mea i iho mai ai, alaila, hoi aku la laua a hiki i Paliuli, a hai aku la i ke kupunawahine i ka laua mea i ike ai.

Ninau mai la ke kupunawahine, "Ua makemake oe i ko kane?"

"Ae," wahi a Laieikawai.

I mai o Waka, "Apopo, ma ka puka ana o ka la, oia ka wa e a-u ai o Kekalukaluokewa i ka heenalu oia wale, ia manawa, e hoouhi aku ai wau i ka noe maluna o ka aina a puni o Puna nei, a maloko oia noe, e hoouna aku no wau ia oe maluna o na manu a hui olua me Kekalukaluokewa me ka ike oleia, aia a pau ka uhi ana o ka noe maluna o ka aina, ia manawa e ike aku ai na mea a pau, o oe kekahi me Kekalukaluokewa e hee mai ana i ka nalu hookahi, oia ka manawa e loaa'i ko ihu i ke keiki Kauai. Nolaila, i kou puka ana mailoko aku nei o kou hale, aole oe e kamailio iki aku i kekahi mea e ae, aole i kekahi kane, aole hoi i kekahi wahine, aia a laa ko ihu ia, Kekalukaluokewa, oia kou manawa e kamailio ai me na mea e ae. Aia a pau ka olua heenalu ana, alaila, e hoouna aku wau i na manu, a me ka noe maluna o ka aina, o kou manawa ia e hoi mai ai me ko kane a loko o ko olua hale, alaila, e hoolaaia ko kino e like me ko'u makemake."

A pau keia mau mea i ka haiia ia Laieikawai, hoi aku la oia ma kona Halealii, oia a me kona kahu.

Ia Laieikawai me kona kahu ma ka hale, mahope iho o ke kauoha ana a kona kupunawahine. Hoouna ae la oia i kona kahu e kii aku ia Mailehaiwale, Mailekaluhea, Mailelaulii, Mailepakaha, a me Kahalaomapuana, kona mau hoa kuka e like me ka lakou hoohiki ana.

A hiki mai la kona mau hoa kuka, kona mau kiai kino hoi, olelo aku la o Laieikawai, "Auhea oukou e o'u mau hoa, ua kuka ae nei au me ke kupunawahine o kakou, e hao wau i kane na'u, nolaila wau i houna aku nei i ko kakou kahu e kii aku ia oukou e like me ka kakou hoohiki ana, mahope iho o ko kakou hui ana maanei. O ka makemake o ko kakou kupunawahine, o Kekalukaluokewa kuu kane, a pehea? Aia i ka kakou hooholo like ana, ina i ae mai oukou, ua pono no, ina e hoole mai, aia no ia i ko kakou manao."

Olelo aku o Kahalaomapuana, "Ua pono, ua hoomoe ae la no ko kakou kupunawahine e like me kona makemake, aohe a makou olelo. Eia nae, a i hoao oe i ke kane, mai haalele oe ia makou e like me ka kakou hoohiki ana; ma kau wahi e hele ai, malaila pu kakou, o oe i ka pilikia, o kakou pu ilaila."

"Aole wau e haalele ia oukou," wahi a Laieikawai.

Eia hoi, ua ike mua ae nei kakou ma na Mokuna mua, he mea mau no ia Laieikawai ka iho i kai o Keaau, ma ka moolelo o Hauailiki, a me ka moolelo o ka hele alua ana o Aiwohikupua i Hawaii, a oia mau no a hiki i ko Kekalukaluokewa hiki ana i Hawaii.

I na manawa a pau o ko Laieikawai hele ana ma Keaau, he mea mau i keia keiki ia Halaaniani ka ike ia Laieikawai ma Keaau, me ka ike ole nae o Halaaniani i kahi e hele mai ai o Laieikawai; mai ia manawa mai ka hoomaka ana o ka manao ino e ake e loaa o Laieikawai, aole nae e hiki, no ka mea, ua alaila mai e ka hilahila, a hiki ole ke pane aku.

A o ua Halaaniani nei, ke kaikunane o Malio, he keiki kaulana ia ma Puna no ke kanaka ui, he keiki *koaka*, nae.

I ka eha o na la hoomalu o Laieikawai, he mea hoohuoi ia Halaaniani ka nalo ana o Laieikawai, aole i hiki hou ma Keaau.

Ia Halaaniani i hookokoke mai ai ma kahi o na kamaaina o Keaau, lohe iho la oia, e lilo ana ua Laieikawai nei ia Kekalukaluokewa.

Ia manawa, hoi wikiwiki aku la oia e halawai me kona kaikuahine me Malio.

Olelo aku la kona kaikunane, "E Malio, i pii mai nei wau ia oe e kii oe i ko'u makemake. No ka mea, i na la a pau a'u e nalo nei, ma Keaau no wau, no ko'u ike mau i keia wahine maikai, nolaila, ua hookonokonoia mai wau e ke kuko e hele pinepine e ike i ua wahine nei. A ma keia la, ua lohe aku nei wau e lilo ana i ke Alii o Kauai i ka la apopo; nolaila, o ko mana a pau maluna iho ia o kaua like e lilo ia'u kela kaikamahine."

I mai la kona kaikuahine, "Aole na he wahine e, o ka moopuna na a Waka, o Laieikawai, ua haawi ae la ke kupunawahine i ke Alii nui o Kauai, popo hoao. Nolaila, a e like me kou makemake, e hoi nae oe a kou wahi, a ma ke ahiahi poeleele pii hou mai, a mauka nei kaua e moe ai, oia ka manawa o kaua e ike ai i ko nele a me ka loaa."

Mamuli o ke kauoha o Malio i kona kaikunane, hoi mai la o Halaaniani a ma kona hale noho ma Kula.

A hiki i ka manawa i kauohaia nona e hele aku i kahi o kona kaikuahine.

Mamua o ko laua manawa hiamoe, olelo aku la o Malio ia Halaaniani, "Ina e moe kaua i keia po, a i loaa ia oe ka moeuhane, alaila, hai mai oe ia'u, a pela no hoi wau."

Ia laua e moe ana, a hiki paha i ka pili o ke ao, ala ae la o Halaaniani, aole i loaa he moe ia ia, a ala mai la no hoi o Malio ia manawa no.

Mokuna XXI

Ninau aku o Malio ia Halaaniani, "Heaha kau moe?"

I aku la o Halaaniani, "Aole a'u wahi moe, i ka hiamoe ana no, o ke oki no ia, aole wau i loaa wahi moe iki a puoho wale ae la."

Ninau aku la hoi o Halaaniani i kona kai kuahine, "Pehea hoi oe?"

Hai mai la kona kaikuahine, "Owau ka mea moe; ia kaua no i moe iho nei, hele aku nei no kaua a ma nahelehele, moe oe i kou puhalaau, a owau no hoi ma ko'u puhalaau; nana aku nei ko'u uhane i kekahi wahi manu e hana ana i kona punana, a pau, lele aku nei no ua manu nei ana i kona punana a pau, lele aku nei no ua manu nei nana ka punana a nalowale. A mahope, he manu okoa ka manu nana i lele mai a hoomoe i ua punana nei, aole nae wau i ike i ka lele ana'ku o ka manu hope nana i hoomoe ua punana nei, a puoho wale ae la wau, aole no hoi i ikeia ka hoi hou ana mai o ka manu nana ka punana."

A no keia moe, ninau aku la o Halaaniani, "A heaha iho la ke ano o ia moe?"

Hai aku la kona kaikuahine i ke ano oiaio o ua moe la, "E pomaikai io ana no oe, no ka mea, o ka manu mua nona ka punana, o Kekalukaluokewa no ia, a o ka punana, o Laieikawai no ia, a o ka manu hope nana i hoomoe ka punana, o oe no ia. Nolaila, ma keia kakahiaka, e lilo ana ka wahine a olua ia oe. Ia Waka e hoouna ae ai ia Laieikawai maluna o ka eheu o na manu, no ka hoao me Kekalukaluokewa; uhi mai auanei ka noe a me ke awa, a mao ae, alaila, ikeia'ku ekolu oukou e ku mai ana ma kuanalu, alaila, e ike auanei oe he mana ko'u e uhi aku maluna o Waka, a ike ole oia i ka'u mea e hana aku ai nou; nolaila, e ku kaua a hele aku ma kahi e kokoke aku ana i kahi e hoao ai o Laieikawai."

A pau ka hoike ana a Malio i ke ano o ke ia mau mea, iho aku la laua a ma kahi kupono ia laua e noho ai.

O malio nae, he hiki ia ia ke hana i na hana mana; a oia wale no kona kumu i hoano ai.

Ia laua i hiki aku ai ma Keaau, ike aku la laua ia Kekalukaluokewa e au ae ana i ka heenalu.

Olelo aku la o Malio ia Halaaniani, "E hoolohe oe i ka'u, ina i hiki oukou ma kulana heenalu, a hee oukou i ka nalu, mai hoopae oe, e hoomake oe i kou nalu, pela no oe e hoomake ai a hala na nalu eha o ko laua hee ana, a i ka lima o ka nalu, oia ko laua nalu pau. Malie o hoohuoi laua i kou pae ole, ninau iho i ke kumu o kou pae ole ana, alaila nai aku oe, no ka maa ole i ka hee ana o ka nalu po kopoko, a i ninau mai i kau nalu loihi e hee ai, alaila hai aku oe o Huia. Ina i maliu ole mai kela i kau olelo, a hoomakaukau laua e hee i ko laua nalu pau, ia laua e hee ai, alaila hopu aku oe i na wawae o Laieikawai, i hee aku o Kekalukaluokewa oia wale. A lilo ia oe kela wahine, alaila ahai oe i ka moana loa, nana mai oe ia uka nei, e au aku ana o Kumukahi iloko o ka ale, alaila o ke kulana nalu ia, alaila pule aeoe ma kuu inoa, a na'u no e hoouna aku i nalu maluna o olua, o kou nalu no ia ko kou makemake, lilo loa ia oe."

Ia laua no e kamailio ana i keia mau mea, uhi ana ka noe a Waka maluna o ka aina. Ia manawa, kui ka hekili, aia o Laieikawai ma kaluna nalu, na Waka ia. Kui hou ka hekili, o ka lua ia, na Malio ia. I ka mao ana ae o ka noe, aia ekolu poe e lana ana ma kulana nalu e ku ana, a he mea haohao ia ia uka i ka nana aku.

E like me ke kauoha a Waka i kana moopuna, "Aole e olelo i na mea e ae, a laa ka ihu ia Kekalukaluokewa, alaila olelo i na mea e ae." Ua hoolohe no kana moopuna i ke kauoha a ke kupunawahine.

A ia lakou ekolu ma kulana heenalu, aole kekahi leo i loheia iwaena o lakou.

I ke ku ana o ka nalu mua, olelo mai o Kekalukaluokewa, "Pae kakou." Ia manawa, hoomoe like lakou i na papa o lakou, make iho la o Halaaniani, pae aku laua la, oia ka manawa i laa ai ka ihu o Laieikawai ia Kekalukaluokewa, e like me ke kauoha a ke kupunawahine.

Ekolu nalu o ka hee ana o lakou, a ekolu no hoi ka pae ana o Laieikawai ma, a e kolu no hoi ka make ana o Halaaniani.

I ka ha o ko laua nalu pae, akahi no a loaa ka ninau a Laieikawai ia Halaaniani, me ka i aku, "Heaha kou mea e pae ole nei? Aha nalu, aole ou pae iki, heaha la ke kumu o kou pae ole ana?"

"No ka maa ole i ka nalu pokopoko," wahi a Halaaniani, "no ka mea, he nalu loloa ko'u e hee ai."

Hai aku la keia e like me ke kauoha a kona kaikuahine.

I ka lima o ka nalu, oia ka nalu pau loa o Laieikawai me Kekalukaluokewa.

Ia Kekalukaluokewa me Laieikawai i hoomaka ai e hoomoe aku i ka nalu, e hopu aku ana o Halaaniani ma na kapuai o Laieikawai, a lilo mai la ma kona lima, lilo aku la ka papa heenalu o Laieikawai, pae aku la nae o Kekalukaluokewa a kau a kahi maloo.

I kela manawa i lilo aku ai o Laieikawai ma ka lima o Halaaniani, olelo aku la ia Halaaniani, "He mea kupanaha, ia oe no ka pae ole ana wau, a lilo aku la ko'u papa."

I aku o Halaaniani, "He lilo no ka papa ou o ka wahine maikai, he kanaka ka mea nana e lawe mai."

Ia laua no e olelo ana no keia mau mea, laweia mai la ka papa heenalu o Laieikawai a hiki i kahi o laua e ku ana.

I aku o Laieikawai ia Halaaniani, "Auhea kau nalu o kau aua ana iho nei ia'u?"

A no ka ninau a ke Alii wahine, au aku la laua, ia manawa a laua e au ana, hai aku la o Halaaniani i kana olelo imua o ke Alii wahine, "Ma keia au ana a kaua, mai alawa oe i hope, imua no na maka, aia no ia'u kulana nalu, alaila hai aku au ia oe."

Au aku la laua a liuliu loa komo mai la iloko o Laieikawai ka haohao; ia manawa, pane aku oia, "Haohao ka nalu au e ke kane, ke au aku nei kaua i kahi o ka nalu ole, eia kaua i ka moana lewa loa, ke hai ka nalu i keia wahi, he mea kupanaha, he ale ka mea loaa i ka moana loa."

I aku o Halaaniani, "E hoolohe pono loa oe, ma ka'u olelo mua ia oe malaila wale no kaua."

Hoolohe aku la no o Laieikawai ma na olelo a kona hoa heenalu.

Ia au ana a laua a hiki i kahi a Halaaniani e manao ai o kulana nalu ia, alaila, olelo aku la o Halaaniani i kona hoa heenalu, "Nana ia o uka."

Pane aku o Laieikawai, "Ua nalo ka aina, ua hele mai nei o Kumukahi a onioni i ka ale."

"O kulana nalu keia," wahi a Halaaniani, "Ke olelo aku nei au ia oe, ina i haki ka nalu mua, aole kaua e pae ia nalu, a i ka lua o ka nalu aole no e pae, a i ke kolu o ka nalu, o ka nalu ia o kaua e pae ai. I haki ka nalu, a i kakala, a i oia oe, mai haalele oe i ka papa o ka mea no ia nana e hoolana; ina e haalele oe i ka papa, alaila aole oe e ike ia'u."

A pau ka laua kamailio ana no keia mau olelo, pule aku la o Halaaniani i ko laua akua ma ka inoa o kona kaikuahine e like me ka Malio kauoha mua.

Pule aku la o Halaaniani a hiki i ka hapalua o ka manawa; ku ana ua nalu, hoomau aku la oia i ka pule a hiki i ka Amama ana. Ku hou ana ua nalu, o ka lua ia, aole i upuupu iho, opuu ana kahi nalu.

Ia wa kahea mai o Halaaniani i kona hoa, "Pae kaua."

Ia manawa, hoomoe koke o Laieikawai i ka papa, o ka pae aku la no ia, ma ke kokua aku o Halaaniani.

I kela manawa, aia no o Laieikawai iloko o ka halehale poipu o ka nalu, a i ka haki maikai ana o ka nalu, i alawa ae ka hana o Laieikawai, aole o Halaaniani me ia. I alawa hou aku o Laieikawai, e kau mai ana o Halaaniani ma ka pea o ka nalu, ma kona akamai nui. Ia manawa ka hoomaka ana o Laieikawai e haawi ia ia iho ia Halaaniani.

Hoi aku la laua mai ko laua heenalu ana, me ka ike mai no o Waka i ko laua hee aku, ua kuhi nae o Kekalukaluokewa ko Laieikawai hoa hee nalu.

A o Malio, ke kaikuahine o Halaaniani, ua ikeia ma kona kuamoo moolelo, he hiki ia ia ke hana i na hana mana he nui, ma ka Mokuna XXII a me ka Mokuna XXIII e ike ai kakou i ka nui o kana mau hana mana.

Mokuna XXII

I kela manawa a Laieikawai me Halaaniani e heenalu ana mai ka moana mai, ua uhiia ko Waka mana e ka mana nui o Malio, a nolaila, ua ike ole o Waka i na mea a pau e hanaia ana o kana moopuna.

I kela manawa, i ke kokoke ana aku o Laieikawai ma e pae i ka honua, oia ka manawa a Waka i hoouna mai ai i na manu maloko o ka noe, a i ka mao ana ae, o na papa heenalu wale no ke waiho ana, aia aku la o Laieikawai me Halaaniani iuka o Paliuli ma ko Laieikawai hale, malaila o Halaaniani i lawe ai ia Laieikawai i wahine hoao nana.

Ia la a po, mai ka po a ao, a awakea, he mea haohao loa ia Waka no kana moopuna, no ka mea, ua olelo mua aku oia i kana moopuna mamua o kona hoouna ana aku e launa me Kekalukaluokewa. Eia ke kauoha:

"Iho oe i keia la, a hui oe me Kekalukaluokewa, hoi mai olua a uka nei, a laa ko kino, alaila, kii ae oe ia'u, na'u no e malama i kou pau no ka hoohaumia ana ia oe." E like me ka mea mau o na kaikamahine punahele.

A no keia haohao o Waka, ma ke awakea o ka lua o ka la o ko Laieikawai la hui me Halaaniani, hele aku la ke kupunawahine e ike i ka pono o kana moopuna.

I ke kupunawahine i hiki aku ai; aia nae ua pauhia laua e ka hiamoe nui, me he mea la ua lilo ka po i manawa makaala na laua e like me ka mea mau i na mea hou.

Ia manawa, iloko o ka wa hiamoe o Laieikawai, i nana iho ka hana o ke kupunawahine, he kane e keia a ka moopuna e moe pu ana, ka mea a ke kupunawahine i ae ole ai.

A no keia mea, hoala ae la o Waka i ka moopuna, a ala ae la, ninau iho la ke kupunawahine, "Owai keia?"

Olelo ae la ka moopuna, "O Kekalukaluokewa no hoi."

I mai la ke kupunawahine me ka inaina, "Aole keia o Kekalukaluokewa, o Halaaniani keia o ke kaikunane o Malio. Nolaila, ke hai aku nei wau i kuu manao paa ia oe, aole wau e ike hou i kou maka e kuu moopuna ma keia hope aku a hiki i kuu la make, no ka mea, ua pale oe i ka'u mau olelo, kainoa wau e ahai nei ia oe ma kahi nalo, e nana mai ana oe ia'u, nolaila, e noho oe me ko kane mamuli o ko wahine maikai, o ko mana, aole ia me oe, he nani ia ua imi aku la no i ke kane, hana pono iho na lima, i kau kane na pono a me kou hanohano."

Mahope iho o keia manawa, hoomakaukau ae la o Waka e hana i hale hou i like me ka hale i hanaia no Laieikawai. A ma ka mana o Waka, ua hikiwawe, ua paa ka hale.

A makaukau ka hale, iho aku la o Waka e halawai kino me Kekalukaluokewa, no ka mea, ua mokumokuahua kona manawa i ke aloha ia Kekalukaluokewa.

A hiki o Waka ma kahi o Kekalukaluokewa, hopu aku la ma na wawae me ka naau kaumaha, a olelo aku la, "He nui kuu kaumaha, a me kuu aloha ia oe e ke Alii, no ka mea, ua upu aku wau i ka'u moopuna o oe ke kane e ola ai keia mau iwi, kainoa he pono ka'u moopuna, aole ka, i ike mai nei ka hana i ka'u moopuna, e moe mai ana me Halaaniani ka mea a ko'u naau i makemake ole ai. Nolaila, i hele mai nei au e noi aku ia oe, e haawi mai oe i waa no'u, a me na kanaka pu mai, e kii wau i ka hanai a Kapukaihaoa, ia Laieiohelohe, ua like no a like laua me Laieikawai, no ka mea, ua hanau mahoeia laua."

A no keia mea, haawi ae la o Kekalukaluokewa hookahi kaulua, me na kanaka pu no, a me na lako a pau.

Mamua o ko Waka kii ana ia Laieiohelohe, kauoha iho la oia ia Kekalukaluokewa, "Ke holo nei wau ekolu anahulu me na po keu ekolu, alaila, hiki mai wau. E nana nae oe, a i ku ka punohu i ka moana, alaila, manao ae oe ua hoi mai wau me ko wahine, alaila, hoomalu oe ia oe a hiki i ko olua la e hoao ai."

Ma ka manao paa o Waka, ua holo mai la oia a hiki i Oahu nei, ma Honouliuli kau na waa, nana aku la no o Waka, e pio mai ana no ke anuenue iuka o Wahiawa.

Lalau iho la oia he wahi puaa, i mea alana aku imua o Kapukaihaoa, ke kahuna nana i malama ia Laieiohelohe, a pii aku la.

Pii aku la o Waka a hiki i Kukaniloko, hookokoke aku la oia ma kahi i hunaia'i o Laieiohelohe, hahau aku la i ka puaa imua o ke kahuna me ka pule ana, a Amama ae la. Kuu aku la i ka puaa imua o ke kahuna.

Ninau mai la ke kahuna, "Heaha ka hana a ka puaa imua o'u? A heaha ka'u e hana aku ai ia oe?"

I aku o Waka, "Ua hewa ka'u hanai, ua pono ole, ua upu aku wau o ke Alii o Kauai ke kane, aka, aole nae i hoolohe i ka'u olelo, ua lilo aku ia Halaaniani; nolaila, i kii mai nei wau i kau hanai i wahine na Kekalukaluokewa, ke Alii o Kauai, i ku kaua i ka moku, ola na iwi o ko kaua mau la elemakule a hiki i ka make. A loaa ia kaua kela Alii, alaila, ku ka makaia o ka'u hanai, i ike ai ia ua hewa kana hana ana."

Olelo mai o Kapukaihaoa, "Ua pono ka puaa, nolaila, ke hookuu aku nei wau i ka'u hanai nau e malama, a loaa ia oe ka pomaikai, a kui mai i o'u nei ka lono ua waiwai oe, alaila, imi aku wau."

Ia manawa, komo aku la o Kapukaihaoa me Waka ma kahi kapu, kahi hoi i hunaia'i o Laieiohelohe, hoonohoia iho la o Waka, a komo aku la ke kahuna ma kahi i hunaia'i. A laweia mai la a mua o Waka, ia manawa, kulou aku la o Waka imua o Laieiohelohe, a hoomaikai aku la.

I ka la i laweia'i o Laielohelohe a kau iluna o na waa, ia manawa, lawe ae la ke kahuna i ka piko o kana hanai a lei iho la ma kona ai. Aka, aole i kaumaha kona manao no Laielohelohe, no ka mea, ua manao no ke kahuna he pomaikai e ili mai ana maluna ona.

I ka manawa i laweia'i o Laielohelohe, aole kekahi o na kanaka hoewaa i ike aku ia ia a hiki wale i Hawaii.

Noho mai la o Kekalukaluokewa me ke kali iloko ka manawa i kauohaia.

I kekahi la ma ke kakahiaka, iloko o ko ke Alii manawa i ala mai ai mai ka hiamoe mai, ike ae la oia i ka hoailona a Waka i kauoha ai. No ka mea, aia ka punohu i ka moana.

Hoomakaukau ae la o Kekalukaluokewa ia ia iho no ka hiki aku o Laielohelohe, me ka manao e ike mua ana laua i ka la e puka aku ai, aole ka!

Ma ka auina la, ike maopopoia aku la na waa, akoakoa ae la na kanaka a pau ma ke awa pae waa e ike i ke Alii, i ka manao e puka aku ana a halawai me ke kane.

I ka hookokoke ana aku o na waa ma ke awa, ia manawa ka uhi ana mai o ke ohu, a me ka noe mai Paliuli mai.

Ia manawa, kailiia'ku la o Laielohelohe me Waka maloko o ka ohu, maluna o na manu a hiki i Paliuli, a hoonoho ia Laielohelohe ma ka hale i hoomakaukauia nona, malaila oia i noho ai a loaa hou ia Halaaniani.

Ekolu mau la o Waka ma Paliuli, mai ka hoi ana mai Oahu aku nei. Iho mai la oia e halawai me Kekalukaluokewa, no ka hoao o na'lii.

Ia Waka i hiki aku ai ma ko Kekalukaluokewa wahi, olelo aku la, "Ua hiki mai ko wahine, nolaila, e hoomakaukau oe i kanaha la, e kuahaua aku i na mea a pau, e akoakoa mai ma ko olua wahi e hui ai, e hana i papai kilu, malaila e hoohilahila aku ai ia Laieikawai, i ike ai oia i ka ino o kana hana."

Ia ka manawa nae i lawe aku ai o Waka i ka mana maluna o Laieikawai, alaila, kukakuka ae la na kaikuahine o Aiwohikupua i ka mea e pono ai ko lakou noho ana; a hooholo ae la ua mau kaikamahine nei i ka lakou olelo e pane aku ai ia Laieikawai.

Hele aku la o Kahalaomapuana a hai aku la imua o Laieikawai, me ka i aku, "Ua kukakuka makou, kou mau kiai kino i ka manawa e pono ana ko olua noho ana me ko kupunawahine, a ua lawe aku nei kela i ka hoopomaikaiia mai a oe aku. Nolaila, e like me ko kakou hoohiki ana mamua, "No kekahi o kakou ka pilikia, malaila pu kakou a pau." Nolaila, ua loaa iho nei ia oe ka pilikia, no kakou pu ia pilikia. Nolaila, aole makou e haalele ia oe, aole hoi oe e haalele ia makou a hiki i ko kakou make ana, oia ka makou olelo i hooholo mai nei."

A lohe o Laieikawai i keia mau olelo, haule iho la na kulu waimaka no ke aloha i kona mau hoa kuka, me ka i aku, "Kuhi au e haalele ana oukou ia'u i ka laweia'na o ka pomaikai mai o kakou aku, aole ka! a heaha la hoi, a i loaa ka pomaikai ia'u ma keia hope aku, alaila, e hoolilo no wau ia oukou a pau i mau mea nui maluna o'u."

Noho iho la o Halaaniani me Laieikawai, he kane, he wahine; a o na kaikuahine no o Aiwohikupua kona mau kanaka lawelawe.

I ka aha malama paha o ko laua noho hoao ana, ma kekahi a awakea, puka ae la o Halaaniani mai loko ae o ka hale, i hele aku iwaho, ia manawa, ike aku la oia ia Laielohelohe e puka ae ana mai loko ae o kona hale kapu. Ia manawa, hiki hou ke kuko i loko o Halaaniani.

Hoi aku la oia me ka manao ino no kela kaikamahine, me ka manao e kii e hoohaumia.

Ia la no, ia laua e noho pono ana me Laieikawai, ia manawa, manao ae la o Halaaniani e kii e hoohaumia ia Laielohelohe, nolaila imi iho la o Halaaniani i hewa no Laieikawai, i mea hoi e kaawale ai laua, alaila, kii aku i kana mea e manao nei.

I ka po iho, olelo hoowalewale aku la o Halaaniani ia Laieikawai, me ka i aku, "Ia kaua e noho nei iuka nei mai ko kaua noho ana iuka nei a hiki i keia manawa, aole he pau o ko'u lealea i ka heenalu, aia awakea, kau mai ia'u ka lealea, pela i na la a pau, nolaila, ke manao nei au apopo kaua iho i kai o Keaau i ka heenalu a hoi mai no hoi."

"Ae," wahi a ka wahine.

Ia kakahiaka ana ae, hele aku la o Laieikawai imua o kona mau hoa kuka, na kaikuahine hoi o Aiwohikupua, hai aku la i ko laua manao me ke kane i kuka ai ia po, a he mea maikai no ia i kona mau hoa kuka.

I aku nae o Laieikawai i ua mau hoa la, "Ke iho nei maua i kai ma ka makemake o ke kane a kakou, i kali ae oukou a i anahulu maua, mai hoohuoi oukou, aole no i pau ka lealea heenalu o ka kakou kane, aka hoi, i hala ke anahulu me ka po keu, alaila ua pono ole maua, alaila, huki ae oukou ia'u."

A hala aku la laua, a hiki i kahi e kokoke aku ana i Keaau, ia manawa, hoomaka o Halaaniani e hana i ke kalohe ia Laieikawai, me ka olelo aku, "E iho mua aku oe o kaua, a hiki i kai e pii ae au e ike i ko kaikoeke (Malio) a hoi mai wau. A ina i kali oe ia'u a i po keia la, a ao ka po, a i po hou ua la, alaila, manao ae oe ua make wau, alaila, moe hou aku oe i kane hou."

A no keia olelo a kana kane, aua aku ka wahine, a i ole, e pii pu no laua, a no ka pakela loa o Halaaniani i ke akamai i ka hoopuka i na olelo pahee, ua puni kana wahine maikai ia ia.

Hala aku la o Halaaniani, iho aku la no hoi o Laieikawai a hiki i Keaau, ma kahi kaawale ae i pili ole aku ia Kekalukaluokewa, noho iho la oia malaila; a po ia la, aole i hoi mai kana kane, mai ia po a ao, aole i hoi mai. Kali hou aku la ia la a po, pale ka pono, alaila, manao ae la o Laieikawai ua make kana kane, alaila, ia manawa, hoomaka aku la ia i ka uwe paiauma no kana kane.

Mokuna XXIII

He mea kaumaha loa ia Laieikawai no ka make ana o kana kane, nolaila i kanikau ai oia hookahi anahulu me elua mau la keu (umikumamalua la), no ke aloha ia ia.

Iloko o keia mau la kanikau o Laieikawai, he mea haohao loa ia i kona mau hoa kuka, no ka mea, ua kauoha mua o Laieikawai mamua o ko laua iho ana i kai o Keaau.

"He umikumamakahi la e kali ai" kona mau hoa ia ia, a i "hoi ole aku" i na la i kauohaia e like me ka kakou kamailio ana ae nei ma ka Mokuna XXII, alaila, maopopo ua pono ole.

A no ka hala ana o ka manawa a Laieikawai i kauoha ai i kona mau hoa, nolaila, ala ae la na kaikuahine o Aiwohikupua i ke kakahiaka nui o ka umikumamalua o ka la iho aku la e ike i ka pono o ko lakou hoa.

A hiki lakou ma Keaau, ia lakou e kokoke aku ana e hiki, ike mua mai la o Laieikawai i kona mau hoa, paiauma mai la me ka uwe.

Aka, he mea haohao nae ia i kona mau hoa ka uwe ana, a ua akaka kana kauoha "ua pono ole, laua." Ma ka uwe ana a Laieikawai, a me na helehelena o ka poina; no ka mea, aia o Laieikawai e kukuli ana i ka honua, a o kekahi limu, ua pea ae la ma ke kua, a o kekahi lima, aia ma ka lae, a uwe helu aku la oia penei:

> *O oukou ia—e, auwe!*
> *Eia wau la,*
> *Ua haalulu kuu manawa,*
> *Ua nei nakolo i ke aloha,*
> *I ka hele o ke kane he hoa pili—e!*
> *Ua hala—e.*

Ua hala kuu lehua ala Kookoolau,
I ka nae kolopua,
Ulili nae o olopua,
Haihai pua o kuu manawa—e.
Ei—e.

Eia wau la ua haiki,
Ua kupu lia halia i ka mana—o—e,
Ke hoopaele mai nei i kuu manawa,
I ke aloha—la,
Auwe kuu ka—ne.

A lohe kona mau hoa i keia uwe a Laieikawai, uwe like ae la lakou a pau.

A pau ka lakou pihe uwe, olelo mai la o Kahalaomapuana, "He mea kupanaha, ia kakou e uwe nei, o ka hamama wale iho no ko'u waha, aole a kahe mai o ka waimaka, o ke kaea pu wale ae la no ia, me he mea la i pania mai ka waimaka."

I mai la na kaikuaana, "Heaha la?"

I aku la o Kahalaomapuana, "Me he mea la aole i poino ka kakou kane."

Olelo mai la o Laieikawai, "Ua make, no ka mea, ia maua no i iho mai ai a mauka ae nei la, o ka hiki mai no hoi ia i kai nei, olelo mai no kela ia'u, 'e iho e oe mamua, e pii ae au e ike i ko kaikoeke, e kali nae oe ia'u a i po keia la, a ao ka po, a po hou ua la, alaila, ua make au,' pela kana kauoha ia'u. Kali iho nei wau a hala kona manawa i kauoha ai, manao ae nei au ua make, oia wau i noho iho nei a hiki wale mai nei oukou la e uwe aku ana wau."

I mai la o Kahalaomapuana, "Aole i make, nanaia aku i keia la, ua oki ka uwe."

A no keia olelo a Kahalaomapuana, kakali aku la lakou a hala na la eha, aole lakou i ike i ke ko o ka Kahalaomapuana mea i olelo ai. Nolaila, hoomau hou aku la o Laieikawai i ka uwe i ke ahiahi o ke kolu o ka la a po, mai ia po a wanaao, akahi no a loaa ia ia ka hiamoe.

Ia Laieikawai i hoomaka iho ai e hookau hiamoe, ku ana no o Halaaniani me ka wahine hou, a hikilele ae la o Laieikawai, he moeuhane ka.

Ia manawa no, ua loaa ia Mailehaiwale he moeuhane, ala ae la oia a kamailio aku la ia Mailelaulii a me Mailekaluhea i keia moe.

E kamailio ana no lakou no kela moe, ia manawa, puoho mai la o Laieikawai, a hai mai la i kana moe.

I aku la o Mailelaulii, "O ka makou no hoi ia e kamailio nei, he moe no Mailehaiwale."

E hahai ana no lakou i na moeuhane, puoho mai la o Kahalaomapuana mai ka hiamoe mai, a ninau mai i ka lakou mea e kamailio ana.

Hai mai la o Mailehaiwale i ka moe i loaa ia ia, "I uka no i Paliuli, hele ae la no o Halaaniani a lawe ae ana no ia oe, (Kahalaomapuana,) a hele aku nei no olua ma kahi e aku, ku aku nei ko'u uhane nana ia olua, hikilele wale ae nei no hoi au."

Hai ae la no hoi o Laieikawai i kana moe, i mai la o Kahalaomapuana, "Aole i make o Halaaniani, kali aku kakou, mai uwe, hoopau waimaka."

A no keia mea, hooki loa ae la o Laieikawai i kana uwe ana, hoi aku la lakou iuka o Paliuli.

(Ma keia wahi, e kamailio kakou no Halaaniani, a maanei kakou e ike ai i kona kalohe launa ole.)

Ma kela olelo a Halaaniani ia Laieikawai e pii e halawai me Malio. Ia laua i hookaawale ai mahope iho o ka Halaaniani kauoha ana ia ia.

Pii aku la oia a halawai pu me Malio, ninau mai la kona kaikuahine, "Heaha kau o uka nei?"

I aku la o Halaaniani, "I pii hou mai nei wau ia oe, e hooko mai oe i ko'u makemake, no ka mea, ua ike hou au he kaikamahine maikai i like kona helehelena me ko Laieikawai.

"Ma ke awakea o nehinei, ia'u i puka ae ai iwaho mai ko maua hale ae. Ike aku la wau i keia kaikamahine opiopio i maikai kona mau helehelena; nolaila, ua pauhia mai wau e ka makemake nui.

"A no ko'u manao o oe no ka mea nana e hoopomaikai nei ia'u ma na mea a'u e makemake ai, nolaila wau i hiki hou mai nei."

I aku o Malio i kona kaikunane, "O Laielohelohe na, o kekahi moopuna a Waka, ua hoopalauia na Kakalukaluokewa, a wahine haoa. Nolaila, a hele oe e makai i ka hale o ua kaikamahine la me ko ike oleia mai, i eha la au e makai aku ai, a ike oe i kana hana mau, alaila, hoi mai oe a hai mai ia'u, alaila, na'u e hoouna aku ia oe e hoowalewale i ua kaikamahine la. Aole e loaa ia'u ma kuu mana, no ka mea, elua laua."

A no keia olelo a Malio, hele aku la o Halaaniani e hoohalua mau mawaho o ko Laielohelohe hale me kona ike oleia mai, kokoke alua anahulu kona hookalua ana, alaila, ike oia i ka Laielohelohe hana, he kui lehua. Hoomau pinepine aku la oia a nui na la, aia no oia e hoomau ana i kana hana he kui lehua.

Hoi aku la o Halaaniani e halawai me ke kaikuahine e like me kana kauoha, a hai aku la i na mea ana i ike ai no Laielohelohe.

A lohe o Malio i keia mau mea, alaila, hai aku la oia i na mea hiki ke hanaia aku no Laielohelohe e kona kaikunane, me ka i aku ia Halaaniani, "E hoi oe a ma ka waenakonu o ka po, alaila, pii mai oe i o'u nei, i hele aku ai kaua ma kahi o Laielohelohe."

Hoi aku la o Halaaniani, a kokoke i ka manawa i kauo haia nona, alaila, ala mai la oia a halawai me kona kaikuahine. Lalau ae la kona kaikuahine i ka pu la-i, a hele aku la me kona kaikunane, a kokoke aku la laua ma kahi a Laielohelohe e kui lehua mau ai.

Ia manawa, olelo aku la o Malio ia Halaaniani, "E pii oe maluna o kekahi laau, ma kahi ou e ike aku ana ia Laielohelohe, a malaila oe e noho ai. E hoolohe mai oe i ke kani aku a kuu pu la-i, elima a'u puhi ana, ina ua ike oe e a-u ana kona maka i kahi i kani aku ai ka pu la-i, alaila ka hoi loaa ia kaua, aka hoi, i aluli ole ae kona mau maka i kuu hookani aku, alaila, aole e loaa ia kaua i keia la."

Ia laua no e kamailio ana no keia mau mea, uina mai ana kahi a ua o Laielohelohe e kui lehua ai, i nana aku ka hana o laua, o Laielohelohe e haihai lehua ana.

Ia manawa, pii ae la o Halaaniani ma kekahi kumu laau a nana aku la. Ia ianei maluna o ka laau, kani ana ka pu la-i a Malio, kani hou aku la o ka lua ia, pela a hiki i ka lima o ke kani ana o ka pu la-i, aole o Halaaniani i ike iki ua huli ae ka maka a hoolohe i keia mea kani.

Kali mai la o Malio o ka hoi aku o Halaaniani e hai aku i kana mea i ike ai, aole nae i hoi aku, nolaila, hoomau hou aku la o Malio i ke puhi i ka pu la-i elima hookani ana, aole no i ike iki o Halaaniani i ka nana o Laielohelohe i keia mea, a hoi wale no.

Hoi aku la o Halaaniani a kamailio aku i kona kaikuahine, i mai la kona kaikuahine, "Loaa ole ae la ia kaua i ka pu la-i, i kuu hano aku ia loaa?"

Hoi aku la laua ma ko laua wahi, a ma kekahi kakahiaka ae, hiki hou no laua i kahi mua a laua i hoohalua ai.

Ia laua nei a hiki iho, hiki ana no o Laielohelohe ma kona wahi mau. Mamua nae o ko laua hiki ana aku, ua hai mua aku o Malio i kana olelo i kona kaikunane penei:

"E haku oe i lehua, e huihui a lilo i mea hookahi, aia lohe oe i kuu hookani aku i ka hano, oia kou wa e hookuu iho ai i kela popo lehua iluna pono ona, malia o hoohuoi kela ia mea."

Pii ae la o Halaaniani iluna o kekahi laau ma kahi kupono ia Laielohelohe. Ia wa no, kani aku la ka hano a Malio, ia wa no hoi ko Halaaniani hoolei ana iho i ka popo lehua mai luna iho o ka laau, a haule pololei iho la ma ke alo ponoi o Laielohelohe. Ia manawa, alawa pono ae la na maka o Laielohelohe iluna, me ka olelo ae, "Ina he kane oe ka mea nana keia makana, a me keia hano e kani nei, alaila, na'u oe, ina he wahine oe, alaila i aikane oe na'u."

A lohe o Halaaniani i keia olelo, he mea manawa ole ia noho ana ilalo e hui me kona kaikuahine.

Ninau mai o Malio, hai aku la oia i kana mea i ike ai no Laielohelohe.

I aku o Malio ia Halaaniani, "E hoi kaua a kakahiaka hiki hou mai kaua ianei, ia manawa e lohe maopopo aku ai kaua i kona manao."

Hoi aku la laua, a ma kekahi kakahiaka ana ae, pii hou aku la, Ia laua i hiki aku ai a noho iho, hiki mai la o Laielohelohe ma kona wahi mau e kui lehua ai.

Ia manawa, hookani aku la o Malio i ka hano ia Laielohelohe e hoomaka aku ana e ako lehua, aole nae e hiki, no ka mea, ua lilo loa o Laielohelohe i ka hoolohe i ka mea kani.

Ekolu hookani ana a Malio i ka hano.

Ia manawa no, pane mai o Laielohelohe, "Ina he wahine oe ka mea nana keia hano, alaila, e honi no kaua."

A no keia olelo a Laielohelohe, hoopuka aku la o Malio imua o Laielohelohe, a ike mai la kela ia ianei, a he mea malihini hoi ia i ko Laielohelohe mau maka.

Ia wa, hoomaka mai la kela e hooko e like me kana olelo mua ma ka honi ana o laua.

A no ka hahai ana mai o Laielohelohe e honi me Malio, i aku o Malio, "Alia kaua e honi, me kuu kaikunane mua oe e honi aku ai, a pau ko olua manawa, alaila, honi aku kaua."

I mai o Laielohelohe, "E hoi oe a kou kaikunane, mai hoike mai ia ia imua o'u, e hoi olua ma ko olua wahi, mai hele hou mai. No ka mea, o oe wale no ka'u mea i ae aku e haawi i ko'u aloha nou ma ko kaua honi ana, aole au i ae me kekahi mea e ae. Ina e hooko au i kau noi, alaila, ua kue wau i ka olelo a ko'u mea nana e malama maikai nei."

A lohe o Malio i keia olelo, hoi aku la a hai i kona kaikunane, me ka i aku, "Ua nele ae nei kaua i keia la; aka, e hoao wau ma kuu mana, i ko ai kou makemake."

Hoi aku la laua a hiki i ka hale, ia manawa, kena ae la oia ia Halaaniani e hele e makai aku ia Laieikawai.

Ia Halaaniani i hiki ai ma Keaau, mamuli o ke kauoha a kona kaikuahine, aole oia i ike a i lohe hoi no Laieikawai.

Mokuna XXIV

Ia manawa nae ana i hiki aku ai, lohe iho la o Halaaniani, he la nui no Kekalukaluokewa, he la hookahakaha, no ka hoao o Laielohelohe me ua Kekalukaluokewa nei. A maopopo iho la ia Halaaniani ka la hookahakaha o na'lii, hoi aku la oia a hai aku i kona kaikuahine no keia mea.

Ia Malio i lohe ai, olelo ae la oia i kona kaikunane, "A hiki i ka la hookahakaha o Kekalukaluokewa me Laielohelohe, oia ka la e lilo ai o Laielohelohe ia oe."

A he mea mau hoi i na kaikuahine o Aiwohikupua ka iho i kai o Keaau e hoohalua ai no ka lakou kane, no ka make a make ole paha.

I ua mau kaikuahine nei o Aiwohikupua e iho ana i Keaau, lohe lakou he la nui no Kekalukaluokewa me Laielohelohe.

I ke kokoke ana aku i ua la nui nei, iho aku la o Waka mai Paliuli aku e halawai me Kekalukaluokewa a olelo aku la o Waka ia Kekaluka luokewa: "Apopo, i ka puka ana o ka la, e kuahaua oe i na kanaka a pau, a me kou alo alii e hele aku ma kahi au i hoomakaukau ai no ka hookahakaha, malaila e akoakoa ai na mea a pau. Ia manawa e hele aku oe e hoike mua ia oe, a kokoke aku i ke awakea, alaila, e hoi oe i kou hale; aia a hiki aku mahope iho o ka auina la, ia manawa, e hoouhi aku wau i ka noe maluna o ka aina, a maluna hoi o kahi e akoakoa ai na kanaka.

"Aia a hoomaka mai ke poi ana o ka noe ma ka aina, alaila, e kali oe ia wa, a lohe oe i ka leo ikuwa a na manu a haalele wale; kali hou aku oe ia wa, a lohe hou oe i ka leo ikuwa hou o na manu a haalele wale.

"A mahope oia manawa, e hoopau aku no wau i ka noe maluna o ka aina. Alaila, e nana oe ia uka o Paliuli, i pii ka ohu a uhi iluna o na kuahiwi, ia manawa e uhi hou ana ka noe e like me mamua.

"E kali oe ia manawa, ina e lohe oe i ke keu a ka Alae, a me ka leo o ka Ewaewaiki e hoonene ana. Ia manawa, e puka oe mai ka hale nei aku, a ku mawaho o ke anaina.

"Hoolohe oe a e kupinai ana ka leo o na manu Oo a haalele, alaila, ua makaukau wau e hoouna mai ia Laielohelohe.

"Aia kupinai mai ka leo o na Iiwipolena, alaila, aia ko wahine ma ke kihi hema o ka aha. A ma ia hope koke iho oia manawa, e lohe auanei oe i ka leo o na Kahuli e ikuwa ana, ia manawa e hui ai olua ma ke kaawale.

"Ia olua e hui ana, hookahi hekili e kui ia manawa, nakolo ka honua, haalulu ka aha a pau. Ia manawa, e hoouna aku wau ia oula maluna o na manu, a mao ae ka ohu a me ka noe, aia olua e kau aku ana iluna o na manu me ko olua nani nui. Ia manawa e ku ai ka makaia o Laieikawai, i ike ai oia i kona hilahila a holo aku me he pio kauwa la."

A pau keia mau mea, hoi aku la o Waka iuka o Paliuli.

Mamua iho nei, ua oleloia ua hiki aku o Halaaniani i Keaau, e ike i ka pono o kana wahine (Laieikawai), a ua oleloia no hoi, ua lohe oia he la hookahakaha no Kekalukaluokewa me Laielohelohe.

I kela la a Waka i hiki ai i Keaau e halawai me Kekalukaluokewa, e like me ka kakou ike ana maluna ae.

Oia no ka la a Malio i olelo aku ai ia Halaaniani e hoomakaukau no ka iho e ike i ka la hookahakaha o Laielohelohe ma; me ka i aku nae o Malio i kona kaikunane, "Apopo, i ka la hookahakaha o Laielohelohe me Kekalukaluokewa, ia manawa e lilo ai o Laielohelohe ia oe, no laua auanei ka hekili ekui, a mao ae ka ohu a me ka noe, alaila, e ike auanei ka aha a pau, o oe a me Laielohelohe ke kau pu mai iluna o ka eheu o na manu."

I ke kakahiaka nui o kekahi la ae, oia hoi ka la hookahakaha o ua mau Alii nei, kiiia aku la o Kihanuilulumoku, a hele mai la imua o na kaikuahine o Aiwohikupua kona mau kahu nana e malama.

A hiki mai la ua moo nui nei, olelo aku la o Kahalaomapuana, "I kiiia aku nei oe e lawe ae oe ia makou i kai o Keaau, e nana makou i ka la hookahakaha o Kekalukaluokewa, aia a hiki i ka auina la a mahope iho oia manawa e kii mai oe a iho aku kakou."

Hoi aku la o Kihanuilulumoku, a hiki i ka manawa i kauohaia'i, a hele mai la.

I ua moo nei i hoomaka ai e hele mai imua o kona mau Haku, aia hoi, ua uhi paaia ka aina i ka noe mai uka o Paliuli a puni ka aina; aka, aole i wikiwiki o Kihanuilulumoku i ka lawe i kona mau Haku, no ka mea, ua maopopo no ia Kihanuilulumoku ka manawa e hui ai na'lii.

A ike o Kekalukaluokewa i keia noe i uhi mua mai maluna o ka aina, alaila, hoomanao ae la ia i ke kauoha a Waka.

Kakali hou aku la no oia i na hoailona i koe. Mahope iho oia manawa, lohe ae la kela i ka leo o ka Ewaewaiki a me ke Kahuli, ia manawa, puka aku la o Kekalukaluokewa mai kona hale aku a ku mawaho o ka aha, ma kahi kaawale.

I kela manawa, oia ka manawa a Kihanuilulumoku i kuu aku ai i kona alelo i waho i noho iho ai o Laieikawai me na kaikuahine o Aiwohikupua.

A i ke kui ana o ka leo o ka hekili, uhi ka ohu a me ka noe, a i ka mao ana ae, i nana aku ka hana o ka aha, aia o Laielohelohe me Halaaniani e kau mai ana iluna o na manu.

Ia manawa no hoi, ikeia mai la o Laieikawai me na kaikuahine o Aiwohikupua e kau mai ana iluna o ke alelo o Kihanuilulumoku ka moo nui o Paliuli.

Ia lakou i hiki ai i kela manawa hookahi me na mea nona ka la hookahakaha; aia hoi ua ike aku la o Laieikawai ia Halaaniani aole i make, alaila, hoomanao ae la oia i ka olelo wanana a Kahalaomapuana.

I kela manawa a Kekalukaluokewa i ike aku ai e kau mai ana o Halaaniani me Laielohelohe iluna o na manu, alaila, manao ae la o Kekalukaluokewa i kona nele ia Laielohelohe.

Ia manawa, pii aku la o Kekalukaluokewa iuka o Paliuli, e hai aku i keia mea ia Waka.

A hai aku la o Kakalukaluokewa ia Waka i keia mau mea, "Ua lilo o Laielohelohe ia Halaaniani, aia oia ke kau pu la me Halaaniani i keia manawa."

I mai la o Waka, "Aole e lilo ia ia, aka, e iho aku kaua a kokoke aku wau i ka aha, ina ua haawi aku oia i kona ihu e honi aku ia Halaaniani, ka mea a'u i kauoha aku ai aole e lilo i ka mea e ae, a ia oe wale no e laa'i ka ihu o kuu moopuna, a laa pu no hoi me konakino, alaila, ua nele kaua i ka wahine ole, alaila, e lawe aku oe ia'u i ka lua me ko minamina ole. Aka hoi, ua hoolohe aku la ia i ka'u kauoha, aole e lilo i kakahi mea e ae, aole no hoi e lilo ka leo ma kona pane ole aku ia Halaaniani, alaila, ua wahine no oe, ua hoolohe no kuu moopuna i ka'u olelo."

Ia laua i kokoke e hiki aku, hoouna aku la o Waka i ka noe a me ka ohu maluna o ka aha, a ike ole kekahi i kekahi.

Ia manawa i hoouna aku ai o Waka ia Kekalukaluokewa maluna o na manu, a i ka mao ana ae o ka noe, aia hoi e kau pu mai ana o Laielohelohe me Kekalukaluokewa iluna o na manu, alaila, uwa ae la ke anaina kanaka a puni ka ha, "Hoao na'lii e! hoao na'lii e!!"

A lohe o Waka i keia pihe uwa, alaila, hiki mai la o Waka imua o ka aha, a ku mai la iwaenakonu o ke anaina, a hoopuka mai la i olelo hoohilahila no Laieikawai.

A lohe o Laieikawai i keia leo hoohilahila a Waka ia ia, walania iho la kona naau, a me na kaikuahine pu kekahi o Aiwohikupua, ia manawa, lawe aku la ke alelo o Kihanuilulumoku ia lakou a noho iuka o Olaa, oia ka hoomaka ana o Laieikawai e hoaaia i kona hilahila nui no ka olelo a Waka, a hele pu no hoi me kona mau hoa.

I kela la, hoao ae la o Kekalukaluokewa me Laielohelohe, a hoi aku la iuka o Paliuli a hiki i ko lakou hoi ana i Kauai. A lilo iho la a Halaaniani i mea nele loa, aole ona kamailio i koe.

A ma ko ke Alii kane manaopaa, e hoi no i Kauai, lawe ae la oia i kana wahine, a me ko laua kupunawahine i Kauai, o na kanaka pu me lakou.

A makaukau lakou e hoi, haalele lakou ia Keaau, hiki mua lakou i Oahu nei, ma Honouliuli, a lawe ae la ia Kapukaihaoa me lakou i Kauai, a hiki lakou i Kauai, ma Pihanakalani, a ili ae la ka hooponopono o na aina, a me ke aupuni ia Kapukaihaoa, a hooliloia iho la o Waka oia ke kolu o ka hooilina o ka noho alii.

(Ma keia wahi, e kamailio kakou no Laieikawai, a me kona loaa ana i ka Makaula ia Hulumaniani.)

Ia Laieikawai ma ma Olaa, e noho ana no oia me kona nani, aka, o ka mana noho iluna o ka eheu o na manu, oia ka mea i kaawale mai o Laieikawai aku, koe no nae kekahi mau kahiko e ae, a me kekahi mau hoailona alii ia ia, mamuli o ka mana i loaa i na kaikuahine o Aiwohikupua, mai a Kihanuilulumoku ae.

Mokuna XXV

Ia Laieikawai ma i hoi aku ai mai Keaau aku, mahope iho o kona hoohilahila ana o Waka, a noho ma Olaa.

Ia manawa, kukakuka ae la na kaikuahine o Aiwohikupua i ka mea hiki ke hooluolu aku i ka naau kaumaha o ke alii (Laieikawai) no kona hilahila i ka olelo kumakaia a Waka.

Hele aku la lakou a hai aku la i ka lakou olelo hooholo i kuka ai imua o Laieikawai me ka i aku:

"E ke Alii wahine o ka lai; ua kukakuka ae nei makou i mea e hoopau ai i kou naau kaumaha no kou hoohilahilaia, aka, aole o oe wale kai kaumaha, o kakou like no a pau, no ka mea, ua komo like kakou a pau no ia pilikia hookahi.

"Nolaila, e ke Alii e, ke noi aku nei makou ia oe, e pono no e hoopauia kou naau kaumaha, no ka mea, e hiki mai ana ia oe ka pomaikai ma keia manawa aku.

"Ua hooholo ae nei makou i pomaikai like no kakou, ua ae ae nei ko kakou kaikaina e kii aku ia Kaonohiokala i kane nau, he keiki Alii e noho la i Kealohilani, ua hoonohoia ma ka pea kapu o kukulu o Tahiti, he kaikunane no no kakou, ko Aiwohikupua mea nana i hoalii mai ia ia.

"Ina e ae oe e kiiia ko kakou kaikunane, alaila, e loaa ia kakou ka hanohano nui i oi aku mamua o keia, a e lilo auanei oe i mea kapu ihiihi loa, me ko launa ole mai ia makou, a oia ka makou i noonoo iho nei, a ae oe, alaila, ku kou makaia, hilahila o Waka."

I mai la o Laieikawai, "Ua ae no wau e hoopau i ko'u kaumaha hilahila, a hookahi a'u mea ae ole, o kuu lilo ana i wahine na ko kakou kaikunane; no ka mea, ke olelo mai nei oukou, he Alii kapu kela, a ina paha e hoao maua, pehea la wau e ike hou ai ia oukou, no ka mea, he Alii kapu kela, a oia ka'u mea minamina loa, o ko kakou launa pu ana."

I aku la kona mau hoa, "Mai manao mai oe ia makou, e nana oe i ka olelo hoohilahila a ko kupunawahine, aia ku kona makaia, alaila pono makou, no ka mea, o oe no ka makou mea manao nui."

A no keia mea, hooholo ae la o Laieikawai i kona ae.

Ia manawa, hai mai la o Kahalaomapuana i kana olelo kauoha ia Laieikawai, a me kona mau kaikuaana, "Ke kii nei au i ko kakou kaikunane i kane na ke Alii, e pono ia oukou ke malama pono i ko kakou Haku, ma kana wahi e hele ai, malaila oukou, na mea ana a pau e makemake ai, oia ka oukou e hooko aku; aka, koe nae ka maluhia o kona kino a hiki mai maua me ke kaikunane o kakou."

Mahope iho o keia mau mea, haalele iho la o Kahalaomapuana i kona mau kaikuaana, a kau aku la maluna o ua moo nui nei (Kihanuilulumoku), a kii aku la ia Kaonohiokala.

(Ma keia wahi, e waiho iki i ke kamailio ana no keia mea. E pono ia kakou e kamailio no Laieikawai, a me kona loaa ana i ka Makaula nana i ike mai Kauai mai, e like me ka mea i oleloia ma na Mokuna mua elua o keia Kaao.)

Mahope iho o ko Kahalaomapuana haalele ana i kona mau kaikuaana, kupu ae la iloko o Laieikawai ka manao makemake e kaapuni ia Hawaii.

A no keia manao o Laieikawai, hooko aku la kona mau hoa i ko ke Alii makemake, a hele aku la e kaapuni ia Hawaii a puni.

Ma keia huakai kaapuni a ke Alii, ma Kau mua, ma Kona, a hiki lakou ma Kaiopae i Kohala, ma ka aoao akau mai Kawaihae mai, aneane elima mile ka loihi mai Kawaihae ae, malaila lakou i noho ai i kekahi mau la, no ka mea, ua makemake iho la ke Alii wahine e hooluolu malaila.

Iloko o ko lakou mau la malaila, ike mai la ka Makaula i ka pio a keia anuenue i kai, me he mea la i Kawaihae ponoi la. I uka nae o Ouli, ma Waimea, kahi a ka Makaula i ike mai ai.

No ka mea, ua oleloia ma na Mokuna mua ae nei, ua hiki ka Makaula ma Hilo, i Kaiwilahilahi; a ua loihi no na makahiki malaila o ke kali ana i kana mea i imi ai.

Aka, no ka hiki ole i ua Makaula nei ke kali no kana mea i imi ai, nolaila, hoopau ae la oia i kona manao kali a me ka imi aku no kana mea i ukali mai ai mai Kauai mai.

Nolaila, haalele keia ia Hilo, a manao ae la oia e hoi loa i Kauai, a hoi aku la. Iloko nae o ko ka Makaula hoi ana, aole oia i haalele i kana mau mea i lawe mai ai mai Kauai mai (oia ka puaa, a me ka moa).

Ma keia hoi ana, a hiki ma Waimea, i Ouli, oia ka ka Makaula ike ana aku i ka pio a ke anuenue i kai o Kawaihae.

A no ka maluhiluhi o ua Makaula nei, aole oia i wikiwiki mai e ike i ke ano o ke anuenue, nolaila, hoomaha iho la oia malaila. A ma kekahi la ae, aole oia i ike hou i kela hoailona.

Ma kekahi la ae, haalele ka Makaula ia wahi, oia la no hoi ka la a Laieikawai ma i haalele ai ia kaiopae, hoi aku la a mauka o Kahuwa, ma Moolau ko lakou wahi i noho ai.

I ka Makaula i hiki mai ai i Puuloa mai Waimea mai, ike aku la oia e pio ana ke anuenue i Moolau, ia manawa, haupu iki ae la ka manao o ka Makaula me ka nalu ana iloko ona iho, "O kuu mea no paha keia i imi mai nei."

Hoomau mai la ka Makaula i kona hele ana a hiki iluna pono o Palalahuakii, alaila, ike maopopo aku la oia i ke ano o ke anuenue, me ka hoomaopopo iloko ona, a ike lea i kana mea e imi nei.

Ia manawa, pule aku la oia i kona akua, e hai mai i ke ano o kela anuenue ana e ike nei; aka, aole i loaa i kona akua ka hookoia o kana pule.

Haalele ka Makaula ia wahi, hiki aku la oia ma Waika a malaila oia i noho ai, no ka mea, ua poeleele iho la.

Ma ke kakahiaka ana ae, aia hoi, e pio ana ke anuenue i kai o Kaiopae, no ka mea, ua iho aku o Laieikawai ilaila.

Ia manawa, iho aku la ka Makaula a hiki i kahi ana e ike nei i ke anuenue, a i ka hookokoke ana aku o ua Makaula nei, ike maopopo aku la oia ia Laieikawai, e kono mau ana i ka lae kahakai. He mea e ka wahine maikai, aia iluna pono o ua kaikamahine nei e pio ana ke anuenue.

Ia manawa, pule aku la ka Makaula i kona akua, e hoike mai ia ia i keia wahine, o kana mea paha e imi nei, aole paha. Aka, aole i loaa ka hoike ana ma ona la, nolaila, aole ka Makaula i waiho i kana mau mohai imua o Laieikawai, hoi aku la ka Makaula a noho mauka o Waika.

I kekahi la ae, haalele ka Makaula ia wahi, hiki aku la keia ma Lamaloloa, a noho iho la malaila. Ia manawa, komo pinepine ae la oia iloko o ka Heiau i Pahauna, malaila oia i pule hoomau ai i kona akua. Ua loihi na la mahope iho o ka noho ana o Laieikawai ma Moolau, haalele lakou ia wahi.

Hele aku la lakou a noho ma Puakea, a no kahi heenalu malaila, noloila, ia lakou malaila e makaikai ana i ka heenalu ana a na kamaaina, ua nanea loa lakou malaila.

Ma kekahi la ae, ma ke awakea, i ka wa e lailai ana ka la maluna o ka aina. Ia wa ka Makaula i puka ae ai mailoko ae o ka Heiau, mahope iho o ka pau ana o kana pule.

Aia hoi, ike aku la oia e pio ana ke anuenue i kai o Puakea, iho aku la ua Makaula nei a hiki ilaila, ike aku la oia, ke kaikamahine no ana i ike mua ai i Kaiopae.

A no keia mea, emi hope mai la oia a ma ke kaawale, pule hou aku la i kona akua e hoike mai i kana mea e imi nei; aka, aole no i loaa ka hoike ana ma ona la. A no ka hooko ole ia o kana mea e noi nei i kona akua, aneane oia e hoohiki ino aku i kona akua; aka, hoomanawanui no oia.

Hoopuka loa aku la a ma kahi o Laieikawai ma e noho ana.

He mea pilikia loa i ka Makaula ka ike ana aku ia Laieikawai, a ia lakou ma kahi hookahi, ninau aku la ka Makaula ia Laieikawai ma, "Heaha ka oukou mea e noho nei maanei, aole he au pu me na kamaaina heenalu mai?"

"He mea hiki ole ia makou ke hele aku," wahi a Laieikawai, "he pono e nana aku i ka na kamaaina heenalu ana."

Ninau hou aku ka Makaula, "Heaha ka oukou hana maanei?"

"E noho ana makou maanei, e kali ana i waa, ina he waa e holo ai i Maui, Molokai, Oahu, a hiki i Kauai, alaila, holo makou." Pela aku o Laieikawai ma.

A no keia olelo, i aku ka Makaula, "Ina e holo ana oukou i Kauai, alaila, aia ia'u ka waa, he waa uku ole."

I aku la o Laieikawai, "A ina e kau makou ma ko waa, aole anei au hana e ae no makou?"

I aku la ka Makaula, "Auhea oukou, mai manao oukou i kuu olelo ana, e kau wale oukou maluna o kuu waa, e hoohaumia aku ana au ia oukou; aka, o ko'u makemake, e lilo oukou i mau kaikamahine na'u, me he mau kaikamahine ponoi la, i lilo ai oukou i mea nana e hookaulana i ko'u inoa, aia a lilo oukou i mea e kaulana ai au, alaila, e ola auanei ko'u inoa. Na Kaikamahine a Hulumaniani, aia la, ola kuu inoa, pela wale iho la no ko'u makemake?"

Ia manawa, imi ae la ka Makaula i waa, a loaa ia ia he kaulua, me na kanaka pu no hoi.

Ma ke kakahiaka o kekahi la ae, kau aku la lakou maluna o na waa, a holo aku la a kau ma Honuaula, i Maui; a mai laila aku a Lahaina, a ma kekahi la ae, i Molokai; haalele lakou ia Molokai, hiki lakou ma Laie, Koolauloa, a malaila lakou i noho ai i kekahi mau la.

Ia la a lakou i hiki ai ma Laie, a ia po iho no, olelo ae la o Laieikawai i kona mau hoa, a me ko lakou makuakane hookama. Eia kana olelo:

"Ua lohe au i ko'u kupunawahine, ianei ko'u wahi i hanau ai, he mau mahoe ka maua, a no ka pepehi o ko maua makuakane i na keiki mua a ko maua makuahine i hanau ai no ka hanau kaikamahine wale no, a ia maua hoi, hanau kaikamahine no, nolaila, ahaiia'i au iloko o ka luawai, malaila ko'u wahi i hanaiia ai e ko'u kupunawahine.

"A o ko'u lua, lilo ia i ke kahuna ka malama, a no ka ike ana o ke Kahuna nana i malama i ko'u kokoolua, i ka Makaula nana i ike mai mai Kauai mai, nolaila, kauoha ai ke Kahuna i ko'u kupunawahine, e ahai loa; a oia ko'u mea i ahaiia'i i Paliuli, a halawai wale kakou."

Mokuna XXVI

A lohe ka Makaula i keia mea, alaila, hoomaopopo lea ae la ka Makaula, o ka mea no keia ana e imi nei. Aka hoi, i mea e maopopo lea ai, naue aku la ka Makaula ma kahi kaawale, a pule aku la i kona akua e hooiaio mai i ka olelo a ke kaikamahine.

A pau kana pule ana, hoi mai la a hiamoe iho la, a iloko a kona manawa hiamoe, hiki mai la ma o ua Makaula nei, ke kuhikuhi ma ka hihio, mai kona akua mai, me ka olelo mai, "Ua hiki mai ka manawa e hookoia'i kou makemake, a e kuu ai hoi ka luhi o kou imi ana i ka loa. Ano hoi, o ka mea nona ke kamailio ana nona iho ia oukou, oia no ua mea la au i imi ai.

"Nolaila, e ala ae oe, a e lawe i kau mea i hoomakaukau ai nona, e waiho aku i kau mohai imua ona, me ka hoomaikai mua me ka inoa o kou akua.

"A pau kau hana, alaila, mai kali, e lawe koke aku ia lakou ma keia po no i Kauai, a hoonoho i na pali o Haena, iuka o Honopuwaiakua."

Ma keia mea, puoho ae la ka Makaula mai kona hiamoe ana, ala ae la oia a lalau aku la i ka puaa a me ka moa, a hahau aku la imua o

Laieikawai, me ka olelo aku, "Pomaikai wau e kuu Haku, i ka hoike ana mai a kuu akua ia oe, no ka mea, he nui ko'u manawa i ukali aku ai ia oe, me ka manao e loaa ka pomaikai mai a oe mai.

"A nolaila, ke noi aku nei au ia oe e ae mai, e malamaia keia mau iwi ma kou lokomaikai e kuu Haku, a e waiho pu ia ka pomaikai me ka'u mau mamo a hiki i ka'u hanauna hope."

I aku o Laieikawai, "E ka makua, ua hala ke kau o ko'u pomaikai nui, no ka mea, ua lawe aku o Waka i ka hoopomaikaiia mai o'u aku nei; aka, ma keia hope aku e kali oe a loaa ia'u he pomaikai oi aku mamua o ka pomaikai a me ka hanohano i loaa mua ia'u, alaila, o oe pu kekahi me makou ia hoopomaikaiia."

A pau keia mau mea, lawe ae la ka Makaula e like me ke kauoha a kona akua, holo aku la ia po a hoonoho i kahi i kauohaia.

I ua Makaula nei me kana mau kaikamahine mauka o Honopuwaiakua, a he mau la ko lakou malaila. He mea mau i ua Makaula nei ke kaahele i kekahi manawa.

Iloko o kona la e hele ana ma kona ano Makaula, ia ia hoi i hiki aku ai i Wailua. Aia hoi, ua hoakoakoaia na kaikamahine puupaa a pau o Kauai, ma o ka poe kaukaualii me na kaikamahine koikoi, mamuli nae o ka olelo kuahaua a Aiwohikupua, e laweia mai na kaikamahine puupaa imua o ke Alii, o ka mea a ke Alii e lealea ai, oia ka wahine a ke Alii (Aiwohikupua).

A hiki aku la ka Makaula iloko o kela akoakoa, aia hoi, ua hoakoakoaia na kaikamahine ma kahi hookahi, e ku ana imua o ke Alii.

Ninau aku la ka Makaula i kekahi poe o ka Aha, "Heaha ka hana a keia Aha? A heaha hoi ka hana a keia poe kaikamahine e ku poai nei imua o ke Alii?"

Haiia mai la, "Ua kuahauaia na kaikamahine puupaa a pau ma ke kauoha a ke Alii, a o ka mea a Aiwohikupua e makemake ai, alaila, e lawe oia elua mau kaikamahine i mau wahine nana, a o laua na mea pani ma ka hakahaka o Poliahu a me Hinaikamalama, a o na makua nana na kaikamahine i laweia i mau wahine na ke Alii, e hoaahuia ka, Ahuula no laua."

Ia manawa, ku ae la ua Makaula nei, a kahea aku la me ka leo nui imua o ke Alii a me ka Aha a pau:

"E ke Alii, ke ike nei au, he mea maikai no ke Alii ka lawe ana i kekahi o keia poe puupaa i mea hoolealea no ke Alii; aka, aole e hiki i kekahi o keia poe kaikamahine puupaa ke pani ma ka hakahaka o Poliahu a me Hinaikamalama.

"Ina i nana iho nei wau i kekahi o keia poe puupaa, ua ane like iki aku ka maikai me ka uha hema o ka'u mau kaikamahine, alaila, e aho la ia. He nani no keia poe, aole nae e like aku me kekahi o ka'u poe kaikamahine."

I mai la o Aiwohikupua me ka leo huhu, "I nahea makou i ike ai he kaikamahine kau?"

A o ua Makaula nei, lilo ae la ia i enemi no ka poe nana na kaikamahine i laweia imua o ke Alii.

A no ka olelo huhu ana mai o ke Alii, i aku ua Makaula nei, "Owau hookahi ka mea i imi ikaika i Haku no ka aina a puni na moku, o ua Haku la o ka aina, oia ua kaikamahine la a'u, a o na kaikamahine e ae a'u, he mau kaikuahine no ia no kuu Haku kane.

"Ina e hele mai ua kaikamahine nei a'u a ku iloko o ke kai, he kaikoo ma ka moana, ina e ku ma ka aina, lulu ka makani, malu ka la, ua ka ua, kui ka hekili, olapa ka uwila, opaipai ka mauna, waikahe ka aina, pualena ka moana i ka hele a kuu kaikamahine Haku."

A no keia olelo a ka Makaula, lilo iho la ia olelo ana i mea eehia no na kanaka a puni ka aha. Aka hoi, o ka poe nana na kaikamahine puupaa, aole o lakou oluolu.

Nolaila, koi ikaika ae la lakou i ke Alii, e hoopaaia iloko o ka hale paehumu (Halepaahao), kahi e hoopaa ai i ko ke Alii poe lawehala.

Ma ka manaopaa o kona poe enemi, hooholoia ae la ua Makaula nei e laweia iloko o kahi paa, a malaila oia e noho ai a make.

Ma ka la o ua Makaula nei e hoopaaia'i, a ma ia po iho, ma ka wanaao, pule aku la oia i kona akua, a ma kona ano Makaula, ua hiki aku ka leo o kana pule imua o kona akua. A ma ka malamalama loa ana ae, ua weheia ka puka o ka hale nona, a hele aku la oia me kona ike oleia mai.

Ia kakahiaka, hoouna aku la ke Alii i kona Ilamuku e hele aku e ike i ka pono o ua Makaula nei maloko o kahi paa o ke Alii.

A hiki aku la ka Ilamuku mawaho o ka hale, kahi i hoopaaia'i ka Makaula, a kahea aku la oia me ka leo nui.

"E Hulumaniani e! E Hulumaniani e!! E ka Makaula o ke akua!!! Pehea oe? Ua make anei oe?" Ekolu hea ana o ka Ilamuku i keia olelo, aole nae oia i lohe i kekahi leo noloko mai.

Hoi aku la ka Ilamuku, a hai aku la i ke Alii, "Ua make ka Makaula."

E hoomakaukau no ka la e Kauwila ai ka Heiau, a kau aku. Ia manawa, kauoha ae la ke Alii i na Luna o ka Heiau, a kau aku i ka Makaula ma ka lele imua o ke kuahu.

A lohe ka Makaula i keia mea ma kahi kaawale aku, a ma ia po iho, lawe aku la oia hookahi pumaia, ua wahiia i ke kapa me he kupapau la, a hookomoia iloko o kahi i hoopaaia'i ua Makaula nei, a hoi aku la a hui me kana mau kaikamahine, a hai aku la i keia mau mea, a me kona pilikia ana.

A kokoke i ka la kauwila o ka Heiau, lawe ae la ka Makaula ia Laieikawai, a me kona mau hoa pu maluna o na waa.

I ke kakahiaka nui hoi o ka la e kauwila ai ka Heiau, kiiia aku la ke kanaka o ka Heiau, a i ke komo ana aku o na Luna o ke Alii, aia hoi, ua paa i ka wahiia, laweia aku la a waiho maloko o ka Heiau.

A kokoke i ka hora e hauia'i ke kanaka ma ka lele, akoakoa ae la na mea a pau, a me ke Alii pu; a hiki ke Alii iluna o ka anuu, laweia mai la ua pumaia la i wahiia a kupono malalo o ka lele.

I aku ke Alii i kona mau Luna, "E wehe i ke kapa o ke kupapau, a kau aku iluna o ka lele i hoomakaukauia nona."

I ka wehe ana ae, aia he pumaia ko loko, aole ka Makaula ka mea i manaoia. "He pumaia keia! Auhea hoi ka Makaula," wahi a ke Alii.

Nui loa iho la ka huhu o ke Alii i na Luna o ka Halepaahao, kahi i hoopaaia'i ka Makaula.

I keia manawa, hookolokoloia iho la kona mau Luna. Ia manawa hoi e hookolokoloia ana na Luna o ke Alii, hiki mai la ua Makaula nei me kana mau kaikamahine maluna o ke kaulua, a lana mawaho o ka nuku o ka muliwai.

Ku mai la ka Makaula ma kekahi waa, a o na kaikuahine o Aiwohikupua ma kekahi waa, a o Laieikawai hoi iluna o ka pola o na waa kahi i ku mai ai, iloko hoi o kona puloulou Alii kapu.

Ia wa a lakou e ku la me Laieikawai, lulu ka makani, malu ka la, kaikoo ke kai, pualena ka moana, hoi ka waikahe o na kahawai a paa i na kumu wai, aole he puka wai i kai. A pau ia, lawe ka Makaula i ka pa-u o Laieikawai a waiho iuka, ia wa, kui ka hekili, hiolo ka Heiau, haihai ka lele.

A pau keia mau mea i ka hoikeia, i nana aku ka hana o Aiwohikupua, a me na mea e ae, e ku mai ana o Laieikawai maloko o ka puloulou Alii kapu iluna o na waa. Ia manawa, kanikani pihe aku la ka aha, "Ka wahine maikai—e! Ka wahine maikai—e! Kilakila ia e ku mai la!"

Ia manawa, naholo mai la na kanaka a ku mauka o kahakai, hehi kekahi maluna o kekahi i ike lea aku lakou.

Ia manawa, kahea aku la ka Makaula ia Aiwohikupua, "Mai hoahewa aku i kou mau Luna, aole wau na lakou i hookuu mai kahi paa mai, na kuu akua i lawe mai ia'u mai kuu pilikia mauwale ana, a kuu Haku.

"He oiaio ka'u olelo ia oe, he kaikamahine ka'u, kuu Haku hoi a'u i imi ai, ka mea nana keia mau iwi."

A no ka ike maopopo ana aku o Aiwohikupua ia Laieikawai, he mea e hoi ka haalulu o kona puuwai, a waiho aku la i ka honua me he mea make la.

A mama ae la ke Alii, kauoha ae la oia i kona Luna e lawe mai i ka Makaula me na kaikamahine pu mai, i pani ma ka hakahaka o Poliahu, a me Hinaikamalama.

Hele aku la ka Luna a kahea aku la i ka Makaula, iluna o na waa, me ka hai aku i ka olelo a ke Alii.

A lohe ka Makaula i keia mea, hai aku la oia i kana olelo i ka Luna, "E hoi oe a ke Alii, kuu Haku hoi, e olelo aku oe, aole e lilo kuu kaikamahine Haku i wahine nana, aia he Alii aimoku, alaila, lilo kuu kaikamahine."

Hoi aku la ka Luna, hoi aku la no hoi ka Makaula me kana mau kaikamahine, aole nae i ike houia ma ia hope iho i Wailua, hoi aku la lakou a noho i Honopuwaiakua.

Mokuna XXVII

Ma keia Mokuna, e kamailio kakou no ke kii ana o Kahalaomapuana ia Kaonohiokala i kane hoopalau na Laieikawai, a me kona hoi ana mai.

A pau ke kauoha a Kahalaomapuana i kona mau kaikuaana, a makaukau hoi kona hele ana.

Ma ka puka ana o ka la, komo ae la o Kahalaomapuana iloko o Kihanuilulumoku, a au aku la ma ka moana a hiki i Kealohilani, eha malama me ke anahulu, hiki keia iloko o Kealohilani.

Ia laua i hiki aku ai, aole laua i ike ia Mokukelekahiki ke kiai nana e malama ko Kaonohiokala waiwai, kona Kuhina Nui hoi iloko o Kealohilani, elua anahulu ko laua kali ana, hoi mai o Mokukelekahiki mai ka mahina mai.

Hoi mai la o Mokukelekahiki, e moe ana keia moo iloko ka hale, i ke poo no piha o loko o ua hale nui nei o Mokukelekahiki, o ke kina no a me ka huelo o ua moo nei, iloko no o ke kai.

He mea weliweli ia Mokukelekahiki ka ike ana i ua moo nei, lele aku la oia a hiki iluna o Nuumealani, ilaila o Kaeloikamalama ke kupua nui nana e pani ka puka o ka pea kapu o kukulu o Tahiti, kahi i hunaia'i o Kaonohiokala.

Hai aku la o Mokukelekahiki ia Kaeloikamalama i kona ike ana i ka moo. Ia manawa, lele aku la o Kaeloikamalama me Mokukelekahiki, mai luna mai o Nuumealani, he aina aia i ka lewa.

Ia hiki ana mai o Mokukelekahiki ma ma ka hale e moe nei ka moo.

Ia manawa, olelo aku la o Kihanuilulumoku (ka moo) ia Kahalaomapuana, "I hiki mai auanei keia mau kanaka e lele mai nei i o kaua nei, alaila, e luai aku wau ia oe a kau ma ka a-i o Kaeloikamalama, a i ninau ae ia oe, alaila, hai aku oe, he kama oe na laua, a i ninau mai i ka kaua hana i hiki mai ai, alaila, hai aku oe."

Aole i upuupu iho mahope iho o ka laua kamailio ana, halulu ana o Mokukelekahiki laua me Kaeloikamalama ma ka puka o ka hale.

I nana aku ka hana o ua moo nei, e ku mai ana o Kaeloikamalama me ka laau palau, o *Kapahielihonua* ka inoa, he iwakalua anana ka loa, eha kanaka nana e apo puni. Manao iho la ka moo he luku keia, aia nae e oniu ana o Kaeloikamalama i ka laau palau i ka welau o kona lima.

Ia manawa, hapai mai la o Kihanuilulumoku i kona huelo mailoko ae o ka moana, pii ke kai iluna, me he poi ana a ka nalu i ke kumu pali, me he akuku nalu la i poi iloko o ka malama o Kaulua, pii ke ehu o ke kai iluna, pouli ka la, ku ka punakea iuka.

Ma ia wa, kau mai la ka weli ia Kaeloikamalama ma, hoomaka laua e holo mai ke alo aku o ua moo nei.

Ia manawa, luai aku ana o Kihanuilulumoku ia Kahalaomapuana, kau ana iluna o ka a-i o Kaeloikamalama.

Ninau ae la o Kaeloikamalama, "Nawai ke kama o oe?"

I aku la o Kahalaomapuana, "Na Mokukelekahiki, na Kaeloikamalama; na kupua nana e malama ka pea kapu o kukulu o Tahiti."

Ninau laua, "Heaha ka huakai a kuu kama i hiki mai ai?"

Hai aku la o Kahalaomapuana, "He huakai imi Lani."

Ninau hou laua, "Imi i ka Lani owai?"

"O Kaonohiokala," wahi a Kahalaomapuana, "ka Lani kapu a Kaeloikamalama laua o Mokukelekahiki."

Ninau hou no laua, "A loaa o Kaonohiokala, heaha ka hana?"

I aku la o Kahalaomapuana, "I kane na ke kaikamahine Alii o Hawaiiakea, na Laieikawai, ke Haku o makou."

Ninau hou no laua "Owai oe?"

Hai aku la keia, "O Kahalaomapuana, ke kaikamahine muli a Moanalihaikawaokele laua me Laukieleula."

A lohe o Kaeloikamalama laua me Mokukelekahiki, he mea e ko laua aloha, ia manawa, kuu iho la mai ka a-i iho, honi aku la i ka ihu o ke kaikamahine.

No ka mea, o Mokukelekahiki, a me Kaelokamalama, he mau kaikunane no Laukieleula ka makuahine o lakou me Aiwohikupua.

I aku la o Kaeloikamalala, "E hele kaua a loaa ke alanui, alaila, pii aku oe."

Hele aku la laua hookahi anahulu, hiki i kahi e pii ai, kahea aku la o Kaeloikamalama, "E ka Lanalananuiaimakua—! kuuia mai ke alanui, i pii aku wa—!! ua hewa o lalo ne—!!!"

Aole i upuupu iho, kuu mai ana o Lanalananuiaimakua i ka punawelewele, hihi pea ka lewa.

Ia manawa, aoao aku la o Kaeloikamalama, "Eia ko alanui, i pii auanei oe a hiki iluna, a i ike oe hookahi hale e ku ana iloko o ka mahina, aia ilaila o Moanalihaikawaokele o Kahakaekaea ia aina.

"I nana aku auanei oe, ka elemakule e loloa ana ka lauoho, ua hina ke poo, o Moanalihaikawaokele no ia. Ina e noho ana iluna, mai wikiwiki aku oe, o ike e mai auanei kela ia oe, make e oe, aole e lohe i kau olelo, kuhi auanei ia oe he mea e.

"Kali aku oe a moe, e huli ana ke alo i lalo, aole i moe, aka, i nana aku oe, a i huli ke alo iluna, ua moe ka hoi, alaila, hele aku oe, mai hele oe ma ka makani, hele oe ma ka lulu, a noho iluna o ka umauma, paa oe a paa i ka umiumi, alaila, kahea iho oe:

"E Moanalihaikawaokele—e!
Eia wau he kama nau,
He kama na Laukieleula,
He kama na Mokukelekahiki,
He kama na Kaeloikamalama,
Na kaikunane o kuu makuahine;
Makuakane, makuakane hoi,
O o'u me o'u kaikuaana,
Me kuu kaikunane o Aiwohikupua hoi.
Homai he ike, he ike nui, he ike loa,
Kuuia mai kuu Lani,
Kuu kaikunane Haku—e.
E ala! E ala mai o—e!!

"Pela auanei oe e hea iho ai, a ina e ninau mai kela ia oe, alaila, hai aku oe i kau huakai i hele mai ai.

"I pii auanei oe, a i uhi ke awa, na ko makuakane ia hana, i hiki mai ke anu ma ou la, mai maka'u oe. Alaile, pii no oe, a i honi oe i ke ala, o ko makuahine no ia, nona ke ala, alaila, palekana, kokoke oe e puka iluna, pii no oe, a i o mai auanei ka kukuna o ka la, a i keehi ka wela ia oe mai maka'u oe, i ike auanei oe i ka oi o ka nohi o ka la, alaila, hoomanawanui aku no oe a komo i ka malu o ka mahina, alaila, pau ka make, o ko komo no ia iloko o Kahakaekaea."

A pau ka laua kamailio ana no keia mau mea; pii aku la o Kahalaomapuana, a ahiahi, paa oia i ke awa, manao ae la keia o ka ka makuakane hana ia, mai ia po a wanaao, honi oia i ke ala o ke kiele, manao ae la keia o ka makuahine ia, mai ia wanaao a kiekie ka la, loaa oia i ka wela o ka la, manao ae la oia, o ka hana keia a kona kaikunane.

Ia manawa, ake aku la keia e komo i ka malu o ka mahina, a ma ke ahiahi, hiki aku la oia i ka malu o ka mahina, manao ae la keia, ua komo i ka aina i kapaia o Kahakaekaea.

Ike aku la oia i keia hale nui e ku ana, ua po iho la, hele aku la oia ma ka lulu, aia no e ala mai ana o Moanalihaikawaokele, hoi mai la oia a ma kahi kaawale, e kali ana o ka moe iho, e like me ke kuhikuhi a Kaeloikamalama. Aoale nae i loaa ka hiamoe ia Moanalihaikawaokele.

A ma ka wanaao, hele aku la keia, iluna ke alo o Moanalihaikawaokele, manao ae la keia ua hiamoe, holokiki aku la keia a paa ma ka umiumi o ka makuakane, kahea iho la e like me ke aoao ana a Kaeloikamalama i hoikeia maluna.

Ala ae la o Moanalihaikawaokele, ua paa kahi e ikaika ai, o ka umiumi, kupaka ae la aole e hiki, ua paa loa ka umiumi ia Kahalaomapuana, o i noke i ke kupaka i o ianei, a pau ke aho o Moanalihaikawaokele.

Ninau ae la, "Nawai ke kama o oe?"

I aku la keia, "Nau no."

Ninau hou kela, "Na'u me wai?"

Hai aku keia, "Nau no me Laukieleula."

Ninau hou kela, "Owai oe?"

"O Kahalaomapuana."

I ae la ka makuakane, "Kuuia ae kuu umiumi, he kama io oe na'u."

Kuu ae la keia, ala ae la ka makuakane, a hoonoho iho la iluna o ka uha, uwe iho la, a pau ka uwe ana, ninau iho ka makuakane, "Heaha kau huakai i hiki mai ai?"

"He huakai imi Lani," wahi a Kahalaomapuana.

"Imi owai ka Lani e imi ai?"

"O Kaonohiokala," wahi a ke kaikamahine.

"A loaa ka Lani, heaha ka hana?"

I aku la o Kahalaomapuana, "I kii mai nei au i kuu kaikunane Haku, i kane na ke kaikamahine Alii o Hawaiiakea, na Laieikawai, ke aikane Alii a makou, ko makou mea nana i malama."

Hai aku la oia i na mea a pau i hanaia e ko lakou kaikunane, a me ka lakou aikane.

I mai la o Moanalihaikawaokele, "Aole na'u e ae aku, na ko makuahine wale no e ae aku, ka mea nana ke Alii, aia ke noho la i kahi kapu, kahi hiki ole ia'u ke hele aku, aia hanawai ko makuahine, alaila, hoi mai i o'u nei, a pau na la haumia o ko makuahine, alaila, pau ka ike ana me a'u, hoi no me ke Alii.

"Nolaila, e kali oe, a hiki i na la mai o ko makuahina, i hoi mai kela, alaila, hai aku oe i kau huakai i hiki mai ai ianei."

Kakali iho la laua ehiku la, maopopo iho la na la e hanawai ai o Laukieleula.

I aku la o Moanalihaikawaokele ia Kahalaomapuana, "Ua kokoke mai ka la e mai ai ko makuahine, nolaila, ma keia po, e hele mua oe ma ka *Halepea*, malaila oe e moe ai, i hiki mai kela i kakahiaka, e moe aku ana oe i ka hale, aole ona wahi e hele e aku ai, no ka mea, ua haumia, ina e ninau ia oe, hai pololei aku no oe e like me kau olelo ia'u."

Ma ia po iho, hoouna aku la o Moanalihaikawaokele, ia Kahalaomapuana iloko o ka Halepea.

Mokuna XXVIII

Ma ke kakahiaka nui, hiki ana o Laukieleula, i nana mai ka hana e moe ana keia mea, aole nae e hiki i ua o Laukieleula ke hookaawale ia ia, no ka mea, ua haumia, o kela hale wale no kahi i aeia nona, "Owai oe e keia kupu, e keia kalohe, nana i komo kuu wahi kapu, kahi hiki ole i na mea e ae ke komo ma keia wahi?" Pela aku ka mea hale.

Hai aku ka malihini, "O Kahalaomapuana au, ka hua hope loa a kou opu."

I aku ka makuahine, "Auwe! e kuu Haku, e hoi oe me ko makuakane, aole e hiki ia'u e ike ia oe, no ka mea, ua hiki mai kuu mau la haumia, aia a pau kuu haumia ana, e launa no kaua no ka manawa pokole a hele aku."

A no keia mea, hoi aku la o Kahalaomapuana me Moanalihaikawaokele, ninau mai la ka makuakane, "Pehea mai la?"

I aku ke kaikamahine, "Olelo mai nei ia'u e hoi mai me oe, a pau ka manawa haumia, alaila hele mai e ike ia'u."

Noho iho la laua ekolu la, kokoke i ka wa e pau ai ka haumia o Laukieleula, olelo aku o Moanalihaikawaokele i ke kaikamahine, "O hele, no ka mea, ua kokoke mai ka wa mau o ko makuahine, hele no oe i kakahiaka nui poeleele o ka la apopo, a noho ma ka luawai, kahi ana e hoomaemae ai ia ia, mai hoike oe, aia a lele kela iloko o ke kiowai, a i luu ilalo o ka wai, alaila, holo aku oe a lawe mai i ka pa-u, a me ke kapa ona i haumia i kona mai, i auau kela a hoi mai ma kapa, aole ke kapa, alaila manao mai ua kii aku au, i hoi mai ai kela i ka hale nei, alaila ki kou makemake.

"Ina i uwe olua a i pau ka uwe ana, a i ninau mai ia'u i ke kapa ona au i lawe mai ai, alaila, hai aku oe, aia ia oe; a e hilahila kela me ka menemene ia oe i ko haumia ana, oia hoi, aole ana mea nui e ae e uku mai ai no kou haumia i kona kapa i hoohaumiaia i kona mai, hookahi wale no mea nui ana o ka Lani au i kii mai nei, aia a ninau kela i kou makemake, alaila, hai aku oe, o ko ike ka hoi ia i ko kaikunane, ike pu me a'u, no ka mea, hookahi wale no a'u ike ana i ka makahiki hookahi, he kiei mai ka, o ka nalo aku la no ia."

A hiki i ka manawa a ka makuakane i olelo ai, ala ae la ke kaikamahine i kakahiaka nui poeleele, a hele aku la e like me ke kauoha a kona makuakane.

Ia ia i hiki aku ai, pee iho la ma kahi kokoke i ke koiwai, aole i upuupu iho, hiki ana ka makuahine, a wehe i ke kapa i hoohaumiaia, a lele aku la iloko o ka wai.

Ia manawa, lawe ae la ke kaikamahine i ka mea i kauohaia ia ia, a hoi aku la me ka makuakane.

Aole keia i liuliu iho, halulu ana ka makuahine, ua hookaawale mua ae o Moanalihaikawaokele ia ia ma ke kaawale, o ke kaikamahine wale no ko ka hale.

"E Moanalihaikawaokele, o kuu kapa i haumia, homai, e lawe ae au e hoomaemae i ka wai." Aole nae he ekemu mai, ekolu ana kahea ana, aole nae he ekemuia mai, kiei aku la keia iloko o ka hale, e moe ana o Kahalaomapuana, ua pulou iho i ke kapa i hoohaumia ole ia.

Kahea iho la, "E Moanalihaikawaokele", homai kuu kapa i haumia i kuu mai, e lawe ae au e hoomaemae i ka wai."

Ia manawa, puoho ae la o Kahalaomapuana, me he mea la ua hiamoe, me ka i aku i ka makuahine, "E kuu Haku makuahine, ua hele aku nei keia, owau wale no ko ka hale nei, a o ko kapa nae i haumia i ko mai, eia la."

"Auwe! e kuu Haku, he nui kuu menemene ia oe i kou malama ana i ke kapa i haumia ia'u, a heaha la auanei ka uku o kuu menemene ia oe e kuu Haku?"

Apo aku la ia i ke kaikamahine, a uwe aku la i ka mea i oleloia ma ka pauku maluna ae nei.

A pau ka uwe ana, ninau iho ka makuahine, "Heaha kau huakai i hiki mai ai i o maua nei?"

"I kii mai nei au i kuu kaikunane i kane na ke aikane a makou, ke Alii wahine o Hawaii-nui-akea, o Laieikawai, ka mea nana i malama ia makou iloko o ko makou haaleleia'na e ko makou kaikunane aloha ole, nolaila, ua hilahila makou, aola a makou uku e uku aku ai no ka malama ana a ke Alii ia makou; a no ia mea, e ae mai oe e iho ae au me kuu kaikunane Lani ilalo, a lawe mai ia Laieikawai iluna nei." O ka Kahalaomapuana olelo keia imua o kona makuahine.

I mai la ka makuahine, "Ke ae aku nei au, no ka mea, aole o'u uku no kou malama ana i kuu kapa i haumia ia'u.

"Ina no la hoi he mea e ka mea nana i kii mai nei, ina no la hoi aole wau e ae aku; o ko kii paka ana mai nei, aole au e aua aku.

"Oia hoi, ua olelo no ko kaikunane o oe hookahi no kana mea i oi aku ke aloha, a me ka manao nui; a nolaila, e pii kaua e ike i ko kaikunane.

"Nolaila, e kali oe pela, e hea ae au i ke kahu manu o olua, a nana kaua e lawe aku a komo i ka pea kapu o kukulu o Tahiti."

Ia manawa, hea aku la ka makuahine,

> *"E Haluluikekihiokamalama—e,*
> *Ka manu nana e pani ka la,*
> *Hoi ka wela i Kealohilani,*
> *Ka manu nana e alai ka ua,*
> *Maloo na kumuwai o Nuumealani.*
> *Ka manu nana i kaohi na ao luna,*
> *Nee na opua i ka moana,*
> *Huliamahi na moku,*
> *Naueue Kahakaekaea,*
> *Palikaulu ole ka lani,*
> *O na kupu, na eu,*
> *O Mokukelekahiki,*
> *O Kaeloikamalama,*
> *Na kupu nana e pani ka pea kapu o kukulu o Tahiti,*
> *Eia la he Lani hou he kana nau,*
> *Kiiia mai, lawe aku i luna i o Awakea."*

Ia wa, kuu iho la ua manu nei i na eheu i lalo, a o ke kino aia no i luna. Ma ia wa, kau aku la o Laukieleula me Kahalaomapuana i luna o ka eheu o ua manu nei, o ka lele aku la no ia a hiki i o Awakea, ka mea nana e wehe ke pani o ka la, kahi i noho ai o Kaonohiokala.

Ia manawa a laua i hiki aku ai, ua paniia aku la ko ke Alii wahi e na ao hekili.

Alaila, kena ae la o Laukieleula ia Awakea, "Weheia mai ke pani o kahi o ke Alii."

Ia manawa, ke ae la o Awakea me kona wela nui, a auhee aku la na ao hekili imua ona. Aia hoi ikeia aku la ke Alii e moe mai ana i ka onohi pono o ka la, i ka puokooko hoi o ka wela loa, nolaila i kapaia'i ka inoa o ke Alii, mamuli oia ano (Kaonohiokala).

Ia manawa, lalau iho la o Laukieleula i kekahi kukuna o ka la a kaohi iho la. Ia manawa, aia mai la ke Alii.

Ia Kahalaomapuana i ike aku ai i kona kaikunane, ua like na maka me ka uwila, a o kona ili a me kona kino a puni, ua like me ka okooko o ke kapuahi hooheehee hao.

Kahea aku la o Laukieleula, "E kuu Lani, eia ko kuahine o Kahalaomapuana, ka mea au e aloha nui nei, eia la ua imi mai nei ia kaua."

A lohe o Kaonohiokala, aia mai la mai kona hiamoe ana, alawa ae la kela ia Laukieleula, e hea aku i na kiai o ka malu. Kahea ae la.

"E ka Mahinanuikonane,
E Kaohukolokaialea,
Na kiai o ka malumalu, kulia imua o ke Alii."

Ia manawa, hele mai la na kiai o ka malu a ku iho la imua o ke Alii. Aia hoi, ua holo ka wela o ka la mai ke Alii aku.

A loaa ka malumalu imua o ko ke Alii wahi moe, alaila, kahea mai la i ke kaikuahine, a hele aku la a uwe iho la, no ka mea, ua maeele kona puuwai i ke aloha no kona kaikuahine opiopio. A he nui no hoi na la o ke kaawale ana.

A pau ka uwe ana, ninau iho la, "Nawai ke kama o oe?"

Pane aku ke kaikuahine, "Na Mokukelekahiki, na Kaeloikamalama, na Moanalihaikawaokele laua o Laukieleula."

Ninau hou mai la ke kaikunane, "Heaha ka huakai?"

Alaila, hai aku la kela e like me kana olelo i ka makuahine.

A lohe ke Alii i keia mau olelo, haliu aku la oia i ko laua makuahine, me ka ninau aku, "Laukieleula, ua ae anei oe ia'u e kii i ka mea a ianei e olelo mai nei i wahine na'u?"

"Ua haawi mua wau ia oe ua lilo, e like me kana noi ia'u; ina o kekahi o lakou kai kii mai nei, ina aole e hiki mai i o kaua nei, i lalo aku la no, hoi; aeia aku ka olelo a kou pokii, no ka mea, nau i wehe mua ke alanui, a na ko kaikuahine i pani mai, aohe he mea mamua ou, a aohe no hoi he mea mahope iho," pela aku ka makuahine.

A pau keia mau olelo, ninau hou mai la o Kaonohiokala ia Kahalaomapuana no kona mau kaikuaana a me kona kaikunane.

Alaila hai aku la o Kahalaomapuana, "Aole he pono o ko makou kaikunane, ua kue ko makou noho ana, o keia wahine no a'u i kii mai nei ia oe. I ka huakai mua ana i kii ai i ua wahine nei; hoi hou ae ia makou; hele no makou a hiki i kahi o ua wahine nei, ke Alii wahine a'u e olelo nei. I ka po, hiki makou i uka, iloko o ka ululaau oia wale no a me kona kupunawahine ko ia wahi. Ku makou mawaho, i nana aku ka hana i ka hale o ua o Laieikawai, ua uhiia mai i ka hulu melemele o ka Oo.

"Kii o Mailehaiwale, aole i loaa, hoole no ua wahine nei, kii aku o Mailekaluhea, aole no i loaa, kii aku o Mailelaulii, aole no i loaa, kii aku o Mailepakaha, aole no i loaa, i ka hoole wale no a pau lakou, koe owau, aole hoi wau i kii, o ka huhu iho la no ia ia makou haalele i ka nahelehele.

"A haalele kela ia makou, ukali aku makou mahope, pakela loa no ko makou kaikunane i ka huhu, me he mea la na makou i hoole kona makemake.

"Nolaila la, hoi hou makou a kahi i haalele mua ia ai, na ua kaikamahine Alii la i malama ia makou, a haalele wale aku la wau, hele mai nei, oia iho la ko makou noho ana."

A lohe o Kaonohiokala i keia mau olelo, he mea e ka huhu. Ia manawa, olelo aku la oia ia Kahalaomapuana, "E hoi oe me ou kaikuaana a me ke aikane Alii a oukou, kuu wahine hoi, kali mai oukou, i nee ka ua ma keia hope iho, a i lanipili, eia no wau i anei.

"I kaikoo auanei ka moana, a i ku ka punakea i uka, eia no wau i anei. Ina e paka makani a hookahi anahulu malie, i kui paloo ka hekili, aia wau i Kahakae kaea.

"Kui paloo hou auanei ka hekili ekolu pohaku, ua hala ia'u ka pea kapu o kukulu o Tahiti, aia wau i Kealohilani, ua pau kuu kino kapu Akua alaila o kuu kapu Alii koe, alaila noho kanaka aku wau ma ko kakou ano.

"Ma ia hope iho, hoolohe mai oukou a i hui ka hekili, ua ka ua, kaikoo ka moana, he waikahe ma ka aina, olapa ka uwila, uhi ka noe, pio ke anuenue, ku ka punohu i ka moana, hokahi malama e poi ai ka ino a mao ae, aia wau ma ke kua o na mauna i ka wa molehulehu o ke kakahiaka.

"Kali mai oukou a i puka aku ka la, a haalele iho i ka piko o na mauna; ia manawa, e ike ae ai oukou ia'u e noho ana wau iloko o ka la, iwaena o ka Luakalai, i hoopuniia i na, onohi Alii.

"Aole nae kakou e halawai ia manawa; aia ko kakou halawai i ka ehu ahiahi; ma ka puka ana mai o ka mahina i ka po i o Mahealani, alaila e hui ai au me kuu wahine.

"Aia a hoao maua, alaila, e hoomaka wau i ka luku maluna o ka aina no ka poe i hana ino mai ia oukou.

"Nolaila, e lawe aku oe i ka hoailona o Laieikawai, he anuenue o kuu wahine ia."

A pau keia mau mea, hoi iho la oia ma ke aia ana i pii aku ai, hookahi malama, a halawai iho la me Kihanuilulumoku, hai aku la i ka hua olelo, "Ua pono kaua, ua waiwai no hoi."

Komo ae la oia iloko o Kihanuilulumoku, au aku la ma ka moana, e like me na la o ka hele ana aku, pela no ka loihi o ka hoi ana mai.

Hiki laua i Olaa, aole a Laieikawai ma, hanu ae la ua moo nei a puni o Hawaii, aole. Hiki laua i Maui, hanu ae la ka moo, aole no.

Hanu aku la ia Kahoolawe, Lanai, a me Molokai, oia ole like no. Hiki laua i Kauai, hanu ae la a puni aole i loaa, hanu ae la i na mauna, aia hoi, e noho ana i Honopuuwaiakua, luai aku la ua o Kihanuilulumoku ia Kahalaomapuana.

Ike mai la ke Alii a me kona mau kaikuaana, he mea e ka olioli. Aka, he mea malihini nae i ka Makaula keia kaikamahine opiopio, a he mea weliweli no hoi i ua Makaula nei ka ike ana i ka moo, aka, ma kona ano Makaula, ua hoopauia kona maka'u.

He umikumamakahi malama, me ke anahulu, me eha la keu, oia ka loihi o ke kaawale ana o Kahalaomapuana mai ka la i haalele ai ia, Laieikawai ma, a hiki i ko laua hoi ana mai mai Kealohilani mai.

Mokuna XXIX

Ia Kahalaomapuana i hoi mai ai mai kana huakai imi Alii, mai Kealohilani mai, hai aku la oia i ka moolelo o ko laua hele ana, a me na hihia he nue, a me na lauwili ana, a me na mea a pau ana i ike ai iloko o kona manawa hele.

Iloko nae o kana manawa e olelo nei no ka olelo kauoha a Kaonohiokala, i mai la o Laieikawai i kona mau hoa, "E na hoa, ia Kahalaomapuana e olelo nei no Kaonohiokala ke kaikunane o kakou, kuu kane hoi, ke kau e mai nei ia'u ka halia o ka maka'u, a me ka weliweli, ke kuhi nei au he kanaka, he Akua nui loa ka! Iahona paha a ike aku, o kuu make no paha ia, no ka mea, ke maka'u honua e mai nei no i kona manawa aole me kakou."

I aku la kona mau hoa, "Aole ia he Akua, he kanaka no e like me kakou, o kona ano nae, a me kona helehelena, he ano Akua. A no kona hanau mua ana, lilo ai oia i hiwahiwa na na makua o kakou, ma ona la i haawiia'i ka mana nui hiki ole ia makou, a o Kahalaomapuana nei, alua wale no mea i haawiia'i ka mana, koe aku nae ke kapu no ko kakou kaikunane, nolaila, mai maka'u oe; aia no hoi paha a hiki mai la, ike aku no hoi paha oe la, he kanaka no e like me kakou."

Mamua aku nae o ko Kahalaomapuana hoi ana mai Kealohilani mai, ua ike mua aku ka Makaula hookahi malama mamua'ku o ko laua hoi ana mai. Nolaila, wanana mua ka Makaula me ka olelo iho, "E loaa ana ka pomaikai ia kakou mai ka lewa mai, aia a hiki aku i na po mahina konane e hiki mai ai.

"Aia a lohe aku kakou i ka hekili kui pamaloo, a me ka hekili iloko o ke kuaua, ia manawa e ike ai ko ka aina nei, he ua me ka uwila, he kaikoo ma ka moana, he waikahe ma ka aina, uhi paaia ka aina, a me ka moana a puni e ka noe, ke awa, ka ohu, a me ke kualau.

"A hala ae ia, a i ka la o Mahealani, ma ka ehu kakahiaka, i ka manawa e keehi iho ai na kukuna o ka la i ka piko o na mauna, ia manawa e ike aku ai ko ka aina, he Kamakahi ke noho mai ana iloko o ka onohi o ka la, he mea like me ke keiki kapu a kuu Akua. E ike auanei ka aina i ka luku nui ma ia hope iho, a nana e kaili aku i ka poe hookiekie mai ka aina aku, alaila, no kakou ka pomaikai, a me ka kakou pua aku."

A lohe kana mau kaikamahine i keia wanana a ka Makaula, nalu iho la lakou iloko o lakou iho ma ke kaawale i keia wanana a ka Makaula, me ka hai ole aku i ua Makaula nei, no ka mea, ua hoomanao wale ae la lakou no ka lakou mea i hoouna ai i ko lakou kaikaina.

Ma kona ano Makaula, ua hiki ia ia ke hele aku e kukala ma Kauai a puni, me ka hai aku i kana mea i ike a no na mea e hiki mai ana mahope.

A no keia mea, kauoha iho la oia i kana mau kaikamahine, mamua o kona haalele ana ia lakou, me ka olelo aku, "E a'u mau kaikamahine ke hele nei au ma kuu aoao mau, e haalele ana wau ia oukou, aole nae e hele loa ana, aka, e hele ana wau e hai aku i keia mea a'u e kamailio nei ia oukou, a hoi mai wau; nolaila, e noho oukou ma kahi a kuu Akua i kuhikuhi ai ia'u, e waiho oukou ia oukou maloko o ka maluhia a hiki i ka hookoia'na o kuu wanana."

Hele aku la ua Makaula nei e like me kona manaopaa, a hele aku la oia imua a na'lii a me ka poe koikoi, ma kahi e akoakoa ai na'lii, malaila oia i kukala aku ai e like me kona ike.

A hiki mua oia i o Aiwohikupua, me ka i aku, "Mai keia la aku, e kukulu mua oe i mau lepa a puni kou wahi, a e hookomo i kau poe aloha a pau maloko.

"No ka mea, ma keia hope koke iho, e hiki mai ana ka luku maluna o ka aina, aole e ikeia kekahi luku mamua aku, e like me ka luku e hiki mai ana, aole hoi mahope iho o ka pau ana ae o keia luku a'u e olelo nei.

"Mamua o ka hiki ana mai o ka mea mana, e hoike mai no oia i hoailona no ka luku ana, aole maluna o na makaainana, maluna pono iho no ou, a o kou poe, ia manawa, e moe ai na mea kiekie o ka aina nei imua ona, a e kailiia aku ka hanohano mai a oe aku.

"Ina e hoolohe oe i ka'u olelo, alaila, e pakele oe i ka luku e hiki mai ana, a oiaio; ano e hoomakaukau oe ia oe."

A no keia olelo a ka Makaula, kipakuia mai la ka Makaula mai ke alo mai o ke Alii.

Pela oia i kukula hele ai imua o na'lii a puni o Kauai, o ka poe alii i lohe i ka ka Makaula, o lakou no kai pakele.

Hele aku oia imua o Kekalukaluokewa, kana wahine, a me ko laua alo a pau.

E like me ka olelo no Aiwohikupua, pela kana olelo ia Kekalukaluokewa, a manaoio mai la oia.

Aka, o Waka, aole oia i hooko, me ka olelo mai, "Ina he Akua ka mea nana e luku mai, alaila, he Akua no ko'u e hiki ai ke hoopakele ia'u, a me ka'u mau Alii."

A no keia olelo a Waka, haliu aku la ka Makaula i ke Alii, a olelo aku la, "Mai hoolohe i ka ko kupunawahine, no ka mea, e hiki mai ana ka luku nui maluna o na'lii. Ano e kukulu i lepa a puni oe, a e hookomo i kau mea aloha maloko o no lepa i kukuluia, a o ka mea e manaoio ole i ka'u, e haule no lakou iloko o ka luku nui.

"A hiki i ua la la, e moe ana na luahine ma na kapua i o ke keiki mana, me ke noi aku i ola, aole e loaa, no ka mea, ua hoole i ka olelo a ka Makaula nei."

A no ka mea, ua ike o Kekalukaluokewa i ke ko mau o kana mau wanana mamua aku, nolaila, ua pale kela i ka olelo a ka luahine.

A hala aku la ka Makaula, kukulu ae la ke Alii i lepa a puni kona Hale Alii, a noho iho la maloko o kahi hoomalu e like me ka olelo a ka Makaula.

A pau ka huakai kaapuni a ka Makaula, hoi aku la oia a noho me kana mau kaikamahine.

No ke aloha wale no o ka Makaula ke kumu o kona hele ana aku e hai i kana mea i ike ai. Hookahi la o kona, noho ana me kana mau kaikamahine ma Honopuuwaiakua, mai kona hoi ana aku mai kaapuni, hiki mai o Kahalaomapuana, e like me ka kakou ike ana mamua ae nei i hoikeia ma neia Mokuna.

Mokuna XXX

Hookahi anahulu mahope iho o ko Kahalaomapuana hoi ana mai mai Kealohilani mai, ia manawa, hiki mai la ka hoailona mua a ko lakou kaikunane, e like me ke kauoha i kona kaikuahine.

Pela i hoao liilii ai na hoailona iloko o na la elima, a i ke ono o ka la, kui ka hekili, ua ka ua, kaikoo ka moana, waikahe ka aina, olapa ka uwila, uhi ka noe, pio ke anuenue, ku ka punohu i ka moana.

Ia manawa, olelo aku ka Makaula, "E a'u mau kaikamahine, ua hiki mai ka hoohoia'na o kuu wanana e like me ka'u olelo mua ia oukou."

I aku la na kaikamahine, "Oia hoi ka makou i hamumu iho nei, no ka mea, ua lohe mua no makou i keia mea ia oe, oiai aole keia (Kahalaomapuana) i hiki mai, a ma ka ianei hoi ana mai nei, lohe hope makou ia ianei."

Olelo mai la o Laieikawai, "He haalulu nui ko'u, a me ka weliweli, a pehea la e pau ai kuu maka'u?"

"Mai maka'u oe, aole hoi e weliweli, e hiki mai ana ka pomaikai ia kakou, a e lilo auanei kakou i mea nui nana e ai na moku a puni, aole kekahi mea e ae, a e noho Alii auanei oukou maluna o ka aina, a e holo aku ka poe hana ino mai ia oukou mai ka noho Alii aku.

"Nolaila wau i ukali ai me ka hoomanawanui iloko o ka luhi, a me ka inea, iloko o na pilikia he nui, a ke ike nei wau, no'u ka pomaikai a no ka'u mau pua, mai ia oukou mai."

Hookahi malama o ka ino ma ka, aina no ka hoailona hope, ma ke kakahiaka, i na kukuna o ka la i haalele iho ai i na mauna. Ikeia aku la o Kaonohiokala e noho ana iloko o a wela kukanono o ka la, mawaena pono o ka Luakalai, i hoopuniia i na anuenue, a me ka ua koko.

I kela wa no, loheia aku la ka pihe uwa a puni o Kauai, i ka ike ana aku i ka Hiwahiwa Kamakahi a Moanalihaikawaokele laua o Laukieleula, ke Alii nui o Kahakaekaea, a me Nuumealani.

Aia hoi he leo uwa, "Ka Hiwahiwa a Hulumaniani—e! Ka Makaula nui mana! E Hulumaniani—e! Homai he ola!"

Mai ke kakahiaka a ahiahi ka uwa ana, ua paa ka leo, o ke kuhikuhi wale iho no a ka lima aohe leo, me ke kunou ana o ke poo, no ka mea, ua paa ka leo i ka uwa ia Kaonohiokala.

Ia manawa a Kaonohiokala e nana mai ana i ka honua nei, aia hoi, e aahu mai ana o Laieikawai i ke kapa anuenue a kona kaikuahine (Kahalaomapuana) i lawe mai ai, alaila, maopopo ae la ia ia o Laieikawai no keia, ka wahine hoopalau ana.

Ma ka ehu ahiahi, ma ka puka ana mai a ka mahina konane o Mahealani, hiki mai la iloko o ke anapuni a ka Makaula.

Ia Kaonohiokala i hiki mai ai, moe kukuli iho la kona mau kaikuahine, a me ka Makaula imua o ka Hiwahiwa.

A o Laieikawai kekahi, i ka Hiwahiwa i ike mai ai ia Laieikawai e hoomaka ana e kukuli; kahea mai la ka Hiwahiwa, "E kuu Haku wahine, e Laieikawai e! mai kukuli oe, ua like no kaua."

"E kuu Haku, he weliweli ko'u, a me ka haalulu nui. A ino i manao oe e lawe i kuu ola nei, e pono ke lawe aku, no ka mea, aole wau i halawai me kekahi mea weliweli nui mamua e like me keia," wahi a Laieikawai.

"Aole au i hiki mai e lawe i kou ola, aka, ma ka huakai a kuu kaikuahine i hiki ae nei i o'u la, a nolaila, ua haawi mai wau i hoailona no'u e ike ai ia oe, a e maopopo ai ia'u o oe kuu wahine hoopalau, a nolaila ua hele mai au e hooko e like me kana kii ana ae nei," pela aku o Kaonohiokala.

A lohe kona mau kaikuhine a me ka Makaula pu, alaila hooho maila lakou me ka leo olioli:

"Amama! Amama! Amama! Ua noa, lele wale, aku la." Ala ae lakou i luna me ka maka olioli.

Ia manawa, kahea iho la oia i kona mau kaikuahine, "Ke lawe nei wau i kuu wahine, a ma kela po e hiki hou mai maua." Alaila, kailiia aku la kana wahine me ka ike oleia e kona mau hoa, aka, o ka Makaula ka mea i ike aweawea aku i ka laweia ana ma ke anuenue a noho i loko o ka Mahina, malaila i hooiaio ai laua i ko laua mau minute oluolu.

A ma kekahi po ae, i ka mahina e konane oluolu ana, i ka wa hapa o ka lai.

Kuuia mai la kekahi anuenue i uliliia mai luna mai o ka mahina a hiki i lalo nei, i ka wa e kupono ana ka mahina i luna pono o Honopuuwaiakua.

Ia manawa, iho mai la na'lii o ka lewa me ko laua ihiihi nui a ku mai la i mua o ka Makaula, me ka olelo iho, "E hele ae oe e kala aku i na mea a pau i hookahi anahulu, e hoohuiia ma kahi hookahi, alaila, e hoopuka aku wau i olelo hoopai no ka poe i hana ino mai ia oukou.

"A pau na la he umi, alaila e hui hou kaua, a na'u no e hai aku i ka mea e pono ai ke hana oe, a me kau mau kaikamahine pu me oe."

A pau keia mau olelo, hele aku la ka Makaula, a hala ia, alaila kaili puia aku la na kaikuahine elima i luna a noho pu me ia i ka olu o ka Mahina.

I ka Makaula i kaapuni ai mamuli o ka olelo a ka Hiwahiwa, aole oia i halawai me kekahi kanaka hookahi, no ka mea, ua pau i uka o Pihanakalani, kahi i oleloia he lanakila.

A pau na la he umi, hiki aku ka Makaula i Honopuwaiakua, aia hoi ua mehameha.

Ia manawa, halawai mai la me ia o Kaonohiokala, a hai aku la i kana olelo hoike no kana oihana kaapuni e like me ke kauoha a ka Hiwahiwa.

Ia manawa kaili puia aku la ka Makaula a noho i ka mahina.

A i ke kakahiaka o kekahi la ae, ma ka puka ana mai o ka la, i ka wa i haalele iho ai na kukuna wela o ka la i na mauna.

Ia manawa ka hoomaka ana o ka Hiwahiwa e hoopai ia Aiwohikupua a me Waka pu.

Haawiia ka make no Waka, a o Aiwohikupua, hoopaiia aku la ia e lilo i kanaka ilihune, e aea haukae ana maluna o ka aina a hiki i kona mau la hope.

Ma ke noi a Laieikawai, e hoopakele ia Laielohelohe a me kana kane, nolaila, ua maalo ae ka pilikia mai o laua ae, a no laua kekahi kuleana ma ka aina ma ia hope iho.

I ke kakahiaka nae, i ka hoomaka ana o ka luku ia Aiwohikupua a me Waka.

Aia hoi, o ke anaina i akoakoa ma Pihanakalani, ike aku la lakou i ke anuenue i kuuia mai ma ka mahina mai, i uliliia i na kukuna wela o ka la.

Alaila, ia manawa akoakoa lakou a pau, ka Makaula, a me na kaikamahine elima e kau mai ana ma ke ala i uliliia, a o Kaonohiokala me Laieikawai ma ke kaawale, a he mau kapuai ko laua me he ahi la. Oia ka manawa a Aiwohikupua a me Waka i haula ai i ka houna, me ka apono i ka olelo a ka Makaula.

A pau ka hoopai a ke Alii no na enemi, hoonoho ae la ke Alii oluna ia Kahalaomapuana i Moi, a hoonoho pakahi aku la i na kaikuahine ona ma na mokupui. A o Kekalukaluokewa no ke Kuhina Nui, a me Laielohelohe, a o ka Makaula no ko lakou mau hoa kuka ma ke ano Kuhina Nui.

A pau ka hooponopono ana no keia mau mea a pono ka noho ana, kaili puia aku la o Laieikawai e kana kane ma ke anuenue iloko o na ao kaalelewa a noho nia kahi mau o kana kane.

Ina e hewa kona mau kaikuahine, alaila na Kahalaomapuana e lawe ka olelo hoopii imua o ke Alii.

Aka, aole i loaa ka hewa o kona mau kaikuahine ma ia hope iho a hiki i ka haalele ana i keia ao.

Mokuna XXXI

Mahope o ko Laieikawai hoao ana me Kaonohiokala, me ka hooponopono i ka noho ana o kona mau kaikuahine, ka Makaula, a me Kekalukaluokewa ma; a pau keia mau mea i ka hooponoponoia, hoi aku la laua iluna o ka aina i oleloia o Kahakaekaea, o noho ma ka pea kapu o Kukulu o Tahiti.

A no ka lilo ana o Laieikawai i wahine mau ma ka berita paa, nolaila, haawiia ae la ia ia kekahi mau hana mana a pau ma ke ano Akua, e like me kana kane; koe nae ka mana hiki ole ke ike i na mea huna, a me na hana pohihihi i hanaia ma kahi mamao, no kana kane wale no.

Mamua nae o ko laua haalele ana ia Kauai, a hoi aku iluna, ua hanaia kekahi olelo hooholo iloko o ko lakou akoakoa ana; ma ka ahaolelo hooponopono aupuni ana.

Oia hoi, i ka la i kuuia mai ai ke alanui anuenue mai Nuumealani mai, a kau aku la o Kaonohiokala, a me Laieikawai maluna o ke ala anuenue i oleloia, a waiho mai la i kona leo kauoha hope i kona mau hoa, ka Makaula, a me Laielohelohe, eia kana olelo:

"E o'u mau hoa, a me ko kakou makuakane Makaula, kuu kaikaina i ka aa hookahi, a me ka kaua kane; ke hoi nei au mamuli o ka mea a kakou i kuka ai, a ke haalele nei wau ia oukou, a hoi aku i kahi hiki ole ia oukou ke ike koke ae; nolaila, e nana kekahi i kekahi me ka noho like, no ka mea, ua hoopomaikai like ia oukou, aole kekahi mea o oukou i hooneleia i ka pomaikai. Aka, oia nei (Kaonohiokala) no ko maua mea e hiki mai i o oukou nei, e ike i ka pono o ko oukou noho ana."

A pau keia mau mea, laweia aku la laua me ko laua ike oleia. A e like me ka olelo, "o Kaonohiokala ka mea iho mai e ike i ka pono o kona mau hoa," oia kekahi kumu i haunaele ai ko Laieikawai ma noho ana me kana kane.

Ia Laieikawai ma ko laua wahi me kana kane, he mea mau ia Kaonohiokala ka iho pinepine mai ilalo nei e ike i ka pono o kona mau kaikuahine, a me kana wahine opio (Laielohelohe), ekolu iho ana i ka makahiki hookahi.

Elima paha makahiki ka loihi o ko laua noho ana ma ka hoohiki paa o ka berita mare; a i ke ono paha o ka makahiki o ko Laieikawai ma noho pono ana me kana kane, ia manawa, haula iho la o Kaonohiokala i ka hewa me Laielohelohe; me ka ike ole o na mea e ae i keia haule ana i ka hewa.

I ka ekolu malama o Laieikawai ma iluna, iho mai la o Kaonohiokala e ike i ka pono o kona mau kaikuahine, a hoi aku la me Laieikawai, pela i kela a me keia hapakolu o ka makahiki, a i ka ekolu makahiki o ko Kaonohiokala huakai makai i ka pono o kona mau kaikuahine; aia hoi, ua hookanaka makua loa ae la kana wahine opio (Laielohelohe), alaila, ua pii mai a mahuahua ka wahine maikai, a oi ae mamua o kona kaikuaana o Laieikawai.

Aole nae i haula o Kaonohiokala ia manawa i ka hewa, aka, ua hoomaka ae kona kuko ino e hana i ka mea pono ole.

I kela hele ana keia hele ana a Kaonohiokala i kana hana niau ilalo nei, a hiki i ka eha makahiki; aia hoi, ua hoomahuahuaia mai ka nani o Laielohelohe mamua o kana ike mua ana, a mahuahua loa ae la ka manao ino o Kaonohiokala; aka, ma kona ano keiki Akua, hoomanawanui aku la no oia e pale ae i kona kuko, hookahi paha minute e lele aku ai ke kuko mai ona aku, alaila, pili mai la no.

I ka lima o ka makahiki, ma ka pau ana o ka hapaha mua o ua makahiki la, iho hou mai la o Kaonohiokala i kana hana mau ilalo nei.

I kela manawa, ua kailiia aku ko Kaonohiokala manao maikai mai ona aku a kaawale loa, a haule iho la oia i ka hewa.

I kela manawa no hoi, ia ia e halawai la me kona, mau kaikuahine, a me ka Makaula hoi, ka pinualua a me ka laua wahine hoi (Laielohelohe), hoomaka ae la o Kaonohiokala e hooponopono hou no ke aupuni, a nolaila, ua hoomaka hou ka ahaolelo.

A i mea e pono ai ko ke Alii manao kolohe, hoolilo ae la oia i kona mau kaikuahine i poe kiai no ka aina i oleloia o Kealohilani, a na lakou e hooponopono pu me Mokukelekahiki i ka noho ana, a me na hana a pau e pili ana i ka aina.

A ike ae la kekahi o kona mau kaikuahine, ua oi aku ka hanohano mamua o keia noho ana, no ka mea, ua hooliloia i mau alii no kahi hiki ole ia lakou ke noho e lawelawe pu me Mokukelekahiki, nolaila, hooholo ae la lakou i ka ae mamuli o ka olelo a ko lakou kaikunane.

Aka, o Kahalaomapuana, aole oia i ae aku e hoi iloko o Kealohilani; no ka mea, ua oi aku kona minamina i ka hanohano mau i loaa ia ia mamua o ka hoi ana i Kealohilani.

A no ko Kahalaomapuana ae ole, hoopuka aku la oia i kana olelo imua o kona kaikunane, "E kuu Lani, ma kou hoolilo ana ae nei ia makou e hoi i Kealohilani, a o lakou no ke hoi, a owau nei la, e noho ae no wau ilalo nei, e like me kau hoonoho mua ana; no ka mea, ke aloha nei wau i ka aina a me na makaainana, a ua maa ae nei no hoi ka noho ana; a ina owau no malalo nei, o oe no maluna mai, a o lakou nei hoi iwaena ae nei, alaila, pono iho no kakou, like loa me ka hanau ana mai a ko kakou makuahine, no ka mea, nau i wahi ke alanui, a o kou mau pokii hoi, hele aku mahope ou, a na'u hoi i pani aku, o ke oki no ia, a oia la."

A no keia olelo a kona kaikuahine muli loa, manao iho la, oia, ua pono ka olelo a kona kaikuahine. Aka, no ke ake nui o Kaonohiokala e kaawale aku oia i kahi e, i mea e ike oleia'i kona kalohe ana, nolaila, hailona aku la oia i kona mai Kaikuahine, a o ka mea e ku ai ka hailona, oia ke hoi iloko o Kealohilani.

I aku la o Kaonohiokala i kona mau kaikuahine, "E hele oukou e u-u mai i pua Kilioopu, aole e hui i ko oukou hele ana, e hele oukou ma ke kaawale kekahi i kekahi, a loaa, alaila, e hoi mai ko oukou mua a haawi mai ia'u, e like me ko hanau ana, pela oukou e heleai, a pela no hoi oukou ke hoi mai, a o ka mea loihi o kana Kilioopu, oia ke hoi i Kealohilani."

Hele aku la kela a me keia o lakou ma ke kaawale, a hoi mai la e like me ka mea i oleloia ia lakou.

Hele aku la ka mea mua, a huhuki mai la elua iniha paha ka loihi o kana, a o ka lua hoi, huhuki mai la, a oki ae la i kana Kilioopu ekolu iniha a me ka hapa paha; a o ke kolu hoi, huhuki mai la i kana Kilioopu, elua iniha paha ka loihi; a o ka eha o lakou hookahi iniha paha ka loihi o kana, a o Kahalaomapuana hoi, aole oia i huhuki mai ma ke Kilioopu loloa, huhuki mai la oia ma ka mea liilii loa, ekolu kapuai paha kona loa; a oki ae la oia i ka hapalua o kana, a hoi aku la, me ka manao o kana Kilioopu ka pokole.

Aka, i ka hoohalike ana, kiola aku la ka mua i kana imua o ko lakou kaikunane, ike aku la o Kahalaomapuana i ka ka mua, he mea kahaha loa ia ia, nolaila, momoku malu ae la oia i kana iloko o kona aahu, aka, ua ike aku la kona kaikunane i kana hana, i aku la, "E Kahalaomapuana, mai hana malu oe, e waiho i kau Kilioopu pela."

Kiola aku la na mea i koe i ka lakou, aka, o Kahalaomapuana, aole i hoike mai, i mai nae "Ua ku ia'u ka hailona."

A no keia mea, koi aku la oia i kona kaikunane e hailona hou; e hailona hou ana, ku hou no ia Kahalaomapuana ka hailona; aole olelo i koe a Kahalaomapuana, no ka mea, ua ku ka hailona ia ia.

Oia hoi, he mea kaumaha nae ia Kahalaomapuana, ke kaawale ana'ku mai kona noho Alii aku, a me na makaainana, no ka mea, ua hoopouliia ko ke Alii wahine naau makemake ole e hoi i Kealohilani e ka hailona.

A i ka la o Kahalaomapuana i hoi ai i Kealohilani, kuuia mai la ke anuenue mai luna mai a hiki ilalo nei.

Ia manawa, hai aku la oia i kana olelo imua o kona kaikunane, me ka i aku, "E ku ke alanui o kuu Lani pela, e kali no na la he umi, e hoakoakoaia mai na'lii, a me na makaainana a pau, i hoike aku ai wau i ko'u aloha nui ia lakou mamua o kou lawe ana aku ia'u."

A ike iho la o Kaonohiokala, ua pono ka olelo a kona kaikuahine hooholo ae la oia i kona manao ae; alaila, lawe houia aku la ke alanui iluna me kona kaikunane pu.

A i ka umi o ka la, kuuia mai la ua alanui nei imua o ke anaina, a kau aku la o Kahalaomapuana iluna o ke alanui ulili i hoomakaukauia nona, a huli mai la me ka naau kaumaha, i hoopihaia kona mau maka i na kulu wai o Kulanihakoi, me ka i mai, "E na'lii, na makaainana, ke haalele nei wau ia oukou, ke hoi nei wau i ka aina a oukou i ike ole ai, owau a me o'u mau kaikuaana wale no kai ike; aole nae no ko'u makemake e hoi ia aina, aka, na ko'u lima no i ae ia'u e haalele ia oukou mamuli o ka hailona a kuu kaikunane Lani nei. Aka hoi, ua ike no wau he mau Akua like ko kakou a pau, aole mea nele, nolaila, e pule oukou i ke Akua, a e pule no hoi wau i ko'u Akua, a ina i mana na pule a kakou, alaila, e halawai hou ana no kakou ma keia hope aku. Aloha oukou a pau, aloha no hoi ka aina, oki kakou la nalo."

Alaila, lalau ae la oia i kona aahu, a palulu ae la i kona mau maka imua o ke anaina, i mea e huna ai i kona manaonao i na makaainana a me ka aina. A laweia'ku la oia ma ke anuenue iloko o na ao kalelewa ma ka Lanikuakaa.

O ke kumu nui o ko Kaonohiokala manao nui e hookawale ia Kahalaomapuana i Kealohilani, i mea e nalo ai kona kalohe ia Laielohelohe; no ka mea, o Kahalaomapuana, aia kekahi ike ia ia, he ike hiki ke hanaia kekahi hana ma kahi malu; a he kaikamahine manaopaa no, aole e hoopilimeai. O manao auanei o Kaonohiokala o haiia kana hana kalohe ana imua o Moanalihaikawaokele, nolaila oia i hookaawale ai i kona kaikuahine, a ma ke ano Akua o Kaonohiokala, na lilo ka hailona ia Kahalaomapuana.

A kaawale aku la kona kaikuahine, a i ka pau ana paha o a hapaha elua o ka lima o ka makahiki, iho hou mai la oia ilalo nei e hooko i kona manao kuko ia Laielohelohe.

Aole nae oia i hooko koke ia manawa; aka, i mea e pono ai oia imua o Kekalukaluokewa nolaila, waiho aku la oia imua o Kekalukaluokewa e pani ma ka hakahaka o Kahalaomapuana; a o ka Makaula no kona Kuhina Nui.

A hoonohoia aku la o Mailehaiwale i Kiaaina paha no Kauai; ia Mailekaluhea no Oahu; o Mailelaulii no Maui a me na moku e ae; ia Mailepakaha no Hawaii.

Mokuna XXXII

A lilo ae la o Kekalukaluokewa i poo kiekie ma ke aupuni, alaila, hoouna aku la o Kaonohiokala ia Kekalukaluokewa e hele e kaapuni ma na mokupuni a pau e lawelawe i kana oihana Moi, a hoonoho iho la ia Laielohelohe ma ko Kekalukaluokewa wahi ma ke ano hope Moi.

A no keia mea, lawe ae la o Kekalukaluokewa i kona Kuhina Nui (ka Makaula), ma kana huakai kaapuni.

I ka la i haalele ai o Kekalukaluokewa ia Pihanakalani, a hele aku la ma kana oihana kaapuni. Ia la no hoi ka haalele ana o Kaonohiokala ia lalo nei.

Ma kela hoi ana o Kaonohiokala, aole nae oia i hiki loa iluna, aka, ua ike nae oia ia la e holo ana na waa o Kekalukaluokewa i ka moana.

A no ia mea, hoi hou mai la o Kaonohiokala mai luna mai a hiki ilalo nei, a launa iho la me Laielohelohe, aole nae i hanaia ka hewa ia manawa.

Ia laua me Laielohelohe e halawai la, noi aku la o Kaonohiokala ia Laielohelohe e hookaawaleia na mea e ae, a ma kona ano Mea Nui, ua hookaawaleia ko ke Alii wahine mau aialo.

Ia Laielohelohe me Kaonohiokala o laua wale no ma ke kaawale, i aku la, "O ka ekolu keia o ko'u mai makahiki (puni) o ka makemake ana ia oe, no ka mea, ua ulu kou nani a papale maluna o kou kaikuaana (Laieikawai). A nolaila, ma na la hope nei, ua hiki ole ia'u ke hoomanawanui e pale aku i ke kuko no'u ia oe mai o'u aku."

"E kuu Lani e," wahi a Laielohelohe, "pehea la e kaawale ai ia kuko ou mai a oe ae? A heaha la ka manao o kuu Lani e pono ai ke hana?"

"E launa kino kaua," wahi a Kaonohiokala, "oia wale no ka mea e pono ai ke hanaia imua o'u."

I aku la o Laielohelohe, "Aole kaua e launa kino e kuu Lani, no ka mea, o ka mea nana i malama ia'u mai kuu wa uuku mai a loaa wale kuu kane, nana ka olelo paa ma o'u la, aole e haawi i kuu kino me kahi mea e ae e hoohaumia; a nolaila, e kuu Lani e, na ka mea nana ka hoohiki paa ia'u e ae aku i kou makemake."

A lohe o Kaonohiokala i keia mea, akahi no a hoomohalaia ke kuko ino iloko, alaila, hoi aku la oia iluna me kana wahine (Laieikawai). Aole nae i anahulu kona mau la i luna, uhi paapu houia mai la oia e na hekili o ke kuko ino, a hiki ole ke hoomanawanui no ke kuko.

A na keia kuko, kaikai kino houia mai la oia mai luna mai e halawai hou me Laielohelohe.

A no ka lohe mua ana o Kaonohiokala "na ka mea nana i malama" ia ia ka "hoohiki paa e ae aku." Nolaila, kii mua aku la oia ma o Kapukaihaoa la, e noi aku e ae mai i ko ke Alii makemake.

A nolaila hoi, hele mua aku la oia a olelo aku ia Kapukaihaoa, "Ua makemake wau e lawe ia Laielohelohe e pili me a'u i keia manawa, aole nae no ke kaili loa mai, aka, i mea e hoomama ae ai i ko'u naau kaumaha i ke kuko i kau milimili, no ka mea, ua noi mua aku wau i ua milimili la au i kuu makemake; aka, ua kuhikuhi mai kela nau e ae aku, a nolaila, kii mai nei wau ma ou la."

I aku o Kapukaihaoa, "E ka lani o na lani, ke ae aku nei wau ma kau noi e kuu Lani, he mea pono nou e komo aku oe me ka'u milimili; no ka mea, ua ike au i ko'u pomaikai ole no ka'u mea i luhi ai, ua upu aku hoi ko maua manao me ka mea nana i malama kau wahine (Laieikawai), o Kekalukaluokewa ke kane a ka'u hanai, ua pono no, aka, i keia noho aupuni ana, ua lilo ka pomaikai i na mea e ae, nolaila, ua nele wau. No ka mea hoi, ua haawi ae nei kela i na moku a pau i ou kaikuahine, koe hoi wau ka mea nana kana wahine i wahine ai, a nolaila e aho hoi ke ka i ka nele lua, a nau ka wahine a olua."

A pau keia mau kamailio a laua ma ke kaawale, hele aku la o Kapukaihaoa me ke Alii pu a hiki o Laielohelohe la.

I aku la, "E kuu luhi, eia ke kane, nohoia, he lani iluna he honua, ilalo, keehi'a kulana a paa, a nana mai i ka mea nana i luhi."

Alaila he mea kanalua ole ia ia Laielohelohe; a lawe ae la o Kaonohiokala ia Laielohelohe, a hui oluolu iho la laua.

Ekolu mau la o laua ma ka laua mau hana, hoi aku la o Kaonohiokala i Kahakaekaea.

A mahope iho oia mau la kaawale, ua aaki paaia ke aloha wela i luna o Kaonohiokala, a ano e kona mau helehelena.

Ia manawa, hoopuka aku la o Kaonohiokala i olelo hoopunipuni i mua o Laieikawai, oia ka ha o na la kaawale o laua, me ka i aku, "Haohao hoi keia po oʻu, aole wau i moe iki, i ka hoopahupahu waleia no a ao wale."

I aku o Laieikawai, "Heaha la?"

I aku o Kaonohiokala, "Ua pono ole paha ka noho ana o lakou la o lalo."

"Ae paha," wahi a Laieikawai, "aole no la hoi e iho."

A no keia hua kena a kana wahine, he mea manawa ole noho ana i lalo nei o Kaonohiokala, a launa no me Laielohelohe. Aka, o Laielohelohe aole i loaa ia ia kona pilikia ma ka manao, heaha la ia mea i kona manao ana.

Ia laua e hui ana ma ka makemake o ke Alii kane, ia manawa, ua ike ole o Laielohelohe i kona aloha ia Kaonohiokala, no ka mea, aole no o ke Alii wahine makemake iki e hana i ka hewa me ke Alii nui o luna; aa hoi, mamuli o ka onou a kona mea nana i malama wale no ka hooko ana.

Hookahi anahulu paha o ko laua hana ana i ka hewa, hoi aku la o Kaonohiokala iluna.

Ia manawa, ulu mai la a mahuahua ke aloha o Laielohelohe ia Kekalukaluokewa no kona haule ana i ka hewa me Kaonohiokala.

I kekahi la ma ke ahiahi, olelo aku la o Laielohelohe ia Kapukaihaoa, "E kuu kahu nana i malama maikai, i keia manawa, ua poino loa iaʻu ka manao no Kaonohiokala iloko o na manawa o maua i hana iho nei i ka hewa, a ke hoomahuahua mai nei ke aloha o kuu kane (Kekalukaluokewa) iaʻu, no ka mea, i ka noho iho nei no ka i ka pono me ke kane, me ko maua maikai, a lalau wale no i ka hewa, aole no koʻu makemake, no kou makemake wale no. Heaha no la hoi kou hewa ke hoole aku, i kuhikuhi aku hoi wau i kou ae ole no kou hoohiki ana, aole au e launa me kekahi mea e ae, kaiona he hoohiki paa kau, aole ka."

I aku o Kapukaihaoa, "I ae aku au e lilo oe i ka mea e, no kuu nele i ka haawina waiwai o ko kane; no ka mea, ma kuu maka ponoi nei no ka waiwai a ko kane i haawi ae ai, a owau no ke ku, nolaila, lilo oe, aole hoi au i manaoia ka mea nana ka wahine i wahine ai oia."

I aku o Laielohelohe i kona kahu nana i hanai, "Ina o kou kumu ia o ka haawi ana i kuu kino e hoohaumia me Kaonohiokala, alaila, ua hewa loa oe; no ka mea, ua ike oe, aole no Kekalukaluokewa i hoonoho na mea maluna o na aina; aka, na Kaonohiokala no, a nolaila, apopo e kau wau maluna o na waa a holo aku e imi i kuu kane."

I ke ahiahi iho, kena'e la oia i na aialo kane ona, na mea malama waa hoi o ke Alii, e hoomakaukau i na waa no ka holo aku e imi i ke kane.

A no ke kumu ole o kona manao ia Kaonohiokala, nolaila huna iho la oia ia ia makolo o na hale kuaaina hiki ole ia ia ke noho, no kona manao o hiki hou mai o Kaonohiokala, hana hou ia ka hewa me kona makemake ole, oia kona pee ma na hale kuaaina, aole nae oia (Kaonohiokala) i hiki mai a hiki i kona hala ana i ka moana ia po iho.

A hala o Laielohelohe i ka moana, a hiki ma Oahu, noho iho la oia ma na hale kuaaina. Pela oia i hele ai a hiki i ko laua halawai ana me Kekalukaluokewa.

Ia Laielohelohe paha i Oahu, a ma kekahi la ae, iho hou mai la o Kaonohiokala e launa hou me Laielohelohe; aka, i kona hiki ana mai, aole o Laielohelohe o ka hale Alii, aole no hoi oia i ninau mai i ka mea nana e malama ka hale Alii, no ka mea, ina e ninau oia, manaoia e hana ana i ka hewa me Laielohelohe; aka, ua hai malu aku nae o Laielohelohe i ke kiai hale Alii i ke kumu o kona hele ana. A no ka nele o ko ke Alii makemake, hoi aku la oia i luna.

O keia haula ana nae a na'lii i ka hewa, ua nakulu aku la keia lohe i ke alo Alii, ma o na aialo wale no nae, a ua lohe puia no hoi ko Laielohelohe makemake ole.

Ia Aiwohikupua e kuewa ana ma ke alo Alii, oia nae kekahi i lohe i keia mau mea. A no ka lohe ana o Aiwohikupua i ko Laielohelohe kumu i holo ai e imi i ke kane; alaila i aku oia i ke kiai hale Alii, "Ina i hoi hou mai o Kaonohiokala, a i ninau mai ia Laielohelohe, i aku oe ua mai ia, alaila aole e hoi hou mai; no ka mea, he mea haumia loa ia ia Kaonohiokala, a me na makua o makou, aia no a pau ka haumia, alaila hana aku ma ka hana o ka hoku Venuka."

Ia iho hou ana mai o Kaonohiokala, ninau i ke kiai hale Alii, alaila haiia aku la e like me ka Aiwohikupua olelo, alaila hoi aku la oia i luna.

Mokuna XXXIII

Ua oleloia ma ka Mokuna XXXII o keia kaao ke kumu o ko Laielohelohe imi ana i kana kane ia Kekalukaluokewa.

Nolaila, imi aku la oia mai Kauai mai a Oahu, a Maui; i Lahaina keia, lohe aia o Kekalukaluokewa i Hana, ua hoi mai mai Hawaii mai.

Holo aku la oia ma na waa a pae ma Honuaula, ilaila lohe lakou o Hinaikamalama ka wahine a Kekalukaluokewa, aole nae i ike ko Honuaula poe o ka Kekalukaluokewa wahine keia.

A no ka lohe ana o Laielohelohe i keia mea, lalelale koke aku la lakou a hiki i Kaupo, a me Kipahulu. Alaila, hoomaopopoia mai la ka lohe mua o lakou i Honuaula, a mailaila aku lakou a kau na waa ma Kapohue, haalele lakou i na waa, hele aku la lakou a Waiohonu, lohe lakou ua hala o Kekalukaluokewa me Hinaikamalama i Kauwiki; a hiki lakou i Kauwiki, ua hala loa aku la o Kekalukaluokewa ma i Honokalani, he nui na la i hala ia lakou ma ia hele ana.

Ia hele ana a lakou a hiki i Kauwiki, ua ahiahi nae, ninau aku la o Laielohelohe i na kamaaina i ka loihi o kahi i koe a hiki i Honokalani, kahi a Kekalukaluokewa e noho ana me Hinaikamalama.

Olelo mai kamaaina, "Napoo ka la hiki."

A hele aku la lakou me ke kamaaina pu, a molehulehu hiki aku la lakou i Honokalani; alaila, hoouna aku la o Laielohelohe i ke kamaaina e hele aku e nana i ka noho ana o na'lii.

Hele aku la ke kamaaina, a ike aku i na'lii e inu awa ana, hoi mai la a hai mai la ia lakou nei.

Alaila, hoouna hou aku la no o Laielohelohe i ke kamaaina e hele hou e nana i na'lii, me ka i aku nae, "E hele oe e nana a ike i na'lii e hiamoe ana, alaila, hoi mai oe a hele pu aku kakou."

A no keia olelo a Laielohelohe, alaila, hele aku la ke kamaaina, a ike aku la, ua hiamoe na'lii, hoi aku la a olelo aku la ia Laielohelohe.

Ia manawa, akahi no a hai aku oia i ke kamaaina, o Kekalukaluokewa kana kane mare (hoao).

Mamua aku nae o ko Laielohelohe halawai ana me Kekalukaluokewa, ua lohe mua aku oia i ka haula ana o Laielohelohe i ka hewa me Kaonohiokala, i lohe no i kahi kahu o Kauakahialii, ka mea i lilo ai i Kuhina Nui ma ka aoao o Aiwohikupua, a no ka lohe ana o ua wahi kanaka nei i ka hewa ana o Laielohelohe, oia kana mea i hele mai ai e hai ia Kekalukaluokewa.

Ia Laielohelohe ma i hiki aku ai ma ka hale a Kekalukaluokewa e noho ana, aia hoi e hiamoe mai ana laua ma kahi hookahi, ua hoouhiia i ka aahu hookahi, e moe ana nae i ka ona a ka awa.

A komo aku la o Laielohelohe, a noho iho la ma ke poo o laua (Kekalukaluokewa ma), honi iho la i ka ihu, a uwe malu iho la iloko ona; aka, ua hoohaniniia na mapuna waimaka o Laielohelohe no ka ike ana iho he wahine e ka kana kane, aole nae e hiki ia laua ke ike ae i keia, no ka mea, ua lumilumiia laua e ka ona a ka awa.

Oia hoi, aole e hiki ia Laieloheolohe ke hoomanawanui i kona ukiuki ia Hinaikamalama; nolaila, komo aku la oia mawaena o laua, a pale aku la ia Hinaikamalama, hoohuli mai la ia Kekalukaluokewa, a apo aku la i kana kane, a hoala aku la.

Ia manawa, puoho ae la o Kekalukaluokewa a ike iho la o kana wahine; ia wa, hikilele mai la o Hinaikamalama mai ka hiamoe mai, a ike iho la he wahine e keia me laua, holo aku la oia mai o laua nei aku, me ka huhu nui, me ka manao hoi aole keia o ka Kekalukaluokewa wahine.

A ike aku la o Kekalukaluokewa ia Hinaikamalama e hele ana me ka maka kukona, alaila, i aku la, "E Hinaikamalama, e holo ana oe i ke aha, me kou maka inaina, mai kuhi oe i keia wahine he wahine e, o ka'u wahine mare (hoao) no keia." Ia manawa, hookaawaleia ae la kona huhu mai ona aku, a paniia iho la ka hilahila a me ka maka'u ma ka hakahaka o ka huhu.

I ka wa nae i ala ae ai o Kekalukaluokewa mai ka hiamoe ona awa ae, a ike mai la i ka wahine, ia Laieloheolohe, honi iho la ma ke ano mau o ka hiki malihini ana.

Alaila, i mai la oia i kana wahine, "E Laieloheolohe, ua lohe iho nei wau nou, ua haule oe i ka hewa me ka Haku o kaua (Kaonohiokala), a nolaila, ua pono aku la no oe me ia, a ua pono no hoi wau ke noho aku malalo o olua, no ka mea, nona mai keia noho hanohano ana a aia no hoi ia ia ka make a me ke ola; Kamailio aku paha auanei wau, o ka make mai kai ala; nolaila, ma kahi a ka Haku o kaua e manao ai, pono no ke hooko aku, aole nae no ko'u makemake ka haawi aku ia oe, aka, no ka maka'u i ka make."

Alaila, i aku la o Laieloheolohe i kana kane, "Auhea oe, kuu kane o ka wa heu ole, ua pololei kou lohe, a he oiaio, ua haule wau i ka hewa me ua Haku la o ka aina, aole nae i mahuahua, elua wale no a maua hana ana i ka hewa; aka, e kuu kane, aole na'u i ae e haawi ia'u e hoohaumia i kuu kino me ua Haku la o kaua; aka, na kuu mea nana i malama ia'u i ae e hana wau i ka hewa; no ka mea, i ka la a oukou i hele mai ai, oia no ka la a ua Haku la o kaua i noe mai ai ia'u e hoohaumia ia maua; aka, no ko'u makemake ole, nolaila, ua kuhikuhi aku wau i ko'u ae ole ia ia; aka, i ka hoi ana iluna a hoi hou mai, nonoi ae la kela ia Kapukaihaoa, a nolaila, ua launa kino maua elua manawa, a no ko'u makemake ole, ua huna wau ia'u iho ma na hale kuaaina, a no ia mea no hoi, ua haalele wau i kahi au i hoonoho ai, a ua imi mai nei wau ia oe; a i ko'u hiki ana mai nei hoi, loaa iho nei oe ia'u me keia wahine. A nolaila, ua pai wale kaua, aole au hana no'u, aole hoi a'u hana aku ia oe; nolaila, ma keia po e hookaawale oe i kela wahine."

A no keia mea, ua pono ka olelo a ka wahine imua o kana kane; aka, ma keia olelo hope a Laielohelohe, ia manawa, ua ho-aia ke ahi enaena o ke aloha wela o Hinaikamalama no Kekalukaluokewa, no ka mea, e kaawale ana laua mai ko laua launa hewa ana.

Hoi aku la o Hinaikamalama i Haneoo, a noho iho la ma kona hale mau; i kela la keia la o Hinaikamalama ma kona Hale Alii, he mea mau ia ia ka noho ma ka puka o ka hale, a huli ke alo i Kauwiki, no ka mea, ua hoopuniia oia e ke aloha wela.

I kekahi la, i ke Alii wahine e hoonana ana i kona aloha ia Kekalukaluokewa, pii ae la oia a me kona mau kahu iluna o Kaiwiopele, a noho iho la malaila, huli aku la ke alo i Kauwiki, nana aku la ia Kahalaoaka, a o ke kau mai a ke ao iluna pono o Honokalani, ia manawa, he mea e ka maeele o ke Alii wahine i ke aloha no kana ipo; alaila, oli ae la oia he wahi mele penei:

"Me he ao puapuaa la ke aloha e kau nei,
Ka uhi paapu poele i kuu manawa,
He malihini puka paha ko ka hale,
Ke hulahula nei kuu maka.
He maka uwe paha—e. Oia—e.
E uwe aku ana no wau ia oe,
I ka lele ae a ke ehukai o Hanualele,
Uhi pono ae la iuka o Honokalani.
Kuu Lani—e. Oia—e."

A pau kana oli ana, uwe iho la oia, a nana i uwe, uwe pu me na kahu ona.

Noho iho la lakou ma ia la a ahiahi, hoi aku la i ka hale, kena mai la na makua a me na kahu e ai, aka, aole loaa ia ia ka ono o ka ai, no ka mea, ua pouli i ke aloha.

A pela no hoi o Kekalukaluokewa, no ka mea, ia Hinaikamalama i haalele aku ai ia Kekalukaluokewa i ka po a Laielohelohe i hiki mai ai, ua pono ole ka manao o ke Alii kane; a nolaila, ua hoomanawanui oia i kekahi mau la mahope mai o ko laua kaawale ana.

A ma kela la i Hinaikamalama i pii ai iluna o Kaiwiopele, a ma ia po iho, hiki oia i o Hinaikamalama la, me ka ike ole o Laielohelohe, no ka mea, ua hiamoe oia.

Ia Hinaikamalama no e ala ana, e hiaa ana no kona aloha, puka ana o Kekalukaluokewa, me ka ike ole oloko o ka Hale Alii ia ianei.

Ia Kekalukaluokewa i hiki aku ai, pololei aku la no oia a ma kahi a ke Alii wahine e hiamoe ana, lalau aku la i ka wahine ma ke poo, a hoala aku la.

Ia manawa, ua hooleleia ka oili o Hinaikamalama me ka manaolana no o kana ipo; aka, i ka lalau ana ae, aia nae o kana mea i manao ai. Ia manawa, kahea ae la oia i na kahu e ho-a ke kukui, a ma ka wanaao, hoi aku la o Kekalukaluokewa me kana hanaukama (Laielohelohe).

Ma ia manawa mai, he mea mau ia Kekalukaluokewa ka hele pinepine i o Hinaikamalama i kela po keia po me kona ike oleia; a hala he anahulu okoa o ko Kekalukaluokewa hoomau ana e hana hewa me Hinaikamalama me ka ike ole o kana wahine; no ka mea, ua uhi paapuia ko Laielohelohe ike e ka ona awa mau, mamuli o ka makemake o kana kane.

I kekahi la, kupu ka manao aloha i kekahi wahine kamaaina no Laielohelohe; noalila, hele mai la ua kamaaina wahine nei e launa me ke Alii wahine.

Ia Kekalukaluokewa me na kanaka ma ka hale kahi-olona, ia manawa i launa ai ka wahine kamaaina me Laielohelohe, me ka i aku ma kana olelo hoohuahualau, "Pehea ko Alii kane? Aole anei he uilani, a kani uhu mai i kekahi manawa no ka wahine?"

I aku la o Laielohelohe, "Aole, he maikai loa maua e noho nei."

Olelo hou ke kamaaina, "Malia paha he hookamani."

"Ae paha," wahi a Laielohelohe, "aka, i ka'u ike aku a maua e noho nei, he oluolu ko maua noho ana."

Ia manawa, olelo maopopo aku la ke kamaaina me ka i aku, "Auhea oe? O ka maua mahinaai aia ma kapa alanui ponoi; i ka wanaao, ala aku la ka'u kane i ka mahiai ma ua mahinaai nei a maua, i kuu kane nae e mahiai ana, hoi mai ana no o Kekalukaluokewa mai Haneoo mai, manao koke ae la no kuu kane me Hinaikamalama no, hoi ae kuu kane a olelo ia'u, aole nae wau i hoomaopopo. A ma ia po mai, i ka puka'na mahina, ala ae la wau me ka'u kane, a iho aku la i ka paeaea aweoweo ma ke kai o Haneoo; ia maua e hele ana, a hiki i ke alu kahawai, nana aku la maua e hoea mai ana keia mea maluna o ke ahua i hala hope ia maua; ia manawa, alu ae la maua e pee ana, aia nae o Kekalukaluokewa keia e hele nei, alaila, ukali aku la maua ma ko iala mau kapuai, a hiki maua ma kahi kokoke i ka hale o Hinaikamalama, aia nae ua komo aku no o Kekalukaluokewa; ia maua i ka lawai-a, a hoi mai maua a ma kahi no a makou i halawai mua ai, loaa iho la maua ia Kekalukaluokewa e hele ana, aole ana olelo ia aole hoi a maua olelo ia ia. Pau ia; i keia la hoi, olelo ponoi mai la ke kahu o Hinaikamalama ia'u, he kaikuahine no kuu kane, anahulu ae nei ka launa ana o na'lii, na'u nae i hoohuahualau aku; a nolaila, hu mai ko'u aloha me ka'u kane ia oe, hele mai nei wau e hai aku ia oe."

Mokuna XXXIV

A no keia olelo a ka wahine kamaaina, alaila, ua ano e ko ke Alii wahine manao, aole nae oia i wikiwiki i ka huhu; aka, i mea e maopopo lea ai ia ia, hoomanawanui no o Laielohelohe. I aku nae oia i ke kamaaina, "Malia i hookina ai kuu kane ia'u i ka inu awa, ia'u paha e moe ana i ka ona awa, hele kela; aka, ma keia po, e ukali ana wau ia ia."

Ia po iho, hoomaka hou o Kekalukaluokewa e haawi i ka awa, alaila, hooko aku la no kana wahine; aka, mahope o ka pau ana o ka inu awa ana, puka koke aku la o Laielohelohe iwaho o ka hale, a hoolualuai aku la, a pau loa ka awa i ka luaiia, aole nae i ike mai kana kane i keia hana maalea a kana wahine; a i ka hoi ana aku i ka hale, haawi mua iho la ua o Laielohelohe ia ia i ka hiamoe nui ma kona ano maalea.

A ike mai la o Kekalukaluokewa, he hiamoe io ko kana wahine no ka ona awa; ia manawa hoomaka hou ke kane i kana hana mau, a hele aku la i o Hinaikamalama la.

A ike o Laielohelohe, ua hala aku la kela, ala ae la oia, a ukali aku la ia Kekalukaluokewa me kona ike oleia.

Ia ukali ana o Laielohelohe, aia hoi ua loaa pono aku la kana kane ia ia e hana ana i ka hewa me Hinaikamalama.

Ia manawa, olelo aku o Laielohelohe ia Kekalukaluokewa, oiai aia ma ko Hinaikamalama wahi moe laua, "E kuu kane, ua puni wau ia oe, malia oe e hookina nei ia'u i ka awa, he hana ka kau, a nolaila, ua loaa maopopo ae nei olua ia'u, nolaila, ke olelo nei wau ia oe, aole e pono ia kaua ke hoomanawanui i ka noho ana maanei, e pono ia kaua ke hoi i Kauai, a nolaila, e hoi kaua ano."

Ike mai la kana kane i ka maikai o ka manao o ke Alii wahine, ku ae la laua a hoi aku la i Honokalani. A ma ia ao ana ae, hoomakaukau koke na waa no ka hooko i ka olelo a Laielohelohe, me ka manao ia po iho e holo ai, aole nae i holo, no ka mea, ua hoomaimai ae la o Kekalukaluokewa, a nolaila, ua hala ia po; a i kekahi po iho, hana hou no o Kekalukaluokewa i kana hana, a no ia mea, ua haalele o Laielohelohe i kona aloha i kana kane, a hoi aku la i Kauai ma kona mau waa, me kona manao hou ole aku ia Kekalukaluokewa.

Ia Laielohelohe ma Kauai mahope iho o kona haalele ana i kana kane; i kekahi la, hiki hou mai o Kaonohiokala mai Kahakaekaea mai, a halawai iho la me Laielohelohe.

A hala eha malama o ko laua hui kalohe ana; he mea haohao nae ia Laieikawai keia hele loihi o Kaonohiokala, no ka mea, eha malama ka loihi o ka nalo ana. A mahope oia manawa haohao o Laieikawai, hoi aku la o Kaonohiokala iluna.

Ninau mai la nae o Laieikawai, "Pehea keia hele loihi ou aha malama, no ka mea, aole oe pela e hele nei."

I mai la o Kaonohiokala, "Ua hewa ko Laielohelohe ma noho ana me kana kane, ua lilo o Kekalukaluokewa i ka wahine e, a oia ka'u mea i noho loihi ai."

A no keia mea, olelo aku o Laieikawai i kana kane, "E kii oe i ko wahine a hoihoi mai e noho pu kakou."

Ia manawa no a laua e kamailio ana no keia mau mea, haalele aku la o Kaonohiokala ia Laieikawai, a iho mai la, me ka manao o Laieikawai e kii ana mamuli o kana kauoha, aole ka!

I keia hele ana o Kaonohiokala, hookahi makahiki; ia manawa, aole o kanamai o ka haohao o Laieikawai no ka hele loihi o kana kane. Ua manao ae o Laieikawai i ke kumu o keia hele loihi, ua pono ole la o Laielohelohe me Kekalukaluokewa.

A no keia mea, ake nui ae la oia e ike i ka pono o kona kaikaina, ia wa, hele aku la o Laieikawai imua o kona makuahonowaikane, me ka ninau aku, "Pehea la wau e ike ai i ka pono o ko'u kaikaina? No ka mea, ua olelo mai nei kuu kane Lani, ua hewa ka noho ana o Laielohelohe me Kekalukaluokewa, a no ia mea, ua hoouna aku nei wau ia Kaonohiokala e kii aku i ka wahine a hoi mai; aka, i ka hele ana aku nei, aole i hoi mai; o ka pau keia o ka makehiki o ka hele ana, aole i hoi mai, nolaila, e haawi mai oe i ike no'u, i ike hiki ke ike aku ma kahi mamao, i ike au i ka pono o ko'u hoahanau."

A no keia mea, olelo mai o Moanalihaikawaokele, kona makuahonowaikane, "E hoi oe a ma ko olua wahi, e nana aku oe i ko makuahonowaiwahine, ina ua hiamoe, alaila, e hele aku oe a komo iloko o ka heiau kapu, ina e ike aku oe i ka ipu ua ulanaia i ke ie, a ua hakuia ka hulu ma ka lihilihi o ke poi oia ua ipu la. O na manu nui e ku ana ma na aoao o ua ipu la, mai maka'u oe, aole ia he manu maoli, he mau manu laau ia, ua ulanaia i ke i-e a hanaia i ka hulu. A i kou hiki ana i kahi o ua ipu la e ku ana, wehe ae oe i ke poi, alaila, hookomo iho oe i ko poo i ka waha o ua ipu la, alaila, kahea iho oe ma ka inoa o ua ipu la, 'E Laukapalili—e, homai i he ike.' Alaila loaa ia oe ka ike, e hiki ia oe ke ike aku i kou kaikaina a me na mea a pau o lalo. Eia nae, i kou kahea ana, mai kahea oe me ka leo nui, o kani auanei, lohe mai ko makuahonowaiwahine o Laukieleula, ka mea nana e malama i ua ipu ike la."

He mea mau nae ia Laukieleula, ma ka po oia e ala ai e malama i ua ipu la o ka ike, a ma ke ao, he hiamoe.

I kekahi kakahiaka, i ka wa e hoomaka mai ai ka mehana o ka La maluna o ka aina, hele aku la oia e makai ia Laukieleula, aia nae e hiamoe ana.

A ike iho la kela ua hiamoe, hooko ae la o Laieikawai i ke kauoha a Moanalihaikawaokele, a hele aku la oia e like me ka mea i aoaoia mai ia ia.

A hiki keia makahi o ka ipu, ka mea i kapaia, "Kaipuokaike," wehe ae la keia i ke poi o ka ipu, a kupou iho la kona poo ma ka waha o ua ipu nei, a kahea iho la ma ka inoa o ua ipu nei, ia wa ka hoomaka ana e ike i na mea a pau i hanaia ma kahi mamao.

Ia awakea, leha ae la na maka o Laieikawai ilalo nei, aia hoi, ua hana o Kaonohiokala i ka hewa me Laielohelohe.

Iloko o keia manawa, hele aku la o Laieikawai a hai aku la ia Moanalihaikawaokele, no keia mau mea, me ka olelo aku, "Ua loaa ia'u ka ike mai a oe mai. Aka, i kuu nana ana aku nei, aia nae ua hewa ka Haku Lani o'u, ua hanaia kekahi hewa me kuu kaikaina, akahi no a maopopo ia'u na kumu a me ke kuleana o kona noho loihi ana ilalo."

A no keia mea, he mea e ka inaina o Moanalihaikawaokele, a lohe pu ae la o Laukieleula, hele aku la kona mau makuahonowai i kahi o ka ipu ike, aia hoi, ike lea aku la laua e hana ana i ka hewa, e like me ka Laieikawai mau olelo.

I kekahi la ae, akoakoa ae la lakou a pau, o Laieikawai me na makuahonowai, e hele e ike i ka pono o Kaonohiokala, a hooholo ae la lakou ia mea.

Ia manawa, kuuia aku la ke alanui mai Kakahaekaea aku a ku imua o Kaonohiokala, ia wa, ua lele koke ka oili o Kaonohiokala, no ke alanui i kuuia mai imua ona. Aole nae i liuliu mahope iho o ko Kaonohiokala haohao ana.

Ia manawa, ua hoopouliia ka lewa, a hoopihaia i na leo wawalo o ka hanehane, me ka leo uwe, "Ua haule ka Lani! Ua haule ka Lani!!"

A i ka pau ana ae o ka pouli ma ka lewa, aia hoi e kau mai ana o Moanalihaikawaokele me Laukieleula a me Laieikawai, iluna o ke alanui anuenue.

A olelo mai la o Moanalihaikawaokele imua o Kaonohiokala, "Ua hewa kau hana, e Kaonohiokala—e, no ka mea, ua haumia loa oe, a nolaila, aole e loaa hou ia oe he wahi noho iloko o Kahakaekaea, a o kou uku hoopai, e lilo ana oe i mea e hoomaka'uka'uia'i ma na alanui, a ma ka puka o na hale, a o kou inoa, he *Lapu*, a o kau mea e ai ai, o na pulelehua, a malaila kou kuleana a mau i kau pua."

Ia manawa, kailiia aku la ke alanui mai ona aku la, mamuli o ka mana o kona makuakane. A pau keia mau mea, hoi aku la lakou i Kahakaekaea.

(Ua oleloia ma keia Kaao, o Kaonohiokala ka *lapu* mua makeia mau moku, a ma ona la na *lapu* e auwana nei i keia mau la, ma ka hoohalike ana i ke ano o ka *lapu*, he *uhane ino*.)

Ia lakou i hoi ai iluna, mahope iho o ka pau ana o ko Kaonohiokala ola, halawai aku la lakou me Kahalaomapuana iloko o Kealohilani, akahi no a lohe lakou aia oia malaila.

A ma keia halawai ana o lakou, hai aku la o Kahalaomapuana i ka moolelo o kona hoihoiia'na e like me ka kakou ike ana ma ka Mokuna XXVII o keia kaao, a pau keia mau mea, laweia'ku la o Kahalaomapuana e pani ma ka hakahaka o Kaonohiokala.

Ia lakou ma Kahakaekaea, i kekahi manawa, nui mai la ke aloha o Laieikawai ia Laielohelohe, aka, aole e hiki ma kona manao, he mea mau nae ia Laieikawai ka uwe pinepine no kona kaikaina, a he mea haohao no hoi i kona mau makuahonowai ka ike aku i ko Laieikawai mau maka, ua ano maka uwe.

Ninau aku nae o Moanalihaikawaokele i ke kumu o keia mea, alaila, hai aku la oia, he maka uwe kona no kona kaikaina.

I mai nae o Moanalihaikawaokele, "Aole e aeia kou kaikaina o noho pu me kakou, no ka mea, ua haumia oia ia Kaonohiokala; aka, ina he manao kou i ko kaikaina, alaila, e hoi oe a e pani ma ka hakahaka o Kekalukaluokewa." Aka, ua ae koke ae la o Laieikawai i keia mau mea.

A ma ka la o Laieikawai i hookuuia mai ai, olelo mai la o Moanalihaikawaokele, "E hoi oe a me kou kaikaina, e noho malu oe a hiki i kou manawa e make ai, a mai keia la aku, aole e kapaia kou inoa o Laieikawai; aka, o kou inoa mau o KAWAHINEOKALIULA, a ma ia inoa ou e kukuli aku ai kou hanauna ia oe, a o oe no ke akua o kou mau hanauna."

A pau keia kauoha, lawe ae la o Moanalihaikawaokele a kau aku la iluna o ke alanui, a kau pu aku la me Moanalihaikawaokele, a kuuia mai la ilalo nei.

Ia manawa, hai aku la o Moanalihaikawaokele i na mea a pau e like me ka mea i oleloia maluna, a pau ia, hoi aku la o Moanalihaikawaokele iluna, a noho ma ka pea kapu o kukulu o Tahiti.

Ia manawa, hooili aku la o Kawahineokaliula i ke aupunu i ka Makaula, o Laieikawai hoi ka mea i kapaia o Kawahineokaliula, ua noho oia ma kona ano akua, a ma ona la i kukuli aku ai ka Makaula, a me kona hanauna e like me ka olelo a Moanalihaikawaokele ia ia. A ma ia ano no o Laieikawai i noho ai a hiki i kona make ana.

A mai ia manawa mai a hiki i keia mau la, ke hoomanaia nei no e kekahi poe ma ka inoa o Kawahineokaliula (Laieikawai).

(HOPENA)

A Note About the Author

S. N. Haleʻole (1819–1866) was a Native Hawaiian writer and historian. Born at a time of monumental change in the Kingdom of Hawaii, Haleʻole was among the first generation of Hawaiians to be educated by American missionaries. He attended Lahainaluna Seminary from 1834 to 1838, studying ancient Hawaiian history under Lorrin Andrews and Sheldon Dibble. After graduation, Haleʻole worked as a teacher in Haiku, Maui, before embarking on a career as a writer and editor. In the last decade of his life, Haleʻole dedicated himself to writing *The Hawaiian Romance of Laieikawai* (1863), a story based on songs from the Hawaiian oral tradition. Upon publication, it became the first work of literature from a Native Hawaiian, securing Haleʻole's status as a leading intellectual among his people and bringing the story of Hawaii to the world stage.

A Note from the Publisher

Spanning many genres, from non-fiction essays to literature classics to children's books and lyric poetry, Mint Edition books showcase the master works of our time in a modern new package. The text is freshly typeset, is clean and easy to read, and features a new note about the author in each volume. Many books also include exclusive new introductory material. Every book boasts a striking new cover, which makes it as appropriate for collecting as it is for gift giving. Mint Edition books are only printed when a reader orders them, so natural resources are not wasted. We're proud that our books are never manufactured in excess and exist only in the exact quantity they need to be read and enjoyed. To learn more and view our library, go to minteditionbooks.com

bookfinity & MINT EDITIONS

Enjoy more of your favorite classics with Bookfinity,
a new search and discovery experience for readers.
With Bookfinity, you can discover more vintage
literature for your collection, find your Reader Type,
track books you've read or want to read,
and add reviews to your favorite books.
Visit www.bookfinity.com, and click on
Take the Quiz to get started.

Don't forget to follow us
@bookfinityofficial and @mint_editions

9 781513 290737